NEW YORK REVIEW B
C L A S S I C S

THE DOLL

BOLESŁAW PRUS (1847–1912) was born Aleksander Głowacki in
the provincial town of Hrubieszów, Poland. His mother died in
1850; his father, an estate steward of noble birth (the author's pen
name is a reference to the family's origin near the Prussian border),
died six years later, leaving him in the care of relatives in Puławy and
Lublin. In 1862, he moved to Kielce with his older brother Leon, a
Polish patriot. The next year, the teenaged Aleksander joined in the
January 1863 uprising against Russian rule. Wounded in battle, he
was imprisoned in Lublin Castle, but released when he was discovered to be underage. He then finished high school and enrolled in
university, but lacked the funds to graduate. Instead, he worked
several odd jobs, including a stint in a metallurgical factory, before
taking up journalism. Prus eventually made a name for himself as a
writer of feuilletons, publishing his much-admired *Kroniki* in the
Kurier Warszawski between 1875 and 1887 and also achieving some
success with his short stories. *The Outpost*, published in 1885, was
the first of four novels that secured his literary reputation. It was
followed by *The Doll* (1890), *Emancipated Women* (1894), and *The
Pharaoh* (1897). A respected but no longer fashionable writer, Prus
dedicated his last years to social reform and philanthropic work.

STANISŁAW BARAŃCZAK is a poet, translator, and literary
critic. He won the 2007 Nike Award for the best work of Polish
literature published in the previous year and the 2009 Silesius
Poetry Award for lifetime achievement. He is a professor of Polish
language and literature at Harvard University.

THE DOLL

BOLESŁAW PRUS

Translated from the Polish by
DAVID WELSH

Revised by
DARIUSZ TOŁCZYK *and* ANNA ZARANKO

Introduction by
STANISŁAW BARAŃCZAK

NEW YORK REVIEW BOOKS

New York

New York Review Books
207 East 32nd Street, New York, NY 10016
www.nyrb.com

Translation and notes © 1996 by Central European Classics Trust
Introduction © 1996 by Stanisław Barańczak
All rights reserved.

First published in Polish as *Lalka*, 1890
First published in English as *The Doll* by Twayne Publishers, Inc., New York, 1972
This edition first published by Central European University Press, 1996

Library of Congress Cataloging-in-Publication Data
Prus, Boleslaw, 1847–1912.
[Lalka. English]
The doll / by Boleslaw Prus ; introduction by Stanislaw Baranczak ; translated by
David Welsh.
    p. cm. — (New York Review Books classics)
ISBN 978-1-59017-383-1 (alk. paper)
1. Poland—Social conditions—19th century—Fiction. 2. Warsaw (Poland)—Social
life and customs—19th century—Fiction. 3. Social classes—Poland—Fiction.
I. Welsh, David J. II. Title.
PG7158.G6L323 2011
891.8'536—dc22

                              2010033548

ISBN 978-1-59017-383-1

Printed in the United States of America on acid-free paper.
10 9 8 7 6 5 4

CONTENTS

Introduction

THE GREATEST realist in the history of the Polish novel suffered all his life from acute agoraphobia. Not that this curious piece of trivia will unlock any mystery about his writing. At first glance, it may even seem that the reader who enters the novelistic world of Bolesław Prus (1847–1912) is in no need of any special key at all, and most certainly not of a psychopathological one. This is the work of a supremely sane mind, produced in an epoch which, while in reality as much affected by human aberration as any other period in recorded history, at least put the principle of sanity relatively high on its list of priorities.

Still, the fact of Prus's agoraphobia *is* curious. The typical narrator in the realistic novel of the nineteenth century was, as a rule, one who blithely defied all the laws of 'realistic' probability by assuming an all-seeing, Olympian view. Prus's critics at the time accused him of a 'myopic' preference to focus on detail rather than seeing the large picture. While not true of his writing, this was true of his life. Venturing into any space broader than his Warsaw apartment or a couple of familiar streets in the neighbourhood made him dizzy. His worst attack of agoraphobia came upon him when, as a thirty-four-year-old man, he took, for the first time in his life, the risk of visiting a fashionable mountain spa. So much for the Olympian viewpoint. And yet, amazingly, if there is any novelist who has succeeded in unfolding a broad and richly detailed panorama of nineteenth-century Polish life while also bringing this picture alive with genuine human drama, it is Bolesław Prus in his *Lalka, The Doll*.

Serialised in a newspaper, starting in 1887, and published in book form in 1890, this novel had to weather a cold reception before it became what it is today, one of the few most loved and continually reread classics of Polish literature. On its first appearance, it had the double disadvantage of being too extraordinary for its critics and too ordinary for its readers. In the eyes of the former, it strayed too much off the beaten path of the genre. 'Chaotic composition' was the most frequently reiterated charge, which particularly infuriated Prus, who thought it his most meticulously planned work of fiction to date. In the eyes of the reader, its appearance was overshadowed and its significance dwarfed by the almost simultaneous serialised publication of two novels by two extremely popular and respected authors for whom Prus at that point seemed to be no competition at all: Henryk Sienkiewicz with the final part of his *Trilogy* and the leading Polish woman writer of that epoch, Eliza Orzeszkowa, with her major work, *On the Banks of the Niemen.* Yet it was not Sienkiewicz, for all the tremendous popular appeal of his historical fables, and not Orzeszkowa, with her respected and influential if overly didactic contemporary novels, but Prus who left behind a work worthy of being called *the* Polish novel of the nineteenth century.

The Doll's initial cold reception resulted from both the critics' and the reading public's confusion about the nature of the work. In fact, the whole course of Prus's career up to 1890 was handicapped by a few popular misconceptions about himself and the nature of his writing. When Polish critics today attempt to give a Western audience some idea of Prus's place in Polish literature, they resort almost unavoidably to portraying him as the Chekhov of Poland. Even though such a comparison usually makes little sense, in this particular case the critics may be on to something. As well as their professional training in medicine or science rather than the humanities, perhaps the most striking analogy between the lives, if not the works, of Chekhov and Prus is that each of them had to struggle for a very long time to convince the public that he was a serious writer rather than a cheap humorist. Ironically, the exquisite sense of humour that these two writers shared was, at the outset of their respective careers, both their greatest asset and their curse. It gave each of them his first foothold in the writing business only to turn into a major obstacle on his creative path. In Prus's case, the condescending labels of 'humorist', '*feuilletonist*', 'journalist' and the like stuck so persistently that they affected the first critical reactions to *The Doll* – which saw the light of day when he was, after all, the forty-year-old author of at least one critically acclaimed and definitely serious novel and a large number of equally serious short stories.

His was an epoch that valued seriousness above all things. The so-called Positivists of his sober-minded, moderate, common-sensical and conciliatory generation resisted Romantic stereotypes of national martyrdom, urged involvement with social reform and generally inclined away from the visionary to the realistic and pragmatic. The typical Positivist critic or writer deplored the literature of the immediately preceding period of Romanticism as foolish flights of fancy. The seeds of the controversy had been sown in 1795, · when Poland's territory was ultimately divided and swallowed up by the three neighbouring empires – Russia, Prussia and Austria. An atmosphere of profound spiritual crisis, caused by the Final Partition (an event almost unanimously perceived by Poles as history's, and perhaps even divine providence's act of supreme injustice) meant it took a quarter of a century for the first Romantic poets to emerge. But when Adam Mickiewicz published his first collection in 1822, the avalanche of Romantic poetry began. Eight years later, a motley band of soldiers and civilians – most of them poets themselves, naturally enough – triggered the so-called November Uprising by staging a legendary assault on the Belweder, the Warsaw residence of the Russian governor of Poland. This band used the title of one of Mickiewicz's most celebrated poems, 'Konrad Wallenrod', as shorthand for what happened that November night: 'The word has become flesh, and Wallenrod has become the Belweder.'

The November Uprising was soon crushed, yet in Polish litera-ture the three decades that followed saw the triumph of the greatest Romantic poets. Since the insurrection's defeat in 1831 all of them, including Mickiewicz, had lived in exile but that did not prevent them from exerting a tremendous influence on the minds of their Polish readers everywhere. Such was Romantic poetry's soul-stirring as well as its lethal potential and, more generally, the preva-lence of the Romantic value system, that a few independent minds issued warnings against possible consequences. Cyprian Norwid, one of the greatest Polish poets but already a post-Romantic, lamented the fate that would await Poland if it continued to be 'a nation where every action is taken too early, and every book comes out too late'. This aphorism, one referring obviously to the Romantic antinomy of the Word versus the Deed, and reversing its usual order of priority, could not, however, slow down the momentum. In January 1863, another uprising against Tsarist oppression started in the Russian-occupied part of Poland. The future author of *The Doll* was then fifteen and a half years of age.

Because all published work in Russian-occupied Poland had to pass the Tsarist censor, Prus tended to avoid any direct mention of the Uprising or his personal involvement. Yet there is no doubt that this was the most powerful formative experience of his youth. Born as Aleksander Głowacki – the pen name Prus was a reference to his family's coat of arms – in the provincial town of Hrubieszów, he was orphaned early and raised by relatives in Puławy and Lublin. In the early 1860s he moved to Kielce in the custody of his older brother Leon, who was deeply involved in patriotic conspiracy. When the uprising broke out, young Aleksander fought in it, was wounded, and spent some time in hospital and prison. After he was released he managed to complete his high school education in Lublin, and moved to Warsaw to study – a significant choice – physics and mathematics at the so-called Main School, which was the Russian authorities' official name for the heavily controlled and downgraded former University of Warsaw.

Prus never graduated from the Main School, yet his interest in science was much more than just a passing fad of the Positivist era: he retained it, as a personal hobby, throughout his life. (Some traces of this interest, bordering on science fiction, also show in *The Doll*; in particular, the fictitious invention of a metal lighter than air.) After dropping out of school he tried to make his living at a number of jobs, even as a manual labourer. He made his début in 1866 with a couple of humorous prose pieces published in the Sunday edition of a Warsaw daily. It was, however, only after 1872 that he began writing and publishing more systematically, initially as a frequent contributor to rather disreputable satirical broadsheets. In 1874 he started contributing to more respected periodicals and his writing shifted towards a more serious genre. It was the classic Central European genre of the *feuilleton*, a half-journalistic, half-essayistic comment on the events of the day. Prus was soon to become a master of it. Columns entitled *Kroniki* ('Chronicles') and published regularly between 1875 and 1887 in the *Kurier Warszawski* (*Warsaw Courier*) brought him wide recognition. And it would be fair to say that the enormous popularity of the *feuilleton* in the literary life of twentieth-century Poland, and the high level of its best examplars, owe a great deal to the standards set by Prus in his 'Chronicles'.

In the mid-1870s Prus's regular writing of *feuilletons* and other mostly journalistic or essayistic pieces began finally to bring him enough income to live on, and even to get married. In 1872 he nevertheless jumped at the chance to take over, as a new editor-in-chief, one of the periodicals he had contributed to, *Nowiny* (*News*). To devote his entire time and energy to this work, he even gave up – as it turned out, for no longer than ten months – his column at the *Kurier*. One is tempted to say that the failure of his ambitious plans to convert *Nowiny*, a run-of-the-mill periodical, into a 'social observatory' was one of the best things that ever happened to Polish literature. After this monumental flop, Prus never returned to editing, and instead focused on writing again. Even more important, his writing from then on included not just the re-started 'Chronicles', but ever more fiction.

Although Prus had written a couple of novels since the mid-1870s, it was the short story that dominated his early *œuvre*. Only after trying out a large number of different narrative approaches and scoring a number of artistic successes in the shorter genre did he feel secure enough to attempt a novel again. As a result, the years

1885–97, the most creative and prolific period in his life, produced four major novels, each of which has a secure place in Polish literary history. *The Doll* was the second of the four, preceded by *Placówka* (*The Outpost*, 1885) and followed by *Emancypantki* (*Emancipated Women*, 1894) and *Faraon* (known in English as *The Pharaoh and Priest*, 1897). Even without taking *The Doll* into account, it would be hard to imagine three realistic novels more different from each other. Suffice it to say that the chief protagonists of *The Outpost*, *Emancipated Women* and *The Pharaoh* are, respectively, an illiterate peasant in the Prussian part of the partitioned Poland, resisting the efforts of German settlers to force him off his land; a well-educated young woman coping with the contradictory expectations of the contemporary social and professional scene, both in Warsaw and in backwater Russian-occupied Poland; and an Egyptian pharaoh engaged in deadly strife with the powerful caste of priests who block his attempts at reforming the state. (Silly as this condensation of its plot may sound, *The Pharaoh*, Prus's only historical novel, is in fact a brilliantly conceived and executed portrayal of the timeless mechanisms of political power; it seems more and more topical, and several critics over the past two or three decades have given this novel even higher marks than *The Doll*. Add *The Doll*'s Stanisław Wokulski, a middle-aged businessman and store owner who has already made it from rags to riches but, spurred by his unreciprocated love for an aristocratic girl, tries unsuccessfully to win the aristocracy's respect as well, and you have a quartet of protagonists truly capable of impressing the reader with their author's range of interest, scope of vision, and depth of psychological insight.

After completing the manuscript of *The Pharaoh*, Prus treated himself – at the age of fifty – to his first longer voyage abroad, to Germany, Switzerland and France. It was to be the only trip of its kind he ever made. His last years were filled mostly with philanthropic and other social work; he helped organise, for instance, a citizens' committee to aid workers fired for their participation in the 1905 strikes and lent his support to initiatives aimed at spreading personal hygiene among the poor. His creative powers, on the other hand, were waning. Around the turn of the century he was also quite palpably losing his grip on his younger readers. Since about 1890, the year of the publication of *The Doll*, the literature of the *fin de siècle* had been dominated by the new generation of 'decadents' and misty symbolists; Prus, a believer in social reform and realistic observer of life, was anomalous. The shock of the revolution of 1905 restored the need for his kind of writing for a while. Prus spent the next two years writing for periodicals, making public appearances, and working on his last completed novel, *Dzieci* (*The Children*), which, as its title clearly indicates, was mostly

focused on portraying the spiritual dilemmas of the young generation. His work on the next novel, entitled, also tellingly, *Przemiany*
(*Changes*), was terminated by his death in 1912.

   If Prus's reaction to the events of 1905 forms the closing bracket
of his creative evolution, the opening bracket must be the failed
uprising of 1863. Of all the major works of Prus, it is *The Doll* that
most needs to be read with the January Uprising in the back of our
minds, even though the novel's action takes place fifteen to sixteen
years after that event and the event itself is seldom mentioned – at
least not directly – by the narrator or the characters. In its first
published version, the text suffered a great deal from the censor's
cuts.

   The present edition follows the twentieth-century Polish critical
editions in restoring all the missing fragments, apart from one
which, for reasons explained on p.ix, is included as an appendix.
The Doll is not only and not even primarily a political novel. It is,
however, a novel about history's impact on individual lives. It
cannot avoid being that since its protagonists are Poles living in the
former capital of their country, which for the past eighty-odd years
had been engrossed by the Russian Empire and which, in living
memory, had experienced two massive and bloodily suppressed
revolts. These defeats loom large: the consequences of the 1863
uprising, in particular, directly affect the lives of many of the
novel's characters, including its chief protagonist, Wokulski. But
the cause is more than the past ordeal of those wronged. The entire
human landscape of *The Doll* is a landscape after a lost battle: after
the defeat of the Polish version of Romantic ideology.

   In the most revealing of his self-commentaries written after *The
Doll*, an extensive letter to the editor published in 1897 in *Kurier
Warszawski*, Prus succinctly defined his intention as the desire 'to
present our Polish idealists against the background of society's
decay'. (The Polish word for 'decay', '*rozkład*', actually has a
number of English possible counterparts in this context, from
'breakdown' and 'disintegration' to 'decay' and 'decomposition'.)
He also offered an alternative title that he considered in 1897, with
the benefit of hindsight, much better than the unintentionally
misleading *Lalka*. After the novel's publication, most critics took its
title either for a one-word summary of the author's opinion about
the chief heroine, the spoiled aristocratic girl and object of
Wokulski's unrequited love, Izabela Łęcka, or an expression of
Prus's more general conviction about our helplessness in the hands
of overpowering Fate: '*lalka*' means both 'doll' and 'puppet'. The
truth, according to Prus, was that he had chosen his title more or
less 'accidentally'. It was supposed to highlight one of the novel's
episodes, in which the alleged theft of a real doll leads to a curious
court trial. The subplot around that event was modelled on a

newspaper story, which was for Prus the moment of 'crystallisation' of his general thematic design.

The less 'accidental' title that he came up with later was *Trzy pokolenia*, *Three Generations*. Such a title would certainly have helped Prus's contemporary reviewers avoid many misreadings and misunderstandings. In particular, the identification of 'the doll' with Izabela can only result in a considerably flattened, one-dimensional image of the novel. It *is*, of course, among other things, also a great novel about a middle-aged man's ill-fated love for a pampered and affected young woman. But Wokulski's infatuation is just part of his psychological profile and is not the only force animating the plot. Wokulski, while *The Doll*'s dominant figure, is flanked by two other characters vital to the novel: the old store-clerk Rzecki and the young scientist Ochocki. These three serve as representatives of the 'three generations' of 'our Polish idealists'. The thoroughly honest and humane but also disarmingly naive Rzecki is a late child of the Napoleonic era, able to think only in outdated, Romantic categories of sacrifice, conspiracy, and Messianic mission. Wokulski is an 'idealist' of the transitional phase in history: from the years he spent in Siberia as a punishment for his involvement in the January Uprising until his current position as a highly successful Warsaw businessman, his life connects the end of the Romantic era with the beginning of the new, Positivist one. (His commercial success actually stems from trade with Russia – one of the novel's many pregnant ironies.) His 'idealism' is incomparably more concrete, active and rational than that of his elderly subordinate and confidant. Wokulski's own Utopia can be built, or so he claims, through wise investment and sound economic policy, for only a nation with economic independence has a right to political independence. Finally, Ochocki is a new type of 'idealist', one of those who, buoyed up by their faith in scientific and technological progress, pin all their hopes on society's intellectual maturation.

Prus's entire novel would be an insufferably uplifting Sunday sermon had any member of this triumvirate triumphed. In fact, all three are, at least in the short run, losers. 'The decay' which, in Prus's own words, forms a background for their dreams and deeds, is not just the decay of the obsolete Romantic ideology. It is also, and perhaps even more so, the decay of Positivist beliefs. The fundamental idea of both Western and Polish Positivists – their concept of society as a gigantic organism, whose parts function harmoniously for the benefit of the whole – could not sound more ridiculous than it does here, when confronted with a starkly realistic picture of contemporary Polish society, chronicled so accurately by Prus the journalist. If this society is a living organism at all, it is the organism of a Colossus with clay feet and a very little brain. It has a disenfranchised, hopelessly vegetating lower class at the base and aristocratic nincompoops, like Izabela's father, at the top. For a former enthusiast of Positivism such as Prus, who had placed so much hope in the enterprising spirit of the middle class, it must have been painful that between the workers and the aristocracy there was little more than isolated figures like Wokulski, whose every effort at lasting social improvement (*not* merely philanthropic improvisation) is doomed to fail. Why? Because each of Wokulski's specific actions is bound to be misinterpreted. His generosity is taken for a *nouveau-riche*'s wish to impress; his sound economic reasoning, for greed; his energy, for pushiness; his caution, for pettymindedness. In a total standstill, every step forward treads on a corn or two. Prus's 'social decay' is a mire of stagnation. Every effort that carries some weight has to sink sooner or later. Only the operations of small-time crooks stay afloat.

This diagnosis sounds even more well-founded since Prus makes it work ingeniously in many dimensions of his novelistic world simultaneously. His keen observation dissects society not merely along its vertical axis. It also moves horizontally, revealing, for instance, the immobilising, destructive results of ethnic animosity. Polish–Russian and Polish–Jewish conflict can find, in the eyes of Prus, neither a rational explanation nor an easy solution. It tears the fabric of society even more irreparably than the class distinctions. Yet another concern is the perennial problem of Poland's place among the civilised nations of the West. Wokulski's trip to Paris makes him – and the reader – realise the enormous distance separating Poland from France, which it claims to have emulated for centuries.

Lastly, the Polish stalemate is scrutinised in historical time. First and foremost a contemporary novel, focused on the present moment in history, *The Doll* is also to some extent a historical novel – a novel whose contemporary plot depends on the backdrop of the historical past. The narrative structure of *The Doll* is affected by the almost compulsive retrospection of at least some of the characters. They either idealise the past or abhor it as the source of present troubles. The most significant of these characters is Ignacy Rzecki. Prus had the brilliant idea of inserting entries from the 'Journal of the Old Clerk' into his narrative. This hybrid – third-person narration with pockets of first-person diaristic narration – crucially affected the novel's narrative and earned the writer much critical abuse. Yet it pays off in more ways than one. It allows him, first of all, to let Rzecki draw his own self-portrait – engaging and sympathetic because expressed in his idiosyncratic style. Second, Rzecki's diary releases a multitude of subtle ironies: the old clerk's naive interpretations of Wokulski's actions diverge from the actual motivations, revealed to the reader in the third-person narrative. But Rzecki's habit of reminiscing, turning back towards the distant historical past at every opportunity, seems to be the chief benefit. It gives the novel a new dimension by demonstrating the extent – one unknown in nations blessed with more peaceful and less absurd histories – to which the burden of the past can mould an individual's as well as an entire society's attitude to the present and vision of the future.

A vision of the future derived from an interpretation of society's past and a critical assessment of its present state – this is actually what Prus's *The Doll* is all about. This is the minimum that this novel demands from successive generations of its readers. It is also an old-fashioned yet still fascinating love story, a historically determined yet still topical diagnosis of society's ills, and a forceful yet subtle portrayal of a tragically doomed man. *The Doll* is all this; but what is most enduring about it has been hinted at already by Prus himself.

In our age of shattered utopias, amidst the overwhelming odour of 'decay', perhaps the most persistent question is the one that this agoraphobic, myopic, yet bold and far-sighted nineteenth-century realist felt compelled to ask: how, without being blindly naive, can one remain an 'idealist' in a 'decayed' world? Or, to put it another way, how to continue in the belief that we can become something better than we are, while almost all available evidence seems to point to the contrary?

Stanisław Barańczak

THE DOLL

I

The Firm of J. Mincel and S. Wokulski
Seen Through a Bottle

EARLY in 1878, when the political world was concerned with the treaty of San Stefano,* the election of a new Pope,* and the chances of a European war,* Warsaw businessmen and the intelligentsia who frequented a certain spot in the Krakowskie Przedmieście* were no less keenly interested in the future of the haberdashery firm of J. Mincel and S. Wokulski.

In a celebrated restaurant where the proprietors of linen stores or wine shops, carriage- and hat-makers, solemn paterfamilias living on their incomes, and the owners of apartment houses with no fixed occupation met to partake of refreshments in the evenings, as much was said of the arming of England as of the firm of J. Mincel and S. Wokulski. Surrounded by clouds of cigar smoke, and sitting over dark bottles, some of the citizens of this neighbourhood bet that England would win – or lose; others bet on Wokulski's likely bankruptcy; some called Bismarck a genius, others declared Wokulski an irresponsible adventurer; some criticised the behaviour of President MacMahon, while others declared that Wokulski was certainly a lunatic, if not something worse. . .

Mr Deklewski, the carriage-manufacturer, who owed all his fortune and position to steady work in one and the same trade, and Councillor Węgrowicz, a lawyer who had for twenty years been member and patron of one and the same charitable institution, had known Wokulski longest and it was they who most vociferously predicted his ruin. 'Ruin and insolvency', said Mr Deklewski, 'must finish off a man who never sticks to a trade and doesn't know how to respect the gifts of Fortune.' Whereas Councillor Węgrowicz added to each of his friend's aphorisms: 'A lunatic . . . a lunatic . . . an adventurer! Joe, another beer there! How many does that make?'

''Tis the sixth, sir . . . Coming!' replied Joe.

'The sixth already . . . How time flies, to be sure. He's a lunatic, that's what,' Councillor Węgrowicz muttered.

To those who ate in the same restaurant as the lawyer, to its proprietor, the clerks and the waiters, the reasons for the disasters about to fall upon Wokulski and his haberdashery store were as clear as the gas-lights that illuminated the establishment. These reasons were rooted in his restless nature, in his adventurous life, not to mention the latest act of this man who – though he had an assured living in his grasp and the opportunity to frequent this respectable restaurant – had nevertheless quit the restaurant of his own free will, left his shop to the care of Providence and gone off with all the cash inherited from his late wife to make a fortune in the Russo-Turkish war.

'Maybe he'll do it . . . Army supplies is good business,' said Szprot the travelling salesman, who was an infrequent visitor here.

'He'll do nothing!' Deklewski retorted, 'and in the meantime a reputable shop is going to the dogs. Only the Germans and the Jews get rich from Army trade; we Poles haven't the brains for it.'

'Maybe Wokulski has.'

'He's a lunatic, a lunatic . . .' the lawyer muttered. 'Here, Joe – another beer! How many does that make?'

'The seventh, sir . . . Coming!'

'The seventh already? . . . How time flies, to be sure . . .'

The travelling salesman, who needed extensive and exhaustive information about trade on account of his calling, carried his bottle and glass over to the lawyer's table and gazed sweetly into the latter's watery eyes as he asked in a low voice: 'Excuse me, I beg . . . why call Wokulski a lunatic? Pray allow me to offer you a cigar . . . I know Wokulski slightly. He always strikes me as a secretive man, a proud man. And in business, secrecy is a great virtue, pride a fault. But I've never seen Wokulski show symptoms of lunacy.'

The lawyer accepted the cigar with no overt signs of gratitude. His red face, with clumps of grey hair on his temples, chin and cheeks, looked like a marrow framed in silver.

'I call him a lunatic,' he replied, as he slowly bit off the end of the cigar and lit up, 'I call him a lunatic because I've known him for – let's see, fifteen, seventeen, eighteen years. That was in 1860 . . . We used to eat at Hopfer's then. Did you know Hopfer, sir?'

'Hm . . .'

'In those days, Wokulski was a waiter in Hopfer's restaurant, and yet he was already over twenty.'

'In the food and drink trade, eh?'

'Just so. And like Joe here, he used to serve me my Beef Nelson* and beer . . .'

'Then he transferred from that line of business to the haberdashery trade?' asked the travelling salesman.

'Not so fast, if you please,' the lawyer interrupted. 'He transferred, certainly, but not to haberdashery. Instead he went to the

Preparatory College and then to the City College – he wanted to become a scholar, d'you see?'

The commercial traveller nodded to express his surprise.

'Just think of that!' he said. 'What put that into his head?'

'Well, it was the same old business – he knew people at the Medical Academy and the School of Fine Arts . . . In those days everyone was crazy with ideas, and he didn't want to be behind the rest of 'em. So by day he waited on customers in the restaurant, and did the accounts, and nights he studied.'

'The service must have gone to the devil?'

'No more than anywhere else,' the lawyer replied, with a deprecatory gesture. 'Except that when he was waiting on you, he was a holy terror: he'd scowl like thunder at the most innocent word . . . It stands to reason we amused ourselves at his expense, and what vexed him most was to be called "Doctor". One fine day he went for a customer and they very nearly tore one another to pieces.'

'Business suffered, of course?'

'Not at all! When the news got around that Hopfer's waiter wanted to go to the Preparatory College, crowds would go there for dinner. It was crowded out with students in particular.'

'And did he get into the College?'

'He did, and he even passed his exam for the City College. Yes, but now,' the lawyer went on, tapping the travelling salesman's knee, 'instead of sticking to his studies till he finished, he left the College in less than a year.'

'What did he do that for?'

'Ah . . . He and the rest of 'em sowed the harvest we're still reaping to this day, and in the end Wokulski finished up somewhere in the neighbourhood of Irkutsk.'*

'Oh my,' sighed the travelling salesman.

'That wasn't all, though . . . In 1870 he came back to Warsaw with what he'd saved. He spent six months looking for work, avoiding the wine and food trade which he hates, until finally the patronage of his present managing clerk Rzecki got him into Mrs Mincel's shop. She'd just become a widow and a year later he married the old girl, who was much older than he.'

'A good move,' the travelling salesman interposed.

'Oh, quite so. At one stroke he acquired a living and a trade he could stick to calmly for the rest of his days. But he had the devil's own work with the old lady.'

'That's often the way.'

'Too true,' said the lawyer. 'But just think of the luck he had! Eighteen months ago the old lady ate too much and died, and Wokulski's hard labour was over, he was free as air, he'd a well-stocked store and 30,000 roubles in cash, for which two generations of the Mincels had toiled.'

'He's a lucky fellow all right.'

'He was,' the lawyer amended, 'but he didn't appreciate it. Another fellow in his place would have married a nice girl and settled down; just think what a shop with a good name means these days – and one in a good location too! But this lunatic threw it all away and went off to do business in the war. It was millions he wanted, that's what.'

'Maybe he'll do it, too,' the commercial traveller remarked.

'Hm . . .' the lawyer grunted. 'Joe, another beer . . . Do you think, my dear sir, that he'll find a richer old lady in Turkey than the late Mrs Mincel? Joe!'

'Coming, sir! The eighth coming up . . .'

'The eighth?' the lawyer echoed. 'It can't be! Just a minute there . . . 'Twas the sixth just now, then the seventh . . . ' and he grunted, covering his face with one hand. 'Maybe it's the eighth after all. How time flies, to be sure . . .'

Despite the mournful prognostications of sober people, the haberdashery store of J. Mincel and S. Wokulski did not collapse into ruin, but even profited. The public was intrigued by the rumours of bankruptcy and visited the store in increasing numbers, and since Wokulski's departure, Russian merchants were coming to his store to order merchandise. Orders increased, credit was available, bills were paid regularly, and the shop was thronged with so many customers that the three clerks could barely cope: of these three, one was a lanky fair youth who looked as if he might become consumptive and die any minute; the second, a dark youth with a philosopher's beard and princely gestures; while the third was a young dandy who wore moustaches the fair sex found fatal and which were perfumed like a chemical laboratory into the bargain.

However, the curiosity of the public, the physical and moral graces of the three clerks, and even the solid reputation of the shop could not have saved it from rack and ruin, had it not been for an employee of the firm for the last forty years, Wokulski's old friend and managing clerk, Ignacy Rzecki.

II

The Reign of an Old Clerk

OR twenty-five years, Ignacy Rzecki had lived in a little room behind the store. During all this time the shop had changed owners and its floor, its cupboards and the window glass, not to mention the scope of its business and its clerks; but Rzecki's room stayed just the same as ever. It still had one dismal window overlooking a dismal yard, with the same bars across it and the same spider-web that had been suspended there perhaps a quarter of a century ago, and the same old curtain, once green, but now faded by the sun.

By the window stood the same black table, covered with a cloth once green, but now merely stained. On it were a large black ink-well and a large black sand-box fastened to the same base, with a pair of brass candlesticks for tallow candles which these days no one ever lit, and steel snuffers with which no one ever snuffed. An iron bed with a very thin mattress, a musket on the wall that no one ever fired, beneath the bed, a box containing a guitar and reminiscent of an infant's coffin, a narrow leather sofa, two chairs also in leather, a large metal wash-basin and a small dark red cupboard – these constituted the furnishings of the room which, because of its length and darkness, looked more like a grave than a dwelling.

In a quarter of a century, neither the room nor the ways of Ignacy Rzecki had changed.

In the mornings he woke at six: for a while he listened to make sure the watch on the chair was still going, and looked at its hands which stood in one straight line. He wanted to get up at leisure, without undue haste: but because his cold feet and somewhat stiff arms were not sufficiently obedient to his bidding, he would jump out of bed, rapidly hop into the centre of the room and, after tossing his nightcap on the bed, run to the big wash-basin by the stove, and wash from tip to toe, neighing and snorting like a thoroughbred remembering a gymkhana.

During the rites of drying himself with a rough towel, he looked down with relish at his skinny calves and hairy chest, muttering: 'I'm putting on weight, that I am . . .'

At the same time his old, one-eyed poodle, Ir, would jump off the sofa, shaking himself vigorously, no doubt to rid himself of dreams, and scratch at the door, behind which someone was heard industriously puffing at the samovar. Still hastily dressing, Rzecki let the dog out, said good morning to the servant, got the tea-pot out of the cupboard, misbuttoned his cuffs, ran into the yard to see what the weather was like, burned his tongue with hot tea, combed his hair without looking into the glass, and was ready by half-past six.

Making sure his tie was on, and his watch and wallet in his pocket, Ignacy took the big key from his table and, stooping a little, ceremoniously unlocked the door of the back shop, which was fastened with an iron bar. He and the servant went in, lit a few little gas-jets and, while the servant was sweeping the floor, Ignacy perused his timetable for the day through his eye-glasses:

'Put 800 roubles into the bank, hm . . . Three albums and a dozen wallets to be dispatched to Lublin . . . That's it! An order to Vienna for 1,200 guldens . . . Fetch the delivery from the railroad depot . . . Tell off that saddler for not sending the cases . . . A mere nothing, to be sure! Write to Staś . . . Oh, a mere nothing . . .'

When he had finished, he would light a few more gas-jets and by their glare would survey the merchandise in the showcases and cupboards.

'Cuff-links, pins, wallets . . . good! . . . Gloves, fans, neck-ties, that's it! . . . Walking-sticks, umbrellas, travelling bags . . . And here, albums, handbags . . . The blue one was sold yesterday, of course . . . Candlesticks, ink-wells, paper weight . . . The porcelain . . . why did they turn that vase around, I wonder? Surely? . . . No, no damage . . . Dolls with genuine hair, the puppetshow, the merry-go-round . . . Must put that merry-go-round in the window tomorrow, the fountain is already out of date . . . Oh, a mere nothing, to be sure! It's almost eight o'clock . . . I'll wager that Klein will be first, and Mraczewski last. Of course! . . . He met some governess or other and bought her a handbag on his account, and with a discount . . . As long as he doesn't start buying without a discount and without a bill . . .'

So he muttered to himself and walked about the shop, stooping, his hands in his pockets, with the poodle following. When his master stopped and eyed an object, the dog would sit down and scratch his thick curls with his hind leg, while the dolls, large, medium and small, blond and brunette, standing in the cupboard in a row, would stare back at them with lifeless eyes.

The passage door squeaked and Klein, the lanky assistant, appeared with a dismal smile on his livid lips.

'Just as I thought. Good morning to you,' said Rzecki 'Paweł! Turn off the lights and open the door!'

The servant shuffled heavily over and turned off the gas. After the rattling of bolts, the creaking of iron bars, daylight, the only customer who never fails, came into the store. Rzecki sat down at the cash desk by the window, Klein took his regular stand at the porcelain.

'The master isn't back yet, haven't you received a letter?' Klein inquired.

'I expect him back in mid-March, within a month at most.'

'Providing another war doesn't keep him.'

'Staś . . . that's to say Mr Wokulski,' Rzecki corrected himself, 'writes to me that there will be no war.'

'But stocks are falling and I read that the British fleet has set out for the Dardanelles.'

'That's nothing, there'll be no war,' Rzecki sighed. 'Besides, how could a war concern us if no Bonaparte takes part in it?'

'The Bonapartes' career is over.'

'Is that so?' Ignacy smiled ironically. 'For whose benefit, pray, did MacMahon and Ducrot arrange that *coup-d'état* last January? Believe me, Mr Klein, Bonapartism is still a power to be reckoned with.'

'There's one that's stronger.'

'What is it?' Ignacy asked crossly. 'Gambetta and the Republic, eh? Bismarck, eh?'

'Socialism . . . ' whispered the starveling clerk, concealing himself behind the porcelain.

Ignacy put his eyeglasses on more firmly and sat up in his chair as if, with one blow, to overturn any new notions that might contradict his views, but was prevented from doing so by the appearance of the second clerk, the one with the beard.

'Good morning to you, Mr Lisiecki,' he turned to the new arrival. 'A cold day, is it not? What's the time, my watch must be fast . . . Surely it is not a quarter after eight yet?'

'For goodness sake! Your watch is always fast mornings but slow evenings,' Lisiecki replied sharply, wiping his frost-covered moustache.

'I'll wager you played whist all last night?'

'But of course! Do you think your haberdashery store and your grey hairs suffice a man for a whole day?'

'Why, sir, I prefer to be a little grizzled than bald,' Ignacy exclaimed indignantly.

'For goodness sake!' Lisiecki hissed. 'My bald spot, if anyone happens to notice it, is a sad family heirloom, while your grey hair and your nagging ways are the fruits of old age, which . . . I suppose I ought to respect.'

The first customer entered: it was a woman in a cape with a kerchief around her head, who wanted a brass spittoon . . . Ignacy bowed and offered her a chair, while Lisiecki disappeared behind the cupboards and came back after a while to hand her the desired object with a dignified gesture. Then he wrote the price of the spittoon on a bill, passed it over his shoulder to Rzecki and retired behind his counter with the air of a banker who has just donated some thousand roubles to charity.

The squabble over grey hair and baldness was laid aside.

Not until nine did Mraczewski enter, or rather rush into the shop; he was a handsome blond young man something over twenty, with eyes like fire, a mouth like coral and a moustache like a poisoned stiletto. He rushed in, bringing a trail of perfume with him, and exclaimed, 'Upon my word, it must be half-past eight! I'm a scatterbrain, a no-good, yes I am . . . I'm a wretch, but I couldn't help it, my mama was taken ill and I had to find a doctor. I tried half a dozen of them . . .'

'The ones you give presents of handbags to?' Lisiecki inquired.

'Handbags? Goodness, no. Our doctor wouldn't even accept a tie-pin. He's an honest man . . . Mr Rzecki, surely it's half-past nine? My watch has stopped . . .'

'It is nearly nine,' said Ignacy, with particular emphasis.

'Is that all? Who'd have thought it? And I'd decided to come first today, even earlier than Mr Klein . . .'

'So as to get away before eight, I daresay,' Lisiecki put in.

Mraczewski fastened upon him his blue eyes, in which the utmost astonishment appeared.

'How did you know?' he asked. 'Well, upon my word, this fellow must be a prophet. It so happens that today, on my word of honour . . . I have to be in town before seven, even if it's the last thing I do, even if . . . I have to give in my notice.'

'You can make a start by doing that,' Rzecki exclaimed, 'and you'll be free before eleven, mark my words! You should have been a lord, not a shop-assistant, and it surprises me you never went in for that calling – you'd always have plenty of time then, Mr Mraczewski. Oh yes, indeed!'

'Come, when you were his age, you ran after skirts too,' Lisiecki remarked. 'Why waste time preaching?'

'I never did!' cried Rzecki, thumping on the counter.

'For once, in a way, he admits he's been useless all his life,' Lisiecki muttered to Klein, who smiled and raised his eyebrows very high at the same time.

Another customer entered and asked for a pair of galoshes. Mraczewski moved forward to meet him.

'Galoshes for the gentleman? What size, may I ask? Ah, the gentleman doesn't recall! Not everyone has the time to remember the size of his galoshes, that is our business. Will the gentleman permit me to measure . . . ? Pray, take a seat. Paweł! Bring the rag, take off the gentleman's galoshes and wipe his shoes for him . . .'

Paweł ran up and hurled himself at the newcomer's feet.

'If you please . . .' the flustered customer began.

'Allow me . . .' said Mraczewski rapidly, 'that is our duty. I think these will do,' he went on, proffering a pair of galoshes tied together. 'Very good, they look fine; you have such a very normal foot, sir, that one can't go wrong as to size. The gentleman will no doubt require his initials added – what are they?'

'L. P.,' the customer muttered, as if drowning in the clerk's rapid flow of eloquence.

'Mr Lisiecki, Mr Klein, pray add the initials. Do you require your old galoshes wrapped, sir? Paweł! Wipe the galoshes and wrap them up . . . But perhaps the gentleman prefers not to carry an unnecessary package? Paweł! Throw the old galoshes away . . . That comes to two roubles fifty. No one will make off with galoshes that have initials on them, and it is always so disagreeable to find quite worn-out rubbish instead of articles one has just purchased . . .'

Before the customer could come to his senses, he was fitted with the new galoshes, given his change and conducted to the door with low bows. He stood for a while in the street, vacantly gazing through the glass, behind which Mraczewski bestowed on him a sweet smile and radiant look. Finally he shrugged and went on his way, no doubt thinking to himself that elsewhere galoshes without initials might only have cost ten zloty.

Rzecki turned to Lisiecki and nodded in a manner that signified admiration and satisfaction. Mraczewski caught this from a corner of his eye, ran over to Lisiecki and said in an undertone:

'Just look, doesn't our boss look like Napoleon III* in profile? That nose . . . that moustache . . . that imperial . . .'

'Napoleon with gallstones,' Lisiecki retorted.

Ignacy grimaced with distaste at this witticism. However, Mraczewski got permission to leave before seven that evening, and a few days later acquired a note in Rzecki's private journal:

'He was at the *Huguenots** in the eighth row of the stalls with a certain Matilda . . .'

Mraczewski might have found some consolation to discover that the same journal contained notes about his colleagues, the cashier, the messenger-boys and even the servant Paweł. How Rzecki knew these and similar details of the lives of his fellow employees is a secret he never confided in anyone.

Towards one o'clock that afternoon, Rzecki handed over the cash-box to Lisiecki whom, despite their continual bickering, he trusted the most, and disappeared into his room to eat dinner brought in from a restaurant. At the same time Klein left, then returned to the shop at two: whereupon he and Rzecki remained on duty while Lisiecki and Mraczewski went for dinner. By three, they were all in their places once more.

At eight in the evening they closed: the clerks went off, and only Rzecki remained behind. He made out the day's accounts, checked the cash, planned his activities for the morrow and wondered whether everything had been done that should have been done that day. For he paid for any neglected duties with insomnia and dismal dreams of the shop in ruins, of the final decline and fall of the Bonaparte dynasty and with the thought that all the hopes he had ever had in his life were only nonsense.

'Nothing will ever happen! We're doomed, and there's no hope,' he groaned, tossing on his hard mattress.

But if the day had gone well, Ignacy was content. Then before going to bed he would read the *History of the Consulate and Empire,** or look at newspaper cuttings of the Italian war of 1859* or sometimes, though less frequently, he would get his guitar out from under the bed and play the Rakoczi March* on it, joining in with his feeble tenor.

Then he would dream of the wide Hungarian plains, the blue and white ranks of armies veiled in clouds of smoke . . . Next morning, however, he was always cross and complained of a headache.

His most agreeable days were Sundays, when he thought over and drew up plans for window displays during the coming week.

His view was that the windows summarised the contents of the store and should at the same time attract the attention of passers-by, either with the smartest merchandise, by handsome window-dressing, or by the use of diverting contrivances. The right-hand windows were earmarked for luxurious articles, usually displaying a bronze bust, a porcelain vase, a whole china set for a boudoir table, around which were arranged albums, fans, wallets and candlesticks accompanied by walking-sticks, umbrellas and innumerable small but elegant objects. In the left-hand window, which contained displays of neck-ties, gloves, galoshes and perfumes, toys, mostly mechanical, occupied the central position.

Sometimes during this solitary task of arranging, the child awoke again in the old clerk. Then he would bring out and set up all the mechanical toys on the table. There was a bear that climbed a post, a cock that crowed, a mouse that ran, a train that ran on rails, a circus clown which trotted along on a horse and pulled another clown behind it, and some couples who waltzed to the strains of indistinct music. Ignacy would wind up these figures and set them all in motion at the same time. And when the cock began to crow, flapping its stiff wings, when the lifeless couples danced jerkily, stopping every now and then, when the leaden passengers in the train began to stare at him in amazement, and when all this world of dolls took on a sort of fantastic life in the flickering gas-light, then the old clerk leaned on his elbow and laughed at them quietly and muttered: 'Ha ha! Where are you off to, you travellers? And you there, acrobat! Why risk your neck in that fashion? And why do you dancers squeeze one another so tightly? The springs will run down and you'll end up back in your boxes again . . . It's vanity, all vanity! Yet all of you, if you could but think, probably believe this is something very splendid.'

After such soliloquies, he would replace the toys hastily and walk about the deserted store, irritable, followed by his shabby dog.

'Trade is vanity . . . politics too . . . that journey to Turkey as well . . . Life is mere vanity and folly, of which we've forgotten the start and don't know the end. Where does the truth lie?'

Because he would sometimes make such remarks aloud and in public, Ignacy was regarded as highly eccentric, and solemn matrons with eligible daughters sometimes declared: 'This is what being a bachelor does to a man!'

Ignacy very rarely left his home, and even then only for short periods, and would usually wander around those streets in which his colleagues and fellow clerks lived. Then his dark-green coat or his tobacco-coloured topcoat, his ash-coloured trousers with the black stripe and his faded top-hat – but most of all his timid manner – attracted general attention. Ignacy knew this and it discouraged him more and more from taking strolls. He preferred to spend holidays lying on the bed and staring for hours at a time at the barred window, behind which could be seen the grey wall of the neighbouring house, adorned by a solitary window, also barred, in which a pot of butter sometimes stood, or the remains of a hare.

But the less he went out, the more frequently he would dream about a long voyage into the countryside or even abroad. More and more often in these dreams he came across green fields and shady woods, through which he wandered, remembering his youth. Gradually a profound yearning awoke within him for these landscapes, and he decided to go off for the whole summer as soon as Wokulski came back.

'At least once before I die, for a few months,' he would tell his colleagues who, for some reason, smiled at these plans.

Voluntarily cut off from nature and humanity, absorbed in the shallow and restricted whirlpool of the shop and its business, he increasingly felt the need to share his thoughts. But because he mistrusted some people and others would not listen to him and because Wokulski was away, Rzecki talked to himself and – with the utmost secrecy – kept his journal.

III

The Journal of the Old Clerk

. . . I have been noticing for some years, with regret, that there are far fewer good clerks and sensible politicians in the world than there used to be, for everyone imitates the latest fashions. A humble clerk will equip himself every quarter with new-fangled trousers, a more original hat, and will fasten his tie differently. In the same way, politicians today change their beliefs every quarter: once they all believed in Bismarck, yesterday it was Gambetta and today it's Beaconsfield, who until recently was a Hebrew.

Evidently they forget that one cannot wear fashionable collars in a shop, but just sell them – otherwise there would be no merchandise for the customers. And politicians should not place their hopes in successful individuals, but in great dynasties. Metternich was once as celebrated as Bismarck, Palmerston more so than Beaconsfield – yet who recalls them today? And the Bonaparte family under Napoleon I made Europe tremble, so did Napoleon III, who today, though some say he's bankrupt, holds sway over the destiny of France through his faithful servants MacMahon and Ducrot.

You'll see what the young Napoleon IV, now quietly studying the art of war in England, will achieve! But enough of that . . . In this journal of mine, I want to talk about myself, not of the Bonapartes, so that people may learn how good clerks are created, not to mention sensible (if not learned) politicians. No academies are required for this purpose, merely a good example, both at home and in the shop.

My father was a soldier when young, and in his old age he was a doorman at the Commission of Internal Affairs. He carried himself as erect as a gold block, had small whiskers and a pointed moustache; he wore a black kerchief around his neck and a silver ring in his ear.

We lived in the Old Town with my aunt, who ironed and mended linen for officials. We had two little rooms on the fourth floor, where there was little luxury but much happiness, at least for me. The most impressive object in our little room was the table at which my father would gum envelopes when he came back from work; in aunt's room, most of the space was taken up by a wash-tub. I remember how I'd fly kites in the street on fine days, or blow soap-bubbles in the apartment when it rained.

The walls of my aunt's room were entirely hung with portraits of saints; but although there were a great many, they did not equal the number of Napoleons adorning my father's room. There was one portrait of Napoleon in Egypt, another at Wagram, a third before Austerlitz, a fourth in Moscow, the fifth on his coronation day, the sixth an apotheosis. But when my aunt, who resented so many secular pictures, hung up a brass crucifix on his wall, my father – not to offend Napoleon – bought himself a bronze bust and placed it over the bed.

'You'll see, you unbeliever,' my aunt sometimes lamented, 'you'll roast in Hell for these notions . . .'

'The Emperor won't let them do me an injustice,' my father replied.

Often my father's old comrades came to see us: Mr Domański, who was also a doorman at the Treasury, and Mr Raczek who had a vegetable stand on the Dunaj. They were simple people (Mr Domański was even fond of absinthe), but thoughtful politicians. All of them, not excluding my aunt, held as firmly as possible to the belief that though Napoleon I had died in captivity, the Bonaparte family would rise again. After the first Napoleon, a second would be found, and even if he came to a bad end, another would come along, until the world had been put to rights.

'We must always be ready for the first summons!' said my father.

'For no one knows the day, nor yet the hour,' Mr Domański would add.

And Mr Raczek, pipe in mouth, signified his approval by spitting as far as my aunt's door.

'Spit in my wash-tub, and I'll give you what for!' my aunt cried.

'I daresay, but I won't take it,' Mr Raczek muttered, spitting in the direction of the fireplace.

'Oh, what ruffians these Grenadiers are . . .' my aunt said crossly.

'You always fancied Hussars, I know, I know . . .'

Later on, Mr Raczek married my aunt.

Wishing me to be quite ready when the hour of justice struck, my father himself worked on my education. He taught me reading, writing, gumming envelopes and – most important – drill. He started me drilling very early, when my shirt was dangling out of my knickerbockers. I remember how my father would shout: 'Right turn!' or 'By the left – quick march!' and would tug me in the proper direction by the tail of that garment.

They were very strict lessons.

Sometimes at night my father would awaken me with the cry 'To arms!' and would drill me then and there despite the cries and sobs of my aunt. He would end by saying: 'Ignacy, be prepared, my child, for we do not know the day nor yet the hour . . . Remember that God sent the Bonapartes to put the world to rights and as long as there is no order and no justice in the world, then the Emperor's last testament will not have been carried out.'

I cannot say that my father's unshakeable trust in the Bonapartes and in justice was shared by his two comrades. Sometimes when Mr Raczek's leg hurt him, he would curse and groan and say: 'Eh, old man, you know we've been waiting too long for a new Napoleon. I'm turning grey and I'm not the man I was, and there's still no sight nor sound of him. Soon they'll turn us all into beggars at the church door, and I daresay Napoleon will join us for vespers.'

'He'll find young men.'

'What kind of young men, eh? The best of them are in their graves and the youngest are – worth nothing. Some have never even heard of Napoleon.'

'My boy has, and will remember,' said my father, winking in my direction.

Mr Domański was still more dispirited.

'The world is going to the dogs,' he declared, shaking his head. 'Food's getting more expensive, a man's wages are gobbled up in rent and even absinthe isn't what it was. In the old days a glass would set a man right, but now you need a whole tumblerful and yet you're still as empty as if you'd been drinking water. Even Napoleon himself wouldn't live to see justice done!'

To this my father would reply: 'Justice will be done even if Napoleon doesn't come. But a Napoleon will be found all the same.'

'I don't believe you,' muttered Mr Raczek.

'And what if he is found, what then?' my father asked.

'We shall not live to see that day.'

'I will,' said my father, 'and Ignacy will live still longer.'

Even then my father's phrases engraved themselves deep in my mind, but later events gave them a miraculous and almost prophetic character.

Mr Raczek visited him every day, and once – looking at his skinny hands and sunken cheeks – whispered: 'Well, old fellow, now surely we shan't live to see Napoleon?'

To this my father calmly replied: 'I'm not going to die until I hear.'

Mr Raczek nodded, and my aunt wiped away her tears and thought my father was rambling. How could they think otherwise if death was already at the door and my father was still awaiting Napoleon?

He was already very sick, had been given the last Sacraments, when Mr Raczek ran in a few days later, strangely agitated, and stopped in the centre of the room to cry: 'Do you know, old fellow, that a Napoleon has turned up?'*

'Where is he?' my aunt cried.

'He's already in France.'

My father rose, then fell back on his pillows again. Only he stretched out his hand to me and looked at me in a way I will never forget, and whispered: 'Remember! Remember everything . . .'

With that, he died.

In later life I confirmed how prophetic my father's views had been. We all saw how the second Napoleon's star rose over Italy and Hungary; and although it sank at Sedan, I do not believe it has been extinguished for ever. What is Bismarck to me, or Gambetta or Beaconsfield, for that matter? Injustice will rule the world until a new Napoleon comes.

A few months after my father's death, Mr Raczek and Mr Domański and my aunt Susanna took council together: what was to be done with me? Mr Domański wanted me to go into his office and slowly rise to a copyist; my aunt advised a trade, and Mr Raczek was all for the vegetable trade. But when they asked me what I wanted to do, I replied: 'Go into a shop.'

'Who knows if that wouldn't be for the best?' Mr Raczek commented. 'And which shop would you like to work in?'

'The one in Podwal Street, that has a sabre over the door and a Cossack in the window.'

'I know,' said my aunt. 'He means Mincel's.'

'We could try,' said Mr Domański. 'We all know Mincel.'

Mr Raczek spat into the fireplace in token of agreement.

'Good gracious,' my aunt cried, 'that booby will start spitting at me next, now that my brother is gone . . . Oh, what an unhappy orphan I am!'

'Big deal!' Mr Raczek exclaimed. 'Get married, my lady, then you won't be one . . .'

'Where shall I find anyone foolish enough to have me?'

'Hm. I might take you myself, as I've no one to rub me with alcohol,' Mr Raczek muttered, leaning heavily over to knock out his pipe.

My aunt burst into tears, then Mr Domański spoke up: 'Why make such a to-do? You've no one to care for you, and he has no housekeeper; get married and look after Ignacy, and you'll have a child ready-made. And a cheap one, too, for Mincel will give him food and lodging; you need only give him clothes.'

'Eh?' asked Mr Raczek, looking at my aunt.

'Well, get the lad apprenticed first, then . . . maybe I'll risk it,' replied my aunt. 'I've always had the feeling I'd end my days badly . . .'

'Let's be off to Mincel's' said Mr Raczek, getting up. 'But mind you don't let me down, now,' he added, shaking his fist at my aunt.

He and Mr Domański went off and returned an hour and a half later, both very red in the face. Mr Raczek was breathing heavily, and Mr Domański had some difficulty in keeping steady on his feet, probably because our stairs were awkward.

'Well?' asked my aunt.

'The new Napoleon has been thrown into prison!'* answered Mr Domański.

'Not prison, the fortress, ow . . . ow . . .' added Mr Raczek and threw his cap on the table.

'Yes, but what about the boy?' asked my aunt.

'He's to go to Mincel's tomorrow with his clothes and his linen,' said Mr Domański.

'Not in the fortress, ow . . . ow . . . but in Ham-ham . . . or is it Cham . . . I don't even know.'

'Why, you're drunk, you fools!' cried my aunt, seizing Mr Raczek by the arm.

'Listen here, no familiarities,' cried Mr Raczek, 'familiarities after the wedding, not now . . . He's to go to Mincel's tomorrow with his clothes and his linen . . . Oh dear, poor Napoleon!'

My aunt pushed Mr Raczek out of the house, then Mr Domański, and threw his cap after him.

'Be off, you tipsy boobies!'

'Long live Napoleon!' cried Mr Raczek, and Mr Domański began singing:

'Passer-by, when your eyes this way you incline,

Come closer and ponder this inscription . . .

Come closer and ponder this inscription . . .'

His voice died away slowly as if he were descending into a well, then silence fell, but that voice reached our ears again from the street. After a while there was an uproar down below, and when I looked out I saw a policeman taking Mr Raczek to the police-station.

Such were the incidents preceding my taking up the trade of shop-keeper.

I had known Mincel's shop for a long time, for my father used to send me there to buy paper, and aunt for soap. I would always hurry there with joyful curiosity to look at the toys in the window. As I recall, there was a large mechanical Cossack in one window, which jumped and waved its arms by itself, and in the doorway were a drum, a sabre and a wooden horse with a real tail.

The interior of the shop looked like a large cellar; I could never see the far end of it because of the gloom. All I know is that pepper, coffee and herbs were sold on the left, at a counter behind which huge cupboards rose from floor to ceiling. But paper, ink, plates and glasses were sold at the counter to the right, where there were glass cupboards, and for soap and washing-powder one went into the depths of the shop, where barrels and piles of wooden boxes were visible.

Even the rafters were loaded. Suspended there were long rows of bladders full of mustard seeds or paint, a huge lamp with a shade, which burned all day long in winter, a net full of corks, and finally a stuffed crocodile, nearly six feet long.

The owner of the shop was Jan Mincel, an old man with a red face and a tuft of grey hair on his chin. At all hours of the day he would sit by the window, in a leather armchair, dressed in a blue fustian robe, a white apron and a white nightcap. In front of him on a table lay a great ledger, in which he kept the accounts, and just above his head was a bunch of canes, intended mainly for sale. The old man took money, gave change, wrote in his ledger and sometimes dozed off, but despite all these tasks, he watched with unbelievable vigilance over the flow of business throughout the entire shop. From time to time, he tugged at the string of the mechanical Cossack for the diversion of passers-by in the street, and also – which pleased us least – he punished us with one of the canes for various offences.

I say 'us' because there were three candidates for corporal punishment: myself, and the old man's two nephews, Franz and Jan.

I became aware of my master's watchfulness and his skill in using the cane on the third day of work at the shop.

Franz was measuring out ten groszy-worth of raisins for a woman. Seeing that one raisin had fallen on the counter (the old man had his eyes closed at this moment), I stealthily picked it up and ate it. I was about to extricate a pit which had got between two teeth when I felt something like the heavy touch of burning iron on my back.

'You rascal!' old Mincel roared, and before I realised what was happening, he had slashed me several times from top to toe with his cane.

I coiled up with the pain, but from that time on I never dared taste anything in the shop. Almonds, raisins, even bread-rolls tasted like dust and ashes to me.

After settling matters with me in this way, the old man hung the cane up, entered the sale of raisins in his ledger and, with the most benevolent look in the world, began to tug at the Cossack by its string. Looking at his half-smiling face and blinking eyes, I could hardly believe that this jovial old gentleman had such power in his arm. And it was not until this moment that I noticed how the Cossack, seen from within the shop, looked less comical than from the street.

Our shop dealt in groceries, haberdashery and soap. The groceries were sold by Franz Mincel, a young man a little over thirty, with red hair and a sleepy face. It was he who most frequently got trouncings from his uncle, for he smoked a pipe, came to work late, disappeared from home at night and, above all, was careless about weighing out goods. However, Jan Mincel – the younger, who was in charge of the haberdashery and, apart from his clumsiness, was distinguished by the mildness of his nature, was beaten for sneaking out coloured paper and writing letters on it to young ladies.

Only August Katz, who sold the soap, never suffered any disciplinary admonition. This underfed weakling of a man was marked by his extraordinary punctuality. He came to work first, cut up the soap and weighed the soap-powder like a machine; he ate whatever was set before him, almost ashamed to betray any physical needs. At ten in the evening he disappeared.

I passed eight years in these surroundings, and each day was as similar to the next as drops of autumn rain. I rose at five, washed and swept the shop. At six I opened the main door and the window, and opened the shutters. At this moment August Katz would appear from somewhere outside, take off his top-coat, put on his apron and take his place in silence between a barrel of grey soap and a column consisting of bricks of yellow soap. Then old Mincel used to hurry in through the yard, muttering: '*Morgen!*', straighten his night-cap, take the ledger out of a drawer, sit down in his armchair and give the mechanical Cossack several tugs. Jan Mincel did not appear until afterwards, then, having kissed his uncle's hand, he would take his place at his counter, where he caught flies in summer and in winter drew figures with his finger.

They usually had to bring Franz into the shop. He came in with his eyes sleepy, yawning, kissed his uncle's hand indifferently and scratched his head all day long in a manner which might have indicated great weariness or great grief. Hardly a morning passed without his uncle, eyeing his tactics, grimacing with derision, asking him: 'Well . . . where did you go, you rascal?'

Meanwhile noises began in the street, and more and more passers-by moved along beyond the shop-window. Now a servant girl, then a woodcutter, then a gentleman in a cap, or a tailor's apprentice, or perhaps a lady wearing a cloak – they passed to and fro like figures in a moving panorama. Carriages, droshkies, carts drove down the street – to and fro . . . more and more people, more carts and carriages, until finally one great flood of traffic was flowing along, from which someone would pop into our shop from time to time on an errand: 'A twist of pepper . . .' 'A pound of coffee, please . . .' 'Rice . . .' 'A half-pound of soap . . .' 'A groszy's worth of bay leaves . . .'

Gradually the shop filled up, mainly with servant girls and poorly dressed women. Then Franz Mincel scowled the most, as he opened or shut drawers, wrapped up groceries in twists of grey paper, ran up his ladder, wrapped things, all with the dismal look of a man forbidden to yawn. Finally, so many customers collected that both Jan Mincel and I often had to help Franz out.

The old man kept writing and giving change, sometimes touching his white night-cap, the blue tassel of which hung down over one eye. Sometimes he tugged at the Cossack, and sometimes seized a cane with the speed of lightning and used it upon one of his nephews. I could rarely understand what was amiss: for his nephews were reluctant to explain the causes of his irascibility.

About eight o'clock the number of customers decreased. Then a fat servant girl would appear out of the depths of the shop with a basket containing rolls and mugs (Franz always turned his back to her), then the mother of our master, a thin old lady in a yellow dress, with a great cap on her head and a jug of coffee in her hand. Putting this vessel on the table, the old lady would squeak:

'*Gut Morgen, meine Kinder! Der Kaffee ist schon fertig . . .*'

And she would pour the coffee into the white mugs.

Old Mincel would go up and kiss her hand, with: '*Gut Morgen, meine Mutter!*'

For this, he obtained a mug of coffee and three rolls.

Then Franz Mincel went up, followed by Jan Mincel, August Katz and at the end me. Each kissed the old lady's dry hand, which was etched with blue veins, and said: '*Gut Morgen, Grossmutter!*'

And each obtained his mug and three rolls.

When we had hastily drunk the coffee, the servant girl carried away the empty basket and the mugs, the old lady her jug, and both disappeared.

The traffic was still passing by outside the window, and a crowd of people moved to and fro; from this, every now and then someone would break away to enter the shop.

'Soap-powder, please . . .' 'Ten groszy's worth of almonds . . .' 'Licorice for a grosz . . .' 'Grey soap . . .'

About midday the business at the grocery counter dropped off, but more and more customers now appeared on the right-hand side of the store, which was Jan's province. They asked for plates, glasses, irons, coffee-mills, dolls and sometimes large greenish-blue or poppy-red umbrellas. These customers, both ladies and gentlemen, were well dressed, sat down on the chairs provided, and asked to be shown a quantity of objects, as they bargained and demanded more.

I recall that when I was tired of going to and fro and of wrapping up groceries on the left-hand side of the shop, what bothered me most on the right-hand side was the thought: what does this customer really want? And does he intend to buy anything? In the end, however, a great deal was sold: the daily income from haberdashery was several times greater than that from groceries and soap.

Old Mincel was in his shop Sundays too. In the morning he said his prayers, and about midday would tell me to come to him for a sort of lesson.

'*Sag mir* – tell me: *was ist das*? What is this? *Das ist Schublade* – this is a drawer.* Look and see what is in the drawer. *Es ist Zimt* – it is cinnamon. What is cinnamon needed for? For soup, for dessert. What is cinnamon? It is bark from a certain tree. Where does the cinnamon tree grow? In India. Look at the globe – India is over here. Give me 10 groszy worth of cinnamon . . . *O, du Spitzub!* If I discipline you ten times, you will know how much cinnamon to sell for 10 groszy . . .'

We would go through each drawer in the shop and he would tell me the story of every article. When he was not tired, he would dictate problems to me and told me to add up the ledger or copy letters.

Mincel was a very orderly old man, who could not endure dust, and would wipe it off even the tiniest object. But he never needed to dust the canes, thanks to his Sunday lessons in accounting, geography and shop-keeping.

Within a few years we had become so used to each other that old Mincel could not do without me, and I even began to regard his canes as quite natural in family relationships. I remember I could not get over my remorse at smashing an expensive samovar, but instead of seizing a cane, old Mincel merely exclaimed: 'What have you done, Ignacy? What have you done?'

I would sooner have felt his cane rather than hear that quavering voice again, or see his fearful look.

Weekdays, we ate our dinners in the shop, first the two young Mincels and August Katz, then my master and I. On holidays we all gathered upstairs and sat down at the same table. Every Christmas Eve Mincel would give us gifts, and his mother used to set up a Christmas tree for us (and her son) in the utmost secrecy. On the first day of each month we were all paid our wages (I got ten zloty). On this occasion, Katz, the two nephews, the servant girl and I had to declare how much he or she had saved. Not saving, or rather not putting away even a few groszy every day was as terrible a crime as stealing in the eyes of Mincel. During my time, several clerks and a number of apprentices came and went in the store, all of whom were dismissed by my master only because they saved nothing. The day on which this came to light was their last with us. Promises, vows, kissing of hands and even falling on one's knees were of no avail. The old man did not stir from his armchair, did not look at the supplicant, only showed him the door with the single word: '*Fort!* . . . *Fort!*' The principle of saving had already grown into a mania with him.

This good man had one fault – he hated Napoleon. He himself never mentioned Napoleon, but at the sound of that name he was seized with a kind of fury: his face grew livid, he spat and shrieked, 'The rogue! *Spitzbub*! Bandit!'

On hearing such shameful words for the first time, I almost swooned away. I felt like saying something very bold to the old man, then taking refuge with Mr Raczek, who was already married to my aunt. Suddenly I saw Jan Mincel put one hand over his mouth, mutter something and grimace to Katz. I pricked up my ears and this is what Jan was saying: 'The old man is raving! Napoleon was a good fellow, even if only because he got rid of those dogs of Krauts! Isn't that so, Katz?'

And August Katz winked and went on cutting up soap.

I was astounded, but at that moment took a great liking to Jan Mincel and August Katz. Later I realised that there were two great factions in the little shop, one of which consisted of old Mincel and his mother who loved the Germans very much, while the other consisted of the young Mincels and Katz, who hated them. As I recall, I was the only neutral person.

In 1846 we heard that Louis Napoleon had escaped from captivity. This year was important to me, because I was promoted and my master, old Jan Mincel, passed away in a somewhat peculiar manner.

The business in our shop decreased that year, on account of the general uneasiness prevailing and also because my master reviled Louis Napoleon too often and too loudly. People began taking a dislike to us, and one day someone – perhaps Katz – even smashed the glass in the shop-window.

But this incident, instead of entirely alienating the public, attracted them to the shop, and for a week we had as big a turn-out as ever; it reached such a point that our neighbours envied us. But a week later, this artificial business boom again decreased and it was empty in the shop.

During my master's absence one evening, in itself an unusual event, a second stone was thrown through the glass. The Mincels in alarm took refuge upstairs and tried to find their uncle. Katz ran into the street to see who was responsible for this outrage, where-upon two policemen appeared dragging along – guess whom?

None other than my master, and they charged him with breaking the glass this time and probably the previous time, too.

The old man denied it in vain: not only had he been caught in the act, but a stone was found on his person . . . So the poor wretch was taken off to the police station.

After a great deal of explaining and talk, the matter was smoothed over naturally enough; but from this time on, the old man lost his spirit entirely and grew thin. One day, he sat in his armchair by the window, and he never rose from it again. He passed away with his chin resting on the ledger, still holding the string that moved the mechanical Cossack.

For some years, his nephews kept the shop going in Podwal Street, and not until 1850 did they split up so that Franz stayed behind with the grocery store, while Jan took the haberdashery and soap and moved to Krakowskie Przedmieście, to the shop we now occupy. A few years after this, Jan married the beautiful Małgorzata Pfeifer and when she (God rest her soul!) became a widow, she bestowed her hand in marriage upon Staś Wokulski, and in this way, he inherited the business, which had been carried on by two generations of Mincels.

My old master's mother survived a long while; when I returned from abroad in 1853, I found her still in the best of health. Every morning she would come into the shop and say: '*Gut Morgen, meine Kinder! Der Kaffee is schon fertig . . .*'

But her voice grew feebler from year to year, until it finally disappeared for ever.

In my time, a man's master was the father and teacher of his apprentices and the most vigilant servant of his shop: his mother or wife was the lady of the house, and everyone in the family worked in the shop. Today, an employer merely takes his profits and usually knows little about the shop, while he is more anxious that his children should not enter trade. I do not refer here to Staś Wokulski, who has wider views, only in general I think a tradesman ought to stick to his shop and create his own staff, if he wants them to be at all decent.

They say Andrássy* has demanded sixty million gulden for unforeseen expenses. So Austria is arming too, and yet Staś writes that there will be no war. He was never one for empty words, so he must be very well-versed in politics. So this means he is not staying in Bulgaria simply for love of business . . .

I wonder what he is doing there? How I wonder . . .

IV

The Return

I T is a wretched Sunday in March; it is nearly noon, but the streets of Warsaw are almost deserted. People stay indoors, or seek shelter in gateways, or flee hunched up before the drenching rain and snow. The rattle of droshkies is rarely heard, for they have stopped running. The drivers have got off their boxes to take refuge under the hoods of their vehicles, while the horses, soaked with rain and bespattered with snow, look as if they would only be too pleased to hide under the shafts and shelter themselves with their own ears.

Despite, or because of, the ugly weather, Ignacy is very cheerful, as he sits in his barred room. Trade is going very well, displays for the windows next week are already planned and, above all, Wokulski is due back any day. Ignacy will at last be able to hand over the accounts and the burden of managing the store, and within two months at most, he will set off on vacation. After twenty-five years of work – and such work – he deserves some respite. He will think of nothing but politics, will walk about, run and jump through fields and woods, whistle and even sing, as he did when he was young. Were it not for his rheumatism which, however, will pass in the country . . .

So, although the rain and snow beat against the window, although it pours so hard that the room is quite dark, Ignacy is in a vernal frame of mind. He takes his guitar out from beneath the bed, tunes it, plucks a few chords, and begins to sing a very romantic air . . .

'Spring is awakening everywhere in nature, greeted by the wistful song of the nightingales! In the green grove by the stream bloom two beautiful roses.'

. . . These magical sounds arouse the poodle Ir as he sleeps on the sofa, and he begins to peer at his master with his one eye. But the sounds do more than this, for they summon a great shadow in the yard, which halts by the barred window and tries to look into the room, thus attracting Ignacy's attention.

'It must be Paweł,' he thinks.

But Ir is of another mind, for he jumps up from the sofa and uneasily sniffs at the door, as if scenting someone unfamiliar.

A noise is heard in the passage. A hand seeks the doorknob, finally the door opens and on the threshold stands someone wrapped in a huge fur coat, spattered with snow and raindrops.

'Who are you?' Ignacy asks, and his face becomes flushed.

'Have you forgotten me already, old fellow?' the visitor asks quietly and slowly.

Ignacy grows confused. He puts on his eyeglasses, then lets them fall, pulls the coffin-like box from under his bed, hastily stows away the guitar and puts the box on his bed.

Meanwhile, the visitor has taken off his great fur coat and sheepskin hat. When one-eyed Ir has sniffed him, he begins to wag his tail, fawn upon him and grovel, whining joyously.

Ignacy approaches his visitor, more uneasy and bent than ever.

'Why, I believe . . .' he says, rubbing his hands together, 'I believe I have had the pleasure . . .'

Then he draws the visitor to the window, blinking at him.

'Staś! . . . For goodness sake . . .'

He claps him on his powerful shoulders, presses both his hands and finally puts his own hand on his head, with its hair cut short, as if to anoint his sinciput.

'Ha! Ha! Ha!' laughs Ignacy. ''Tis Staś himself . . . Staś back from the wars . . . What, had you forgotten your shop and your old friend?' he adds, striking him forcefully on the shoulder. 'Why, if you aren't more like a soldier or sailor than a merchant . . . He hasn't been near the shop in eight months . . . What a chest! . . . What a head! . . .'

The visitor smiled too. He grasped Ignacy by the shoulders, embraced him warmly and kissed him on the cheeks, to which the old clerk submitted, though without returning the embrace.

'What's the latest news here, old fellow?' the visitor exclaimed. 'You're thinner, paler . . .'

'On the contrary, I am putting on weight.'

'You've turned grey . . . How are you?'

'Very well. And things are going well in the shop too, we have increased the sales a little. In January and February we took twenty-five thousand roubles . . . My dear Staś! Eight months . . . But that's over and done with . . . Why don't you sit down?'

'Of course,' the visitor replied, sitting down on the sofa, upon which Ir immediately placed himself, his head on Staś's knee.

Ignacy brought up a chair.

'Something to eat? I've ham and a little caviar.'

'Very well.'

'Something to drink too? I have a bottle of reasonable Hungarian wine, but only one wine glass that is not broken.'

'I'll drink from a tumbler,' replied the visitor.

Ignacy began to scuttle around the room, opening the cupboard chest and table-drawer in turn.

He produced the wine, put it away again, then set out ham and bread on the table. His hands and cheeks were quivering and a good deal of time passed before he was sufficiently himself to get together all the provisions he had previously mentioned. Not until he had partaken of a small glass of the wine did he regain his much-shaken equilibrium.

Meanwhile, Wokulski was eating.

'Well, and what's the latest news?' asked Ignacy, in the coolest tone imaginable, tapping his visitor's knee.

'I suppose you mean in politics?' replied Wokulski. 'There will be peace.'

'Then why is Austria arming?'

'At a cost of sixty million gulden? She wants to seize Bosnia and Herzegovina.'

Ignacy opened his eyes very wide.

'Austria wants to seize . . .' he echoed. 'How so?'

'How so?' Wokulski smiled. 'Because Turkey cannot prevent her.'

'And what about England?'

'England will get compensation.'

'At Turkey's expense?'

'Of course. The weak always pay the costs of any conflict between the strong.'

'And justice?' exclaimed Ignacy.

'Justice lies in the fact that the strong multiply and increase, and the weak perish. Otherwise the world would become a charitable institution, which would indeed be unjust.'

Ignacy shifted his chair.

'How can you say such things, Staś? Seriously, joking aside . . .'

Wokulski turned his calm gaze upon him.

'Yes,' he replied. 'What is so strange in it? Doesn't the same law apply to me, to you, to all of us? . . . I've wept for myself too often to feel for Turkey . . .'

Ignacy lowered his eyes and was silent. Wokulski went on eating.

'Well, and how did things go with you?' asked Ignacy in his normal voice.

Wokulski's eyes gleamed. He put down the bread and leaned against the arm of the sofa.

'Do you remember,' he asked, 'how much money I took with me when I went abroad?'

'Thirty thousand roubles, in cash.'

'And how much do you suppose I've brought back?'

'Fifty . . . perhaps forty thousand roubles . . . Am I right?' asked Rzecki, looking at him uncertainly.

Wokulski poured a glass of wine and drank it slowly.

'Two hundred and fifty thousand roubles, mostly in gold,' he said distinctly. 'And since I told them to buy banknotes, which I'll sell when the peace is signed, I shall have over three hundred thousand roubles . . .'

Rzecki leaned towards him, his mouth open.

'Don't be alarmed,' Wokulski went on, 'I made it honestly, by hard, very hard, work. The secret was that I had a rich partner and was satisfied with four or five times less profit than others. So my capital, while continually growing, was in constant circulation. Well,' he added after a time, 'I was very lucky too . . . Like a gambler who backs the same number ten times running at roulette. High stakes? . . . nearly every month I risked my entire fortune, and my life every day.'

'Was that the only reason you went there?' Ignacy asked.

Wokulski looked at him mockingly.

'Surely you didn't expect me to turn into a Turkish Wallenrod?'*

'But to risk your neck for money, when you had a good living . . .' Ignacy muttered, shaking his head and raising his eyebrows.

Wokulski shuddered and jumped up.

'That good living,' he said, clenching his fist, 'was stifling me and had stifled me for six years . . . Don't you remember how many times a day I was reminded of the two generations of Mincels or of the angelic goodness of my late wife? Was there anyone among my closest or not so close acquaintances – except you – who did not torment me with a word, gesture or look? How often was it said of me, and almost to me, that I was tied to my wife's apron-strings, that I owed every penny to the industry of the Mincels, and nothing, nothing at all to my own efforts, though it was I who built up the shop and doubled its profits . . .

'The Mincels, it was always the Mincels! Why don't they compare me to the Mincels now? In six months I've made ten times the money that two generations of Mincels made in a half-century. A thousand Mincels in their shops and night-caps would have to sweat their hearts out to make what I've made amidst bullets, knives and typhus. Now I know how many Mincels I'm worth, and I swear I'd risk it all again for this result! I'd sooner fear bankruptcy and death than owe it to the people who buy umbrellas in my store, or than kiss the hands of people who deign to equip themselves in my store with water-closets . . .'

'You're still the same,' Ignacy murmured.

Wokulski cooled down. He put one hand on Ignacy's arm and

looked into his eyes as he mildly said: 'You're not angry, old fellow?'

'Why? As if I didn't know that a wolf doesn't look after sheep . . . Naturally enough . . .'

'What's the latest here – tell me!'

'Precisely what I told you in my reports. Business going well, goods arriving, still more orders coming in. We need another clerk.'

'We'll hire two, we'll expand the store, it will be splendid.'

'Fancy that . . .'

Wokulski glanced sideways at him and smiled to see that the old man had regained his good humour.

'But what is going on in town? Things must be going well as long as you are in the shop.'

'In the town?'

'Have any of my regular customers quit business?' Wokulski interrupted, now pacing about the room.

'No one! New ones have appeared . . .'

Wokulski stopped, as if hesitating. He poured another glass of wine and tossed it off.

'Is Łęcki buying at our store?'

'Mostly on credit . . .'

'Ah . . .' Wokulski sighed with relief. 'What is his financial position?'

'They say he's quite bankrupt and that his apartment house will be put up for auction later this year.'

Wokulski leaned over and began to play with Ir.

'Well . . . And Miss Łęcka isn't married yet?'

'No.'

'Isn't she engaged?'

'I doubt it. Who today would marry a girl with expensive tastes and no dowry? She's getting older too, though she's still pretty. Naturally enough . . .'

Wokulski straightened his back and took a deep breath. His stern face bore a strangely tender expression.

'My dear old fellow,' he said, taking Ignacy by the hand, 'my honest old friend! You can't begin to guess how glad I am to see you again, still here in this room. Do you recall how many evenings and nights I've spent here? . . . how you used to give me dinner . . . how you gave me clothes . . . Remember?'

Rzecki looked at him attentively and thought the wine must have been good to unlock Wokulski's lips so.

Wokulski sat down on the sofa, leaned his head against the wall, and spoke as if to himself: 'You've no idea what I suffered, far away from everyone, never knowing whether I should ever see them again, so terribly alone. For, don't you see, the worst loneliness is not the one that surrounds a man, but the emptiness within himself, when he has not carried away with him even a warm look or a friendly word or spark of hope from his homeland . . .'

Ignacy shifted on his chair, to protest: 'Allow me to remind you that at first I wrote very friendly letters, perhaps even excessively sentimental ones . . . Your brief replies upset me.'

'Am I blaming you?'

'No, but you can blame the others still less, for they don't know you as I do.'

Wokulski looked up.

'I don't bear any resentment against them. Perhaps – a trifle – towards you, because you used to write so very little about . . . the town. Besides, the newspapers were often lost in the post, there were gaps in the news and I was tormented by awful forebodings.'

'Of what? There was no war here!' Ignacy replied in amazement.

'That's so . . . You even managed to divert yourselves very well, as I recall. You had splendid tableaux in December. Who took part in them?'

'Well, I don't go to such nonsense.'

'That's so. But I'd have given – oh, ten thousand roubles, just to see them. How absurd! Isn't it?'

'Certainly, though loneliness and boredom explain a good deal . . .'

'Perhaps yearning too,' Wokulski interrupted. 'It poisoned my every free moment, my every hour of rest. Pour me some wine, Ignacy.'

He drank it, again began to walk about the room and speak in a stifled voice: 'It came upon me first during a passage across the Danube that lasted from dusk till late at night. I was alone, with only a gipsy guide. We could not talk, so I watched the scenery. In that place, I saw sandbanks just like those here. Then it occurred to me that I was so far away from home that the only link between myself and all of you were these stars, but that probably none of you were looking at them at that moment, no one was thinking of me, no one! . . . I felt as though torn asunder, and not until that moment did I realise how deep was the wound in my soul . . .'

'Truly, the stars have never interested me,' Ignacy whispered.

'From that day on, I suffered a strange sickness,' Wokulski said. 'As long as I was writing letters, doing accounts, inspecting goods, dispatching my agents or watching out for thieves, I had relative calm of mind. But when I tore myself away from business, and even when I momentarily laid down my pen, I felt a pain – do you understand me, Ignacy? – as if there were grit in my heart. It became so that I'd walk about, eat, talk, think reasonably, look at the scenery, even laugh and be cheerful, yet all the time I'd feel this dull pain, this uneasiness, this interminable disquiet . . .

'This chronic state, indescribably agonising, was blown into a tempest by the slightest circumstance. A tree of familiar outline, some rocky hill, the colour of a cloud or flight of a bird, even a breath of wind, with no other reason, woke such insane despair within me that I fled from other people. I sought out a solitary refuge to fall to the ground and howl like a dog, unheard by anyone . . .

'Sometimes, in this flight from myself, night would overtake me. Then dark shadows with sunken eyes would appear to me in the undergrowth, among the fallen tree-trunks, and would shake their heads sorrowfully. And all the rustling leaves, the distant noise of carts passing by, the trickling water would blend into one mournful voice, which asked: "Passer-by, what has become of you?"

'Yes, what had become of me? . . .'

'I don't understand,' Ignacy interrupted. 'What sort of madness was it?'

'Yearning . . .'

'For what?'

Wokulski shivered.

'Well, for everything . . . for home . . .'

'Why didn't you come back home, then?'

'What would my return have meant? . . . Anyhow, I couldn't.'

'You could not?' Ignacy echoed.

'I could not – and *basta*! I had nothing to return for,' Wokulski replied impatiently. 'It was all the same whether I died here or there . . . more wine!' he finished suddenly, reaching out his hand.

Rzecki looked at his feverish face and drew the bottle out of reach.

'Let it be – you're excited enough as it is.'

'That's why I want to drink . . .'

'And that is why you should not drink,' Ignacy interrupted. 'You are talking too much . . . perhaps more than you would have wished,' he added, emphatically.

Wokulski drew back. He reflected, then answered with a shake of the head: 'You are wrong.'

'I'll prove it to you,' said Ignacy in a stifled voice, 'You didn't go abroad merely to make a fortune . . .'

'Of course not,' said Wokulski, after a pause.

'For what use are three hundred thousand roubles to you, when a thousand is ample for a year?'

'That is so.'

Rzecki approached his lips to Wokulski's ear.

'What's more . . . you didn't bring this money back for yourself.'

'Who knows but what you're right?'

'I guess a great deal more than you may think.'

Suddenly Wokulski laughed.

'Aha, so that's what you think?' he exclaimed. 'I assure you, you old dreamer, that you know nothing.'

'I fear your sobriety, which makes you talk like a madman. Do you understand me, Staś?'

Wokulski went on laughing.

'You're right, I'm not used to drink and the wine has gone to my head. But I've collected myself now. I'll tell you simply that you are mistaken. And now, to spare me becoming tipsy, drink up – to the success of my plans.'

Ignacy poured a glass, and pressing Wokulski's hand firmly said: 'To the success of your great plan!'

'Great to me, but in reality very humble.'

'So be it,' said Ignacy. 'I'm so old I prefer to know no more. I'm so old that I only want a decent death. Give me your word that when that time comes . . .'

'When that time comes, you'll be my best man.'

'I already was, once – and unhappily,' said Ignacy.

'With the widow Mincel, seven years ago?'

'Fifteen years ago.'*

'Yes, you're still the same as ever,' laughed Wokulski.

'So are you. To the success of your plans, then. Whatever they may be, I know one thing they must be worthy of you. And now – I say no more . . .'

At this, Ignacy drank his wine and threw the glass to the floor. It shattered with a crash which awoke Ir.

'Let's go into the shop,' said Ignacy. 'There are conversations after which it is good to talk business.'

He took the key and they went out. In the passageway wet snow engulfed them. Rzecki opened the door and lit some gas-jets.

'What a fine display,' Wokulski exclaimed. 'Surely everything is new?'

'Almost everything. You'd like to see . . . This porcelain. Pray observe . . .'

'Later. Give me the ledger.'

'Income?'

'No, the debtors.'

Rzecki opened the bureau, took out the ledger and drew up a chair. Wokulski sat down and glanced down the list of names, seeking one name in it.

'A hundred and forty roubles,' he read aloud. 'Well, that is not a great deal.'

'Who's that?' Ignacy inquired. 'Ah – Łęcki.'

'Miss Łęcka has an account too . . . very good,' Wokulski continued, peering at the page as if the writing were indistinct. 'Hm . . . hm . . . the day before yesterday she bought a purse . . .

Three roubles? . . . Surely you overcharged her?'

'Not at all,' said Ignacy. 'It was a first-rate purse, I picked it out myself.'

'What kind was it?' Wokulski asked carelessly, as he closed the ledger.

'One of these. Look, how elegant . . .'

'She must have deliberated a great deal among them . . . She is said to be very particular in her tastes.'

'Not at all, why should she deliberate?' Ignacy replied. 'She looked at this one . . .'

'This one . . .'

'And wanted to take that one . . .'

'Ah, that one . . .' Wokulski whispered, taking it up.

'But I suggested another, in this style.'

'This is a nice piece of work, all the same.'

'The one I chose was still finer!'

'I like this one very much. You know . . . I'll take it myself, for mine is quite worn out . . .'

'Wait, I'll pick you a better one,' Rzecki exclaimed.

'Never mind. Show me other things, perhaps something else will come in useful.'

'Cuff-links? A tie, galoshes, an umbrella . . . ?'

'I'll take an umbrella . . . and a tie. Choose them yourself. I'll be your only customer, and will pay cash.'

'A very good method,' Rzecki said, pleased. He rapidly took a tie out from a drawer and an umbrella from the window and handed them to Wokulski with a smile. 'With your discount,' he said, 'as trade, you owe seven roubles. An excellent umbrella . . . Goodness me . . .'

'Let us go back to your room,' said Wokulski.

'Won't you look around the shop?'

'Ah, what concern is . . . ?'

'Your own shop, this fine shop, of no concern to you?' Ignacy asked in surprise.

'How can you suppose that? . . . But I'm rather tired.'

'Of course,' said Rzecki, 'you're right. Let us go.'

He turned out the lights and closed the shop, letting Wokulski go first. In the passage, they met the wet snow again, and Paweł bringing dinner.

V

The Democratisation of a Gentleman and Dreams of a Society Lady

MR TOMASZ Łęcki, his only daughter Izabela and his cousin Flora, did not live in their own house, but rented an apartment of eight rooms near Aleje Ujazdowskie. There he had a drawing-room with three windows, his study, his daughter's boudoir, a bedroom for himself, a bedroom for his daughter, a dining room, a room for Flora and a dressing-room, not to mention the kitchen and quarters for servants, who consisted of the old butler Mikołaj, his wife, the cook, and a maid, Anna.

The apartment had many advantages. It was dry, warm, spacious, light. It had marble stairs, gas, electric bells and taps. Each room could be linked with the others if required, or form an entity by itself. The furniture was adequate, neither too much nor too little, and each piece was distinguished by comfortable simplicity rather than striking ostentation. The sideboard made one feel certain that the silver would not disappear; the beds brought to mind well-deserved repose; the table might groan, and the chairs could be sat on without fear of their collapsing, while anyone might doze in the armchairs.

Anyone who entered moved about freely: no one needed to fear that something would get in the way, or that he might break something. No one was bored while waiting for the master of the house, for he was surrounded by things well worth looking at. All in all, the sight of antique objects still able to serve several more generations instilled a solemn mood in the beholder.

Its inhabitants stood out against this background.

Mr Tomasz Łęcki was a man of over sixty, not tall, but stout, full-blooded. He wore a small white moustache, his hair was white and brushed upwards. He had grey, understanding eyes, an upright posture and walked briskly. People made way for him in the street, and simple people said: 'He must be a real gentleman . . .'

And it was true that Mr Łęcki could number whole crowds of senators in his family. His father had owned millions of roubles, and he himself, when young, had had thousands. Later, however, a part of his fortune had been engulfed by political events, and the rest by travelling in Europe and mixing in high society. Before 1870, Mr Łęcki had been in attendance at the Court of France, then at the court in Vienna and in Rome. Charmed by the beauty of Łęcki's daughter, Victor Emmanuel had honoured him with friendship and even wished to bestow the title of Count upon him. It is understandable, therefore, that Mr Łęcki wore mourning crêpe on his hat for two months after the death of that amiable monarch.

But for some years now Mr Łęcki had not left Warsaw, for he no longer had the money to sparkle in royal Courts. But his apartment became a gathering-place for the elegant world and remained so until a rumour began to spread to the effect that Tomasz had lost not only his fortune but also Izabela's dowry.

The first to withdraw were the marrying men, then the ladies with plain daughters, whereupon Mr Tomasz himself broke with the rest and restricted his acquaintance exclusively to members of his family. But when he saw a coolness here too, he withdrew entirely from society and even (to the dismay of many worthy persons), as an owner of a tenement house in Warsaw, joined the merchants' social club. They wanted to make him president, but he declined.

But his daughter went on frequenting the home of the old Countess Karolowa and a few of the latter's female friends, and this in itself started the rumour that Tomasz still had his fortune and that he had quit society partly through eccentricity, partly to find out who his true friends were, and to choose for his daughter a husband who would love her for herself and not for her dowry.

So once again a crowd of admirers began to gather around Miss Łęcki, and piles of visiting cards lay on the little table in her boudoir. Visitors were not received, however, but this did not arouse much annoyance, for a third rumour now started, to the effect that Łęcki's house was to be put up for auction.

At this, confusion prevailed in society. Some vowed that Mr Łęcki was bankrupt, others were ready to swear that he had merely concealed his fortune to assure the happiness of his only child. Marriageable men and their relatives were agonisingly uncertain. Neither to risk anything nor to lose anything, they paid their tributes to Miss Izabela without involving themselves too much, and quietly left cards at her home, praying they would not be invited there before the situation had cleared.

There was no question of Mr Łęcki paying return visits. People explained this as due to his eccentricity and grief over the death of Victor Emmanuel.

Meanwhile Mr Łęcki walked in Aleje Ujazdowskie every day and played whist at the club in the evenings. His expression was always so tranquil, his attitude so haughty, that the admirers of his daughter lost their heads entirely. The most sensible of them waited, but the boldest began once more to bestow upon her their veiled glances, their quiet sighs or a trembling pressure of the hand, to which the young lady responded with an icy, often contemptuous indifference.

Izabela was an uncommonly pretty woman. Everything about her was original and perfect. More than average in height, a very shapely figure, copious blonde hair with an ash tint, a straight nose, a somewhat supercilious mouth, pearly teeth, ideal hands and feet. Her eyes were especially impressive, being sometimes dark and dreamy, sometimes full of light and merriment, or sometimes clear blue and as cold as ice.

The play of her features was striking. When she spoke, her lips, brows, nostrils, hands, her whole figure seemed to speak too – and above all her eyes spoke, and seemed to want to pour out her soul into that of her interlocutor. When she listened, she seemed to long to drink up the speaker's soul. Her eyes knew how to fondle, caress, weep without tears, to burn and freeze. Sometimes one would think she was about to put her arms around someone and lean her head on his shoulder: but when the fortunate man melted in delight, she would suddenly make a gesture which said she was not to be caught, for she would either disappear or thrust him away, or simply tell a footman to turn her admirer out of doors . . .

Izabela's soul was a curious phenomenon.

If anyone had asked her point-blank what this world is, and what she herself was, she would certainly have replied that the world is an enchanted garden full of magical castles, and that she herself was a goddess or nymph imprisoned in a body.

From her cradle, Izabela had lived in a beautiful world that was not only superhuman but even supernatural. For she slept in feathers, dressed in silks and satins, sat on carved and polished ebony or rosewood, drank from crystal, ate from silver and porcelain as costly as gold.

The seasons of the year did not exist for her, only an everlasting spring full of soft light, living flowers and perfumes. The times of day did not exist for her either, since for whole months at a time she would go to bed at eight in the morning and dine at two at night. There was no difference in geographical location, since in Paris, Vienna, Rome, Berlin or London she would find the same people, the same manners, the same objects and even the same food – soups from Pacific seaweed, oysters from the North Sea, fish from the Atlantic or Mediterranean, animals from every country, fruits from all parts of the globe. For her, even the force of gravity did not exist, since her chairs were placed for her, plates were handed, she herself was driven in carriages through the streets, conducted inside, helped upstairs.

A veil shielded her from the wind, a carriage from the rain, furs from the cold, a parasol and gloves from the sun. And thus she lived from day to day, month to month, year to year, above other people and even above the laws of nature. Twice in her life she experienced a terrible storm, once in the Alps, later in the Mediterranean. The bravest shrank in terror, but Izabela smiled as she listened to the thunder of the battering waves and the shuddering of the boat, never even considering the danger. Nature was staging a splendid spectacle for her, with thunderbolts, waves and chaos, just as on another occasion it had shown her the moon over the Lake of Geneva, or had drawn aside clouds veiling the sun over a Rhine waterfall. For mechanics in the theatre did the same every day, and even nervous ladies were not alarmed.

This world of everlasting spring, where silks rustled, only sculptured trees grew and where clay was covered with artistic paintings – this world had its own population. Its proper inhabitants were princesses and princes, dukes and duchesses and very old and wealthy aristocrats of both sexes. It also included wealthy women and married men who played hosts, matrons who watched over elegant manners and behaviour, and elderly gentlemen who took their place at the top table, spoke kindly to young people, blessed them and played cards. There were also bishops, the likenesses of God in this world, high officials whose presence protected this world from disturbances and earthquakes, and finally there were children, little angels sent from Heaven so that their elders could arrange Kinderbale.

Amidst the permanent population of this enchanted world an ordinary mortal would sometimes appear, who had succeeded in reaching the heights of Olympus on the wings of fame. He might be an engineer who had linked two oceans or drilled through mountains, or a captain who had lost his entire company in a battle with savages and, although gravely wounded, had himself been spared by the love of a Negro princess. He might be a traveller who was said to have discovered a new part of the globe, had been shipwrecked on a desert island and even tasted human flesh.

There were also eminent painters and in particular there were inspired poets who wrote charming verses in the albums of the princesses, poets who might fall hopelessly in love and render the charms of their cruel goddess immortal, first in the newspapers then in slim volumes printed on vellum.

All these people, among whom there carefully moved a crowd of uniformed footmen, female companions, poor cousins and relatives seeking promotion – all these people were on a permanent holiday.

From midday they visited one another and returned visits, or drove to the shops. In the evenings, they amused themselves before, at and after dinner. Then they drove to a concert or the theatre, there to see another artificial world, in which heroes rarely ate or worked, but frequently talked to themselves, where the infidelity of a woman caused tremendous catastrophes and where a lover, slain by the husband in Act Five, would rise from the dead next day to perpetrate the same mistakes and talk to himself without being heard by the person standing next to him. On leaving the theatre, they gathered in drawing-rooms again, and servants carried cold or warm drinks about, artistes sang, young married ladies listened to the wounded captain talk about his Negro princess, unmarried young ladies talked to the poets about affinities of the soul, elderly gentlemen gave the engineers their views on engineering and middle-aged ladies fought one another with hints and glances for the sake of the traveller who had eaten human flesh. Then they sat down to supper, at which mouths ate, stomachs digested and little shoes under the table talked about the feelings of frozen hearts and the dreams of unfeeling heads. Then they would separate, to regain their strength for the dream of life in real sleep.

Outside this enchanted world was yet another world – the ordinary one.

Izabela knew of its existence, and even liked gazing at it from the window of her carriage or boudoir. Framed thus, and at a distance, that world seemed picturesque, even charming. She saw farm labourers slowly ploughing the earth, great wagons drawn by broken-down nags, hawkers of fruit and vegetables, an old man breaking stones at the roadside, messengers hurrying by, pretty and impudent flower-girls, a family consisting of father, stout mother and four little children holding hands in pairs, a dandy of the lower world travelling in a droshky and behaving quite absurdly – and sometimes a funeral. And she told herself that this world, though inferior, was charming; it was even more charming than paintings of low life, for it moved and changed.

And Izabela also knew that just as flowers bloomed in hot-houses and vines in vineyards, so things necessary to her grew in that inferior world. It was from that world that loyal Mikołaj and the maid Anna came, it was there that people made carved chairs, porcelain, crystal and curtains, it was there that polishers, upholsterers, gardeners and the girls who made her dresses were born. Once in a modiste's, she had asked to be shown the tailoring shop and it was so interesting to see a dozen girls cutting, tacking and fitting garments on busts. She was certain this gave them great pleasure, for the girls who took her measurements were always smiling and so anxious that the dress be well cut. And Izabela knew that in that inferior world there existed some people who happened to be unhappy. So she gave instructions that any poor person she met should be given a few złoty. Once, meeting a poor woman with a child as pale as wax at her breast, Izabela gave her a bracelet of her own, while she always bestowed sweets on beggar-children and kissed them piously. For it seemed to her that Christ might be hidden in one of these poor people, or perhaps in each one of them, and they had crossed her path so she might have the opportunity of doing a good deed.

On the whole she felt benevolent towards the people of this inferior world. The words of the Bible came to her mind: 'thou shalt labour in the sweat of thy brow,' and obviously they had committed some grave sin, since they were condemned to labour. Angels such as she could not but pity their fate. Such as she, whose greatest labour was that of touching an electric bell or giving an order.

Once only did that inferior world make a powerful impression upon her.

She visited an iron foundry in France one day. While travelling down from the mountains into a region of woods and fields under a sapphire sky, she saw an abyss of black smoke and white steam, and heard the dull rattling, creak and hiss of machinery. Then she saw the foundries, like the towers of medieval castles breathing flame, powerful wheels that revolved as fast as lightning, great scaffolds that moved on rails, streams of molten iron glowing white, and half-naked labourers like bronze statues with sombre expressions. Over it all was a blood-red glow, the sound of rumbling wheels, bellows panting, the thundering of hammers and impatient breathing of furnaces, and underfoot the terrified earth trembled.

Then it seemed to Izabela that she had descended from the heights of Olympus into the hopeless chasms of Vulcan, where the Cyclops were forging thunderbolts that might shatter Olympus itself. She recalled legends of rebellious giants, of the end of this splendid world of hers, and for the first time she the goddess, before whom senators and marshals bowed their heads, was afraid.

'These are terrible people, papa,' she whispered to her father.

He did not say a word, but pressed her arm more closely.

'Surely they won't harm a woman?'

'No, not even they,' Tomasz replied.

Then Izabela was ashamed to think she was only concerned about herself, and she hastily added: 'If they won't harm a woman, they won't harm you either . . .'

Mr Łęcki smiled and shook his head. At the time much was being said of the coming end of the old world, and Mr Łęcki felt this particularly, for he was experiencing great difficulty in extracting funds from his agents.

This visit to the iron foundry was an important epoch in Izabela's life. Piously she read the poem by a distant cousin of hers, Zygmunt, and thought that she had this day found an appropriate illustration to his 'Un-Divine Comedy'.* From this time on, she often dreamed at twilight that the bastions of the Holy Trinity Fortress stood on that sunlit mountain from which her carriage had driven down to the iron foundry, and that the rebel democrats had their encampment in the valley below, veiled in smoke and steam, ready to set out to storm and overthrow her beautiful world.

Only now did she realise how much she loved her spiritual homeland, where crystal chandeliers replaced the sun, carpets the earth, statues and columns the trees. This other homeland included the aristocracy of all nations, the elegance of every age and the finest blessings of civilisation.

And was all this to collapse and perish, perhaps be scattered to the winds? . . . These elegant young men who sang with such feeling, danced delightfully, would fight a duel for a smile or jump headlong into a lake for a flower? And all these charming girls who gave her thousands of caresses, or confided so many little secrets in her or who wrote such very long letters in which sensitive feelings were mingled with very dubious spelling – were they all to perish too?

And the servants who behaved as though they had sworn undying love, loyalty and obedience to their masters? And the modistes who always greeted her with smiles and could remember the smallest details of her toilettes, who knew all about her triumphs in society? And the noble horses, whose flight a swallow might envy, and the clever dogs, just as attached as people, and the gardens where human hands had raised hills, poured streams, fashioned trees? . . . Was all this to vanish?

These thoughts gave Izabela's face another expression – one of tranquil sorrow, which made her still more lovely. People said she had quite grown up now.

Understanding quite well that the great world is a superior world, Izabela slowly learned that people could only attain these heights and remain there with the help of two wings – those of birth and wealth. And birth and wealth were associated with certain chosen families, like the flower and fruit of the orange tree. It was also very likely that the good God, seeing two souls with celebrated names linked in the bonds of holy matrimony, would increase their income and also send them a little angel to look after, who would in due course carry on the eminence of the family by his virtues, good manners and beauty. Hence the duty of making sensible marriages, of which old ladies and gentlemen were the best informed. A proper choice of name and fortune meant everything. For love – not the wild love poets dream of, but genuine Christian love – appears only after the Sacrament, and it is quite enough if the wife knows how to behave prettily at home, and if the husband accompanies her ceremonially into society.

Thus it had been in the past and it had been good, according to all the matrons. But today this principle had been forgotten, and things were bad: misalliances were increasing, and the great families were in decline.

'And there is no happiness in marriage,' Izabela added quietly, for young ladies had imparted not a few of their domestic secrets to her.

As a result of these tales, she had acquired a great horror of marriage, and a slight contempt for men.

For a husband in his dressing-gown, yawning in his wife's presence, kissing her with a mouth still tainted with cigar smoke, often exclaiming 'Oh, let me be . . .' or even 'You're a fool!', who makes a scene at home over a new hat but will spend his money away from home on carriages for an actress – this is not at all an attractive creature. What was worse, every one of these men before his marriage had been a warm admirer of his lady, had wasted away if unable to see her, had blushed when they met and more than one had even threatened to shoot himself for love of her.

So, at the age of eighteen, Izabela knew how to tyrannise men with her coldness. When Victor Emmanuel kissed her hand one day, she told her father she wished to leave Rome at once. In Paris, a wealthy French duke had proposed marriage; she replied that she was Polish, and would not marry a foreigner. She rejected a Podolian magnate with the remark that she would only yield her hand to a man she loved, and that he had not yet appeared, while she rejected the proposals of an American millionaire with a burst of laughter.

Within a few years, this behaviour had created a desert around Izabela. She was admired and adored, but from a distance; no one wanted to risk a mocking refusal.

When her first distaste had passed, Izabela realized that marriage must be accepted as it is. She was already determined to marry, but on condition that she liked her future husband, that he had a good name and appropriate fortune. And she often met handsome men, wealthy and titled; unfortunately none of them combined the three conditions, so – more years passed.

Suddenly rumour had it that Mr Łęcki's affairs were in a deplorable state, and Izabela found herself with only two suitors remaining from a whole battalion: these were a certain Baron and a certain marshal, both of them wealthy but old.

Now Izabela saw the ground was slipping away from beneath her feet, so she decided to lower her standards. But since the Baron and the marshal, in spite of their fortunes, aroused an unconquerable aversion in her, she postponed her final choice from one day to the next. Meanwhile, Mr Łęcki had quit society. The marshal could not wait for a reply and left for his country estate, while the heartbroken Baron went abroad – and Miss Izabela remained entirely alone. Of course, she knew that either of them would return if she summoned him, but which was she to choose, how could she stifle her aversion? What concerned her most of all, though, was whether it was possible to make such a sacrifice as this without any assurance that one day she might again acquire a fortune and would again be free to make her own choice. This time she would make her choice fully realising how difficult it was for her to live outside drawing-room society . . .

One thing greatly facilitated her marriage for rank. The fact was that Izabela had never been in love. This was due to her cold nature, and her belief that marriage survives with no poetic adjuncts, and finally an ideal love, the most extraordinary ever heard of.

Once in an art gallery, she had seen a statue of Apollo, which made such a strong impression upon her that she bought a fine copy, and had it placed in her boudoir. She would gaze at it for hours, would think of him . . . and who can tell how many kisses had warmed the hands and feet of the marble god? And a miracle came to pass: caressed by a loving woman, the clay had come to life. When one night she went to sleep weeping, the immortal stepped down from his pedestal and came to her in a laurel wreath, gleaming with a mystic glow.

He sat on the edge of her bed, gazed at her with eyes from which eternity looked out, then took her in his powerful embrace and brushed away her tears and cooled her fever with kisses from his pallid lips.

Henceforward he visited her more and more often, and as she swooned in his embraces, the god of light would whisper to her secrets of heaven and earth which had never before been uttered by a human tongue. And for love of her he wrought a still greater miracle, for his heavenly likeness was revealed to her in the features of men who at any time had made an impression on her.

Once he resembled a general (somewhat younger), who had won a battle and gazed upon the deaths of thousands of warriors. On another occasion he reminded her of the features of a celebrated tenor, to whom women threw flowers and whose carriage had been unharnessed by a crowd. Then he was a witty and handsome prince of the blood, a member of one of the oldest ruling families; or he was a brave fireman who won the Légion d'honneur for saving three persons from the fifth floor; or he was a great painter who had startled the world with the scope of his imagination; and sometimes he was a Venetian gondolier, or a circus acrobat of great charm and strength.

For a while, each of these men had captured Izabela's secret thoughts, to each of them she had devoted the most silent of sighs, knowing that for one reason or another she could not love him – and each had appeared to her in the shape of the god, in dreams that were half-real. From these visions, Izabela's eyes took on a new expression – a supernatural brooding. Sometimes her eyes would gaze far above other people, and beyond this world; and when the golden and ash-coloured hair on her temples was disordered, as if dishevelled by a mysterious breath, then the observers seemed to behold an angel or saint.

A year earlier, at one such moment, Wokulski had seen Izabela. From that time onward his heart had known no peace.

Almost simultaneously, Tomasz had broken with society and joined the merchants' club as a sign of his revolutionary sympathies. He used to play whist there with persons he had formerly despised, such as tanners, brush-makers and distillers, telling all and sundry that the aristocracy had no right to wall themselves up in exclusive society, but should lead the way for the enlightened bourgeois and, through them, for the whole nation. In return, the tanners, brush-makers and distillers all agreed that Mr Łęcki was the one aristocrat who was carrying out his duties towards the country, and doing so in a conscientious manner. They might have added daily, from nine in the evening till midnight.

While Mr Łęcki thus shouldered the burden of his position, Izabela passed her time in the solitude and silence of her fine apartment. Sometimes Mikołaj would be dozing in an armchair, Flora fast asleep with her ears plugged with cotton-wool, yet sleep would not come to Izabela's boudoir, it was driven away by memories. And she would rise from her bed to pace for hours, wearing only a light robe, through the drawing-room where the carpet deadened her steps and the only light was that of two dim street-lamps.

As she paced about the great room, her mournful thoughts gathered about her, and she saw a procession of all the people who had ever been there. Here the old Countess was nodding her head; two duchesses were inquiring from a prelate whether or not a child might be christened with rose water? A swarm of young men cast longing glances upon her or attempted to arouse her interest by feigned coldness; a garland of young ladies caressed her with their gaze, admiring or envying. The room seemed full of lights, rustling silks, conversations, and the greater part, like butterflies around a flower, framed Izabela's beauty. Wherever she was, everything else paled; other women were her background, and men her slaves.

Yet all this had passed . . . and today it was cold, dark, empty in the drawing-room . . . There was only herself and that invisible spider of sorrow, which always spins its grey web in those places where we have been happy and from which happiness has fled. Has fled! . . . Izabela pressed her hands together to stifle the tears of which she was ashamed even in solitude and at night.

The Doll

They had all deserted her, except Countess Karolowa who, whenever she was in a bad temper, would come and spread her skirts over the sofa to sigh and preach: 'Yes, Bela dear – you must admit you have made some quite unforgivable blunders. I'm not referring to Victor Emmanuel, for that was but the fleeting caprice of a king – a rather liberal king, too, and anyhow he was terribly in debt. For relationships such as that one needs – I won't say "tact", but experience,' the Countess went on, modestly casting down her eyes. 'But to let slip – or, if you prefer it, reject – the Duke of St Auguste – my dear! A young man, wealthy, very well thought of, and with such a promising career before him . . . Only now he's leading a deputation to the Holy Father and will certainly obtain a special benediction for the whole family . . . and Prince Chambord calls him *cher cousin* . . . Oh, my dear!'

'I think it is too late to regret anything now, aunt,' Izabela put in.

'Do you suppose I want to upset you, poor child? As it is, misfortunes lie in store for you which only profound faith can alleviate. You probably know that your father has lost everything, even what was left of your dowry?'

'What can I do?'

'But only you can help him, and so you should,' said the Countess emphatically. 'Admittedly the marshal is not an Adonis, but . . . if one's duties were easy to carry out, there would be no need for self-sacrifice. Anyhow, my dear, who can stop us from having some ideal in the depths of our hearts, the thought of which can sweeten the most difficult times? Finally, I can assure you that the position of a pretty woman with an old husband is by no means the worst imaginable. Everyone takes an interest in her, they all talk about her, pay tribute to her devotion and yet again an old husband is less demanding than one of middle age.'

'But, aunt . . .'

'No exaltation, Bela, if you please! You are not sixteen any longer and must take life seriously. You cannot, after all, sacrifice your father's very existence, not to mention that of Flora and your servants for a mere whim! Finally, do remember how much good you – with your noble heart – might do in controlling a large fortune.'

'But, aunt – the marshal is hideous. It isn't a wife he needs, but a nursemaid to wipe his mouth for him . . .'

'I don't insist on the marshal, but the Baron . . .'

'The Baron is still older, he paints his face and there are revolting marks on his hands.'

The Countess rose from the sofa.

'I don't insist, my dear, I am no match-maker; leave that to Mrs Meliton. I merely wish to point out that disaster is hanging over your father's head.'

'We still have the house.'

'Which they will sell by midsummer so that even your share will decrease.'

'How so? . . . A house that cost a hundred thousand to be sold for sixty thousand?'

'It's not worth more, your father spent too much on it. I know this from the builder who surveyed it for the Baroness Krzeszowska.'

'But we still have the dinner-service and silver,' Izabela exclaimed, wringing her hands.

The Countess kissed her several times.

'My dear, dear child,' she said with a sob, 'to think I must hurt you so . . . Listen to me! Your father still has debts in the form of bills of exchange – several thousand roubles. But these debts – mind this – these bills have been bought up by someone – a few days ago, at the end of March. We think it may have been Krzeszowska . . .'

'How vile!' Izabela whispered. 'But less of this . . . My dinner-service and the silver will cover these few thousand roubles.'

'They are worth far more, but who will buy such costly things nowadays?'

'In any case, I will try,' said the feverish Izabela. 'I'll ask Mrs Meliton to handle it for me . . .'

'Just think, though – is it not a pity to dispose of such fine heirlooms?'

Izabela laughed.

'Ah, aunt – so I am to hesitate between selling myself and the dinner-service? For I should never permit our furniture to be taken away . . . Ah, that Krzeszowska . . . buying up father's bills of exchange . . . how monstrous!'

'Well, perhaps it was not she.'

'So some other enemy has turned up, worse than Krzeszowska?'

'Perhaps it was Aunt Honorata,' the Countess soothed her. 'I don't know. Perhaps she wants to help Tomasz by threatening him. But goodbye, dear child, adieu . . .'

At this point the conversation ceased; it had been in Polish, copiously ornamented with French, which made it resemble a face disfigured by a rash.

VI

How New People Appear on the Old Horizon

IT IS the beginning of April, one of those months which bridge winter and spring. The snow has already gone, but green leaves have not yet appeared; the trees are black, the grass-plots grey and the sky grey as marble cut across with silver and gilt veins.

It is about five in the afternoon. Izabela is in her boudoir, reading Zola's latest novel, *A Page of Love*. She reads inattentively, every now and then raising her eyes to gaze out of the window, half-consciously thinking that the branches of the trees are black and the sky grey. Then she reads on, or looks round the boudoir and half-consciously thinks that her furniture, covered with that sky-blue material, and her blue gown have a sort of greyish tinge, and that the loops of the white curtains are like great icicles. Then she forgets what she was thinking and wonders: 'What was I thinking of? . . . Ah, the Easter collection . . .' Then suddenly she feels like taking a carriage drive, and at the same time regrets that the sky is so grey, that its gilded veins are so narrow . . . She is tormented by almost imperceptible uneasiness and expectancy, but is not sure what it is she is waiting for: whether for the clouds to part, or for the footman to come in with a letter inviting her to take part in the Easter collection. It is very soon now, but she has not yet been invited to take part.

She goes on with the novel, that chapter when Mr Rambaud repairs little Joanne's broken doll one starry night, when Helene melts into futile tears and Father Jouve advises her to marry. Izabela shares Helene's grief and who knows whether, if stars instead of clouds had been in the sky, she too might have burst into tears at this moment? After all, it is but a few days to the Easter collection, and they still have not invited her to take part. She knew she would be invited, but why the delay.

'Those women who seem to seek God so feverishly, are sometimes unhappy beings whose hearts are shattered by passion. They attend church to adore a man there,' says Father Jouve.

'The good priest wanted so much to calm poor Helene,' thought Izabela, and suddenly threw the book aside. Father Jouve has reminded her that for two months she has been embroidering a sash for a church bell, and has not yet finished it. She rises and draws a small table with embroidery frame and box of silks to the window, unwinds the sash and begins feverishly to embroider it with roses and crosses. Calmed by her work, she feels more courageous. No one who serves the Church as she does will be forgotten at the Easter collection. She chooses silks, threads, needles, and continues to sew. Her eye goes from pattern to material, her hands rise and fall, but in her thoughts the question of her dress for the collection and her toilette for Easter begins to arise. This question soon fills her attention entirely, she blinds her eyes and stops her hand. Her dress, hat, cloak and parasol must all be new, but there is so little time left, they are not even ordered, let alone chosen!

Here she recalls that her dinner-service and the silver are already at the jewellers, already a buyer may be considering them and today or tomorrow they will be sold. Izabela feels a constriction of the heart for her dinner-service and the silver, but gains some relief at the thought of the Easter collection and her new toilette. She will wear a very splendid one, no doubt, but what is it to be?

She pushes the embroidery frame aside and takes *Le Moniteur de la Mode* from a little table on which lie Shakespeare, Dante, an album of European celebrities and several journals, and begins to look through it attentively. Here is a dinner gown: here spring outfits for young girls, unmarried ladies, wives and their mothers; here there are afternoon gowns, dinner dresses, walking-out dresses; half a dozen new hat designs, a dozen different materials and dozens of different colours . . . Which is she to choose? It is impossible to make her choice without the advice of Flora and the modiste . . .

Izabela, frustrated, lets the fashion magazine fall and reclines on the *chaise-longue*. Her hands, clasped as if in prayer, rest on the arm and she looks at the sky dreamily. The Easter collection, the new toilette, the clouds – all blend together in her mind's eye against a background of remorse for the dinner-service and a slight feeling of shame at having sold it.

'Oh, never mind . . .' she tells herself, and again she wishes the clouds would part, even if only for a while. But the clouds thicken and within her heart remorse, shame and uneasiness increase. Her gaze falls on the little table by the *chaise-longue*, and on a prayer-book bound in ivory. Izabela picks it up and slowly, page by page, seeks the 'Acte de resignation' and when she has found it, she begins to read: '*Que votre nom soit béni à jamais, bien qui avez voulu m'éprouver par cette peine.*' As she reads, the grey sky lightens and at the last words '*et d'attendre en paix votre divin secours . . .*' the clouds break asunder, a fragment of bright blue appears. Izabela's boudoir fills with light and her soul with tranquillity. Now she is certain that her prayers have been heard, that she will have the most splendid toilette and smartest church for the Easter collection.

At this moment the boudoir door softly opens: Flora appears, tall, in black, timid, holding a letter between two fingers and saying softly: 'From Countess Karolowa.'

'Ah, about the collection,' Izabela replies with a charming smile. 'You haven't been to see me all day, Flora.'

'I didn't want to interrupt.'

'My boredom?' Izabela asks. 'Who knows if it mightn't be more amusing to bore ourselves together?'

'The letter . . .' says the woman in black timidly, holding it out to Izabela.

'I know what it says,' Izabela interrupts. 'Sit here with me for a while and, if it is not too much trouble, read me the letter.'

Flora shyly sits down, carefully takes a paper-knife from the bureau and slits the envelope very carefully. She replaces the paper-knife then puts down the envelope, unfolds the letter and reads a letter in French in a quiet and melodious voice:

Dear Bela, forgive me for referring to a matter which only you and your father have the right to decide. I know, my dear, that you are disposing of your dinner-service and the silver, since you told me so yourself. I also know that a purchaser has been found, who offers five thousand roubles. In my opinion this is not enough, though nowadays it will be difficult to expect more. After a conversation I have had with Mme Krzeszowska, however, I begin to fear lest these heirlooms may not have fallen into the wrong hands.

I should like to prevent this, so I propose to offer you three thousand roubles as a loan, with the dinner-service and silver as security. I think the things will be better in my possession, since your father is in such difficulties. You may have them again whenever you wish, and without repaying the debt, in the event of my death.

I do not insist, merely suggest this. Consider which will be the more convenient to you, and think above all of the consequences.

I know you well enough to understand you would be painfully hurt should you hear at some time in the future that our family heirlooms adorn the table of some banker, or form part of his daughter's dowry.

A thousand kisses from

Joanna

P.S. Imagine how fortunate my orphanage has been! Yesterday in the celebrated Wokulski's shop, I alluded to a small donation for the orphans. I hoped for ten roubles or so, but he – believe it or not! – gave me a thousand, one thousand roubles, and said he would not have ventured to give me a lesser sum. A few more like Wokulski, and I feel I might become a democrat in my old age!'

Flora finished the letter but dared not raise her eyes. Finally she plucked up courage and looked: Izabela was seated on the *chaise-longue*, pale, her fists clenched.

'What have you to say to that, Flora?' she asked presently.

'I think,' said Flora quietly, 'that your dear aunt makes her position very clear.'

'How humiliating!' Izabela whispered angrily, striking her hand on the *chaise-longue*.

'It is humiliating to offer three thousand roubles when other people offer five. But I see no other cause for humiliation.'

'How she treats us! We must be ruined already . . .'

'Not at all, Bela,' Flora interrupted, with animation. 'This unkind letter proves we are not ruined. Aunt likes being unkind but also knows how to spare the unfortunate. If you were threatened by ruin, she would be a sensitive and kindly comforter.'

'I would not thank her for it.'

'You need have no fear. Tomorrow we shall obtain five thousand roubles with which we can keep going for six months . . . well, three months. A month or two . . .'

'They will auction our house.'

'That is merely a formality. You may profit by it, since nowadays a house is merely a burden. And you are to inherit a hundred thousand roubles from Aunt Hortensja. Moreover,' Flora added presently, raising her eyebrows, 'I am not at all sure but that your father may not still have a fortune. Everyone believes he has . . .'

Izabela leaned forward to seize Flora's hand.

'Flora,' she said in a low voice, 'why tell me such things? Do you regard me as a marriageable woman who sees and understands nothing? You think I don't know', she added, still more softly, 'that for a month now you have been borrowing money for the house-keeping from Mikołaj? . . .'

'Perhaps it is your father's wish.'

'And does he ask you to slip a few roubles into his purse every morning?'

Flora looked her in the eyes and shook her head.

'You know too much,' she replied, 'but that is not the whole of the matter. For the last two weeks or so your father has ten roubles and more every day.'

'So he is contracting debts . . .'

'No, your father never contracts debts in town. The money-lenders come to the apartment with the cash, and your father transacts his business with them in his study. You don't know him in this respect.'

'So where is he getting this money from?'

'I don't know. All I know is that he has money, and has always had some.'

'But why is he permitting me to sell the silver?' Izabela asked.

'Perhaps to vex the family.'

'And who has bought up his bills of exchange?'

Miss Flora made a gesture of resignation.

'It was not Krzeszowska,' she said, 'I know that for certain. It was either Aunt Hortensja, or . . .'

'Or . . .'

'Your father himself. You know how often your father has done things to vex the rest of the family and laugh at them afterwards . . .'

'Why should he want to vex you and me?'

'He thinks your mind is at rest. A daughter should trust her father implicitly!'

'Ah, I understand . . .' said Izabela, pondering.

Her black-robed cousin slowly rose and went out softly.

Izabela began to look around her room again, at the black boughs waving outside the windows, at a few sparrows chirping and perhaps building a nest, at the sky which had become uniformly grey without any bright streaks. The question of the Easter collection and her new toilette haunted her, but both matters seemed so trivial to her now, almost laughable, that while thinking of them she imperceptibly shrugged.

She was tormented by other questions: should she not hand the dinner-service over to her aunt? And where was her father getting that money? If he had had it before, why did he allow debts to be contracted from Mikołaj? And if he had none, where was he able to obtain it? If she let her aunt have the dinner-service and silver, she might lose the last opportunity of disposing of them at a profit; but if she sold them for five thousand, these heirlooms might in reality be acquired by the wrong sort of people, just as the Countess said.

Suddenly she broke off: her quick ear had caught a sound in the other rooms. It was a man's footsteps, level, measured. The carpet in the drawing room stifled them, but in the dining room they again grew louder, and softer again in her bedroom, as if someone were tip-toeing.

'Come in, papa,' Izabela said, hearing a tap on her door.

Tomasz came in. She rose from the *chaise-longue*, but her father made her sit down again. He embraced her, kissed her forehead, then seated himself beside her, glancing at the large looking-glass on one wall. There he observed his own handsome features, his grey moustache, irreproachable black waistcoat and smooth trousers which looked as if they had just come from the tailor, and saw that all was well.

'I hear', he told his daughter with a smile, 'that you have been receiving correspondence that has upset you.'

'Oh papa, if you only knew the tone aunt uses . . .'

'Probably the tone of a woman with disordered nerves. You should not be vexed with her.'

'If it were only that . . . But I am afraid she may be right, and that our silver may find its way to the table of some banker or other.'

She leaned her head on her father's shoulder. Tomasz glanced involuntarily at the mirror and admitted to himself that they formed a remarkably fine couple. The uneasiness on his daughter's face made a particularly striking contrast with his own tranquillity. He smiled.

'Bankers' tables!' he echoed. 'Our ancestral silver has already graced the table of Tartars, Cossacks and rebellious peasantry – far from disgracing us, this has only brought us honour. He who fights must risk losing.'

'They were lost in wars . . .' Izabela interposed.

'And is there no war on today? It is the weapons that have changed, that's all. Instead of an axe or scythe or scimitar, they fight with roubles. Joanna understood this very well when she sold her family estate – not merely a dinner-service – and demolished the ruins of her castle to build granaries.'

'So we have lost . . .' Izabela whispered.

'No, my child,' said Tomasz, straightening his back. 'We are just beginning to win, and that no doubt is what my sister and her coterie are afraid of. They are so fast asleep that they take fright at every sign of vitality, every bold step I take,' he added as if to himself.

'You, papa?'

'Yes. They thought I would beg them for help. Joanna would be glad to make me her plenipotentiary. But I declined a pension with thanks, and have drawn closer to the bourgeoisie. I have gained their respect, and this is beginning to alarm our little world. They expected me to go under, but now they see I may go forward to the top.'

'You, papa?'

'Yes, I. Hitherto I said nothing, for I lacked suitable partners. But today I met a man who understands my ideas, and I shall begin to act.'

'Who can he be?' Izabela looked at her father in surprise.

'A certain Wokulski, a tradesman, a man of iron. With his help I plan to organize our bourgeoisie and form a company for trading with the East. In this way I will support our industry . . .'

'You, papa?'

'And then we shall see who will get to the top, albeit, perhaps, through elections to the city council . . .'

Izabela listened to this with wide-open eyes.

'Is not this man of whom you speak, papa,' she whispered, 'is he not a speculator, an adventurer?'

'So you do not know him?' Tomasz inquired. 'He is one of our tradesmen.'

'Yes, I know his shop, it is very elegant,' said Izabela, thoughtfully. 'There's an old clerk who looks eccentric but is really very civil . . . Ah, I believe I met the proprietor too. He looks like a boor . . .'

'Wokulski a boor?' asked Tomasz in surprise. 'I agree he is somewhat stiff in his manners, but he is most civil.'

Izabela shook her head.

'He's a disagreeable man,' she replied animatedly. 'Now I remember him. When I was in his shop on Tuesday I asked him the price of a fan. You should have seen how he looked at me! He didn't answer, but beckoned with that huge red hand of his to a clerk (quite an elegant young man), and muttered in a voice in which I could hear his anger: "Mr Morawski . . . or Mraczewski" (I don't recall) "this lady wants to know the price of this fan." Oh, you have picked on a very disappointing partner, papa,' Izabela smiled.

'He's a man of extraordinary energy, a man of iron,' replied Tomasz. 'Such men behave like that. You will make their acquaintance, for I plan to hold a few evening parties here, at home. They're all originals, but he is more so than the rest.'

'You intend to receive these men, papa?'

'I must have talks with some of them. And as for our own people,' he added, looking his daughter in the eye, 'I promise you that when they learn who has been here, not one of them will be absent from my drawing-room.'

At this moment Flora entered to announce dinner. Tomasz gave his hand to his daughter and the three went into the dining-room; the tureen and Mikołaj were already there, the latter in a frock coat and large white tie.

'I can't help smiling at Bela,' said Tomasz to Flora, who was serving soup from the tureen, 'just think, Flora – Wokulski makes the impression of a boor on her! Do you know him?'

'Everyone knows Wokulski nowadays,' Flora replied, handing Mikołaj a plate for his master. 'He is not elegant, I agree – but he's a striking man.'

'Like a tree-trunk with red hands,' Izabela interposed with a smile.

'He reminds me of Trosti, that Colonel of the Rifles, in Paris,' said Tomasz.

'And he makes me think of the statue of the victorious gladiator,' said Flora in a melodious tone. 'Do you remember, Bela – the one with the uplifted sword that we saw in Florence. A stern face, even fierce – but handsome.'

'And his red hands?' Izabela asked.

'He got them frozen in Siberia,' Flora said significantly.

'Repenting the enthusiasm of his youth,'* said Tomasz. 'We can forgive him that.'

'So he's a hero too?'

'And a millionaire,' Flora added.

'That too? I am beginning to think, papa, that you have chosen well in taking him as a partner. And yet . . .'

'And yet?' her father repeated.

'What is the world going to say to the combination?'

'He who has power in his hands has the world at his feet.'

Mikołaj had just brought in the roast pork when the bell rang in the hall. The old butler went out and presently reappeared with a letter on a silver or perhaps nickel-plated tray.

'From the Countess,' he said.

'For you, Bela,' added Tomasz taking the letter. 'Allow me to swallow this new pill for you.'

And he opened the letter, began reading it, then said with a smile: 'Here you have Countess Karolowa all over! Nerves, nerves . . .'

Izabela pushed her plate aside and uneasily glanced through the letter. But her face gradually cleared.

'Listen, Flora,' she said, 'this is interesting.'

My dear Bela (my aunt writes) forget my previous letter, my angel. After all, your dinner-service is of no concern to me, and we will find you another when you get married. But I am most anxious that you should attend the Easter collection with me and no one else, and that was really what I meant to write about in my previous note, not about the dinner-service. My wretched nerves! If you do not want to upset me entirely, you must accept my invitation. The arrangements in our church will be quite splendid. My good, honest Wokulski is giving us a fountain, artificial singing-birds, music boxes that play solemn music and a number of fine carpets. Hozer will supply the flowers, and some amateurs are arranging a concert for the organ, violins, cellos and soloists. I am so pleased, but if you were absent amidst these wonders, I should be quite ill. So what is your reply to be?

Affectionately, and with a thousand hugs and kisses,

Joanna.

Post scriptum. Tomorrow we will visit the stores and order a spring outfit for you. I shall die if you do not accept.

Izabela was radiant. The letter fulfilled all her hopes.

'Wokulski is incomparable!' said Tomasz, smiling. 'He has won her over and she will not only recognise him as my partner but even fight me for him.'

Mikołaj was serving the chicken.

'He really must be something of a genius,' Flora observed.

'Wokulski? Well, no,' said Tomasz. 'He's a man of tremendous energy, but as for the gift of foresight – no, I would not say he has that in any very high degree.'

'Yet he is proving it.'

'These things are nothing but proof of his energy,' Tomasz replied. 'The gift of foresight, of working out brilliant ideas can be seen in other fields, such as . . . gambling. I often play whist with him, where foresight is essential. The result is that I would lose from eight to ten roubles, but win about seventeen, although I lay no claim to genius,' he added modestly.

Izabela dropped her fork. She turned pale and put one hand to her temples, whispering:

'Oh . . . oh! . . .'

Her father and Flora rose from their places.

'What is it, Bela?' asked Tomasz anxiously.

'Nothing,' she replied, also rising. 'Migraine. I felt it coming on . . . It is nothing, papa.'

She kissed her father and went to her boudoir.

'A sudden attack of migraine should pass very soon,' said Tomasz. 'Go to her, Flora. I must go out for a while, but will be home early. In the meantime, look after her, my dear Flora, I beg you,' said Tomasz with the tranquil air of a man whose instructions can set all the world to rights.

'I'll go to her when I have tidied up here,' replied Flora, to whom order in the household was a more important matter than anyone's migraine.

Already night had fallen . . . Izabela was alone in her boudoir again; she reclined on the *chaise-longue* and covered her face with both hands. Her tiny slippers and a fragment of stocking appeared beneath the cascade of fabrics she wore, but no one saw and she did not think of it. At this moment her soul was again torn with anger, remorse and shame. Her aunt had invited her, she would attend the Easter collection in the smartest church in Warsaw and would wear the finest toilette; but she was unhappy . . . She felt as if she had entered a crowded drawing-room and suddenly noticed a great greasy stain of hideous shape and colour on her new gown, as though it had been soiled on some kitchen stairs. The thought was so hateful that her mouth filled with a bad taste.

What a terrible position, to be sure! For a month they had been getting into debt with their butler, and for two weeks her father had been winning money at cards for his day-to-day expenses . . . It is permissible to win money at cards, of course: men win thousands of roubles . . . but not for day-to-day expenses, and certainly not from tradesmen. If only she could fall at her father's feet and beg him not to play cards with such people, or at least not just now, when their financial state was so precarious. In a few days, when she obtained the money for the dinner-service, she herself would hand her father a few hundred roubles so he could lose them to this Wokulski, so he could reward him generously, even more generously than she would reward Mikołaj for the debts incurred with him.

But was it proper to do so, or even mention it to her father?

'Wokulski, Wokulski . . .' Izabela whispers. Who is this Wokulski who had suddenly appeared on all sides, and in various aspects? What does he have to do with her aunt, with her father?

Now she recalls hearing about this man several times in the past weeks. Some merchant or other had recently donated several thousand roubles to charity, but she was uncertain whether he dealt in ladies' gown or in furs. Then people talked of a merchant who had made a great fortune in the Bulgarian war, but she had not paid attention to whether he was a shoemaker from whom she purchased her shoes, or her hairdresser. Only now did she realise that this merchant who had donated money to charity and the man who had made the great fortune were one and the same person, none other than this Wokulski who had also lost money at cards to her father, and whom her aunt, the notoriously proud Countess Karolowa, called 'my good honest Wokulski'.

At this moment she even recalled the face of this man, who had refused to speak to her in his shop and had withdrawn behind a huge Japanese vase to eye her sombrely. How he had looked at her!

One day, she and Flora had gone into a café for chocolate, just for a lark. They sat by the window, behind which several ragged children gathered. The children looked in at her, at the chocolate and the cakes with the curiosity and greed of starving animals, and this shop-keeper had looked at her in the same manner.

A slight shudder ran through Izabela. And he was to be her father's partner? . . . What for? . . . How had it crossed her father's mind to establish a commercial company, think up extensive plans he had never even dreamed of before? He hoped to rise to the forefront of the aristocracy with the help of the bourgeoisie; he hoped to be elected to a town council which never existed and probably never would . . .

Surely this Wokulski was nothing more than a speculator, perhaps a cheat, who needed an eminent name as shield for his enterprises? Such things happened. How many eminent names of the German and Hungarian aristocracy had been bedraggled in trade operations which Izabela did not understand, and of which her father hardly knew more.

It had grown quite dark; the lamps had been lit in the street, and their light outlined the window frame and folds of the curtain upon the ceiling of Izabela's boudoir. The shadows looked like a cross against a dark background which was slowly being submerged by a dense cloud.

'Where have I seen a cross like that, such a cloud and such brightness?' Izabela asked herself. She began to recall places seen in her life – and to dream.

It seemed to her she was travelling by carriage in some familiar spot. The landscape was like a huge ring of forests and green mountains, and her carriage was on the edge of the ring, descending into it. Would it go down? For it was neither coming nor going, but seemed to be motionless. Yet it was moving: this was evident from the face of the sun reflected in the polished sides of the carriage, trembling slightly as it moved backwards. Moreover, the wheels could be heard . . . Or was it the rattle of a droshky in the street? . . . No, it was the roar of machinery somewhere far below, in the depths of that ring of mountains and trees. She could even see, down there, what looked like a lake of black smoke and white steam, framed in greenery.

Now Izabela caught sight of her father sitting by her, inspecting his finger-nails attentively, glancing from time to time at the landscape. The carriage continued to stand on the edge of the ring, as if motionless, and only the face of the sun, reflected in the polished wings of the carriage, slowly moved backwards. This apparent rest or mysterious movement irritated Izabela to a high degree. 'Are we moving or standing still?' she asked her father. But he said nothing, as though he had not heard: he was inspecting his fine nails, and sometimes glanced out at the surroundings . . .

Then (the carriage went on trembling and the rattling could still be heard) the figure of a man half emerged from the depths of the lake of black smoke and white steam. He had close-cropped hair, a swarthy face which reminded her of Trosti, the Colonel of Rifles (or was it perhaps the Florentine gladiator?), and huge red hands. He wore a pitch-stained shirt, his sleeves were rolled up above his elbows: in his left hand, against his chest, he held some cards arranged in a fan, while in his right hand, which was raised above his head, he held one card, clearly with the intention of throwing it upon the front seat of the carriage. The rest of his figure could not be seen through the smoke.

'What is he doing, father?' Izabela asked fearfully.

'Playing whist with me,' her father replied, also holding cards.

'But he is dreadful, papa!'

'Even men such as he will not harm a woman,' Tomasz replied.

Only now did Izabela notice that the man in the shirt was looking at her with a peculiar expression as he continued to hold the card above his head. The smoke and steam, boiling in the valley, sometimes concealed his open shirt and stern features: he was sinking into them, he was gone. Only from behind the smoke, she could still see the pale glitter of his eyes, and his arm, naked to the elbow – and the card – rising above the smoke.

'What does that card mean, papa?' she asked her father.

But her father was calmly looking at his own cards, and did not answer, as if he did not hear her.

'When are we going to leave this place . . . ?'

But although the carriage shuddered and the sun reflected in the wings was still drawing backwards, the lake of smoke was still visible below and in it, the submerged man with his hand above his head – and that card.

Izabela was overcome with nervous agitation, she summoned all her powers of recollection, marshalled all her thoughts in order to guess: that card the man was holding, what did it mean? . . . Was it the money he had lost to her father at whist? Surely not . . . Or perhaps the sum he had contributed to the Charitable Society? Not that either. Or the thousand roubles he had given her aunt for the orphanage, or perhaps a receipt for the fountain, birds and carpets to adorn the church at Easter? But no, it was not them either: for none of these things would alarm her.

Gradually Izabela was filled with a great dread. Perhaps it was her father's bills of exchange, which someone recently bought up? If so, she would take the money for the dinner-service and silver, and would pay off this debt first and free herself from such a creditor. But the man submerged in smoke was still looking into her eyes and had not yet played his card. So perhaps . . . Oh!

Izabela jumps up, stumbles in the darkness against a stool and rings the bell with a hand that trembles. She rings again, no one answers, so she runs into the hall and in the doorway meets Flora, who seizes her hand and asks in surprise: 'What is the matter, Bela?'

The light in the hall brings Izabela to her senses somewhat. She smiles. 'Flora, bring a lamp to my room. Is Papa in?'

'He just went out.'

'And Mikołaj?'

'He'll be back directly, he took a letter for delivery. Is your headache worse?' asks Flora.

'No,' Izabela smiles. 'I dozed off, and had a dream.'

Flora takes the lamp and Bela goes with her cousin into the boudoir. Izabela sits down on the *chaise-longue*, shields her eyes from the light with one hand, and says: 'You know, Flora, I have changed my mind. I won't sell my silver to a stranger. It might get into the wrong hands. Sit down at my desk, if you will, and write to my aunt that . . . I accept her offer. Let her lend us three thousand roubles and take the dinner-service and silver.'

Flora looks at her in the utmost surprise, then says:

'That is impossible, Bela.'

'Why?'

'Fifteen minutes ago I had a note from Mrs Meliton saying the dinner-service and silver have already been sold.'

'Already? . . . Who has bought them?' Izabela cries, seizing her cousin's hand.

Flora is taken aback.

'Apparently some merchant from Russia . . .' she says, but it is clear she is not telling the truth.

'You know something, Flora! Please tell me . . .' Izabela implores. Her eyes fill with tears.

'Very well, only don't give the secret away to your father.'

'Who was it? Who has bought them?'

'Wokulski,' Flora replies.

In a moment Izabela's eyes became dry and took on a steely tint. She rejects her cousin's hand angrily, walks to and fro in the boudoir, sits down in a small chair opposite Flora. She is no longer an alarmed and upset beauty, but a great lady who intends to reprimand, perhaps dismiss, one of her servants.

'Tell me, cousin,' she said in a splendid contralto voice, 'what is the meaning of this silly plot you are all hatching against me?'

'Me? . . . a plot?' Flora echoed, pressing her hands to her bosom. 'I don't understand you, Bela . . .'

'Yes – you, Mrs Meliton and this . . . amusing hero . . . this Wokulski.'

'Wokulski and me?' Flora exclaims. This time her amazement is so sincere that it cannot be doubted.

'Well, perhaps you are not plotting,' Izabela goes on, 'but you know something, all the same.'

'Of Wokulski I know what everyone else knows. He owns that shop in which we sometimes buy things, he made a fortune in the war . . .'

'And he is involving my father in a trade company, haven't you heard?'

Flora's expressive eyes grew very large.

'Involving your father?' she said, shrugging. 'What sort of trade company can Wokulski involve him in?'

But at this moment her own words alarm her.

Izabela could not doubt Flora's innocence; she walked to and fro a few times like a caged lioness, then suddenly asked: 'At least tell me what you think of this man?'

'Wokulski? I think nothing of him, except perhaps that he is seeking notoriety and useful contacts.'

'So it was for notoriety that he donated a thousand roubles to the orphanage?'

'Of course. He gave twice that to charity.'

'Why did he buy up my dinner-service and the silver?'

'So that he can sell them again at a profit,' Flora replied. 'Things like that are in demand in England.'

'And why . . . why did he buy up papa's bills of exchange?'

'How do you know it was he? He would have no reason for doing so.'

'I know nothing,' Izabela snapped feverishly, 'but I feel, I understand everything. This man is trying to draw close to us . . .'

'He has made your father's acquaintance, after all,' Flora said.

'Then it is me he wants to approach,' exclaimed Izabela, with another outburst. 'I saw that by . . .'

She was ashamed to add 'the way he looked at me'.

'Aren't you exaggerating, Bela?'

'No. What I feel at this moment is not exaggeration, but clairvoyance. You can't even guess how long I have known – or rather how long he has been pursuing me. Only now I recall there was no new play at the theatre, no concert, no lecture at which I did not encounter him, and yet only now does that . . . that automaton seem terrible to me . . .'

Flora almost rose from her little chair as she whispered: 'Do you think he may dare . . . ?'

'To be infatuated with me?' Izabela interrupted with a sudden laugh. 'I wouldn't dream of preventing that. I'm neither so naive nor so falsely modest as not to know that I am attractive . . . even to servants, Heaven help me! . . . It used to irritate me, like a beggar who stops one in the street, or rings the door-bell or writes begging letters. But now – I've learned to understand the phrase "Of him who has much, much shall be required".

'In any case,' she added, with a shrug, 'men honour us in such unceremonious ways with their adoration that I am no longer surprised by their importunity or impertinent looks, but would be surprised if it were otherwise. If I meet a man in a drawing-room who does not refer to his affection for me and his suffering on my account, or does not fall gloomily silent in a manner betraying still greater affection and suffering, or who fails to display icy coldness meant to signify the utmost affection and suffering, why then – I feel something is wanting, as if I had forgotten my fan or handkerchief . . . Oh, I know them very well! All these Don Juans, poets, philosophers, heroes, all these sensitive, disinterested, suffering, dreamy or powerful souls . . . I know this masquerade through and through, and it amuses me very much, I assure you. Ha ha ha! How diverting it all is . . .'

'I don't understand you, Bela,' Flora interposed, clasping her hands.

'Then you are no woman.'

Flora made a gesture of denial, then of uncertainty.

'Listen,' Izabela exclaimed. 'A year ago we lost our position in society. No, don't deny it, for it is so, everyone knows it. Today we're ruined . . .'

'You exaggerate . . .'

'Flora, don't console me, don't lie to me . . . Didn't you hear at dinner that even those few roubles my father has were won at cards from . . .'

As she spoke, Izabela shuddered from top to toe. Her eyes glittered, her face flushed.

'And at such a time this . . . this tradesman comes, acquires our bills of exchange, our dinner-service, binds my father and aunt to him, in other words – surrounds me on all sides with his snares, like a hunter trapping an animal. He's no mournful admirer, not a suitor for my hand who can be rejected, but – a conqueror! He doesn't sit and sigh, but wheedles his way into my aunt's good graces, binds my father's hands and feet, and hopes to make off with me by force, if he cannot make me yield myself to him . . . Don't you understand this subtle villainy?'

Flora was horrified. 'If this is so, you have one very simple recourse. Tell . . .'

'Tell whom what? My aunt, who is only too ready to support this man in the hope of marrying me off to the marshal? Or perhaps I should tell my father, and alarm him and so hasten the disaster? I'll do one thing: I shall not let my father be drawn into any kind of commercial undertaking with this man, even if I have to go on my knees to him, even if I have to forbid it in the name of my dead mother.'

Flora gazed at her with admiration. 'Really, Bela,' she said, 'you exaggerate. With your will-power, your ingenuity . . .'

'You do not know such people, but I have seen them at work. They can crush iron bars in their bare hands. They are terrible. They know how to move all earthly powers which we are not even aware of, to suit their own ends. They can smash us, snare us, grovel before us, risk everything and even – wait patiently . . .'

'You talk like a novel.'

'I speak from the knowledge of my own forebodings, which warn me . . . they cry out that this man went to the wars to acquire me. And hardly has he returned than he lays siege to me on all sides . . . But let him beware! He wishes to buy me, does he? Well, let him . . . He will find out that I am very expensive . . . He wishes to trap me in his snares? Let him lay them . . . I will elude him even if it means yielding to the marshal . . . Good God, I had not even guessed the depths of the abyss into which we are descending until I saw this . . . From the drawing-rooms of the Quirinal – to a tradesman's shop. This is more than a decline; it is shame; it is humiliation.'

She sat down on the *chaise-longue*, covered her face with both hands, and sobbed.

VII

The Dove Goes Out to
Encounter the Serpent

THE dinner-service and the silver of the Łęcki family were
already sold, and the jeweller had brought Tomasz the
money, deducting a hundred or so roubles for his services.
Nevertheless, Countess Karolowa did not cease loving Izabela; on
the contrary, the energy and self-sacrifice Izabela had displayed in
selling the heirlooms aroused a new source of family affection in
the old lady's heart. Not only did she persuade Izabela to accept a
beautiful gown, not only did she call on her every day or invite her
to her house, but (proof of inconceivable favour!) she even offered
her the carriage for the whole of Holy Wednesday.

'Drive around the town, my angel,' said the Countess, kissing
her niece, 'and make your purchases. Only remember that during
the collection you must look charming . . . as charming as only you
know how . . . I beg you . . .'

Izabela made no reply, but her gaze made it evident that she was
only too glad to indulge her aunt.

Exactly at eleven on the morning of Holy Wednesday Izabela
was already seated in the open carriage with her devoted Flora.
Spring breezes were blowing along the Boulevard, wafting that
peculiar sharp scent which precedes the bursting out of leaves on
the trees and the appearance of the first primroses; the grey grass-
plots had taken on a greenish tinge; the sun shone so warmly that
the ladies put up their parasols.

'A beautiful day,' Izabela sighed, looking at the sky that was
scattered here and there with white clouds.

'Where to, madame?' asked the footman, as he slammed the
carriage door.

'To Wokulski's shop,' Izabela replied with nervous haste.

The footman jumped on to his box and the stout bay horses
moved off at a ceremonial trot, neighing and tossing their heads.

'Why Wokulski's, Bela?' asked Flora, somewhat startled.

'I want some French gloves, some perfume . . .'

'We could get it elsewhere.'

'I want to go to Wokulski's,' said Izabela drily.

For some days she had been haunted by a peculiar uneasiness which she had already experienced once before in her life. Years ago, in a zoological garden abroad, she had seen a tiger asleep in one of the cages, against the bars in such a way that part of its head and one ear was outside.

Izabela had had an irresistible desire to seize the tiger by that ear. The stench of the cage horrified her, the powerful paws of the animal made her shrink with indescribable fear, but all the same she felt she must at least touch the ear of the tiger.

This strange impulse had struck her as both dangerous and absurd. So she forced herself to go on further; but after a few minutes she had returned. Again she retreated, looked at other cages, tried to think of something else. But in vain. She went back once more, and even though the tiger was no longer asleep, but growling and licking its terrible paws, Izabela had run over to the cage, put out her hand and – trembling, pale – touched the tiger's ear.

A little later she had been ashamed of her foolishness, but at the same time she felt that bitter satisfaction known to those who obey the voice of instinct in an important matter.

Today she had awakened with a similar longing. She despised Wokulski; her heart faltered at the mere thought that this man might have paid more for the silver than it was worth, yet she felt an irresistible desire to go into his shop, look into Wokulski's eyes and pay him for a few trifles with the money that had come from him. Fear seized her at the thought of this encounter, but an inexplicable instinct drove her on.

In Krakowskie Przedmieście she caught sight in the distance of the sign 'J. Mincel & S. Wokulski' and saw a new, still-unfinished shop with five windows of plate-glass next to it. Several craftsmen and labourers were working there, some wiping the glass from within, others gilding and painting the door and shop-front, yet others putting great brass bars across the windows.

'What is that shop they are building?' she asked Flora.

'It is probably for Wokulski, I hear he has taken a larger site.'

'That shop is for me!' thought Izabela, fidgeting with her gloves.

The carriage stopped, the footman jumped down and helped the ladies descend. But when he opened the door into Wokulski's shop with a crash, Izabela shrank so that her legs almost gave way under her. For a moment she wanted to go back to the carriage and flee; but she controlled herself and went in, her head high.

Rzecki was already standing in the centre of the shop to greet her, rubbing his hands and bowing low. In the depths, Lisiecki was stroking his splendid beard and exhibiting a bronze candelabra to a

woman seated in a chair. The slender Klein was choosing a
walking-stick for a young man who rapidly armed himself with
eye-glasses at the sight of Izabela – while Mraczewski, scented with
heliotrope, eyes ablaze, was twirling his moustache at two blushing
young ladies accompanied by elderly ladies, inspecting toilet
articles.

Wokulski, bent over accounts, was seated to the right of the
door, at a desk.

When Izabela entered, the young man inspecting walking-sticks
straightened his collar, the two young ladies glanced at one another,
Lisiecki broke off half-way through a rounded phrase about the
style of the candelabra, though he retained an elegant pose, and
even the lady listening to his discourse turned in her chair. For a
moment the shop was silent, then Izabela asked in a beautiful
contralto voice:

'Is Mr Mraczewski here?'

'Mr Mraczewski!' Ignacy cried.

Mraczewski was already before Izabela, blushing like a cherry,
scented like a censer, his head bowed like a clump of rushes.

'We have come for some gloves.'

'Size five and a half,' Mraczewski replied, already holding the
box which trembled a little under Izabela's gaze.

'Not those . . .' she interrupted, smiling. 'Five and three-quarters
. . . You have forgotten already!'

'Madam, there are things a man never forgets . . . If, however,
you desire size five and three-quarters, I will serve you, in the hope
you will soon grace our establishment again with your presence.
Because gloves size five and three-quarters', he added with a soft
sigh, putting other boxes forward, 'will certainly be too large . . .'

'He's a genius,' Ignacy whispered softly, winking at Lisiecki, who
shrugged contemptuously.

The lady in the chair turned back to the candelabra, the two girls
to their toilet articles, the young man in eye-glasses went on
selecting his walking-stick – business reverted to its calm progress.
Only Mraczewski feverishly darted up and down ladders, opened
drawers, brought out more and more boxes, explaining to Izabela
in Polish and French that she could not wear any other size of
gloves but five and a half, or use any perfumes except Atkinson's
original, or adorn her dressing-table with anything but French
oddments.

Wokulski bent over his desk so that the veins stood out on his
forehead, and kept counting to himself: '29 and 36 is 65, and 16
makes 80 and 73 is . . .'

Here he broke off and looked furtively towards Izabela as she
was talking to Mraczewski. Both had their profiles towards him, so
he could see the burning gaze of the clerk fixed upon Izabela and

the way in which she was replying with smiles and kindly encouragement.

'29 and 36 is 65, and 15 . . .' Wokulski thought, but suddenly the nib of his pen broke. Without looking up, he got a new one from the drawer and at this moment, without knowing why, he asked himself: 'Am I supposed to be in love with her? What nonsense! A year ago I had a disordered brain, and it seemed to me I was in love . . . 29 and 36 . . . 29 and 36 . . . I never dreamed she could mean so little to me . . . How she looks at that fool! Well, she is obviously a woman who flirts even with clerks, and probably with carriage-drivers and footmen too . . . Now for the first time I'm calm . . . Good God! And I longed for it so . . .'

A few more persons entered the shop and Mraczewski reluctantly turned to them as he slowly tied up Izabela's packages.

Izabela approached Wokulski and, pointing in his direction with her parasol, said distinctly: 'Flora, kindly pay that gentleman. We are going home.'

'The cash desk is over here,' Rzecki exclaimed, hurrying to Flora. He took the money and both withdrew into the depths of the shop.

Izabela moved slowly towards the desk at which Wokulski was seated. She was very pale. The sight of this man seemed to exert a magnetic effect upon her.

'Am I addressing Mr Wokulski?'

Wokulski arose and replied indifferently: 'At your service.'

'So it was you who bought our dinner-service and silver?' she said in a stifled voice.

'Yes, madam.'

Now Izabela hesitated. But presently a pale glow returned to her face. She continued: 'I expect you intend to sell them.'

'That is why I bought them.'

Izabela's flush intensified.

'Does the future purchaser live in Warsaw?' she asked.

'I do not sell such things here, but abroad. There . . . they give better prices . . .' he added, noticing a question in her eyes.

'Do you expect to make a great deal of profit?'

'I bought them for that purpose.'

'Is that why my father does not know that the silver is in your possession?' she asked ironically.

Wokulski's lips quivered.

'I bought the dinner-service and silver from a jeweller. I make no secret of it. I brought no third party into the transaction because one does not do that in trade.'

Despite these gruff replies, Izabela sighed with relief. Her eyes even darkened somewhat and lost their gleam of hatred.

'If my father were to change his mind and wish to buy these

objects back, what price would you ask?'

'The price I paid. With a percentage of from six . . . to eight per annum, of course.'

'So you would forgo the profit you expected? Why is that?' she interrupted quickly.

'Because, madam, trade does not depend merely on profit but on the circulation of cash.'

'Goodbye and . . . thank you for the explanation,' said Izabela, seeing that Flora had finished paying.

Wokulski bowed and seated himself at the ledger again.

When the footman had taken the packages and the ladies were seated in the carriage, Flora reproachfully asked: 'Did you speak to that man, Izabela?'

'Yes, and I do not regret having done so. He lied all the time, but . . .'

'What do you mean by that "but"?' asked Flora uneasily.

'Don't ask me . . . Don't speak to me unless you want me to burst into tears in public . . .'

Presently she added in French: 'Perhaps I did wrong in going there, but . . . it is all the same to me.'

'Bela, I think,' said her companion gravely, pouting, 'that it would have been proper to discuss it with your father or aunt first.'

'You mean,' Izabela interposed, 'that I must discuss it with the marshal or Baron? There will be time for that; today I still lack the courage.'

The conversation broke off. Silent, the ladies returned home. Izabela was irritable all day.

When Izabela had left the shop, Wokulski returned to his accounts and added up two long columns of figures without a single error. Half-way down the third column, he stopped and marvelled at the calm in his soul. How could he be so indifferent after a whole year of feverish yearning and outbursts of madness? Had he been cast from a ballroom into a forest, or from a stifling prison cell into cool, expansive fields, he could not have known more profound astonishment.

'Obviously I have been almost insane for a year,' Wokulski thought. 'There was no risk, no sacrifice I would not have made for her – yet scarcely do I set eyes on her, than I am no longer even interested . . .

'And the way she spoke to me! That contempt for a wretched tradesman . . . "Pay that gentleman!" . . . These great ladies are quite amusing: an idler, a card-sharp, even a criminal would be acceptable to them in society, providing he had a fine name, even though his features were those of his mother's footman rather than his father. But a merchant is a pariah . . . However, what concern is it of mine: let them all rot . . .'

He added up another column without even noticing what was happening in the shop.

'How does she know', he went on to himself, 'that it was I who bought the dinner-service and the silver . . . ? And how anxious she was to find out whether I had paid more than it was worth! I would gladly have made her a present of this little trifle. I owe her a lifelong debt of gratitude, for had I not been insane about her, I would never have made a fortune but would have mouldered away behind a counter. But now perhaps I'll miss all that misery, despair and hope . . . What a stupid life! . . . We're all of us chasing a dream in our hearts and it is not until the dream escapes us that we realise it was an illusion . . . Well, I would never have believed there could be such a miraculous cure. An hour ago I was poisoned, but now I'm as calm as – and somehow empty, too, as if my soul and innards had left me with nothing but skin and my clothing. What shall I do now? What shall I live for . . . ? Maybe I'll go to the Paris Exhibition and afterwards the Alps . . .'

At this moment Rzecki tiptoed over to him and whispered: 'That Mraczewski is splendid, isn't he? He knows how to talk to women!'

'Like an impertinent barber,' said Wokulski, without looking up.

'Our customers have made him so,' said the old clerk, but when he saw he was interrupting his master, he retired. Wokulski sank into a brown study again. He glanced imperceptibly at Mraczewski and suddenly noticed that the young man had something peculiar in his face.

'Yes,' he thought, 'he is insufferably stupid and that is no doubt why women like him.'

He wanted to laugh both at the looks Izabela had given the handsome young man and at his own delusions, which had left him so suddenly.

Then he shuddered: he heard the name of Izabela and noticed there were no customers in the shop.

'Well, today you didn't even have to conceal your devotion,' said Klein to Mraczewski, with a dismal smile.

'The way she looked at me, oh my!' Mraczewski sighed, one hand on his heart, the other twisting his moustache. 'I am positive,' he said, 'that in a day or two I'll get a scented note. Then – the first rendezvous, then "for your sake I'll break the rules I've been brought up in", and then "now you despise me?" Beforehand it is all very delightful, but later on a man has trouble with 'em . . .'

'What are you talking about?' Lisiecki interrupted. 'We know your conquests: they are all called Matilda and you impress them with a pork chop and glass of beer.'

'The Matildas are for every day, ladies for holidays. But Bela will be the greatest holiday of all. I give you my word that no woman has ever made such an impression on me . . . And how keen she was on me!'

The door slammed and a grey-haired gentleman entered: he asked for a watch-guard, but shouted and banged his stick so fiercely that one would have thought he wanted to buy up all the trinkets in the shop.

Wokulski listened to Mraczewski's boasting but did not move. He felt as if a burden had fallen upon his head and shoulders.

'All in all, it is no concern of mine,' he whispered.

After the grey-haired gentleman, a lady came in for a parasol, then a middle-aged man for a hat and a young man who wanted a cigar-case, followed by three young ladies, one of whom asked for a pair of Szok's gloves, and only Szok's, for she wore no others.

Wokulski put aside the ledger, rose slowly and reached for his hat, then went towards the door. He was out of breath and his head was reeling.

Ignacy stopped him.

'Are you going out? Perhaps you'll glance into the other shop,' he said.

'No, I'm tired,' Wokulski replied, without looking at him.

When he had gone, Lisiecki nudged Rzecki.

'The old man looks as if he's on his last legs,' he whispered.

'Well,' said Ignacy, 'organising that deal with Moscow was not a mere trifle. That's obvious.'

'What is he going into that for?'

'To increase our wages,' replied Ignacy sternly.

'Then I hope he organises a hundred business deals, even with Irkutsk, if he puts our wages up every year,' said Lisiecki. 'I won't quarrel with that. But anyhow I think he's devilishly changed, particularly today. The Jews,' he added, 'when they get an inkling of what he's up to, they'll give him a licking.'

'What are you talking about?'

'The Jews, I say! . . . They all keep together and won't let any Wokulski get in their way, for he's no Jew, not even a convert.'

'Wokulski is making connections with the nobility,' Ignacy replied, 'and that is where the money is.'

'Who knows which is worse – the Jews or the nobility?' put in Klein and raised his eyebrows in a very lamentable manner.

VIII

Meditations

IN THE STREET, Wokulski stood on the pavement as if wondering which way to go. He was not drawn in any particular direction. Not until he happened to glance to the right, at his recently finished shop, in front of which people were already stopping, did he turn away with distaste and go to the left.

'It's odd how little it all concerns me,' he said to himself. Then he thought of the dozen people he gave work to, and of the dozens more he was to employ after 1 May, of the hundreds whom he was to supply with work in the coming year, and the thousands who would be able to better their wretched lot with his cheap merchandise – and he felt that at this moment none of these people and their families concerned him.

'I'll give up the shop and the company and go abroad,' he thought.

'But what about the disappointment you will cause these people who have placed their hopes in you?'

'Disappointment? . . . Haven't I too been disappointed?'

He felt uncomfortable as he walked along, then realised he was irritated by continually stepping aside for the passers-by; so he crossed the street, where there was less traffic.

'But that Mraczewski is infamous!' he thought. 'How can he say such things in the shop? "In a few days I'll get a note and then – a rendezvous . . ." Ha, she has only herself to blame, one should not flirt with fools. Ah well, it is all the same to me.'

He felt a strange emptiness in his soul and, at its very depths, something like a drop of stinging bitterness. No force, no desires, nothing – only that drop, so small that it could barely be perceived, and so bitter that the whole world could be poisoned by it.

'A momentary apathy, exhaustion, lack of stimulation . . . I think too much about business,' he said.

He stopped and looked around. It was the eve of a holiday and the fine weather had enticed many people out on to the city's streets. A string of carriages and a motley, undulating crowd between the statues of Copernicus and Zygmunt III looked like the flock of birds which were rising at that very moment above the town, heading north.

'How singular,' he said. 'Every bird above and every man below imagines that he goes where he pleases. And only someone observing from the sidelines sees that everyone is being pushed forward together by some ill-starred current, stronger than their expectations and desires. Perhaps the very one that tosses up the streaks of sparks blown out at night by the locomotive? They glitter for the twinkling of an eye, only to be extinguished for all eternity, and that is called life. "Human generations pass like waves on a wind-tossed sea; and their joys leave no memories, and their sorrows are beyond recall." Where did I read that? . . . No matter.'

The constant rumbling and murmuring was intolerable to Wokulski, and terrible his internal emptiness. He wished to occupy himself with something and remembered that one of the foreign capitalists had requested his opinion regarding the question of avenues along the banks of the Vistula. He had already formed his opinion: the whole vastness of Warsaw was weighing and shifting down towards the Vistula. If the banks were to be reinforced with avenues, it would become the most beautiful part of the city: buildings, shops, boulevards . . .

'I must go over and see how it would look.' Wokulski murmured and turned into Karowa.

By the gate leading in that direction he saw a barefoot porter, all hung about with string, drinking straight from the water fountain. He had splashed himself from head to toe but had a most pleased expression and laughing eyes.

'There's someone who has what he desired. Scarcely have I approached my source, when I see that not only has it disappeared, but my very desires begin to wither. And yet I am envied and he is to be pitied. What a monstrous misunderstanding!'

He rested a moment on Karowa. It seemed to him that he was like the chaff already discarded by the mill of big city life, and that he was floating slowly downwards in the gutter between these ancient walls.

'And what of the avenues?' he thought. 'They may stand for a time, then they will begin to crumble, overgrown and dilapidated, like these walls here. Those who laboured so to build them had other aspirations also: health, security, wealth, and fun, perhaps, caresses. And where are they now? . . . a few cracked walls is all that's left of them, like the shell of a long-gone snail. And the only profit this heap of bricks and a thousand other heaps will bring will be to some future geologist who will describe them as the human stratum, just as today we refer to coral reefs or chalk as the protozoan strata. "And what does a man's toil profit him? . . . And all his labours commenced under the sun? . . . Nothing – his works are fleeting, his life the flicker of an eye." Where did I read that? No matter.'

He stopped half-way along the road and looked at the district between Nowy Zjazd and Tamka Street, stretching out at his feet. He was struck by its resemblance to a ladder, one side formed by Dobra Street, the other by a line from Gabarska to Topiel, with several alleys across, forming rungs. This ladder leads nowhere. It's a sick place, a wild place. And he thought bitterly that this area of riverside earth, strewn with the refuse of the whole city, had given birth to nothing but two-storey houses coloured chocolate and bright yellow, dark green and orange. To nothing but black and white fences separating empty spaces, in which a several-storey apartment house rose here and there like a pine tree spared in a forest laid waste by the axe and uneasy at its own solitude.

'Nothing, nothing . . .' he repeated, wandering through the alleys with their shacks sunk below street level, roofs overgrown with moss, buildings with shutters and doors nailed shut, with tumbledown walls, windows patched with paper or stuffed with rags. He walked along looking through dirty window-panes into dwellings, and absorbed the sight of cupboards without doors, chairs with only three legs, sofas with torn seats, clocks with one hand and cracked faces. He walked along and silently laughed to himself to see labourers interminably waiting for work, craftsmen employed only at patching old clothes, women whose entire property was a basket of stale cakes – and to see ragged men, starving children and unusually dirty women.

'This is a microcosm of Poland,' he thought, 'where everything tends to make people wretched and to extinguish them. Some perish through poverty, others through extravagance. Work is taken from other people's mouths to feed the useless; charity breeds insolent loafers, while poverty is unable to acquire tools and is beseiged by perpetually hungry children, whose greatest virtue is to die a premature death. Individuals with initiative are of no use here, for everything conspires to chain initiative and waste it in a vain struggle – for nothing.'

Then his own story rose up before him in broad outline. As a child he had yearned for knowledge – they had put him to work in a shop and restaurant. As a clerk he had been killing himself with night work – everyone mocked him, from the kitchen-hands to the intelligentsia getting drunk in the shop. When he finally reached the university – they tormented him with the dishes he had recently served up to customers.

He only breathed freely when he reached Siberia. There he had been able to work, had gained the recognition and friendship of

Czerski, Czekanowski, Dybowski.* He returned to Poland almost a scholar, but when he sought employment in that field, he had been laughed at and scorned and sent into trade . . . 'A good living, in times like these!'

So he had gone back to trade, but then people exclaimed he had sold himself and was living on his wife, on the Mincels' work.

It had so happened that after a few years his wife died, leaving him a quite sizeable fortune. After burying her, Wokulski withdrew somewhat from the store and again took to his books. And perhaps the haberdashery merchant might have become a good natural scientist, had he not been once to the theatre and seen Izabela there. She was sitting in a box, with her father and Flora, wearing a white gown. She was looking not at the stage, which was holding the attention of everyone else, but at somewhere before her, who knows where or at what? Was she, perhaps, thinking of Apollo? . . .

Wokulski gazed at her all the time. She made a peculiar impression upon him. It seemed he had seen her before, and knew her well. He gazed still more intently into her dreaming eyes and recalled, without knowing why, the limitless tranquillity of the Siberian steppe, where sometimes it was so hushed that you could almost hear the rustle of souls flying back to the West. Not until later did he realise he had never before seen her anywhere, yet it was somehow as if he had been awaiting her for a long time.

'Are you she – or not?' he asked in his soul, unable to look away from her.

Henceforth he concerned himself little with the store or his books, but kept seeking opportunities to see Izabela at the theatre, concerts or lectures. He would not have called his feelings 'love', and in fact was not sure whether human language had a word to express them. All he knew was that she had become a mystic point where all his memories, longings and hopes coincided, a hearth without which his life would have neither sense nor meaning. His work in the grocery store, the university, Siberia, marriage to Mincel's widow, finally his involuntary visit to the theatre when he had not in the least wanted to go – all these were but pathways and stages through which fate had led him to catch sight of Izabela.

From then on, his time consisted of two phases. When he was looking at Izabela he felt completely calm and somehow greater; away from her, he thought about her and yearned for her. Sometimes it seemed there was a sort of error deep within his feelings, and that Izabela was not the centre for his soul at all, but an ordinary and perhaps even very commonplace eligible young lady. But then a strange plan came into his head.

'I shall make her acquaintance, and ask her point-blank: "Are you she for whom I have been waiting all my life? If not, I will go away without bearing you any grudge or being unhappy."'

A little later he saw that this plan showed mental aberration on his part. So he laid aside his inquiry as to what she was or was not and decided, come what may, to make the acquaintance of Izabela. Then he realised there was no one among his acquaintances able to introduce him into the Łęcki home. Worse still: Mr Łęcki and the young lady were customers in his store, but this relationship, instead of facilitating a meeting, made it more difficult.

Gradually he formulated the conditions required for making Izabela's acquaintance. In order simply to talk frankly to her, he must not be in trade, or be a very rich merchant; must be of genteel birth at least, and be acquainted with aristocratic circles; above all, however, he must have a great deal of money.

It had not been difficult to prove his genteel birth. Last May he set about the matter, which his journey to Bulgaria had expedited so that by December he already had the necessary certificate. It had been more difficult to make a fortune, but Fate had helped.

At the beginning of the Eastern War, a rich Muscovite, Suzin, a friend of Wokulski's from Siberia, passed through Warsaw. He called on Wokulski and forcefully urged him to go in for army supplies. 'Get together as much money as you can, Stanisław Piotrovich,' he had said, 'and I give you my word you'll make a million.' Then, in an undertone, he revealed his plans.

Wokulski had listened. He wanted nothing to do with some of them, others he accepted, though hesitantly. He regretted leaving the city where he at least saw Izabela from time to time. But when she left Warsaw in June for her aunt's estate, and when Suzin began urging him on with telegrams, Wokulski made up his mind, and drew out all his late wife's cash, amounting to thirty thousand roubles, which the lady had kept untouched in her bank.

Some days before his departure, he visited a doctor of his acquaintance, Szuman, whom he rarely saw despite a mutual liking. The doctor was Jewish, an old bachelor, yellow and tiny, with a black beard and the reputation of an eccentric. As he had private means, he practised medicine for nothing, and only as much as was necessary for his ethnographical studies; to his friends, however, he would give a piece of advice, once and for all: 'Take any medicine you like, from the smallest dose of castor oil to the largest of strychnine, and it'll help you somehow – even if you have glanders.'

When Wokulski rang the doctor's doorbell, the doctor was busy classifying the hair of various individuals of the Slavic, Teutonic and Semitic races, measuring the largest and smallest cross-sections through a microscope.

'So it's you . . .' he said to Wokulski, looking round. 'Light your pipe if you want to, and sit down on the sofa, if you can find room.' His visitor did as instructed, the doctor went on with his own business. For a time both were silent, then Wokulski said:

'Tell me this: does medical science know of a state of mind in which it seems to a man that all his previously scattered knowledge . . . and feelings have become concentrated, as it were, into one organism?'

'Of course. Continuous mental work and good food can form new cells in the brain or join together old ones. And then one unity is formed out of the various sections of the brain and various spheres of knowledge.'

'But what is the meaning of that state of mind in which a man grows indifferent to death, or begins to feel the need of legends of eternal life?'

'Indifference to death,' the doctor replied, 'is a trait of mature minds, and the desire for an eternal life is the sign of approaching old age.'

Again they fell silent. The visitor smoked his pipe, the doctor concerned himself with the microscope.

'Do you think,' Wokulski asked, 'that it's possible . . . to love a woman ideally, without desiring her?'

'Of course. It is a kind of mask, in which the instinct to preserve the species likes to disguise itself.'

'Instinct . . . species . . . the instinct for preserving something, and – preserving the species . . .' Wokulski repeated. 'Three phrases and four pieces of nonsense.'

'Make a sixth,' said the doctor, not looking away from his eye-piece, 'and get married.'

'The sixth?' asked Wokulski, rising, 'where's the fifth?'

'You have already done it; you have fallen in love.'

'Me? At my age?'

'Forty-five years old – that is the period for a man's last love, and the most serious.'

'Experts say first love is the worst,' Wokulski murmured.

'Not so. After the first, a hundred others are waiting, but after the hundredth there's nothing. Get married; that is the only cure for your ailment.'

'Why didn't you ever marry?'

'My fiancée died,' the doctor answered, leaning back in his chair and eyeing the ceiling. 'So I did all I could: I took chloroform. This was in the provinces . . . But God sent me a good colleague, who broke down the door and saved me. The worst kind of charity! I had to pay for the door he smashed, and my colleague inherited my practice by pronouncing me insane.'

He turned back to the hairs and the microscope.

'But what moral significance am I to draw from your remarks about last love?'

'That one should never interfere with a suicide,' the doctor replied.

Wokulski stayed another fifteen minutes, then rose, put his pipe away, and leaned over to embrace the doctor. 'Goodbye, Michał.'

The doctor rose. 'Well?'

'I am leaving for Bulgaria.'

'What for?'

'To go in for military supplies. I have to make a large fortune,' Wokulski replied.

'Or else . . . ?'

'Or else – I shall not come back.'

The doctor gazed into his eyes, and shook his hand firmly.

'*Sit tibi terra levis*,' he said calmly. He took him to the door and returned to his work.

Wokulski was already on the stairs when the doctor ran after him and called over the banister: 'If you come back, don't forget to bring me specimens of hair: Bulgarian, Turkish and so on, of both sexes. But remember – in separate packets, with notes. You know how it's done . . .'

. . . Wokulski aroused himself from these old memories. The doctor and his house weren't there, and he had not even seen either of them for ten months. This was muddy Radna Street, and that was Browarna. Above him, behind the naked trees, the yellow buildings of the university were looking down: below were one-storey houses, empty spaces and fences, and further off – the Vistula.

Near him, a man with a red beard, in a worn greatcoat, had halted. He took off his hat and kissed Wokulski's hand. Wokulski looked at him more closely.

'Wysocki?' he said. 'What are you doing here?'

'We live here, sir, in this house,' said the man, pointing to a low shack.

'Why have you stopped coming for carting jobs?' Wokulski asked.

'How could I, sir, when my horse died at New Year?'

'So what are you doing?'

'Well – nothing. We spent the winter at my brother's; he's a guard on the Vienna railroad. But things are going badly for him, they've transferred him from Skierniewice to near Częstochowa. He had three acres of land at Skierniewice, and lived like a rich man, but today he's badly off and his land is going from bad to worse without anyone to look after it.'

'Well, but what about you yourselves?'

'My wife does a little laundry, but for people who can't pay much, and I . . . well, there it is . . . We're going from bad to worse, sir – not the first, and not the last either. In Lent a man keeps up his spirits by saying "Today you'll fast for the souls of the dead, tomorrow to commemorate Christ eating nothing, the day after in the hope that God will cure evil." But after the holiday there won't even be a way to explain to the children why they're not eating . . . But you look poorly, sir. Evidently the time has come for us all to perish . . .' the destitute man sighed.

Wokulski reflected. 'Is your rent paid?' he asked.

'We haven't any rent to pay, for they are turning us out, sir.'

'Why on earth didn't you come to the shop, to Rzecki?' Wokulski asked.

'I dared not. My horse has gone, the Jews have my cart, my coat is like a beggar's . . . How could I come and bother other people?'

Wokulski produced his wallet. 'Here,' he said, 'ten roubles for the holiday. Tomorrow afternoon, go to the shop and get a note for Praga. There you will choose a horse yourself from the dealers, and come for work. You will get three roubles a day from me, so you can easily repay your debt. In any case, you will manage.'

The poor man trembled as he took the money. He listened attentively to Wokulski, and the tears flowed down his lean face.

'Did someone tell you, sir,' he asked after a moment, 'that things are like this with us? For someone,' he added in a whisper, 'sent a nun, a month back. She said I must be a loafer, and gave us paper for a sack of coal. Did you, maybe, sir . . . ?'

'Go home, and come to the shop tomorrow,' Wokulski replied.

'I will, sir,' said the man, bowing low.

He left, but kept stopping, obviously pondering over his unexpected good fortune.

At this moment Wokulski felt a peculiar sense of foreboding.

'Wysocki!' he called, 'what's your brother's first name?'

'Kasper, sir,' the man replied, running back.

'What station does he live near?'

'Częstochowa, sir.'

'Go home. Maybe they'll transfer Kasper back to Skierniewice.'

But the other man came closer, instead of going away. 'Excuse me, sir,' he said timidly, 'but what if someone asks me where I got this money?'

'Tell them it was on account from me . . .'

'I understand, sir . . . God . . . may God . . .'

But Wokulski was no longer listening; he was walking towards the Vistula, thinking: 'How fortunate they are, all these people whose apathy is caused merely by hunger, and who only suffer from the cold. And how easy it is to make them happy! With even my small fortune I could elevate several thousand such families. It's unlikely, yet it is so.'

Wokulski reached the Vistula bank, and looked about in surprise. Here, occupying several acres of space, was a hill of the most hideous garbage, stinking, almost moving under the sun, while only a few dozen yards away lay the reservoirs from which Warsaw drank.

'Here,' he thought, 'is the centre of all infection. What a man throws out of his house today he drinks tomorrow. Later he's moved to the Powazki cemetery, and then again from the other side of the city he infects those of his dear ones who are still alive . . . A boulevard here, drains and water from the hill-top – several thousand people could be saved from death, and tens of thousands from diseases . . . Not much work, but an inestimable profit; nature would know how to compensate for it.'

On the side and in the ravines of the hideous hill he saw what looked like people. Several drunkards, or criminals, were dozing in the sun, there were two women street-sweepers and a loving couple, consisting of a leprous woman and a consumptive man without a nose. They looked like phantoms of diseases unearthed here, rather than human beings, that had dressed themselves in rags. All these individuals sniffed the scent of an intruder: even the sleepers lifted their heads and gazed at the visitor with the look of mad dogs.

Wokulski smiled. 'Had I come here by night, they would certainly have cured me of melancholia. Tomorrow I'd be resting under this garbage which, after all, is as comfortable a grave as any. In the town there'd be a fuss, these honest folk would be run to earth and excommunicated – yet they might have done me a favour . . .

'For they do not know, as they slumber in their tombs, the heavy cares of this life, and their souls no longer struggle with desires, yearning, powerless . . .

'But am I really growing sentimental? My nerves must be thoroughly disordered. But a boulevard wouldn't do away with these Mohicans: they'd move over the river to Praga or beyond, go on with their business, make love like that pair, even increase and multiply. What fine children you will have, my homeland, born and brought up in this garbage heap, with a mother covered in sores and a father with no nose! . . .

'My own children would be different; they would have her beauty, my strength . . . Yes, but they will never be. In this country only disease, poverty and crime find a marriage bed and shelter for their offspring. It is terrible to think what will happen here within a few generations. Yet there is a simple remedy: compulsory labour, properly renumerated. That alone can bring forth better individuals and wipe out evil without a fuss . . . We would have an active population where today we have hungry or sick people . . .'

Then, without knowing why, he thought: 'What does it matter if she flirts a little? Coquetry in a woman is like colour in flowers. It's their nature to want to please everyone, even a Mraczewski . . .

She flirts with everyone else, but for me there's only "Pay that gentleman!" . . . Perhaps she thinks I cheated them in buying the silver? That would indeed be amusing!'

A heap of planks was lying on the very edge of the Vistula. Wokulski felt tired, sat down and gazed around. The Saska Kępa district, already turning green, and the houses of Praga with their red roofs, were reflected on the smooth surface of the water. A barge stood motionless in the centre of the river. A ship Wokulski had seen on the Black Sea last summer motionless because its engines had broken down, had looked no bigger. 'It was travelling along like a bird, then suddenly broke down; the engine had failed. I asked myself then, what if I too sometime come to a halt? And now I have done so. What commonplace engines they are that cause movement in the world: a little bit of coal moves a ship, a little bit of heart – a man.'

At this moment a premature yellow butterfly passed over his head, in the direction of the town, 'Where did it come from, I wonder?' Wokulski thought. 'Nature has her caprices sometimes – and analogies,' he added. 'There are butterflies in mankind, too: prettily coloured, flitting over the surface of life, feeding on sweets without which they perish – such is their occupation. As for the worms – they undermine the earth and make it ready for sowing. The butterflies play; you labour: space and light exist for them – your only privilege is growing together again if someone carelessly steps on you . . .

'Are you sighing for a butterfly, you fool? And surprised because you disgust her? What bond can exist between her and me? . . . Well, a caterpillar resembles a worm until it becomes a butterfly. Ah, so you are to become a butterfly, are you – you haberdasher! Why not, though? Continuous improvement is a natural law, and just consider how many merchant families in England have become Your Lordships.

'In England! There a creative era still exists in society; there, everything is improving and moving up to a higher level. There, even the higher levels of society continue to attract new forces to themselves. But here the higher level has solidified like water in frost, and has not only created a peculiar species not connected with the rest and has a feeling of physical repulsion towards them, but even hampers all movement below by its own dead weight. Why deceive myself? She and I are two different species, just like the butterfly and the worm. Am I to leave my hole in the ground and the other worms for the sake of her wings? These are my people – lying here on the garbage. And perhaps they are poor and will be poorer because I want to squander some thirty thousand roubles a year for playing with the butterfly . . . Stupid tradesman, vile man that you are . . .

'Thirty thousand roubles means as much as sixty small workshops or stores, which whole families could live on. And am I to destroy their existence, suck the human souls out of them and drive them to this garbage heap?

'Very well – but if it were not for her, would I have this fortune now? Who knows what would have become of me and this money had it not been for her? Perhaps it is precisely because of her that the money will acquire creative properties; maybe at least a dozen families will benefit by it.'

Wokulski turned and suddenly caught sight of his own shadow on the ground. Then he recalled that his shadow went before, after or beside him always and everywhere, just as the thought of this woman accompanied him always and everywhere, awake or dreaming, interfused with all his aims, plans and acts.

'I can't give her up,' he whispered, clasping his hands together as if explaining to someone.

He rose from the planks and went back to town.

Walking along Oboźna Street he recalled the driver Wysocki, whose horse had fallen and been destroyed, and it seemed to him he could see a whole row of carts, in front of which lay fallen horses, with a whole row of drivers in despair over them, each with a group of wretched children and a wife who washed linen for people who couldn't pay.

'A horse?' Wokulski whispered, and somehow his heart ached. Once, last March, as he had been crossing Aleje Jerozolimskie, he had seen a crowd of people, a black coal-wagon standing across the street by a gate, and an unharnessed horse a few feet away. 'What's happened?' 'Horse broke its leg,' one of the passers-by replied cheerfully; he had a violet scarf on, and kept his hands in his pockets.

Wokulski looked at the culprit as he passed. It was a lean nag with its ribs showing, and kept lifting its back leg. Tied to a small tree, it stood quietly, looked with its rolling eye at Wokulski and gnawed in its pain at a branch covered with hoar-frost.

'Why should I be reminded of that horse just now?' Wokulski thought. 'Why do I feel this pity?'

He walked thoughtfully up Oboźna and felt that, in the course of the few hours spent by the river, a change had come upon him. Formerly – ten years ago, a year ago, even yesterday – while walking about in the streets he never met anything unusual. People passed by, droshkies drove along, shops opened their doors hospitably for customers. But now a new kind of feeling had come to him. Each ragged man looked as if he were shouting for help, the more loudly because he said nothing but only cast a fearful glance, just as that horse with the broken leg had done. Each poor woman looked like a washerwoman, supporting her family on the

brink of poverty and decline with her worn hands. Each pitiful
child seemed condemned to premature death or to spending days
and nights on the garbage heap in Dobra street.

It was not only people who concerned him. He shared the
weariness of horses pulling heavy carts along, and the sores where
their horse-collars had drawn blood. He shared the fright of a lost
dog barking in the street for his master and the despair of a starving
bitch as she ran from one gutter to the next, seeking food for
herself and her puppies. And on top of these sufferings he was even
pained by the trees with their bark cut, the pavements like broken
teeth, dampness on broken pieces of furniture and ragged garments.
It seemed to him that every object like this was sick or wounded,
complaining: 'See how I suffer . . .', and that he alone heard and
understood their laments. And this peculiar capacity for feeling the
pain of others had been born in him only today, an hour ago.

Strange! After all, he had the reputation of an established philan-
thropist. Members of the Charitable Society, in their frock-coats,
had thanked him for his offerings to their ever-hungry institutions;
Countess Karolowa talked in drawing-rooms of all the money he
had donated to her orphanage; his servants and clerks spread his
fame for raising their wages. But these things caused Wokulski no
pleasure, for he himself attached no significance to them. He tossed
thousands of roubles to charity to buy fame, without ever asking
what was to be done with the money.

Not until today, when he had extricated a man from destitution
by a mere ten roubles, which no one would tell the rest of the
world of, not until today had he recognised what sacrifice meant.
Not until this day had a new, hitherto unknown part of the world
risen up before his eyes – poverty, which must be helped.

'Yes, but did I not notice poverty before?' Wokulski whispered.
And he recalled whole throngs of ragged people, poor, looking for
work, throngs of starving horses, hungry dogs, trees with broken
bark and broken branches. He had encountered all these things
without emotion. It was not until now, when a great personal pain
had fallowed and harrowed his soul, had fertilized it with his own
blood and tears unseen to the world, that this strange plant had
grown within him: this mutual sympathy encompassing everything
– people, animals, even inanimate objects.

'The doctor would say a new cell has been formed in my brain,
or that several old ones had joined together,' he thought. 'Yes –
but what now?'

Hitherto he had had only one aim: to approach Izabela. Now he
acquired another: to extricate Wysocki from destitution.

'A small thing!'

'And transfer his brother to Skierniewice,' a voice added.

'A mere nothing!'

But behind these two people were several others, with still others behind them, then a huge crowd struggling with all kinds of poverty and finally – a whole ocean of suffering which must be mitigated as far as his powers allowed, or at least stopped from spreading.

'Visions . . . abstractions . . . nervous exhaustion!' Wokulski whispered.

That was one way. At the end of the other, however, he saw a real and well-defined aim – Izabela.

'I'm not Christ, to sacrifice myself for mankind.'

'So – forget the Wysockis to begin with,' the inner voice retorted.

'Well, this is nonsense. Even though I'm excited today, I mustn't make a fool of myself,' Wokulski thought. 'I'll do what can be done, but I won't renounce my own happiness, that's too much . . .'

At this moment he stopped at the door of his shop and went in.

Inside, Wokulski found only one customer. It was a tall lady in black, of indeterminate age. Before her was a pile of dressing-cases – wooden, leather, plush, metal, plain and fancy, the most expensive and the cheapest – and all the clerks were attending to her. Klein kept proffering more, Mraczewski was praising the cases, while Lisiecki accompanied him with gestures. Only Ignacy came forward to greet his principal.

'There's a delivery from Paris,' he told Wokulski, 'I think we shall have to collect it tomorrow.'

'As you like . . .'

'And orders from Moscow for ten thousand roubles, for early May.'

'I expected them.'

'Two hundred from Radom, but the driver wants payment by tomorrow.'

Wokulski shrugged. 'We must have done with this huckstering trade once and for all,' he exclaimed. 'There's no profit in it and the demands are too heavy.'

'Break with our provincial trade?' Rzecki asked in surprise.

'Break with the Jews,' Lisiecki put in in an undertone; 'the boss is quite right to get out of those wretched deals. Sometimes I'm ashamed to give change, the money smells so of garlic . . .'

Wokulski did not reply. He sat down at his accounts and pretended to be reckoning, but in reality he did nothing; he had not the energy. He recalled his recent dream of making mankind happy and decided he must be in a very nervous state. 'Sentiment and imagination triumphed over,' he thought. 'It's a bad sign. I may become a laughing-stock, be ruined . . .'

He mechanically eyed the unusual countenance of the lady

choosing a dressing-case. She was modestly dressed, her hair drawn back smoothly. Deep sorrow was etched upon her face, which was both white and yellowish; bad temper lurked in her tight lips, and anger or sometimes humiliation glittered in her downcast eyes. She was speaking in a low and mild voice, but bargaining more than any miser. This case was too expensive, that too cheap; this plush would fade, the leather would wear off that, and here rust was showing on the fittings. Lisiecki had already retreated, Klein was resting, and only Mraczewski was talking to her as if he knew her.

Just then the door of the shop opened and a still more original individual appeared. Lisiecki was to say of him that he looked like a consumptive whose whiskers and moustache had begun to sprout in his coffin. Wokulski noticed that this customer had a gaping mouth and large eyes behind dark spectacles, from behind which still greater absent-mindedness peered.

This customer entered while terminating a conversation with someone outside in the street, and at once withdrew to bid goodbye to his companion. Then he came in again, only to retire once more, raising his head as if to read the sign over the door. He glanced accidentally at the lady – and his dark spectacles dropped.

'Oh!' he exclaimed.

But the lady turned away convulsively to the dressing-cases, then sank into a chair.

Mraczewski hurried over to the newcomer and, smiling ambiguously, inquired: 'What can we do for His Excellency?'

'Cufflinks, d'you see . . . ordinary cufflinks, gold or metal . . . Only, d'you see, they must be shaped like a jockey's cap and – with a whip.'

Mraczewski opened the case containing cufflinks.

'A glass of water!' the lady cried in a feeble voice.

Rzecki poured some from the carafe and handed it to her sympathetically. 'Madam is ill? Perhaps a doctor . . . ?'

'I'm better . . .' she retorted.

The Baron was inspecting cufflinks, his back ostentatiously turned towards the lady. 'Perhaps links in the form of a horse-shoe would be better, sir?' Mraczewski asked. 'I think these would suit Your Excellency, or these . . . Sporting gentlemen only wear sporting emblems, but they like a change too . . .'

'Tell me, please,' the lady suddenly turned to Klein, 'what use are horse-shoes to a person who cannot afford to keep horses?'

'Here, young man,' said the Baron, 'please select a few more trifles in the shape of horse-shoes.'

'Perhaps an ash-tray?' Mraczewski inquired.

'Very well,' said the Baron.

'And perhaps an elegant inkwell, with a saddle and a little jockey and hunting-crop on it?'

'I will take the inkwell with the saddle and jockey on it . . .'

'Tell me, young man,' said the lady to Klein, raising her voice, 'are you not ashamed to stock such expensive trifles when our country is ruined? Is it not shameful to buy race-horses?'

'Young man,' said the Baron equally loudly to Mraczewski, 'pray pack all these trifles – the ash-tray, the inkwell – and send them to me at home. You have a most elegant selection of goods here. Good-day to you! Adieu!'

And he hurried out of the door, turning back several times to look at the sign over it.

After the exit of the eccentric Baron, silence reigned in the store. Rzecki gazed at the door, Klein at Rzecki, and Lisiecki at Mraczewski who, being behind the lady, was able to make a very ambiguous grimace.

The lady rose slowly from her chair and approached the cash-desk at which Wokulski was seated.

'May I inquire,' she said in a trembling voice, 'how much that gentleman who has just left owes you?'

'The account of that gentleman in this store, madam, if he has one, is his business and mine,' said Wokulski with a bow.

'Sir!' the fretful lady went on, 'I am Krzeszowska, and that man is my husband. His debts concern me, for he has appropriated my estate over which a law-suit is progressing at this very time . . .'

'Forgive me, madam,' Wokulski interrupted, 'but relations between husband and wife are no concern of mine.'

'Ah, so? No doubt that is most convenient – for a tradesman. Adieu.'

And she left the shop, slamming the door.

A few minutes after her departure, the Baron hurried in. He glanced out into the street a few times, then approached Wokulski.

'My apologies,' he said, trying to keep his eye-glasses in place, 'but as a regular customer, I venture to inquire in confidence what that lady who has just left said to you? I apologise for my boldness, but in confidence . . .'

'She said nothing that would bear repetition,' Wokulski replied.

'For, d'you see, she is – alas! – my wife. You know me – Baron Krzeszowski . . . She's a devilishly fine woman, very polished and all that, but the death of our daughter has somewhat upset her and sometimes . . . d'you see . . . So – nothing . . . ?'

'Nothing.'

The Baron bowed, and exchanged glances with Mraczewski, who winked at him. 'So that's how it is?' the Baron said, looking sharply at Wokulski. And he hurried out into the street.

Mraczewski turned to stone and flushed up to the roots of his hair. Wokulski went a little pale but sat down again at his accounts.

'Who are those eccentric individuals, Mraczewski?' Klein asked.

'It's a long story,' said Mraczewski, glancing sideways at

Wokulski. 'That was Baron Krzeszowski, a great eccentric and his
wife, who is a trifle off her head. They're related to me, of course,
but what of it?' he sighed, gazing into the mirror. 'I haven't any
money, I have to serve behind a counter; they still have some, so
they patronise me . . .'

'They have money without working for it . . .' Klein put in. 'A
fine state of affairs, isn't it?'

'Well, never mind . . . Don't drag me into your affairs,'
Mraczewski replied. 'The Baron and Baroness have been at war
together for a year. He wants a divorce, but she doesn't; she wants
to dislodge him from managing her property, to which he won't
agree. She won't let him keep horses, particularly one race-horse;
and he won't let her buy the Łęcki house, in which the Baroness
lives and where she lost her daughter. Odd people! Everyone
laughs at their antics . . .'

He spoke lightly and moved around with the air of a young
gentleman who merely dropped in for a few moments but would be
leaving directly. Wokulski changed colour as he sat at his accounts;
he could not endure Mraczewski's voice a moment longer.

'The Krzeszowskis' cousin . . .' he thought. 'He'll be getting a
love-letter from Izabela. . . . Ah, the scoundrel . . .'

He turned back to his ledger with an effort. More people began
coming into the store, selecting goods, bargaining, and paying. But
Wokulski, absorbed in his work, only saw their shadows. And as he
added up more columns, reached greater totals, the more he felt
some indescribable rage boiling up within him. What was it about?
And against whom? Never mind . . . enough that someone would
pay for it, as soon as the occasion arose.

By seven, the shop was decidedly emptier, the clerks were
chatting together, Wokulski still reckoning. Then he again heard
the insufferable voice of Mraczewski, saying in an arrogant tone:
'What are you trying to confuse me for, Klein? All Socialists are
criminals, because they are out to divide up other people's property
– and they're hangmen, for they have one pair of boots between
two and don't believe in using pocket-handkerchiefs.'

'You wouldn't say that,' Klein replied mournfully, 'if only you'd
read a few pamphlets, even short ones.'

'Rubbish . . .' Mraczewski interrupted, putting his hands in his
pockets. 'You expect me to read pamphlets that are out to destroy
the family, religion and property! Well, you won't find such stupid
people in Warsaw.'

Wokulski closed the ledger and put it into the desk. At this
moment three ladies came into the store for gloves. Their purchase
lasted fifteen minutes. Wokulski sat and stared out of the window;
when the ladies had gone he called in a very calm voice: 'Mr
Mraczewski!'

'Sir?' asked the handsome young man, skipping up to the cash-desk.

'From tomorrow you will look for another post,' said Wokulski abruptly.

Mraczewski turned to stone. 'Why, sir? Why?'

'Because there is no job for you here.'

'But what's the reason, sir? After all, surely I haven't done anything wrong? Where shall I go if you dismiss me so suddenly?'

'You'll get good references,' Wokulski replied. 'Mr Rzecki will pay your wages for the next quarter – or for five months. The reason is that you and I don't get on . . . We don't get on at all. Ignacy, pay Mr Mraczewski until the first of October.'

With that, Wokulski rose and went into the street.

Mraczewski's dismissal made such an impression that the other clerks said not a word to one another, and Rzecki told them to close the shop, though it was not yet eight o'clock. He at once hurried to Wokulski's house, but did not find him there. He went again at eleven, but the windows were dark and Ignacy went despondently home.

Next day, Maundy Thursday, Mraczewski did not appear in the shop. His colleagues were depressed and sometimes conferred quietly together.

Wokulski came in about one o'clock. But before he could sit down at his desk, the door opened and Baron Krzeszowski hurried in with his usual hesitant step, attempting to fix his eye-glasses in place.

'Mr Wokulski,' he exclaimed distractedly, almost at the door, 'I have just heard . . . I am Krzeszowski . . . I hear that poor Mraczewski has been dismissed on my account. But, Mr Wokulski, I was not in the least vexed with you yesterday . . . I respected the discretion you showed in the matter of myself and my wife . . . I know that you replied to her as becomes a gentleman . . .'

'Baron,' said Wokulski, 'I have not asked you for a certificate of respectability. Apart from that – what can I do for you?'

'I have come to ask forgiveness for poor Mraczewski, who even . . .'

'I am not vexed with Mr Mraczewski, though he should apply to me himself . . .'

The Baron bit his lip. He was silent a moment, as if stunned by the brusque reply; finally he bowed and with a quiet 'Excuse me', left the shop.

Messrs Klein and Lisiecki retired behind the cases, and after a short conference returned into the shop, casting sad but eloquent glances at one another from time to time.

At about three o'clock, Baroness Krzeszowska appeared. She seemed paler, greener and still more sombrely dressed than the previous day. She looked fearfully around and, catching sight of Wokulski, approached his desk: 'Sir,' she said quietly, 'today I heard that a certain young man, Mraczewski, lost his post here on my account. His unhappy mother . . .'

'Mr Mraczewski no longer works here, and will not be doing so,' Wokulski replied with a bow, 'so what can I do for you?'

Evidently Baroness Krzeszowska had a long speech prepared. Fortunately, she looked into Wokulski's eyes and . . . with the phrase 'Excuse me', left the shop.

Messrs Klein and Lisiecki winked at each other more eloquently than hitherto, but made do with an unanimous shrug.

Not until nearly five did Rzecki approach Wokulski. He leaned on the desk and said in a low voice: 'Mraczewski's mother, Staś, is a very poor woman . . .'

'Pay his wages until the end of the year,' Wokulski replied.

'I think . . . Staś, I don't think one should punish a man for having political opinions different from ours . . .'

'Political opinions?' Wokulski repeated in such a tone that a cold shiver ran up Ignacy's spine.

'Besides,' Ignacy went on, 'it's a shame to let such a clerk go. He's a handsome young man, the ladies like him . . .'

'Handsome?' Wokulski replied. 'Then let him go and become a kept man, if he's so handsome . . .'

Ignacy withdrew. Messrs Klein and Lisiecki did not even glance at one another.

An hour later, a certain Mr Zięba came into the shop, and Wokulski introduced him as the new clerk.

Mr Zięba was about thirty; he was perhaps as handsome as Mraczewski, but looked far more serious and discreet. Before the shop closed, he had already made the acquaintance of and even gained the friendship of his colleagues. Rzecki discovered he was a fervent Bonapartist; Lisiecki had to admit that he himself was a very pale anti-Semite in comparison with Zięba, and Klein decided that Zięba must be at least a bishop of Socialism.

In a word, all were pleased, and Zięba was content.

IX

Footbridges on which People of Various Worlds Meet

ARLY ON Good Friday, Wokulski recalled that on this day and the next, Countess Karolowa and Izabela would be accepting charitable offerings in church.

'I must go and give them something,' he thought, and took five golden half-imperials from the safe. 'Although,' he added after a moment, 'I have already sent them carpets, stuffed birds, a music box and even a mechanical fountain . . . Surely that will suffice to save one soul. I won't go.'

But in the afternoon he told himself that perhaps Countess Karolowa was expecting him. And in that case it would not do to decline or offer only five half-imperials. So he took five more from the safe and wrapped them all up in tissue paper.

'Yet,' he told himself, 'Izabela will be there, and it wouldn't do to offer her only ten half-imperials.' So he undid the roll, added ten more gold pieces and still debated whether to go or not.

'No,' he said, 'I won't join that charitable market-place.'

He threw the roll into the safe and did not go to the ceremony that Friday.

But on Easter Saturday the matter presented itself to him in a very different light. 'I was insane,' he said. 'If I don't go to church, then where else shall I meet her? How can I draw attention to myself if not with money? I'm losing my wits . . .'

But still he hesitated, and not until about two in the afternoon, when Rzecki had ordered the store closed on account of the holiday, did Wokulski take from the safe twenty-five half-imperials and go in the direction of the church. He did not go in directly, however; something held him back. He wanted to see Izabela, but at the same time he was afraid to, and was ashamed of his half-imperials. 'To throw down a pile of gold . . . How impressive in these days of paper money and – how bourgeois! Well, but what am I to do if they are waiting for money? Maybe it won't be enough . . .'

He walked to and fro in the street opposite the church, unable to take his gaze from it.

'I'll go in,' he thought. 'Just a moment, though . . . Oh, what has come over me?' he added, feeling that his distraught soul could not accomplish even as simple an act as this without hesitation.

Then he recalled how long it had been since he had been in church. 'When was it? My wedding was once . . . my wife's funeral another . . .'

But in neither case had he been fully aware of what was happening; so now he looked at the church as if it were something completely new to him.

'What's that huge building, which has towers instead of chimneys, in which no one lives, where only the remains of the dead sleep? Why that waste of space and walls; for whom does the light burn night and day; why do crowds of people gather there? They go to the market for food, to the shops for goods, to the theatre for entertainment, but why here?'

Involuntarily he compared the smallness of the pious people standing near the church with the huge dimensions of the sacred edifice, and a peculiar notion came into his mind. Just as, once upon a time, powerful forces had raised mountain chains from the flat plains, so once upon a time another immeasurable force had existed in mankind, which had raised up this kind of building. Contemplating such buildings, a man might think that giants had lived in the depths of our planet who had undermined the earth's crust and left traces of their activities in the form of impressive edifices.

'Where did they go to, those giants? To another, higher world, perhaps. And if the tides of the sea prove that the moon is not merely an illusory gleam, but genuine reality, then why should not these strange buildings confirm the existence of another world? Do they not attract human souls as powerfully as the moon attracts the waves of the sea?'

He went into the church and was struck by another sight. Some mendicants, male and female, were begging for the charity which God would repay to the charitable in the next world. Some of the faithful were kissing the feet of a Christ who had been tortured and put to death by the Roman State, while others had fallen on their knees on the threshold and were raising up their hands and eyes as if gazing at a supernatural vision. The church was plunged in gloom, which could not be dispelled by the glow of several hundred tapers in silver candelabra. Here and there, on the floor of the chapels, could be seen indistinctly the shapes of people lying outstretched or crouching down to conceal their piety and humility. Looking at these motionless bodies, a man might think their souls had left them for a time and flown to some better world.

'Now I understand,' thought Wokulski, 'why visiting a church intensifies faith. Here everything is arranged so as to remind us of eternity.'

His gaze shifted from these shadows absorbed in prayer towards the light. In various parts of the church he saw tables spread with carpets, on them trays full of bank-notes, silver and gold, and near them were ladies seated in comfortable chairs, dressed in furs, feather and velvet, surrounded by cheerful young people. The most pious were accosting passers-by, all were talking and enjoying themselves as if they were at a ball. It seemed to Wokulski that at this moment he could distinguish three worlds. One (which had long since departed from the earth) had prayed and erected powerful buildings to the glory of God. The second, poor and humble, knew how to pray but only erected cottages – while, the third built palaces for itself, but had forgotten how to pray and made God's House into a place for fashionable gatherings, like carefree birds that build their nests and sing on the graves of dead heroes.

'And I? What am I – a stranger to them all?'

'Perhaps you are an eye of the iron sieve into which I cast all these people to divide the chaff from the grain,' replied a voice.

Wokulski looked round. 'The illusion of a disordered imagination.' Simultaneously he caught sight at a fourth table in the depths of the church of Countess Karolowa and Izabela. Both were seated by a tray with money, and were holding books, probably prayer-books. A servant in black livery was standing behind the Countess's chair.

Wokulski went towards them, past the kneeling people, avoiding other tables where they tapped insistently for his attention. He approached the tray and bowed to the Countess, then put down his roll of half-imperials.

'My God . . .' he thought, 'how stupid I must look with this money.'

The Countess put her book aside. 'How are you, Mr Wokulski?' she said. 'You know, I thought you were not coming, and I may tell you that I was rather disappointed.'

'I told you he would come, aunt, and with that sack of gold into the bargain,' Izabela interposed in English.

The Countess flushed and perspired. Her niece's words alarmed her, for she supposed that Wokulski understood English. 'Please, Mr Wokulski,' she said hastily, 'sit down here for a while, our companion has deserted us. Allow me to put your imperials on top, to shame those gentlemen who prefer squandering their money on champagne . . .'

'Don't be so anxious, aunt,' Izabela interrupted, again in English, 'he certainly doesn't understand.'

This time Wokulski blushed.

'Please, Bela,' said the Countess in a ceremonial tone, 'Mr Wokulski . . . has given so generously to our cause . . .'

'So I've heard,' Izabela replied in Polish, lowering her eyelashes in token of greeting.

'Your ladyship', said Wokulski rather facetiously, 'seeks to deprive me of my deserts in the next world by praising deeds I may well have done with a view to profit in this . . .'

'I guessed as much,' whispered Izabela in English.

The Countess nearly swooned, feeling certain that Wokulski must have guessed the meaning of her niece's words even if he knew no languages at all. 'You may, Mr Wokulski,' she said in feverish haste, 'you may easily obtain your deserts in the next world if only by . . . forgiving insults . . .'

'I always do,' he replied, somewhat surprised.

'You should not say "always",' the Countess continued. 'I'm an old woman, and your friend, Mr Wokulski,' she added with emphasis, 'so you must make certain allowances for me.'

'I am at your service.'

'Recently you dismissed one of your . . . employees, a certain Mraczewski . . .'

'Why was that?' Izabela suddenly exclaimed.

'I don't know,' said the Countess. 'Apparently it was to do with a difference in political opinions or something of the sort . . .'

'So that young man has opinions?' Izabela exclaimed. 'Interesting!'

She said this in such a diverting fashion that Wokulski felt his dislike for Mraczewski diminish. 'It was not his opinions that were in question, Countess,' he said, 'but his tactless comments on customers in our shop.'

'Perhaps the customers themselves behaved tactlessly,' Izabela put in.

'That is their privilege, they pay for it,' Wokulski replied calmly. 'We do not.'

A strong flush appeared on Izabela's face. She picked up her book and began reading.

'However that may be, let me persuade you to be merciful,' said the Countess. 'I know the boy's mother, and believe me it is pitiful to see her despair . . .'

Wokulski pondered. 'Very well,' he replied, 'I'll give him a position, but in Moscow.'

'And his poor mother?' asked the Countess, imploringly.

'I'll increase his wages by two – three hundred roubles,' he replied.

At this moment some children approached the table, and the Countess began distributing sacred pictures. Wokulski rose from his chair and, to avoid interrupting the pious occupation of the Countess, went across to Izabela.

Izabela looked up from her book and, gazing strangely at Wokulski, asked: 'Do you never change your mind?'

'No,' he replied. But at that moment he lowered his gaze.

'Suppose I were to plead for this young man?'

Wokulski glanced at her in surprise. 'In that case, I would reply that Mr Mraczewski lost his position because he spoke indiscreetly of persons who had honoured him by their condescension . . . However, if you order . . .'

Now Izabela lowered her eyes, highly confused.

'Oh . . . oh, it is all the same to me where this young man goes. He may as well go to Moscow.'

'So he will,' Wokulski replied. 'Pray accept my respects, ladies,' he added, bowing.

The Countess gave him her hand. 'Thank you, Mr Wokulski, for remembering us, and please come to me for the Easter meal. Please do, Mr Wokulski,' she added, with emphasis.

Suddenly catching sight of movement inside the church, she turned to the servant. 'Ksawery, please go to the Duchess and ask her to allow us the use of her carriage. Say our horse is sick.'

'For when, your ladyship?' asked the servant.

'In an hour and a half . . . Bela, we shan't stay longer, shall we?' The servant went across to a table by the door.

'So until tomorrow, Mr Wokulski,' said the Countess. 'You will meet many acquaintances at my house. There will be some gentlemen from the Charitable Society . . .'

'Hm . . .' Wokulski thought as he said goodbye to the Countess. However, he felt so grateful to her that he would have devoted half his fortune to her cause just then.

Izabela nodded distantly to him and again glanced at him in a manner which struck him as unusual. But when Wokulski had disappeared into the obscurity of the church, she said to the Countess: 'You were flirting with that man, aunt. Really, it is beginning to look rather suspicious . . .'

'Your father is right,' the Countess replied, 'this man can be useful. Anyhow, such social relations are *comme il faut* abroad.'

'What if they turn his head?' Izabela asked.

'That would prove he had a weak head,' the Countess replied shortly, reading her prayer-book.

Wokulski did not leave the church, but turned into a side nave near the door. Just by Christ's Grave, opposite the Countess's table, an empty confessional stood in one corner. Wokulski went into it, shut the door and began unseen to watch Izabela.

She was holding a book, glancing now and then towards the church door. Weariness and boredom were depicted in her face.

Sometimes children approached the table for pictures; Izabela herself distributed a few, with a gesture which said: 'Oh, when will this end?'

'She is doing all this not out of piety or love for children, but for notice and to acquire a husband,' Wokulski thought. 'Well, and I too,' he added, 'do much for self-advertisement and marriage. The world is well arranged, to be sure! Instead of simply asking "Do you love me or not?" or "Do you want me or not?" I throw away hundreds of roubles while she bores herself for hours on end and feigns piety.'

'Suppose she said she didn't love me? All these ceremonies have one good aspect: they give us time and the opportunity to become acquainted. But it is bad not to speak English . . . Today I'd have known what she thinks of me; for I am certain she was speaking of me to her aunt. I must learn it . . .

'Or take such a trivial thing as a carriage . . . If I had one, I could have sent her home with her aunt in it, and another bond would have formed between us. It would cost a thousand roubles a year, but that can't be helped. I must be prepared for all eventualities . . . A carriage, English lessons . . . more than two hundred roubles for one Easter offering! And I am doing all this, I who despise it. However, what am I to spend my money on, if not to ensure my own happiness? What do theories of economics mean to me when my heart aches?'

His thoughts were interrupted by a sorrowful melody. It came from a musical box, and was followed by the singing of stuffed birds; when they fell silent the whispering of the fountain and the sighs of the pious could be heard.

Crouched and kneeling figures were visible in the nave, near the confessional, in the doors of chapels. Some crawled along the floor to the Crucifix and kissed it, then placed small coins extricated from handkerchiefs in the tray.

A white Christ figure, surrounded by flowers, lay in the depths of a chapel, under a flood of light. It seemed to Wokulski that its face had come alive under the influence of the flickering rays, taking on an expression of severity, or mercy and forgiveness. When a musical box played tunes from *Lucia di Lammermoor*, or when the clatter of money and exclamations in French came from the centre of the church, the features of the Christ darkened. But when a poor man approached the Crucifix and told the Crucified One of his sufferings, then Christ opened His dead lips and, against the tinkling of the fountain, repeated blessings and promises: 'Blessed are the meek . . . Blessed are they who mourn . . .'

A young, painted girl went up to the tray. She placed a silver coin in it, but did not venture to touch the Cross. Those kneeling near looked askance at her velvet coat and gaudy hat. But when the Christ whispered: 'Let him who is without sin cast a stone at her . . .' she sank to the floor and kissed His feet as Mary Magdalene once did.

'Blessed are they who seek justice . . . Blessed are they who mourn . . .'

Deeply touched, Wokulski watched the crowd in the gloom of the church who had been waiting with such patient faith for eighteen centuries for the heavenly promises to be fulfilled.

'When will that be?' he thought.

'The Son of Man will send His angels and they will bear away all suffering and those who commit injustices, as if gathering weeds, and will consume them with fire . . .'

Wokulski looked around the church mechanically. By the table, the Countess was taking a nap, and Izabela yawning; at a further table three unknown young ladies were laughing at the stories of an elegant young man.

'It is another world . . . another world,' Wokulski thought. 'What fatality is driving me in their direction?'

At this moment, a young woman, very neatly dressed and accompanied by a little girl, stopped then knelt down by the confessional. Wokulski looked at her and noticed she was unusually beautiful. The expression of her face was what struck him most, it was as if she had come to the grave not to pray, but to question and lament. She crossed herself, then saw the tray for offerings and brought out a small purse.

'Helusia,' she said to the little girl in an undertone, 'go and put this on the tray, and kiss the Lord Jesus.'

'Where am I to kiss Him, mama?'

'On His hands and feet.'

'Not on His mouth?'

'No, that is not allowed.'

'Well, fancy . . .' and she ran to the tray, then crouched over the cross.

'Mama,' she cried, coming back, 'I kissed Him, but the Lord Jesus didn't answer.'

'Now, be a good girl,' said her mother, 'kneel down and say your prayers.'

'Which prayers?'

'Three Our Fathers, then the Hail Mary . . .'

'Oh, what long prayers . . . and I am only a little girl.'

'Well, say one . . . But kneel down . . . and look over there.'

'Hail Mary, full of Grace . . . Mama, what are those birds singing?'

'They're stuffed birds. Say your prayer.'

'Stuffed, mama?'

'Say the first rosary . . .'

'I forget where I got to . . .'

'Say after mama: "Hail Mary . . ."'

'. . . to our death, amen,' the little girl concluded. 'What are those stuffed birds made of, mama?'

'Helusia, shush, or I won't give you a kiss,' her mother whispered distractedly. 'Here's a prayer-book, look at the pictures of how the Lord Jesus was crucified.'

The little girl sat down with the book on the confessional steps and fell silent.

'What a pretty child,' Wokulski thought. 'If she were mine, then surely I'd regain control of my senses which I'm losing from one day to the next. And her mother is a pretty woman, too. Her hair, profile, eyes . . . She's praying to find happiness again . . . Beautiful but unhappy . . . she must be a widow.

'Ha – if I'd met her a year ago! What kind of order is there in the world? Just a pace away are two unhappy people: one seeking love and a family; the other perhaps struggling with poverty and indifference. Either might find what he or she needs in the other – but they'll never meet. One comes here to beg God's mercy; the other throws away money in order to make social contacts. Who knows but that a few hundred roubles mightn't mean happiness to that woman? Yet she won't get them: nowadays God doesn't hear the prayers of the oppressed . . .

'Suppose I were to find out who she is? Perhaps I could help her? Why shouldn't the high-sounding promises of Christ be fulfilled, even by such an unbeliever as I, since the pious are otherwise engaged?'

At this moment Wokulski flushed . . . An elegant young man had approached the Countess's table and placed something in the tray. Seeing him, Izabela blushed and her eyes took on that strange expression which always made Wokulski wonder.

The elegant young man sat down at the Countess's invitation in the same chair Wokulski had occupied, and a lively conversation ensued. Wokulski could not hear what was said, but he felt the picture of the group burning into his brain. The costly carpet, the silver tray strewn with his handful of imperials, the two candelabra with ten flames, the Countess in deep mourning, the young man gazing at Izabela and she – radiant. Nor did it escape his notice that the Countess's cheeks, the tip of the young man's nose, and Izabela's eyes were all glowing in the light of the flames.

'Are they in love?' he thought. 'If so, why don't they marry? Perhaps he has no money . . . If he hasn't, what does that look of hers mean? She looked at me like that, today. It is true that an eligible young lady must have several or several hundred admirers and attract them all, in order to sell herself to the highest bidder . . .'

Their companion arrived. The Countess rose, as did Izabela and the handsome young man, and all three went towards the door with a great deal of rustling, stopping at the other tables. Each young man assisting there greeted Izabela cordially, while she bestowed upon them the same, the very same gaze, which had made Wokulski's reason totter. Finally all became silent; the Countess and Izabela had left the church.

Wokulski roused himself and looked around. The pretty woman and the child had gone. 'A pity,' he whispered, and felt a light pressure upon his heart.

Meanwhile, the young girl in the velvet jacket and gaudy hat was still kneeling on the ground by the Cross. When she turned her gaze upon the illuminated grave, something glistened on her rouged cheeks. She kissed Christ's feet once more, rose wearily and went out.

'Blessed are they who mourn . . . May the dead Christ keep his promise to you at least,' Wokulski thought, and followed her out.

He saw the girl giving money to the beggars in the porch. And a cruel pain came upon him when he thought of these two women, one of whom wanted to sell herself for a fortune, while the other was already selling herself from poverty; the latter, covered though she was in shame, might well be the better and the purer before some higher tribunal.

In the street he caught up with her, and asked: 'Where are you going?'

There were traces of tears on her face. She raised her apathetic gaze to Wokulski, and replied: 'Your way, if you like.'

'So? Come then.'

It was not yet five o'clock, broad daylight: some passers-by looked around after them. 'I must be mad to do anything like this,' Wokulski thought, going in the direction of the store. 'Never mind the scandal, but what sort of ideas have I got into my head? Evangelism? It's the height of absurdity. However, I don't care. I am only carrying out the will of another . . .'

He turned into the gate of the block in which his shop was, and went into Rzecki's room, the girl following. Ignacy was in and, seeing the extraordinary pair, raised his hands in amazement.

'Can you leave us alone for a few minutes?' Wokulski asked him. Ignacy said not a word. He took the key from the back door and left the room.

'Both of you?' the girl murmured, taking out her hat-pin.

'One moment,' Wokulski interrupted. 'You were in church just now, miss, weren't you?'

'You saw me?'

'You were praying and crying. May I ask why?'

Surprised, the girl shrugged as she answered, 'Are you a priest, then, to ask me that?' And looking more attentively at Wokulski, added: 'Ah – all this fuss! It's silly.'

She moved as if to go, but Wokulski stopped her: 'Wait. Someone would like to help you, so don't be in a hurry and just answer me openly.'

Again she gazed at him. Suddenly her eyes lit up and a flush came into her face. 'I know!' she cried, 'you must be from that old gent! He promised to look after me, several times. Is he very rich? Of course he is, very . . . He rides in his own carriage and sits in the front row at the theatre.'

'Listen,' Wokulski interrupted, 'and answer me; why were you crying in the church?'

'Well, you see . . .' the girl began, and told him such a bold tale of some squabble with her landlady that Wokulski turned pale as he listened: 'The animal . . .' he whispered.

'I went to have a look at those graves,' the girl went on, 'I thought it might keep my mind off things. But not likely – when I remembered the old hag I had to cry out of sheer rage. And I asked the Lord God to afflict the old hag with sickness, or to help me get away from her. And God must have heard me, if that gent wants to look after me . . .'

Wokulski sat motionless. Finally he asked: 'How old are you?'

'I usually say I'm sixteen, but I'm nineteen really.'

'Do you want to get away from it?'

'Oh, to Hell even. They've treated me so hatefully . . . but . . .'

'Well?'

'Nothing will come of it. If I leave today, then they'll take me back after the holidays is over and treat me like they did after New Year, when I was sick for a week . . .'

'They won't . . .'

'How so? I'm in debt . . .'

'Much?'

'Hm . . . about fifty roubles. I don't know how it came about, but they make me pay double for everything. There it is though . . . It's always so with the likes of us. And when they hear that the old gent has money, then they'll say I stole from them and will slander me as they choose.'

Wokulski felt his boldness ebbing away. 'Tell me, do you want to get work?'

'Doing what?'

'You might learn to sew.'

'That's no use. I worked in a laundry once. But no one can manage on eight roubles a month. Besides, I'm not that worthless yet, so I can do without sewing for anyone.'

Wokulski looked up: 'Do you want to leave that place?'

'Yes, I do!'

'Then make up your mind. Either you go to work, because no

one can expect to live for nothing in the world . . .'

'That isn't true,' she interrupted. 'That old gent don't work, but he has money. Sometimes he told me I wouldn't have to worry my head no more . . .'

'You won't go to that man, but to the Magdalenes instead. Or – back to where you came from.'

'The nuns won't take me. I'd have to pay my debts first, and have a recommendation.'

'If you go there, everything will be arranged.'

'How?'

'I'll give you a letter, which you will take with you, and you can stay there. Do you want to – or not?'

'Ha – give me the letter first. Then I'll see what it is like.'

She sat down and gazed about the room. Wokulski wrote the letter, told her where to go and added: 'Here's money for the trip, and for moving your things. If you are a good girl, and industrious, they will be good to you; but if you don't take advantage of this opportunity – then do what you want. You may go.'

The girl laughed out loud: 'The old woman will be mad! I'll show her . . . Ha ha! But . . . may be you're only putting me on?'

'Go,' said Wokulski, indicating the door.

She glanced inquiringly at him once again, and went out with a shrug.

Presently Ignacy appeared: 'What kind of an acquaintance was that?' he asked sourly.

'You're right . . .' said Wokulski thoughtfully. 'I never yet saw such an animal, though I know many beasts.'

'Thousands in Warsaw alone,' Rzecki replied.

'I know. It is no use condemning them, though, for they are continually being reborn and, in consequence, society will sooner or later have to be reconstructed from top to bottom. Or perish.'

'Hm . . .' Rzecki whispered, 'I thought as much.'

Wokulski said goodbye to him. He felt like a man with fever over whom cold water had been thrown.

'But before society can re-create itself,' he thought, 'I can see that the sphere of my philanthropy will narrow down very much. My fortune will not suffice to ennoble inhuman instincts. I prefer yawning ladies seeking charity to weeping and praying monsters . . .'

The picture of Izabela appeared to him, surrounded by an aureole even brighter than before. The blood rose to his head and he blamed himself inwardly for comparing her with such a creature! 'I'd sooner throw away money on carriages and race-horses than on that sort of wretch!'

On Easter Sunday, Wokulski drove to the Countess's house in a hired carriage. There he found a long line of carriages of all kinds and elegance. There were smart droshkies serving gilded youths, ordinary droshkies hired by the hour by retired persons; old carriages, old horses, old equipment and servants in worn livery; and new little barouches direct from Vienna, whose footmen had flowers in their button-holes and whose drivers laid their whips across their thighs like marshals' batons. There were even fantastic Cossacks dressed in trousers so baggy that their masters might have placed all their hopes within them.

In passing he also noticed that in the crowd of drivers, the servants of great gentlefolk behaved in a very dignified manner, while those of bankers wished to run the whole show (for which they were much abused), but that the droshky-men were the most resolute. However, the drivers of the hired carriages kept close together, despising the rest and being despised by them.

When Wokulski entered the vestibule, a grey-haired doorkeeper with a black ribbon around his neck bowed low and opened the door to the cloakroom, where a gentleman in a black frock-coat relieved him of his overcoat. At the same time, the Countess's butler Józef hurried up: he knew Wokulski well, and he had brought the music-box and singing-birds from the store to the church. 'Her Excellency expects you,' said Józef.

Wokulski reached into his waistcoat pocket and handed him five roubles, feeling he was behaving like a parvenu. 'How stupid of me,' he thought. 'No – not stupid – merely a *nouveau riche* who has to pay everyone at every step he takes in this society. Well, it costs more to convert women who have sinned.'

He went up the marble staircase that was decorated with flowers, Józef in front. On the first landing he had his hat on his head, on the second he took it off, not knowing whether he was behaving properly or not. 'I might have gone in to join them with my hat on,' he said to himself.

He noticed that although Józef was past middle age, he darted up the stairs like a young goat, and had already disappeared, so that Wokulski was left alone, not knowing which way to go nor to whom he should announce himself. It was only a moment, but anger began boiling up within him.

'What conventions do they safeguard themselves with, then?' he thought. 'Oh – if only I could overthrow all this . . .'

And for ten seconds or so he saw that between himself and this respectable world of elegant conventions a struggle must ensue in which either this world must collapse – or he perish. 'All right – let me perish . . . but I'll leave behind a memory of myself . . .'

'You will leave behind forgiveness and mercy,' a voice whispered to him.

'Am I then – so vile?'

'No, you are noble.'

He pulled himself together – before him stood Mr Tomasz
Łęcki. 'How are you, Stanisław,' he said majestically, 'I welcome
you even more warmly since your arrival is linked with a very
agreeable event in our family . . .'

'Can Izabela have become engaged?' Wokulski thought, and
there was a blackness before his eyes.

'Imagine, my dear sir, that on the occasion of your visit . . .
Are you listening, Stanisław? . . . On the occasion of your call I
have reached agreement with my sister Joanna . . . But you turn
pale? . . . Come, you will find many acquaintances here. Pray do
not suppose the aristocracy is quite so alarming . . .'

Wokulski pulled himself together: 'Mr Łęcki,' he said, coldly, 'in
my tent near Plevna even greater gentlefolk used to visit me. And
they were so agreeable towards me that I do not easily become
excited at the sight of such gentry as . . . one meets in Warsaw.'

'Upon my word . . .' Mr Łęcki murmured and bowed.

Wokulski was taken aback: 'There's a flunkey for you,' went
through his head, 'And I . . . I was apprehensive of such people as
this?'

Mr Łęcki took him by the arm and conducted him in a very
ceremonial manner into the first drawing-room, where there were
only men.

'You see, my dear sir – the Count . . .' Tomasz began.

'I know him,' Wokulski said, adding inwardly, 'He owes me
some three hundred roubles . . .'

'The banker . . .' Tomasz then explained. But before he could
utter the banker's name, the banker himself came up, saluted
Wokulski and said: 'Upon my word, there's a great deal of excitement in Paris about those boulevards. Have you replied?'

'I wanted to speak to you first,' Wokulski replied.

'Let us meet somewhere, then. When are you at home?'

'I have no fixed time, and would prefer to come to your house.'

'Pray call on me next Wednesday, then, for lunch, and we will
finish with the matter once and for all.'

They said goodbye. Tomasz pressed Wokulski's arm more
warmly: 'The general . . .' he began. Seeing Wokulski, the general
shook him by the hand and they greeted one another like old
acquaintances.

Tomasz became increasingly affectionate toward Wokulski and
began to be surprised, seeing that this tradesman knew so many of
the most eminent persons in town, and not only those distinguished by unearned titles and fortunes.

When they went into the second drawing-room, where there
were a number of ladies, the Countess Karolowa came over to
them. Józef, the butler, was hovering in the background.

'They have set up a sentry,' Wokulski thought, 'so as not to compromise the *nouveau riche* tradesman. Considerate of them, but . . .'

'I am so pleased, Mr Wokulski,' said the Countess, taking him over from Tomasz, 'so pleased that you have done as I asked. There is someone here who wishes to make your acquaintance.'

The appearance of Wokulski had caused something of a sensation in the first drawing-room: 'General,' said the Count, 'Countess Karolowa is beginning to introduce us to tradespeople. This Wokulski . . .'

'Is as much a tradesman as you or I,' the general replied.

'Prince,' said another Count, 'how on earth did that Wokulski get invited here?'

'Our hostess invited him,' the Prince retorted.

'I have no prejudice against tradespeople,' the Count went on, 'but Wokulski has been involved in military supplies and made a fortune . . .'

'Yes, yes . . .' the Prince interrupted. 'That sort of fortune is usually suspect, but I can vouch for Wokulski. The Countess spoke to me of him, and I have asked officers who served in the war, including my own nephew. The general opinion is that the supplies Wokulski was concerned with were honest. Even the men, when they got good bread, used to say it must have been baked with Wokulski's flour. Furthermore,' the Prince went on, 'Wokulski came to the attention of some very highly placed personages indeed and had some very attractive propositions made to him. In January this year he was offered two hundred thousand roubles merely for his signature in a certain enterprise, but he refused.'

The Count laughed and said: 'No doubt he might have held out for more than two hundred thousand . . .'

'Yes, but then he would not have been here today,' the Prince replied and moved away with a nod.

'Old fool,' the Count whispered, looking after the Prince contemptuously.

In the third drawing-room, which Wokulski now entered with the Countess, there was a buffet and many small and large tables, at which guests sat in couples, threes or even foursomes. Servants were handing round food and wine, and Izabela was directing them, evidently taking the place of the hostess. She wore a pale blue gown, and had large pearls at her throat. She was so beautiful, her gestures so queenly, that Wokulski turned to stone as he looked at her. 'How can I even so much as dream of her?' he thought in despair.

At the same moment, he caught sight in a window-seat of the young man who had been in church the previous day, and who was now sitting alone at a small table, without taking his eyes off Izabela. 'Of course, he loves her . . .' Wokulski thought, and he felt as though the chill of the grave had enveloped him. 'I am lost . . .' he added, to himself.

All this lasted only a few seconds.

'Do you see that old lady between the bishop and the general?' the Countess asked Wokulski. 'That is Duchess Zasławska, my best friend, who insists on meeting you. She is very interested in you,' the Countess went on, smiling, 'she has no children, and several pretty grand-daughters. Make a good choice! Meanwhile, keep your eye on her, and when those gentlemen go away I will introduce you. Ah, Prince!'

'How do you do,' the Prince said to Wokulski, 'may I, cousin?'

'Of course,' the Countess replied. 'Here is a vacant table for you both . . . Allow me to leave you for a moment.'

'Let us sit down, Mr Wokulski,' said the Prince. 'This is indeed convenient, as I have an important matter to discuss with you. Pray imagine that your plans have caused a tremendous upheaval among our cotton manufacturers . . . Isn't that the word: "cotton"? . . . They insist you want to kill the industry. Is the competition you are creating really so dangerous?'

'It is true', Wokulski replied, 'that I have three or even four million roubles credit with the Moscow manufacturers, but I do not yet know whether their products will suit our market.'

'A huge sum of money, to be sure,' the Prince murmured. 'Do you not see a genuine threat to our factories in it?'

'Not in the least. I see only an insignificant decrease in their own immense profits, which are no concern of mine. My duty is to concern myself with my own profits and give my customers good value; for our goods will be cheaper.'

'Have you reflected upon this problem as a citizen?' the Prince asked, pressing his arm. 'As things are, we have so little to lose . . .'

'It seems to me it is enough for a citizen to provide cheap products for consumers and to smash the monopoly of factory owners, who have nothing in common with us except that they exploit our customers and workers . . .'

'You think so? I hadn't considered that. However, I'm not concerned with factory owners but with our country, our unhappy country . . .'

'What may I offer you?' asked Izabela, suddenly approaching. The Prince and Wokulski rose.

'How pretty you look today, cousin,' said the Prince, taking her hand. 'I much regret that I am not my own son . . . Although perhaps it is just as well. For if you were to turn me down, which is very likely, I should be very unhappy . . . I beg your pardon!' the Prince added, 'allow me, cousin, to introduce Mr Wokulski. An active man, an active citizen . . . That is recommendation enough, is it not?'

'We have met,' Izabela whispered in response to Wokulski's

bow. He looked into her eyes and saw there such horror, such wretchedness, that he was once again overcome by despair. 'Why did I come here?' he thought. He glanced at the window and again noticed the young man, who was still sitting there alone with an untouched plate, covering his eyes with one hand. 'Why did I come here, wretched man that I am . . .' thought Wokulski, feeling as if his heart were being torn out of him with pincers.

'Would you care for some wine?' Izabela inquired, eyeing him with surprise.

'If you like,' he replied mechanically.

'We must become better acquainted, Mr Wokulski,' said the Prince. 'You must join our sphere in which, believe me, there are sensible and noble hearts – but a lack of initiative.'

'I am a *nouveau riche*, I have no title,' Wokulski replied, merely for the sake of answering.

'On the contrary, you have one title at least – work: the second, honesty; the third – talent; the fourth – energy . . . We need these for the rebirth of our country, so give us them and we will take to you as to a brother . . .'

The Countess approached. 'May I, Prince?' she said, 'Mr Wokulski . . .' She gave him her hand and both went over to the Duchess's armchair.

'This, Duchess, is Mr Stanisław Wokulski,' said the Countess to an old lady in black, covered with costly lace.

'Sit down, please,' said the Duchess, indicating the chair by her. 'Your first name is Stanisław, then? And which branch of the Wokulskis do you belong to, pray?'

'A branch . . . unknown to anyone,' he replied, 'and least of all to you, I am sure.'

'Didn't your father serve in the army?'

'My uncle, but not my father.'

'Do you not recall where he served? Wasn't his first name Stanisław?'

'It was. He was a lieutenant, later a captain in the Seventh Infantry regiment.'

'The first brigade of the second division,' the Duchess interrupted. 'You see, young man, that you are not so unknown to me. Is he still alive?'

'He died five years ago.'

The Duchess's hands began trembling. She opened a tiny flask and inhaled it. 'He died, you say? God rest his soul . . . Did he not leave behind a souvenir of any kind?'

'A gold cross.'

'Yes, a gold cross . . . Nothing more?'

'A miniature of himself, taken in 1828, on ivory.'

The Duchess kept sniffing the tiny flask: her hands trembled more and more. 'A miniature,' she repeated. 'Do you happen to know who painted it? Did he not leave anything else?'

'There was a bundle of letters and another miniature.'

'What has become of them?' the Duchess inquired, still more agitated.

'My uncle sealed them up some days before he died and asked that they should be put into his coffin.'

'Ah . . . ah . . .' the old lady whispered, and burst into tears.

There was a stir in the drawing-room. Izabela anxiously hastened over, then the Countess. They took the Duchess by the hand and slowly led her into another room. All eyes were upon Wokulski. People began whispering.

Seeing that everyone was looking at him and talking about him, Wokulski grew embarrassed. In order to give the impression that this peculiar popularity did not concern him, he drank two glasses of wine in rapid succession from a table, then realised that one glass of Hungarian wine had been that of the general, and the other, of red wine, the bishop's.

'I am doing very nicely indeed,' he said to himself. 'They will say I offended the old lady in order to get at her neighbours' wine.'

He rose, meaning to leave, and grew hot at the thought of proceeding across two drawing-rooms in which a gauntlet of stares and whispers awaited him. But the Prince stopped him.

'You and the Duchess were no doubt talking about the old days, and that has distressed her. Am I right? To revert to the subject we were discussing when we were interrupted. Do you think it would be a good thing to establish a Polish factory of cheap linen?'

Wokulski shook his head: 'I doubt if it would succeed,' he replied. 'It is difficult to conceive of large factories for people unable to make small improvements in those already in existence . . . In other words . . . I am referring to mills,' Wokulski went on, 'in a few years we shall even be importing flour, for our millers are reluctant to replace the stones they use with steam rollers.'

'Unheard of ! . . . Let us sit down,' said the Prince, drawing him to a wide alcove, 'and tell me what you have in mind.'

Meanwhile people were talking in the drawing-rooms.

'There is something enigmatic about that man,' said a lady in French, wearing diamonds, to a lady wearing peacock feathers, 'I never before saw the Duchess crying.'

'It's a love story, of course,' said the befeathered lady, 'and it was a malicious trick on someone's part to introduce that individual . . .'

'Do you think that . . . ?'

'I'm quite sure,' she replied, with a shrug. 'One only has to look at him. Very bad manners, but what features, what pride of bearing! Noble birth cannot be concealed, not even by rags . . .'

'How extraordinary,' said the lady in diamonds, 'and that fortune of his, allegedly made in Bulgaria?'

'Of course. That helps explain why the Duchess, despite her wealth, spends so little on herself . . .'

'And the Prince so very civil to him . . .'

'That was the least he could do . . . Just to look at the pair of them is enough . . .'

'Yet I wouldn't say there was any likeness . . .'

'Perhaps not, but – that pride, that self-confidence . . . and how very freely they talked to one another . . .'

At another table three men were conferring: 'Well, the Countess has achieved a real *coup d'état*!' said a dark man with a forelock.

'And it succeeded. Wokulski is somewhat on the stiff side in his manners, but there's something about him for all that,' replied a grey-haired man.

'Of course he's in trade . . .'

'Trade is no worse than banking . . .'

'But a tradesman in haberdashery, he sells pocket-books,' the dark man insisted.

'We sell coats of arms sometimes,' put in the third, a lean old man with grey whiskers.

'On top of this he wants to marry here . . .'

'So much the better for our girls . . .'

'I'd let him have my daughter. I hear he's respectable, wealthy, he won't gamble her dowry away.'

The Countess passed by them swiftly: 'Mr Wokulski,' she said, and stretched out her fan in the direction of the alcove.

Wokulski hastened to her side. She gave him a hand, and they left the drawing-room together. Men at once surrounded the Prince, some asked to be introduced to Wokulski. 'It is worth while,' said the Prince, gratified. 'There has never yet been such a man among us. Had we drawn closer to them long ago, our unhappy country would be different today . . .'

Izabela, who was passing, heard this and turned pale. The young man who had been with her in the church approached. 'You are tired?' he said.

'A little,' she replied, with an unhappy smile. 'An odd question has just occurred to me,' she added, after a pause, 'I wonder whether I too am capable of struggling?'

'Against your own heart?' he asked. 'It is not worth while.'

Izabela shrugged: 'Not that. I am thinking of a real struggle, with a powerful enemy.' She pressed his hand and left the drawing-room.

Conducted by the Countess, Wokulski passed through a long series of rooms. From one, far away from the other guests, came the sounds of singing and a pianoforte. When they entered, he was confronted by an unusual sight. A young man was playing the piano, one very handsome young woman standing by him was pretending to play a violin, and another a trumpet: to this music several couples were dancing, with only one man among them.

'Naughty things!' the Countess scolded. They replied by a burst of laughter, but did not pause in their diversions.

They passed through this room and came to a staircase.

'That,' said the Countess, 'was the highest aristocracy. Instead of sitting in the drawing-rooms, they have taken refuge here to misbehave themselves . . .'

'How sensible of them,' Wokulski thought. And it seemed to him that life passed more simply and more entertainingly among those people than among the pompous bourgeoisie or gentry seeking to enter aristocratic circles.

Upstairs, in a room well away from the tumult, and somewhat dark, sat the Duchess in an armchair.

'I'll leave you here,' said the Countess. 'Have a talk, for I must go back to the guests.'

'Thank you, Joanna,' the Duchess replied. 'Please sit down,' she turned to Wokulski.

When they were alone, she added: 'You cannot know how many memories you have brought back to me.'

Only then did Wokulski realise that some unusual relationship must have existed between this woman and his uncle. He was overcome with uneasy surprise. 'Thank God,' he thought, 'that I'm the legal child of my parents . . .'

'Now,' the Duchess began, 'you say your uncle is dead. Where is his grave?'

'At Zasław, where he lived after returning from abroad.'

The old lady raised a handkerchief to her eyes: 'Is it so? How ungrateful of me . . . Were you ever at his home? Did he say nothing to you? Did he not show you . . .? For there, on a hill-top, is a ruined castle, is there not? Are the ruins still standing?'

'My uncle went to the castle every day for his walk, and I used to sit there with him for hours at a time, on a big rock.'

'Really? I know that rock; we both sat there together, and watched the river, and the clouds that passed taught us that happiness passes, just like they do. I only feel that now . . . And is the well inside the castle still as deep as ever?'

'It is very deep. But access to it is difficult, for ruins have covered the way in. It was not until my uncle showed me the way that . . .'

'Do you know', said the Duchess, 'that when we last said good-bye, we wondered if we should throw ourselves into that well . . . No one would ever have found us, and we would have been together for ever . . . As always – the follies of youth . . .'

She touched her eyes, and went on: 'I . . . I loved him very much, and think that he too loved me – a little, when he looked back. But he was a poor officer and I, unfortunately, was a rich heiress and related to two generals. So they separated us. Perhaps we were too virtuous . . . But no matter, no matter,' she added, smiling and crying. 'Such things can only be spoken of by a woman in her seventies . . .'

A sob interrupted her. She sniffed at the little flask, paused, then went on again: 'Great crimes are always being committed in this world of ours, but surely the greatest is to murder love. So many years have passed, almost half a century; everything has gone, my fortune, title, youth, happiness . . . Only grief has not passed and remains as fresh as though it were yesterday. Ah, were it not for my faith in another world, where this world's injustices are rewarded, who knows but that life and its conventions might not have been cursed . . . But you do not understand me, for you people nowadays have stronger though colder hearts than we . . .'

Wokulski sat with downcast eyes. Something was stifling him, tearing at his heart. He pressed his fingernails in his palms and wondered how to get away as fast as he could, so as not to listen to these laments which renewed his own most painful wounds.

'Has a gravestone been erected on his tomb?' the Duchess asked presently. Wokulski flushed. It had not occurred to him that the dead required anything more than a clod of earth over them.

'No?' the Duchess continued, noticing his embarrassment. 'But I am not surprised at you, my child, for forgetting a gravestone – rather do I reproach myself for having forgotten the man.'

She paused again, and putting her thin, trembling hand on his arm, suddenly said in a low voice: 'I have a request to make. Please say you will do it.'

'Of course,' Wokulski replied.

'Let me have a gravestone erected for him. But as I cannot see to it myself, you will do it. Take a stonemason with you, and tell him to make use of that rock, the one we used to sit on in the castle, and let one half be placed on his grave. Pay whatever it costs, and I shall return it to you with my eternal gratitude. Will you do this?'

'I will.'

'Good, I thank you . . . I think he will rest more easily under that stone which once heard us talking and which saw our tears . . . Oh, how painful it is to recollect . . . As for the inscription,' she went on, 'when we parted he left me a few verses from Mickiewicz. You must have read them: "Like a shadow that lengthens as the mournful wheel turns – so will remembrance of me . . . The further it flees, the more profound will be the mourning that bedims thy soul. . . ." How true that is! And I would like to commemorate in some way the well that was to have joined us . . .'

Wokulski roused himself and gazed wide-eyed into the distance.

'What is the matter?' the Duchess asked.

'Nothing,' he replied with a smile, 'death just looked into my eyes.'

'That should not surprise you; death is very near an old woman like me, so my neighbours cannot help seeing it. But you will do as I ask?'

'Yes.'

'Call on me after the holiday and . . . come often. Perhaps you will find it tedious, but even I perhaps, infirm as I am, may be useful to you in some way. Now, be off with you, be off . . .'

Wokulski kissed her hand, she kissed his forehead several times, then touched the bell. A servant entered. 'Take this gentleman to the drawing-room,' she said.

Wokulski was stunned. He did not know which way he was going, did not realise what he had been talking about with the Duchess. He only sensed that he was in a maze of huge chambers, ancient portraits, soft footfalls, undefined perfume. He was surrounded by costly furniture, people of great sensibility and taste such as he had never dreamed of. But above all this, the presence of that aristocratic old woman wafted like a poem, imbued with sighs and tears.

'What kind of a world is this? What kind of a world?'

Yet he felt the absence of something. He wanted to look upon Izabela once more. 'Well, I will see her in the drawing-room . . .'

The footman opened the door to the drawing-room. Again, all heads turned towards him and talk died down like the rustle of a bird flying away. A moment of silence followed in which everyone looked at Wokulski, but he saw no one, only sought feverishly for that pale blue gown. 'She isn't here . . .' he thought.

'Just look how unconcerned he is by all of us,' whispered the old man with grey whiskers, smiling.

'She must be in the second drawing-room,' Wokulski told himself.

He caught sight of the Countess, and went over to her.

'Well, have you finished your conference?' the Countess inquired. 'The Duchess is a charming person, is she not? . . . You have a true friend in her, though not more than you have in me. Let me introduce you . . . Mr Wokulski!' she added, turning to the lady in diamonds.

'I will come to the point immediately,' said the lady, looking at him loftily. 'Our orphans need several rolls of linen . . .' The Countess blushed slightly.

'Only several?' Wokulski echoed, and he looked at the lady's diamonds, which represented the value of several hundred rolls of the very finest quality linen. 'After the holiday,' he went on, 'I will have the honour of sending you the linen by the Countess.'

He bowed as if anxious to depart: 'You wish to say goodbye to us?' the Countess asked, somewhat embarrassed.

'But he is impertinent!' said the lady in diamonds to her companion in peacock feathers.

'Goodbye, Countess, and thank you for the honour you have been kind enough to confer on me,' said Wokulski, kissing the hand of his hostess.

'But it is only *au revoir*, Mr Wokulski, isn't it? We shall have a great deal of business together.'

Izabela was not in the second drawing-room either. Wokulski felt uneasy: 'I must see her . . . Who knows how long it will be before we meet again under such circumstances . . .'

'Ah, there you are,' the Prince cried. 'Now I know just what sort of a plot you and Łęcki have been hatching. A company for trading with the East – an excellent notion. You must let me in on it . . . We must get better acquainted. . .' But seeing that Wokulski said nothing, he added: 'I'm a great bore, Mr Wokulski, am I not? But that cannot be helped: you must join us; you and the likes of you – and we shall forge ahead together. Your firms are coats of arms, while our coats of arms are also firms which provide a guarantee of honesty in business dealings . . .'

They shook hands and Wokulski said something, though without knowing what. His uneasiness was mounting: he sought Izabela in vain.

'Surely she is further on,' he whispered fearfully, going into the last of the drawing-rooms.

Here Mr Łęcki stopped him with signs of unusual affection: 'Are you leaving already? Well, goodbye, my dear sir. The first meeting after the holiday will be at my house, and with God's blessing we shall begin work.'

'She's not here!' Wokulski thought, bidding goodbye to Tomasz.

'You know, sir,' Łęcki whispered, 'you have made a tremendous impression. The Countess is quite beside herself with glee, the Prince speaks only of you . . . And that incident with the Duchess, too! Quite marvellous . . . No one could wish for a better position. . .'

Wokulski was already on the threshold. Once again his glassy eyes travelled around the drawing-room – and he went out with despair in his heart. 'Perhaps I ought to go back and say goodbye to her? After all, she was taking the hostess's place . . .' he thought, going slowly down the stairs. Suddenly he stopped, hearing the rustle of a dress in the long gallery: 'There she is!'

He looked up, and saw the lady in diamonds.

Someone handed him his overcoat. Wokulski went into the street, staggering as though intoxicated: 'What is a fine position to me – if she is not there?'

'Mr Wokulski's carriage!' the porter shouted from the porch, devoutly clutching a three-rouble piece. His bleary eyes and somewhat hoarse voice bore witness that this citizen, despite his responsible position, had nevertheless been celebrating the first day of Easter. 'Mr Wokulski's carriage! . . . Wokulski's carriage . . . Drive up, Wokulski!' the drivers called.

Two lines of carriages were slowly moving along the Boulevard to and from the Belvedere palace. Someone passing caught sight of Wokulski standing on the pavement and bowed. 'An acquaintance!' Wokulski whispered, and he flushed. When his carriage was brought, he went to get in, but changed his mind: 'Go home, my man,' he said to the driver, tipping him.

The carriage drove off towards town. Wokulski joined the passers-by and went towards Aleje Ujazdowskie. He walked slowly and eyed the people in carriages. He knew many of them personally. There went a saddler who supplied him with leather goods, out for a ride with his wife who resembled a sugar-sack, and their rather plain daughter, whom they wanted to marry off to him. There went the son of a butcher, who had at one time supplied Hopfer's shop with pork. There was a wealthy carpenter with his family. The widow of a distiller, who had a large fortune of her own and was equally ready to bestow her hand on Wokulski . . . Here a tanner, there two clerks in the textile trade, then a tailor, a bricklayer, a jeweller, a baker – and here was his competitor, a haberdasher, in an ordinary carriage.

Most failed to see Wokulski, but some did, and bowed: but there were also those who saw him and did not bow, and even grinned maliciously. Of all these merchants, industrialists and tradesmen, equal to him in position, some wealthier and longer established in Warsaw – he alone had been invited to the Countess. None of them, only he!

'I'm having incredibly good fortune,' he thought. 'In six months I've made a fortune of thousands, in a few years I may have millions. Even earlier . . . Already today I have the entrée to drawing-rooms, and with a year – what? I might have waited on some of those people with whom I rubbed shoulders this evening – seventeen years ago, in the shop: the only reason I did not, was that none of them would enter such a place. From the cellar of a shop to the boudoir of a Countess! What a leap . . . But am I not advancing too fast?' he added, with secret uneasiness in his heart.

He had reached the wide Aleje Ujazdowskie, where a fair was being held in the southern portion. The sound of barrel-organs mingled with the blowing of trumpets and the uproar of a crowd of several thousands enveloped him like the wave of an incoming tide. He could very clearly see the long line of swings rocking from right to left, like great pendulums. Then another line of swiftly revolving canopies, striped in different colours, where hideous monsters glowed and brightly dressed clowns, or huge dolls, were standing. And in the centre were two lofty poles, up which men competing for frock-coats or cheap watches were scrambling. An excited crowd was swarming among all these temporary and dirty stands.

Wokulski recalled his childhood. How he used to enjoy a roll and a sausage, when he was starving! How he had imagined himself to be a famous bold warrior, as he rode on a merry-go-round! What wild intoxication he had felt flying on a swing! What a delight it had been to think he did not have to go to work in the morning – his holiday for the whole year! And what could compare with the certainty that tonight he could go to bed at ten o'clock, and tomorrow, if he wished, he could also get up at ten o'clock after sleeping twelve solid hours!

'Was that really me?' he asked himself in amazement. 'Was I so pleased with things that now only disgust me? . . . So many thousands of merry-making poor people all around me – while I, a wealthy man in comparison – what do I have? . . . Uneasiness and ennui, ennui and uneasiness . . . Just when I might possess that which I once dreamed of, I have nothing, for my former dreams have evaporated. Yet I believed so firmly in my exceptional good fortune! . . .'

At this moment a loud cry rose from the crowd. Wokulski roused himself, and saw a human figure at the top of a pole: 'Aha, the winner,' Wokulski said to himself, keeping his balance with difficulty in the crowd that was running, applauding, cheering, pointing to the hero, asking his name. It looked as if they were about to carry the winner of the frock-coat into the town, but the enthusiasm languished. People ran more slowly, even stopped, the cries died down, finally ceased completely. The winner climbed down from the summit and in a few minutes was forgotten.

'A warning for me . . .' Wokulski whispered, wiping the sweat from his forehead. The square and the excited crowd sickened him. He went back to town.

Droshkies and carriages were driving along the Boulevard. In one, Wokulski caught a glimpse of a pale blue dress: 'Izabela? . . .' His heart began to beat violently: 'No, it isn't her . . .'

A few hundred feet away he caught sight of a pretty face and distinguished gestures: 'She? . . . No. How could it be?'

And he walked along the entire Boulevard, through Alexander Square across Nowy Świat, continually gazing at people and continually disappointed. 'So this is my good fortune?' he thought. 'I don't desire what I could have, and fret for what I don't have. So this is good fortune? . . . Who knows, perhaps death is not the great evil that people imagine.'

And for the first time he yearned for heavy, dreamless sleep undisturbed by any desire, or even hopes.

At the same time, Izabela had returned home from her aunt's and called to Flora almost from the threshold: 'You know who was at the reception?'

'Who?'

'Well, that Wokulski . . .'

'Why not, since he was invited?' Flora replied.

'But it was impertinence! Unheard of ! . . . And to crown it all, just fancy that my aunt is fascinated by him; the Prince speaks of no one else, and everyone regards him as something quite exceptional . . . What have you to say to that, pray?'

Flora smiled sadly: 'I know it all. The hero of a season. Last winter there was that Mr Kazimierz, and a decade ago – I myself,' she added quietly.

'But who is he, after all? A tradesman . . . a tradesman!'

'Bela,' Flora replied, 'I can remember seasons when our world was thrilled by circus acrobats. It will pass . . .'

'I'm afraid of that man,' Izabela murmured.

X

The Journal of the Old Clerk

SO – HERE we have a new store: five windows in front, two warehouses, seven clerks and a door-keeper. We also have a carriage that gleams like newly polished boots, a pair of brown horses, a driver and a footman in livery. And all this came upon us in early May, when England, Austria and even battered Turkey were arming as fast as they could!

'My dear Staś,' I said to Wokulski, 'all the merchants are laughing at us for spending so much in such uncertain times.'

'My dear Ignacy,' Wokulski replied, 'we shall laugh at them when more certain times come. Today is just the time for doing business.'

'But a European war,' I said, 'is just around the corner. In that case bankruptcy is inevitable.'

'Think nothing of it,' said Staś, 'all this uproar will die down in a few months, and in the meanwhile we shall have left our competitors far behind.'

Well, and there was no war. In the shop, the rush is like a market, goods come and go from our warehouses as if they were mills, and money flows like water into the safe. Anyone who didn't know Staś would say he was a merchant of genius: but as I know him, I cannot refrain from asking myself what it is all for. '*Warum hast Du denn das getan?*'

It's true I've been asked this myself. Can it be that I am already as old as the late Grossmutter, and do not understand either the spirit of the times or the intentions of men younger than I? It can't be as bad as that . . .

I recall that when Louis Napoleon (later the Emperor Napoleon III) escaped from prison in 1848, all Europe was in a ferment. No one knew what was going to happen. But all sensible people prepared for something, and my uncle Raczek (who had married my aunt) kept saying: 'I told you Bonaparte would come to the top and cause them trouble! The worst of it is that my legs ain't what they was . . .'

The years 1846 and 1847 passed in great excitement. All sorts of pamphlets kept appearing, while people disappeared.* Sometimes I'd wonder whether it wasn't time to venture out into the great world? And when doubts and uneasiness came upon me, after the store was closed, I would go to my uncle Raczek and tell him what was troubling me, asking him to advise me as my father would have done: 'You know,' my uncle said, thumping his lame leg with his fist, 'I shall advise you like a father. If you want to be off – then off with you: if you don't – why then, stay here!'

Not until 1848, when Louis Napoleon was already in Paris, did my late father appear to me one night, looking as I'd seen him in his coffin. His coat was buttoned up to the chin, there was the earring in his ear, his moustaches were waxed up to a point (Mr Domanski did this so that my father should not appear at the Seat of Judgement looking like nothing on earth). He stopped in the door of my little room and said only: 'Remember what I taught you, young scamp!'

'Dreams deceive, in God believe . . .' I reflected for several days afterwards. But the shop already disgusted me. I even lost my interest in the late Małgosia Pfeifer, and felt so cramped in my lodgings that I couldn't bear it. So I went to my uncle Raczek for advice again. I recall that he was in bed, covered up with my aunt's quilt, drinking herb tea to bring on the sweats. But when I told him the whole story he said: 'Well, I'll advise you just like your father would have. Go if you want to – if you don't, why then – stay here. As for me, though, if it wasn't for my poor old leg, I'd have been off long ago. Because your auntie, you know,' and here he lowered his voice, 'carries on so that I'd sooner listen to a battery of Austrian cannons than to her chattering. What she gives with her plasters and such, she takes away with her chatter . . . Have you any money?' he asked after a pause.

'I can lay my hands on a few hundred złoty.'

My uncle Raczek told me to lock the door (my aunt was out), then reached under his pillow for a key: 'Here,' he said, 'open that there leather trunk. You'll find a small box in it, on the right-hand side, and in it there's a small purse. Give it to me . . .' I brought out a thick, heavy purse. My uncle Raczek took it and, sighing, counted out fifteen half-imperials. 'Take this money,' said he, 'for your journey, and if you must go – then be off with you. I'd give you more, but maybe my time is near . . . In any case, something must be left for the old lady so that she can find another husband if she has to . . .'

Weeping, we said goodbye. My uncle managed to raise himself in bed and, turning my face to the candle, whispered: 'Let's have another look at you . . . Because, you know, not everyone comes

back from this kind of a ball. Besides, I'm getting past it, and a
man's fancies can kill as well as bullets . . .'

When I went back to the shop, despite the late hour, I talked to
Jan Mincel, giving in my notice and thanking him for his hospitality. As we had been talking over these things for a year already,
and he had always encouraged me to go and fight the Germans, it
seemed to me that my plan would give him great pleasure.
However, Mincel somehow grew sad. Next day he paid me the
money he had been holding for me, even gave me a tip, promised
to look after my bed-linen and trunk just in case I never came
back. But his usual belligerence had evaporated and not once did
he utter his favourite cry: 'Ah, I'd give it to the Krauts if it weren't
for this shop of mine . . .'

But when, at about ten that evening, wearing my half-jerkin and
thick boots, I embraced him, and lifted the latch to leave the room
where we had lived together for so long, something strange came
over Jan. Suddenly he got up from his chair, pressed his hands
together and cried: 'You blackguard . . . where are you off to?'
And he threw himself down on my bed, sobbing like a child.

I fled. In the passage, lit dimly by an oil-lamp, someone stopped
me. I almost jumped out of my skin. It was August Katz, dressed as
befitted a March journey: 'August, what are you doing?' I asked.

'Waiting for you.' I thought he wanted to see me off: so we
went to Grzybowski Square in silence, for Katz never had anything
to say. The Jew's cart I was to travel in was awaiting us. I embraced
Katz and he me.

I got in . . . he followed: 'Let's go together,' he said.

Then, when we had already passed Mitosna, he added: 'It's
devilish hard and shaking so a man can't sleep . . .'

Our journey lasted unexpectedly long, right up to October
1849* – do you remember, Katz, my never-to-be-forgotten friend?
Do you recall long marches in parching heat, when we sometimes
drank water from puddles: or that march through a bog, when we
got our powder wet: or those night bivouacs in forests or meadows,
when one of us would push the other's head off the kit-bag and
secretly tug over the coat that served as covering for us both? Do
you remember the baked potatoes and bacon which four of us
cooked in secret, away from the rest of the platoon? I have often
eaten potatoes since, but none ever tasted so good. Even today I
can smell them, the fragrance of the steam from the saucepan and I
see you, Katz, as you said your prayers, ate the potatoes and lit your
pipe at the fire simultaneously, so as not to waste time.

Katz, if there is no Hungarian infantry or baked potatoes in
Heaven, then you will have hastened there in vain. And do you
remember the battle which we looked forward to so, as we rested
after a skirmish? I will never forget it to my dying day and if the

Lord God ever asks me why I lived in the world, I will answer 'So as to experience such a day as that!' Only you, Katz, understand me, because we both saw it. Yet at the time it seemed – nothing . . .

Our brigade halted a day and a half beforehand near a Hungarian village, the name of which I forget. It was a sight for sore eyes to see how they regaled us. A man might have washed himself in the wine (though it was not very good), and we were so sick of pork and paprika that no one would have eaten it, had there been anything else. But the music and the girls! The gipsies play wonderfully, and the Hungarian girls are really stunning. There must have been twenty of them, and yet tempers grew so hot that our men stabbed and hacked three peasants to pieces, and the peasants killed one of our hussars with a pole.

God knows how this fine entertainment would have ended had not a gentleman driving a four-in-hand covered with foam ridden up to headquarters during the greatest uproar. Some minutes later the news spread that a great crowd of Austrians was in the vicinity. They blew bugles for parade, the uproar died down, the Hungarian girls disappeared and men began whispering in the ranks of a battle.

'At last!' you said to me.

That same night we moved on a mile, and next day another mile. Couriers were riding in every few hours, and later every hour. This showed that our headquarters was in the neighbourhood and that something big was in the air. That night we slept in the open, without even stacking our rifles. As soon as it was dawn, we moved on: first a squadron of cavalry with two light cannons, then our battalion, then a whole brigade with artillery and four guns, flanked by strong patrols. Couriers were dashing in every half-hour.

When the sun came up we saw the first traces of the enemy along the highway: remains of straw, stamped-out campfires, buildings that had been demolished for fuel. Then we began to meet more and more refugees: a gentleman with his family, priests of various denominations, finally peasants and gipsies. Fear was evident on all their faces: nearly all shouted in Hungarian, pointing in the direction from which they came.

It was close on seven when cannon shots were heard to the south-west. A murmur flew along our ranks: 'Oho, it is beginning . . .'

'No, that was a signal . . .'

Two more shots were fired, then two more. The squadron riding ahead of us stopped, two cannons and two tumbrils galloped past, several riders spurred their horses up the hill. We stopped and for some time there was a silence in which we could hear the hoofs of the adjutant's mare catching up with us. Then she flew by, panting hard, her belly almost scraping the earth. This time a dozen or more cannons were to be heard, some closer, others further away; each shot could be distinguished from the others. 'They're feeling their distance,' the old major exclaimed. 'There must be about fifteen cannons,' Katz muttered, becoming as always more talkative at such moments, 'and as we have twelve, there will be some fun!'

The major turned to us on his horse and smiled under his grizzled whiskers. I understood what this meant when I heard a whole arpeggio of shots, as if someone were playing on an organ. 'There are more than twenty . . .' I said to Katz.

'You asses . . .' the captain laughed, and spurred on his horse.

We were on a hill where we could see the brigade coming up behind. A red cloud of dust marked them as they moved along the highway for two or three kilometres. 'What a huge crowd!' I whispered, 'where will they find room for them all?'

Trumpets sounded and our battalion broke up into four companies, flank to flank. The first platoons moved ahead, we remained in the rear. I looked back and saw that two more battalions had moved away from headquarters; they had left the highroad and were running across the fields, one to our right, the other to our left. Within fifteen minutes they drew level with us, halted for another fifteen minutes, then all three battalions moved on, in step.

Meanwhile the cannonade had intensified so that two or even three shells could be heard exploding simultaneously. To make things worse, a sort of stifled voice rose with them, like continuous thunder. 'How many cannons are there, comrade?' I asked a non-commissioned officer, in German, as he came up behind me.

'Must be a hundred, nearly,' he replied, shaking his head, then added, 'but they're doing good business, for they all fired off together.'

We were pushed off the highroad along which two squadrons of hussars and four cannons then passed at a canter; a few minutes later, the tumbrils followed. Then some of the men in my column began crossing themselves: 'In the name of the Father . . .' Here and there others drank from water-bottles.

To our left the noise grew louder: single shots could no longer be distinguished. Suddenly there was shouting in the forward ranks: 'Infantry! . . . Infantry! . . .' I automatically seized my rifle, thinking the Austrians had appeared. But there was nothing ahead except a hillock and some sparse undergrowth. However, against the background of the cannon shots which had almost stopped worrying me, I now caught the sound of a crash like a heavy downpour of rain, only much more powerful. 'The battle! . . .' someone in front shouted out, in a wailing voice. I felt my heart stop beating for a moment, not from terror, but as though in response to those two words which had made such a strange impression on me ever since my childhood.

Although we were still marching, the ranks grew restless. Wine went from hand to hand, rifles were cleaned, someone said that in half an hour at most we should be under fire and, above all, the Austrians were mocked in a coarse manner, because they were not doing well just then. Someone began whistling, another hummed under his breath; even the stiff formality of our officer gradually changed into comradely intimacy. We did not quiet down until the command 'March at attention' was given.

We fell silent and the somewhat straggling ranks drew up. The sky was clear, only here and there was a motionless white cloud: not a leaf was stirring in the undergrowth as we passed, not a single startled lark was heard over the fields of new grass. Only the heavy tread of the battalion was audible, the swift breathing of the men, sometimes the clank of rifles jarring or the penetrating voice of the major as, riding ahead, he shouted to the officers. And there to our left, a herd of cannons was roaring, and a rain of bullets falling. A man who has not heard such a storm out of a clear sky, brother Katz, knows nothing about music! . . . Do you remember how strange we felt just then? It wasn't fear, but something more like grief and also curiosity. . .

The battalion's flanks were getting further away from us; finally, the right-hand flank disappeared over a hilltop, while the left-hand one dived into a broad ravine a few hundred feet away from us, where their bayonets gleamed from time to time. The hussars and cannons had disappeared somewhere, as had the reserve battalion trailing along behind, so our battalion was alone, ascending one hill only to be confronted by another. Now and then, from the front, rear or side, a courier would fly past, with a dispatch or order for the major. It was really quite remarkable that he did not get confused with so many orders!

It was already nearly nine when we came out upon the last of the hills, which was covered with thick undergrowth. A new order was given: they began to disperse the platoons one alongside the other. When we came to the hilltop, they ordered us to crouch, lower our rifles, then kneel.

Katz, do you remember Kratochwil, who was kneeling beside us, as he poked his head up between two young pines and whispered: 'Look there!' From the top of our hill, to the south, as far as the horizon, stretched a valley and over it, like a river, lay a column of white smoke, several hundred feet wide and perhaps a mile long.

'That's riflemen,' said an old corporal. On both sides of this strange river were to be seen several black and some dozen white clouds, boiling up on the earth. 'Those are batteries, and villages burning,' the corporal explained.

By looking more closely, it was possible to discern square blotches here and there on either side of this long ribbon of smoke: they were dark on the left, white on the right. They looked like great hedgehogs with gleaming bristles: 'These are our regiments –

those the Austrians . . .' said the corporal, and added, 'Even headquarters won't have a better view.'

The ceaseless clatter of rifle firing reached us from this long river of smoke, and the thunder of cannons roared from those white clouds. 'Ooooh! . . .' Katz exclaimed, 'so this is a battle, is it? Is this what I was supposed to be afraid of?'

'Just you wait,' the corporal muttered.

'Rifles at the ready . . .' was heard along the ranks. Kneeling, we began to get out our bullets and warm them up. The clatter of steel ramrods and rifles being cocked was heard . . . We tipped powder into our pans and again there was silence.

Opposite us and perhaps a kilometre away were two hills, with a highroad winding between them. I noticed that some white blotches had appeared against this green background, which soon formed into a white line and then into a white smudge. At the same time, soldiers dressed in blue emerged from the ravine a few hundred feet to our left, and quickly formed into a blue column. At this moment a cannon was heard to the right of us, and a grey puff of smoke appeared over the white Austrian unit. A few minutes pause followed, then another shot and another little cloud over the Austrians. Half a minute later, another shot and the cloud again . . . 'Herr Gott!' the old corporal exclaimed, 'just look how our lads are firing . . . General Bem* or the devil himself must be in command . . .'

From this time on a shot from our side followed every shot of theirs, until the earth shook, while the white smudge on the highroad grew larger. At the same time, smoke gleamed on the opposite hill, and a snarling shell flew in the direction of our battery. Another smoke-cloud . . . a third . . . a fourth . . . 'Clever devils!' the corporal muttered. 'Battalion, forward march!' our major roared in a tremendous voice . . . 'Company, forward march! . . . Platoon, forward march! . . .' officers echoed in different tones.

Again they deployed us differently. The four central platoons remained in the rear, four went ahead to the right and left respectively. We pulled out our knapsacks and took up our arms as we pleased. 'Up and at 'em!' Katz exclaimed. At this moment a shell flew high over our heads and burst with a great bang somewhere in the rear. Then a peculiar notion came to me: surely battles are merely noisy spectacles, arranged by armies for the benefit of people at home, but not intended to harm anyone. For what I could see before me looked very fine, as though it was not so terrible after all.

We went down into the plain. A hussar flew from our battery to report that one of the cannons had been blown to bits. At the same time a shell fell to the left of us; it ploughed into the earth without going off. 'They are beginning to get our scent,' said the old corporal. A second shell exploded overhead, and a piece of shrapnel fell at Kratochwil's feet. He went pale, then laughed. 'Aha! . . . Ah!' men shouted in the ranks.

Confusion started in the platoons which were marching about a hundred yards ahead of us, to the left; when the column moved on, we saw two men, one lying face downwards, stretched out like a piece of cord, the other sitting up, holding his stomach with both hands. I caught the stench of gun-powder: Katz said something to me, but I did not hear him, for there was a roaring in my right ear as if a drop of water had got into it.

The corporal went over to the left, we followed. Our column separated into two long lines. Smoke was boiling up a few hundred feet ahead. They trumpeted something but I did not understand the signal; however, I heard shrill screaming overhead and past my left ear. Something hit the ground a few feet away, bespattering me with sand on my face and chest. My neighbour fired: two men behind, almost at my back, levelled their rifles and fired, one after the other. Entirely deafened, I fired too. I loaded and fired again. In front, someone's helmet and rifle fell, but we were surrounded by such a dense cloud of smoke that I could see nothing more. All I could see was Katz, who kept on firing, looking like a madman, with froth in the corners of his mouth. The roaring in my ears intensified so that finally I could hear neither the rattling of rifles nor the cannons.

Finally the smoke grew so thick and intolerable that I felt I had to get out of it at any price. I moved away, slowly at first, then running, surprised to see that other men were doing the same. Instead of two long lines I now saw a mass of fleeing men. 'Why the devil are they running away?' I thought, hastening my step. It was no longer a run but a gallop. We paused half-way up the hill, and not until now did we notice that our position on the battle-field had been taken by another battalion, and they were firing cannons from the hill-top.

'Reserves into action! . . . Forward, you scoundrels! . . . You swine-herds, you sons of dogs!' the officers were shouting, black with smoke, furious, aligning us into ranks again and striking anyone who came within reach.

The major was not among them. Gradually the soldiers who had been bewildered by the retreat found they were back in their platoons; the deserters were caught and the battalion returned to order. However, some forty men were missing.

'Where have they gone?' I asked the corporal.

'Ah, they've bolted,' he replied gloomily. I dared not think they had been killed.

Two soldiers came driving down from the hill-top: each was accompanied by a horse loaded with packs. Our corporal ran to meet them, and soon came back with packets of bullets. I took eight, for so many were missing in my pouch, and I wondered how I had happened to lose them. 'You know,' said Katz to me, 'it's past eleven o'clock already.'

'Just fancy,' I replied, 'I can't hear anything . . .'

'Fool, you can hear me, can't you?'

'Yes, but I can't hear the cannons. Or rather – of course I can,' I added, concentrating. The roar of the cannons and rattling of rifles had merged into one huge rumbling, no longer deafening, but stupefying. Apathy overcame me. In front, perhaps half a kilometre away, a broad column of smoke was surging, which the wind sometimes broke up. Then it was possible to catch sight of a long row of legs or of helmets, with bayonets gleaming. Shells were whistling over that column and over ours, being exchanged between the Hungarian battery firing from our rear and the Austrians, replying from the opposite hills. The river of smoke stretching along the valley to the south billowed more and more violently, and was very much curved to the left where the Austrians were gaining ground, and to the right where the Hungarians were winning. On the whole the river of smoke curved more to the right, as if our men were already driving the Austrians back. A delicate blue mist was spreading along the entire valley. It was odd that the roaring, though now stronger than before, no longer made any impression on me; I had to listen intently in order to hear it. However, the clash of rifles being loaded, or the crash of cocks reached me clearly.

The adjutant ran up, bugles sounded, officers began shouting.

'Lads!' our lieutenant cried at the top of his voice (he had run away not long before from a seminary), 'we retreated because there were more Huns but now we will have a go at that column on the flank, d'you see? . . . The third battalion and the reserves will support us . . . Long live Hungary! . . .'

'I'd like to live a bit, too!' Kratochwil muttered.

'Half turn to the right – forward!'

We went on like this for several minutes, then made a half-turn to the left and began descending into the valley, trying to gain the right flank of the column that was fighting in front of us. The area was rocky: through the mist ahead we could see fields overgrown with stalks and a small wood beyond them. Suddenly I caught sight of a dozen or so small bursts of smoke among these stalks, as if men were lighting pipes at various points: simultaneously bullets began whistling overhead. I thought that the whistling of bullets, which poets have sung the praises of, was not at all poetic, but rather vulgar. One could sense the malice of inanimate objects in it.

A string of men in scattered battle array broke from our column and ran towards the stalks. We kept on marching as though the bullets flying from the flank were not meant for us at all. At this moment the old corporal marching on the right flank whistling the Rakoczy march dropped his rifle, threw up his hands and staggered as though tipsy. I saw his face for a moment: on the left side was the shattered visor of his helmet, and there was a red stain on his forehead. We went on marching: another corporal, a young, fair-haired fellow, appeared on the right flank.

We were now coming up level with the fighting column and could see the empty gap between the smoke of infantry and that of the Austrians, when a long row of white uniforms appeared. This row moved up and down and very quickly, their legs twinkled as if they were on parade. The row halted. Above it, gleamed a band of steel glistening like brand-new needles, which was then lowered, and I saw about a hundred rifles aimed at us. Then it grew smoky, there was a rattling noise like a chain being dragged along iron bars, and a storm of bullets flew past us. 'Halt! . . . Fire! . . .' I fired as fast as I could, wanting to shield myself if only in the smoke. Despite the uproar, I heard something like the blow of a stick striking a man behind me: someone fell, clutching at my pack. Anger and desepration overwhelmed me: I felt I would perish if I did not kill the unseen enemy. I loaded my weapon and fired at random, lowering the rifle a little and thinking with crazy glee that my bullets would not go over *their* heads. I did not look to the side nor downward: I was afraid to see a man lying there.

Then something unexpected happened. Near us, drums rattled and fifes shrilled in a terrifying manner. The same behind us. Someone yelled 'Forward!' and goodness knows how many voices echoed the cry like groans or howls. The column moved forward slowly, then faster, began running . . . The firing almost ceased and only single shots were heard . . . I hit my chest against something hard, men pushed me from all sides, I pushed too . . .

'Kill the Huns!' Katz shrieked in an inhuman voice, rushing ahead. As he could not extricate himself from the throng, he raised his rifle and brought its butt down on the packs of comrades in front. Finally it grew so crowded that my chest began giving way and I could not breathe. I was lifted up, then let fall, and I realised I was not even standing on the ground, but on a man who was gripping my leg.

At this moment the shouting crowd moved ahead and I fell down, my left hand sliding in blood. By me an Austrian officer was lying on his side, a young man, with very aristocratic features. He looked at me, his eyes darkening with inexpressible grief, and he whispered hoarsely: 'No need to kick . . . We Germans are human beings too . . .' He put one hand to his side and groaned pitifully.

I ran after the column. Our men were already on the hill where the Austrian batteries had stood. Climbing up after the others, I saw one cannon on its side, the other harnessed and surrounded by our men. I came upon an unusual scene. Some of our men were clutching the cannon wheels, others pulling it off the carriage: Katz stabbed a horse of the first pair with his bayonet, and an Austrian bombardier was trying to hit him on the head with a cleaning-rod. I seized the bombardier by his collar and hurled him to the ground. Katz wanted to stab him. 'What are you doing, you madman?' I shouted, pushing his bayonet away.

Then Katz hurled himself furiously at me, but an officer nearby knocked his bayonet away with a sabre. 'What are you interfering for?' Katz shrieked at the officer, 'What are you interfering for?'

The two cannons were captured, the hussars hurried after the others. Far ahead our men were standing singly and in groups, firing after the retreating Austrians. Now and then a wandering enemy bullet whistled over our heads or tore into the earth, with a little cloud of dust. The buglers blew the 'Fall-in'.

An hour later, the regimental bands were playing at various points of the huge battlefield. The adjutant hurried over to congratulate us. The buglers and drummers struck up the call for prayers. We took off our helmets, the ensign bearers raised the banners and the entire army, weapons at their feet, thanked the Hungarian God for victory.

Gradually the smoke died away. As far as the eye could see we saw what looked like scraps of white or navy-blue paper scattered in disorder on the trampled grass in various places. Several carts were moving around the field, and some people were placing these scraps in them. The rest remained. 'So this is what they were born for,' Katz sighed, leaning on his rifle, overcome by melancholy.

This was just about the last of our victories. From this time on the banners bearing the three rivers went in front of, rather than behind, the enemy, until finally at Vilagos, they fell from their poles like autumn leaves.

When he learned this, Katz threw his sword on the ground (we were both officers by then) and said that he would now shoot himself. I recalled, however, that Napoleon was already installed in France. So I encouraged him, and we crept over to Komorna. We watched for relief for a month: from Hungary, France, even Heaven. Finally Komorna surrendered.

On that day, I remember Katz prowling around the gunpowder store with the same look on his face as when he had wanted to stab the recumbent bombardier. Several of us seized him and took him out of the fortress. 'What's this?' one of his comrades whispered to him, 'instead of going into exile with the rest of us, you want to steal a march, do you? Eh, Katz, Hungarian infantry does not take fright or break its word even . . . to the Huns.'

Five of us got away from the rest of the army, smashed our swords, disguised ourselves as peasants and set off in the direction of Turkey with our revolvers hidden in our clothing. But Haynau's* pack of hounds caught up with us. Our journey across the pathless plains and woods lasted three weeks. Mud underfoot, autumn rains overhead, patrols before and behind – eternal exile – these were our travelling companions. Nevertheless we were cheerful. Szapary kept saying Kossuth* would still think of something; Stein was certain Turkey would declare war on our side; Liptak longed for a night's rest and a hot dinner, and I said no matter what happened, Napoleon would not desert us. The rain melted our clothes like butter, we struggled through marshes up to our knees, our soles dropped apart and our boots squeaked like so many bugles: the local people were afraid even to sell us a jug of milk, and peasants chased us away from one village with their hoes and scythes. Despite all this, we were cheerful, and Liptak, as he plunged along beside me so the mud splashed, breathlessly exclaimed: '*Eljen Magyar*! . . . We'll have a good night's sleep . . . Oh, for a night-cap of slivovica . . .'

Of all this cheerful company of ragged men who were enough to scare the crows, only Katz was depressed. He needed to rest more than anyone, and somehow grew thinner more rapidly: he was parched all the time, and had a pale glittering in his eyes. 'I'm afraid he may have camp fever,' said Szapary to me.

Not far from the Sava river on I don't know which day of our wanderings, we found some huts in a lonely neighbourhood, where we were received very hospitably. Dusk had fallen, we were exhausted, but a good fire and a bottle of slivovica brought us more cheerful thoughts. 'I vow,' Szapary exclaimed, 'that by March at the latest Kossuth will summon us back to the ranks. We were foolish to break our swords . . .'

'Maybe in December the Turkish army will start moving,' Stein added. 'If only it heals up by that time . . .'

'My dear fellows,' Liptak groaned, wrapping himself up in a heap of pea-pods, 'go to bed for the devil's sake, otherwise neither Kossuth nor the Turks will ever wake us . . .'

'That they won't,' Katz muttered. He was sitting on a bench by the hearth, looking sadly into the fire.

'Katz, you will soon stop believing in heavenly justice,' Szapary exclaimed, frowning.

'There is no justice for those who don't know how to die with their rifles in their hands,' Katz exclaimed, 'you are fools and so am I. Will France or Turkey risk their necks for the likes of us? Why didn't you stick your own out?'

'He's feverish,' Stein whispered, 'we'll have trouble with him on the way . . .'

'Hungary! Hungary doesn't exist any longer!' Katz muttered, 'equality! There never was equality . . . Justice! There never will be any. . . . A pig doesn't mind taking a bath in a bog: but a man with guts. . . . It's no use, Mr Mincel, I shall never cut up soap for you again.'

I could see that Katz was very sick. I went to him and made him lie down on the pea-pods: 'Come, August, come . . .'

'Where to?' he replied, conscious for a moment. Then he added: 'They have driven us out of Hungary, I won't join the Huns . . .' Nevertheless he lay down. The fires went out. We finished off the liquor, then lay down in a row, our pistols within reach. The wind howled through the cracks of the hut, as if all Hungary was weeping, and sleep overcame us.

I dreamed I was a little boy again, and it was Christmas. A tree was glittering on the table, as poor in decoration as we were, and around it were my father, aunt, Mr Raczek and Mr Domański, singing in high-pitched voices the carol: 'God is born, the powers tremble . . .'

I awoke sobbing for my childhood. Someone tugged at my arm. It was a peasant, the owner of the hut. He pulled me out of the heap of pea-pods, pointed in alarm to Katz and said: 'Look there, Mr Soldier . . . something is wrong . . .' He picked up a twig from the hearth and lit it. I looked. Katz was lying hunched up, with his spent pistol in one hand. Red flashes flew before my eyes and it seems I fainted.

I came to my senses in a cart, just as we were arriving at the Sava river. Day was breaking, a clear day was coming: a penetrating dampness rose out of the water. I rubbed my eyes, counted . . . There were four of us in the cart, and the fifth was the driver. But there ought to be five . . . no, six! I looked for Katz, but could not see him. I did not inquire about him: a sob caught my throat and I thought it would choke me. Liptak was dozing, Stein rubbing his eyes and Szapary was looking away, whistling the Rakoczy march though he kept hitting wrong notes.

Eh, Katz, what did you do? Sometimes now it seems to me you have found the Hungarian infantry and your platoon in Heaven . . . Sometimes I hear again the rattle of drums, the brisk rhythm of the march, and the order: 'Present arms!' and I think it must be you, Katz, going to change the guard before the Heavenly Throne . . . For He would be a poor Hungarian God if he did not recognise you . . .

. . . But I have been wandering, for goodness sake . . . I was thinking about Wokulski, yet here I am writing about myself and Katz. So I will now return to my subject.

A few days after Katz's death, we reached Turkey and for two years I – alone now – wandered through Europe. I was in Italy,

France, Germany, even England, and everywhere I was troubled with poverty and devoured by home-sickness. Sometimes it seemed to me I would go out of my mind listening to the flood of foreign tongues and seeing faces that were not ours, costumes not ours, earth not ours. Sometimes I'd have given my life just to see a pine wood and some straw-thatched huts. Sometimes I cried out in my sleep like a child: 'I want to go home . . .' and when I awoke, bathed in tears, I would dress and run along the streets, for it seemed to me that these streets just certainly led to the Old City or Podwale. I might even have done away with myself in despair, had it not been for frequent news of Louis Napoleon, who had become President and was thinking of becoming Emperor. It was easier for me to bear poverty and to stifle outbursts of grief when I heard of the triumphs of a man who was to execute the will and testament of Napoleon I, and bring back order into the world. Admittedly he did not succeed in doing so – but he left his son. And Rome, after all, was not built in a day . . .

Finally I could bear it no longer and in December 1851 I crossed Galicia and stopped at the Tomaszow frontier post. Only one thought troubled me: 'Suppose they drive me away from here too?' I shall never forget my joy when I heard I could travel on to Zamość. Not that I travelled much, for I walked mostly, yet what a relief it was!

I stayed over a year in Zamość.* And because I was handy at chopping wood, I was in the open air every day. I wrote a letter to Mincel, and got a reply from him, even some money: but with the exception of the receipt, I do not recall details of this incident. It seems, however, that Jan Mincel did something more, though to his dying day he never referred to it, and did not want to mention it. He visited several generals who had fought in the Hungarian campaign, and told them that after all they ought to save a comrade in misfortune. And so they did: in February 1853 I was allowed to travel to Warsaw. Even my officer's patent was returned to me: the one souvenir I brought back from Hungary, not counting two wounds in my chest and leg. The officers even gave me a dinner, at which we drank copiously to the health of the Hungarian infantry. From that time, I have always believed that the closest friendships are formed on the battlefield.

Hardly had I left my temporary abode in Zamość, as penniless as a Turkish beggar, when an unknown Jew stopped me and handed me a letter with money in it. It said:

My dear Ignacy,

I am sending you herewith two hundred złoty for your journey. Come straight to my shop in the Krakowskie Przedmieście, not to Podwale. Heaven forbid you should go there as that scoundrel

Franz is living there, whom a self-respecting dog would not shake
hands with.

My regards,

Jan Mincel,

February 16, 1853.

P.S. Old Raczek who married your aunt, you know he died, and
she too, only before him. They left you some furniture and a few
thousand złoty. Everything is at my place, only your sister's coat is
a little damaged because silly Kasia forgot the moth-balls. Franz
sends you his greetings. Warsaw, February 18, 1853.

The Jew took me to his house, where I was given a bag
containing a change of linen, clothes and shoes. They fed me goose
soup, then stewed goose, then roast goose, which I could not digest
until I had reached Lublin. He also presented me with a bottle of
excellent mead, led me to a cart that was waiting but would not
hear of any reward for his pains. 'I'd be ashamed, that I would, to
take money from a person back from exile,' he replied to all my
urging. Not until I was about to climb into the cart did he draw me
aside and look around to see whether anyone was listening before
whispering: 'I'll buy Hungarian ducats, sir, if you have any. I'll pay
a good price, I need 'em for my daughter, who's getting married
after the New Year . . .'

'I have no ducats,' I said.

'In the Hungarian war but no ducats?' he said, in surprise.

I had no sooner set my foot on the cart step when the same Jew
again drew me aside: 'Maybe you have some jewellery then? . . .
Rings, watches, bracelets? I'll pay you well, that I shall – it's for my
daughter. . . .'

'Brother, I have none, I give you my word . . .'

'No?' he echoed, his eyes wide open, 'well, why did you go to
Hungary then?'

We moved off but he stayed where he was, clutching his beard
and shaking his head sorrowfully.

The cart had been engaged for me alone. But as soon as we
turned the corner, the driver met his brother, who had urgent
business to attend to in Krasnystaw. 'Allow me to take him,
honoured sir,' he begged, doffing his cap to me. 'If the road is bad,
he will walk . . .'

The passenger got in. Before we had reached the fortress gate, a
Jewish woman with a bag stopped us and began conferring noisily
with the driver. It turned out that she was his aunt, who had a sick
child in Fajslawice. 'Allow her to get in, honoured sir . . . she is a
very light person . . .' the driver said.

Once past the city gate, three more relatives of the driver
appeared at various points on the highroad, and he picked them all

up on the pretext that the journey would be merrier. Somehow they edged me over the back axle of the cart, trod on my toes, smoked vile tobacco and squealed like the possessed. Nevertheless, I would not have exchanged my crowded corner for the most comfortable seat in a French stagecoach or an English coach-and-four. I was home.

For four days I seemed to be sitting in a metaphorical temple. At every halt, whenever a passenger got off, another took his place. Near Lublin a heavy bundle fell on me: it was a miracle I wasn't killed. Near Kurów we stopped several hours on the roadside, because someone's trunk had gone astray and the driver had to go back to a tavern for it, on horseback. During the entire journey I felt as though the quilt over my knees was more densely populated than Belgium.

On the fifth day we reached Praga at dusk. But as there were so many carts, and the swing bridge was crowded, it was not until nearly ten that we drove into Warsaw. I must add that all my fellow travellers disappeared like ether in Bednarska Street, leaving a powerful odour behind. But when I mentioned them to the driver upon settling accounts he opened his eyes very wide. 'What passengers would they be, sir?' he exclaimed in surprise, 'You was the passenger – them was only kikes. When we stopped on the corner, even the watchman reckoned two of 'em at a złoty apiece. And you was thinkin' they was passengers?'

'So there was no one else?' I replied, 'yet where did all the fleas come from, that crept all over me?'

'From the dampness, I daresay,' replied the driver.

Convinced in this manner that there had been no one but myself in the cart, I of course paid for the entire journey myself, which so affected the driver that, when he learned my address, he promised to bring me smuggled tobacco every two weeks. 'Even now,' he whispered, 'I've a hundred kilograms of it in the cart. Will I bring you a few pounds, sir?'

'Go to the devil,' I muttered, seizing my bag, 'it would be the last straw if I were to be arrested for smuggling . . .'

Hurrying along the street, I looked about at the city, which struck me as dirty and crowded after Paris, and the people wretched. I found the shop of J. Mincel in Krakowskie Przedmieście easily enough; but the sight of the familiar places and signs made my heart pound so that I had to rest a while.

I gazed at the shop – almost as it had been in Podwale: the tin sabre and the drum (perhaps the very one I had seen as a child) – the window containing plates, the horse and the jumping Cossack . . . Someone opened the door and inside I saw the bladders of paint, the nets full of corks and even the stuffed crocodile.

Behind the counter and near the window was sitting Jan Mincel in his old chair, pulling at the string of the Cossack . . . Trembling like jelly I went in and stopped in front of Jan. Catching sight of me (he was already growing fat), he rose heavily from the chair and blinked. Suddenly he shouted to one of the shop-boys: 'Wicek! Run and tell Małgosia the wedding will be just after Easter . . .' Then he stretched out both hands to me over the counter and we embraced lengthily in silence.

'You gave them Krauts a good hiding! I know, I know,' he whispered in my ear. 'Sit you down,' he added, showing me a chair. 'Kazik! Run and tell Grossmutter that Mr Rzecki is here!'

I sat down and again we said nothing. He shook his head mournfully, I looked away. We were both thinking of poor Katz and our deluded hopes. At length Mincel blew his nose noisily and, turning to the window, muttered: 'Well now, just fancy . . .'

Wicek, out of breath, came back. I noticed that the lad's topcoat was shiny with grease. 'Did you go there?' Mincel asked him.

'I did. Miss Małgorzata said all right.'

'So you are getting married?' I asked Jan.

'Humph . . . what else can I do?'.

'And how is Grossmutter?'

'The same as ever. She only falls sick when they break one of her coffee-pots.'

'And Franz?'

'Don't mention that scoundrel to me!' Jan Mincel exclaimed, 'only yesterday I vowed never to set foot in his house again . . .'

'Why, what has he done this time?'

'The cowardly Kraut keeps making fun of Napoleon! He says he broke his promise to the Republic, that he's nothing more than a conjurer whose tame eagle has spit in his top-hat . . . No,' said Jan Mincel, 'I can't get on with the man at all.'

During our conversation, the two lads and the clerk were serving customers to whom I paid no attention. Then the back door of the shop squeaked and an old lady in a yellow dress emerged from behind the cupboards, with a little jug in one hand: '*Gut Morgen, meine Kinder . . . Der Kaffee is schon . . .*'

I hurried to her, unable to utter a word, and kissed her dry little hands: 'Ignaz! . . . *Herr Jesas!* . . . Ignaz! . . .' she exclaimed, embracing me, '*wo bist Du so lange gewesen, lieber Ignaz?*'

'You know perfectly well, Grossmutter, that he's been away at the wars. Why ask him where he's been?' Jan interrupted.

'*Herr Jesas! . . . Aber Du hast noch keinen Kaffee getrunken? . . .*'

'Of course he didn't,' Jan replied on my behalf.

'*Du lieber Gott! Es ist ja schon zehn Uhr . . .*'

She poured me a mug of coffee, handed me three fresh rolls and disappeared as always.

Then the main door opened with a bang and in ran Franz

Mincel, fatter and redder than his brother: 'How are you, Ignacy?' he shouted embracing me.

'Don't shake hands with that fool, he is the disgrace of the Mincel family,' Jan said to me.

'Oj! Oj! what kind of a family is this?' Franz replied with a smile, 'our father came here with nothing but a barrow and two dogs . . .'

'I'm not speaking to you!' Jan bellowed.

'And I'm not speaking to you either, but to Ignacy,' Franz retorted.

'Our uncle,' he went on, 'was such a blockhead of a Hun that he crept out of his coffin to get his night-cap, which they'd forgotten to put on him . . .'

'You are insulting me in my own house!' Jan shouted.

'I didn't come to your house, but to the shop, to buy something . . . Wicek!' Franz turned to the boy, 'give me a groszy worth of corks . . . Wrap them up nicely in paper . . . Goodbye, my dear Ignacy, come and see me this evening, we will talk over a bottle of good wine. And perhaps that gentleman will come with you,' he added from the threshold, pointing to Jan who was livid with rage.

'I will not set foot in the house of a rotten Hun!' Jan shouted. But this did not prevent him from being with me that evening at Franz's.

I ought to mention that not a week went by without the Mincel brothers quarrelling and making up at least twice. What was even odder was that the cause of their disagreements had never anything to do with matters of a business nature. Despite their squabbles, the two brothers always guaranteed each other's receipts, lent one another money and paid their debts together. The cause was rooted in their natures.

Jan Mincel was romantic and enthusiastic, Franz was phlegmatic and bad-tempered; Jan was an enthusiastic Bonapartist, Franz a republican and special foe of Napoleon III. Finally, Franz admitted his German origin, whereas Jan solemnly declared that the Mincels were descended from the ancient Polish family of Mientuses, who had settled among the Germans perhaps under the Jagiellon dynasty or under the elected kings.

A single glass of wine sufficed to set Jan Mincel banging the table or his neighbours' backs with his fists, and bellowing: 'I feel ancient Polish blood in my veins! No German woman could have given birth to me! Besides, I have proof . . .' And he would show very trusted persons two old documents, one of which referred to a certain Modzelewski, a merchant in Warsaw in the Swedish times, and the other to a certain Miller, a lieutenant in Kosciuszko's army. What sort of link there was between these persons and the Mincels — to this day I still do not know, though I heard the explanation more than once.

A disagreement even arose between the brothers on account of Jan's marriage: he had equipped himself for the ceremony in an amaranthine overcoat with split sleeves, yellow top-boots and a sabre, whereupon Franz announced he would not tolerate such a masquerade at a wedding, even if he had to complain to the police. On this, Jan vowed he would kill the informer if he caught him, and for the wedding breakfast he donned the attire of his ancestors, the Mientuses. Yet Franz was present at the ceremony and at the breakfast, and though he would not speak to his brother, he danced the latter's wife off her feet and drank himself silly on his wine.

Even Franz's death from a boil in 1856 did not pass without an angry scene. During the last three days, both brothers vowed twice in a very solemn manner to disinherit one another. Nevertheless, Franz bequeathed all his property to Jan and for several weeks afterwards Jan pined away with grief for his brother and assigned half the fortune he had inherited (about twenty thousand złoty) to three orphans whom he looked after to the end of his days.

A strange family, indeed!

But here again I have wandered from my subject: I meant to write about Wokulski, but am writing about the Mincels. If I didn't feel as breezy as I do, I might suspect myself of the loquacity which is a symptom of old age.

I have said that I do not understand many things in the behaviour of Staś Wokulski, and every time I want to ask: 'What is it all for?'

When I went back to the shop, we gathered in Grossmutter's room upstairs almost every evening: Jan and Franz Mincel, and sometimes Małgosia Pfeifer. Małgosia and Jan used to sit in the window seat and hold hands as they gazed at the stars; Franz would drink beer from a large tankard (which had a metal lid); the old lady knitted socks and I used to tell tales of my few years spent abroad. Most often, we naturally talked about the yearnings of exile, the discomforts of a soldier's life, or of battles. At such times, Franz would drink twice as much beer; Małgosia snuggled up to Jan (no one has ever snuggled up to me in that way . . .) and Grossmutter would drop stitches. When I had finished, Franz would sigh as he sat sprawling on the sofa; Małgosia kissed Jan and he her, while the old lady would shake her head and say: '*Herr Jesas! . . . wie ist das schrecklich . . . Aber, sag mir, lieber Ignaz, wozu also bist Du denn nach Ungarn gegangen?*'

'Oh goodness me, surely you understand he went there to fight, Grossmutter!' Jan interrupted crossly.

But the old lady would shake her head in amazement and mutter: '*Der Kaffee war ja immer gut und zu Mittag hat er sich doch immer vollgegessen . . . Warum hat er denn das getan? . . .*'

'Oh, you think of nothing but coffee and dinner,' Jan told her impatiently.

As when I spoke of the last moments and terrible death of Katz, the old lady burst into tears admittedly, for the first time since I had known her. Yet when she had wiped the tears away and set to work on her knitting again, she would whisper: *'Merkwürdig! Der Kaffee war ja immer gut . . . Warum hat er denn das getan?'*

Even so, today, almost every hour, I wonder the same thing about Staś Wokulski. He had a good living after his wife's death, so why did he go to Bulgaria? He made a fortune there so he would wind up the shop; so why has he now enlarged it? He had an excellent income from the new shop, so why is he creating a new trading company? Why has he rented a huge apartment? Why has he bought a carriage and horses? Why is he striving to get into the aristocracy and avoiding tradesmen, who will never forgive him for it? And why has he concerned himself with the carter Wysocki and his brother, the railwayman? Why has he established workshops for several poor apprentices? Why is he taking care of that harlot who, although she lives at the Magdalenes, is doing his good name so much harm?

And how quick-witted he is! When I heard at the Stock Exchange of Hodl's attempt to assassinate Emperor Wilhelm, I came back to the shop and, looking into his eyes sharply, said: 'You know, a certain Hodl has shot at the Emperor Wilhelm . . .'

He, as if unconcerned, replied: 'A madman, evidently.'

'But,' say I, 'they will cut the madman's head off.'

'And quite rightly,' he replied, 'he will not live to increase the lunatic species . . .'

Not even a muscle quivered as he said this. I turned to stone in the face of such sang-froid.

Dear Staś, you are quick-witted, but I am not a blockhead either. I know more than you suppose, and it only pains me to see you have no confidence in me. The advice of a friend and an old soldier might protect you from more than one folly, if not from stains on your reputation . . . But why should I express my own views? Let events speak for me.

Early in May we moved into the new store, which occupies five huge rooms. In the first, to the left, are Russian textiles: calico, cretonnes, silks and velvets. The same textiles occupy half the second, and oddments of apparel the other half: hats, collars, ties, umbrellas. In the front room are the most elegant goods: bronzes, majolicaware, crystals, ivory. The next room, to the right, holds toys, wood and metal merchandise, and in the last room, to the right, are rubber and leather goods.

I arranged it this way myself; I do not know if I did it properly,

but, as God is my witness, I meant well. Then I asked Staś
Wokulski his views: but instead of advising me, he merely shrugged
and smiled as if to say: 'What does it have to do with me?'

Strange man! A plan of genius comes into his head, he carries it
out in a general way, but does not care in the least for the details.
He had the shop moved, made it a centre for trade in Russian
textiles and foreign haberdashery; he organised the entire administration. But since this was done, he has never interfered in the
shop; instead, he pays calls on great gentlefolk, or drives in his
carriage to the Łazienki park, or disappears somewhere without
trace, appearing in the shop for only a few hours each day. In
addition, he is absent-minded, irritable, as if he were waiting for
something or afraid of something.

But what a kind heart he has, all the same!

I am ashamed to admit I was rather reluctant to move into the
new store. That was not all: I certainly prefer to serve in a huge
store, on the Parisian model, rather than in a booth like our
previous shop. What I regretted was my room, where I had lived
twenty-five years. As our old lease was good until July, I stayed in
my little room to mid-May, looking at its walls, the grating which
reminded me of agreeable times in Zamość, and at the old furniture. 'How can I move all these things, how shall I get away,
merciful Heaven?' thought I.

But one day about the middle of May (rumours of peace were
circulating just then), Staś came to me just before the store closed,
and said: 'You, know, old man, it's time to move to your new
abode.' I felt my blood turn to water. Then he went on: 'Come
along, I'll show you the new apartment I have rented for you in
this very house.'

'How so?' I asked, 'I must first discuss the rent with the landlord.'

'It's already paid,' he replied. So he took my arm and led me
through the back door of the shop into the hall.

'But,' said I, 'this is rented . . .'

Instead of replying, he opened a door on the far side of the hall
. . . I go in . . . my goodness! . . . a drawing-room! . . . Furniture
covered in tapestry, albums on the tables, flower-pots in the
window . . . a book-case by the wall . . . 'Here,' said Staś, showing
me richly bound books, 'three histories of Napoleon I, the lives of
Garibaldi and Kossuth, the history of Hungary . . .'

I was delighted with the books but I must admit that the
drawing-room made a disagreeable impression. Staś noticed this
and suddenly, with a smile, opened another door.

My goodness me! . . . this second room was *my* room, the room
where I had lived twenty-five years. Barred windows, the green
curtain, my black table . . . and by the wall opposite, was my iron
bed, my rifle and the box containing my guitar. 'How is this?' I

asked Staś, 'so they have moved me already?'

'Yes,' Staś replies, 'every single thing, even Ir's sheet . . .'

It may seem comical, but I had tears in my eyes . . . I looked at his stern face and unhappy eyes, and could hardly believe that this man could be so thoughtful and have such delicacy of feeling. For I had never breathed a word to him . . . He himself had guessed that I might pine for my former abode, and had himself supervised the moving of my bits and pieces. Happy will be the woman he marries (I even have a suitable party in mind for him): but he won't marry, for sure. Some kind of wild dreams possess him, but they are not, alas, concerned with marriage . . . Goodness knows how many respectable people come into our shop, purportedly to buy something but in reality matchmaking for Staś – yet nothing comes of it. There is Mrs Sperling, who has a hundred thousand roubles in cash and a distillery. What hasn't she bought in our store, all in order to inquire: 'Well, isn't Mr Wokulski getting married, then?' 'No, madam.' 'That's a shame,' said Mrs Sperling with a sigh, 'a fine store, a big fortune, but it will all go to rack and ruin for want of a lady in the house. Now, if Mr Wokulski were to choose a respectable and well-to-do lady, his credit would even go up.' 'Madam, you never said a truer word,' I said. 'Adieu, Mr Rzecki,' said she (putting twenty or fifty roubles on the cash desk), 'but pray do not mention to Mr Wokulski that I said anything about marriage, he may think the old girl is after him . . .' 'On the contrary, I will not omit to mention it . . .'

And I thought to myself that if I were Wokulski, I'd marry this rich widow in a moment. That figure of hers, my goodness!

Or there is Schmetterling, the saddler. How often, when paying his bills, has he not said: 'Why, sir, couldn't such a man as Wokulski, sir, get married? A fine fellow, sir, spirited, sir, shoulders like a bull. May the devil take me if I wouldn't let him have my own daughter and ten thousand a year dowry, sir . . . Hm?'

Or Councillor Wroński. Not wealthy, quiet, yet he buys a pair of gloves every week, and each time he says: 'Good God, how can Poland help going to the dogs when a man like Wokulski doesn't marry? Good God, he's a man who doesn't even need a dowry, so he could find a young lady who can play the piano, look after the house-keeping and knows foreign languages . . .'

Dozens of such suitors pass through our store. Some mothers, aunts or fathers simply bring their eligible young ladies to us. The mother, aunt or father will buy something for a rouble, and meanwhile the young lady walks about the store, sits down, shows off her figure, puts forward her right foot, then her left, displays her hands . . . All with the aim of trapping Staś, who, more often than not, isn't even in the store, or – if he is – doesn't even look at the property, as much as to say: 'Mr Rzecki is in charge of appraisals . . .'

Poor Staś is not liked, except by families with grown-up daughters, widows and eligible young ladies, who seem bolder than Hungarian infantry. Not surprising, though – he has set all the silk and wool manufacturers, and the tradesmen who sell their own products, against him.

One Sunday (this rarely happens), I went to a café for my breakfast. A glass of anisette and a portion of herring at the counter, then a small portion of tripe and a carafe of porter at my table – quite a feast! I paid nearly a rouble, but how much smoke I swallowed, and what I overheard! It was enough to keep me going for several years.

In a room as stuffy and dark as a smoked-herring factory, where they served me my tripe, some six gentlemen were sitting around a table. They were portly and well-dressed individuals; certainly tradesmen, landowners or perhaps manufacturers. Each looked as if he had from three to five thousand roubles income a year.

As I did not know any of these gentlemen, and they certainly did not know me, I cannot accuse them of deliberately bedevilling me. However, just fancy the coincidence – at the moment I entered, they were talking about Wokulski! I could not see who was speaking on account of the smoke, and I dared not look up from my plate.

'He done very well for himself,' said a coarse voice. 'When he was young, he used to wait on the likes of us, but now he's doing well he prefers to dance attendance on great gentlefolk.'

'These gentlemen of today,' an asthmatic individual put in, 'are no better than he is. Would they have been at home to an ex-tradesman at a Count's house in the old days? And an ex-tradesman who made his fortune by marrying . . . Why, it's laughable . . .'

'Never mind about the marrying,' the coarse voice replied, after coughing a little, 'a good marriage is nothing to be ashamed of. But those millions he made in war supplies have an unsavoury smell about them.'

'Yet he apparently never cheated anyone,' a third remarked, in an undertone.

'That's the only way to make millions,' the bass voice thundered, 'and anyhow why does he turn up his nose at the likes of us? . . . why try to elbow his way among the aristocracy?'

'People say', another voice added, 'that he wants to form a trading company of nobility alone . . .'

'Aha! He'll skin them, then bolt,' the asthmatic individual interrupted.

'No,' said the bass, 'he'll never wash off the stain of those war supplies, not even with kitchen soap. A haberdasher in military supplies, indeed! A Warsaw tradesman going to Bulgaria, indeed!'

'Yet your brother, the engineer, went even further after profit,' said the undertone.

'Of course,' the bass interposed, 'but at least he never imported calico from Moscow . . . Confound the man, he's ruining our industry.'

'Ha ha!' chuckled a voice hitherto silent, 'that is no longer any concern of a tradesman. A tradesman's aim is to import cheaper goods and make more profit for himself. Isn't that so? Ha ha!'

'However that may be, I wouldn't give you a penny for his patriotism,' the bass declared.

'Yet it seems to me,' the low voice said, 'that Wokulski has shown his patriotism by more than words . . .'

'So much the worse for him,' said the bass, 'he showed it when he was penniless, but has cooled off now that he has roubles in his pocket . . .'

'Come now, do you always have to accuse people either of treachery to Poland or dishonesty? That's not nice . . .' the low voice said, vexed.

'How is it that you stand up for him so strongly?' asked the bass, pushing back his chair.

'I defend him because I've heard a little about him,' the low voice replied, 'a certain Wysocki, who drives carts for me, was starving to death until Wokulski put him on his feet.'

'With money he made from military supplies in Bulgaria? There's a benefactor for you!'

'Other people, my dear sir, enriched themselves on Polish money – and nothing was said. So there!'

'In any case, he's a dubious character,' the breathless voice concluded, 'he's always rushing here and there, importing calico, not looking after his shop, as if to coax the gentry . . .'

As the waiter was bringing them more bottles, I quietly bolted. I did not interrupt their conversation, because – knowing Staś since his boyhood as I do – I could only have said three words: 'You abject creatures!' And there they were talking like this while I was in fear and trembling for his future, while I asked myself morning and evening: 'What is he doing? What is he doing it all for? And what will come of it?'

And to think that they can say such things about him today, in my presence, after I'd seen the carter Wysocki kneel at his feet only yesterday to thank him for arranging the transfer of his brother to Skierniewice, and for giving him help . . . He's a simple man, yet how honest. He'd brought his ten-year-old son with him and pointed to Wokulski as he said: 'Look at the gentleman, Pietrek, he is our greatest benefactor . . . If he ever asks you to cut off your right hand for him, do it, though even then you will not have repaid him . . .'

Or consider the girl who wrote to him from the Magdalenes: 'I have remembered a childhood prayer so as to pray for you . . .'

These are simple people, immoral girls: yet do they not possess more nobility of feeling than we in our frock-coats, extolling ourselves all over town for virtues none of us believes in? Staś is right to concern himself with these poor people, though I wish he would do so in a less excitable manner.

The truth is that his new acquaintances alarm me. I recollect, early in May, a very dubious individual (red whiskers, hateful eyes) came into the shop, placed his visiting card on the cash desk and said in broken Polish: 'Pray tell Mr Wokulski I come seven o'clock . . .' And that was all.

I glanced at his card, which read 'William Collins, teacher of English'. What kind of a joke was this? Surely Wokulski is not going to learn English? But I understood it all when news arrived the next day of Hödl's assassination.

Not to mention another acquaintance, a certain Mrs Meliton, who has been honouring us with visits ever since Staś returned from Bulgaria. She's a skinny creature who chatters away like the proverbial mill-race, though you feel she is only saying what she wants to say. She called once at the end of May: 'Is Mr Wokulski here? Of course not, I thought as much . . . Am I addressing Mr Rzecki? I thought so . . . What a charming dressing-case . . . Fine wood, I appreciate such things. Pray tell Mr Wokulski to send it to me, he knows my address – and tell him to be in the Łazienki park tomorrow, around one o'clock.'

'Where did madam say?' I asked, vexed by her effrontery.

'You're a fool . . . in the park,' said the lady.

Well, and Wokulski sent her the case and went to the park. When he came back, he said that a congress was to meet in Berlin, to bring the Eastern war to an end – and so it did!

The same lady called a second time on – as I recall – June the first. 'Ah!' she exclaimed, 'what a charming vase . . . Majolica, I'll be bound, I appreciate such things . . . Tell Mr Wokulski to send it (and here she added in a whisper) also tell him that the day after tomorrow, around one o'clock . . .'

When she had gone, I said to Lisiecki: 'You may be sure that we shall have important political news the day after tomorrow.' 'On the third of June?' he replied with a smile. Pray imagine our expressions when news came of Nobiling's assassination in Berlin. I thought I would drop dead on the spot. Lisiecki has since stopped making unsuitable jokes about me, and what is worse, now always asks me for political news . . . It is true that a great reputation can indeed be a terrible thing. For ever since Lisiecki has started appealing to me as an 'informed source' I have stopped sleeping and lost what was left of my appetite. And as for what must be happening to poor Staś, who is in constant touch with this Mr Collins and Mrs Meliton! . . . Heaven help us!

As I have gone on this far (I am becoming quite a gossip, to be sure) I may as well add that an unhealthy unrest prevails in our emporium. Apart from myself, there are now seven clerks altogether (would old Mincel ever have dreamed of this?) – but there is no unity among them. Klein and Lisiecki, as the seniors, keep together and treat the rest of their colleagues in a manner which I can hardly call contemptuous, but which is certainly rather haughty. And the three new clerks, in the haberdashery, metal and rubber departments respectively, only mix with one another, and are stiff and sulky towards the others. Admittedly, honest Zięba, in his desire to bring them together, trots from old to new and seeks to placate them, but the poor man has such a heavy hand that the opponents merely glower at one another still more fiercely after each attempt at placation.

Perhaps if our emporium (it certainly is an emporium and a first-rate one into the bargain) had developed gradually, if we had taken on one new clerk a year, the new man would have mingled with the old and there would be harmony. But to take on five new clerks at once, so that one will often get in the way of another (for the merchandise cannot be properly arranged, nor the sphere of each man's duties defined in such a short time) – why then, it is natural enough that disagreements would occur. But why should I criticise my principal's activities, and he a man who has more sense than the rest of us put together . . .

Only on one point do the old and the new gentlemen agree, and here Zięba is even a help – in teasing our seventh clerk, Szlangbaum. This Szlangbaum (I have known him for years) is of the Hebraic persuasion, but an honest fellow for all that. Small, dark, bent, unshaven – in a word, you would not give tuppence for him when he sits at the cash desk. But as soon as a customer comes in (Szlangbaum works in the department of Russian textiles), good gracious, how he twirls like a top! Now he is at the highest shelf on the right, now at the lowest on the left. When he begins hurling rolls of cloth about, he resembles a steam-engine rather than a man; when he begins unfolding and measuring, I think he has three pairs of hands. Also he is a born salesman, and when he starts recommending goods, making suggestions, guessing taste, all in an exceedingly grave tone, then I give my word that not even Mraczewski comes anywhere near him. It is too bad, though, that he is so small and plain; we shall have to get him a stupid but handsome young man as assistant with the ladies. For although it is true that ladies linger longer with a handsome clerk, yet they also complain and bargain less. (Heaven protect us from lady customers! Perhaps I lost my taste for marriage by seeing ladies in the shop all the time. The Creator, when He formed that miracle of Nature known as Woman, cannot have realised the misfortune He would bring down upon tradesmen.)

Thus, though Szlangbaum is a decent citizen in the fullest sense, yet no one likes him since he has the misfortune to be a Hebrew . . . In general, I have noticed over the last year or two that dislike of the Hebrews is increasing; even people who, a few years ago, called them Poles of the Mosaic persuasion, now call them Jews. And those who recently admired their hard work, their persistence and their talents, today only see their exploitation and deceit.

When I hear such things, I sometimes think a spiritual twilight is falling on mankind, like night. By day all is nice, cheerful and good; at night, all is dark and dangerous. I think this, but can say nothing; for what does the opinion of an old clerk matter in the face of well-known journalists who can prove that Jews use Christian blood on their matzos, and should have their rights restricted. The bullets overhead, Katz, whistled a very different tune . . .

This state of affairs affects Szlangbaum in a peculiar manner. Only a year ago, he called himself Szlangowski, he celebrated Easter and Christmas, and I am sure the most pious Catholic did not eat as much sausage-meat as he. I remember he was once asked in a café: 'Don't you care for ice-cream, Mr Szlangowski?'

And he replied: 'I prefer sausages, but without garlic. I can't abide garlic.'

He came back from Siberia with Staś and Dr Szuman, and at once found work in a Christian shop, though Jews offered him better pay. From that time on he has always worked for Christians, and not until this year was he sacked. Early in May he came to ask a favour of Staś.

'Staś,' he said humbly, 'I will drown in Nalewki Street unless you help me.'

'Why didn't you come to me before?' Staś asked.

'I did not dare. I was afraid they might say of me that a Jew will creep in anywhere. And I would not have come today but for my children.' Staś shrugged and at once took Szlangbaum on at wages of fifteen hundred roubles a year.

The new clerk set to work at once, but half an hour later Lisiecki muttered to Klein: 'What in the world stinks so of garlic, Mr Klein?' Then, fifteen minutes after that, I don't know why he added: 'How these swines of Jews creep into the Krakowskie Przedmieście! Why don't they stay in Nalewki or Świętojerska?'*

Szlangbaum was silent, though his red eyelids quivered. Fortunately Wokulski overheard both taunts. He rose from his desk and said in a tone which, I must say, I didn't like: 'Mr . . . Mr Lisiecki! Mr Henryk Szlangbaum was my colleague at a time when things were going very badly. So why not allow him to be my colleague today, when things are somewhat better?' Lisiecki was embarrassed, realising that his job hung on a thread. He bowed, muttered something, then Wokulski went over to Szlangbaum and embraced him; 'My dear Henryk, do not take these little things too much to heart, for we here appreciate each other as colleagues. I assure you that if you ever quit this store it will be with me.'

Szlangbaum's situation at once improved; today the others would sooner taunt (even insult) me than him. But has he found a defence against insinuations, looks and glances? . . . And all this is poisoning the poor fellow's existence, so he sometimes tells me with a sigh: 'If I weren't afraid my children would become Jewish, I'd go and settle down in Nalewki once and for all.'

'Then why, Henryk,' I asked him, 'don't you get christened and have it over with?'

'I'd have done so years ago, but not now. Today, I understand that as a Jew I am only despised by Christians, but as a convert I'd be despised by Christians and Jews alike. After all, I must live somewhere. Anyway,' he added, more quietly, 'I have five children and a rich father, whose heir I am . . .'

This is strange. Szlangbaum's father is an usurer, but his son, so as not to take a penny-piece from him, stays poor and works as a clerk.

Sometimes I talk frankly about him to Lisiecki: 'Why do you persecute him?' I ask. 'He conducts his house in a Christian manner and even has a Christmas tree for his children.'

'Because he thinks', said Lisiecki, 'that it is more profitable to eat matzo with sausage than by itself.'

'He was in Siberia, exposed to danger . . .'

'Yes, but for profit . . . And it was for profit that he called himself first Szlangowski, and now Szlangbaum, because his old man has asthma.'

'You mocked him for dressing up in peacock feathers, so he went back to using his old name.'

'For which he'll get a hundred thousand roubles when his father dies,' Lisiecki replied.

Then it was my turn to shrug and fall silent. It was wrong to call himself Szlangbaum, but Szlangowski was just as bad: wrong to be a Jew, wrong to be a convert . . . Night is falling: a night in which everything looks grey and uncertain . . .

Moreover, Staś suffers for this. Not only did he take Szlangbaum into the shop, but he also supplies goods to Jewish merchants and has let several Jews into his firm. Our own people protest and threaten, but Staś is not to be frightened: he is determined and will not yield, even if they boiled him in oil. How will this all end, for goodness sake?

But in straying thus from my subject I have forgotten several very important details. I have in mind Mraczewski, who has for some time either been thwarting my plans or deliberately leading

me into error. The lad was dismissed from our shop because he was
rather insulting about Socialists in the presence of Wokulski. Later,
however, Staś allowed himself to be persuaded and immediately
after Easter he sent Mraczewski to Moscow and even raised his
wages. For more than one evening I have pondered over the
meaning of this journey, or rather exile. But when, three weeks
ago, Mraczewski came thence to collect goods, I comprehended
Staś's plan at once.

Physically, the young man had changed little: always talkative
and handsome, but perhaps somewhat paler. He said he liked
Moscow, particularly the local women, who had more experience
and spirit, and fewer prejudices than ours. I too, when young, used
to think that women had fewer prejudices than today.

All this is merely an introduction. For Mraczewski brought with
him three very dubious individuals, whom he called 'prikashchiki',*
and a whole package of pamphlets. The 'prikashchiki' were
supposed to see about something or other in the shop, but they did
so in such a manner that none of us caught sight of them. They
wandered about the town for days at a time, and I would take my
oath they were preparing the way for a revolution in our country.
Seeing that I had my eye on them, they always feigned drunkenness
whenever they came near the shop, and talked to me about
nothing but women, claiming – despite Mraczewski – that Polish
women were 'stunning' – only very like Jewesses. I pretended to
believe everything they said, and discovered by means of skilful
questioning that the districts they knew best were those around the
Citadel prison.* It was there that they conducted most business.
And that my guesses were well founded was shown by the fact that
these 'prikashchiki' even attracted the attention of the police.
Within ten days at most, they have been taken three times to
police-stations. Clearly, they must have important contacts, for they
were freed.

When I communicated my suspicions of these 'prikashchiki' to
Staś, he merely smiled and replied: 'This is only the beginning! . . .'
From this, I conclude that Staś must have gone far in his relations
with the nihilists.

But, pray picture my amazement when, having invited Klein
and Mraczewski to my room for tea, I discovered that Mraczewski
is a worse Socialist than Klein . . . This Mraczewski who lost his
position in our shop for insulting Socialists! I was struck dumb
with amazement for the entire evening; only Klein was quietly
gratified, while Mraczewski talked. I have never heard anything
like it in all my life! This young man proved to me, by quoting
very clever people, that all capitalists are criminals, that the earth
ought to belong to those who cultivate it, that factories, coal-
mines and machines ought to be the property of everyone, that

there is no God or Soul which priests invented to trick people into paying tithes. He added that when they start the revolution (he and the three 'prikashchiki'), then we shall all work only eight hours a day, and enjoy ourselves for the rest of the time, even though everyone will have a pension when old, and a free funeral. Finally he said that paradise will not come to this world until everything is held in common: the earth, buildings, machines and even wives.

As I am a bachelor (people even call me an old one) and am writing this journal honestly, I must confess that this communality of wives rather pleased me. I must even say that I gained some sympathy for Socialism and the Socialists. But why do they have to have a revolution, when people might have wives in common without it? This was what I thought, but Mraczewski himself cured me and at the same time thwarted my plans very badly.

In passing, I must say I sincerely wish Staś would marry. If he had a wife, he would not consult so often with Collins and Mrs Meliton, and if children came along he might break off his dubious contacts. For how can a man like him, with his military nature, be in contact with people who will certainly never go openly into battle against the armed enemy? Neither Hungarian nor any other infantry would fire at a disarmed opponent. But times are changing. So I very much want Staś to marry and I think I have found him a partner.

Sometimes our emporium (as was our shop) is visited by a lady of extraordinary charm. Dark-haired, with grey eyes, wonderfully beautiful features, imposing stature and tiny hands and feet – perfection itself! I once saw her getting out of a droshky, and must say that what I caught sight of made me quite feverish . . . Oh, honest Staś would find great comfort in her, for she is well proportioned, her lips like ripe berries . . . and her bosom! When she comes in, dressed up to the nines, I think an angel has entered, its wings folded over its bosom . . .

I believe she is a widow, for I never see her with a husband, only with her little daughter Helena, who is pretty as a picture too. If Staś marries her, he would have to break once and for all with the Nihilists, because any time left over from looking after his wife, would be spent caressing her child. But such a wife would not leave him much free time.

I had already formulated my plan and was wondering how to make the lady's acquaintance and introduce Staś to her, when suddenly the devil brought Mraczewski back from Moscow. Pray imagine my vexation when, on the day after his arrival, the young scamp came into the shop with my widow! And how he fussed around her, how he rolled his eyes, how he strove to guess her every thought . . . Fortunately I am not a stout man, for this impudent flirtation would surely have brought on an apoplectic stroke.

When he came in again a few hours later, I asked him with the most indifferent expression in the world who the lady had been. 'You like her?' he said, 'champagne . . . not a woman,' he added, winking shamelessly, 'but she's not for you, she's wild about me . . . Oh, my dear sir, what temperament, what a figure! If you knew what she looks like in a peignoir.'

'I thought as much, Mr Mraczewski,' I replied, sternly.

'But what have I said?' he protested, rubbing his hands in a manner that struck me as lustful, 'I'm saying nothing! The greatest virtue a man can have, Mr Rzecki, is discretion, particularly in the more confidential relationships . . .'

I interrupted him, feeling I would despise him if he went on. What times these are, what people! For had I the good fortune to attract the attentions of such a lady, I would not even dare to think of such things, let alone shout them at the top of my voice in a store the size of ours. But when in addition, Mraczewski unfolded to me his theory of the communality of wives, I at once thought: 'Staś a nihilist, and Mraczewski a nihilist too . . . So let the first marry and the second will then introduce communality . . . But it would be a shame for Mraczewski to get a woman like that.'

At the end of May Wokulski decided to have our shop blessed. On this occasion I noticed once again how times are changing. In my young days too, merchants used to have their shops blessed, making sure that the ceremony was carried out by an elderly and pious priest, that there was genuine holy water, a new censer and an organist fluent in Latin. After the ceremony, during which almost every cupboard and object was sprinkled and prayed over, a horseshoe would be nailed over the threshold of the shop to attract customers. Only then did they think of something to eat and drink – usually a glass of vodka, sausages and beer. But nowadays (what would the contemporaries of old Mincel have had to say?) the first question is how many cooks and footmen will be required, how many bottles of champagne, how much wine and what sort of a dinner will be served? For the dinner was the main attraction of the ceremony, since the guests were not concerned with who is to perform the blessing, but what would be served at the dinner.

The evening before the ceremony, a dumpy, sweating individual rushed into the shop: I could not say whether his collar had dirtied his neck, or vice versa. He produced a thick notebook from his worn overcoat, put on a greasy pince-nez and began walking about with an expression that alarmed me. 'What the devil? . . .' thought I, 'can he be from the police, or is he the landlord's secretary making an inventory?' I crossed his path in order to ask him, as civilly as could be, what he wanted.

But the first time he muttered: 'Please don't interrupt,' and the second he unceremoniously pushed me aside. My amazement was all the greater, for some of our gentlemen bowed to him very politely and rubbed their hands, as though in the presence of a bank-manager at least, and explained everything to him.

'Well,' said I to myself, 'the poor devil can hardly be from the insurance company. They don't employ such shabby fellows.'

Finally Lisiecki whispered to me that the gentleman was a very eminent journalist, who was going to describe us in the newspaper. I grew excited to think that I might see my own name in print, something which has only happened once before, when it appeared in the *Police Gazette* after I lost my identity papers. In a moment I realised that everything about this man was great: a great head, a great notebook and a very great hole in the sole of his left shoe. But he kept walking about the shop, puffed up like a turkey-cock, and writing away . . .

At length he said: 'Hasn't there been any kind of incident here lately? A small fire, a burglary, an embezzlement, a fight?'

'God forbid,' I ventured to put in.

'That is a shame,' he replied, 'the finest advertisement for a shop would be if someone were to hang himself in it . . .'

I turned to stone on hearing this. 'Perhaps the gentleman', I ventured with a bow, 'would select some small object or other which we shall send without obligation . . .'

'A bribe?' he asked, eyeing me as if I were Copernicus's statue, 'we are in the habit,' he added, 'of buying what we fancy: we take bribes from no one.' He put on his greasy top-hat and walked out, with his hands in his pockets, like a minister. But when he was on the other side of the street I could still see the hole in his shoe.

I must revert to the blessing ceremony. The main part of the proceedings, i.e. the dinner, took place in the great hall of the Europejski Hotel.* The hall was adorned with flowers, huge tables placed in a horseshoe, music brought, and at six that evening, some hundred and fifty people gathered. Who was not present! Mainly merchants and manufacturers from Warsaw, the provinces, Moscow, even Vienna and Paris. There were also two counts, a prince and a quantity of gentlefolk. I will not mention the drink, for I do not know which there was more of – leaves on the vegetation adorning the hall, or bottles. The entertainment cost us three thousand roubles, but the sight of so many people eating was truly impressive.

When the Prince rose and drank Staś's health, when the music struck up (I don't know what the tune was, but something very pretty), and a hundred and fifty people roared: 'Long live Wokulski!' then I had tears in my eyes. I hurried to him and whispered as I congratulated him: 'See how they love you!'

'They love the champagne,' he replied. I saw that the cheers meant nothing to him. He did not even smile when one of the speakers (who must have been a literary gentlemen, for he said a great deal and made no sense) said that either in his own name or that of Wokulski (I forget which) this was the finest day of his life. I noticed that Wokulski mostly stayed near Łęcki, who is said to have frequented European royalty before his bankruptcy . . . Always these wretched politics . . .

At the start of the banquet everything was very seemly: now and then one of the guests rose and made a speech, as if to talk off the wine he had drunk and the food he had eaten. But as more and more empty bottles were removed, so the decorum disappeared in proportion, and finally there was so much din that it almost drowned the band. I was as cross as the devil himself, and wanted to scold someone, even if only Mraczewski. Drawing him away from the table I only managed to say: 'What is all this for?'

'For?' he echoed, gazing blankly at me, 'it's for Miss Łęcka . . .'

'Are you mad? What's for Miss Łęcka?'

'These business deals . . . the store . . . this dinner . . . all for her . . . And it was because of her that I was kicked out of the shop,' said Mraczewski, leaning on me for he couldn't keep his feet.

'What?' I asked, seeing he was quite tipsy, 'so you were kicked out of the shop on her account, were you? And perhaps it was on her account that you were sent to Moscow?'

'Of course it was . . . of course. She whispered one little word. . . . And I got three hundred roubles a year more. Iza can make the old man do anything she wants.'

'Come, off to bed with you,' I said.

'Certainly not . . . I'm going to join my friends . . . Where are they? They'd handle Iza better . . . She wouldn't lead them a dance as she does the old man . . . Where are my friends?' he began shouting. Naturally I had him taken to a room upstairs. I suspect, though, he was only pretending to be tipsy in order to bedevil me.

By midnight the hall was like a mortuary or hospital; they kept having to take people upstairs or out to a droshky. Finally I found Dr Szuman, who was sober too, and took him to my room for tea.

Dr Szuman is a Hebrew, but an unusual man for all that. He was once to have been christened, for he fell in love with a Christian girl, but as she died he left matters alone. People even say he poisoned himself from grief, but was saved. Today he has quite abandoned his medical practice. He has a large fortune, and busies himself with investigating people and their hair. A small, yellow man, he has an alarming gaze before which nothing can be hidden. But as he has known Staś for years, he must know all his secrets.

After the noisy banquet I was curiously troubled and wanted to loosen Szuman's tongue a little. If he did not tell me something about Staś, then surely I would never know. When we reached my room and the samovar had been brought, I remarked: 'Tell me frankly, doctor – what do you think of Staś? He is making me uneasy. I can see that for a year he has been throwing himself into all sorts of things. That trip to Bulgaria, and today this store . . . the trading company . . . his own carriage . . . There is a peculiar change in his character.'

'I see none,' Szuman replied, 'he always was a man of action who carried out whatever came into his head. He decided to go to the university, and went; he decided to make a fortune, and did so. If he has got some folly or other into his head, he will not hesitate to commit it. It's his character.'

'But for all that,' I said, 'I see many contradictions in his behaviour . . .'

'That is hardly to be wondered at,' the doctor interrupted, 'for two men are merged in him: a Romantic of the pre-1863 kind, and a positivist of the '70s.* What onlookers find contradictory is perfectly consistent with Wokulski himself.'

'But has he not been involved in any new . . . incidents?' I asked. 'I know of none,' Szuman replied drily.

I fell silent and it was a moment before I began again: 'What will become of him in the long run?'

Szuman raised his eyebrows and clasped his hands: 'Nothing good,' he replied. 'People like him either reconcile themselves to everything, or come up against a great obstacle and break their heads open on it. Hitherto things have gone well with him . . . but no man wins every time in his life.'

'What then?' I asked.

'So we may well be witnesses of a tragedy,' Szuman concluded. He drank a glass of tea, then went home.

I could not sleep that night. Such terrible predictions on what should have been a day of triumph . . . But the Lord knows more than Szuman and surely He will not let Staś go to waste . . .

XI

Old Dreams and New Acquaintances

MRS MELITON had been through a hard school in life, where she even learned to despise all generally accepted notions. When she was young, it had been a truth universally acknowledged that a pretty and virtuous girl could marry even if she had no money; yet she did not marry. Later on, it was said – also in a general way – that an educated governess would acquire her pupils' affection and their parents' respect. She was an educated, even devoted governess, yet her pupils teased her to distraction and their parents derided her from morning to night. Then she read a great quantity of novels, in which it was a universally acknowledged truth that princes, counts or barons in love are noble persons in the habit of bestowing their hands upon a poor governess in exchange for her heart. So she surrendered her heart to a young and noble count, yet she never acquired his hand in marriage.

She was already over thirty when she married an elderly tutor, Meliton, solely in order to effect the moral elevation of a man who had taken somewhat to drink. After marriage, the bridegroom drank more than before, and sometimes beat his wife, as she elevated him morally, with a thick stick. When he died in the street one day, Mrs Meliton had him taken off to the cemetery, and once she was sure he was well and truly buried, got herself a dog: for it was a truth universally acknowledged that a dog is the most affectionate of all creatures. And so it was, until it went mad and bit a servant girl, which brought a serious illness upon Mrs Meliton herself. She stayed in the hospital six months, in a private room, alone and forgotten by her pupils, their families and the count she had bestowed her heart upon. It gave her time to reflect. And when she emerged as a thin, elderly woman with grey and thinning hair, people began to declare that illness had changed her beyond recognition.

'I have learned sense,' Mrs Meliton retorted.

She was no longer a governess, but recommended them; she did not think of marriage, only acted as go-between for young couples; she gave her heart to no one, only facilitated lovers' meetings in her own house. And as everyone had to pay her for everything, she acquired a little money and lived on it.

At the start of her new career she was solemn and even cynical. 'A priest', she would tell her confidantes, 'gets his income from marriages – I from engagements. A count . . . takes money for arranging things between horses, I for facilitating acquaintances between people.'

In time, however, she became more moderate in her tone, and sometimes even moralised, for she noticed that giving voice to universally acknowledged opinions and views affected her income.

Mrs Meliton had known Wokulski for years. And since she enjoyed public events and was in the habit of watching everything, she soon noticed that Wokulski was observing Izabela much too reverently. Having made this discovery, she shrugged: what concern was it of hers if a tradesman in haberdashery was in love with Miss Łęcka? If he had taken a fancy to some wealthy tradesman's widow, or the daughter of some manufacturer, then Mrs Meliton would have had the opportunity of acting as go-between. But as it was . . .

Not until Wokulski returned from Bulgaria with a fortune, of which people gave miraculous accounts, did Mrs Meliton herself approach him with regard to Izabela, and offer him her services. And a tacit agreement came into being: Wokulski paid generously, while Mrs Meliton provided him with all sorts of information concerning the Łęcki family and the fashionable persons who associated with them. It was through her that Wokulski had acquired Łęcki's promissory notes and Izabela's silver. On this occasion Mrs Meliton had visited Wokulski at home to congratulate him: 'You are setting about it very sensibly,' she said, 'though admittedly you will get little pleasure from the dinner-service and the silver, but it was a master-stroke to buy up Łęcki's promissory notes. The mark of a real tradesman!'

Hearing this compliment, Wokulski opened his desk, looked about inside and presently produced a bundle of promissory notes: 'These?' he asked, showing them to Mrs Meliton. 'Yes – I'd like to have the money they represent,' she replied with a sigh.

Wokulski took the packet in both hands and ripped it up. 'The mark of a tradesman?' he asked.

Mrs Meliton looked at him curiously and muttered: 'I am sorry for you.'

'Why so, pray?'

'I am sorry for you,' she repeated, 'I am a woman and I know women are not to be gained by sacrifice, but by power.'

'Is that so?'

'The power of looks, health, money . . .'

'Intelligence . . .' Wokulski interrupted in the same tone of voice.

'Not so much intelligence as brute force,' Mrs Meliton added with a derisive laugh, 'I know my own sex, and have had occasion more than once to pity masculine innocence . . .'

'Pray do not trouble to do so on my account . . .'

'You think it will not be necessary?' she asked, looking into his eyes.

'My dear lady,' Wokulski replied, 'if Miss Łęcka is what I think she is, she may appreciate me at some future time. If she isn't I shall have time to disillusion myself.'

'Do it sooner than that, Wokulski – sooner,' she said, rising, 'for believe me it is easier to throw away a thousand roubles than to dislodge affection from the heart. Particularly when it is already established there. But do not forget to invest my little capital profitably. You would not have torn up those thousands of roubles, had you known how hard they must sometimes be worked for . . .'

In May and June the visits of Mrs Meliton grew more frequent, much to the dismay of Rzecki, who suspected a plot. He was not mistaken, either. There was a plot, but it was directed against Izabela; the elderly woman used to provide Wokulski with important information, but it concerned only Izabela. In other words, she used to tell him on what days the Countess planned to walk with her niece in the Łazienki park. When this happened, Mrs Meliton would call at the shop, reward herself with a trifle worth a few roubles or more, then would tell Rzecki the appointed day and hour.

These were strange periods for Wokulski. On being told that the ladies would be in the Łazienki park on the morrow, he became restless today. He grew indifferent to business, became irritable; time seemed to stop and tomorrow was never coming. His night was full of wild dreams; sometimes, half awake, he would mutter: 'In the end – what is it all for? Nothing! Oh, what a brute I am . . .'

But when the morning came, he feared to look out of the window lest he saw a cloudy sky. And the morning dragged so that all his life might have been anchored in it, poisoned with a dreadful poison. 'Can this possibly be love?' he asked himself in despair.

In a state of fever he would order the carriage for noon. At every moment it seemed to him he was about to meet the Countess's carriage on its way back, or that his horses, chafing at the bit, were going too slowly.

In the Łazienki park he jumped out of the carriage and hurried to the pond where the Countess usually walked, as she liked feeding the swans. He arrived too early, sank on a bench, drenched in cold sweat, and sat motionless, gazing towards the palace, oblivious of the whole world. Finally, two female figures appeared at the end of the path, one in black, the other in grey. The blood rushed to Wokulski's head: 'There they are! Will they speak to me? . . .'

He rose from the bench and went towards them like a madman, breathless. Yes, it was Izabela; she was with her aunt, talking to her. Wokulski stared at her, and thought: 'Well, what is there about her that is so extraordinary? She's a woman like any other . . . Surely I am unnecessarily crazy about her? . . .'

He bowed, the ladies bowed. He walked by without turning his head, so as not to betray himself. Finally he glanced back; both ladies had disappeared into the shrubbery.

'I'll go back,' he thought, 'I'll look at her again . . . No – it wouldn't do.' And at this moment he felt the glittering water of the pond was drawing him with irresistible power: 'Oh, if only I could be sure that death is forgetfulness. Suppose it is not? . . . No, there is no pity in nature. Is it right to equip wretched human hearts with an infinity of yearning, without at least giving them the consolation that death means oblivion?'

At the same time, the Countess would be saying to Izabela: 'I am becoming increasingly convinced that money does not bring happiness, Bela. That Wokulski has made himself a fine career by his standards, but what good is it? He doesn't work in his shop any more, but bores himself here in the Łazienki park . . . Didn't you see how bored he looked?'

'Bored?' Izabela echoed, 'he strikes me most of all as comical.'

'I wouldn't have said that,' the Countess was surprised.

'Well – unpleasant,' Miss Izabela corrected herself.

Wokulski lacked the courage to leave the park. He walked along the other side of the pond and watched that grey dress fluttering among the trees. Not until later did he realise he was watching two grey dresses and a third, blue one, none of which belonged to Izabela: 'I am abysmally stupid,' he thought. Yet this did not help.

One day in the first half of June, Mrs Meliton let Wokulski know that Izabela would be out walking the next day with the Countess and the Duchess. This small incident might well have capital significance. For Wokulski had visited the Duchess several times since that memorable Easter, and knew that the old lady was extremely well disposed towards him. He usually listened to her tales of olden times, talked about his uncle and recently had even discussed erecting a gravestone for him. During these talks, the name of Izabela appeared in some unexplained manner, so unexpectedly that Wokulski was not able to conceal his emotion: his face changed; his voice darkened.

The old lady put on her spectacles and looked at Wokulski, then asked: 'Am I right in thinking you are not indifferent to Miss Łęcka?'

'I hardly know her . . . I have only spoken to her once in my life,' Wokulski explained, in confusion.

The Duchess fell to pondering, nodded and murmured: 'Ah . . .'

Wokulski bade her goodbye but that 'Ah . . .' remained in his mind. In any case, he was sure he did not have an enemy in the Duchess. And now, less than a week since that conversation, he had learned that the Duchess was going to the Łazienki park with the Countess and Izabela. Could she have found out that the ladies sometimes encountered him there? Perhaps she wanted to bring them together?

Wokulski looked at his watch: it was three in the afternoon. 'So it's to be tomorrow,' he thought, 'within twenty-four hours . . . No, not so many . . . how many?' He could not estimate how many hours would flow between three o'clock and one o'clock next afternoon. He was overwhelmed with nervousness; he ate no dinner; his imagination rushed ahead, but cold common sense put the brake on it: 'Let us see what tomorrow brings. Perhaps it will rain, or one of the ladies will be ill.'

He hurried out into the street and wandered about aimlessly, repeating: 'Well, we shall see what tomorrow brings . . . Perhaps they won't even stop? In any case, Izabela is a pretty woman, even unusually pretty, but she is only a woman, not a supernatural being. Thousands of equally pretty women walk about this world, yet I don't dream of attaching myself to their skirts. What if she rejects me? So be it! I shall fall into the clutches of another, still more frantically . . .'

In the evening he went to the theatre, but left after the first act. Again he wandered about the town, and wherever he went, was haunted by the thought of the walk tomorrow and by an obscure premonition that it would bring him closer to Izabela.

That night passed, and dawn came. At noon, he ordered the carriage to be harnessed. He wrote a note to the shop that he would come later, and ripped a pair of gloves to shreds. At last the servant came in: 'The horses are ready!' He reached for his hat. 'The Prince!' said the servant.

Everything grew dark before Wokulski's eyes: 'Announce him . . .'

The Prince entered: 'Good morning, Mr Wokulski,' he cried, 'are you going out? To the shops or the railway, I'll be bound. But none of that! I hereby place you under arrest and am taking you off to my house. I will even be uncivil enough to commandeer your carriage, as I didn't bring mine today. However, I am sure you will forgive me in view of the splendid news . . .'

'Please be seated . . .'

'Well, just for a moment. Pray imagine,' said the Prince, as he took a chair, 'that I have teased our fraternal gentlemen – was not that neatly phrased? – until they have promised to come to my house and listen to the plans for your partnership. So I will take you at once, or rather I shall come along with you, and we shall be off to my house.'

Wokulski felt like a man who has fallen from a height and lies stunned. His confusion did not escape the Prince's attention, and he smiled, attributing it to delight at this visit and invitation. It never even entered his head that a ride to the Łazienki park was more important to Wokulski than any Prince or trading partnership.

'Are we ready, then?' the Prince inquired, rising. It was only a matter of a second for Wokulski to say he was not going, and wanted nothing to do with any partnership. But at this moment he thought: 'The outing – that's for me; the partnership – for her.'

He took his hat and went with the Prince. It seemed to him that the carriage was not driving along the street but over his own brains. 'Women are not gained by sacrifice, but by brute force . . .' he recalled Mrs Meliton's phrase. Influenced by this aphorism, he felt like seizing the Prince by the scruff of the neck and throwing him bodily into the roadway. But this lasted only a moment.

The Prince was looking at him through half-closed eyes, and seeing Wokulski turn red, then white, thought: 'I never dreamed I would give this honest fellow so much pleasure. Yes, one should always extend a hand to new people . . .'

Among his peers, the Prince had the reputation of a fervent patriot, almost a chauvinist; elsewhere, he enjoyed the reputation of an excellent citizen. He very much enjoyed speaking Polish, and even his conversations in French concerned matters of public interest. He was an aristocrat from top to toe, in his soul, heart and blood. He believed that society consisted of two elements: the ordinary crowd, and the chosen few. The ordinary crowd was the work of Nature, and might well be descended from monkeys, as Darwin maintained, despite Holy Scripture. But the chosen few had some higher origin, and were descended, if not from gods, then at least from heroes related to them – Hercules, Prometheus, or in the last resort Orpheus. The Prince had a good friend in France (infected to the greatest possible degree by the democratic disease) who scoffed at the divine origins of the aristocracy.

'Cousin mine,' he would say, 'I think you fail fully to understand the question of stock. What are the great houses? They are made up of those whose ancestors were hetmans, senators, governors, or, in today's terms, marshals, members of the upper house, or departmental prefects. Well – we know such gentlemen, do we not? There's nothing unusual about them . . . They eat, drink, play cards, court women, amass debts – like any other mere mortal, whom they occasionally surpass in stupidity.'

A sickly flush suffused the Prince's face.

'Cousin,' he retorted, 'have you ever met a prefect or marshal with a majestic expression such as those we see in the portraits of our forefathers?'

'There is nothing odd in that,' laughed the plague-stricken Count. 'Artists endowed their paintings with expression never dreamt of by the original sitters, just as heraldists and historians told fabulous legends about them. All lies, my cousin! . . . These are only the scenery and costumes that make of one Jack a prince and of another a ploughman. In reality they are merely miserable actors both.'

'Derision, cousin, makes a poor debating partner!' fulminated the Prince and escaped. He hurried home, lay down on the *chaise-longue* with his hands clasped behind his head and, gazing at the ceiling, watched as figures of superhuman strength, courage, reason, disinterestedness passed before him. These were his ancestors, and those of the Count, except that the latter denied them. Could he possibly have some mixed blood? . . .

The prince did not despise ordinary mortals, but was even benevolently disposed towards them, had contact with them and was concerned with their needs. He saw himself as a Prometheus who performed the honourable duty of bringing fire down from Heaven for the benefit of the poor people. Moreover, religion required him to sympathise with the humble, and the Prince blushed to think that most members of high society would eventually stand before the seat of Heavenly Judgement without ever having performed this kind of good deed. So, in order to avoid bringing shame upon himself, he frequented and even invited to his house various committees, spent twenty or even a hundred roubles on various charitable public causes and above all, he continually grieved over the unhappy position of his country, ending all his speeches with the phrase: 'Gentlemen, let us first of all consider how to elevate our unhappy country . . .' And as he said this, a weight would fall from his heart, and the weight varied in proportion as to the number of listeners he had, or the amount he had spent on good deeds.

He believed it was a citizen's duty to hold committee meetings, to encourage trade and to grieve, grieve continually over his unhappy country. Had he been asked whether he ever planted a tree to provide shade for people or the earth, or whether he ever removed a stone from a horse's hoof, he would have been frankly astonished. For he felt, thought, yearned and grieved for millions. He had never done anything useful. He thought that continual fretting about the whole country was far more valuable than wiping the nose of a grubby child.

In June, the character of Warsaw undergoes a marked change. The hotels, hitherto empty, fill and put up their prices; advertisements appear on many houses: 'Furnished Apartments to Let for a Few Weeks'. All droshkies are hired, all the messengers run hither and thither. Figures not to be met with at other times are now encountered in the streets, parks, theatres, restaurants, exhibitions, shops and stores selling ladies' dresses. Among them are stout and ruddy men in blue peaked caps, in boots too wide and gloves too tight, wearing suits in styles invented by provincial tailors. They are accompanied by ladies not distinguished either for beauty or Warsaw chic, and by equally numerous crowds of clumsy children, glowing with health.

Some of these rural visitors bring wool for the market; others come for the races; yet others to see both the wool and the races; some to meet neighbours who live but a mile away; others to refresh themselves with the cloudy water and the dust of the city, and yet others wear themselves out by travelling several days without knowing why.

The Prince took advantage of these gatherings to bring together Wokulski and some landowners.

The Prince occupied a huge apartment on the second floor of his own palace. That part which consisted of the master's study, library and smoking room was used for meetings of gentlemen, at which the Prince would introduce his own or other people's plans concerned with matters of public interest. This happened several times a year. The previous spring session had been devoted to the question of paddle-boats on the Vistula river, at which three sides had made themselves very clear. The first, consisting of the Prince and his personal friends, absolutely demanded the introduction of paddle-boats, although the second, the bourgeois – while admitting the plausibility of the plan, considered it premature and did not want to spend money on it. The third side consisted only of two men – a certain technician who declared that paddle-boats could not navigate on the Vistula, and a certain deaf magnate, who always replied to any appeal addressed to his pocket: 'A little louder, pray, I cannot hear a word . . .'

The Prince and Wokulski arrived at one o'clock, and a quarter of an hour later other members of the committee began gathering. The Prince greeted everyone with agreeable familiarity, introduced Wokulski, then checked off the arrival's name on his list of members with a very long and very red pencil.

One of the first guests was Mr Łęcki; he drew Wokulski aside, and once again asked him about the aim and significance of the partnership, to which he already belonged heart and soul, though he could never remember quite what it was all about.

Meanwhile, the other gentlemen eyed the intruder and commented in lowered voices: 'Looks like a bull!' whispered a stout marshal, indicating Wokulski with his eyes, 'the tufts on his

head stick up like a bison's, as for his chest . . . my word! And sharp
eyes . . . He wouldn't soon get tired out hunting.'

'And that face!' added a Baron with the features of Mephistopheles, 'his forehead, my dear sir! His whiskers! His imperial, my
dear sir . . . features somewhat . . . hm, but all in all . . .'

'Let us wait and see how he gets on in business,' put in a
somewhat round-shouldered Count.

'He's bold, he takes risks, oh dear me, yes,' another Count
exclaimed, as though speaking out of a deep cellar, as he sat stiffly
in a chair, looking – with his luxuriant whiskers and glassy eyes –
for all the world like an Englishman in the *Journal amusant*.

The Prince rose from his armchair and coughed: everyone fell
silent, so it was possible to catch the end of the marshal's anecdote:
'We were all looking hard into the forest, when something squeaks
under our horses' hoofs. Just fancy, my dear sir, one of the dogs
was throttling a hare . . .' With this, the marshal with an immense
hand, clapped one thigh, out of which both a secretary and his
assistant might have been hewed.

The Prince coughed again; the marshal wiped his forehead in
embarrassment with an unusually large silk handkerchief.
'Gentlemen,' said the Prince, 'I have taken the liberty of bringing
you here in a certain . . . very important connection, which as we
all know must always stand on guard over public interests . . . I
mean . . . of our ideas . . . that is to say . . .' The Prince seemed
flustered. Suddenly, however, he got his second wind and went on:
'It is in connection with trade . . . that is to say it is a plan . . . or
rather a project of forming a partnership to facilitate trade . . .'

'In wheat,' said someone in a corner.

'To be precise,' said the Prince, 'not wheat exactly, but . . .'

'Spirits,' the same voice said, hastily.

'Not at all! Trade, or rather the facilitating of trade between
Russia and abroad in goods . . . While it is highly desirable that our
city should become the centre of any such . . .'

'What sort of trade?' asked the round-shouldered Count.

'The professional side of the question will be graciously
explained by Mr Wokulski, a man . . . a professional,' the Prince
said, adding, 'Let us never forget the duties which our concern for
public interest and this unhappy country . . . lay upon us . . .'

'To be sure! I will contribute ten thousand roubles at once,' the
marshal cried.

'What for?' asked the Count who feigned to be a genuine
Englishman.

'No matter!' the marshal replied in a huge voice, 'I said I'd spend
fifty thousand in Warsaw this summer, so ten thousand will go to
charity, as our dear Prince speaks wonderfully . . . sincerely, I assure
you, yes – and sensibly . . .'

'Excuse me, gentlemen,' Wokulski exclaimed, 'this is not a charitable partnership, but one to ensure financial profit.'

'That's it,' the round-shouldered Count interposed.

'Oh dear me, yes,' the 'English' Count agreed.

'What sort of profit will ten thousand roubles bring me?' the marshal countered, 'I'd be begging in the streets with such profits as that.'

The round-shouldered Count burst out: 'Allow me to ask whether small profits should be ignored? That attitude will ruin us, gentlemen!' he exclaimed, tapping with a fingernail on the arm of his chair.

'Count,' the Prince interrupted sweetly, 'Mr Wokulski is speaking . . .'

'Oh dear me, yes,' the 'English' Count joined in, caressing his luxuriant whiskers.

'Let us then ask Mr Wokulski,' said another voice, 'that he be kind enough to present to us, with his own inimitable clarity and brevity, this matter of public interest which has brought us together here in the hospitable apartments of His Excellency . . .'

Wokulski glanced at the person who thus acknowledged his clarity and brevity. He was an eminent lawyer, the friend and the right-hand man of the Prince; he liked speaking in a flowery manner, beating time with one hand and listening to his own phrases, which he always found splendid.

'Providing we all understand it,' someone muttered in the corner occupied by some gentry who hated the magnates.

'You gentlemen know', Wokulski began, 'that Warsaw is a trading post between Western and Eastern Europe. Here part of the French and German merchandise intended for Russia is collected and passed through our hands . . . We might have certain profits from this trade . . .'

'Were it not in the hands of the Jews,' said someone in an undertone from the table where merchants and industrialists were sitting.

'Not at all,' Wokulski retorted, 'the profits would accrue if our trade were properly handled . . .'

'It cannot be properly handled with Jews . . .'

'But nowadays,' the Prince's lawyer interrupted, 'Mr Wokulski is giving us the opportunity of replacing Jewish by Christian capital . . .'

'Mr Wokulski is himself bringing Jews into trade,' muttered an opponent on the merchants' side.

It became quiet.

'I must decline giving anyone an account of my way of doing business,' Wokulski went on. 'I am putting before you gentlemen a way to establish Warsaw's foreign trade. This is the first half of my plan, and should be one source of profit for Polish investments.

The second source is trade with Russia. Goods in demand here, can be obtained there cheaply. A partnership which dealt with these goods might make fifteen or twenty per cent annually on invested capital. I would mention textiles in the first place . . .'

'That would undermine our own industry,' an opponent in the group of merchants cried.

'I am not concerned with manufacturers but with consumers,' Wokulski replied.

The merchants and manufacturers began whispering together in a manner not at all favourable towards Wokulski.

'So we have come to the question of public interest,' the Prince exclaimed in an emotional tone of voice, 'and the problem appears to be whether Mr Wokulski's projects would be advantageous for our country. You, sir . . .' and the Prince turned to his lawyer, feeling the need for the latter's aid in this somewhat awkward situation.

'My dear Mr Wokulski,' cried the lawyer, 'pray be good enough to explain to us – with your own inimitable thoroughness – whether the importation of textiles from such a distance might harm not our own manufacturers . . .'

'In the first place,' Wokulski said, 'the factories are not ours, but German . . .'

'Oho!' exclaimed someone in the merchant group.

'I am quite ready', Wokulski went on, 'to enumerate for you factories in which the entire administration and all the better-paid workers are Germans, in which the capital is German, and the managing directors all reside in Germany; in which our workers have no opportunities of bettering themselves, but are badly paid labourers, badly treated and totally Germanised.'

'That is important,' the round-shouldered Count interposed.

'Oh dear me, yes,' the 'English' Count muttered.

'Goodness me, it stirs me just to listen to you . . .' the marshal exclaimed, 'I never thought it possible to be so taken by a conversation . . . I will be back directly,' and he left the room, the floor almost sinking under his weight.

'Shall I enumerate them?' Wokulski inquired. The group of merchants and industrialists hastily proved their moderation by not asking for any names.

The lawyer rose swiftly from his chair, rubbed his hands and exclaimed: 'I think we may now pass from the question of local factories to the next point on the agenda. Now, Mr Wokulski, will you – with your inimitable brevity – be so kind as to explain what positive advantages your project will bring . . .'

'Our unhappy country . . .' the Prince interposed.

'Gentlemen,' said Wokulski, 'if a yard of my calico were to cost only two pennies less than it does today, then there would be a general saving of ten thousand roubles for every million yards purchased.'

'What does ten thousand roubles matter?' the marshal asked. He had just come back into the room, but had not yet caught up with the course of the debate.

'A great deal, a very great deal,' the round-shouldered Count cried, 'we must learn once and for all to respect profits in terms of pennies.'

'Oh dear me, yes . . . a penny saved is a pound made,' added the Count posing as an Englishman.

'Ten thousand roubles is the basis for a reasonable standard of living for at least twenty families,' Wokulski went on.

'A drop in the ocean,' one of the merchants muttered.

'But there is yet another aspect,' Wokulski added, 'which only concerns capitalists. I have at my disposal merchandise worth three to four million roubles a year . . .'

'My word!' the marshal murmured.

'That is not my fortune,' Wokulski continued, 'mine is much more modest.'

'Upon my word, I like such men,' said the round-shouldered Count.

'Oh dear me, yes,' added the 'Englishman'.

'That three to four million is my personal credit and brings me in a very small interest as middle-man,' said Wokulski, 'but I must point out that if cash could replace this credit, then the interest would amount to fifteen to twenty per cent, perhaps more. This aspect of the matter concerns you gentlemen who invest your money in banks at low rates of interest. Others use this money and draw interest for themselves. I am offering you the opportunity to use it directly and increase your own incomes. That is all.'

'Excellent,' the round-shouldered Count exclaimed, 'but would it not be possible to have more details?'

'I can only discuss them with my partners,' Wokulski replied.

'You may rely on me,' said the round-shouldered Count, and gave Wokulski his hand.

'Oh dear me, yes,' the pseudo-Englishman added, giving him two fingers.

'Gentlemen,' exclaimed a clean-shaven individual from the group of gentry who hated the magnates, 'you have been referring to the calico trade, which does not interest us . . . But, gentlemen, we have corn in our granaries,' he added in a tearful voice, 'we have spirits in our warehouses, which the middle-men take advantage of to exploit us in a way I can only describe as . . . deplorable.' He looked around the study. The group of gentry who hated the magnates cheered him on.

The face of the Prince, glowing with discreet joy, lit up at this moment with a flash of genuine inspiration: 'But, gentlemen,' he exclaimed, 'today we have been referring to the calico trade, but what is to prevent us debating on other matters tomorrow or the day after?'

'Goodness me, how well the dear Prince talks, to be sure,' the marshal exclaimed.

'Go on, go on!' the lawyer urged, forcefully showing that he was trying to put a brake on his own enthusiasm for the Prince.

'Well, gentlemen,' the Prince went on, moved, 'I propose further meetings: one to discuss the corn trade, another the spirits trade . . .'

'And credit for the farmers?' asked one of the disunited gentry.

'A third on credit for farmers,' said the Prince, 'a fourth . . .'

'The fourth and fifth,' the lawyer hurried on, 'to be devoted to solving the general economic problems . . .'

'Of our unhappy country,' the Prince concluded, almost with tears in his eyes.

'Gentlemen,' the lawyer cried, blowing his nose in excitement, 'let us honour our host, the well-known citizen, the most respected of men . . .'

'Ten thousand roubles, my goodness!' the marshal exclaimed.

'. . . by rising!' the lawyer hastily finished.

'Bravo! Long live the Prince!' everyone cried, to the accompaniment of the scraping of feet and chairs. The group of magnate-hating gentry cheered loudest of all.

The Prince began embracing his guests, no longer restraining his emotion; assisted by the lawyer, he embraced everyone and wept copiously.

Some men gathered around Wokulski. 'I shall come in with fifty thousand roubles at first,' said the round-shouldered Count, 'next year though . . . let us wait and see.'

'Thirty, sir, thirty thousand roubles, my dear sir . . .' added the Baron who looked like Mephistopheles.

'And I – thirty thousand, oh dear me, yes,' added the 'English' Count, nodding his head.

'And I'll contribute twice – no, three times as much as our dear Prince. Goodness me!' said the marshal.

A few opponents from the merchant group also approached Wokulski. They said nothing, but their appreciative glances were a hundred times more eloquent than the most affectionate words. Then Wokulski was approached by a young man, shabby, with a thin beard and evident traces of premature decay in his entire aspect. Wokulski had encountered him at various public events and in the street too, riding by in the fastest droshkies.

'I am Maruszewicz,' said the decayed young man with a charming smile, 'forgive me for introducing myself in this informal manner, and at our first meeting, too – but I would like to ask you . . .'

'I am at your service.'

The young man took Wokulski's arm and led him to the window: 'Allow me to place my cards on the table at once – it is the only way with men like yourself. I am not wealthy, but have good intentions and would like to find some occupation. You are forming a partnership, would it not be possible for me to work under your direction?'

Wokulski eyed him attentively. The proposal he had just heard did not, somehow, suit the decayed aspect and uncertain looks of the young man. Wokulski felt distaste, but said: 'What can you do? What is your profession?'

'Well, I have not yet chosen a profession, but I have great talents and can undertake anything.'

'What wages do you expect?'

'A thousand . . . two thousand roubles,' the young man replied, embarrassed.

Wokulski shook his head involuntarily: 'I doubt whether we shall have any posts suited to your requirements. However, please call on me one day . . .'

The round-shouldered Count began speaking from the middle of the room: 'And so, gentlemen, we are agreed in principle to enter into the partnership proposed by Mr Wokulski. I therefore take pleasure in inviting those of you who wish to take part to come to my house tomorrow, at nine in the evening.'

'I'll be there, my dear Count, goodness me,' the stout marshal exclaimed, 'and will probably bring a few Lithuanians. But tell me please, why should we form a partnership? Why don't the merchants? . . .'

'If only,' the Count replied, enthusiastically, 'to prevent other people from saying we do nothing but stay at home and count our dividends.'

The Prince asked to be heard: 'In any case,' he said, 'we have in mind two more partnerships – in the grain and the spirits trades . . . Anyone who does not wish to belong to one can join the other . . . Besides, let us invite Mr Wokulski to be kind enough to take part in our committee meetings.'

'Oh dear me, yes,' the would-be English Count interposed.

'And to illuminate our problems with his own inimitable talent,' the lawyer concluded.

'I doubt whether I can be of any use to you, gentlemen,' Wokulski replied, 'I have certainly had dealings in grain and spirits, but under very different circumstances. I was concerned with large quantities and speed of delivery, not price. Besides, I am not familiar with the local grain trade.'

'There will be specialists, my dear Mr Wokulski,' the lawyer interrupted, 'they will provide details which you need only be kind enough to put in order and illuminate with your own inimitable talents . . .'

'Pray do so!' the Count exclaimed, and they were echoed still more loudly by the gentry who hated the magnates.

It was almost five o'clock, and they began to take leave. At this moment, Wokulski saw Mr Łęcki approaching him from the other room, accompanied by the same young man he had seen in the company of Izabela at the Easter collection and at the Countess's house.

'Mr Wokulski, allow me', said Łęcki, 'to introduce Mr Julian Ochocki . . . Our cousin, you know . . . a trifle eccentric, but there . . .'

'I have long wanted to meet you,' said Ochocki, shaking hands.

Wokulski looked at him silently. The young man was not yet thirty, and was distinguished by his unusual appearance. He seemed to have the features of Napoleon, veiled by clouds of dreaminess.

'Which way are you going?' the young man asked Wokulski, 'may I join you?'

'Please do not trouble . . .'

'Oh, I have plenty of time,' the young man replied.

'What does he want of me?' Wokulski wondered, and said: 'We might go in the direction of the Łazienki park, then?'

'Certainly,' Ochocki replied, 'I'll just say goodbye to the Prince and will catch up with you.'

Hardly had he gone, than the lawyer stepped up to Wokulski. 'I congratulate you on a complete triumph,' he said in a low voice, 'the Prince is quite taken with you, both the Counts and the Baron too . . . They are all somewhat scatterbrained, as you will have noticed, but they're men of good will . . . They want to do something, they're intelligent and educated – but they lack energy. A sickness of the will, my dear sir, their whole class is affected by it . . . They have everything – money, titles, respect, even success with women, so they want nothing. But without that urge, Mr Wokulski, they cannot help becoming tools in the hands of new and ambitious men . . . We, my dear sir, we still want many things,' he added in a still lower voice, 'they are lucky to have found us . . .'

As Wokulski did not answer, the lawyer began to regard him as a very skilled diplomat, and secretly regretted being so outspoken. 'Anyway,' he thought, looking furtively at Wokulski, 'even if he repeats this to the Prince, what could the Prince do to me? I'll say I wanted to test him . . .'

'What kind of ambitions does he suspect me of?' Wokulski asked himself privately.

He bade farewell to the Prince, promised to come to all future meetings and, going into the street, sent his carriage home. 'What does this Ochocki want of me?' he thought, suspiciously, 'of course he is worried about Izabela . . . perhaps he means to frighten me away from her? . . . Fool! If she loves him, then he need not waste words; I will go away of my own accord . . . But if she does not love him, then let him beware of trying to remove me . . . I have committed one capital folly in my life, for Izabela's sake. I hope it does not come down upon him, I should be sorry for the lad.'

Hasty footsteps sounded in the gateway: Wokulski turned and saw Ochocki. 'Were you waiting? I'm sorry,' the young man cried.

'Shall we go to the Łazienki?' Wokulski asked.

'By all means.'

They walked for some time in silence. The young man was thinking; Wokulski was on edge. He made up his mind to take the bull by the horns: 'You are a close relative of the Łęckis, then?' he asked.

'Fairly,' the young man replied. 'My mother was a Łęcka,' he explained ironically, 'though my father was merely an Ochocki. This has very much weakened any family ties . . . I would not be acquainted with Tomasz, who is a sort of second cousin, were it not that he has lost his money.'

'Miss Łęcka is a very distinguished person,' said Wokulski, gazing ahead.

'Distinguished?' Ochocki echoed, 'say rather a goddess! When I am talking to her, I think she could fill my whole life for me. Only with her do I feel at peace and forget the uneasiness that haunts me. But there! I could not sit all day long with her in a drawing-room, nor could she stay with me in my laboratory.'

Wokulski stopped: 'Are you interested in physics or chemistry?' he asked in surprise.

'Oh, what am I not interested in?' Ochocki replied, 'physics, chemistry, technology . . . I graduated in the natural sciences at the university and in mechanical engineering at the polytechnic. I am interested in everything: I read and work from morning to night – but do nothing. I have been able to improve the microscope a trifle, to build a new kind of electric lamp . . .'

Wokulski's surprise intensified: 'So you are Ochocki the inventor?'

'Yes,' the young man replied, 'but what does that signify? Nothing. When I think that at the age of twenty-eight I have only achieved this, then despair overcomes me. I feel like smashing up my laboratory and plunging head-first into polite society, to which people are trying to attract me – or putting a bullet through my head. Ochocki's electric lamp – how absurd! To rush headlong through life and finish up with an electric lamp – that is terrible. To reach the middle of life and not find even a trace of the road along which one wants to travel – what despair!'

The young man fell silent and, as they were now in the Botanical Gardens, took off his hat. Wokulski looked at him attentively, and made another discovery. Though the young man looked elegant, he was not at all smart: he even seemed careless of his appearance. He had tangled hair, his tie was somewhat crooked, and a button was undone on his shirt. It seemed as if someone looked after his linen and clothes very carefully, while he himself treated them carelessly, and it was precisely this carelessness which gave him his individual charm. His every movement was involuntary, casual, but graceful. Equally graceful was his manner of looking and listening – or rather not listening – and even of disposing of his hat.

They went to the hillock from where the round well can be seen. Strollers surrounded them on all sides, but Ochocki did not mind them and, indicating a bench with his hat, said: 'I have often read that a man with great aspirations is happy. I myself have unusual aspirations which only make me ludicrous and offend my nearest and dearest. Look at this bench . . . Here, at the beginning of June, I was sitting with my cousin and Flora. Some moon or other was shining, and even some nightingales were singing. I was thinking of something else. Suddenly my cousin said: 'Do you know anything about astronomy, cousin?'

'A little . . .'

'Well then, tell me what star that is . . .'

'I don't know,' I told her, 'but one thing is certain – we shall never reach it. Man is fastened to the earth like an oyster to a rock. At this moment,' Ochocki went on, 'an idea or notion came to me. I forgot my beautiful cousin and began thinking about flying machines. And because I have to walk about when thinking, I got up and left my cousin without a word . . . Next day Flora called me impertinent; Mr Łęcki said I was eccentric and my cousin refused to speak to me for a week . . . And if only I had thought of something! But nothing came, nothing at all, though I could have sworn that before I reached the well a general sketch of the flying machine would come to me . . . Stupid, wasn't it?'

'So they spend evenings here by moonlight and with nightingales singing?' Wokulski thought, and felt a terrible anguish in his heart. Izabela is already in love with this Ochocki, or if she isn't, it is only on account of his eccentricities. Well, she is right – he is a handsome man, and an unusual one.

'Of course,' Ochocki went on, 'I said not a word of this to my aunt who, whenever she sews a button on my shirt, says: "Julian dear, please try to please Izabela, she is exactly the wife for you . . . Clever and beautiful: she alone can cure you of your visions." But I wonder what sort of wife she would make me? If at least she could help me, then it would not be so bad . . . But as if she could leave a drawing-room for my laboratory! She is right, that is her proper environment: a bird needs air, a fish water . . . What a fine evening it is,' he added after a moment, 'I am excited tonight as rarely happens. But what is wrong, Mr Wokulski?'

'I am rather tired,' Wokulski replied dully. 'We might sit down over there . . .'

They did so on the slope of the hillock, near the edge of the park. Ochocki leaned his chin on his knees and began pondering. Wokulski eyed him with a feeling in which admiration mingled with hatred: is he stupid or cunning? Why has he told me all this? Wokulski thought. But he had to admit that Ochocki's talk had the same frankness and extravagance as his gestures and all his person. They had just met for the first time, yet already Ochocki was talking to him as if they had known one another since childhood.

'I'll get this over with,' said Wokulski to himself, and he asked aloud, with a deep sigh: 'So you are going to marry her, Mr Ochocki?'

'I'd be insane if I did . . .' the young man muttered with a shrug.

'How so? After all, you like your cousin.'

'Very much indeed, but that is not all. I'd marry her if I were certain that I would never achieve anything in science.'

In addition to hatred and admiration, joy now radiated within Wokulski's heart. At this moment Ochocki rubbed his forehead as if waking up, looked at Wokulski and suddenly exclaimed: 'But there . . . I was forgetting I had an important question to ask you.'

'What does he want?' Wokulski thought, privately admiring the wise look of his rival and his sudden change of tone. It was as though another man were speaking now.

'I want to ask you a question – no, two questions, very personal, perhaps even offensive,' said Ochocki, 'will you be offended?'

'Well?' Wokulski replied.

Had he been standing on a scaffold he would not have experienced such a terrible feeling as he did at this moment. He was certain it concerned Izabela and that his fate was about to be decided on this spot.

'You were once interested in natural sciences?' Ochocki asked.

'Yes.'

'And also you were enthusiastic. I know what you went through, I have long respected you for that . . . No, this is inadequate: I must add that for a year recollections of the difficulties you encountered have encouraged me. I told myself I would do at least as much as that man, and since I was faced with such obstacles, I would go even further . . .'

Listening to this, Wokulski thought he was dreaming or listening to a madman: 'How do you know all this?' he asked Ochocki.

'From Dr Szuman.'

'Ah, Szuman . . . But what is it all leading up to?'

'I shall tell you,' Ochocki replied. 'You were an enthusiast of the natural sciences, but in the end you rejected them. At what age did your interest in this field weaken?'

Wokulski felt as though he had been struck by an axe. The question was so bitter and so unexpected that for a moment he could not reply or even collect his thoughts. Ochocki repeated the question, watching his companion sharply.

'At what age?' Wokulski said, 'a year ago . . . I am now forty-six.'

'So I have fifteen years until complete indifference sets in. That encourages me,' said Ochocki, as if to himself.

After a moment he added: 'That was one question; here's the second, but please don't be offended. At what age do men begin to feel . . . indifferent to women?'

A second blow. For an instant Wokulski felt like seizing the young man and throttling him. But he controlled himself and replied with a faint smile: 'I think they never do. In fact, women come to look increasingly desirable . . .'

'That's bad,' Ochocki whispered, 'ha – we shall see who is the stronger.'

'Women are, Mr Ochocki . . .'

'Surely that depends, my dear sir,' the young man replied, pondering again.

He began speaking as though to himself: 'Woman – there's a precious topic for you! I've been in love – let me see, how often? Four . . . six . . . about seven, yes, seven times. It takes up a great deal of time, and can lead a man into desperate thoughts. Love's a foolish thing. You meet, you love, you suffer . . . Then you grow bored or are betrayed . . . And then you find another woman. Yes, I was bored twice and betrayed three times. Then you find a different woman, better than the others – and she behaves just like the others. Oh, what an abject race of creatures women are . . . They play with us, though their limited minds can't even understand us. Well, it's true that even a tiger can play with a man . . . Abject, but how delightful . . . But never mind this! For when an idea gains domination over a man, it will never desert him, never deceive him . . .'

He put one hand on Wokulski's arm, looked at him with a sort of ecstatic and dreamy gaze, then asked: 'You once had the idea of a flying machine, didn't you? Not a guided balloon, which is lighter than air, for that is nothing – but of the flight of a heavy machine, weighed down like a battleship. Do you appeciate what a turning-point for the world such an invention would be? . . . No more forts, armies, frontiers . . . Nations will disappear, while beings like angels or classical gods in heavenly vehicles will inhabit the earth. We have already harnessed the wind, heat, light, the thunderbolt. Do you not think, my dear sir, that the time has come for us to liberate ourselves from the bonds of gravity? It's an idea which is still in the womb of time . . . Other men are already working on it; it has only just seized me, but it holds me enthralled. What's my aunt to me, with all her good advice and laws of decorum? What are marriage, women, even microscopes and electric lamps? I'll either go mad – or give mankind wings . . .'

'Suppose you do – what then?' Wokulski asked.

'Fame – such as no man has ever yet attained,' Ochocki replied, 'and that's the wife, the woman for me. Goodbye, I must go . . .' He shook Wokulski's hand, ran down the hill and disappeared between the trees.

Dusk was already falling on the Botanical Gardens and the Łazienki park. 'Madman or genius?' Wokulski whispered, feeling highly unstrung, 'what if he were a genius?' He rose and walked into the depths of the park, amidst the strollers. It seemed to him that a divine terror was lurking on the hillock from which he had fled.

The Botanical Gardens were almost crowded: streams, groups or at least rows of promenaders crowded every alley, each bench groaned under a throng of persons. They stepped in Wokulski's way, trod on his heels, elbowed him; people were talking and laughing on every side. The Aleje Ujazdowskie, the wall of the Belvedere park, the fences on the hospital side, the less frequented alleys, even the fenced-off paths – everywhere was crowded and lively. As nature grew darker, so it grew noisier and more crowded amidst the people.

'Already there's beginning to be no room in the world for me,' he murmured.

He reached the Łazienki park and found a calmer refuge here. Some stars were glittering in the sky, through the air from the Boulevard came the rustle of passers-by, and dampness rose from the lake. Sometimes a noisy cockchafer flew overhead, or a bat flitted silently by; a bird was mournfully chirping in the depths of the park, calling in vain to its mate; the distant splash of oars and the laughter of young women hung over the lake. Opposite, he saw a couple close together, whispering. They moved off and hid in the shadows.

He was overcome with pity and derision: 'Happy lovers, those,' he thought, 'they whisper and glide away like criminals. The world is well arranged, to be sure! I wonder how much better it would be if Lucifer were king? Or if some robber stopped me and killed me here, in this corner?'

And he imagined how agreeable the cold of a knife would be, plunged into his feverish heart. 'Unfortunately,' he sighed, 'people aren't allowed to kill other people nowadays, only themselves:

providing it is done at one blow, and well done.'

The recollection of such an effective means of escape calmed him. Gradually he fell into a sort of solemn mood; it seemed to him that the time was coming when he would have to reckon with his conscience, or draw up a general balance sheet of his life.

'Were I the highest judge of all,' he thought, 'and if I were asked who is more worthy of Izabela – Ochocki or Wokulski – I would have to admit that Ochocki is. Eighteen years younger than I am (eighteen years! . . .) And handsome . . . At the age of twenty-eight, he has graduated from two faculties (at that age I had only just begun studying . . .) and has already three inventions to his credit (I – none!). Above all, he is the instrument by which a great invention is to come. Odd – a flying machine: yet he has found the only possible point of departure – by genius! A flying machine must be heavier than air, not lighter, like a balloon is: for everything which flies, from insects to an enormous vulture, is heavier than air. He has the right starting-point: a creative mind, as he has proved by his microscope and lamp, so who knows but that he will succeed in building a flying machine? If he does, he will be more significant in the history of mankind than Newton and Napoleon together . . . Am I to compete with him? If the question ever arises as to which of us ought to back down, then should I hesitate? What hell it would be to tell myself that I must sacrifice my nullity to a man who, in the end, is like myself – mortal, suffering illnesses, committing errors and, above all, so naive – for he talked like a child . . .'

Indeed, it was odd. When Wokulski had been a clerk, in the grocery store, he dreamed of perpetual motion: a machine that would operate by itself. But when he entered the Preparatory College, he discovered that such a machine was out of the question, whereupon his most secret and favourite ambition had been to invent some way of guiding balloons. What had been only a fantastic notion for Wokulski, as he strayed along false tracks, had already acquired the form of a practical problem for Ochocki.

'The cruelty of fate!' he thought bitterly. 'Two people have been given the same aspirations, but one was born eighteen years earlier than the other: one born in poverty, the other in wealth; one could not even scramble up to the first floor of knowledge, the other lightly stepped up two floors. . . . He will not be diverted from his path by political storms as I was; he will not be interrupted by love, which he regards as a plaything; but for me, who spent six years in the wilderness, that feeling is essential and is salvation. Even more than that! . . .

'Well – he is surpassing me in every sphere, though after all I have the same feelings, the same awareness of my predicament, and my work is certainly greater . . .'

Wokulski knew men, and often compared himself to them. But

wherever he was, he always saw himself as a little better than the rest. Whether as a clerk, who spent his nights studying, or as a student who strove for knowledge despite his poverty, or as a soldier under a rain of bullets, or as an exile who studied science in a snow-covered hut – he always had an idea in his soul that reached beyond the next few years. Others lived from day to day, to fill their bellies or pockets.

Not until today had he met a man higher than he was, a madman who wanted to build a flying machine.

'But don't I too today have an idea for which I have been working over a year? Have I not acquired a fortune, do I not help people and make them respect me? . . . Yes, but love is a personal feeling: all good deeds accompanying it are merely fish caught in a cyclone. If that one woman and my memories of her were to disappear from the earth, then what would I be? . . . Nothing but a capitalist who plays cards at the club out of sheer boredom. Whereas Ochocki has an idea which will always draw him on, unless his mind gives way . . .

'Very well, but suppose he does nothing and finishes up in a lunatic asylum instead of building a flying-machine? I will at least accomplish something and that microscope or electric lamp will certainly not signify more than the hundreds of people to whom I give an existence. Whence this ultra-Christian humility in me, then? Who knows what any man will accomplish? I am a man of action; he a dreamer. Let us wait a year . . .'

A year! Wokulski awoke. It seemed to him that at the end of the road called a 'year' he saw only a bottomless abyss, which engulfed everything but contained nothing . . . Nothing? . . . Nothing!

He looked around instinctively. He was in the depths of the Łazienki park, on a pathway to which no sound penetrated. Even the clumps of immense trees were silent.

'What's the time?' a hoarse voice suddenly asked.

'The time?' Wokulski rubbed his eyes.

A shabby man appeared before him out of the dusk. 'When you're asked politely,' said the man, and came closer, 'you should answer politely.'

'Kill me, you will see for yourself,' Wokulski retorted. The shabby man drew back. A few human shapes became visible to the left of the path.

'You fools!' Wokulski cried, walking on, 'I have a gold watch and some hundred roubles cash. I won't defend myself . . .'

The shapes drew among the trees and one of them said in a stifled voice: 'The likes of him turns up, confound him, just where he ain't wanted . . .'

'You animals! Cowards!' Wokulski shouted almost madly. The thunder of retreating footsteps was the only reply.

Wokulski pulled himself together: 'Where am I? In the Łazienki . . . But – whereabouts? I have to go the other way . . .' He had turned several times and no longer knew which direction he was going. His heart began beating violently; a cold sweat broke out on his forehead, and for the first time in his life he was afraid of the night and of losing his way . . . For a few minutes he hurried along aimlessly, almost breathless: wild notions whirled through his brain. Finally he saw a wall to his left, then a building: 'Ah, the Orangery . . .'

Then he came to a small bridge, where he rested and leaned on the parapet, thinking: 'So I have come to this, then? A dangerous rival . . . my nerves in disorder . . . It seems to me that today I might write the last act of this comedy . . .'

A straight path led to the lake, then to the Łazienki palace. Twenty minutes later he was on Aleje Ujazdowskie and got into a passing droshky; within a quarter of an hour he was in his own apartment. At the sight of the traffic and lights in the streets he regained his good spirits, even smiled and muttered: 'What sort of vision was all that? Ochocki or someone . . . suicide . . . folly! I have got among the aristocracy after all, and as for what comes next – we shall see.'

When he entered his study, the servant gave him a letter, written on his own paper by Mrs Meliton: 'The lady was here twice,' said the faithful servant, 'once at five, then at eight o'clock . . .'

XII

Travels on Behalf of Someone Else

WOKULSKI opened Mrs Meliton's letter slowly, thinking of the recent incidents. It seemed to him that he could still see in the dark part of his study the thick clumps of trees in the Łazienki park, the vague outlines of the shabby men who had accosted him, and the hillock with the well, where Ochocki had confided in him. But the obscure pictures disappeared when he saw the lamp, with its green shade, a pile of papers and the bronze ornaments on his desk, and for a moment he thought that Ochocki with his flying-machine and his own despair were only a dream after all.

'What sort of genius is he?' Wokulski asked himself. 'He's only a dreamer . . . And Izabela is a woman like all the others. If she marries me – well and good; if she doesn't, it won't kill me.'

He opened the letter and read:

Dear Sir, Important news: in a few days, Łęcki's house will be put up for sale, and the only purchaser will be Baroness Krzeszowska, their cousin and enemy. I know for certain she is only prepared to pay sixty thousand roubles for the house, in which case what is left of Izabela's dowry, amounting to thirty thousand roubles, will be lost. The moment is very advantageous since Izabela, caught between poverty and marriage to the marshal, will gladly agree to any other solution. I suppose that you will not treat this coming opportunity as you did Łęcki's promissory notes, which you tore up in my presence. Remember this: women like being embraced so much that it is sometimes necessary to trample them underfoot in order to intensify the effect. The more ruthless you are in this, the more certainly she will fall in love with you. Remember this! . . .

In any case, you can do Bela a small favour. Baron Krzeszowski, pressed by need, has sold his wife a favourite race-horse, which is soon to race and which he greatly counted on. As far as I know their feelings about one another, Bela would be sincerely pleased if neither the Baron nor his wife were to own this horse on the day of the races. The Baron would be ashamed of having sold it, and the Baroness in despair if the horse wins and someone else profits by it. This gossip of the fashionable world is very subtle, but try to make use of it. Moreover, the opportunity will present itself, for I hear that a certain Maruszewicz, friend of both Krzeszowskis, is to propose the purchase of this horse to you.

Remember that women are only the slaves of those who can hold them fast – and indulge their caprices.

I am really beginning to think that you must have been born under a lucky star. Sincerely, A.M.

Wokulski drew a deep breath: both pieces of information were important. He read the letter again, considering Mrs Meliton's harsh style and smiling at the comments she made on her own sex. It was in Wokulski's nature to grasp people or opportunities fast: he would grasp everyone and everything by the scruff of the neck – except Izabela. She alone was a being whom he wanted to have absolute freedom, if not domination.

He glanced up: the servant was at the door. 'Go to bed,' he told him.

'I'm just going, sir, only there was a gentleman here,' the servant replied.

'Who was it?'

'He left his card, it's on your desk . . .'

On the desk lay Maruszewicz's visiting-card. 'Aha . . . and what did he say?'

'Nothing – that's to say, he asked when you would be home. So I says about ten in the morning, then he says he'll come tomorrow at ten, for a minute or two.'

'Very well – goodnight to you . . .'

'Goodnight, sir, thank you kindly.' The servant went out.

Wokulski felt completely sober. Ochocki and his flying-machine had lost their significance. Once again he felt an influx of the energy he had felt before leaving for Bulgaria. Then he had been going to make his fortune, but today he had the opportunity of throwing away his share for Izabela's sake. Mrs Meliton's phrase stuck in his memory: '. . . caught between poverty and marriage to the marshal . . .' No, she would never find herself in that situation . . . And she would not be elevated by some Ochocki or other, with the help of a machine, but by himself . . . He felt such strength within him that had the ceiling started to collapse, he could have kept it in place with his own two hands.

He took his notebook out of the desk and began reckoning: 'A race-horse – nothing to it . . . I'll spend a thousand roubles at most, of which at least part will return . . . The house is sixty thousand, Izabela's dowry thirty thousand, making a total of ninety thousand. A trifle . . . almost a third of my fortune. Still, I'll get back sixty thousand roubles for the house, if not more. Well! I must persuade Łęcki to entrust me with the thirty thousand, I'll pay him five thousand a year interest. Surely that will be sufficient for him? I'll put the horse out to stables, they can enter it for the race. Maruszewicz will be here at ten, at eleven I'll go to the lawyer . . . I'll get the money at eight per cent – seven thousand two hundred a year: and will certainly get fifteen per cent. Yes, and the house will bring in some income . . . But what will my partners say? As if that mattered! I have forty-five thousand a year, which will decrease by twelve or thirteen thousand, leaving thirty-two thousand roubles. My wife need never be bored . . . During the year I'll dispose of the house again, even if I lose thirty thousand – which in any case will not be a loss, but her dowry . . .'

Midnight. Wokulski began undressing. Influenced by this clearly defined aim, his tense nerves calmed down. He turned off the light, lay down and looked at the curtains, which were stirred by a breeze passing through the open windows, then fell asleep like a log.

He rose at seven, so brisk and cheerful that the servant noticed it as he began moving about the room. 'What is it?' Wokulski asked.

'Nothing, sir . . . only, if you please, the porter – he don't dare trouble you to be godfather to his child at the christening.'

'Ah! Did he ever ask if I wanted him to have the child?'

'He never asked because you was at the war then.'

'Very well, I'll be godfather.'

'Perhaps then sir, you'll give me that old frock-coat, otherwise how can I go to the christening?'

'Very well, take the frock-coat . . .'

'And the mending of it, sir?'

'Oh, don't bother me . . . have it done, though I don't know what . . .'

'You see, sir, I want a velvet collar . . .'

'Then have a velvet collar put on it, and go to the devil . . .'

'You don't have to be angry, sir, it's in your honour not mine,' the servant replied, and slammed the door as he went out. He felt that his master was in an exceptionally good humour.

Dressed, Wokulski sat down to his accounts and drank tea. When he had finished, he wrote a telegram to Moscow for a bill for a hundred thousand roubles, and another to his agent in Vienna, instructing him to postpone certain purchases.

A few minutes before ten Maruszewicz came in. The young man looked still more run-down and bashful than the day before. 'Allow me', said Maruszewicz after a few words of greeting, 'to lay my cards on the table. This is concerned with an original proposition.'

'I am prepared to listen to even the most original . . .'

'Madame the Baroness Krzeszowska (I am a friend of both her and the Baron)', said the run-down young man, 'wishes to dispose of a race-horse. I at once guessed that you, with your social life, may wish to own a good horse. There's an excellent chance of winning, for only two other horses, much weaker, are running in the race.'

'Why does not the Baroness race the horse herself?'

'She? . . . She's a mortal enemy of racing!'

'Why did she buy the horse, then?'

'For two reasons,' the young man replied, 'firstly, the Baron needed money to pay off a debt of honour, and vowed to shoot himself if he didn't get eight hundred roubles, even if it meant selling his beloved horse – and secondly, the Baroness doesn't want her husband to have anything to do with horse-racing. So she bought the horse, but today the poor woman is quite ill with shame and despair, and is ready to dispose of it at any price.'

'In other words?'

'Eight hundred roubles,' the young man replied, looking away.

'Where is the horse?'

'At Miller's stables.'

'And the papers?'

'Here they are,' the young man replied more cheerfully, taking a packet of papers from his coat-pocket.

'Perhaps we can finish the transaction at once?' Wokulski asked, glancing through them.

'Immediately . . .'

'And after lunch we might go and have a look at the horse.'

'Oh, by all means . . .'

'Please sign this receipt,' Wokulski said, and took money out of his desk.

'Eight hundred? Of course . . .' the young man said. He took a sheet of paper and began writing. Wokulski noticed that the hands of the young man were trembling slightly and that his expression had altered. The receipt was written out formally. Wokulski laid down eight hundred roubles and put away the papers.

A little later the young man, still embarrassed, left the study. As he ran downstairs he thought, 'I am a wretch, a wretch . . . But in a few days I'll give the old woman the two hundred roubles and say Wokulski added them when he saw the qualities of the horse. After all, he'll never meet – either the Baron or his wife, not that . . . tradesman. He told me to write the receipt myself – capital! How easy it is to recognise a tradesman and a parvenu. Oh, I am being cruelly punished for all my foolishness . . .'

At eleven, Wokulski went out, intending to call on his lawyer. But scarcely had he emerged from the gate than three droshky drivers whipped up their horses at the sight of his light-coloured topcoat and white hat. One was driving a hackney-cab, another an open droshky, while the third, as he tried to pass them, almost knocked over a porter carrying a heavy cupboard. An uproar started, a fight with whips, the whistling of policemen, people ran up, and in consequence, the two most spirited drivers were taken off in their own droshkies to the police-station. 'A bad omen . . .' Wokulski thought, then suddenly clapped a hand to his forehead. 'A fine business,' he said to himself, 'I'm on the way to see the lawyer and buy a house without knowing what the house looks like, or even where it is.'

He went back to his apartment and, with his hat on and walking stick under his arm, began to go through the street-directory. Fortunately he had heard that the Łęckis' house was somewhere in the vicinity of Aleje Jerozolimskie; nevertheless, several minutes passed before he found the street and number. 'I should have looked well,' he thought, going downstairs, 'one day I am persuading people to entrust their money to me, and on the next buying a pig in a poke. Of course I would at once have embarrassed either myself – or Izabela.'

He jumped into a passing droshky and told the driver to go towards Aleje Jerozolimskie. He got out on a corner and walked down one of the side-streets.

The day was fine, the sky almost cloudless, the pavements free of dust. The windows of houses were open, some just washed: a lively breeze teased the skirts of servant girls, making it plain to see that the servant-girls of Warsaw find it easier to clean windows on the third floor than to wash their own feet. In many apartments pianos were playing; in many yards barrel-organs or the monotonous cries of sand-vendors, sweepers, rag-and-bone men and other street traders were to be heard. Here and there a door-keeper in a blue blouse was yawning in a gateway; several dogs trotted down the street (there was no traffic); little children were playing at pulling the bark off the chestnut trees, whose bright green leaves had not yet darkened.

All in all, the street looked clean, peaceful and gay. At the far end a fragment of the horizon and a clump of trees could even be seen; but this rural landscape, inappropriate to Warsaw, was veiled by scaffolding and a brick wall.

As he walked along the right-hand pavement, Wokulski caught sight, more or less half-way down the street, of a house on the left side of unusually bright yellow. Warsaw has many yellow houses; it is probably the yellowest city in the world. However, this house seemed more yellow than the others, and would certainly have gained first prize in an exhibition of yellow objects (such as we may expect to see, one day). Going closer, Wokulski realised he was not alone in paying attention to this particular house: even the dogs, here more than on any other wall, had left their visiting-cards.

'Well I never,' he murmured, 'I believe this is the very house . . .'

And in fact it was the Łęcki property.

He began to survey it. The house had three floors; it had a few iron balconies and each floor was in a different style. The architecture of the gate was dominated by a single motif, to wit − a fan. The upper part of the gate was in the form of an open fan, which an antediluvian giantess might have used for cooling herself off. On both sides of the gate were sculptured enormous squares, which were also adorned with open fans. But the finest adornment of this gate were two sculptures in the centre of its wings, representing nail-heads so enormous that it looked as if they nailed the gate to the house and the house to Warsaw.

The entrance passage was peculiar in that it had a wretched floor but fine landscapes painted on the walls. There were so many hills, woods, rocks and streams that the tenants of the house need never go away for the summer. The yard inside, surrounded by the three-storey wings, looked like the bottom of a deep well, full of smelly air. In every corner was a door, in one there were even two: a dustbin and waterpump stood under the window of the caretaker's apartment.

Wokulski glanced up the main staircase, to which a glass door led. The stairs looked very dirty; however, there was a niche at the side, holding a broken-nosed nymph with a jug on her head. As the jug was purple in colour, the nymph's face yellow, her bosom green and legs blue it was plain to see that she was standing opposite a stained-glass window.

'Well, well . . .' Wokulski murmured in a tone which did not express very much relish.

At this moment a pretty woman with a little girl came out of the right-hand block. 'Are we going to the park now, mama?' the child asked.

'No, dear, we're going to the store, and to the park after lunch,' the lady replied in a very agreeable voice. She was a tall brunette with grey eyes and classical features. She and Wokulski glanced at each other, and the lady turned pink.

'Where have I seen her before?' Wokulski wondered, going out into the street again. The lady looked around, but turned away again when she saw him. 'Yes,' he thought, 'I saw her in church in April, and later in the store. Rzecki drew my attention to her, and said she has pretty legs. So she has . . .'

He went back into the gate-way again and began reading the list of tenants: 'What's this? Baroness Krzeszowska on the second floor! And Maruszewicz in the left-hand block, on the first floor? A strange coincidence, indeed. Third-floor front − students. Who can that attractive woman be? Right-hand block, first floor – Mrs Jadwiga Misiewicz, retired, and Helena Stawska and daughter. That must be she.'

He went into the yard and looked around. Almost all the windows were open. In the rear block, on the ground floor, was a laundry describing itself as 'Parisian', on the third floor could be heard the beating of a shoemaker's hammer, and below, on a parapet, a couple of pigeons were cooing, while on the second floor of the same block the monotonous sounds of a pianoforte and a shrill soprano singing scales could be heard: 'Do re me fa . . .'

High above, on the third floor, Wokulski heard a strong masculine bass voice, which said: 'There, she's been taking cascara again . . . The tape-worm's coming out . . . Marysia, come up here!'

At the same time, the head of a woman looked out of a second-floor window, shouting: 'Marysia, come back at once . . . Marysia!'

'That must be Mme Krzeszowska,' Wokulski thought.

Then he heard an unmistakable sound, and a stream of water poured down from the third floor, hitting the outstretched head of the Baroness and splashing all over the yard. 'Marysia, come up here!' the bass voice shouted.

'You cads!' Baroness Krzeszowska cried, looking upwards. Another stream of water shot out of the third-floor window and cut off her words in midstream.

Simultaneously a young man with a black beard leaned out and, catching sight of Mme Krzeszowska's countenance, exclaimed in a bass voice: 'Oh it's you, madam – pardon me, I beg . . .'

He was answered from within Mme Krzeszowska's apartment by the spasmodic sobbing of a female voice: 'Oh woe is me! I vow it was that scoundrel himself who set those bandits upon me . . . He repays me thus for saving him from poverty, for buying that horse of his . . .'

Meanwhile, down below, the laundry-women ironed linen, the shoemaker was hammering on the third floor, and in the second-floor back, the pianoforte resounded and a shrill scale was heard: 'Do re mi fa . . .'

'A cheerful house, no doubt about it,' Wokulski thought, shaking off the drops of water which had fallen on his sleeve. He went out into the street, looked once again at the property of which he was to become owner, then turned back to Aleje Jerozolimskie. Here he took a droshky and drove to the lawyer's.

In the lawyer's waiting room, he found a couple of shabby Jews and an old woman with a kerchief around her head. Through the open door to the left were visible cupboards full of documents, three clerks writing rapidly and some city visitors, one of whom looked like a criminal, and the other two who looked very bored.

An old usher with grey whiskers and suspicious look took

Wokulski's coat, and asked: 'Will your business take long, sir?'

'No, a very short time.'

He showed Wokulski into a room to the right: 'Whom shall I announce?' Wokulski gave him his card and was left alone.

The room contained furniture covered in purple tapestry, as in first-class railway carriages, some ornamental cupboards with richly bound books which looked as though no one had ever read them, and a few magazines and albums on the table, which everyone had apparently handled. In one corner was a plaster statue of the goddess Temida, with bronze lips and grubby knees.

'This way please,' said a servant. The eminent lawyer's study contained furniture covered in brown leather, with brown curtains in the windows and brown paper on the walls. He himself was dressed in a brown frock-coat, and was holding a very long pipe in one hand, with an amber stopper and a little feather.

'I thought I would have the honour of welcoming you here, my dear sir,' said the lawyer, drawing an armchair towards Wokulski and straightening the carpet, which was slightly crumpled, with one foot. 'In a word,' the lawyer went on, 'we may count on contributions of some three hundred thousand roubles for the partnership. And you may be sure we shall go to the notary public as fast as possible and obtain the cash down to the last penny.' He said this, laying emphasis on the more important words, pressed Wokulski's arm, then observed him narrowly.

'Ah yes – the partnership,' Wokulski echoed as he sat down, 'but it is the business of the other gentlemen as to how much cash they can lay hands on . . .'

'Well, it is always capital, you know,' the lawyer interposed.

'I have capital without the partnership . . .'

'Proof of confidence, then . . .'

'My own word suffices . . .'

The lawyer fell silent and hastily began puffing smoke out of his pipe.

'I have a request to make,' Wokulski said after a moment. The lawyer fixed him with a look, seeking to divine what it was. His manner of listening would depend on its nature. But he evidently divined nothing dangerous, since his visage took on an expression of grave but cordial benevolence.

'I wish to buy a house,' Wokulski went on.

'So soon?' the lawyer inquired, raising his brows and lowering his head, 'I congratulate you, indeed I do . . . A business house is not called a 'house' for nothing. To a tradesman a house is like a stirrup to a rider; it helps to stick firmly to business. Trade which is not based on a real foundation (such as a house provides) is merely street-trading. What house have you in mind, since you have been good enough to confide in me this far?'

'The Łęcki property is to be auctioned within the next few days . . .'

'I know it,' the lawyer interrupted, 'the walls are quite solid, the woodwork will have to be altered gradually, the garden is in reserve . . . Baroness Krzeszowska is prepared to pay up to sixty thousand for it, no other competition – we shall get it for seventy thousand at most.'

'For ninety thousand, perhaps even more,' Wokulski put in.

'How so?' the lawyer sat up in his chair, 'the Baroness will not go beyond sixty thousand, nobody is buying houses these days . . . A very good stroke of business . . .'

'As far as I'm concerned, it would be good business at ninety thousand . . .'

'Better at sixty thousand, though . . .'

'I do not want to rob my future partner.'

'Your partner?' the lawyer exclaimed, 'but Mr Łęcki is a confirmed bankrupt; you would simply harm him by giving him several thousand roubles. I know the views of the Countess, his sister, on this matter. As soon as Łęcki is without a penny to his name, his charming daughter – whom we all adore – will marry the Baron or the marshal . . .

Wokulski's eyes gleamed so strangely that the lawyer stopped short. He eyed him, pondered . . . Suddenly he clapped one hand to his forehead: 'My dear sir,' he said, 'you are determined to give ninety thousand roubles for that hovel?'

'Yes,' Wokulski replied heavily.

'Sixty thousand from ninety thousand . . . Miss Łęcka's dowry,' the lawyer muttered, 'aha . . .' His face and attitude changed out of all recognition. He puffed a great cloud of smoke out of the big amber pipe, settled back in his chair and, with a gesture in Wokulski's direction, said: 'We understand one another, Mr Wokulski. I admit that only five minutes ago I suspected you – goodness knows what of, for your business dealings are always above-board. But now, believe me, you have in me only a well-wisher and – an ally.'

'I do not understand you now,' Wokulski whispered, looking away. Brick-red spots appeared on the lawyer's cheeks. He rang, the servant came in. 'Let no one in till I call,' he said.

'Very good, sir,' said the gloomy servant.

Again they were left alone.

'Stanisław . . .' the lawyer began, 'you know, don't you, what our aristocracy and their hangers-on are? They're a few thousand people who are sucking our entire country dry, squandering money abroad, bringing back the worst vices imaginable and infecting the middle classes with them, as if they were healthy, and they themselves are inevitably dying out – economically, physiologically and morally. If they could be forced to work, if they could be cross-bred with other levels of society – there would perhaps be some advantage to be gained from them, for after all they are more subtle organisms than the rest of us. You see, my dear sir – cross-breeding, yes . . . but not throwing away thirty thousand roubles to support the likes of them. As for the cross-breeding – I'll help you: but as for throwing away thirty thousand roubles – no!'

'I do not understand you,' said Wokulski quietly.

'You understand me, but do not trust me. Mistrust is a great virtue, I would not cure you of it. Let me say this much: Łęcki, the bankrupt, may become the relative even of a tradesman, and still more of a tradesman with genteel connections . . . But not Łęcki with thirty thousand roubles in his pockets!'

'My dear sir,' Wokulski interrupted, 'will you take part in the auction of this house on my behalf?'

'I shall, but I'll only go a few thousand roubles above the amount Mme Krzeszowska will pay. Forgive me, Mr Wokulski, but I am not going to bid against myself.'

'Suppose a third bidder can be found?'

'Ha! In that case I will outdo him, in order to humour your whim.'

Wokulski rose. 'Thank you,' he said, 'for your few frank words. You are right, but I have right on my side, too. I'll bring you the cash tomorrow – now, goodbye.'

'I am sorry for you,' said the lawyer, shaking his hand.

'How so?'

'Because, my dear sir, a man who wants to win must conquer and suppress his antagonist, not feed him from his own granary. You are making a mistake which is more likely to remove you from your aim, than bring you near it.'

'You are wrong . . .'

'A romantic, a romantic!' the lawyer repeated, with a smile.

Wokulski hurried from the lawyer's house and took a droshky, telling the driver to go Elektoralna. He was vexed that the lawyer had discovered his secret and had criticised his manner of proceeding. Naturally a man who wants to conquer must suppress his antagonist, but in this case the prize was – Izabela . . .

He got out in front of a modest little shop, over which was a black sign with a yellowish inscription: 'S. SZLANGBAUM: Promissory Notes & Lottery.' The shop was open: an elderly Jew with bald head and grey beard, apparently glued to the *Courier*, was sitting behind the tin-covered counter, separated from the public by wire-netting.

'Good day, Mr Szlangbaum,' Wokulski cried.

The Jew looked up, and brought his spectacles down from his

forehead to his nose: 'Ah, it is you, my good sir,' he replied, shaking Wokulski by the hand, 'what does this mean, are you in need of money too?'

'No,' Wokulski replied, throwing himself into a cane chair by the counter. But because he was ashamed to explain immediately why he had come, he asked: 'What's the news, Mr Szlangbaum?'

'Things are bad,' the old man replied, 'they are starting to persecute the Jews. Perhaps it is as well. When they kick and spit on us, and torture us, then perhaps the young Jews like my Henryk who dress up in frock-coats and do not observe their religion will begin to understand.'

'Who is persecuting you?' Wokulski countered.

'You want proof?' the Jew asked, 'you have it here, in the *Courier*. I sent them a charade the other day . . . Can you play charades? I sent this one: my first is a Company in short, my second a bag, my whole is terrible in battle. Do you see it? My first is 'Co', my second 'sack', and my whole is 'Cossack'. Do you know what they replied? Just a moment . . .'

He picked up the *Courier*, and read: '"Answers from the Editor. Mr W: The Orgelbrand encyclopedia says . . ." Not that . . . "Mr Motyk: A frock-coat is worn . . ." No, not that. Here it is. "Mr S. Szlangbaum: Your political charade is not grammatical." I ask you, my dear sir: what is political about it? If I'd written a charade on Disraeli or Bismarck, that would be political, but one about Cossacks is surely not political, but military . . .'

'But where does the persecution of the Jews come into this?' Wokulski asked.

'Let me explain. You yourself had to protect my Henryk from persecution: I know all about it, though he did not say a word to me. As to the charade — when I took my charade to Mr Szymanowski six months ago, he said: "Mr Szlangbaum, we are not going to print your charades, though I suggest you would be better off writing charades than charging interest."

'So I said: "Mr Editor, if you will pay as much for charades as I get from charging interest, then I shall write them."

'But Mr Szymanowski said: "Mr Szlangbaum, we have no money to pay for your charades." That is what Mr Szymanowski himself said, d'you hear? And today they say in the *Courier* that it is political and ungrammatical! Six months ago they spoke differently. But what they say in the papers about the Jews, nowadays . . .'

Wokulski listened to the tale of the persecution of the Jews, gazing at the wall, on which a lottery list was hanging, drumming his fingers on the counter. But he was thinking of something else, and was hesitant.

'So you still busy yourself writing charades, Mr Szlangbaum?' he inquired.

'Not only me,' the old Jew replied, 'I've a grandson, nine years old, and pray listen to what he wrote to me the other week. "Dear Grandad," little Michael wrote, "I made up this charade: my first is part of the body, my second you put on, and my whole is a garment." And he wrote, "Dear Grandad, if you guess it, please send me six roubles for such a garment." I burst into tears, Mr Wokulski, when I read it . . . For the answer is trousers. I wept, Mr Wokulski, that such a clever child must go without trousers through Henryk's stubbornness. But I wrote back: "My dearest one. I am pleased indeed that you have learned how to write charades from your old Grandad. But so that you should also learn thrift, I am sending you only four roubles for this corduroy garment. But if you study hard, then, after the vacation, I will buy you this charade: "My first means lips in German, an hour is my second. The whole is bought for a child when he begins the gymnasium." The answer is: *mund-ur* *; you guessed it at once, Mr Wokulski?'

'So all your family plays charades?' Wokulski interrupted.

'Not only my family,' Szlangbaum replied, 'but among us Jews, when young people meet together, they do not waste time as you do with dances, compliments, fine clothes or other nonsense, but they study accounts or learned books, or quiz one another or solve charades and chess problems. Among us, the intellect is always at work, and that is why we Jews have intellect and why – don't be offended – we are conquering the world. Among you, everything is done by emotional excitement and wars, while we use wisdom and patience.'

The last words struck Wokulski. He, after all, would win Izabela by wisdom and patience . . . Some comfort entered his heart, so that he ceased hesitating and suddenly said: 'I have a request to make of you, Mr Szlangbaum.'

'Your requests are my commands, Mr Wokulski.'

'I want to buy the Łęcki house.'

'I know that house. It will go for sixty thousand.'

'I want it to go for ninety thousand, and need someone to bid up to that sum.'

The Jew opened his eyes wide: 'How so? You want to pay thirty thousand roubles more?' he asked.

'Yes . . .'

'Excuse me, but I do not understand you. If you were selling the house, and Łęcki wanted to buy it, then it would be in your interest to send the price up. But if you are buying it, then it is in your interest to lower the price.'

'It is in my interest to pay more.'

The old man shook his head and after a moment said: 'If I did not know you, I should think you were doing bad business, but because I know you, I think you are doing – strange business. You are not only immobilising cash and losing some ten per cent interest annually, but on top of that you want to pay thirty thousand roubles extra. Mr Wokulski,' he added taking him by the hand, 'do not do such a foolish thing. I, old Szlangbaum, beseech you . . .'

'Believe me when I say that good will come of it.'

The old Jew suddenly put one finger to his nose. His eyes sparkled and so did his pearly teeth: 'Aha,' he cried, 'well, this just shows how old I am – not to guess it directly! You give Mr Łęcki thirty thousand roubles, and he does business with you worth perhaps a hundred thousand . . . Gut! I shall find you a bidder who will send up the price – and for the fee of only fifteen roubles. A very respectable gentleman, a Catholic too, only one must not give him an advance on the fee . . . I shall also provide you with some very respectable ladies, who will bid for you too . . . I can also give you a couple of Jews, at five roubles each . . . It will be such an auction that you could pay a hundred and fifty thousand for that house, and nobody would be any the wiser.'

Wokulski was rather embarrassed: 'In any case, the matter will remain confidential?' he said.

'Mr Wokulski,' replied the Jew solemnly, 'you had no need to say that. Your secret is mine. You protected my little Henryk; you do not persecute the Jews . . .'

They said good-day, and Wokulski went home. There he found Maruszewicz, with whom he went to the riding-school to inspect the horse he had purchased.

The riding-school consisted of two connected buildings arranged in the form of a diamond-cutter. The round part held the school, the long part the stables. When Wokulski and Maruszewicz entered, a riding lesson was in progress. Four gentlemen and a lady were riding one behind the other around the wall of the ring; in the middle stood the director of the establishment, a man with a military air, wearing a blue jacket, tight white breeches and high boots with spurs. This was Mr Miller; he was instructing the riders and assisting himself in this activity with a long whip, which he cracked from time to time in the direction of a clumsily handled horse, whereupon its rider grimaced. Wokulski noticed first that one of the men, riding without stirrups, with his right hand behind his back, looked like a villain; that the second was trying to occupy a seat on his horse somewhere between its neck and tail, while the fourth looked as if he were continually on the verge of dismounting, and would never, no matter how long he lived, master the equestrian art. Only the lady in a riding-habit rode boldly and competently, making Wokulski think that, in the whole world, no position was uncomfortable or dangerous for a woman.

Maruszewicz introduced his companion to the director. 'I was waiting for you, gentlemen, and am at your service . . . Mr Schultz!'

Mr Schultz ran in, a young fair-haired man also wearing a blue jacket, but still taller top-boots and tighter breeches. He took the emblem of directorial power with a military bow and before Wokulski left the ring, he saw that despite his youth, Schultz could yield the whip still more energetically than the director himself. For the second gentleman puffed, and the fourth began protesting querulously.

'Sir,' said the director to Wokulski, 'you are taking over the Baron's horse with all appurtenances: saddles, blankets and so forth?'

'Of course . . .'

'Then I must ask you for sixty roubles for stabling, which Baron Krzeszowski has not paid.'

'It can't be helped . . .'

They went into a small stable as airy as a living-room, even adorned with carpets, though not valuable ones. The stall was brand-new and full, and the ladder too; fresh straw was lying on the ground. All the same, the director's sharp eye observed something wrong, for he shouted: 'What does this mean, Mr Ksawery? . . . Upon my soul! D'you keep such things in your bedroom at home, then?'

A second assistant appeared for a moment. He took a look, disappeared, then in the corridor shouted: 'Wojciech! What the devil's this? Clean it up at once, or I will make you eat it . . .' 'Stefan, you booby,' came a third voice from behind a partition, 'if you leave the stable in this state once more, you young puppy, I'll make you lick it up . . .' Several loud thumps were heard at the same time, as if someone had seized someone else's head and was banging it against a wall. Soon Wokulski saw through the stable window a young man with metal buttons on his jacket, who ran into the yard for a broom and, having found one, accidentally struck a staring Jew on the head with it. Being a natural scientist, Wokulski was surprised by this variation on the law of the preservation of energy, by which the director's anger was vented upon a person not connected with the riding-school at all.

Meanwhile, the director ordered the horse to be brought into the passage. It was a beautiful animal with slim legs, small head and eyes which looked both clever and wistful. As she came out, the mare turned her head to Wokulski, sniffing at him, and snorting, as if she recognised her master.

'She knows you already,' said the director, 'give her a lump of sugar . . . A beautiful mare!' With this, he brought a piece of some grubby substance, smelling rather of tobacco, out of his pocket.

Wokulski gave it to the mare, who ate it without more ado.

'I'll wager fifty roubles she will win,' the director cried, 'are you game?'

'Of course,' Wokulski replied.

'She is bound to win. I'll give her a first-rate jockey, and have him ride according to my instructions. Had she remained the property of Baron Krzeszowski – devil take me, but she'd have come in last, mark my words. But then, I would not have kept her in the stables, even.'

'The director is still upset,' Maruszewicz interrupted with a sweet smile.

'Upset!' the director cried, flushing with rage, 'let Mr Wokulski judge whether I could keep on good terms with anyone who tells people I sold a horse in Lublin which had cholera! Such things,' he exclaimed raising his voice still more, 'are not easily forgotten, Mr Maruszewicz. And if the Count had not smoothed the matter over, then Baron Krzeszowski would have a bullet in his rump today . . . Me sell a horse with cholera! Even if I have to pay a hundred roubles out of my own pocket, that mare will win . . . Even if she is going to die . . . the Baron will see for himself . . . A horse with cholera, indeed! Ha ha ha!' and the director burst into a fiendish laugh.

After looking at the mare, the gentlemen went into the office, where Wokulski settled the account, vowing privately never to refer to any horse as having cholera.

On leaving, he said: 'Would it be possible to race the horse anonymously?'

'It will be done . . .'

'But . . .'

'Pray put your mind at rest,' the director replied, pressing his hand, 'discretion is a gentleman's middle name. I expect Mr Maruszewicz too . . .'

'Yes indeed,' Maruszewicz confirmed, nodding and gesticulating in such a way as to make it clear that the secret was buried in his breast.

Returning past the ring, Wokulski heard the cracking of the whip again, whereupon the fourth rider began complaining to the director's deputy. 'That is indelicate, my good man!' the fourth rider cried, 'my breeches will split . . .' 'Not them,' Mr Schultz replied phlegmatically, cracking his whip in the direction of the second rider.

Wokulski left the riding-school. When he had said goodbye to Maruszewicz and was getting into a droshky, a strange thought occurred to him: 'If the mare wins, then Izabela will fall in love with me . . .'

Suddenly he turned back; the mare, a matter of indifference a little while ago, had now become sympathetic and interesting. Going back into the stable, he again heard the unmistakable thump of a human head being banged against a wall. Just then a very red-faced stable-boy Stefan ran out of the next stall, his hair standing on end as if someone's hand had just been removed from it, and immediately after him, the coachman Wojciech appeared too, rubbing his somewhat grubby hands on his jacket. Wokulski gave the elder three roubles and a rouble to the younger, and promised them a tip in future, providing no harm came to the mare. 'Sir, I will look after her better than if she was my own wife,' Wojciech replied with a low bow, 'no harm will come to her, sir – of course not. And in the race, sir, she'll go like the wind . . .'

Wokulski went into the stable and contemplated the mare for a quarter of an hour. Her fine, delicate legs made him uneasy and he was alarmed to see shivers passing across her velvet skin, for he thought perhaps she was falling ill. Then he put an arm around her neck and when she leaned her head on his shoulder, he kissed her and whispered:

'If only you knew how much depends upon you . . . If only you knew . . .'

After that he visited the ring several times a day, fed the mare with sugar and caressed her. He felt that something not unlike a superstition was beginning to take shape in his practical mind. When the mare greeted him gaily, he took it as a good omen: but when she was unhappy, then unease troubled his heart. For, on the way to the stables he said to himself: 'If I find her cheerful, then Izabela will fall in love with me.'

Sometimes common sense awoke within him; then anger gained hold of him, and self-contempt: 'What is this?' he thought, 'is my life to depend on the caprices of one woman? Will I not find a hundred others? Has not Mrs Meliton promised to introduce me to three or four equally beautiful women? Once and for all, I must wake up!' But instead of waking up, he plunged still more deeply into his obsession. It seemed to him in moments of awareness that witches must still exist on the earth, and that one had cast a spell on him. And then he thought fearfully: 'I am not the man I was . . . I am becoming someone else . . . It is as if someone had changed my soul . . .'

Then again, the naturalist and psychologist spoke within him: 'Here', their voices whispered somewhere in the depths of his mind, 'this is how nature is revenged for violations of her laws. As a young man, you despised your heart, you mocked love, you sold yourself as husband of an old woman – and now look at you! Your capital, hoarded over many years, is coming back to you with interest today!'

'Very well . . .' he thought, 'but if this is so, then I ought to change into a libertine; why is it that I think only of her?'

'The devil alone knows,' his antagonists answered, 'perhaps it is precisely this woman who suits you best. Perhaps it is true, as the legend says, that once, centuries ago, your souls were one?'

'In that case, she should love me too,' Wokulski said. Then he added: 'If the mare wins the race, that will be a sign that Izabela will fall in love with me . . . Oh, you old fool, madman . . . what are you coming to?'

A few days before the races, the 'English' Count he had met during the gathering at the Prince's house paid him a call. After the customary salutations, the Count sat down stiffly on a chair and said: 'This visit has another purpose too. Dear me, yes! May I go on?'

'Pray do, Count.'

'Baron Krzeszowski,' the Count continued, 'whose mare you have bought, very correctly of course – dear me, yes – ventures to ask you very kindly to let him have her back . . . The price is of no consequence. The Baron has placed large bets. . . He will offer twelve hundred roubles.'

Wokulski turned cold: Izabela might despise him if he were to sell the mare. 'What if I have my own plans for the horse, Count?'

'In that case, you have priority, dear me, yes,' the Count lisped.

'You have decided the matter for me,' Wokulski said with a bow.

'Really? I am very sorry for the Baron, but you have prior rights.'

He rose from his chair like a dummy on springs and added, as he said goodbye: 'When are we to go to the notary with our partnership, my dear sir? On thinking matters over, I have decided to contribute fifty thousand roubles . . . dear me, yes.'

'It all depends on you gentlemen.'

'I very much hope to see our country flourishing and so, my dear Mr Wokulski, you have all my sympathy and respect, dear me, yes, despite the disappointment you will cause the Baron. I was quite sure you would yield the mare to him . . .'

'I cannot.'

'I understand you,' the Count concluded, 'a true gentleman, even under the skin of a tradesman, cannot but reveal himself on such an occasion. However, if you will pardon my boldness, you are primarily a gentleman, and in the English style too, such as each one of us should be.'

He shook him warmly by the hand and left. Wokulski admitted to himself that this eccentric, who pretended to be a dummy, had many likeable qualities, nevertheless. 'Yes,' he thought, 'it is more agreeable to live with these gentlemen than with tradespeople. They really are beings made from a different clay.'

Then he added: 'Is it surprising that Izabela despises a man like me – brought up, as she has been, among men like these? Yet what good do they do in the world and for the world? They respect people who can give them fifteen per cent on investments . . . But that is not of merit, after all.

'The devil take it,' he muttered, cracking his fingers, 'but how do they know I've bought the mare? Never mind. . . After all, I bought it from Baroness Krzeszowska through Maruszewicz . . . Besides, I frequent the stables too much, they all know me there . . . Yes, I am beginning to commit follies, I am incautious . . . I didn't care for that Maruszewicz, though.'

XIII

Gentlefolk at Play

T LAST the day of the races came, it was fine but not too hot: just as it should be. Wokulski rose at five and at once went to visit his mare. She received him somewhat indifferently, but was well, and Mr Miller was full of encouragement.

'What's this?' he laughed, digging Wokulski in the ribs, 'you're excited, eh? The sportsman in you is coming out. The likes of us, my dear sir, are in a fever throughout the racing season. Our little bet of fifty roubles still stands, eh? It's like having the money in my pocket already – you might as well pay me now.'

'I'll pay it with the greatest of pleasure,' Wokulski replied, and thought: 'Will the mare win? Will Izabela ever fall in love with me? Suppose something happens? What if the mare breaks a leg?'

The morning hours dragged as if harnessed to snails. Wokulski called at the shop for a moment only, could not eat his lunch, then went to Saski park, continually thinking: 'Will the mare win and Izabela fall in love with me?' But he mastered his excitement, and did not leave home until five o'clock.

There was already such a throng of carriages and droshkies in Aleje Ujazdowskie that in places they had to crawl: at the toll-gate a real jam occurred, and he had to wait fifteen minutes, devoured by impatience, before his carriage finally turned into the Mokotow race-course.

At the gate Wokulski leaned out and surveyed the track through a cloud of yellowish dust which was settling heavily on his face and clothes. Today the stadium seemed immeasurably large and disagreeable, as if the phantom of uncertainty were looming over it. Far ahead, he saw a long line of people in a semi-circle which was continually increasing as newcomers arrived. Finally he gained his place, and then some ten minutes passed before his servant came back with a ticket.

A throng of non-paying spectators pressed around his carriage, and the uproar of a thousand voices made it seem to Wokulski that they were all talking of nothing but his mare and were mocking this tradesman playing at horse-racing.

At last his carriage was admitted into the ring. Wokulski jumped out and hurried to find his mare, trying to preserve the aspect of an indifferent spectator. After a long search he saw her in the centre of the enclosure, with Messrs Miller and Schultz beside her, as well as a jockey with a large cigar in his mouth, wearing a blue and yellow cap and a greatcoat over his shoulders.

His mare, against the background of this huge place and innumerable crowds, seemed to him so small and pitiful that, in despair, he was ready to toss away everything and go home. But Messrs Miller's and Schultz's countenances were illuminated with hope. 'Here you are, at last,' the director of the riding-school cried, and with a glance at the jockey, added: 'May I introduce you – Mr Young, the best jockey in the country – Mr Wokulski.'

The jockey lifted two fingers to his blue and yellow cap, then, removing the cigar from his mouth with his other hand, he spat through his teeth. 'Just tell us, Mr Young, shall she win?' the director asked.

'Ach,' the jockey replied.

'The other two horses aren't bad, but our mare is first-rate.' said the director.

'Ach,' the jockey agreed.

Wokulski took him aside and said: 'If we win, I'll owe you fifty roubles over and above the agreement.'

'Ach,' the jockey replied, then, after eyeing Wokulski, he added: 'You're a real sportsman, but you're still a bit too excited. Next year you'll take it easier.' He spat the distance of a horse and went off toward the grandstand, while Wokulski, saying goodbye to Messrs Miller and Schultz and patting the mare, went back to his carriage.

Now he began looking for Izabela.

He walked down a long line of carriages placed along the track, eyed the horses, servants, peeped under parasols at ladies, but could not find Izabela. 'Perhaps she isn't coming,' he thought, and it seemed to him that the whole place full of people might as well sink into the ground, taking him along with it. Fancy throwing away so much money – if she was not going to be there! Perhaps Mrs Meliton, the old intriguer, had lied to him in a plot with Maruszewicz?

He went up the steps leading to the judges' stand and looked around in all directions. In vain . . . When he was coming down, two gentlemen with their backs to him were barring the way: one was tall, with the bearing of a sportsman, and he was saying in a loud voice: 'I've been reading for the past ten years how they accuse us of extravagance so I was ready to mend my ways and sell off my stable. Then I see that a man who made his money yesterday is running a horse in the races today . . . So I think to myself, aha – that is the sort of bird you are, is it? You preach to us, but when you succeed you behave just as we do . . . So I refuse to mend my ways, will not sell my stable, will not . . .'

Catching sight of Wokulski, his companion nudged the speaker, who suddenly broke off. Taking advantage of the opportunity, Wokulski sought to pass them, but the tall gentlemen prevented him: 'Excuse me,' he said, touching his hat, 'for venturing to make such a remark . . . My name is Wrzesinski . . .'

'I was pleased to hear it,' Wokulski replied with a smile, 'for I say the same things privately. In any case, I am entering a race for the first and last time in my life . . .'

He shook hands with the tall sportsman, who muttered, when Wokulski had gone a few yards, 'A spirited fellow, that . . .'

Only now did Wokulski buy a programme, and it was with a feeling of something like shame that he read that in the third race the mare Sultanka, out of Ali by Klara, owned by X.X., was ridden by the jockey Young (yellow shirt and blue sleeves). Prize: three hundred roubles: the winning horse to be put up for sale on the spot.

'I was crazy,' Wokulski muttered, going towards the stand. He thought that Izabela would surely be there, and planned to go straight back home if he did not find her.

He became pessimistic. The women looked ugly, their colourful dresses barbarous, their flirtations hateful. The men were stupid, the crowd vulgar, the band out of tune. Entering the stand, he sneered at its squeaking steps and old walls, stained with rain leaks.

Acquaintances bowed to him, women smiled at him, here and there people whispered: 'Look! . . . Look! . . .' But he did not notice. He halted on the top level of the stand, and looked through his field-glasses at the variegated and noisy crowds on the road, right as far as the corner, but saw only clouds of yellow dust.

'What purpose do these stands serve for the rest of the year?' he wondered. And it seemed to him that every night, on these rotting benches, dead bankrupts, remorseful coquettes, all kinds of idlers and wastrels took their seats, having been expelled from Hell, and that by the sorrowful light of the stars, they watched the races of skeleton horses who had perished on this course. It seemed to him that even at this moment he could see mouldering garments and smell the stench of decay.

He was aroused by a shout from the crowd, the ringing of a bell and cheers. The first race was over. Suddenly he looked at the course, and saw the Countess's carriage driving up to the barriers. The Countess was sitting with the Duchess, and Mr Łęcki and his daughter were behind.

Wokulski himself did not know when he ran down from the stand or when he entered the enclosure. He pushed someone, someone asked for his ticket . . . He ran straight across and at once came up to the carriage. The Countess's footman bowed to him from the box, and Mr Łęcki exclaimed: 'Here is Mr Wokulski . . .'

Wokulski greeted the ladies, whereupon the Duchess pressed his hand in a significant manner, and Łęcki asked: 'Is it true, Mr Wokulski, that you have bought Krzeszowski's mare?'

'Yes, it is . . .'

'Well, you know you have played a fine trick on him, and given my daughter a pleasant surprise.'

Izabela turned to him with a smile: 'I have made a wager with my aunt,' she cried, 'that the Baron would not keep his mare for the races, and I won — now I have wagered the Duchess that the mare will win . . .'

Wokulski went around the carriage and approached Izabela, who continued: 'Really, the Duchess and I only came for this race. For aunt pretends that the races only make her cross. Oh, you must win . . .'

'I shall — if you desire it,' Wokulski replied, looking at her with admiration. She had never before seemed so beautiful as in this outburst of excitement. Nor had he ever dreamed she would talk to him so kindly.

He looked at the others. The Duchess was cheerful, the Countess smiling, Mr Łęcki beaming. The Countess's coachman on the box was making a bet with the driver that Wokulski would win. Laughter and joy were all around them. He delighted in the crowd, the stands, the carriages; the women in their colourful dresses were pretty as flowers, lively as birds. The music was out of tune, but gay: the horses neighed, sportsmen placed bets, hawkers cried their beer, sausage-rolls and oranges for sale. The sun was joyful, so were the sky and the earth, and Wokulski felt in such a strange mood that he wanted to embrace everything and everyone.

The second race was over, the music struck up again. Wokulski ran across to the stands, and meeting Young who was carrying his saddle and had just left the weighing-in, he whispered: 'Mr Young, we must win . . . a hundred roubles over and above our agreement. Even if it kills the mare . . .'

'Ach,' the jockey muttered, eyeing him with a touch of cool surprise.

Wokulski had his carriage brought closer to that of the Countess and went back to join the ladies. He was surprised to see that no one was standing near them. Admittedly, the Baron and the marshal had approached the carriage, but on being coldly received by Izabela, had soon withdrawn. But young men merely bowed from a distance and passed by.

'I understand,' Wokulski thought, 'the news that the house is to be auctioned off has cooled them down. But now,' he added inwardly, looking at Izabela, 'you will see who really loves you, not your money.'

The bell rang for the third race. Izabela stood up on the seat; a blush appeared on her face. A few yards away Young passed mounted on Sultanka, with the expression of a man who is bored. 'Run well, you beautiful creature!' Izabela cried.

Wokulski jumped into his carriage and opened his field-glasses. He was so absorbed by the race that for a moment he forgot Izabela. The seconds dragged like hours: it seemed to him he was bound to the three horses which were going to race, and every unnecessary movement they made caused him a prickling sensation. He thought that his mare was lacking in fire and that Young was too blasé. He listened involuntarily to the conversations around him: 'Young will walk away with it . . .' 'But. . . just look at the bay!' 'I'd give ten roubles if Wokulski were to win. He'd wipe the smiles off the faces of those Counts.' 'Krzeszowski would be furious . . .'

The bell rang. The three horses set off at a gallop: 'Young's in the lead!' 'Nonsense . . .' 'They've passed the corner. . .' 'The first corner, but the bay is just behind . . .' 'Now the second!' 'He's moved ahead again!' 'The bay is coming up! . . .' 'The red jacket is falling back! . . .' 'The third corner!' 'But Young is not troubled by them!' 'The bay is catching up!' 'Look, look! The red jacket is coming up after the bay!' 'The bay is last! You've lost your bet!' 'The red jacket is catching up with Young! . . .' 'He won't overtake him, he's already whipping the horse!' 'No, no . . . Bravo, Young! Bravo, Wokulski! The mare is going like the wind! Bravo! Bravo! Bravo! . . .'

The bell. Young had won. The tall sportsman took the mare by the bridle, led her to the judges' stand and cried: 'Sultanka! Ridden by Young. Owner – anonymous!'

'Anonymous, indeed! Wokulski . . . Bravo, Wokulski!' the crowd roared. 'The owner is Mr Wokulski,' the tall gentleman repeated, and sent the mare to be put up for auction.

Wild enthusiasm for Wokulski arose among the crowd. No race had excited the spectators so much; there was rejoicing that a Warsaw tradesman had beaten two Counts.

Wokulski approached the Countess's carriage. Mr Łęcki and the elderly ladies congratulated him; Izabela was silent. At this moment the tall sportsman ran up; 'Mr Wokulski,' he said, 'here is the money – three hundred roubles prize, eight hundred for the mare, which I have bought . . .'

Wokulski turned with the packet of banknotes to Miss Izabela: 'Will you permit me to hand you this for your charities?' Izabela accepted the packet with a smile and beautiful glance.

Then someone pushed against Wokulski. It was Baron Krzeszowski. Pale with rage, he approached the carriage, stretched out his hand to Izabela and exclaimed in French: 'I am pleased, dear cousin, that your admirers are triumphant . . . I'm sorry it had to be at my expense, though. How do you do, ladies?' he added, bowing to the Countess and Duchess.

The Countess's face clouded over; Mr Łęcki was embarrassed, Izabela turned white. The Baron put on his pince-nez in an impertinent manner and, gazing fixedly at Izabela, said: 'Yes, indeed – I have the devil's own luck with your admirers, cousin . . .'

'Baron . . .' the Duchess interrupted.

'Surely I have not said anything wrong, have I? I merely said I have the devil's own luck . . .'

Wokulski, standing behind, touched his arm: 'A word, Baron,' he said.

'Oh, it is you, is it?' the Baron replied, eyeing him. They stepped aside.

'You pushed me, Baron . . .'

'I beg your pardon . . .'

'That is not enough . . .'

'Surely you don't expect satisfaction from me?' the Baron asked.

'Precisely so . . .'

'In that case, I'm at your service,' said the Baron, looking for a visiting-card, 'oh, confound it, I didn't bring any . . . Perhaps you have a notebook and pencil, Mr Wokulski?'

Wokulski handed him a pencil and notebook, in which the Baron wrote his name and address, not omitting to add a flourish to it. 'I shall be delighted,' he said, bowing to Wokulski, 'to finish off the accounts for my Sultanka.'

'I shall endeavour to give you full satisfaction.' They parted with an exchange of the most elegant bows.

'A quarrel, upon my word,' said the mortified Mr Łęcki, who had seen this exchange of civilities. The Countess, vexed, ordered the carriage to go home without waiting for the races to finish. Wokulski barely had time to catch up with the carriage and bid goodbye to the ladies.

Before the carriage moved away, Izabela leaned out, gave Wokulski the tips of her fingers and whispered: 'Merci, monsieur . . .'

Wokulski was dazed with joy. He stayed until the last race without knowing what was going on around him; then, taking advantage of a pause, left the course.

Wokulski went straight from the races to Dr Szuman. The doctor was sitting by an open window, wearing a ragged, padded dressing-gown, proofing a thirty-page pamphlet on ethnography, which had taken over a thousand observations and four years of time to write. It was an article on the colour and form of hair of people living in the Polish kingdom. The learned doctor told everyone that a few dozen copies of the work would be published at most, but had secretly ordered the printing of four thousand copies, and was certain a second edition would be called for. Despite his jokes on his own beloved subject and complaints that no one was interested, Szuman believed in the depths of his soul that everyone in the civilised world would be extremely interested in the question of the colour of hair and relation between length and radius. At this very moment he was wondering whether it would be proper to head his article with the motto: 'Show me your hair, and I shall tell you what you are.'

When Wokulski entered and sank wearily onto a sofa the doctor began: 'How these proofreaders desecrate everything! Here I have a few hundred figures of three decimal places – but half of them are wrong! They think a thousandth or even a hundredth part of a millimetre is of no consequence, and do not realise – the ignoramuses! – that this is the whole point. Upon my word, it would have been impossible to invent or even print logarithmic tables in Poland. Your true Pole starts to sweat at the second decimal place, at the fifth he runs a temperature, and at the seventh has a stroke. . . . What have you been up to?'

'I am going to fight a duel,' Wokulski replied.

The doctor jumped up and ran over to the sofa so hastily that the wings of his dressing-gown gave him the look of a bat. 'What? A duel?' he cried, eyes flashing, 'perhaps you think I'll accompany you to serve as doctor? I am to stand and watch two fools shoot at one another's heads, and perhaps attend one of them into the bargain? I wouldn't dream of being involved in such tomfoolery!' he exclaimed, both hands at his head, 'and in any case I'm no surgeon, I gave up practising medicine long ago.'

'Come as my second, then, if you won't come as a doctor . . .'

'Ah, that is another matter,' the doctor replied without hesitation, adding, 'who are you to fight this duel with, pray?'

'Baron Krzeszowski.'

'He's a good shot,' the doctor muttered, his lower lip protruding, and he went on, 'what is it all about?'

'He pushed me at the races . . .'

'At the . . . ? And what in Heaven's name were you doing at the races?'

'I had a horse running, and even won a prize.'

Szuman struck the back of his head with one hand, suddenly raised first one, then the other, of Wokulski's eyelids and began examining his pupils carefully.

'Do you think I have gone mad?' Wokulski asked him.

'Not yet. Is this supposed to be a joke,' he added after a moment, 'or are you serious?'

'Very serious. I want no reconciliation and ask that strict conditions be observed.'

The doctor returned to his desk, sat down, leaned his chin on one hand and, after some consideration, said: 'A woman, eh? Even turkeys will only fight for . . .'

'Szuman, mind what you say,' Wokulski interrupted in a stifled voice, straightening his back.

The doctor again eyed him searchingly: 'So this is how things are?' he muttered, 'very well . . . I'll be your second. If you are so anxious to smash open your skull, you may as well do so in my presence: perhaps I may even be able to help, somehow . . .'

'I'll send Rzecki to see you at once,' Wokulski declared, shaking him by the hand.

From the doctor's house he went back to his shop, spoke briefly to Ignacy, returned to his apartment and went to bed before ten o'clock. As before, he slept like a log. Strong emotions were essential to his leonine nature; only when experiencing them did his spirit, torn apart by passion, regain its equilibrium.

Next day, at about five, Rzecki and Szuman called on the 'English' Count, who was Krzeszowski's second. On the way, both Wokulski's friends remained silent: only once did Ignacy remark: 'Well, and what have you to say to all this, doctor?'

'Only what I have already said,' Szuman replied, 'we're approaching the fifth act. Either this is the end of a gallant man, or the start of a whole series of follies . . .'

'And of the worst sort, for they will be political,' Mr Rzecki interposed. The doctor shrugged and looked the other way: Ignacy with his everlasting politics struck him as insufferable just then.

The 'English' Count was awaiting them with another gentleman who kept looking out of the window at the clouds, and moving his Adam's apple every few minutes as if he were gulping something down with difficulty. He looked only semi-conscious: but in fact he was an unusual man, a lion-hunter and profound scholar of Egyptian antiquities.

In the middle of the 'English' Count's study was a table covered with a green cloth and surrounded by four high chairs: on the table lay four sheets of paper, four pencils, two pens and an ink-well of such dimensions that it might have been meant for a hip-bath. When all had sat down, the Count began: 'Gentlemen, Baron Krzeszowski admits he may have pushed Mr Wokulski, for he is absent-minded. Dear me, yes . . . In consequence, at our insistence . . .' Here the Count glanced at his companion who had just gulped with a ceremonious air, 'at our insistence,' the Count went on, 'the Baron is prepared to apologise, even in writing, to Mr Wokulski, whom we all respect – dear me, yes. What have you to say to this?'

'We are not authorised to take any steps for reconciliation,' replied Rzecki, in whom the former Hungarian officer had come to life again. The learned Egyptologist opened his eyes wide and gulped twice. Amazement flashed across the Count's face; however, he controlled himself and replied in a tone of dry politeness: 'In that case may we know the conditions?'

'You gentlemen may state them,' Rzecki replied.

'Oh no, not at all,' said the Count.

Rzecki coughed: 'In that case, I venture to suggest . . . the opponents to stand at twenty-five paces, take five paces . . .'

'Dear me, yes . . .'

'Pistols to be loaded . . . First blood . . .'

'Dear me, yes . . .'

'The time, if convenient, tomorrow morning . . .'

'Dear me, yes . . .'

Rzecki bowed without getting up. The Count took out a sheet of paper, and amidst a general silence, prepared a document which Szuman at once copied. Both documents were witnessed, and within forty-five minutes the matter was done. Wokulski's second bade farewell to their host and his companion, who again lost himself gazing at the clouds.

In the street, Rzecki said to Szuman: 'Very agreeable people, these gentlemen of the aristocracy . . .'

'May the devil take them! May the devil take you all, with your silly conventions . . .' the doctor exclaimed, shaking his fist.

That evening, Ignacy took the pistols and called on Wokulski. He found him alone, at tea. Rzecki poured himself some, and exclaimed: 'Mind you, Staś, they are perfectly honourable people. The Baron who, as you know, is very absent-minded, is prepared to apologise to you . . .'

'No apologies.'

Rzecki fell silent. He drank the tea and dabbed his forehead with a handkerchief. After a long pause he said: 'Of course, you will have considered the store. . . In the event of . . .'

'No accident will befall me,' Wokulski replied angrily.

Ignacy sat for another quarter-hour in silence. He did not like the tea, his head ached. He finished it, looked at his watch, then left his friend's house, saying farewell: 'Tomorrow we leave at half-past seven in the morning.'

'Very well . . .'

When Ignacy had gone, Wokulski sat down at his desk, wrote a few lines on a piece of notepaper and put Rzecki's address on the envelope. It seemed to him he could still hear the Baron's unpleasant voice: 'I am pleased, cousin, that your admirers have triumphed . . . I'm sorry it was at my expense, though . . .' And wherever he looked, he saw Izabela's beautiful face flushed with shame.

Unutterable rage was fuming within his heart. His hands were becoming like iron bars, his body taking on such strange rigidity that surely any bullet would rebound from it. The word 'death' crossed his mind and for a moment he smiled. He knew death does not attack the bold; it merely confronts them like a mad dog, and glares with green eyes, waiting for a muscle to twitch.

That night, as every night, the Baron was playing cards. Maruszewicz, who was also at the club, reminded him at midnight, then again at one and two o'clock, that he ought to go to bed as he was to get up at seven next morning. The absent-minded Baron answered: 'Presently! Presently!' but sat on until three, at which time one of his partners exclaimed: '*Basta*, Baron! Sleep a few hours, for your hands will tremble and you'll miss your mark.'

These words, and even more his partners' desertion of the table, sobered the Baron. He left the club, went home and told his valet Konstanty to wake him at seven.

'Your excellency must have gone and done something silly again,' muttered his servant, crossly undressing the Baron.

'You booby!' said the Baron, vexed, 'do you expect me to explain it all to you? I'm to fight a duel, so there . . . Because I choose to. At nine o'clock I am to shoot some wretched boot-maker or barber . . . Do you forbid me, then?'

'You can shoot the devil himself,' Konstanty replied, 'all I would like to know is – who is to pay off your promissory notes? And the rent? And the housekeeping money? Just because you have a matter to see to at the cemetery, the landlord will put the bailiffs in and I'm afraid I'll starve to death . . . A fine business, and no mistake!'

'Then be off with you,' roared the Baron, seizing a gaiter and throwing it at the retreating valet. The gaiter struck the wall and almost brought down a bronze statuette of Sobieski.

Having settled with his faithful servant, the Baron went to bed and began pondering on his wretched situation: 'Just my confounded luck to have a duel with a tradesman,' he thought. 'If I hit him, I'll look like a hunter who goes out for a bear and gets a peasant's cow instead. If he hits me, it will be as though a droshky driver had hit me with his whip. If we both miss . . . No, we are to shoot for first blood. Damn appearances – I'd almost have preferred to apologise to this jackanapes in a notary's office, dressed up for the occasion in a frock-coat and white tie . . . Oh these damnable liberal times! My father would have had such an impudent scoundrel whipped by his dog-keepers, but I have to give him satis-faction, as if I were a dealer in cinnamon myself . . . If only this confounded social revolution would come and finish us or the liberals off!'

He began dozing and dreamed Wokulski had killed him. He saw two messengers bringing his corpse to his wife, how she swooned away and threw herself on his blood-stained breast . . . How she paid all his debts and set aside a thousand roubles for his funeral . . . how he rose from the dead and took the thousand roubles for personal expenses. . . A blissful smile played over the Baron's decrepit face, and he fell asleep like a baby.

At seven, Konstanty and Maruszewicz could hardly wake him. The Baron simply would not get up, muttering that he preferred disgrace and dishonour to getting out of bed so early. Only a carafe of cold water brought him to his senses.

The Baron jumped out of bed, boxed Konstanty's ears, cursed Maruszewicz and vowed inwardly to kill Wokulski. But when he was dressed, he went out into the street, saw the beautiful weather and imagined he was seeing the sunrise – then his hatred for Wokulski diminished, and he decided only to shoot him in the leg.

'That's it,' he added after a moment, 'I'll graze him, and he will limp for the rest of his life and tell people he got his mortal wound in a duel with Baron Krzeszowski! That would take care of me . . . What have my dear seconds made of all this? If some merchant or other gets it into his head that he must shoot at me, at least let him do so when I am out for a walk, not in a duel . . . What a frightful position to be in! I can imagine my dear wife will tell everyone I fight duels with the tradesmen . . .'

The carriages drove up. The Baron and the 'English' Count got into one, the silent Egyptologist with the pistols and a surgeon into the second. They set off for Bielany, and a few minutes later were overtaken by the Baron's valet, Konstanty, in a droshky. The faithful servant swore by heaven and earth, and promised he would charge his master double the expense of this jaunt. Yet he was uneasy.

In the Bielany woods, the Baron and his three companions found the other party already there, and they set off in two groups towards the thickets immediately overlooking the Vistula bank. Dr Szuman was irritable, Rzecki stiff, Wokulski gloomy. The Baron stroked his thin beard, eyed him attentively, and thought: 'He must eat well, that tradesman fellow . . . Compared to him, I look like an Austrian cigar beside a bull. May the devil take me, though, if I don't shoot over the fool's head, or even not at all . . . That would be best.'

Then he suddenly recollected that the duel was for first blood, fell into a rage and decided to kill Wokulski on the spot, without more ado: 'Let these Philistines learn once and for all not to challenge the likes of us to duels,' he said to himself.

Some dozen paces away, Wokulski was walking to and fro between the pine-trees, like a pendulum. He was not thinking of Izabela now: he could hear the twittering birds which crowded the whole wood, and the splashing of the Vistula along its bank.

Against the background of nature's tranquil serenity, the rattle of
the pistols and snap of drawn bolts resounded strangely. A ferocious
animal had awakened in Wokulski: the whole world disappeared
from before his eyes, all that remained was this one man, the
Baron, whose corpse he was to drag to the feet of the insulted
Izabela.

They took up their stand. The Baron was still troubled by uncertainty about what to do to this tradesman fellow, and finally
decided to shoot him in the hand.

Such wild fury was depicted on Wokulski's face that the
'English' Count thought in surprise: 'This is more than a question
of the mare, or even of a push at the races!' The Egyptologist,
hitherto silent, gave the word. The antagonists moved off, their
pistols levelled. The Baron aimed at Wokulski's left elbow, lowered
his pistol and lightly touched the trigger. In the last moment his
pince-nez slipped, the pistol shifted a hair's breadth, went off – and
the bullet flew several centimetres wide of Wokulski's arm. The
Baron covered his face with the barrel of his pistol, and looking
around it, thought: 'The fool will miss . . . He is aiming at my
head.'

Suddenly he felt a powerful blow on his temple: there was a
roaring in his ears, black dots flickered before his eyes. He dropped
his pistol and groaned. 'In the head!' someone shouted.

Wokulski threw down his pistol and left the spot. All ran to the
kneeling Baron who, however, instead of giving up the ghost, said
in a squeaky voice: 'A most extraordinary accident, to be sure . . . I
have a hole in my cheek, a tooth gone, but no bullet anywhere.
Surely I haven't swallowed it?'

The Egyptologist picked up the Baron's pistol and examined it:
'Ah,' he exclaimed, 'I see . . . the bullet went into the pistol, and
the catch entered your cheek. The pistol is wrecked – a most interesting shot . . .'

'Is Wokulski satisfied?' the 'English' Count asked.

'Yes.' The surgeon bandaged the Baron's face. Alarmed,
Konstanty ran up from among the trees. 'What's this?' he cried,
'didn't I say his Excellency would catch it?'

'Silence, you ninny,' the Baron roared, 'be off with you to the
Baroness and tell the cook I am gravely wounded . . .'

'Now, if you please,' said the 'English' Count gravely, 'will you
two gentlemen shake hands?'

Wokulski approached the Baron and did so. 'A fine shot, Mr
Wokulski,' said the Baron with some difficulty, shaking him firmly
by the hand, 'it surprises me that a man of your trade . . . but
perhaps that offends you?'

'Not at all . . .'

'That a man of your trade – highly respected, of course, should shoot so well. Where is my pince-nez? Ah, here . . . Mr Wokulski, a word in your ear, if you please.'

He leaned on Wokulski's arm and they went a few yards into the wood. 'I am disfigured,' said the Baron, 'I look like an old monkey with the mumps . . . I don't want another quarrel with you, for I see you have good luck on your side. So tell me please – why have I been wounded? Not for pushing you,' he added, looking straight at him.

'You insulted a lady,' Wokulski answered quietly.

The Baron took a step back: '*Ah, c'est ça . . .*' he said, 'I understand. I apologise once more and, as for that, know what I must do.'

'And pray forgive me, Baron,' Wokulski rejoined.

'It is nothing . . . don't mention it . . . never mind,' said the Baron, shaking his hand, 'the disfigurement will pass, and as for the tooth . . . Where is my tooth, doctor? Please wrap it up in a bit of paper . . . As for my tooth, I should have had false ones long ago. You would scarcely believe, Mr Wokulski, what a state my teeth are in.'

Much pleased, they all parted. The Baron was surprised that a man in trade should be such a good shot, the would-be Englishman looked more than ever like a dummy, and the Egyptologist began observing the clouds again. In the other party, Wokulski was thoughtful, Rzecki delighted by the spirits and civility of the Baron, and only Szuman was cross. Not until their carriage had gone down the hill past the Camaldolite monastery did the doctor glance at Wokulski and mutter: 'What savages! And to think I did not call the police about such fools . . .'

Three days after the strange duel, Wokulski was sitting locked in his study with a certain Mr William Collins. The servant, long intrigued by these conferences, which were held several times a week, was dusting in the next room, and from time to time would put his ear or eye to the key-hole. He could see some books on the table, his master writing in a note-book; he could hear the visitor put questions to Wokulski, who replied sometimes loudly and at once, sometimes in an undertone, shyly . . . But the servant could not imagine what they were talking about in this peculiar fashion, for the conversation was conducted in a foreign language: 'It ain't German, though,' the servant muttered, 'for in German they say "*Bitte mein Herr,*" and it ain't French neither, for they don't say "*Monsieur bonjour*" . . . and it ain't Hebrew neither, nor no language whatsoever, so what is it? The old man must be thinking up some first-rate speculation altogether, if he talks so the devil himself wouldn't understand him . . . And he's found himself a partner too . . . May the devil take 'em . . .'

The bell rang. The watchful servant withdrew on tiptoe from the study door, went noisily into the hall and after a minute returned to knock at his master's door.

'What is it?' asked Wokulski impatiently, looking out.

'That gent has come, what comes here,' the servant replied, and peered into the study. But apart from the note-book on the table and the red whiskers on Mr Collins's countenance, nothing of any interest met his eye.

'Why didn't you say I am not at home?' Wokulski asked crossly.

'I forgot,' said the servant, frowning and shrugging.

'Ask him into the hall, you fool,' said Wokulski, and he slammed the study door.

Soon Maruszewicz appeared in the hall. He was already embarrassed, and became even more so when he saw that Wokulski received him with evident disfavour: 'Excuse me . . . am I interrupting? Perhaps you have important business?'

'I am doing nothing at the moment,' Wokulski replied sullenly, and he flushed slightly. Maruszewicz noticed this. He was certain something was going on in the apartment – perhaps a woman was there. In any case, he regained his composure, which he always possessed in the presence of embarrassed people.

'I will take only a moment of your valuable time,' said the rundown young man more boldly, waving his cane and hat ingratiatingly.

'Well, what is it?' said Wokulski. He sat down heavily in an armchair and indicated another to his visitor.

'I have come to apologise, my dear sir,' said Maruszewicz affectedly, 'because I am unable to be of any service in the auction of the Łęcki property.'

'How do you know of the auction?' Wokulski was openly startled.

'Can't you guess?' asked the agreeable young man with the utmost self-possession, blinking imperceptibly, for he was still not quite sure of his facts, even yet, 'can't you guess, my dear sir? It was honest old Szlangbaum . . .'

Suddenly he fell silent, as if the unfinished phrase had been bitten off inside his open mouth, while his left hand holding the cane and his right hand with the hat sank to rest on the arms of his chair. Meanwhile Wokulski did not move, but fixed a clear stare upon him.

He traced the almost imperceptible shades of expression moving across Maruszewicz's features as a hunter watches startled hares running over a fallow field. He eyed the young man and thought: 'So this is the respectable Catholic gentleman Szlangbaum is hiring for the auction, at a fee of fifteen roubles – which he advised me not to pay in advance. Aha! And when he took the eight hundred for Krzeszowski's mare he was somehow confused . . . Hm . . .

And it was he who spread the news I had bought the mare . . . He is serving two masters: the Baron, and the Baron's wife. . . . Yes, but he knows too much about my affairs . . . Szlangbaum has been careless.'

Thus thought Wokulski as he coolly eyed Maruszewicz. But the decayed young man, who was moreover very nervous, wilted under the gaze like a dove eyed by a spotted snake. First he turned a little pale, then sought to rest his weary eyes on some indifferent object, which he looked for in vain on the walls and ceiling of the room, until finally, drenched in a cold sweat, he knew his wandering gaze could not escape Wokulski's influence. It seemed to him that the sombre merchant had caught hold of his soul with grappling-irons, and there was no resisting him. So he shifted his head a few times more, then finally sank with complete surrender into Wokulski's gaze.

'My dear sir,' he said sweetly, 'I see I must lay all my cards on the table . . . So I will tell you at once . . .'

'Please do not trouble, Mr Maruszewicz, I know all I need to know already.'

'But, my dear sir, you have formed an unfavourable opinion of me, you have been misled by gossip. On my word of honour, I have the best intentions . . .'

'Believe me, Mr Maruszewicz, I do not base my opinions on gossip.'

He rose from his chair and looked away, which enabled Maruszewicz to come back to his senses somewhat. The young man hastily bade Wokulski farewell, left the house and, as he ran hastily downstairs, thought: 'Unheard of, upon my soul! A street-trader like that trying to impress me! There was a moment, I swear it, when I wanted to strike him with my cane . . . The impudence of the fellow, upon my soul . . . He is ready to think I'm afraid of him, upon my soul if he isn't! Oh God, how gravely You are punishing me for my frivolity! Wretched usurers are setting the bailiffs on me; I have a debt of honour due in a day or two, and that tradesman, that scoundrel . . . I'd like to know what he thinks, what he imagines about me? Nothing but that . . . Upon my soul, he must have killed someone, for no decent man has such a look in his eyes. Of course he almost killed Krzeszowski. Ah, the contemptible bully! He dared look at me like that – at me, for goodness sake!'

Nevertheless, he called on Wokulski again the next day, but as he did not find him in, he told the droshky to go to the store. Ignacy greeted him in the store, spreading out his hands as if putting the entire stock at his disposal. An inner voice told the old clerk, however, that this customer would not buy anything costing more than a few roubles and even then would have it charged to his account, very likely.

'Is Mr Wokulski in?' Maruszewicz asked, without removing his hat.

'He'll be in directly,' Ignacy replied with a low bow.

'Directly? What does that mean?'

'Within fifteen minutes at most,' Rzecki answered.

'I'll wait . . . Have them give my driver a rouble,' said the young man, carelessly sinking into a chair. But his legs turned to water at the thought that the old clerk might refuse to give the driver a rouble. However, Rzecki obeyed the instructions, though he gave up bowing to the customer.

Wokulski entered within a few minutes. Seeing the detestable figure of the merchant fellow, Maruszewicz experienced such a variety of sensations that he hardly knew what he was saying, let alone what he was thinking. All he remembered was that Wokulski took him into the office behind the store, where the iron safe was kept, and that he told himself the feelings he experienced at the sight of Wokulski were contempt mingled with loathing. Later, he remembered that he had tried to mask these feelings with refined civility, which even in his own eyes looked more like humility.

'What can I do for you?' Wokulski asked, when they were seated (Maruszewicz could not precisely indicate the point in time when he performed the act of taking his seat in space).

Despite this, he began, somewhat hesitantly: 'I wanted to give you proof, my dear sir, of my goodwill . . . Madame the Baroness Krzeszowska, as you know, is anxious to buy the Łęcki property . . . Now, her husband has placed a veto on a certain part of her funds, without which the purchase cannot take place . . . Now . . . today . . . the Baron is in temporary difficulties . . . He needs . . . he needs a thousand roubles . . . he wants to effect a loan, without which . . . without which, d'you see, he will not be able to thwart his wife's wishes with sufficient force . . .'

Seeing that Wokulski was again eyeing him searchingly, Maruszewicz wiped the sweat from his forehead.

'So the Baron needs money?'

'Yes,' the young man replied hastily.

'I will not give him a thousand roubles – but three, perhaps four hundred. And only against a receipt with the Baron's own signature.'

'Four hundred?' the young man repeated automatically, and suddenly added: 'I will bring you the Baron's receipt within an hour. Will you be here?'

'I shall.'

Maruszewicz left the office and came back with a receipt signed by Baron Krzeszowski inside of an hour. Wokulski read the document, put it in the safe and gave Maruszewicz four hundred roubles in exchange.

'The Baron will try as soon as possible . . .'

'There is no hurry,' Wokulski replied, 'apparently the Baron is ill?'

'Yes . . . a little . . . He is leaving tomorrow or the day after . . . He will repay the money as soon as . . .'

Wokulski dismissed him with a very indifferent nod.

The young man quickly left the shop, forgetting to repay Rzecki the rouble for the driver. When he was in the street, he took a deep breath and began thinking: 'Ah, the wretched tradesman! He had the impertinence to give me four hundred roubles instead of a thousand . . . God, how terribly You are punishing me for my frivolity . . . If I were to win, then upon my soul, I'd throw these four hundred roubles back into his face and the two hundred as well . . . God, how low I have sunk . . .'

He thought of waiters in various restaurants, billiard-markers and hotel porters, from whom he had extracted money in many various ways. But not one of them struck him as as hateful and contemptible as Wokulski: 'On my word of honour,' he thought, 'I have put myself into his hateful paws involuntarily. . . God, how You are punishing me for my frivolity . . .'

But after Maruszewicz had gone, Wokulski was very pleased: 'He looks to me,' he thought, 'like a scamp of the first degree and cunning into the bargain. He wanted a position with me, but found himself one spying on me, and informing others. He might make things awkward for me, were it not for those four hundred roubles he's taken, on a forged signature, I am sure. Krzeszowski, for all his eccentricity and laziness, is an honest man (can an idler be honest? . . .). He would never sacrifice his wife's affairs or caprices for a loan from me . . .'

He felt it was all very unpleasant; he leaned his head in his hands and went on brooding, his eyes closed: 'But what am I doing? I have deliberately helped a scoundrel to commit a villainy . . . Were I to die today, Krzeszowski would have to repay the money to my estate. No, Maruszewicz would be sent to prison. Well, that awaits him anyhow . . .'

After a while, still blacker pessimism overtook him: 'Four days ago I almost killed a man; today I have built a bridge to prison for another, and all in return for that '*Merci* . . .' of hers. Well, it was for her that I made my fortune, that I give work to several hundred people, and am increasing the country's prosperity . . . For what should I be, were it not for her? A small dealer in haberdashery . . . Whereas now all Warsaw is talking about me . . . A lump of coal moves a ship bearing the destinies of hundreds of people, and love drives me on . . . But what if it consumes me so I am reduced to a handful of ash? Oh God, what a wretched world this is . . . Ochocki was right: a woman is a wretched creature – she will play with things she cannot even begin to understand . . .'

He was so preoccupied with his painful thoughts that he did not
hear the door open and rapid footsteps behind him. He did not
waken until he felt the touch of someone's hand. He looked up
and saw the eminent lawyer of the Prince, with a large briefcase
under one arm and a solemn look on his face.

Wokulski jumped up in embarrassment, seated his visitor in a
chair; the eminent lawyer then put one hand on the desk and,
quickly rubbing the back of his neck with one finger, said in a low
voice: 'My dear sir . . . Mr Wokulski . . . My dear Stanisław . . .
What is this? What are you up to? I protest . . . I deny it . . . I
appeal to Mr Wokulski, a frivolous fellow – to dear Stanisław, who
from being a shop-boy became a scholar, and was to reform our
foreign trade for us . . . Stanisław – this cannot be!'

As he spoke, he rubbed the back of his neck and grimaced as if
his mouth were full of quinine. Wokulski looked away: the lawyer
went on: 'My dear sir, in a word – bad news! Count Sanocki – you
remember him, he was in favour of saving pennies – wishes now to
withdraw entirely from the partnership. And do you know why?
For two reasons: first, you enjoy yourself at the races, and second,
because your horse beat his. His horse ran against your mare – and
lost. The Count is extremely vexed, and keeps muttering: "Why
the devil should I invest capital with him? To enable a tradesman to
race against me and seize the prize from under my very nose?" I
tried in vain to dissuade him,' the lawyer went on, after a pause for
breath, 'and reminded him that races are as good a business as any
other, after all, and even better, since within a few days you made
three hundred roubles on eight hundred; but the Count silenced
me immediately. "Wokulski," said he, "gave away all the prize
money and the sum obtained for the horse to some ladies, for
charity, and goodness knows how much he gave Young and
Miller. . ."'

'May I not even do that?' Wokulski interrupted.

'Of course, of course,' the eminent lawyer agreed, affably, 'you
may indeed, but in doing so, you are only repeating former sins,
which in any case are better committed by others. But that was not
why I and the Prince and these Counts appealed to you, merely to
warm up old dishes – but so that you should show us new ways.'

'Let them quit the partnership, then,' Wokulski muttered, 'I am
not forcing them . . .'

'They will do so,' said the lawyer, with a gesture, 'if you make
just one more mistake. . .'

'Anyone would think I had already committed so many . . .'

'Upon my word, you take the biscuit,' the lawyer said angrily,
striking his knee, 'do you know what Count Liciński, that would-
be Englishman, with his "Dear me, yes," is saying ? He says:
"Wokulski is a perfect gentleman, he shoots like Nimrod – but he

is no director for commercial enterprises. One day he throws millions into industry, but tomorrow or the next day he will challenge someone to a duel, and risk everything . . ."'

Wokulski almost pushed his chair back. This charge had not even occurred to him. The lawyer saw the effect of his own words and decided to strike while the iron was hot: 'So, my dear Stanisław, if you don't want to spoil such a promising beginning, pray do not go on like this. Above all – do not buy the Łęcki property. If you invest ninety thousand roubles in it, then the partnership will melt away like smoke. If people see you investing a large sum at six or seven per cent, they will lose confidence in the interest you promised them, and even . . . you understand me . . . they are ready to suspect . . .'

Wokulski jumped up from the desk: 'I want no partnerships,' he cried, 'I want no favours from anyone, it is I who grant them to others. If anyone does not trust me, let him check the entire business. He will find out I have not deceived him – but he will be no partner of mine. Counts and Princes have no monopoly of dreams . . . I have mine too, and do not like anyone interrupting them . . .'

'Hush, hush, pray calm yourself, my dear Stanisław,' the lawyer implored, replacing him in his chair, 'but you will not refrain from making the purchase?'

'No, that property is of more value to me than any partnership with all the gentlemen in the world . . .'

'Very well, very well . . . Then perhaps you will let someone else act for you? In the last resort I could even recommend an agent to you, so there would be no risk in securing the property. Most important, though, is not to discourage people. Once the aristocracy have gained an appetite for public affairs, they may become attached to them – and in a year or six months, you may become the nominal owner of the property too. Do you agree?'

'So be it,' Wokulski replied.

'Yes,' said the lawyer, 'that will be best. If you buy the property yourself, you would even find yourself in an awkward position *vis-à-vis* the Łęckis. As a rule, we dislike those who are going to inherit anything from us – that's one thing. Then again – who would take his oath that various notions haven't begun taking shape in his heir's head? Suppose they thought he paid too much or too little for it? If too much – how dare he patronise us? If too little – he has insulted us . . .'

Wokulski scarcely heard the lawyer's last words, for he was absorbed by other thoughts, which dominated him still more strongly after the lawyer's departure. 'So that's it,' he said to himself, 'the lawyer is right. People are judging me, even passing sentence upon me; but they are doing it behind my back. I know nothing of it. Not until today have many details come to light. For a week already the merchants associated with me have had sour looks, and my opponents are triumphant. Something is amiss in the store, too – Ignacy walks about looking miserable, Szlangbaum is preoccupied. Lisiecki has grown more impertinent than ever before, as if he expects to leave soon. Klein has a wretched expression (a Socialist! He's angry on account of the races and the duel . . .), while that nincompoop Zięba is already beginning to fawn upon Szlangbaum . . . Perhaps he divines the future owner of the store in him? Oh, charming people, indeed . . .'

He stopped on the threshold of the office and beckoned to Rzecki; the old clerk was indeed somewhat abstracted, and did not look his master in the eye. Wokulski gave him a chair and after sitting a while in the cramped little room, he said: 'Old fellow! Tell me frankly – what are people saying about me?'

Rzecki folded his arms: 'Oh my, what aren't they saying? . . .'

'Tell me outright,' Wokulski encouraged him.

'Outright? Very well. Some say you are going out of your mind . . .'

'Bravo!'

'Others, that . . . others that you are about to commit a swindle . . .'

'What the devil? . . .'

'And everyone agrees you are going bankrupt, and very soon, too.'

'As always,' Wokulski interrupted, 'but what about you, Ignacy, what do you yourself think?'

'I think,' he replied unhesitatingly, 'that you have got yourself involved in some terrible trouble, from which you will not escape whole – unless you retreat in time, which, after all, you have enough sense to do . . .'

Wokulski burst out: 'I will not retreat!' he exclaimed, 'a thirsty man does not draw back from a well. If I am to perish, let me at least perish drinking . . . In any case, what is it you all want from me? Since childhood I have lived like a caged bird – in service, in prison, even in that unhappy marriage I sold myself into. But today, when my wings are opening, you all begin to hoot after me, like domestic geese at a wild one which has taken flight . . . What is some stupid shop or partnership to me? I want to live, I want . . .'

At this moment there was a knock at the study door. Łęcki's butler Mikołaj appeared with a letter. Wokulski seized it feverishly, tore the envelope open and read:

Dear Mr Wokulski,
My daughter insists on making your closer acquaintance. A woman's wish is sacred; therefore, I invite you to our house

tomorrow for dinner (about six o'clock), and you must not even attempt to decline.

Kind regards,

T. Łęcki.

Wokulski felt so shaken he had to sit down. He read the note a second, third, fourth time . . . Finally he came to his senses. He replied to Mr Łęcki, and gave Mikołaj five roubles.

Ignacy had hurried into the shop for a few minutes, but when Mikołaj had gone, he returned to Wokulski and said, as if to start the conversation again: 'All the same, dear Staś, consider the situation, and perhaps you will yourself draw back . . .'

Whistling softly to himself, Wokulski put on his hat and, with one hand on his old friend's arm: said, 'Listen. Even if the earth were to give way before my feet – do you understand? Even if the heavens collapsed – I shall not draw back, do you understand? I would give my life for such happiness . . .'

'What happiness?' Ignacy asked.

But Wokulski had already left by the back door.

XIV

Girlish Dreams

SINCE Easter, Izabela had often thought about Wokulski, and in all her ponderings, one unusual feature had impressed her: this man kept appearing in an ever different light.

Izabela had many acquaintances and possessed a good deal of wit at characterising people. All her acquaintances, hitherto, had had the quality of being definable in a single word. The Prince was a patriot; his lawyer shrewd; Count Liciński posed as an Englishman; her aunt was proud; the Duchess was good; Ochocki was an eccentric, and Krzeszowski a card-player. In a word: a man was a talent or a vice, sometimes a merit, more often a title or fortune – which had a head, arms and legs, and dressed itself more or less fashionably.

On meeting Wokulski, she had for the first time made the acquaintance, not only of a new personality, but also of an unexpected phenomenon. It was impossible to define him in a single word, or even in several hundred words. He was unlike everyone else, and if it was at all possible to compare him to anything, then perhaps it was to a place through which one travels all day, and where valleys and mountains, woods and lakes, water and desert, villages and towns are to be found. And where too, beyond the mists of the horizon, some vague landscapes appear, unlike anything known before. She was amazed and wondered whether this was the play of an excited imagination – or was he really a supernatural being, or at least a super-drawing-room one.

Then she began to enumerate her experiences with him.

The first time she had not seen him at all, had only felt the approach of some immense shadow. He was someone who threw away a few thousand roubles for her aunt's charities and orphanages; then someone who played cards with her father at the club, and lost every day; then someone who bought up her father's promissory notes (perhaps that wasn't Wokulski, though?), then her dinner-service, and had then provided various items to decorate Christ's Grave at Easter.

This 'someone' was a bold parvenu, who had pursued her for a year, staring at her in theatres and at concerts. He was a cynical brute who had made a fortune in dubious speculation in order to purchase a reputation for himself in society, and buy her, Miss Izabela Łęcka, from her father.

Of this period, she only recalled his coarse looks, red hands and brusque manners, which had seemed insufferable in comparison with the civility of other tradespeople, and simply laughable against that background of fans, travelling-bags, parasols, canes and haberdashery. He was a cunning, insolent tradesman who posed as a fallen minister in that shop of his. He was hateful, unspeakably hateful, for he had presumed to help them by buying the dinner-service and providing her father with money at cards.

Thinking of this today, Izabela plucked nervously at her dress. Sometimes she would throw herself upon the sofa and beat it with her fists, murmuring: 'Scoundrel! Scoundrel!'

It filled her with despair to confront the poverty into which her house was now plunged. And to make matters worse, someone had torn the veil from her most intimate secrets, and had dared tend the wounds she would sooner have kept hidden from God Himself. She could have forgiven anything but this blow to her pride.

Now came a change of scene. A different man appeared, and told her frankly, without a shade of ambiguity, that he had bought the dinner-service to make money. In other words, he felt he had no right to support Izabela Łęcka, and if he did, it was not to seek fame or gratitude, or even to dare to think of the matter.

The same man had driven Mraczewski from his shop because he had ventured to speak maliciously of her. In vain had Izabela's enemies (Baron and Baroness Krzeszowski) set themselves up behind this young man; in vain had her aunt, the Countess, spoken for him – she, who rarely even said 'Thank you' and still more rarely asked for anything! Wokulski had not yielded . . . But one little word from her, Izabela, had vanquished this inflexible man: not only did he yield, but he even gave Mraczewski a better post. Such submission is made not to a woman if she is not honoured . . .

All the same, it was a pity that at almost the same time a conceited parvenu had revealed himself in her admirer, when he tossed down that roll of imperials at the collection. How very mercantile that was! He did not understand English, either; he had no conception of a language that was fashionable!

Now – the third phase. She had seen Wokulski in her aunt's drawing-room on the first day of Easter, and noticed that he stood a whole head and shoulders above the rest of the company. The most aristocratic persons had sought his acquaintance, while he, that brutal parvenu, had actually avoided them. He had moved clumsily yet boldly, as if the drawing-room were his unquestioned property, and listened gloomily to compliments bestowed upon him. Then the Duchess, that most respectable of matrons, had summoned him to her and, after a few minutes of conversation, had burst into floods of tears . . . Could that have been the same parvenu, with the red hands?

Only now had Izabela noticed that Wokulski's face was unusual. He had clear and decisive features, hair that seemed to stand angrily on end, a small moustache and beard, the figure of a statue, a clear and penetrating look . . . Had this man possessed a large estate, instead of a shop, then he would have been very handsome: had he been born a prince, he would have been tremendously handsome. As it was, he reminded her of Trosti, of the colonel in the Rifle Brigade and – truly! – of her statue of the victorious gladiator.

By this time, almost everyone had drawn away from Izabela.

Admittedly, elderly gentlemen still heaped compliments upon her for her beauty and elegance, but the young men, particularly those with titles, or the rich, treated her very coldly and brusquely; and when she grew tired of solitude and banal phrases, and spoke to anyone in a more lively fashion, then he would glance at her with evident alarm, as if afraid she was about to seize him by the scruff of the neck and drag him to the altar there and then.

Izabela loved the world of drawing-rooms to distraction; she could only quit it for the grave, but as each year and month passed by, she despised people more and more: she found it inconceivable that a woman as beautiful, virtuous and well-bred as herself could be deserted by that world, simply because she had no money.

'Dear God, such people!' she sometimes whispered, looking through the curtains at the passing carriages of dandies who turned away their heads from her windows on various pretexts, so as not to bow. Did they think, then, that she was awaiting them? Well, admittedly, she was . . . But then, hot tears came into her eyes: she bit her beautiful lips in fury and wrenched at the cords to pull the curtains across. 'Dear God, such people!' she repeated, reluctant nevertheless to call them anything worse because, after all, they belonged to the great world. In her opinion, only Wokulski could properly be called a base wretch.

To intensify the mockery of Fate, only two admirers were now left of all her former suitors. She had no illusions about Ochocki: he was more interested in some flying-machine or other (what folly!) than in her. It was the marshal and the Baron who danced attendance upon her, though without intruding excessively. The marshal reminded her of a pig's carcass, such as she had sometimes seen in butchers' wagons in the street; while the Baron resembled some sort of untanned animal hide, great heaps of which might also be seen in carts. These two constituted her suite, perhaps even her wings if, as was said, she was an angel. . .

The terrible combination of these two old men haunted Izabela night and day. Sometimes it seemed to her she was doomed, and that Hell had opened up for her while she was still alive.

At such times Izabela thought of Wokulski much as a drowning man looks towards a light on the distant shore. And in her unutterable bitterness, she felt a touch of relief to know that an unusual man, much spoken of in society, was, after all, mad about her. Then she recalled famous travellers, or wealthy American industrialists who had laboured years in mines and had sometimes been pointed out to her at a distance in Parisian drawing-rooms.

'Look there,' some Countess or other, recently let out of a convent school, would twitter, tipping her fan in a certain direction, 'do you see that man who looks just like an omnibus conductor? He's said to be a great man who discovered something or other, though I don't know what – a gold mine, or the North Pole . . . I don't recollect his name, but a margrave from the Academy assures me that this man lived ten years at the Pole – or no, he lived underground. A terrible man! In his shoes I'd have died of fright, I assure you! Wouldn't you?'

If only Wokulski had been such a traveller, or at least a miner who had made millions by living underground for ten years! But he was only a tradesman, and in haberdashery at that! He did not even know English; the parvenu in him was continually being shown up, and as a youth he had served food to restaurant customers. Such a man might at best be a good adviser, perhaps an invaluable friend (in private, when there were no visitors). Perhaps even . . . a husband, for people do suffer the most terrible misfortunes. But as a lover – that was simply absurd. If necessary, even the most aristocratic of ladies will take a mud-bath: but only a madman would enjoy it.

The fourth phase. Izabela met Wokulski several times in the Łazienki park, and had even deigned to return his bow. Amidst the greenery and beside the statues, this coarse man seemed yet again different from the man behind a shop counter. Suppose he had an estate, with a park, palace, and lake? Admittedly he was a parvenu, but he was supposed to be gentry all the same, the nephew of an Army officer. Compared with the marshal or the Baron, he looked like Apollo, the aristocracy were talking about him more and more, and what of that outburst of tears by the Duchess?

Moreover, the Duchess was obviously lending him her support with her friend the Countess and her niece Izabela. Those hour-long strolls with her aunt in the Łazienki park were terribly tedious, and the gossip about fashions, charities and the marriages forthcoming in society was so trying that Izabela was even rather sorry Wokulski did not come up to her during the strolls and talk for fifteen minutes or so. For it is interesting for people in society to talk to that kind of person, and to Izabela even peasants, for example, looked as if they might be amusing, with their different way of speaking and thinking.

Of course, a haberdashery salesman, and one who had his own carriage, would not be as amusing as a peasant . . .

Be that as it may, Izabela was not disagreeably surprised to hear one day from the Duchess that she was to go with her and the Countess to the Łazienki park, and that she was going to stop Wokulski. 'We are bored, let him amuse us,' the old lady said.

And as they were driving to the park at one o'clock, the Duchess said to Izabela, with a meaningful smile: 'I have a premonition we shall meet him somewhere here. . .'

Izabela blushed a little, and decided not to speak to Wokulski at all, or at least to treat him haughtily, so he would not imagine things. Of course there could be no mention of love in those 'imagining things'. Izabela did not even wish to appear affable, however, 'Fire is all very well, especially in winter,' she thought, 'but only at a distance.'

However, Wokulski was not in the park. 'Can it be,' Izabela said to herself, 'that he didn't wait? Or is he ill?' She did not suppose that Wokulski had any more urgent business in the world than to meet her; if he were late, she decided not only to treat him haughtily, but even to show her displeasure. 'If punctuality is the politeness of kings,' she thought, 'then it should be at least the obligation of a tradesman.'

Half an hour passed, an hour, then two . . . It was time to go home, but Wokulski had not appeared. Finally the ladies got into their carriage; the Countess, cold as always, the Duchess rather thoughtful, and Izabela vexed. Her indignation did not diminish when her father told her that evening that he had attended a meeting in the afternoon at the Prince's, where Wokulski had put forward his plan for a vast commercial partnership, and aroused something very close to enthusiasm among the blasé magnates.

'I have been feeling for a long time,' Mr Łęcki concluded, 'that this man's help will free me from the tender care of my relatives, and I shall take my rightful place in society again.'

'For the partnership, father,' said Izabela, shrugging slightly, 'money is required . . .'

'That is why I am having my house put up for auction; I know my debts will consume some sixty thousand roubles, but even so, I will have at least forty thousand left.'

'Aunt says that no one will pay more than sixty thousand for the house.'

'Oh, your aunt . . .' Tomasz was cross, 'she always says things to hurt or humiliate me. Krzeszowska, who doesn't care two bits for us, will give sixty thousand — that middle-class creature! But naturally your aunt agrees with her, because it is a matter touching my house, my position . . .'

He flushed and began breathing heavily; but as he did not want to lose his temper in his daughter's presence, he kissed her on the brow and went to his study.

'Perhaps my father is right,' Izabela thought, 'perhaps he really is more practical than all the people who judge him so harshly. After all, it was father who first made the acquaintance of that . . . Wokulski. But what a boor he is! He didn't come to the Łazienki, though the Duchess must have engaged him to do so. Still, perhaps it was better so: we should have made a picture, if an acquaintance had seen us walking about with a haberdashery salesman . . .'

During the next few days, Izabela heard of nothing but Wokulski. The drawing-rooms resounded with his name. The marshal vowed Wokulski must be descended from an ancient family, and the Baron – an expert on masculine looks (he spent half his time at a looking-glass) – declared that Wokulski was 'really quite . . . quite . . .' Count Sanocki wagered that he was the first sensible man in the country, and Count Liciński said this tradesman modelled himself on English industrialists, while the Prince rubbed his hands and smiled, saying 'Aha!'

Even Ochocki, visiting Izabela one day, told her he had been for a stroll with Wokulski in the Łazienki park.

'What did you talk about?' she asked in surprise, 'not about flying-machines, surely?'

'Bah!' her thoughtful cousin muttered, 'Wokulski is probably the only man in Warsaw with whom it would be possible to do so. He's a regular fellow. . .'

'The only sensible man . . . the only tradesman . . . the only man who can talk to Ochocki?' Izabela thought. 'So – what is he, really? Ah, I know . . .'

It seemed to her she had found Wokulski out. He was an ambitious speculator, who wished to penetrate into good society, and had bethought himself of marrying her, the impoverished daughter of an eminent family. It was for this purpose and no other that he had gained the respect of her father, of the Countess her aunt, and of the entire aristocracy. Then, deciding he could make his way into the society of great gentlefolks without her, he suddenly cooled off and did not even come to the Łazienki.

'I must congratulate him,' she told herself, 'he has all the virtues required to make a career for himself: not plain, capable, energetic and above all – shameless and abject. How dare he pretend to be in love with me, and with such facility? Really, these parvenus are outdistancing even us in their deception . . . What an abject man!'

Offended, she wanted to tell Mikołaj never to admit Wokulski to her drawing-room. At the most he might be permitted into the

master's study, if he came on business. But recollecting that
Wokulski never called, she blushed.

Then she learned from Mrs Meliton of the latest disagreement
between Baron Krzeszowski and his wife, and that the Baroness
had bought the mare from him for eight hundred roubles, but
would certainly give her back, because the races were to be held in
a few days, and the Baron had placed some large bets.

'Perhaps even this precious pair will be reconciled on this
occasion,' Mrs Meliton remarked.

'Oh, what wouldn't I give if the Baron didn't acquire the mare
and were to lose his bets!' Izabela cried.

A few days later she heard as a great secret from Flora that the
Baron would not get his mare back, for Wokulski had bought it . . .
The secret was still so well-kept that when Izabela called on her
aunt she fount the Countess and the Duchess in council, wondering
how to bring about a reconciliation between the Krzeszowskis with
the help of the mare.

'Nothing will come of it,' Izabela interrupted with a smile, 'the
Baron will not get his mare back.'

'Would you care to wager?' the Countess asked coldly.

'Certainly, if I win that sapphire bracelet, aunt.'

The bet was accepted. Consequently, the Countess and Izabela
were extremely interested in the races.

For a little while, Izabela was frightened; it was said the Baron
was offering Wokulski four hundred roubles compensation, and
that Count Liciński had undertaken to mediate between them. In
the Countess's drawing-room, it was even whispered that
Wokulski would have to agree to this arrangement, not for the
money, but for the Count's sake. Then Izabela thought: 'If he is a
greedy parvenu, he'll agree: but he won't if . . .'

She dared not complete the phrase. Wokulski did it for her. He
did not sell the mare, and even entered her for the race, 'He is not
so abject after all,' she said to herself. And under the influence of
this idea, she spoke very affably to Wokulski at the races.

Yet Izabela reproached herself inwardly for even this small
manifestation of benevolence. 'Why should he know we are interested in his race? No more than in the others . . . Why did I tell
him he "must win"? And what did he mean by replying "I shall
win if you want me to"? He forgets who he is. Never mind though
– if a few civil words can make Krzeszowski fall ill with rage.'

Izabela hated Krzeszowski. Once he had flirted with her: then
rejected, had taken his revenge. She knew he called her an ageing
spinster, who would marry her own footman. This was something
to remember for the rest of her life. But the Baron had gone still
further than this unlucky phrase, and had even behaved cynically in
her presence, mocking her elderly admirers and dropping hints

about her ruined estate. And because Izabela had reluctantly felt obliged to refer to his middle-class wife, whom he had married for money though he never managed to get any out of her, a regular and even fierce battle was in progress between them.

The day of the races was a triumph for Izabela, and one of defeat and humiliation for the Baron. Admittedly he had driven up to the course and pretended to be very gay: but he was fuming inwardly. When he saw Wokulski hand the prize and the money for the horse to Izabela, he had lost control of himself, run over to the carriage and made a scene.

The impudent look of the Baron and his openly calling Wokulski her 'admirer' was a terrible blow to Izabela. She would have killed the Baron on the spot, if that had been a proper thing for a well-bred woman to do. Her suffering was all the worse because the Countess had listened to his outburst quite calmly, the Duchess with embarrassment, and her father had not even spoken, for he had long regarded Krzeszowski as a lunatic who should not be provoked but treated mildly.

It was at a time like this (when people had started glancing at them from the other carriages) that Wokulski had come to the aid of Izabela. Not only did he interrupt the flow of the Baron's resentment, but had also challenged him to a duel. No one doubted this: the Duchess was quite alarmed for her favourite, but the Countess pointed out that Wokulski could not have done anything else, because when the Baron approached the carriage, he had pushed him and not apologised.

'But just tell me,' said the Duchess in dismay, 'whether it is right to fight a duel over such a trifle. After all, everyone knows that Krzeszowski is absent-minded and a fool. The best proof of that is what he himself said to us . . .'

'I agree,' Tomasz exclaimed, 'but after all Wokulski was not to know that, his attention had to be drawn to it.'

'They'll be reconciled,' the Countess put in carelessly, and gave the order to drive home.

It was then that Izabela committed the worst infringement of her own notions of decorum, and pressed Wokulski's hand in a significant manner. Even before they reached the corner she knew that it had been unforgivable. 'How was it possible to do such a thing? What will a man like that think?' she asked herself. But then the sense of justice awoke within her, and she had to admit that this man was not just anybody. 'To give me pleasure (for he certainly had no other reason), he had tripped up the Baron by buying his mare. He had given all the prize money (a proof of disinterestedness) to charity, and through me (the Baron saw that). Above all, he challenged him to a duel as if he had guessed my thoughts. Well, duels nowadays usually finish with champagne: but all the same, the Baron will find out I am not yet an old . . . Yes, there's something about this Wokulski . . . It's a great pity he's a haberdashery salesman. It would be pleasant to have such an admirer, if . . . if he had a different position in society.'

On returning home, Izabela told Flora of the incidents at the races, and had forgotten them within the hour. However, when her father reported later that night that Krzeszowski had chosen as his second Count Liciński, and that the latter was unconditionally demanding that the Baron apologise to Wokulski, Izabela made a contemptuous pout: 'Fortunate man,' she thought, 'they insult me, but are to apologize to him. If anyone insulted my beloved in my presence, I would not accept an apology. He will, of course.'

When she had gone to bed and was falling asleep, a new thought suddenly came to her: 'Suppose Wokulski doesn't want an apology? After all, Count Liciński also intervened with him over the mare, but got nowhere. Oh Heavens, what am I thinking of?' She answered her own question with a shrug and fell asleep.

Next afternoon, her father, herself and Flora were certain Wokulski would come to terms with the Baron, and that it would not even be proper if he did not. Tomasz did not go into town until afternoon, and returned very troubled.

'What is it, father?' Izabela asked, struck by his expression.

'A wretched business,' Tomasz replied, throwing himself into a leather arm-chair, 'Wokulski has rejected the apologies and his seconds have made strict conditions.'

'When is it to be?' she asked more quietly.

'Tomorrow, before nine o'clock,' Tomasz replied, and wiped the sweat from his brow. 'A wretched business,' he went on, 'there is confusion among our partners, for Krzeszowski is a good shot. If this man dies, all my calculations will go for nothing. I'd lose my right hand . . . he's the only man who could possibly carry out my plans . . . There's no one else I would entrust my capital to, and I am certain I would get at least eight thousand a year . . . Bad luck is haunting me, no doubt about it.'

The bad temper of the master of the house affected the others; no one ate any dinner. Afterwards Tomasz shut himself up in his study and walked about, which was a sure sign of unusual excitement. Izabela went to her room also, and lay down on her *chaise-longue*, as she always did in anxious times. Dreary thoughts oppressed her.

'My triumph was short-lived,' she told herself, 'Krzeszowski really is a good shot. If he kills the only man who concerns himself with me nowadays, then what? Duelling is indeed a barbarous business. For Wokulski (taking him from a moral standpoint) is worth more than Krzeszowski, yet he may die. The last man in whom my father has placed his hopes . . .'

But here family pride spoke up in Izabela: 'Still, my father doesn't need Wokulski's favours after all; he would entrust his capital to him, provide him with support and he in return would pay interest. But it is a pity . . .'

She recalled the old manager of their former estate who had served them thirty years and whom she had much loved and trusted; Wokulski might have taken the place of the dead man for both of them, and become her sensible confidant – but he was going to die!

She lay with her eyes closed for some time, not thinking of anything: then extraordinary notions began coming into her head: 'What a peculiar coincidence,' she told herself. Tomorrow two men who had mortally offended her were going to fight for her sake – Krzeszowski, with his malicious remarks and Wokulski, with the sacrifices he had dared make for her. She had already almost forgiven him the purchase of the dinner-service and the promissory notes, and the money lost at cards to her father, on which the entire household had lived for several weeks . . . (No, she had not yet forgiven him that, and never would!)

So heavenly justice was, in a way, looking after the insult to her. Who would perish on the morrow? Perhaps both . . . In any case, he who had presumed to offer financial assistance to Izabela Łęcka. Such a man, like the lovers of Cleopatra, must not live . . .

Thus she reflected, sobbing: she was sorry for a devoted servant and perhaps confidant, but she humbled herself before the judgement of Providence, which does not forgive an insult to Miss Łęcka.

Had Wokulski been able to look into her soul just then, he would have fled in alarm and been cured of his obsession.

Izabela did not sleep all that night. She saw before her the picture by a French painter which represents a duel. Two men in black were taking aim at one another with pistols, under a group of green trees. Then (this was not in the picture) one of them fell, struck by a bullet. It was Wokulski. Izabela did not even attend his funeral, as she did not wish to betray her emotion. But she wept several times, at night. She was sorry for the unusual parvenu, this faithful slave, who was paying for his crimes towards her by his death.

She did not fall asleep till seven in the morning, then slept like a log till noon. Then she was awakened by an excited tapping at her bedroom door. 'Who is it?'

'It is I,' her father replied joyfully, 'Wokulski is unharmed, the Baron wounded in the face.'

'Is that so?'

She had a migraine, and stayed in bed till four in the afternoon. She was pleased the Baron had been wounded, and surprised that Wokulski, whom she had mourned, was not dead. As she had risen so late, Izabela went out for a short stroll in the Boulevard before dinner. The sight of the clear sky, the beautiful trees, the birds flying about and the cheerful passers-by erased all traces of her nocturnal visions, and when she was noticed and greeted from several passing carriages, satisfaction awoke within her.

'God is merciful, all the same,' she thought, 'since He has spared a man who may be useful to us. My father counts on him so, and I, too, am gaining confidence in him. I'd have experienced far fewer disappointments in my life if I'd had a sensible and energetic friend . . .'

She did not care for the word 'friend', though. A 'friend' of Izabela's would have to own an estate at least. A haberdashery salesman only qualified as adviser and administrator.

On returning home, she saw at once that her father was in an excellent humour. 'You know,' he said, 'I went to congratulate Wokulski. He's a splendid fellow, a real gentleman! He has forgotten the duel already, and even seems sorry for the Baron. No two ways about it – genteel blood always tells, no matter what a man's social position.'

Then, taking his daughter into his study, and glancing several times into the looking-glass, he added: 'Now, who said one cannot trust in heavenly protection? The death of this man would have been a serious blow to me – and he has been spared! I must enter into closer contact with him, then we shall see who comes out best – the Prince with his great lawyer, or I with my Wokulski. What do you think?'

'I was thinking the very same thing just now,' Izabela replied, struck by the analogy between her own feelings and those of her father, 'you really must have a capable and trustworthy man at your side.'

'And one who is in addition attracted to my service,' Tomasz added, 'and a sharp man! He understands that he will do more and gain a better reputation by helping an ancient family to rise again than if he were to rush ahead by himself. A very intelligent man,' Tomasz repeated, 'and although he had temporarily acquired the support of the Prince and the entire aristocracy, he is showing greater attachment to me. And he will not regret it, once I regain my position in the world.'

Izabela gazed at the gee-gaws arranged on his desk and thought that her father was deluding himself all the same in thinking that Wokulski was attracted into his service. However, she did not correct his error, but on the contrary admitted privately that it would be quite proper to draw a little closer to this tradesman and overlook his social position. A lawyer . . . a merchant . . . it came to almost the same thing; and if a lawyer could have a prince's confidence, then why should not a tradesman (oh, how vulgar!)

become a man of confidence in the Łęcki household?

Dinner that evening, and the next few days too, passed very pleasantly for Izabela. She was struck by one circumstance, namely – that they were visited by more people during this short time than had called during a whole month. There were hours when the sound of laughter and conversation resounded in the formerly empty drawing-room, until the well-rested furniture itself was surprised by the throng, and in the kitchen it was whispered that Mr Łęcki must have laid his hands on a large sum of money. Even the ladies who had failed to recognise Izabela at the races, now called on her. As for the young men, although they did not call, they recognised her in the street, and bowed respectfully.

Tomasz had visitors too. Count Sanocki called, to urge that Wokulski stop attending race-meetings and playing at duels, and should instead concern himself with the partnership. Count Licinski called and told amazing stories of Wokulski's gentlemanliness. Most important of all was that the Prince called several times to tell Tomasz that, despite the incident with the Baron, Wokulski should not grow discouraged about the aristocracy and should bear his unfortunate country in mind.

'And, cousin, pray dissuade him from fighting duels,' the Prince concluded. 'It is quite unnecessary – all very well for young men, but not for serious and respectable citizens.'

Tomasz was delighted, particularly when he thought that all these agreeable ovations were greeting him on the eve of selling the apartment-house; a year ago, the proximity of such an event would have frightened people away. . .

'I am beginning to regain my proper position in the world,' Tomasz murmured, and suddenly looked up. It seemed to him that Wokulski was standing before him. So, to calm himself, he repeated several times: 'I will reward him, indeed I will . . . He can be sure of my support.'

On the third day after Wokulski's duel, Izabela received a costly box and a letter which startled her. She recognised the Baron's hand:

Dear cousin, If you will forgive my unfortunate marriage, I in return will forgive your references to my wife, who has already teased the life out of me. As a material symbol of eternal peace between us I am sending you the tooth which Wokulski shot because of what – I think – I ventured to say to you at the races. I assure you, my dear cousin, that it is the very same tooth with which I have in the past bitten you, and that I will no longer bite. You can throw it away, but pray keep the box as a souvenir. Accept this trifle from a man who is rather ill today, and is not, believe me, a bad man, and I hope you will at some time be able to forget my clumsy malice, Your affectionate and respectful cousin, Krzeszowski.

P.S. If you do not throw my tooth away, pray send it back to me, so I can present it to my neglected spouse. She will have something to think about for a few days, which the doctors are supposed to have recommended to the poor soul. Your Mr Wokulski is a very agreeable and distinguished man, and I admit I have grown sincerely fond of him, though he did me such an injury.

Inside the costly box was a tooth, wrapped in tissue. After some thought, Izabela wrote the Baron a very affable letter, declaring she was no longer cross and acknowledging the box, while she was sending back the tooth, with all due respect, to its owner.

She could no longer doubt it was only thanks to Wokulski that the Baron had come to terms with her and asked her pardon. Izabela was not a little moved by her triumph, and felt something not unlike gratitude toward Wokulski. She shut herself up in her boudoir and began day-dreaming.

She dreamed that Wokulski sold his store and bought a landed estate, but remained director of the trading partnership, which brought in vast profits. All the aristocracy received him in their homes while she, Izabela, made him her right-hand man. He restored their fortune and brought it back to its former splendour; he executed all her orders; he took risks when necessary. Finally he found her a husband, suitable to the eminence of the Łęcki family.

He did all these things because he loved her with an ideal love, more than his own life. And he was completely happy if she smiled at him, looked at him kindly, or if – after some exceptional service – pressed his hand sincerely. If the good Lord were to give them children, then he would find nursemaids and governesses, would increase their fortune and finally, when she herself died (at this point tears came to Izabela's beautiful eyes), he would shoot himself at her tomb . . . Or no – the delicate feelings she had developed in him would make him shoot himself a few tombs away.

The entrance of her father interrupted the course of her fantasies. 'So Krzeszowski has written to you?' Tomasz asked with curiosity. His daughter showed him the letter on her bureau, and the golden box. Mr Tomasz shook his head as he read, and finally said: 'Always a lunatic, though a good fellow at heart. But . . . Wokulski has done you a real service; you have conquered a mortal foe.'

'Father, I think it would be proper to invite this gentleman to dinner . . . I should like to be better acquainted with him . . .

'For some days I have been wanting to ask you the same thing,' Tomasz replied, gratified, 'it is not right to stick too closely to etiquette with such a useful man.'

'Naturally,' Izabela put in, 'after all, we admit faithful servants to some degree of intimacy . . . '

'I adore your common sense and tact, Bela,' Tomasz exclaimed, and in his delight he kissed her, first on the hand, then on the brow.

XV

*How a Human Soul is Devastated by Passion
and by Common Sense*

A FTER Wokulski received Łęcki's invitation to dinner, he hurried out into the street.

The little office had stifled him, and the conversation with Rzecki, in which the clerk warned him and commented, seemed perfectly fatuous: for was it not fatuous that a frigid old bachelor, who believed in nothing but the shop and the Bonapartes, should accuse him of madness? 'Am I wrong, then,' Wokulski thought, 'in loving her? Perhaps it has come a little too late, but I have never allowed myself such a luxury in my life. Millions of other people fall in love, the whole sensate world loves, why should I alone be forbidden this? And if this is justified, then surely so is everything I do. Any man who wants to marry must have a fortune, so I have acquired one. A man must draw close to the woman he has chosen; I have done so. He must be concerned for her material well-being, and protect her from enemies; I am doing both. Have I harmed anyone in this fight for happiness? Have I neglected my duties to society or my neighbours? Those well-beloved neighbours of mine are also society – which has never concerned itself with me, but has put up all sorts of obstacles, and keeps demanding sacrifices from me . . .

'But it is precisely what they call 'madness' that makes me carry out these otherwise imaginary duties. Were it not for this, I'd be wrapped up in my books like a worm, and several hundred people would have less income. So what do they expect of me?'

Walking in the open air calmed him; he reached Aleje Jerozolimskie and turned towards the Vistula. The brisk east wind enveloped him and aroused certain indefinable feelings reminiscent of childhood. Walking along Nowy Świat he felt he was a child again, and could feel the surging pulse of youthful blood. He smiled to see a sand-carter and his load weighing down a wretched nag and its long cart, while a spectre begging seemed to him a very pleasant old lady. He enjoyed the whistle of a factory, and would have liked to talk to a crowd of delightful little boys who were throwing stones at passing Jews from a roadside hill.

He stubbornly pushed away any thoughts of the letter and tomorrow's visit to the Łęckis; he wanted to stay level-headed, yet his passion overwhelmed him: 'Why have they invited me?' he wondered, feeling a slight inward uneasiness. 'Izabela wants to get to know me better . . . But surely what they are doing is making it clear that I may marry her! They would be blind or idiots if they hadn't noticed what my feelings are towards her.'

He began to shiver so that his teeth chattered: but then common sense stirred within him: 'Just a moment, pray! It's a long way from one dinner-party and one visit to a close acquaintance. After all, less than one close acquaintance in a thousand leads to a proposal of marriage: and less than one proposal in ten is accepted, and of these only half end in marriage. A man would therefore have to be an out-and-out lunatic to think, even during close acquaintance with a woman, of marriage, when there is only one chance in twenty thousand of it coming off. Is that clear, or not?'

Wokulski had to admit it was. If every acquaintance led to marriage, then every woman would have some dozen husbands, every man some dozen wives, priests would not be able to handle the ceremonies, and the whole world would become a lunatic asylum. Whereas he, Wokulski, was still not even a close friend of Miss Łęcka, but was only on the threshold of making her acquaintance.

'So what have I gained,' he wondered, 'from the risks I took in Bulgaria, at the races here or in the duel?'

'You have acquired a better opportunity,' common sense told him. 'A year ago you had perhaps one-hundred-millionth or one-twenty-millionth chance that she would marry you, and within a year you may have a one-twenty-thousandth chance . . .'

'Within a year?' Wokulski echoed, and again a sort of severe chill struck him. He cast it aside, however, and asked: 'Suppose Izabela falls in love with me – or has already done so?'

'First, you must find out whether Izabela is capable of loving anyone . . .'

'Is she not a woman?'

'There are women with moral defects who are incapable of loving anyone or anything except their own fleeting caprices, just as there are such men; it is a defect like deafness, blindness or paralysis, only less obvious.'

'Let us suppose . . .'

'Very well,' the voice went on, reminding Wokulski of the sarcastic advice Dr Szuman had given him, 'if this woman is capable of loving anyone, the second question arises – will she fall in love with you?'

'I'm not repulsive, after all . . .'

'On the contrary, you may be, just as the most superb of lions is repulsive to a cow, or an eagle to a goose. You see, I am even complimenting you by comparing you to a lion or eagle, which – despite all their good qualities – nevertheless arouse horror in the females of other species. So you should avoid females of a species different from yourself.'

Wokulski came to and looked around. He was now not far from the Vistula, near some wooden barns, and passing carts were bespattering him with black dust. He turned back quickly towards town, and began considering: 'There are two men in me,' he thought, 'one quite sensible, the other a lunatic. But I am not concerned with that any longer . . . What shall I do, though, if the sensible man wins? What a terrible thing it would be to possess a great fund of emotion, yet be unable to lay it at the feet of a female of another species: a cow, a goose, or something even worse! How humiliating it would be to smile at the triumph of a bull or goose, yet at the same time to have to weep because one's own heart is torn to shreds, shamefully trampled underfoot . . . Would life be worth living under such conditions?'

Wokulski felt a longing for death at the mere thought – but a death so oblivious that even his ashes would not remain on this earth. Gradually he calmed down, however, and on returning home began to consider quite coolly whether to wear a frock-coat or a tail-coat for the next day's dinner-party. Would some unforeseen obstacle occur to prevent him yet again from drawing closer to Izabela? Then he completed his accounts of the latest commercial transaction, sent a few telegrams to Moscow and St Petersburg, and wrote a letter to old Szlangbaum, suggesting he should use his name for acquiring the Łęcki property.

'The lawyer was right,' he thought, 'it would be better to buy the house in someone else's name. Otherwise they may suspect me of wanting to take advantage of them or – still worse – think I mean to do them a favour.'

However, a storm was brewing within him behind the façade of these trivial duties. Common sense shouted aloud that tomorrow's dinner-party meant nothing, and prophesied nothing. Yet hope whispered softly, very softly, that – perhaps he was loved, or might be . . . But so softly, that Wokulski had to listen to its whisper with the utmost attention.

The next day, so significant to Wokulski, was not marked by anything unusual either in Warsaw or in Nature. Here and there in the streets, dust was stirred up by door-keepers' brooms; droshkies rushed wildly along or stopped for no particular reason, and an endless stream of passers-by moved this way and that, merely to get in the way of the traffic. Sometimes ragged people shuffled along under walls, stooping, hands hidden in their sleeves as if it was not June, but January. Sometimes a peasant cart rolled by in the street, loaded with rubbish, driven by a bold-faced old lady in a blue coat and red kerchief.

The throngs passed between two long walls of variegated coloured houses, over which loomed the high façades of churches. Two monuments stood at either end of the street, watching over the city like sentries. At one end was King Zygmunt, standing on what looked like an enormous candle, inclined towards the Bernadine church as if he wanted to communicate something to the passers-by. At the other end, Copernicus, holding a motionless globe in one hand, turned his back on the sun which rose every day behind the Karas Palace, ascended over the Society of Friends of Art and went down behind the Zamoyski Palace, as much as to contradict the saying: 'He stopped the sun – and made the earth rotate.'

Wokulski, who was looking in that direction from his balcony, sighed involuntarily, remembering that the astronomer's only friends had been porters and sawyers, not distinguished (as we know) by any precise knowledge of Copernicus's services to mankind. 'Much good it did him,' he thought, 'to be called the "pride of the nation" in a few books . . . I can understand working for happiness, but working for a fiction calling itself society, or fame – no, I wouldn't undertake that. Let society think of itself, as for fame . . . What prevents me from thinking I may be famous on Syrius, say? Yet Copernicus is in no better position today regarding the earth, and is about as much concerned with statues in Warsaw as I am with pyramids on Vega. I'd gladly give three centuries of fame for a brief period of happiness, and am surprised I was ever so stupid as to think otherwise . . .'

As if in response to this, he noticed Ochocki on the opposite side of the street, head bowed, hands in pockets, walking slowly along. This plain coincidence startled Wokulski. For a moment he even believed in premonitions, and thought in joyful amazement: 'Does not this mean that he will have the fame of Copernicus – and I happiness? Go, build your flying-machines, but let me have your cousin! Yet – what superstition is this?' he reflected after a moment, 'I – and superstition!'

All the same he was much pleased by the notion that Ochocki might have immortal fame while he himself possessed the living Izabela. He felt encouraged. He could not help laughing at himself, but felt calmer and encouraged nevertheless.

'Let us suppose,' he thought, 'that despite all my efforts – she rejects me. Well, then? Upon my word, I'll take a mistress at once, and sit with her in a box next to the Łęckis. The worthy Mrs Meliton and perhaps . . . Maruszewicz – will find me a woman

with looks like hers: even that can be found for a few thousand
roubles. I'll dress her up in lace from head to foot, I'll lavish jewels
upon her – then we'll see whether Izabela doesn't pale beside her.
Let her marry the marshal or Baron if need be . . .'

But the thought of Izabela's marriage overcame him with rage
and despair. At this moment he would gladly have packed the earth
with dynamite and blown it sky-high.

But he came to his senses yet again: 'Well, what should I do if it
pleased her to marry? Or even if it pleased her to take lovers – my
clerk, some officer or other, a waggoner or footman . . . What
could I do about it?'

Respect for the personality and individuality of other people was
so great in him, that even his madness yielded before it. 'What
should I do? What?' he repeated, clutching his fevered brow with
both hands.

He called at the store for an hour, did some business, then went
home: at four o'clock the valet produced linen from a wardrobe,
and a barber came to shave and trim his hair for him. 'Well, what's
the news, Mr Fitulski?' he asked the barber.

'Nothing, and it will get worse. The Berlin congress is thinking
of suppressing Europe, Bismarck hopes to suppress the congress,
and the Jews hope to skin us alive . . .' said the young artist, who
was handsome as a seraphim and as neat as if he had just stepped
out of a fashion-plate.

He tied a towel around Wokulski's neck, and as he soaped his
chin with lightning rapidity, went on: 'The town, sir, is pretty
quiet just now. I was at a party in Saska Kepa last night, but oh my!
what common young people they were, sir. They got to fighting
while we were dancing, and just think . . . Head a trifle higher, *s'il
vous plaît* . . .'

Wokulski raised his head and noticed that his barber had gold
links in his very grubby cuffs.

'Fighting, sir, while we were dancing,' the dandy went on,
flashing a razor before Wokulski's eyes, 'and just think, one of
them struck a lady as he was trying to kick someone else – just to
show off! There was a hullaballoo, a duel . . . I was naturally
chosen as second, but I really was in a fix today, only having the
one pistol, when half an hour ago up comes the offender and said it
would be stupid to fight, and that he might yield for once, seeing as
how . . . Head a trifle to the right, *s'il vous plaît* . . . Well, and
would you believe it, sir, I was so vexed I took him by the scruff of
the neck, put my knee to his posterior and – off with him through
the door. A genuine gent wouldn't fight such a booby, sir, now
would he? Face to the left, *s'il vous plaît* . . .'

He finished the shave, washed Wokulski's face and, wrapping
him up in a cloth like a criminal's shroud, went on: 'Fancy that

now, but I never yet saw a trace of a lady in your house, sir, though I come at all times of day . . .' He took out a brush and comb, and began combing his hair for him: 'All times of day, sir, and I've an eye for such things, sir, I do assure you. But never a sight of a skirt, not to mention bloomers or a scrap of ribbon. Yet there was a time when I saw a pair of stays – in a Canon's house, it was! True, he found them in the street and was going to post them (anonymously) to the newspaper. But, my dear sir, at the officer's quarters, especially them hussars . . . (Head a fraction lower, *s'il vous plaît* . . .) Oodles of them! At one officer's I met four young ladies, laughing their heads off, too. From then on I always bow to him in the street, mark my words, though he dropped me and still owes five roubles. But if I can afford six roubles a seat at the Rubinstein concert, then I'm not going to begrudge five roubles to such a virtuoso, now am I? Should I darken the hair a trifle, *je suppose que oui?*'

'No, thanks,' Wokulski replied.

'I thought not,' the barber sighed, 'there isn't a scrap of affectation about you, sir – but that's bad! I know several ballet girls who'd be delighted to enter relations with you, sir. It would be worthwhile, upon my word! Splendidly built, muscles like iron, bosoms like spring mattresses, ever so graceful and not at all stuck-up, particularly when they're still young. For the older a woman is, the more expensive she'll be, no doubt that's why no one wants an old thing of sixty, she'll be too expensive. She'd make Rothschild go bankrupt! But you can give a beginner three thousand roubles a year, some little presents, and she'll be faithful to you . . . Ah, the ladies, God bless 'em . . . They gave me the sciatica, but I can't be cross with 'em . . .'

He finished his task, bowed according to the rules of etiquette and left, smiling; from his splendid appearance and the bag in which he carried his brushes and razors, you'd have taken him for an official from the Ministry.

After he had gone, Wokulski did not even think twice of the young and undemanding ballet girls. He was preoccupied by a very profound question, which could be paraphrased in two words: to wit, frock-coat or tail-coat? 'If I wear a tail-coat I'll look like a snob conforming to the conventions, which in the end do not bother me. But if I wear the frock-coat, I may offend the Łęckis. Besides, suppose someone else is present? Well, there's no help for it – as I have my own carriage and race-horse, I must wear the tail-coat.'

Meditating thus, he could not help smiling at the depths of naivety into which his acquaintance with Izabela had thrust him: 'Would old Hopfer or any of my university and Siberian friends ever imagine me worrying about such matters?' he thought.

He put on his evening clothes, stood at the mirror and felt gratified. The close-fitting garments revealed his athletic frame to the best advantage.

The horses had been waiting fifteen minutes, and it was already five-thirty. Wokulski put on a light top-coat and left the house. As he climbed into the carriage he was very pale but calm, like a man going out to encounter danger face to face.

XVI

'She', 'He' and the Others

ON THE DAY Wokulski was expected to dinner, Izabela came home from the Countess's at five. She was somewhat vexed and very languid and altogether perfectly lovely.

This day had brought her good fortune and disappointment. The great Italian tragedian, Rossi, whom she and her aunt had known in Paris, was in Warsaw for some performances. He called on the Countess at once, and asked anxiously about Izabela. He was to call again, and the Countess invited her niece. However, Rossi did not come; instead, he sent a letter to apologise for the disappointment and to excuse himself because of an unexpected visit from a high-ranking personage.

In Paris some years ago Rossi had been Izabela's ideal; she fell in love with him, and did not even conceal her feelings – as far as possible for a young lady of her social standing, of course. The celebrated actor knew this, called at the Countess's home every day, performed and recited everything Izabela asked for, and when he left for America, presented her with an Italian version of *Romeo and Juliet*, with a dedication: 'Heaven is here where Juliet lives . . .'

The news that Rossi had come to Warsaw and had not forgotten her excited Izabela. By one o'clock that afternoon, she was with her aunt. Every now and again she went to the window, every rattle hastened the beating of her heart, she jumped every time the bell rang: she forgot what she was talking about, bright blushes appeared on her face . . . But Rossi did not come.

And today she was beautiful. She had dressed especially for him, in a silk dress of cream colour (from a distance it looked like crushed linen), she had diamond earrings (no bigger than pea-seeds) and a red rose at her throat. And nothing came of it. But let Rossi be the one to regret not coming . . .

After waiting four hours she came home offended. Despite her fury, she picked up the copy of *Romeo and Juliet*, looked through it, and thought: 'Suppose Rossi were suddenly to come here . . . It would be even better here than at the Countess's.' With no witnesses present, he could whisper feverish phrases to her; he would learn how she treasured his souvenir, and above all would find (as the looking-glass so clearly declared) that in this dress, with this rose, and seated in this gleaming blue armchair, she looked heavenly.

She recalled that Wokulski was coming to dinner, and shrugged involuntarily. The haberdashery tradesman seemed so ludicrous in comparison with Rossi, whom the whole world admired, that she was quite simply overcome with pity for him. Had Wokulski been on his knees to her at this moment, she might even have stroked his hair, played with him as she would with a big dog, and read Romeo's complaint to Lawrence:

> 'Heav'n is here
> Where Juliet lives; and every cat and dog
> And little mouse, every unworthy thing,
> Live here in Heaven and may look on her;
> But Romeo may not: more validity.
> More honourable state, more courtship lives
> In carrion flies than Romeo: they may seize
> On the white wonder of dear Juliet's hand,
> And steal immortal blessing from her lips:
> . . . Flies may do this, but I from this must fly;
> They are free men, but I am banished.
> . . . O friar! the damned use that word in hell;
> Howlings attend it; how hast thou the heart,
> Being a divine, a ghostly confessor,
> A sin-absolver, and my friend professed,
> To mangle me with that word "banished"?'

She sighed: – who knows how often the celebrated exile had thought of her while saying these lines? Perhaps he did not even have a confidant. Wokulski might be such a confidant; surely he knew how to yearn for her, since he had risked his life for her sake.

Turning a few pages back, she read:

> 'O Romeo, Romeo, wherefore art thou Romeo?
> Deny thy father and refuse thy name;
> Or, if thou wilt not, be but sworn my love
> And I'll no longer be a Capulet. . .
> 'Tis but thy name that is my enemy;
> Thou art thyself though, not a Montague.
> . . . What's in a name? that which we call a rose
> By any other name would smell as sweet;
> So Romeo would, were he not Romeo call'd,
> Retain that dear perfection which he owes

Without that title. Romeo, doff thy name;
And for thy name, which is no part of thee,
Take all myself.'

What a strange likeness there was between the two of them – Rossi
the actor, and she, Miss Łęcka. Refuse thy name . . . Yes, but what
would be left? Yet even a princess might marry Rossi, and the world
would only admire her sacrifice. To marry Rossi . . . to look after his
theatrical wardrobe, perhaps sew buttons on his night-shirts? Izabela
was taken aback. To love him hopelessly – that sufficed. To love him
and sometimes talk to someone about this tragic love . . . Perhaps to
Flora? No, she hadn't enough feeling. Much better talk to Wokulski.
He would look into her eyes, would suffer both for himself and for
her, she would tell him and mourn over her own and his sufferings,
and in this manner the hours would pass very agreeably. A haberdasher for a confidant! One could forget his trade, of course . . .

Simultaneously, Tomasz was twirling his grey whiskers and
walking about in his study, thinking: 'Wokulski's a very clever and
energetic fellow. If I'd had such a right-hand man (he sighed) I
should not have lost my fortune. But it can't be helped, and I have
him today. The sale of the house should leave me with forty – no,
fifty – thousand, perhaps sixty thousand roubles . . . Well, let us not
exaggerate: say fifty thousand, or only forty thousand . . . I'll let
him have it, he will pay me some eight thousand roubles a year
interest, and the rest (if matters prosper in his hands as I trust), I'll
have him invest the rest of the interest. The sum will double in five
or six years, and in ten may be quadrupled . . . Because money
increases fantastically in commerce. But what am I saying? If
Wokulski is really a businessman of genius, he ought and certainly
will get a hundred per cent. In that case, I'll look him in the eye
and tell him point-blank: 'You can pay others fifteen or twenty per
cent yearly, but not me, for I understand these matters.' And he, of
course, seeing whom he is dealing with, will yield at once and may
even produce an income beyond my wildest dreams . . .'

The bell in the vestibule rang twice. Tomasz retired into the
depths of his study and sat down, taking a volume of economics by
Supinski for the occasion. Mikołaj opened the door and in a
moment Wokulski appeared.

'Ah, how are you?' Tomasz exclaimed, stretching out a hand.
Wokulski bowed low before the white hair of the man he would
have been glad to call 'Father'.

'Sit down, Stanisław. A cigarette? . . . Pray do . . . What's the
latest? I'm just reading Supinski's book – a clever fellow, that! Yes
indeed – nations who do not know how to work and economise
must disappear from the face of the earth . . . Economy and work,
that's the ticket! All the same, our partners are beginning to look
sour, you know.'

'Let them do as they choose,' Wokulski replied, 'I am not profiting by a single rouble of theirs.'

'I shall never desert you, Stanisław,' said Tomasz, in a firm tone, adding after a moment: 'I am selling or at least having my house sold in a few days. I've had a great deal of trouble with it; the tenants don't pay their rent, the caretakers are rascals, and I had to satisfy the mortgagees out of my own pocket. It's not surprising that in the end it grew tedious.'

'Of course not,' Wokulski interposed.

'And I hope,' Tomasz went on, 'that fifty or at least forty thousand roubles will be left to me.'

'How much do you hope to get for the house?'

'Oh, a hundred, or up to a hundred and twenty thousand. And I'll place whatever I get in your hands, Mr Stanisław.'

Wokulski nodded in agreement, and thought that all the same Tomasz was not going to get more than ninety thousand for his house. This was the amount he had at his disposal just then and he could not incur debts without damaging his credit.

'And I will place it all in your hands, Stanisław,' Mr Łęcki went on, 'I merely wanted to inquire if you will accept?'

'Certainly . . .'

'And what interest will you give me?'

'I can guarantee twenty, and more if business picks up,' Wokulski replied, adding privately that he would not have been able to pay anyone else more than fifteen.

'A sharp fellow, this,' Tomasz thought, 'he himself gets a hundred per cent, but only pays me twenty . . .' However, he went on aloud: 'Very well, my dear Stanisław. I accept twenty per cent, providing you pay it in advance.'

'I'll pay in advance – every six months,' Wokulski replied, fearing Łęcki would spend the money too fast.

'Very good,' said Tomasz very affably, adding with some emphasis, 'But all the profits above twenty per cent – please do not pay them to me, not even if I beg you to . . . d'you understand me? Add it to the capital. Let it grow, isn't that the idea?'

'The ladies are waiting,' said Mikołaj, appearing at this moment in the study door. Mr Tomasz rose gravely from his armchair and ceremoniously conducted his guest into the drawing-room.

Later on, Wokulski tried several times to remember that drawing-room and the manner in which he had entered it; but he could not recollect all the details. He remembered bowing several times to Tomasz on the threshold, and that later he was engulfed in an agreeable perfume, as a result of which he bowed to a lady in a cream-coloured gown with a red rose at her throat, then to another lady, tall and dressed in black, who eyed him in alarm. At least, so it seemed to him.

Not for a while did he realise that the lady in the cream-coloured dress was Izabela. She was seated in an armchair and, turning with incomparable charm to him and looking kindly into his eyes, said: 'My father will have to have a good deal of practice before he will satisfy you as a partner. I ask for your tolerance on his behalf.' She stretched out one hand, which Wokulski scarcely dared touch.

'As a partner,' he replied, 'Mr Łęcki need only have a trustworthy lawyer and book-keeper, who will check his account from time to time. The rest is our business.' It struck him he had said something very stupid, and flushed.

'You must have a great deal to do in such a large store.' said Flora in her black dress, and she became still more agitated.

'Not really. My business is to provide the capital, and make contact with suppliers and purchasers. But the kinds of goods and the pricing are done by the shop staff.'

'But is it possible to rely on other people?' Miss Flora sighed.

'Yes, I have an excellent manager who is also a friend, and who looks after the business better than I could.'

'You are fortunate, Stanisław,' Mr Łęcki exclaimed, catching the phrase, 'and are you not going abroad this year?'

'I should like to go to the Paris Exhibition . . .'

'Oh, I envy you,' Izabela cried, 'I have thought of nothing but the Exhibition for the past two months, but somehow papa doesn't show any desire to go.'

'Our trip depends entirely on Mr Wokulski,' her father replied, 'so I advise you to invite him to dinner as often as possible and serve delicious food to put him in a good humour.'

'I promise that whenever you favour us, I'll peep into the kitchen myself. Will good intentions suffice this time?'

'I am most grateful for your offer,' Wokulski replied, 'but that cannot affect the date of the departure of you both for Paris, because that depends entirely on your wishes.'

'*Merci*,' Izabela whispered.

Wokulski bowed his head: 'I know that "*Merci*" of hers,' he thought, 'it has to be paid for in bullets . . .'

'Shall we go in?' Flora murmured. They went into the dining room, where a round table set for four stood in the centre. Wokulski found himself between Izabela and her father, facing Flora. He was already perfectly calm, so calm that he was uneasy. His madness of love had left him, and he even asked himself if this was the woman he loved? For was it possible to love as he did, and yet feel such tranquillity in his soul, such extreme tranquillity, when sitting only a pace away from the cause of his madness? His thoughts were so free that he not only saw every expression on the countenances of his companions but (which was really rather amusing), he looked at Izabela and made the following calculations:

'That dress – fifteen yards of silk at a rouble: fifteen roubles . . . Lace at ten roubles, and work fifteen or so . . . Forty roubles altogether for the dress, about a hundred and fifty for the necklace, and the rose – ten groszy.'

Mikołaj began serving. Though not in the least hungry, Wokulski ate some spoonfuls of consommé, drank port-wine, then tried the sirloin and drank beer with it. He smiled without knowing why and, in an onset of boyish audacity, decided to commit some *faux-pas* at table.

First he placed his knife and fork on a small stand by his plate after tasting the sirloin. Miss Flora very nearly winced, but Tomasz began talking very vivaciously about an evening at the Tuileries, where he had danced a minuet with some marshal's wife at the request of the Empress Eugenie.

A dish of pike was served next, and Wokulski attacked it with his knife and fork. Flora very nearly swooned, Izabela glanced at her neighbour with indulgence, while Tomasz began eating the fish with his knife and fork too.

'How stupid you all are,' Wokulski thought, feeling something not unlike contempt for his companions awakening within him. To make matters worse, Izabela exclaimed (though without even a trace of malice): 'Papa, you must show me how to eat fish with a knife one of these days.'

This struck Wokulski as simply vulgar: 'I see I shall fall out of love with her before dinner is over,' he told himself.

'My dear,' said Tomasz to his daughter, 'not eating fish with one's knife is merely a convention. Isn't that so, Mr Wokulski?'

'A convention? I couldn't say,' Wokulski replied, 'it is merely the transference of a custom from conditions which it suits to conditions where it does not.'

Tomasz actually fidgeted in his seat. 'The English regard it as almost an insult,' Flora declared.

'But the English have sea-fish, which can only be eaten with a fork: they would eat our bony fresh-water fish in another manner . . .'

'Oh, the English never go against conventions,' Flora said defensively.

'That is so,' Wokulski agreed, 'they do not under ordinary circumstances, but in less usual ones they adopt the rules, "do what is most convenient". I myself have seen very distinguished peers eating mutton and rice with their fingers, and taking soup from basins.'

The lesson struck home. Nevertheless, Tomasz heard it with satisfaction, and Izabela with something bordering on surprise. This merchant, who had eaten mutton with peers and clung so boldly to his theory of using a knife for fish had gained stature in her imagination. Who knows but this theory did not seem of more importance to her than the duel with Krzeszowski?

'So you are an enemy of etiquette?' she inquired.

'No, but I do not want to be its slave.'

'Yet there are societies in which it is always observed.'

'I can't say. But I have seen the highest society where – under certain circumstances – it has been forgotten.'

Tomasz bowed his head slightly; Flora had turned blue in the face; Izabela looked almost cordially at Wokulski. Even more than 'almost' . . . There were moments in which she dreamed of Wokulski as some sort of Haroun al Raschid, disguised as a merchant. Admiration, even liking, awoke in her heart. This man might certainly be her confidant; she would be able to talk to him about Rossi.

After the ice-cream, Flora remained in the dining-room, entirely flabbergasted, but the others went into the master's study for coffee. Just as Wokulski had finished, Mikołaj brought Tomasz a letter on a tray, saying: 'They are waiting for an answer, sir.'

'Ah, from the Countess . . .' said Tomasz, glancing at the superscription, 'will you excuse me?'

'We might go into the drawing-room,' Izabela interposed, smiling at Wokulski, 'and in the meantime my father will write a reply.' She knew Tomasz had written that letter to himself, for he simply had to have a half-hour nap after dinner.

'You forgive me?' asked Tomasz, pressing Wokulski's hand.

Wokulski left the study with Izabela, and they went into the drawing-room. She sat down in an armchair with her own inimitable grace, indicating another only a few feet away to him. When Wokulski found himself alone with her, the blood surged to his head. His emotion intensified when he saw that Izabela was looking at him in a strange way, as if she sought to penetrate to his depths and chain him to her. This was no longer the Izabela of the Easter ceremonies nor even of the races; this was an intelligent and feeling being, who was about to ask him seriously about something, and wanted to speak frankly.

Wokulski was so curious about what she was going to tell him and had lost so much control over himself, that he would certainly have killed anyone who interrupted them at this moment. He looked at Izabela in silence, and waited.

Izabela was confused; for a long time she had not experienced such chaotic feelings as now. Phrases ran through her mind: 'He bought the dinner service . . . He deliberately lost at cards to my father . . . He insulted me . . .' and then 'He loves me . . . He bought the race-horse . . . He had a duel . . . He has eaten mutton with peers of the realm . . .' Contempt, anger, admiration, liking – all created a turmoil in her soul, like drops of heavy rain: at the heart of this storm, however, there was the need for confiding her daily cares and her various doubts and her tragic love for the great actor to somebody else.

'Yes, he could be – he will be – my confidant,' thought Izabela, plunging a sweet look into Wokulski's startled eyes and leaning forward slightly as if to kiss him on the brow. Then she was seized by irrational shame; she retreated into the depths of her armchair, blushed and slowly let her eyelashes sink, as if sleep were coming upon her. Watching the play of her features, Wokulski was reminded of the miraculous waves of a northern dawn, and of those strange melodies without words or music which sometimes resound in the human soul like echoes from a better world. Dreaming, he listened to the feverish tick of the grandfather clock and to the throbbing of his own pulses, and was surprised that two such rapid phenomena nevertheless dragged in comparison with the speed of his own thoughts.

'If there is such a place as Heaven,' he told himself, 'then even the blessed cannot know greater happiness than I do at this moment.'

The silence persisted so long that it began to be improper. Izabela came to herself first: 'You had a misunderstanding,' she said, 'with Baron Krzeszowski?'

'About the races,' Wokulski said hastily, 'the Baron could not forgive me for buying his mare.'

She looked at him for a moment with a kindly smile: 'After that, you had a duel which . . . made us very anxious,' she added more softly, 'and then the Baron apologised to me,' she concluded quickly, looking away. 'In the letter he wrote me on that occasion, the Baron spoke of you with great respect and friendship . . .'

'I am very . . . very gratified . . .' Wokulski stammered.

'Why so, pray?'

'That the circumstances should work out in such a manner . . . The Baron is a distinguished person.'

Izabela stretched out one hand and placed it for an instant in Wokulski's feverish palm: 'Despite the Baron's unquestioned virtues, it is you alone I have to thank . . . Thank you . . . There are services which are not soon forgotten, and in truth,' (here she began speaking more slowly and softly), 'in truth, you would relieve my conscience by asking me for something that might compensate for your . . . civility.'

Wokulski let her hand go and straightened his back. He was so confused that he did not pay attention to the word 'civility'.

'Very well,' he replied, 'if you so wish, I'll admit even to . . . services. But might I in return, make a request of you?'

'Yes . . .'

'Well, then,' he said in a state of fever, 'I ask for one thing – to serve you as long as my strength permits. Always, in everything . . .'

'Oh come,' Izabela interrupted, with a laugh, 'that really is a stratagem. I want to repay one favour, you want to make me incur others. Is that right?'

'What is wrong in it? Do you not, after all, accept services from servants?'

'They are paid for it,' she replied, looking into his eyes playfully.

'So there is one difference only between them and me – they are paid, and it is not proper to pay me. Impossible, even . . .'

Izabela shook her head.

'What I am asking,' Wokulski continued, 'does not exceed the boundaries of the most commonplace human relationships. Ladies always give orders – we carry them out, that's all. People in your social sphere do not even have to ask for favours: they take them as a right. On the other hand, I have fought my way to it, and am now begging you for it, because it would be a sort of distinction for me to carry out your orders. Merciful Heaven! If coachmen and footmen can wear your colours, why should not I deserve that honour?'

'Ah, so that is what you mean? It is not necessary to give you my scarf – you have already taken it by force. But as for taking it back . . . It's too late, even if only on account of the Baron's letter.'

She gave him her hand again, which Wokulski respectfully kissed. Footsteps were heard in the next room, and Tomasz came in, beaming after his nap. His handsome face wore such a cordial expression that Wokulski thought: 'I'd be a scoundrel if your thirty thousand roubles didn't bring you in ten thousand a year, you honest old man.'

They sat together another fifteen minutes, talking of an entertainment for charitable purposes held in the 'Swiss Valley', of Rossi's arrival and of the trip to Paris. Finally Wokulski regretfully left his agreeable companions, promising to come more often and to travel to Paris with them.

'You will see how amusing it is there,' said Izabela in farewell.

XVII

Germination of Certain Crops – and Illusions

IT WAS eight-thirty in the evening when Wokulski returned home. The sun had just set, but a strong eye could already have perceived the larger stars glittering in the blue and gold sky. The merry cries of passers-by were audible in the streets; joyful tranquillity had taken up its abode in Wokulski's heart.

He recalled Izabela's every movement, every smile, every glance and every expression, seeking with anxious concern for a shadow of dislike or pride in them. In vain. She had treated him as an equal and a friend, had invited him to visit them more often, and had even demanded that he ask a favour . . . 'Suppose I had proposed to her at that moment?' he thought, 'then what?' And he attentively considered the image of her features which filled his soul; but again he could perceive no shadow of dislike. Instead – a playful smile. 'She'd have replied,' he thought, 'that we still do not know each other well enough, that I ought to deserve her hand . . . Yes, that is certainly what she would have replied,' he repeated, continually recalling to mind those unmistakable signs of liking.

'On the whole,' he thought, 'I have been unjustly prejudiced against high society. After all, they are men and women like the rest of us: perhaps they have greater sensibility. Knowing that we are boors chasing after profits, they avoid us. But when they discover our honest hearts, they attract us to them . . . What a delicious wife such a woman would make! Of course I ought to deserve her, first. Of course!'

Influenced by these thoughts, he felt a great benevolence awaken within him, encompassing first the Łęcki household, then their relatives, then his own store and all the people who worked in it, then all the tradesmen he had dealings with, finally the entire country and all mankind. It seemed to Wokulski that every passer-by in the street was his blood-relative, nearer or more distant, whether cheerful or mournful. And he very nearly stopped on the pavement to accost people, like a beggar, and to ask them: 'Is there anything you need? Ask me, command me, please – in her name . . .'

'Life has gone badly for me hitherto,' he told himself. 'I was an egoist. Ochocki – now, there is a splendid soul: he wants to fix wings upon mankind, and can forget his own happiness for that idea. Fame is nonsense, of course, but work for the general good – that's the foundation.' Then he added with a smile: 'This woman has already made me a rich man, and a well-known man, but if she persists, she will make me – goodness knows what! Perhaps a holy martyr, who devotes his work, even his life, to the good of others. Of course I'd do that, if she wanted me to.'

His shop was closed, but a light twinkled through an opening in the shutters: 'They're still busy,' Wokulski thought.

He turned into the gate, and entered the shop through the back door. On the threshold he met Zięba, who said goodnight and bowed low; there were still several people inside the shop. Klein was ascending a ladder to straighten something on the shelves; Lisiecki was putting on his overcoat, and behind the cash-desk was Rzecki, with a ledger in front of him, and a man, weeping, standing before him.

'The boss!' Lisiecki exclaimed. Shading his eyes with one hand, Rzecki glanced up at Wokulski; Klein bowed to him several times from the top of the ladder, while the weeping man suddenly turned around and sank at his feet with a loud groan.

'What's this?' Wokulski asked in surprise, recognising the old cashier Oberman.

'He has lost over four hundred roubles,' Rzecki replied sternly, 'of course there was no fraud, I'll take my oath on that, but even so the firm cannot be the loser, particularly as Mr Oberman has several hundred roubles saved with us. So – one of two things,' Rzecki went on crossly, 'either Mr Oberman pays up, or Mr Oberman loses his position. We'd do good business, indeed, if all our cashiers were like Mr Oberman.'

'I'll repay the money, sir,' said the cashier, sobbing, 'I'll pay it back, but let me spread it over a few years at least. The five hundred roubles I have saved with you is my whole fortune. My boy has finished school and wants to study for a doctor, and old age is just around the corner . . . God knows – and so do you, sir – how a man has to work before he can put by so much money. I'd have to be born again to make as much . . .'

Klein and Lisiecki, both dressed to leave, awaited the verdict of their principal.

'Yes,' Wokulski exclaimed, 'the firm cannot be the loser. Oberman must repay.'

'Very well, sir,' the unhappy cashier murmured.

Messrs Klein and Lisiecki said goodnight and left. Sighing,

Oberman started to go after them. But when the three of them were alone, Wokulski hastily added: 'Oberman, repay the money and I'll refund it to you . . .'

The cashier sank at his feet. 'Come, come,' Wokulski interrupted, 'if you say a single word to anyone about this arrangement, I shall take my gift back – mind that, Oberman? . . . Otherwise they'll all decide to lose us some money. So go home and say nothing . . .'

'I understand, sir. May God send you the very best of everything,' the cashier replied and went out, trying in vain to conceal his joy.

'He already has,' Wokulski said, thinking of Izabela.

Rzecki was not pleased: 'You know, Staś,' he exclaimed, when they were alone, 'you would do better not to interfere in the running of the shop. I knew in advance you would not make him repay the whole amount, I wouldn't have asked that myself. But the booby ought to have paid a hundred roubles or so, as punishment . . . In the end, the devil take it, he might have been forgiven the whole amount; but he should have been kept in suspense at least a few weeks . . . Otherwise we might as well shut up shop once and for all.'

Wokulski laughed: 'I'd be afraid of the anger of Heaven,' he replied, 'had I done anyone an injustice on a day like this.'

'A day like what?' Rzecki asked, opening his eyes widely.

'Never mind – only today do I see how necessary it is to be merciful.'

'You always were, and too much so,' Ignacy said irritably, 'and you'll find out that other people will not be the same towards you.'

'They already are,' Wokulski said, and gave him his hand in farewell.

'They already are?' Ignacy repeated, mimicking him, 'they already are? I hope you never have to put their sympathy to the test, that's all.'

'I have it without that. Goodnight.'

'Hm! We'll see how it looks if the need arises. Goodnight, goodnight . . .' said the old clerk, noisily putting his ledgers away.

Wokulski walked home and thought: 'I really must pay a call on Krzeszowski. I'll go tomorrow . . . He apologised to Izabela like the decent fellow he is. Tomorrow I'll thank him and – may the devil take me if I don't try to help him. Though it will be difficult to do anything for such an idle and frivolous fellow. Never mind, I can only try . . . He has apologised to Izabela, I'll free him from his debts.'

Feelings of tranquillity and unshakeable certainty so dominated all others in Wokulski's soul just now that when he got home, instead of dreaming (as usually happened), he set to work. He brought out a thick exercise-book, already nearly full, then a book with Polish–English exercises, and began writing down sentences, pronouncing them in an undertone and trying to imitate his teacher, Mr William Collins, as closely as possible.

But during pauses of several minutes, he thought either of tomorrow's visit to Baron Krzeszowski and how to free him from his debts, or of Oberman, whom he had saved from ruin. 'If a blessing is of any value,' he told himself, 'then I cede to her the whole capital of Oberman's, together with added interest . . .'

Then it occurred to him that this was not a very splendid gift for Izabela – making only one man happy! He could not do it for the whole world: but it would be worth elevating at least a few people in order to celebrate getting to know Izabela better. 'Krzeszowski will be the second,' he thought, 'though it is no service to save such fellows. Aha!' He struck his forehead and, putting aside his English exercises, brought out the file of his private correspondence. This was a morocco case, in which incoming letters were filed according to date, with an index in the front.

'Aha!' he said, 'the letter of my penitent and her guardian . . . page 603 . . .'

He found the page and read the two letters attentively: one was elegantly written, the other as if scrawled by a childish hand. The first informed him that Maria So-and-So, formerly a girl of loose conduct, was now learning to sew and make dresses, and was behaving piously, obediently, modestly and nicely. In the second letter, Maria herself . . . thanked him for his help and asked only to be found some occupation:

'Dear and Respected Sir,' she wrote, 'since God has given you so much money, do not spend it on a sinner like me. For now I can earn my own living, if I find something to set my hands to, but there are many people in Warsaw whose need is greater than mine, unhappy and disgraced though I am . . .'

Wokulski was sorry this request had been unanswered for several days. He replied at once and called the servant. 'Have this letter delivered in the morning,' he said, 'at the Magdalenes.'

'Very good, sir,' the servant replied, trying to stifle a yawn.

'And bring the carter Wysocki to me, the man in Tamka Street, d'you know him?'

'Course I do . . . But have you heard, sir . . . ?'

'Be sure he comes in the morning, that's all.'

'Why shouldn't I, sir? But have you heard Oberman lost a lot of money? He was here this evening, he swore he would kill himself or do himself an injury if you didn't forgive him. So I said to him, "Don't be silly," I said, "don't kill yourself, wait a bit . . . the old man's got a soft heart." And he says, "That's what I thought, but even so there will be a row, and even if he cuts my wages, my son is going to be a doctor, and old age is just around the corner . . ."'

'Come now, be off to bed with you,' Wokulski interrupted.

'All right, sir, all right,' the servant replied, crossly, 'though working for the likes of you is worse than being in prison, that it is . . . A man can't even go to bed when he chooses . . .' He took the letter and went out.

Next day, about nine in the morning, the servant awoke Wokulski and told him Wysocki was waiting. 'Tell him to come in.'

The carter entered next moment. He was respectably dressed, had a ruddy complexion and cheerful look. He approached the bed and kissed Wokulski's hand.

'Wysocki, I understand there's a room vacant in your house?'

'Indeed there is, sir, for my uncle has died and those beasts of tenants wouldn't pay the rent so I turned 'em out. The scoundrels could always find money for vodka, but never for the rent . . .'

'I'll rent the room from you,' said Wokulski, 'but you must clean it out first.'

The carter looked at Wokulski in surprise.

'A young seamstress will be living there,' Wokulski continued, 'she can board with you, your wife can launder for her . . . Let her see what more she'll need. I'll give you money for furniture and linen . . . Then you must watch to see she doesn't bring anyone into the house . . .'

'Not likely,' the carter exclaimed excitedly, 'whenever you need her, sir, I'll bring her . . . but that anyone from the town – no, that wouldn't do. In such a business you might get into bad company.'

'You're a fool, Wysocki. I don't mean to see her at all. Let her do as she pleases, provided she is well-behaved, modest and industrious. But don't let anyone visit her. Do you understand? The walls in the room must be painted, wash the floor, buy some cheap furniture – but new and good – you know what I mean.'

'Of course, sir. I've been carting such furniture all my life.'

'Very well. And let your wife ascertain what the girl needs in linen and clothes, then let me know.'

'I understand, sir,' said Wysocki, kissing his hand again.

'But what about your brother? How is he?'

'Not doing so badly, sir. He's back in Skierniewice, thanks be to God and to you, sir; he has his plot of land; he's taken on a farm-hand, and now he's quite the gentleman. In a few years' time he'll buy more land, because he has a railway-guard and two firemen boarding with him. And the railway has even increased his wages.'

Wokulski said goodbye to the carter and began dressing: 'I'd like to be able to sleep through the time until I see her again,' Wokulski thought.

He did not feel like going to the shop. He picked up a book and read, deciding to call on Baron Krzeszowski between one and two. At eleven, the door-bell and the sound of a door opening were heard from the vestibule. The servant came in: 'A lady is waiting . . .'

'Ask her in,' said Wokulski.

A woman's dress rustled in the hall. Wokulski, on the threshold, saw his penitent. The extraordinary changes in her astounded him. The girl was dressed in black, had a pale but healthy complexion and a timid expression. Catching sight of Wokulski, she blushed and began trembling.

'Take a seat please, miss,' he exclaimed, indicating a chair. She sat down on the edge of a velvet chair, still more embarrassed. Her eyelids fluttered rapidly, she gazed at the carpet and drops of tears glittered on her lashes. Two months earlier she had looked very differently.

'So you have learned sewing, miss?'

'Yes.'

'And where do you plan to settle?'

'Maybe in some shop . . . or in service in Russia . . .'

'Why there?'

'Because people say it's easier to get work there, and here . . . who will employ me?' she whispered.

'But would it not pay you to stay here, if some shop were to buy work from you?'

'Oh yes . . . But a girl must have her own sewing-machine, and a place to live, and everything . . . A girl who hasn't got these things must go into service.'

Even her voice had altered. Wokulski eyed her attentively, and finally said: 'You will stay in Warsaw for the time being. You will live with the Wysocki family in Tamka. They are very good people. You will have your own room, you can board with them, and the sewing-machine and everything necessary will be provided too. I'll give you a reference to a store and in a few months' time, we'll see whether you can support yourself by this work. Here is Wysocki's address. Please go there at once, buy some furniture with Mrs Wysocka and make sure they have put the room in order. I'll send you the sewing-machine tomorrow . . . And here is some money for settling in. It's a loan: you can pay me back by instalments when work starts coming in.'

He gave her a few dozen roubles wrapped in a note to Wysocki. When she hesitated to take them, he pressed the twist of paper into her hand and said: 'Please go to Wysocki at once. He'll bring you a letter for the linen shop in a few days. Please call upon me in case of urgent need. Goodbye now . . .'

The girl stayed a little longer in the centre of the hall; then she wiped away her tears and went out, filled with a kind of sublime astonishment.

'We'll see how she gets on in her new surroundings,' Wokulski said to himself, and took to his reading again.

At one o'clock that afternoon, Wokulski set off to call on Baron Krzeszowski, reproaching himself on the way that he had procrastinated so in visiting his former antagonist. 'Never mind,' he consoled himself, 'after all, I could not intrude when he was ill. And I sent in a visiting-card.'

As he approached the house in which the Baron was lodging, Wokulski could not help noticing that the walls of the house were as unhealthily greenish as Maruszewicz was unhealthily yellowish, and that the blinds were up in Krzeszowski's apartment. 'Evidently he has recovered,' he thought, 'all the same, it won't do to ask about his debts right away. I'll mention them on my second or third visit; then I'll pay off the usurers and the poor Baron will be able to breathe again. I cannot be indifferent towards a man who has apologised to Izabela.'

He went up to the second floor, and rang the bell. Steps were audible inside the apartment, but there was evidently no urgency about opening the door. He rang again. The footsteps and even the moving about of objects went on inside, but still no one came. In his impatience, he pulled the door-bell so hard he nearly wrenched it off. Only then did someone come to the door and start unfastening the chain in a phlegmatic manner, then turned the key and pulled back the bolt, muttering: 'One of us, obviously . . . No Jew would ring like that . . .'

Finally the door opened and the footman Konstanty appeared.

Seeing Wokulski, he blinked, thrust out his lower lip and asked: 'Well?' Wokulski guessed he was not in the faithful servant's good books, as the latter had been present at the duel.

'Is the Baron at home?' he asked.

'The Baron's in bed, poorly and is not receiving anyone because the doctor is with him.'

Wokulski produced his card and two roubles: 'When will it be possible, more or less, to call?'

'Not at present, not at all,' Konstanty replied, somewhat more mildly, 'my master is ill of a bullet wound, and the doctors have told him to go to warm countries, or leave town today or tomorrow.'

'So it will not be possible to see him before he goes?'

'Not at all. The doctors have forbidden him to see anyone. He's feverish all the time.'

Two card tables, one with a broken leg and the other with a thickly bescribbled cloth, as well as two candlesticks with the stumps of wax candles, made Wokulski doubt the accuracy of Konstanty's diagnosis. Nevertheless, he added another rouble and left, not at all pleased with his reception: 'Perhaps the Baron simply didn't want me to call? Then let him pay off the usurers himself, and keep them out by chaining, locking and bolting the door . . .'

He went home.

The Baron really intended to leave for the countryside and was not well, though he was not so poorly either. The wound in his cheek was very slow in healing: not because it was serious, but because the Baron's health was very much undermined.

During Wokulski's call, the Baron had been wrapped up like an old woman against the cold, but was not in bed, sitting instead in an armchair while with him, was not the doctor, but Count Liciński. He was just complaining to the Count of his state of health: 'May the devil take this wretched way of life,' he said, 'my father left me nearly half a million roubles, but four diseases too, each worth a million. How inconvenient it is to be without eye-glasses! And just think, Count – the money has all gone but I still have the diseases. And as I have caught a few more diseases myself, and made new debts – the situation is clear. I'd have to send for the notary and for a coffin if I even scratched myself . . .'

'Dear me, yes,' the Count exclaimed, 'though I don't think you should waste money on notaries in such a situation.'

'It's the rent collectors who are really the ruin of me . . .'

The Baron irritably overheard the echoes reaching him from the hall as he talked, but could not make out who it was. Not until he heard the door close, the bolt drawn and the chain put up, did he suddenly bellow: 'Konstanty!'

In a moment the servant entered, though without undue haste. 'Who was that? Goldcygier, I daresay . . . I told you not to have anything to do with that scoundrel, just grab him and throw him downstairs. Just think,' and he turned to Liciński, 'that damned Jew is pestering me with a forged promissory note for four hundred roubles, and has the impudence to demand payment.'

'You should start a law-suit against him, dear me, yes . . .'

'I don't start law-suits. I am not a public prosecutor, it isn't my duty to chase after forgers. In any case, I don't want to take the initiative in ruining some poor wretch who's killing himself with work running down other people's signatures. So I'm waiting for Goldcygier to start an action, and then will declare that it is not my signature, though without accusing anyone.'

'As it happens, it wasn't Goldcygier,' Konstanty remarked.

'Then who was it? The councillor? Or the tailor, I suppose . . .'

'No, it was this person,' said the servant, handing a visiting card to Krzeszowski, 'a respectable person but I sent him away like you said.'

'What!' the Count asked in surprise, glancing at the card, 'didn't you give orders to receive Wokulski?'

'No, I didn't,' the Baron agreed, 'a low person, and certainly not fit for society.'

Count Liciński sat up in his chair rather significantly: 'I never expected to hear such a remark about that gentleman . . . from you. Oh dear me, no . . .'

'Pray don't take what I said as derogatory,' the Baron explained hastily, 'Mr Wokulski has done nothing to be ashamed of, only . . . a minor dirty trick which may pass in trade, but not in society.'

Both the Count in his armchair and Konstanty on the threshold eyed the Baron attentively. 'Judge for yourself,' the Baron went on, 'I yielded up my mare to Baroness Krzeszowska (my legal spouse before God and man) for eight hundred roubles. Madame Krzeszowska – to spite me (I've no idea why!) – decided to sell it. So a purchaser was found in Mr Wokulski who, by taking advantage of a woman's weakness, thought he would make a profit out of the mare – two hundred roubles – as he only gave six hundred for her.'

'He was in the right, dear me, yes,' the Count interposed.

'Well, I suppose so . . . Yes, I know he was. But a man who throws away thousands of roubles just for show, and then makes twenty-five per cent profit in an underhand manner and out of hysterical females – such a man is not behaving with the best of taste. He isn't a gentleman. He committed no crime, but . . . he's as unbalanced in his relations with other people as someone who gives presents of carpets and shawls to his friends, but would take a handkerchief away from a stranger. You can't deny it . . .'

The Count said nothing; not for a while did he exclaim, 'Dear me . . . But are you positive of it?'

'Absolutely. The arrangement between Madame Krzeszowski and that . . . gentleman was made by my Maruszewicz, and I know it from him.'

'Dear me. However that may be, Wokulski is a good tradesman, and is in charge of our partnership.'

'Just as long as he doesn't cheat you . . .'

Konstanty, still on the threshold, had begun to nod his head condescendingly, then impatiently exclaimed: 'Eh! Whatever are you talking about? Pah! You're no better than a little child, to be sure . . .'

The Count glanced at him curiously, and the Baron burst out: 'Why, you fool, who asked your opinion?'

'Why shouldn't I give it, when you chatter and behave like a little child . . . I'm only a footman, but I'd sooner trust a man who gives me two roubles when he calls than one who borrows three and is in no hurry to repay it. That's it – Mr Wokulski gave me two roubles today, but Mr Maruszewicz . . .'

'Be off with you!' the Baron roared, seizing a carafe, at the sight of which Konstanty saw fit to put the thickness of the door between himself and his master.

'That flunkey is a knave,' the Baron added, evidently very vexed.

'Do you have a weakness for this Maruszewicz fellow?' the Count inquired.

'He's an honest young man . . . He's got me out of all kinds of scrapes . . . He's given me ever so many proofs of his dog-like attachment . . .'

'Dear me,' the Count muttered thoughtfully. He stayed a few minutes longer without speaking, then bade the Baron goodbye.

On his way home, Count Liciński's thoughts reverted several times to Wokulski. He considered it quite natural that a tradesman should profit even on a race-horse: at the same time, he felt some distaste for such transactions and was displeased that Wokulski should hobnob with Maruszewicz, a dubious individual to say the least. 'As usual, a newly rich parvenu,' the Count muttered, 'we took to him prematurely, though . . . he may manage the partnership . . . under strict control, of course, by us.'

A few days later, at about nine in the morning, Wokulski received two letters: one from Mrs Meliton, the other from the Prince's lawyer. He opened the first impatiently: in it, Mrs Meliton wrote only these words: 'In the Łazienki park today at the usual time.' He read it several times, then reluctantly took up the lawyer's, which also invited him at eleven in the morning to a conference about the Łęcki house purchase. Wokulski sighed deeply; he had the time.

At eleven prompt, he was in the lawyer's office, where he found old Szlangbaum. He could not help noticing that the grey-haired Jew looked very grave against the background of the brown furniture and tapestry, and that it suited the lawyer, in his brown morocco slippers, very well.

'You are lucky, Mr Wokulski,' Szlangbaum exclaimed, 'no sooner do you want to purchase a house than the price of houses goes up. Upon my word, in six months you will make your deposit on this house, and then some over! And me too . . .'

'You think so?' Wokulski replied carelessly.

'I don't think, I'm making money already,' said the Jew, 'yesterday Baroness Krzeszowska's lawyer borrowed ten thousand roubles from me until New Year, and paid me eight hundred roubles interest in advance.'

'What's that? Is she short of money already?' Wokulski asked the lawyer.

'She has ninety thousand in the bank, but the Baron has frozen it. Fine marriage articles, I must say,' the lawyer smiled, 'the husband freezes money which is indubitably the property of his wife, against whom he is starting an action for separation. It's true

that I never write such marriage articles, ha ha . . .' the lawyer
laughed, puffing smoke from his great amber pipe.

'Why did the Baroness borrow ten thousand from you, Mr
Szlangbaum?' Wokulski asked.

'Don't you know?' the Jew replied, 'houses are going up, and
the lawyer told the Baroness she would not get the Łęcki house for
less than seventy thousand. She'd like to buy it for ten thousand, of
course, but what can she do?'

The lawyer sat down at his desk and said: 'So, my dear Mr
Wokulski, the Łęcki house is to be bought not (he nodded) in my
name but that of (he bowed) Mr S. Szlangbaum.'

'I'll buy it, to be sure,' the Jew murmured.

'But for ninety thousand roubles,' Wokulski interrupted, 'not a
penny less, and by auction,' he added emphatically.

'Why not? It ain't my money! If you want to pay, there will be
others to outbid you . . . If I had as many thousands as there are
respectable Catholic people to be found for the purpose here in
Warsaw, why then, I'd be richer than Rothschild.'

'So your opponents at the sale will be respectable people,' the
lawyer repeated, 'very well. Now I'll give Mr Szlangbaum the
money.'

'No need,' the Jew put in.

'Then we will draw up a nice little document, authorising Mr S.
Szlangbaum to draw ninety thousand on Mr S. Wokulski, and this
will ensure him the newly acquired apartment house. If, however,
Mr Szlangbaum has not repaid the money by 1 January, 1879 . . .'

'And I won't!'

'Then, Mr Łęcki's apartment house, purchased by him, will
become the property of Mr S. Wokulski.'

'It could do so now . . . I won't even look at it,' the Jew replied
with a gesture.

'Excellent,' the lawyer exclaimed, 'we'll have the document by
tomorrow and the house within a week or ten days. I hope to
goodness you don't lose a few thousand on it, my dear Stanisław.'

'I shall profit,' Wokulski replied, and bade goodbye to the lawyer
and Szlangbaum.

'But . . . but . . .' the lawyer exclaimed, as he accompanied
Wokulski out, 'our Counts are forming a partnership, except that
they are decreasing their contributions and demanding a very
detailed account of the transaction.'

'They are quite right.'

'Count Liciński is proving particularly shrewd. I can't think what
has come over him . . .'

'He is providing money, so he is cautious. As long as he was only
giving his word, he could afford to be rash.'

'Not at all,' the lawyer interposed, 'there's more to it than that, and I am investigating. Someone is interfering . . .'

'Not with you, but with me,' Wokulski smiled, 'yet I don't care, and would not mind at all if these gentlemen didn't join our partnership.'

He bade farewell to the lawyer once more and hurried to the store. There he found several important matters which detained him longer than he expected. He was not in the Łazienki park until one-thirty.

The harsh chill of the park excited rather than calmed him. He hurried so that sometimes he wondered whether he was attracting the attention of passers-by. Then he slowed down and felt that his chest would burst with impatience: 'Surely I won't meet them now,' he repeated desperately.

Just by the lake, he caught sight of Izabela's ash-coloured wrap against a background of green shrubs. She was standing on the bank with the Countess and her father, throwing crumbs to the swans, one of which had even waddled out of the water and stood at Izabela's feet.

Tomasz was first to notice him: 'What a fortunate coincidence,' he exclaimed to Wokulski, 'you in the Łazienki at this time of day!'

Wokulski bowed to the ladies, noticing the blush on Izabela's face with a sensation of delighted surprise: 'I come here whenever I am overworked . . . which is quite often.'

'Take care of yourself, Mr Wokulski,' Tomasz warned, shaking a finger at him gravely, 'and apropos,' he added in an undertone, 'just think – Baroness Krzeszowska wants to give me seventy thousand for my house. I shall certainly get a hundred thousand, perhaps a hundred and ten thousand. Thank goodness for auction sales.'

'I see you so rarely, Mr Wokulski,' the Countess interposed, 'that I must get down to business immediately.'

'I am at your service, madam.'

'My dear sir,' she exclaimed, pressing her hands together with mock humility, 'I entreat you for a roll of calico for my orphans. Just see how I have learned to beg for charity.'

'Will you deign to accept two rolls?'

'Only if one is of thick linen . . .'

'Aunt, you are going too far,' Izabela interrupted with a smile, 'if you do not want to lose your entire fortune,' she added to Wokulski, 'you had better run away. I'll take you in the direction of the Orangery, and the others can rest here awhile . . .'

'Bela, aren't you afraid? . . .' her aunt exclaimed.

'Surely you don't suppose, aunt, that anything bad can happen to me in the company of Mr Wokulski?'

The blood ran to Wokulski's head; an imperceptible smile flitted across the Countess's lips.

It was one of those moments when Nature puts a brake on her

immense powers, and suspends her eternal labours to emphasise the happiness of small and insignificant beings. The breeze was scarcely blowing, and then only to cool the fledgelings in their nests and help insects winging their way to nuptial festivities. The leaves on the trees stirred so gently that it was as if they were moved not by a material breath, but by the shifting sun-beams. Here and there, in the moisture-drenched undergrowth, colourful dew drops shimmered like the particles of a rainbow from Heaven. Thus everything was appropriate: the sun and trees, the light and shade, the swans on the lake, the swarms of mosquitoes hovering over the swans, even the glittering waves on the blue water. At this moment it seemed to Wokulski that time itself had quit the earth, leaving behind only a few white streaks in the sky – and that from now on nothing would change: everything would remain the same forever and ever – he and Izabela would walk forever through radiant meadows, both surrounded by green clouds of trees, in which the curious eyes of a bird would glitter here and there, like a couple of black diamonds – that he would be filled with immeasurable silence, and she always so dreamy and blushing, that those two white butterflies, kissing in the air, would be before them forever, as now.

They were half-way to the Orangery when Izabela, evidently embarrassed by the tranquillity in Nature and between them, began to say: 'A beautiful day, is it not? It's so hot in town, but here it is delightfully cool. I love the Łazienki at this time of day; there are hardly any people, so everyone can find a corner entirely for himself. Do you like solitude?'

'I have grown used to it.'

'Have you seen Rossi?' she added, blushing still more, 'have you?' she insisted, looking into his eyes in surprise.

'No, but I'm going to.'

'My aunt and I have already been to two performances.'

'I shall go to them all . . .'

'Oh, that is splendid! You'll see what a great artist he is. He plays Romeo particularly well – although he is no longer in his first youth. Aunt and I know him personally, we met in Paris . . . He's a most charming man, but a great tragedian primarily. He mingles very faithful realism in his acting with the most poetic idealism.'

'He must be very great,' Wokulski said, 'if he arouses so much admiration and sympathy in you.'

'Yes, you are right. I know I shall never do anything extraordinary, but at least I know how to appreciate unusual people. In every walk of life . . . even on the stage . . . Just think, though, that Warsaw doesn't appreciate him as it should.'

'Is that possible? After all, he's a foreigner . . .'

'You are malicious,' she replied, with a smile, 'but I put it down to Warsaw, not to Rossi. Really, I am ashamed of our city. If I were the public (of the male sex), I'd overwhelm him with bouquets, and my hands would be quite swollen from applauding. Here, though, the applause is rather sparing, and no one thinks of bouquets. We are still barbarians, really . . .'

'Applause and bouquets are such small things that . . . at Rossi's next performance he may well have too many, rather than not enough,' said Wokulski.

'Are you sure?' she asked, looking eloquently into his eyes.

'Quite sure . . . I guarantee it . . .'

'I shall be so pleased if your prophecy comes true; but now perhaps we ought to go back to the others?'

'Anyone who pleases you deserves the highest thanks . . .'

'Oh come,' she interrupted, smiling, 'you have just paid yourself a compliment . . .'

They turned back from the Orangery.

'I can just picture Rossi's surprise,' Izabela went on, 'if he has an ovation. He's already dubious and almost regrets coming to Warsaw. Artists, even the greatest, are peculiar people; they cannot live without fame and tributes, just as we cannot do without food and air. Work, no matter how productive, or tranquillity or sacrifice – are not for them. They simply must be in the forefront, hold everyone's gaze, dominate the hearts of thousands . . . Rossi himself says he would rather die a year sooner, on the stage before a full and crowded house, than a year later, with only a few people. How strange that is!'

'He is right – if a full theatre is his greatest happiness.'

'You think there are kinds of happiness, for which it is worth paying by a shorter life?' Izabela asked.

'Yes, and unhappinesses that it is worth avoiding in a like manner,' Wokulski replied.

Izabela pondered, and from that time both walked on in silence.

Meanwhile, the Countess was seated by the lake, still feeding the swans and talking to Tomasz: 'Haven't you noticed,' she said, 'that this Wokulski is somehow interested in Bela.'

'Oh, I think not.'

'Very much so, indeed; tradesmen nowadays know how to make daring plans.'

'It is a great distance from making a plan to carrying it out,' Tomasz replied rather irritably, 'though even if it were so, it has nothing to do with me. I don't control Mr Wokulski's thoughts, and am easy as regards Bela . . .'

'I have nothing against it,' the Countess added, 'and whatever happens, I accept God's will, if the poor benefit. They continually do . . . My orphanage will soon be the first in the town, simply because that man has a weakness for Bela.'

'For goodness sake! They're coming back . . .' Tomasz interrupted.

Izabela and Wokulski had just appeared at the end of the path.

Tomasz eyed them attentively and only now did he notice that these two people looked well together, both in height and movement. He, a head taller and powerfully built, stepped like an ex-military man; she, somewhat slighter, but more graceful, moved as if gliding. Even Wokulski's white top-hat and light overcoat matched Izabela's ash-coloured wrap.

'Where did he get that white top-hat?' Tomasz wondered resentfully. Then a strange notion occurred to him: that Wokulski was a parvenu who ought to pay him at least fifty per cent on the capital lent him, in return for the right to wear a white top-hat. But in the end he only shrugged.

'How beautiful those paths are, aunt,' Izabela exclaimed as she drew nearer, 'we have never been in that direction. The Łazienki park is only pleasant when one can walk a long way, and fast.'

'In that case, please ask Mr Wokulski to keep you company more often,' the Countess replied in a tone of peculiar sweetness. Wokulski bowed, Izabela frowned imperceptibly and Tomasz said: 'Perhaps we should go home . . .'

'I think so,' said the Countess, 'are you staying here, Mr Wokulski?'

'Yes. May I see you to your carriage?'

'Please do. Bela, your hand.'

The Countess and Izabela went in front, Tomasz and Wokulski following. Tomasz felt so much resentment, spleen and gall at the sight of that white top-hat that he forced himself to smile in order not to be disagreeable. Finally, wishing to divert Wokulski in some way or other, he began talking about his house again, from which he hoped to gain forty or fifty thousand roubles clear profit. These figures reacted unfavourably on Wokulski, as he had told himself he was not in a position to add anything over thirty thousand.

Not until the carriage came up and Tomasz, after handing in the ladies, cried: 'Drive on!' did Wokulski's feeling of distaste disappear and yearning for Izabela awaken.

'It was so brief,' he thought, looking with a sigh at the Łazienki alley along which the green water-cart of a park-keeper was now rolling, sprinkling the gravel.

He went in the direction of the Orangery again, along the same path as before, gazing at Izabela's footsteps in the fine sand. But something was different. The wind now blew stronger, it ruffled the water of the lake, had scattered the butterflies and the birds and was also driving up more clouds, which kept eclipsing the sunshine: 'How boring it is here,' he thought, and went back to the main alley.

He got into his carriage and, with his eyes closed, relished its slight rocking motion. It made him think of a bird on a branch, which the wind blows to left then right, up then down, but he suddenly smiled to think that this slight rocking motion was costing him about a thousand a year. 'I'm a fool, a fool,' he repeated, 'why am I pushing my way in among people who either fail to understand the sacrifices I am making, or who laugh at my clumsy efforts? Why do I have to keep this carriage? Couldn't I use a droshky, or that rattling omnibus with its canvas curtains?'

When he stopped in front of his house, he recalled the promise he had given Izabela concerning Rossi's ovation. 'He will get his ovation, mark my words! There's a performance tomorrow . . .'

Towards evening, he sent his servant to the shop for Oberman. The grey-haired cashier hurried over at once, asking himself in alarm whether Wokulski had changed his mind and was going to order him to repay the lost money . . .

However, Wokulski greeted him very affably and even took him into the study, where they talked for nearly half an hour. What about? The question very much intrigued the footman. 'About the lost money, surely?' . . . Worried, he put his ear and eye to the key-hole in turn, saw and heard a great deal, but could make nothing of it all. He saw Wokulski give Oberman a whole bundle of five-rouble notes and heard such phrases as: 'In the Grand Theatre . . . the balcony and gallery . . . a bouquet by the doorman . . . a bouquet across the orchestra . . .'

'What the devil is the old man up to now? Dealing in theatre tickets, or what?'

Hearing the sound of farewells in the study, the servant took refuge in the vestibule in order to catch Oberman there. When the cashier emerged he exclaimed: 'Well, is it over with the money, then? I took a lot of my breath to make the old man have mercy on you, Oberman, but finally I forced him to say "We'll see, we'll do what we can . . ." And now I see you've done well for yourself, Mr Oberman. Is the old man in a good temper, then?'

'Like always,' the cashier replied.

'You had a nice talk with him, didn't you? It must have been about more than the money . . . I daresay it was about the theatre, for the old man likes the theatre. . . .'

But Oberman glared at him wolfishly and went out without answering. At first the servant gasped in astonishment, but then he cooled down and shook his fist: 'You wait,' he muttered, 'I'll pay you back . . . A great gentleman, just look at him . . . Steals four hundred roubles but he won't even talk to a fellow . . .'

XVIII

Surprises, Delusions and Observations
of the Old Clerk

ANOTHER period of uneasiness and surprises had come upon Ignacy Rzecki. This same Wokulski, who had rushed off to Bulgaria a year ago and had amused himself like a lord a few weeks back at horse-races and duels, had today developed an extraordinary fondness for theatrical performances. It would not have been so bad if they'd been in Polish – but in Italian! And Wokulski did not understand a word of Italian.

This new mania had already lasted almost a week, much to the surprise and chagrin of other people as well as Ignacy. Once, for instance, old Szlangbaum had been looking for Wokulski for half a day, obviously in connection with some important business. He tried the shop, but Wokulski had just left, after ordering a large vase of Saxon porcelain to be delivered to the actor Rossi. He hurried to Wokulski's apartment – Wokulski had just left, and gone to Bardet's flower-shop. With a grimace, the old Jew took a droshky in an attempt to catch up with him; but as he offered the driver one złoty and eight groszy for the drive, instead of forty groszy, Wokulski had already left the flower-shop by the time they finished arguing.

'D'you know where he went?' Szlangbaum asked the gardener, who was sowing destruction among his finest blooms with a crooked knife.

'How should I know? To the theatre, I daresay,' the gardener replied, looking as if he would like to cut Szlangbaum's throat with that crooked knife.

The very same notion had occurred to the Jew, who retreated as hastily as possible from the Orangery and jumped into the droshky like a stone from a sling. But the driver (who had obviously come to an agreement with the cannibal gardener) declared he would not go any further unless the merchant paid him forty groszy for the drive and repaid the two groszy deducted the first time.

Szlangbaum felt palpitations around his heart, and at first wanted

either to get out or to call the police. Recalling, however, that
malice, injustice and greed were now prevailing towards Jews in
the Christian world, he agreed to all the conditions of the outra-
geous driver and drove to the theatre, groaning.

There – he did not know whom to address, then nobody would
speak to him, but he finally ascertained that Mr Wokulski had been
there, but at that moment left for Aleje Ujazdowskie. The wheels
of his carriage could still be heard in the gate . . .

Szlangbaum gave up in despair. He went back on foot to
Wokulski's store, taking the opportunity for the hundredth time of
cursing his son for calling himself 'Henryk', wearing a frock-coat
and eating non-kosher food, then he finally went to expatiate on
his woes to Ignacy:

'Now!' he said in a lamenting voice, 'whatever is Mr Wokulski
up to, for goodness sake? I had a transaction he could have made
three hundred roubles on within five days . . . I'd have made a
hundred myself . . . But no! He goes riding around the town, and I
had to spend two złoty and twenty groszy on droshkies. O my!
What brigands those droshky-men are!'

Rzecki of course authorised Szlangbaum to transact the business
and not only refunded the money he had spent on the droshky, but
even had him driven to Elektoralna Street at his own expense,
which so touched the old Jew that as he went out he lifted the
parental curse from his son and invited him for the Sabbath supper.

'All the same,' said Rzecki to himself, 'this theatre business is
going too far, mainly because Staś is neglecting his work . . .'

Then again, the widely respected lawyer and right-hand man of
the Prince, the legal adviser of the entire aristocracy, called at the
store to invite Wokulski to his office for an evening meeting.
Ignacy did not know where to seat this eminent person, nor how
to appreciate the honour paid his Staś by the lawyer. But Staś was
not only unmoved by the grand invitation for the evening, but
simply refused it, which somewhat upset the lawyer, who left at
once and said goodbye to them very coolly.

'Why didn't you accept?' the despondent Rzecki asked.

'Because I have to go to the theatre tonight,' Wokulski replied.

But genuine alarm seized Rzecki when on that same day the
cashier Oberman came to him before seven and asked him to do
the day's figures: 'Later on . . . after eight o'clock,' Ignacy replied,
'there isn't time now.'

'But I shan't have time after eight,' Oberman replied.

'How so? What do you mean?'

'Just that I have to go with the master to the theatre at seven-
thirty,' Oberman muttered, shrugging imperceptibly.

At the same moment in came Zięba, smiling, to say goodnight.

'Are you going already, Mr Zięba? At six-fifteen?' asked Ignacy in amazement, his eyes opening very wide.

'I'm taking the bouquets for Rossi,' the polite Zięba whispered, with a still more agreeable smile.

Rzecki clutched his head with both hands: 'They've gone mad over this theatre!' he cried, 'perhaps they'll even try to get me involved too . . . Not likely, though . . .'

Feeling that Wokulski might well try and persuade him to go as well, he rehearsed a speech in which he declared he would not go to the Italians and even made Staś think twice about it, in more or less these words: 'For goodness sake, give over, please! What's all this nonsense?' and so on.

But instead of trying to persuade him, Wokulski came into the store around six, found Rzecki at the accounts and said: 'My dear fellow, Rossi is playing Macbeth tonight, be so kind as to sit in the front row of the stalls (here's your ticket) and hand him this album after the third act . . .'

And without more ado or even explaining, he handed Ignacy an album containing views of Warsaw and local young ladies, which must have cost fifty roubles!

Ignacy felt deeply hurt. He rose, frowned and had opened his mouth to protest, when Wokulski abruptly left the shop without so much as another look at him. So of course Ignacy had to go to the theatre, to avoid hurting Staś's feelings.

In the theatre a whole series of surprises lay in wait for Ignacy. First of all, he went in by the gallery stairs, his usual entry in the good old days. An attendant had to remind him he had a ticket for the front row of the stalls and in doing so cast a look at him as if to say that Mr Rzecki's dark-green frock-coat, the album under his arm and even his countenance à la Napoleon III appeared highly suspect to the lower hierarchy of the theatre authorities. Embarrassed, Ignacy went down to the front vestibule, clutching the album under his arm and bowing to all the ladies he had the honour of passing. This politeness, to which the good people of Warsaw were not at all accustomed, created quite a stir in the vestibule. People began asking who he was; and although no one recognised him, everyone at once noticed that his top-hat was ten years old, his tie five, while his dark-green frock-coat and striped trousers dated from an even earlier epoch. On the whole they took him for a foreigner; but when he asked an attendant the way to the stalls, people burst out laughing: 'He must be a squireen up from Wolyn,' the dandies said, 'but what is that under his arm? His supper, I daresay – or a pneumatic cushion.'

Scourged by derision, drenched in cold sweat, Ignacy finally gained the much-longed for stalls. It was only just after seven, and the audience had barely started coming in: here and there people came to their seats with hats on, the boxes were empty, and only in the balcony was there a seething mass of people, while up in the gallery, the police were already being called for.

'It looks as if the audience is going to be very lively,' muttered the unhappy Ignacy with a pallid smile, taking his seat in the front row.

At first he gazed fixedly at the right-hand hole in the curtain, vowing he would not remove his eyes from it. However, a few minutes later his agitation cooled down, and he even plucked up enough courage to begin looking around. The auditorium looked rather small and dirty, and it was not until he began pondering over the reasons for this, that he realised he had last been in the theatre more or less sixteen years ago, to see Dobrski in *Halka*.*

Meanwhile the auditorium was filling, and the sight of pretty women taking their places in the boxes completely emboldened Ignacy. The old clerk even brought out a small pair of opera-glasses and began gazing at their countenances: whereupon he made the sad discovery that he too was being looked at from the amphitheatre, from the stalls behind and even from the boxes . . . When he transferred his psychic talents from eye to ear, he caught phrases flying over his head like so many wasps: 'Who on earth is that eccentric?'

'Someone up from the provinces . . .'

'But where in the world did he acquire that frock-coat?'

'And just look at the trinkets on his watch-chain! How disgraceful!'

'Whoever does his hair like that nowadays?'

Ignacy very nearly left his album and top-hat and fled bareheaded from the theatre. Fortunately he caught sight in the eighth row of a piemaker of his acquaintance, who left his seat in response to a bow from Ignacy and approached the front row.

'For goodness' sake, Mr Pifke,' he whispered, drenched in sweat, 'take my place and let me have yours . . .'

'With pleasure, I'm sure,' the red-faced pie-maker replied loudly, 'what, don't you like it? A splendid seat . . .'

'Yes, it's excellent, but I prefer being further back. It's so hot . . .'

'It's the same back there, but I'll change with you. What's that packet you have?'

Only now did Rzecki recollect his duty: 'Look, my dear Mr Pifke, an admirer of this . . . this Rossi . . .'

'Bah, who isn't an admirer of Rossi?' Pifke replied, 'I have the book of words to *Macbeth*, would you care for it?'

'Certainly . . . but this admirer, you see, bought an expensive album from us and asked me to hand it to Rossi after the third act.'

'I'll do it with pleasure,' the stout Pifke exclaimed, squeezing himself into Rzecki's seat.

Ignacy passed a few more disagreeable moments. He had to

extricate himself from the front row of the stalls, where dandies
eyed his frock-coat and tie and his velveteen waistcoat with ironical
smiles. Then he had to get into the eighth row of the stalls where,
admittedly, they looked at his costume without any irony, but
where he had to press the knees of seated ladies.

'A thousand pardons,' he said, embarrassed, 'but it's so tight . . .'

'No need to use such expressions,' one of the ladies replied, in
whose rather painted eyes Ignacy observed quite the opposite of
vexation for his squeezing. He was so embarrassed he would
willingly have gone to confession, if only he could purify his soul
of the stains left by those squeezes.

Finally he found his place and breathed again. Here at least no
one paid any attention to him, partly because the theatre was
already full and the performance was beginning.

The acting at first did not interest him, so he looked around the
auditorium and caught sight of Wokulski. He was in the fourth
row and was not gazing at Rossi at all, but at a box occupied by
Izabela, Tomasz and the Countess. Rzecki had seen hypnotised
people a few times in his life and he thought that Wokulski looked
like a man hypnotised by that box. He was sitting there motionless,
like a man asleep with his eyes wide open.

What could have charmed Wokulski so? Ignacy had no idea. He
also observed something else; whenever Rossi was not on stage,
Izabela gazed indifferently around the theatre or talked to her aunt.
But when Rossi-Macbeth entered, she half-screened her face with a
fan and seemed to be devouring the actor with those magnificent,
dreaming eyes of hers. Sometimes the white feathers of her fan sank
to her lap, and then Rzecki perceived on Izabela's face the same
hypnotised look which had so surprised him on Wokulski's.

He saw something else too. When Izabela's beautiful face
expressed greatest admiration, then Wokulski rubbed the top of his
head with one hand. And then, as if in response to an order, violent
applause and noisy shouts were heard from the balcony and gallery:
'Bravo, bravo Rossi!' It even seemed to Ignacy that somewhere in
the chorus he could distinguish the weary voice of Oberman the
cashier, which began yelling first and was the last to fall silent.

'Upon my soul,' he thought, 'can Wokulski be directing a
claque?'

But he at once abandoned this unworthy thought. For Rossi
acted splendidly and everyone applauded with equal vigour. Mr
Pifke, the jolly pie-maker, applauded most of all and, in accordance
with the agreement, handed Rossi the album with a great deal of
to-do after the third act. The celebrated actor did not even nod to
Pifke, but he made a very deep bow in the direction of the box in
which Izabela was sitting and perhaps – in that direction alone.

'It's a delusion! A fancy!' thought Ignacy as he left the theatre after the last act, 'after all, Staś would not be so stupid as to . . .'

In the end, however, Ignacy was not displeased with his visit to the theatre. Rossi's acting delighted him; some scenes, such as the murder of King Duncan and the appearance of Banquo's ghost had made a powerful impression on him, and he had also been quite delighted by the way Macbeth fought with his sword. So, as he left the theatre, he was not so vexed with Wokulski; on the contrary he even began wondering whether his dear Staś had invented all that business of handing Rossi a gift merely in order to give him pleasure. 'He knows, does my honest Staś,' he thought, 'that I'd only go to the Italian actors if I were forced to. Well, and it turned out nicely after all. That fellow acts wonderfully well, I must see him again . . . Besides,' he added after a moment, 'anyone with as much money as Staś can give presents to actors if he chooses . . . I must say I'd prefer some nicely built actress, but I'm a man of another age; they even call me a Bonapartist and a Romantic . . .'

Thinking this, he muttered softly to himself, for he was fretted by another thought which he wanted to suppress: 'Why had Staś stared so oddly at the box in which the Countess, Mr Łęcki and Miss Łęcka were sitting? Could it possibly be . . . ? Oh, for goodness sake . . . Surely Wokulski had too much sense to suppose that anything could come of that . . . Any child could see that that girl, usually as cold as ice, was crazy about Rossi . . . How she looked at him, how she even sometimes forgot herself, and in the theatre too, in the presence of a thousand other people. No, that is nonsense. They are quite right to call me a Romantic . . .'

And he tried yet again to think about something else. He even went (despite the lateness of the hour) into a restaurant, where a band consisting of fiddles, a pianoforte and a harp was playing. He ate roast meat with potatoes and cabbage, drank a tankard of beer, then another, then a third and a fourth . . . not to mention a seventh. He even grew bold enough to put two 40-groszy pieces in the harpist's tray and begin humming. Then it occurred to him he simply must introduce himself to four Germans eating tripe and onions at the next table. 'But why should I introduce myself to them? Let them introduce themselves to me,' thought Ignacy.

At this moment he was preoccupied by the idea that those four gentlemen ought to introduce themselves to him, because he was an older person, also a former officer of the Hungarian infantry which had well and truly defeated the Germans. He even summoned the waitress for the express purpose of sending her over to those four gentlemen eating tripe and onions, when all at once the band of fiddles, harp and pianoforte struck up – the 'Marseillaise'!

Ignacy was reminded of Hungary, of the infantry, of August Katz and, feeling tears coming into his eyes, so that at any moment he would burst into sobs, he seized his antiquated top-hat from the table and throwing down a rouble, rushed from the restaurant. Not until the fresh air in the street enveloped him did he lean against a lamp-post and ask: 'For goodness sake, am I tipsy? Impossible! Seven beers . . .'

He went home, trying to walk as straight as possible, and only now did he discover that Warsaw pavements are unusually uneven; for at every few yards he had to step aside into the gutter, or towards the house walls. Then (to convince himself that his intellectual capacities were unimpaired) he began counting the stars in the sky: 'One . . . two . . . three . . . seven . . . seven what? Ah seven tankards of beer . . . Can I possibly? . . . What did Staś send me to the theatre for?'

He found his way home and reached for the bell. But after ringing for the door-keeper seven times, he felt the urge to lean against the corner between gate and wall, and tried to count – not because he had to, but just for his own benefit – how many minutes would pass before the door-keeper opened. With this in mind, he brought out his watch which had a second hand, and realised it was half-past one o'clock.

'Confounded door-keeper,' he muttered, 'I have to get up at six, yet here he is keeping me out in the street at half-past one . . .' Fortunately the door-man opened the gate at once, Ignacy passed through with a perfectly steady tread (it was more than steady, it was very steady) and crossed the entire yard, aware that his top-hat was a little crooked, though only a little.

Having found the door of his dwelling with no difficulty whatsoever, he tried several times to insert the key in the lock. He could feel the key-hole, he clutched the key as firmly as he could, but even so he could not get in: 'Can I possibly . . . ?'

At this moment the door opened, and at the same time his one-eyed poodle Ir barked several times: 'Yap . . . yap . . . yap!' 'Shut up, confounded thing,' Ignacy muttered and he undressed and went to bed without even lighting the lamp.

He had awful dreams. He dreamed, or had the illusion, that he was still in the theatre and could see Wokulski with his wide-open eyes, staring at a certain box. In this box the Countess, Mr Łęcki and Izabela were sitting. It seemed to Rzecki that Wokulski was looking at Izabela in that same manner as before: 'It can't be,' he muttered, 'Staś isn't so stupid . . .'

Meanwhile (in his dream) Izabela rose from her seat and went out of the box, with Wokulski following her, still gazing like someone mesmerised. Izabela left the theatre, crossed Theatre Square and ran lightly up the Town Hall tower, with Wokulski following, still gazing like someone mesmerised. Then Izabela rose into the air like a bird and flew over the theatre, while Wokulski tried to fly after her but instead fell ten storeys to the ground.

'Goodness! Goodness me!' Rzecki exclaimed, starting up in bed.

'Yap, yap . . .' Ir barked in his sleep.

'Well, obviously I am quite drunk,' Ignacy muttered, lying down again and impatiently pulling up the quilt, under which he lay shivering. He kept his eyes open several minutes and again fancied he was in the theatre, just after the third act, when the pie-maker Pifke was to hand the album of Warsaw and its beauties to Rossi.

Ignacy watched closely (Pifke was his deputy, after all) and saw with the utmost horror that instead of the costly album, the infamous Pifke was handing the Italian some sort of a parcel done up in brown paper and carelessly tied with string.

And Ignacy saw something worse. For the Italian smiled ironically, untied the string, unwrapped the paper and in full view of Izabela, Wokulski, the Countess and a thousand other spectators – revealed a pair of yellow nankeen pantaloons with an apron attached in front and little straps on the bottom. Just like the ones Ignacy had worn at the time of the famous Sebastopol campaign!

To make these horrors still worse, the infamous Pifke bawled at the top of his voice: 'This is a gift from Stanisław Wokulski and Ignacy Rzecki, his manager!' The entire theatre burst out laughing: all the eyes, all the pointing fingers were directed at the eighth row of the stalls and at the very seat occupied by Ignacy. The culprit rose to protest, but felt his voice freeze in his throat, and that – to make matters even worse – he himself was falling. He was falling into a limitless, bottomless ocean of nothingness, in which he would rest forever and ever, without once being able to explain to the audience that the nankeen pantaloons with the little apron and straps had been stolen from his collection of personal souvenirs.

After a night restlessly spent, Rzecki did not wake till a quarter to seven. He could hardly believe his own eyes when he looked at his watch, though in the end he had to. He even had to believe that last night he had been somewhat tipsy, to which a slight headache and general heaviness of his limbs attested.

But all these sickly symptoms alarmed Ignacy less than one terrible symptom: he didn't feel like going to the shop. And, even worse, he felt not only lazy, but even completely lacking in pride, for instead of being ashamed of his decline and struggling against his slothful instincts, he, Rzecki, kept finding reasons for staying in his room as long as he possibly could.

First it seemed to him that Ir was poorly, then that his never-used rifle was rusty, then that there was something wrong with the green curtain that screened the window, and finally that his tea was too hot, and must be drunk more slowly than usual.

Consequently, Ignacy was forty minutes late to work and he sidled into the office with a lowered gaze. It seemed to him that each of the 'gentlemen' (as if to spite him, each had been punctual that day!) was staring with the utmost contempt at his bloodshot eyes, earth-coloured skin and slightly trembling hands.

'Very likely they are thinking I have given myself up to dissipation altogether,' the unhappy Ignacy sighed.

Then he brought out the ledgers, dipped his pen and made as if he were reckoning. He was certain he smelled of beer like an old barrel turned out of a vaults, and began very seriously to consider whether he ought not to resign from the store after having committed such a series of shameful acts . . .

'I got drunk . . . came home late . . . got up late . . . I was forty minutes late to work . . .'

At this moment Klein came up with a letter: 'It says "Very Urgent" so I opened it,' said the starveling clerk, giving Rzecki the envelope. Ignacy took it and read:

'Stupid man – or vile! Despite so many benevolent warnings you are nevertheless set on buying a house which will prove the tomb of your dishonestly gained fortune . . .'

Ignacy glanced at the last line but there was no signature: the letter was anonymous. He looked at the envelope; it was addressed to Wokulski. He went on reading:

Bad luck has placed you in the path of a certain genteel lady whose husband you have almost slain and today you seek to snatch away from her the house in which her beloved daughter expired . . . Why are you doing this? Why are you going to pay – if it is true – ninety thousand roubles for a house not worth more than sixty thousand? These are the secrets of your own black soul which Heavenly justice will at some future date lay bare and which respectable persons will punish with contempt.

Ponder what you are about, while there is yet time. Do not destroy your soul and your fortune, and do not poison the tranquillity of a respectable lady whose unconsolable grief at the death of her daughter can only be consoled by the possibility of spending a little time in the room where her unfortunate child breathed her last. Recollect yourself, I charge you!

A Well-wisher.

When he had read it, Ignacy shook his head: 'I don't understand a word of it,' he said, 'though I am very doubtful as to the good intentions of this lady.'

Klein looked nervously around, then, seeing that no one was watching, whispered: 'Sir, our old man is said to be buying the Łęcki house, which his creditors are to sell by auction tomorrow.'

'Staś – that's to say Mr Wokulski – is buying a house?'

'Yes, yes,' Klein nodded, 'but not in his own name, only

through old Szlangbaum. At least that's what people are saying in the house where I live.'

'For ninety thousand roubles?'

'Exactly so. But Baroness Krzeszowska wants to buy the house for seventy thousand, so very likely the anonymous letter is from her. I'd even lay a bet on it, for she's a regular demon of a woman.'

A customer, entering the store to purchase an umbrella, took Klein away. Very peculiar notions began circulating in Ignacy's head: 'If I', he told himself, 'brought about as much confusion in the shop by wasting one evening, then what sort of confusion will Staś cause in the business, spending days and weeks at the Italian actors and even – goodness knows what else.'

At this moment, however, he recalled there was not so much confusion in the shop on Wokulski's behalf, and that business was going very well on the whole. It was even true that despite his strange way of life, Wokulski was not neglecting the duties of the head of the establishment.

'But why should he want to lock up ninety thousand roubles in bricks and mortar? And how do these Leckis come into it? For goodness sake, Staś isn't such a fool . . .'

All the same, the purchase of the house alarmed him: 'I'll ask Henryk Szlangbaum,' he thought, getting up.

In the cloth department the little hunchbacked Szlangbaum with his red eyes and a fierce look on his face was moving about as usual, jumping up and down ladders, or pouncing between rolls of calico. He was so accustomed to his feverish labours that although there were no customers, he kept bringing out one roll or another, then unrolling and rolling them up again so as to replace in its proper place on the shelf.

Seeing Ignacy, Szlangbaum interrupted his pointless labours and wiped the sweat from his brow: 'Hard work, ain't it?' said he.

'What are you bringing all that stuff down for, when there aren't any customers in the store?' Rzecki asked.

'Well, if I didn't, I'd forget where things are . . . My joints would get rusty. Besides, I'm used to it . . . Do you have some business with me?'

Rzecki hesitated a moment: 'No . . . I just wanted to see how things were going,' Ignacy replied, blushing as much as was possible at his age.

'Can he be suspecting me, watching me?' passed through Szlangbaum's mind swiftly, and rage seized him: 'Yes, my father is right . . . Everyone is against the Jews today. Soon I'll have to let my hair grow and put on a skull-cap . . .'

'He knows something!' Rzecki thought, and said aloud: 'Apparently your respected father is buying a house tomorrow – the Łęcki house.'

'I know nothing about that,' Szlangbaum replied, looking away. Inwardly he added: 'My old man is buying the house on Wokulski's behalf, and they think and no doubt say 'Look there – another Jew, a usurer, has ruined a Catholic and real gentleman . . .'

'He knows something but won't talk,' Rzecki thought, 'that's a Jew all over.'

He fidgeted about a little longer, which Szlangbaum took for more suspicion and spying, then went back to his own place, sighing: 'It's awful – Staś trusts Jews more than he trusts me . . . But why is he buying the house, why is he taking up with the Łęckis? Perhaps he isn't going to buy it? Perhaps this is only a rumour?'

He was so alarmed at the thought of ninety thousand being locked up in bricks and mortar that he thought of nothing else all day. There was a moment when he thought of asking Wokulski directly, but he lacked courage: 'Staś,' he told himself, 'is taking up with gentlefolk but he confides in Jews. What does old Rzecki mean to him?'

So he decided that next day he would go to the auction and see whether in fact old Szlangbaum bought the Łęcki house and whether, as Klein had said, he bid up to ninety thousand roubles. If that happened, it would be a sign that everything else was going to follow.

In the afternoon, Wokulski dropped by the store and began talking to Rzecki, questioning him about the theatre the previous evening, why he had quit the front row of the stalls and had let the album be handed to Rossi by Pifke. But Ignacy's heart was so full of sorrow and doubts about his dear Staś, that he replied in an undertone and with a sulky look on his face.

So Wokulski fell silent too, and left the shop with bitterness in his soul: 'They are all turning away from me,' he told himself, 'even Ignacy. Even he . . . But you will be my reward,' he added in the street, looking in the direction of Aleje Ujazdowskie.

When Wokulski had left the store, Rzecki cautiously asked the 'gentlemen' in which court-room and at what time the auctions of houses took place. Then he asked Lisiecki to deputise for him next day between ten in the morning and two in the afternoon, and set about his accounts with redoubled fervour. Mechanically (though without a mistake) he added up columns of figures as long as Nowy Świat Street, and in the intervals he thought: 'I have wasted nearly an hour today, tomorrow I'll waste about five, and all because Staś trusts Szlangbaum more than me. What does he want an apartment house for? Why the devil is he taking up with that bankrupt Łęcki? What put it into his head to rush off to the Italian company and on top of it all to give expensive gifts to that strolling player Rossi?'

He sat at the cash-desk till six o'clock without looking up from the ledgers, and was so absorbed that he not only declined to take money but did not even see or hear the customers who flocked in and made a noise in the store like so many bumble-bees in a hive. He did not even notice a most unexpected visitor whom the 'gentlemen' greeted with loud cries and embraces. Not until the newcomer stopped in front of him and shouted into his ear: 'Ignacy, it's me!' did Rzecki awaken, raise his head, brows and eyes and perceive Mraczewski.

'Ha?' Ignacy inquired, eyeing the young dandy, who had got sunburned, grown manlier and – above all – plumper.

'Well, what's the news?' Ignacy went on, shaking his hand, 'what about politics?'

'Nothing new,' Mraczewski replied, 'the Berlin congress is doing its job, the Austrians will take Bosnia . . .'

'Well, well, jokes – that's all. But what's the news about young Bonaparte?'

'He's studying at a military school in England and they say he's in love with some actress or other.'

'There, he falls in love right away,' Ignacy repeated, 'why doesn't he go back to France? What do you think? And what are you doing here? Come, let's hear it!' Rzecki exclaimed cheerfully, taking him by the arm, 'when did you arrive?'

'It's a long story,' Mraczewski replied, throwing himself into a chair, 'Suzin and I arrived at eleven . . . We were at Wokulski's from one to three, and after that I called on my mother and on Mrs Stawska . . . A fine woman, ain't she?'

'Stawska? Stawska? . . .' Rzecki recollected, frowning

'Go on – you know her! That pretty woman with the little daughter. The one you took such a fancy to . . .'

'Oh her . . . I know . . . It wasn't that I took a fancy to her,' Rzecki sighed, 'only I thought she'd make a good wife for Staś.'

'You're a card, you are,' Mraczewski laughed, 'she's already got one husband.'

'Already got one?'

'Certainly. Besides, the name is well-known. Four years ago the poor devil ran away abroad, for they accused him of murdering that . . .'

'Yes, I remember. So that's the man? Why didn't he come back, after all it turned out he wasn't guilty.'

'Of course he wasn't,' Mraczewski agreed, 'but anyhow, since he got away to America there has been no word of him to this day. I daresay the poor wretch has perished somewhere and Mrs S. is left neither a spinster nor a widow. Awful fate! To keep a household going by embroidery, piano lessons, English lessons . . . To work all day like a horse and still not to have a husband . . . Poor woman! We wouldn't remain virtuous so long, would we, Ignacy, eh? That old madman . . .'

'Who's a madman?' Rzecki asked, astonished by the sudden change in the conversation.

'Who – if not Wokulski?' retorted Mraczewski, 'Suzin is going to Paris and insists on taking him along too, as he is going to make some huge purchase there. Our old man wouldn't have to pay a penny for the trip, he'd live like a prince, for the further Suzin is from his wife, the more money he spends. And on top of all this – he'd make some ten thousand roubles profit.'

'You mean Staś – our boss – would make ten thousand roubles?' Rzecki asked.

'Of course! But now that he's grown so silly . . .'

'Oh come, Mr Mraczewski,' said Ignacy threateningly.

'Upon my word, he has! For I know he's going to the Paris Exhibition any week now.'

'Yes, that's so.'

'So why doesn't he choose to go with Suzin, without spending his own money, and he'd make so much into the bargain. For two weeks Suzin has been begging him: "Come with me, Stanisław Piotrowicz!" He begged and prayed, but all in vain. Wokulski just won't . . . He says he has some business here . . .'

'Well, so he has,' Rzecki interrupted.

'Has he, though?' Mraczewski mocked him, 'his main business is not to vex Suzin, who helped him make a fortune, allows him huge credit and sometimes said to me he would not settle down until Stanisław Piotrowicz had made at least a million roubles. And to refuse such a friend such a small favour, when it's well paid into the bargain!' Mraczewski burst out.

Ignacy opened his mouth, then bit his lip. At this moment he very nearly said that Wokulski was buying the Łęcki house, and had given Rossi expensive gifts.

Klein and Lisiecki approached the cash-desk. As they were not busy, Mraczewski began talking to them, and Ignacy was again left alone over his ledger. 'What a misfortune,' he thought, 'why doesn't Staś go to Paris for nothing, and when Suzin asks him to? Some evil spirit has bound him to these Łęckis. Can it possibly be true that . . . ? No, he isn't so stupid . . . All the same, it's a pity about the trip and the ten thousand roubles . . . My goodness, how people change, to be sure . . .'

He bowed his head and, his finger moving up and down, added up columns of figures as long as Nowy Świat and Krakowskie Przedmieście. He calculated without making a single error, though he softly muttered and at the same time thought to himself that his Staś was on the brink of some fatal precipice.

'It's all in vain,' a voice hidden in the very depths of his soul whispered to him, 'Staś has got himself involved in some important affair . . . It must be political, for a man like that wouldn't go off his head for a woman, even if she were that Miss . . . herself . . . Oh, for goodness sake, I've made a mistake . . . He refuses, he despises ten thousand roubles – he who eight years ago had to borrow ten roubles a month from me to eat like a beggar . . . And now he's throwing away ten thousand, bricking up ninety thousand, making presents worth dozens of roubles to actors . . . For goodness sake, I don't understand it at all! And yet he's supposed to be a positivist, a man who thinks realistically . . . They call me an old romantic, yet I wouldn't commit such follies . . . Well, however, if he has got himself involved in politics . . .'

These meditations filled in the time until the closing of the store. His head ached a little, so he went for a stroll to Nowy Zjazd, and went to bed early when he reached home.

'Tomorrow,' he told himself, 'I'll find out what is really going on. If Szlangbaum buys the Łęcki house and pays ninety thousand roubles, that will mean Staś has really supplied him and is already completely off his head. But what if Staś don't buy the house, what if it's only gossip?'

He fell asleep and dreamed he saw Izabela in the window of a big house, and Wokulski, who was beside him, wanted to hurry to her. Ignacy tried to prevent him in vain, until sweat bathed his entire body. Wokulski tore himself away and disappeared into the gateway of the house. 'Staś, come back!' Ignacy cried, seeing the house begin to collapse. And in fact, it caved in altogether. Izabela, smiling, flew out of it like a bird, but there was no trace of Wokulski.

'Perhaps he ran into the yard, and is safe,' thought Ignacy and he woke up with his heart beating fiercely.

Next morning, Ignacy awoke a few minutes before six; he recalled that this was the day of the auction of the Łęcki house and that he was to watch the spectacle, so he jumped out of bed like a goat. He ran barefoot to the big hand-basin, poured cold water all over himself, looked at his spindly legs and muttered: 'It looks to me as if I've gained some weight.'

During the intricacies of his toilet, Ignacy made so much noise that he woke Ir. The grubby poodle opened the only eye he had left, and on seeing his master's unusual activity, jumped from his box to the floor. He stretched, yawned, put out first one back leg then the other, and sat down for a while at the window, outside which were heard the painful consequences of a hen having its neck wrung; then, seeing that nothing had really happened, Ir went back to bed. Meanwhile he was so discreet or perhaps so vexed with Ignacy on account of the false alarm, that he turned his back on the room, nose and tail to the wall, as much as to say: 'I prefer not seeing your bony shanks . . .'

Rzecki dressed in the twinkling of an eye and drank his tea up like lightning, without looking either at the samovar or at the servant who brought it. Then he hurried to the store, which was still closed, did accounts for three hours without paying any attention to the customers or the conversation of the 'gentlemen', and at ten precisely said to Lisiecki: 'Mr Lisiecki – I'll be back at two.'

'Unheard of!' Lisiecki muttered, 'something very unusual must have happened for the old fellow to go into the town at this time of day . . .'

Upon reaching the pavement in front of the store, Ignacy was seized with remorse. 'What am I up to?' thought he, 'what concern of mine is the auctioning of palaces, not to mention an apartment house?' And he hesitated whether to go to the court or return to the store. At this moment he saw a droshky passing along Krakowskie Przedmieście, with a tall, thin, ill-looking woman in a black dress inside. The lady was just looking at their store and in her sunken eyes and slightly livid lips, Rzecki saw a look of profound hatred. 'Goodness, it's Baroness Krzeszowska,' Ignacy muttered, 'of course she's on her way to the auction. There's going to be an unpleasant scene . . .'

However, doubts awoke within him. Who knows whether the Baroness was really going to the court? Perhaps it was only gossip. 'It would be worth making sure,' thought Ignacy and he forgot his duties as manager and senior clerk, and began following the droshky.

The wretched nag ambled along so slowly that Ignacy was able to keep the vehicle in sight along the entire boulevard to the Zygmunt Column. At this point the driver turned left and Rzecki thought: 'Obviously the old girl is going to Miodowa Street. It would come cheaper if she rode a broom-stick . . .'

Rzecki, too, got to Miodowa by passing the front of Retzler's café (which reminded him of his recent spree) and through Senatorska Street. Here, passing Nowicki's tea warehouse, he stepped in for a moment to say good-day to the proprietor, then hastily fled, muttering: 'What will he think to see me in the street at this hour? Of course he'll think I'm the most wretched of managers, who wanders around the town instead of staying in the shop. What a fate!'

Ignacy's conscience troubled him for the remainder of the way to the court-house. It took the form of a bearded giant in a yellow silk jacket and yellow trousers who eyed him affably and at the same time ironically, and said: 'Tell me, Mr Rzecki, what respectable tradesman wanders around the town at this hour of the day? You're as much of a merchant as I am a ballet-dancer . . .' And Ignacy felt he could not reply a single word to his stern judge. He blushed, sweated and was on the verge of going back to his ledgers (making sure Nowicki would see him), when he suddenly beheld the former Pac Palace.

'The auction will be held here,' said Ignacy and forgot his scruples. The bearded giant, in a yellow silk jacket, dissolved before the eyes of his soul like mist.

On considering the situation, Ignacy noticed first of all that two huge gates and a double door led into the building. Then he saw four different sized groups of Hebrews with very solemn faces. Ignacy did not know which way to go, but approached the door at which most of the Hebrews were standing, guessing that the auction would be held there.

At this moment a carriage drove up to the building with Mr Łęcki inside. Ignacy was unable to restrain his feelings of respect for those fine grey whiskers and of admiration for Łęcki's good humour. Mr Łęcki did not at all look like a bankrupt whose property was being auctioned off, but more like a millionaire come to his notary to take up the small sum of a hundred and more thousand roubles.

Mr Łęcki got ceremoniously out of the carriage, approached the court door with a triumphant step and at the same moment an individual who looked like an idler, but who was in reality a lawyer ran up to him. After a very brief and even casual greeting, Mr Łęcki asked this individual: 'Well – what and when?'

'In an hour or so, perhaps a little longer,' the individual replied.

'Just imagine,' said Łęcki, with a benevolent smile, 'that a week ago an acquaintance of mine got twice as much for a house which had cost him a hundred and fifty thousand. As mine cost a hundred thousand, I ought to get some hundred and twenty-five, in proportion.'

'Hm . . . hm . . .' muttered the lawyer.

'You'll no doubt laugh,' Tomasz went on, 'when I tell you (for you love laughing at premonitions and dreams) that today I dreamed my house went for a hundred and twenty thousand. Pray notice I'm telling you this before the auction! In a few hours you'll see that dreams are not to be laughed at. There are more things in Heaven and earth . . .'

'Hm . . . hm . . .' the lawyer replied, and both went through the first door of the building.

'Thank goodness,' thought Ignacy. 'If Łęcki gets a hundred and twenty thousand for his house, that will mean Staś won't pay ninety thousand for it.'

Just then someone touched his arm slightly. Ignacy looked around and saw old Szlangbaum behind him. 'Looking for me, eh?' asked the venerable Jew, eyeing him sharply.

'No, no . . .' Ignacy replied in confusion.

'You have no business matter to see me about?' Szlangbaum repeated, blinking his red eyelids.

'No, no . . .'

'*Gut*,' Szlangbaum muttered, and went off to join his co-religionists.

Ignacy felt chilly; Szlangbaum's presence in this place aroused new suspicions within him. To dispel them, Ignacy asked the doorman where the auctions were held. The doorman showed him the stairs.

Ignacy hurried up them into a hall. He was impressed by a crowd of Jews listening to a speech with the utmost attention. Rzecki realised that at this moment a case was being heard, that the prosecutor was speaking and that it concerned fraud. It was stuffy in the court-room; the prosecutor's speech was somewhat drowned by the rattle of droshkies outside. The magistrates looked as if they were dozing, the lawyer yawned, the accused looked as if he would be delighted to defraud the judges of the supreme court, the Hebrews were eyeing him with sympathy and listened to the charges with attention. Some grimaced and murmured: 'Oh my!' at the prosecutor's more powerful charges.

Ignacy left the court-room; he had not come for this case. Finding himself in a vestibule, Ignacy thought of ascending to the second floor; at the same moment, Baroness Krzeszowska passed him, accompanied by a man who looked like a bored teacher of dead languages. However, he was a lawyer, as was shown by a silver badge in the lapel of his very shabby frock-coat; and the grey trousers of this high priest of justice were as baggy at the knees as if their owner were in the habit of making proposals to the goddess Temida, instead of defending clients.

'If it is not for an hour,' said Mme Krzeszowska in a plaintive voice, 'I shall go to the Capucines. Do you not think? . . .'

'I don't think a visit to the Capucines will influence the course of the auction,' replied the lawyer, bored.

'But if you sincerely want it to go well . . .'

The lawyer in the baggy trousers made an impatient gesture: 'Dear lady,' said he, 'I have already run about so much in the business of this auction that today at least I deserve a rest. Furthermore, I have a murder trial in a few minutes . . . Do you see those fine ladies yonder? They're coming to listen to my speech of defence. An interesting case!'

'So you are deserting me?' cried the Baroness.

'I'll be in court,' the lawyer interrupted, 'I'll be there for the auction, but pray leave me a few minutes at least to think about my murderer . . .'

And he rushed through an open door, forbidding the doorman to let anyone in.

'Good God!' said the Baroness, aloud, 'a wretched murderer has a defender, but a poor lone woman seeks a man to defend her honour, peace of mind, property – in vain!'

As Ignacy did not want to be this man, he hurriedly fled downstairs, elbowing the fine, young and elegant ladies brought here by the wish to attend a celebrated murder trial. It would be better than the theatre: for the performers in this official spectacle act more realistically, if not better, than stage players.

The lamentations of Baroness Krzeszowska resounded on the stairs along with the laughter of the fine, young and elegant ladies hastening in to see the murderer, his bloodstained garments, the axe with which he slew his victim, and the sweating judges. Ignacy fled from the vestibule to the other side of the street; on the corner of Kapitulna and Miodowa Streets he hastened into a café and hid himself in such a dark corner that even Baroness Krzeszowska would not have noticed him. He ordered a cup of foaming chocolate, hid behind a torn newspaper and saw that in this small room was another, still darker corner, in which was placed a certain ostentatiously plump individual and a hunchbacked Jew. Ignacy took the stately personage for a Count and the owner of great estates in the Ukraine at least, and the Jew for his agent; however, he overheard the conversation going on between them.

'Sir,' said the hunchbacked Jew, 'were it not that no one in Warsaw knows Your Excellency, I wouldn't even give you ten roubles for the business. But as it is, you'll make twenty-five . . .'

'And stand an hour in a stuffy court-room!' the personage muttered.

'That's so,' the Jew went on, 'it's hard to stand up in this age of ours, but such money doesn't go on foot either. And how your reputation will go up when people find you wanted to buy a house for eighty thousand roubles!'

'So be it. But I want the twenty-five roubles in cash, here and now.'

'Heaven forbid,' the Jew responded, 'you'll get five roubles now and twenty will go towards paying off your debts to the unfortunate Selig Kupferman, who hasn't seen a penny of yours in two years, though he got a court order.'

The stately personage banged the table-top and made to depart. The hunchbacked Jew caught him by the coat-tails, sat him down at the table again and offered six roubles in cash. After bargaining several minutes, both sides agreed on eight roubles, of which seven would be paid after the auction and a rouble now. The Jew resisted, but the majestic gentleman did away with his hesitation by a single argument: 'After all, I have to pay for the tea and cakes we've had!'

The Jew sighed, pulled an excessively crumpled little piece of paper from his greasy wallet, straightened the paper out and placed it on the marble table-top. Then he rose and lazily left the dark little room, whereupon Ignacy recognised old Szlangbaum through a hole in his newspaper.

Ignacy hurriedly drank up his chocolate and fled into the street. He was already sick and tired of the auction, with which his ears and head were crammed. He wished to pass the remaining time in some way, and seeing the Capucine church open, went towards it, certain he would find tranquillity in its walls, and an agreeable coolness and that above all he would at least not hear about the auction.

He went into the church and really did find silence and coolness there, not to mention a dead body on a catafalque, surrounded by unlit candles and flowers which had lost their smell. For some time past, Ignacy had disliked the sight of coffins, so he turned left and saw a woman in black kneeling on the ground. It was the Baroness Krzeszowska, humbly bowed to the earth: she was beating her breast and dabbing her eyes with a handkerchief now and then.

'I'm positive she's praying that the Łęcki property will go for sixty thousand roubles,' thought Ignacy. But as the sight of Baroness Krzeszowska held no attraction, he withdrew on tip-toe and went over to the right-hand side of the church. Here he found only a couple of women: one was saying her rosary in an undertone, the other sleeping. There was no one else – except that from behind a pillar there appeared a man of medium height, erect despite his grey hair, whispering a prayer with bowed head. Rzecki recognised Mr Łęcki, and thought 'He, of course, is praying that his house fetches a hundred and twenty thousand . . .'

Then he hastily left the church, wondering how the good Lord would satisfy the contradictory pleas of Baroness Krzeszowska and Tomasz Łęcki.

As he had not found what he was looking for either in the café or in the church, Ignacy began walking about in the street near the court. He was much confused: it seemed to him that every passer-by looked into his face mockingly, as much as to say: 'Wouldn't you be better employed, you old scamp, looking after the shop?' or that one of the 'gentlemen' was about to leap out of every passing droshky to tell him the shop had burned down or collapsed. So again he wondered whether it would be better to give up the whole idea of the auction as a bad job, and go back to his ledgers and office – when he suddenly heard a desperate shriek.

It was some Jew or other, leaning out of a window of the court and shouting something to the crowd of his co-religionists, who in turn all rushed to the door, pushing, thrusting tranquil passers-by aside and stamping their feet impatiently, like a frightened flock of sheep in a crowded byre.

'Aha – the auction has started,' said Ignacy to himself, following them up the stairs.

At this moment he felt someone take hold of his arm and, turning, saw that same majestic gentleman who had obtained a rouble on account from Szlangbaum in the café. The stately personage was obviously in a hurry, for he was making way for himself with both fists among the packed mass of the Hebrews' bodies, shouting: 'Out of my way, Yids! I am going to the auction . . .'

Against their custom, the Jews drew aside and looked at him with admiration: 'What money he must have!' one muttered to his neighbour.

Ignacy, infinitely less presumptuous than the stately individual, yielded himself up to the favour and disfavour of fate, rather than push. The stream of Hebrews surrounded him on all sides. In front he saw a greasy collar, dirty neckerchief and still dirtier neck: behind, he could smell the odour of fresh onion: to the right, a grizzled beard pressed against his collar-bone, and to the left a powerful elbow was squeezing his ribs almost unbearably.

They thronged about, pushed, clutched at his coat. Someone grabbed his legs, another reached into his pocket, someone thumped him between the shoulder blades. It reached the point where Ignacy thought they would entirely crush his chest. He raised his eyes to Heaven, and saw he was already within the door . . . Now! Now! They were stifling him . . . Suddenly he felt an empty space before him, struck his head on someone's personal charms not very carefully veiled in a frock-coat and was inside the court-room.

He breathed again. Behind him resounded the shrieks and curses of the would-be bidders and from time to time the comments of the door-man: 'Gents, why are you pushing so? What's this, gents? Are you a flock of sheep, then?'

'I never thought it would be so hard to get into an auction sale,' Ignacy sighed.

He passed two court-rooms, so empty that there was not even a chair to be seen on the floor, nor a nail in the wall. These rooms formed the vestibule to one of the departments of justice, but were light and cheerful all the same. Floods of sun-beams and the warm July breeze, imbued with Warsaw dust, poured through the open windows. Ignacy could hear the twitter of sparrows and the cease-less rattle of droshkies, and felt a curious sensation of disharmony: 'Is it possible,' thought he, 'that a court should look as empty as an unrented apartment and yet be so cheerful?'

It seemed to him that barred windows, grey damp walls and suspended handcuffs would be much more appropriate to a court-room in which people were sentenced to everlasting or at least lifelong imprisonment.

But here was the main court-room, into which all the Hebrews were hastening, and where the whole business of the auction was concentrated. It was such a large room that forty people might have danced a mazurka in it – were it not for the low barrier which divided it into two sections, for civil cases and for auctions. In the civil portion were carved benches, in the auction part was a platform, with a table on it, circular and covered with green baize. Behind the table Ignacy saw three officials with chains around their necks and senatorial dignity on their faces: they were the auctioneers. In front of each official lay a heap of documents concerning the properties for sale. Between the table and barrier, immediately in front of the latter, was a crowd of would-be buyers. All had their heads raised and were gazing at the officials with a spiritual absorption that inspired ascetics gazing at a holy vision might have envied.

Although the windows were open, a smell midway between the scent of hyacinths and aged putty prevailed in the court. Ignacy guessed it was the smell of Jewish gabardines.

Except for the rattle of droshkies, it was quite quiet in the courtroom. The auctioneers were silent, absorbed in their documents, the buyers equally silent, gazing at the auctioneers: the remainder of the public, gathered in the civilian portion of the hall and separated into groups, was certainly murmuring, but softly. It was not in their own interests to be overheard.

Consequently the groan of Baroness Krzeszowska sounded all the louder as, clutching her lawyer by the lapel of his frock-coat, she cried feverishly: 'Do not leave me, I beg you! I'll pay you anything you ask . . .'

'Please, Baroness – no threats,' replied the lawyer.

'I'm not threatening you in the least, but don't leave me,' the Baroness exclaimed with genuine feeling.

'I'll come back for the auction, but just now I have to go to my murderer . . .'

'So! A wretched murderer arouses more of your sympathy than a deserted woman, whose property, honour, peace of mind . . .'

The importuned lawyer fled so fast that his trousers looked even shinier around the knees than they really were. The Baroness began to run after him, but at this moment she fell into the embrace of an individual who wore very green spectacles and had the countenance of a sacristan.

'Dear lady, what is wrong?' the individual in green spectacles asked sweetly, 'no lawyer vill inflate the price of your house . . . That is vat I am here for. Gif me one per cent for every thousand roubles over the initial sum, and twenty roubles for expenses . . .'

The Baroness Krzeszowska started away from him and, recoiling like an actress in a tragic role, uttered a single word: 'Satan!' The individual in green spectacles realised he had missed the boat and withdrew in discomfiture. At the same time, his path was crossed by a second individual with the features of a confirmed scoundrel, who whispered to him for a few moments, making very lively gestures. Ignacy was certain these two gentlemen would come to blows, but they parted quite peaceably and the individual who looked a scoundrel drew near the Baroness Krzeszowska and said in a low voice: 'If the Baroness is not careful, we may even not let the price reach seventy thousand . . .'

'My saviour!' cried the Baroness, 'you see before you a wronged and deserted female, whose property, honour and peace of mind . . .'

'What's honour to me?' said the individual with the visage of a scoundrel, 'will you give me ten roubles deposit?'

Both went off into the furthest corner of the room and were lost to Ignacy's gaze behind a group of Hebrews. In the group were old Szlangbaum and a young, beardless Jew who was so pale and emaciated that Ignacy suspected he must very recently have entered into the bonds of matrimony. Old Szlangbaum was holding forth to the emaciated little Jew, whose eyes grew more and more sheepish; but just what he was holding forth about, Ignacy could not imagine.

So he turned to the other side of the room and caught sight of Mr Łęcki with his lawyer, a few paces away; the latter was clearly bored and wanted to be off. 'If only a hundred and fifteen . . . or a hundred and twenty thousand,' said Mr Łęcki, 'after all, you must know some method . . .'

'Hm . . . hm . . .' said the lawyer, looking longingly at the door, 'you're asking too much . . . A hundred and twenty thousand roubles for a house that cost sixty thousand . . .'

'But, my dear man, it cost me a hundred thousand . . .'

'Yes, but . . . you paid rather too much . . .'

'Yet,' Mr Łęcki interrupted, 'I'm only asking a hundred and ten thousand. It strikes me you ought to help me, no matter what. Surely there are ways of which I know nothing, since I'm not a lawyer . . .'

'Hm . . . hm . . .' the lawyer muttered.

Fortunately one of his colleagues (also in a frock-coat with badge) called him from the room: a moment later the individual in green spectacles with the look of a sacristan approached Mr Łęcki and said: 'Vhat is the matter, Your Excellency? No lawyer will outbid you for the house. That is vat I am here for. Gif me tventy roubles for expenses and one per cent per thousand above sixty thousand . . .'

Mr Łęcki eyed the sacristan with vast contempt: he put both hands in his trouser pockets (which struck even himself as odd) and declared: 'I'll pay one per cent per thousand over a hundred and twenty thousand . . .'

The sacristan in green spectacles bowed, shrugged his left shoulder and replied: 'You must excuse me, Excellency . . .'

'Wait!' Mr Łęcki interrupted, 'over a hundred and ten . . .'

'Excuse me . . .'

'Over a hundred, then!'

'Excuse me . . .'

'May the devil take you! How much do you want?'

'One per cent on any sum over seventy thousand, plus twenty roubles for expenses,' said the sacristan, bowing low.

'Will you take ten?' asked Mr Łęcki, purple with fury.

'I won't say no even to a rouble . . .'

Mr Łęcki produced a splendid wallet, took a whole bundle of rustling ten-rouble notes from it and gave one to the sacristan who bowed: 'You'll see, Your Excellency,' the sacristan whispered.

Two Jews were standing near Ignacy: one was tall and swarthy, with a beard so black as to be blue, while the other was bald, with such long whiskers that they reached down to the lapels of his frock-coat. Catching sight of Łęcki's ten-rouble notes, the gentleman with the whiskers smiled and said in an undertone to the handsome dark man: 'See the bank-notes yonder gent has? Listen how they rustle . . . They're glad to see me. You understand me, Mr Cynader?'

'Łęcki is your client, then?' asked the handsome dark man.

'Why not?'

'He has . . . a sister in Cracow who is bequeathing to his daughter . . .'

'Suppose she doesn't, though?'

The gentleman with whiskers was taken aback for a moment: 'Don't talk such nonsense to me! Why shouldn't his sister in Cracow make a will, seeing she's sick?'

'I don't know nothin' about that,' the handsome dark man replied (Ignacy had to admit he had never before seen such a handsome man).

'But he has a daughter, Mr Cynader,' said the owner of the flowing whiskers uneasily, 'you know his daughter Izabela, don't you, Mr Cynader? I'd give her – well, a hundred roubles and no questions asked.'

'I'd give her a hundred and fifty,' said the handsome dark man, 'though of course that Łęcki is a doubtful case.'

'Doubtful? And what about Mr Wokulski?'

'Mr Wokulski? Ah – that's big business,' replied the dark man, 'but she's stupid and Łęcki is stupid and so are they all. And they will destroy Wokulski, and he can't do anything about it.'

Ignacy saw red: 'Good God!' he thought, 'so they even talk about Wokulski at auction-sales, and about her. And they even predict she will destroy him. Good God!'

Some confusion had occurred at the table occupied by the auctioneers; all the spectators surged in that direction. Old Szlangbaum approached the table, nodded on the way to the emaciated Jew and winked imperceptibly at the stately individual to whom he had been talking in the café. At the same moment, Baroness Krzeszowska's lawyer hurried in, took his place in front of the table without so much as looking at her and muttered to the auctioneer: 'Be quick, be quick, for goodness sake, I have no time to waste . . .'

A new group of persons entered the court a few moments after the lawyer. They consisted of a married couple apparently in the butchering line of business, an old lady with a teenage grandson and two gentlemen: one was stout and grey-haired, the other curly-haired and consumptive-looking. Both had humble expressions and shabby clothing but on catching sight of them, the Jews began whispering together and pointing at them with expressions of admiration and respect. Both stopped so near Ignacy that he involuntarily overheard some comments the grey-haired gentleman made to his curly-haired companion: 'Do as I do, Ksawery. I am in no hurry, I assure you. I've been going to buy a nice little house for three years now, something costing a hundred thousand or so, for my old age – but I'm in no hurry. I see in the papers what houses are up for auction, I read them slowly, I work it all out in my head, then I come here to see what offers people make. And now that I've gained experience and want to buy a property – the prices all go up in a most impractical way, damnation take them, and I have had to start all my calculations over again. But when we start, I assure you we'll beat down the prices . . .'

'Silence!' someone at the table shouted. The court-room grew quiet, and Ignacy listened to the description of an apartment house situated in so-and-so street, with three wings and three floors, a driveway, garden and the like. During this important event, Mr Łęcki went pale then pink by turns, and Baroness Krzeszowska kept sniffing a crystal flask in a gold case.

'Why, I know that house!' the individual in green glasses like a sacristan, suddenly exclaimed, 'I know that house! It's worth a hundred and twenty thousand roubles at least . . .'

'What d'you mean?' exclaimed the gentleman with the look of a scoundrel, next to the Baroness Krzeszowska, 'what sort of a house is it? It's a positive ruin, it's a morgue . . .'

Mr Łęcki turned very pink. He nodded to the sacristan and asked in a whisper: 'Who is that scoundrel?'

'Him?' asked the sacristan, 'he'll be hanged one day . . . Don't pay no attention, Your Excellency.' And he added loudly: 'Upon my word, a man could safely pay a hundred and thirty thousand for it.'

'Who is that scoundrel?' the Baroness asked the individual with a wicked look on his face, 'who's that in the green spectacles?'

'Him?' asked the man, 'he's a well-known criminal . . . he left jail not so long ago. Don't pay any attention to him, madam. Not worth spitting on . . .'

'Silence, there!' an official voice called from the table.

Smiling in a familiar manner, the sacristan winked at Mr Łęcki and pushed his way between the bidders to the table. There were a total of four: the Baroness's lawyer, the stately individual, old Szlangbaum and the emaciated Jew, next to whom the sacristan stopped.

'Sixty thousand and five hundred roubles,' said Baroness Krzeszowska's lawyer.

'Good God! It's not worth a penny more,' put in the individual with the face of a scoundrel. The Baroness glanced triumphantly at Mr Łęcki.

'Sixty-five thousand,' said the majestic individual.

'Sixty-six . . .' added Szlangbaum.

'Seventy thousand!' cried the sacristan.

'O! O! O!' the Baroness burst into tears, collapsing on the shabby sofa. Her lawyer hastily quit the table and hurried off to defend his murderer.

'Seventy-five thousand!' shouted the stately individual.

'This is killing me!' the Baroness groaned.

There was a stir in the court-room. An aged Lithuanian took the Baroness by the arm, of which Maruszewicz (who had appeared from Heaven knows where for this solemn occasion) relieved him. Sobbing, leaning on Maruszewicz, the Baroness left the court-room, calling down curses upon her lawyer, the court, the bidders and the auctioneers. Mr Łęcki smiled faintly and meanwhile the emaciated Jew was saying: 'Eighty thousand and one hundred roubles . . .'

'Eighty-five,' interposed Szlangbaum.

Mr Łęcki was all eyes, all ears. His eyes perceived nothing but the three bidders and his ears caught the words of the stately individual: 'Eighty-eight thousand . . .'

'Eighty-eight thousand and one hundred roubles,' said the emaciated Jew.

'Ninety thousand, then!' concluded old Szlangbaum, banging the table with his fist.

'Ninety thousand roubles,' said the auctioneer, 'going . . .'

Forgetting his manners, Mr Łęcki leaned over to the sacristan and whispered: 'Bid! Make a bid, sir!'

'What are you fighting for?' the sacristan asked the emaciated Jew.

'What are you fussing about?' another auctioneer addressed the sacristan, 'are you buying the property then? Be off with you!'

'Ninety thousand roubles . . . going . . .' shouted the auctioneer.

Mr Łęcki's face turned grey.

'Ninety thousand roubles . . . gone!' the auctioneer cried, and struck the green baize with his little hammer.

'Sold to Szlangbaum!' some in the court exclaimed.

Mr Łęcki gazed dully around and only now did he notice his lawyer: 'My dear sir,' he said in a trembling voice, 'this isn't right . . .'

'What isn't?

'No, it isn't right . . . it's dishonest . . .' Mr Łęcki repeated indignantly.

'What isn't right?' his lawyer echoed, rather vexed, 'after paying off your mortgage you'll make thirty thousand . . .'

'But that house cost me a hundred thousand, and might have fetched more, if more care had been taken – a hundred and twenty thousand.'

'Yes,' the sacristan confirmed, 'that house is worth about a hundred and twenty thousand.'

'D'you hear that, my good man?' Mr Łęcki said, 'if only more care had been taken . . .'

'My dear sir, no recriminations, please! You have been taking the advice of crooked dealers, of scoundrels from jail . . .'

'Come, now!' the sacristan replied, offended, 'not everyone who has been to jail is a scoundrel. As for advice . . .'

'Yes, that house was worth a hundred and twenty thousand,' exclaimed the scoundrel-like individual, unexpectedly coming to Łęcki's aid.

Mr Łęcki gazed at him glassily, but could not yet realise the situation fully. He did not bid his lawyer good-bye, put his hat on in the court-room and as he went out, muttered: 'Through Jews and lawyers I have lost thirty thousand roubles . . . I might have got a hundred and twenty thousand.'

Old Szlangbaum was leaving too: then he was accosted by Mr Cynader, the handsome dark man Ignacy had seen just before: 'What sort of business are you up to, Mr Szlangbaum?' he asked him, 'you might have bought that house for seventy-one thousand. It's worth no more today.'

'Not to some, perhaps, but to another it is: I do always good business,' said the pensive Szlangbaum.

Finally Rzecki too left the court, in which another sale was taking place and another audience had already collected. Ignacy went downstairs slowly and thought: 'So Szlangbaum bought the house, and for ninety thousand, as Klein predicted. But Szlangbaum is not Wokulski, after all . . . Staś wouldn't do anything so silly! No! As for Izabela, it's all nonsense, gossip . . .'

XIX

First Warning

I T WAS one o'clock in the afternoon when Ignacy drew near to
the store, feeling ashamed and uneasy. How could anyone waste
so much time . . . precisely when the most customers were in
the shop? And hadn't some disaster occurred? What pleasure was
there to be gained from wandering about the streets amidst the
heat, dust and smell of roasting asphalt? The day really was remarkably hot and glaring; the pavements and buildings gave off a glow;
metal signs and lamp-posts could not be touched and because of the
excess of light, tears came into Mr Ignacy's eyes and black spots
danced across his field of vision. 'If I were the Lord,' he thought,
'I'd save half the heat of July for use in December . . .'

Suddenly he noticed the store's display windows (he was just
passing) and was astounded. The display had not been changed for
two whole weeks. Here another week had passed without the
display being changed! The same bronzes, vases, fans, the same
travelling bags, gloves, umbrellas and toys. Had anyone ever seen
anything so dreadful?

'I'm a wretch,' he muttered, 'first I got drunk, today I'm
wandering about . . . The devil will get me, sure as fate . . .'

Hardly had he entered the store, uncertain which burdened him
most – his heart or his feet – than Mraczewski seized on him. His
hair had been trimmed in the Warsaw style, he was combed and
perfumed as before, and was serving customers out of sheer
pleasure, for he himself was a customer and from foreign parts too.
The local ladies could not get over their admiration.

'For goodness sake, Ignacy,' he exclaimed, 'I've been waiting
three hours for you! You must all have gone off your heads!' He
took him by the arm and without paying any attention to a couple
of customers, who stared at them in amazement, hurriedly drew
Rzecki into the office where the safe was kept. Here he thrust the
old clerk who had gone grey in service into a hard chair and stood
before him, ringing his hands like a desperate Germont before

Violetta, as he said: 'You know what? I realised that after I'd left here the business would go to pieces, but I never expected it to happen so soon . . . The fact that you don't stay in the store doesn't matter so much – it won't run away. But as for the stupidities the old man is committing – that's a disgrace!'

Ignacy's eyebrows seemed about to disappear from his forehead altogether in amazement. 'I beg your pardon!' he exclaimed, jumping up. But Mraczewski made him sit down again.

'Not a word!' the perfumed young man interrupted, 'do you know what is going on? Suzin is leaving tonight for Berlin to see Bismarck, and then on to Paris for the Exhibition. It is essential – essential, d'you hear? – that we persuade Wokulski to go with him. But that blockhead . . .'

'Mr Mraczewski! How dare you . . . ?'

'It's my nature, and Wokulski is mad! Only today did I find out the truth . . . D'you know how much the old man might make in this Paris business with Suzin? Not ten, but fifty thousand roubles, Mr Rzecki! And that booby not only refuses to go, but even says he doesn't know whether he will go at all. He doesn't know, yet Suzin can only wait a few days at the most for the deal.'

'How about Suzin?' asked Mr Ignacy, genuinely perturbed.

'Suzin? He's angry and – what's worse – bitter. He says Stanisław Petrovich is no longer the man he used to be, that he despises him – in a word, they disagree! Fifty thousand roubles profit and the trip free. Well, just tell me whether St Stanisław himself wouldn't have gone to Paris on such terms?'

'Certainly,' Ignacy muttered, 'where's Staś – that's to say Mr Wokulski?' he added, rising.

'In your apartment, writing accounts for Suzin. You'll find out for yourself how much you stand to lose by this folly . . .'

The office door opened and Klein appeared, a letter in his hand. 'Łęcki's butler brought this for the old man,' he said, 'maybe you'll hand it to him, for he's rather bad-tempered today.'

Ignacy took the pale blue envelope adorned with a pattern of forget-me-nots, but hesitated. Meanwhile Mraczewski glanced over his shoulder at the superscription: 'A letter from little Bela!' he exclaimed, 'here's a go!' and he hurried out of the office, laughing.

'Devil take it,' Ignacy muttered, 'can all these rumours be true, then? So it's for her that he is spending ninety thousand roubles on buying that house, and losing fifty thousand from Suzin? A total of a hundred and forty thousand roubles! And that carriage, and the races, and those donations to charity! And . . . and that Rossi who stared at Miss Łęcka as fervently as a Jew at Moses' tablets! Ach – away with ceremony!'

He buttoned up his jacket, straightened his back and went to his room with the letter. Not until this moment did he notice that his shoes were squeaking somewhat, and felt a sort of relief.

Wokulski was sitting in Ignacy's room over a pile of papers, without his coat and waistcoat, writing. 'Here you are,' he said, looking up at Rzecki's entry, 'you won't mind me using your place as though it were mine?'

'The boss being formal!' exclaimed Mr Ignacy, bitterly, 'here's a letter from . . . from them, from the Łęckis.'

Wokulski glanced at the superscription, feverishly tore open the envelope and pored over the letter – once, twice, thrice he read it. Rzecki upset something on the desk, then noticing that his friend had finished reading and was thoughtfully resting his head on one hand, said drily: 'Are you going to Paris with Suzin today?'

'Certainly not.'

'I hear it's an important deal . . . fifty thousand roubles.'

Wokulski did not say a word.

'So you'll be going tomorrow or the next day, for apparently Suzin is prepared to wait for you a day or two?'

'I don't know whether I'll be going at all.'

'That's too bad, Staś. Fifty thousand roubles is a fortune, a pity to let it slip. If people hear you have let such an opportunity go by . . .'

'They will say I've gone mad,' Wokulski interrupted.

Again he fell silent, then suddenly exclaimed: 'Suppose I have a more important duty to fulfil than making fifty thousand roubles?'

'Is it politics?' Rzecki asked quietly, with alarm in his eyes and a smile on his lips.

Wokulski handed him the letter: 'Read this,' he said, 'you will see there are better things than politics.'

Ignacy took the letter with some hesitation, but on Wokulski's renewed command, read it:

'The wreath is perfectly beautiful and I thank you in Rossi's name for this gift. Placing emeralds between the golden leaves was incomparably tasteful. You simply must come to us for dinner tomorrow so we may discuss Rossi's farewell performance, and our trip to Paris too. Papa told me yesterday we shall be leaving within a week at the latest. We shall of course travel together, since without the pleasure of your company the journey would lose half its charm for me. Au revoir. Izabela Łęcka.'

'I don't understand,' said Ignacy, indifferently casting the letter to the table, 'no one throws fifty thousand roubles – if not more – into the mud for the pleasure of travelling to Paris with Miss Łęcka and even talking about presents for her . . . her admirers.'

Wokulski rose and, leaning both hands on the table, asked: 'What if it suited me to throw my entire fortune in the mud for her sake – what then?'

The veins stood out on his forehead, his shirt-front heaved fever-ishly. The same sparks which Rzecki had noticed during the duel with the Baron glittered and died away in his eyes.

'What then?' Wokulski repeated.

'Then – nothing,' Rzecki replied calmly, 'I'd merely admit that I was mistaken for I don't know how often in my life . . .'

'What about?'

'About you. I thought that a man who had risked death . . . and gossip to acquire a fortune would have some higher aim . . .'

'Don't mention higher aims to me,' Wokulski cried, banging the table, 'I know what I have done for those higher aims, but what have they done for me? Is there no end to the demands of the oppressed who allow no rights to *me*? I want for the first time to do something for myself . . . My head's full to overflowing with clichés that no one ever puts into action . . . Personal happiness – that's my obligation now . . . otherwise I'd shoot myself, if I didn't see something for myself ahead, other than monstrous burdens. Thousand of people are idle, but one man has his "duty" towards them . . . Did you ever hear anything more abominable?'

'Wasn't the ovation for Rossi a burden?' Mr Ignacy asked.

'I didn't do it for Rossi . . .'

'Merely to please a woman, I know. Of all savings banks, a woman is the least secure,' Rzecki replied.

'Mind what you say!' Wokulski hissed.

What I have said, rather . . . You seem to think you have only just invented love. I know about it, too – hm! A few years back, I, like a half-wit, fell in love, and yet my Heloise was carrying on all the time with other men. My God! How much all those glances tortured me as I saw them exchanged . . . In the end embraces were exchanged in my presence, even . . . Believe me, Staś, I am not as naive as some people think. I have seen a great deal in my life, and have come to the conclusion that we put too much heart into the game called love.'

'You say that because you don't know her,' Wokulski interrupted stormily.

'Every woman is exceptional, until she breaks your heart. It's true I don't know her, but I know others. To gain a great victory over a woman one must be both ruthless and shameless: two virtues you haven't got. That is why I am warning you – do not risk much, for you will be outdistanced, if you haven't been already. I have never spoken to you of such things before, have I? I don't even look like a philosopher. . . . But I feel you are threatened by danger, so I repeat – beware! Do not engage your heart in a shameful game, for with her at your side you will be derided by every Tom, Dick and Harry. And I must tell you that when that happens a man feels such bitterness that . . . better not live to see it, God knows!'

Wokulski, on the settee, clenched his fist but kept silent. At this moment there was a knock on the door and Lisiecki appeared: 'Mr Łęcki to see you. Shall I bring him in here?'

'Ask him to step in,' Wokulski replied, hastily buttoning his waistcoat and jacket.

Rzecki got up, shook his head mournfully and left the room. 'I thought things were bad,' he muttered in the passage, 'but never that they were this bad . . .'

Hardly had Wokulski collected himself than Mr Łęcki entered, followed by the door-man. Mr Łęcki had bloodshot eyes and livid patches on his cheeks. He threw himself into an armchair, leaned back and breathed heavily. The door-man lingered on the threshold with an embarrassed expression and waited for orders, twiddling with the metal buttons on his livery.

'Forgive me, Stanisław, but . . . a little water and some lemon juice, if you please . . .' Tomasz whispered.

'Soda water, lemon and sugar. Be quick!' said Wokulski to the door-man. The latter went out, catching his great buttons on the door-handle.

'It's nothing,' said Tomasz with a smile, 'I have a short neck, then the heat and vexation . . . I'll rest a moment . . .'

Concerned, Wokulski took off his tie for him and undid his collar. Then he soaked a towel in eau de cologne which he found in Rzecki's desk and bathed the sick man's neck, face and temples with filial concern. Tomasz pressed his hand: 'I am better . . . Thank you,' and he added in an undertone, 'I like you as a ministering angel. Bela couldn't have done it more delicately . . . Well, she was born to be served . . .'

The door-man brought a syphon and lemons. Wokulski made lemonade and gave it to Tomasz, from whose face the livid stains were gradually disappearing.

'Go to my house,' said Wokulski to the door-man, 'and tell them to harness the horses. Bring the carriage around to the shop.'

'Good of you . . . good of you . . .' said Tomasz, pressing his hand and looking gratefully at him with bloodshot eyes, 'I am not used to so much trouble being taken, for Bela knows nothing of such things . . .'

Izabela's inability to look after sick people struck Wokulski disagreeably. But only for a moment.

Tomasz slowly regained strength. The copious sweat left his forehead, his voice grew stronger and only the network of little veins in his eyes bore witness to the attack. He even walked about the room, stretched and began: 'Oh, you can have no idea, Stanisław, how vexed I was today. Will you believe that my house was sold for ninety thousand?'

Wokulski flinched.

'I was positive,' said Mr Łęcki, 'that I'd get at least a hundred and ten thousand. In the court I heard people saying the property was worth a hundred and twenty . . . But what of it? A Jew had set his heart on buying it, a miserable usurer, that Szlangbaum . . . He came to terms with his competitors and who knows but with my lawyer too, and I lost twenty or thirty thousand.'

Now Wokulski looked apoplectic, but he said nothing.

'I'd reckoned,' went on Mr Łęcki, 'that on the fifty thousand you'd pay me some ten thousand a year. Household expenses are six or eight thousand, so Bela and I could go abroad every year on the remainder. I even promised the child we'd go to Paris next week. Confound it! Six thousand roubles will barely suffice for a wretched existence and there's no question of travelling . . . Wretched Jew! Wretched society, so subservient to usurers that no one dares to come into conflict with them even at an auction-sale. But what pains me most is the fact that some Christian, perhaps even an aristocrat, may be concealed behind this Szlangbaum.'

His voice grew more breathless and again livid colouring appeared on his cheeks. He sat down and drank some water: 'Scoundrels . . . scoundrels . . .' he whispered.

'Please be calm,' Wokulski said. 'How much cash will you be able to let me have?'

'I asked the Prince's lawyer (for my own is a scoundrel) to collect the money due and hand it all to you, Stanisław . . . Thirty thousand altogether. And as you have promised me twenty per cent I'll have six thousand roubles a year for my entire upkeep . . . It's poverty, poverty!'

'With that amount,' Wokulski replied, 'I can invest in a better business. You'll get your ten thousand a year.'

'Is that possible?'

'Yes. I have a special opportunity.'

Tomasz jumped up: 'My saviour! My benefactor!' he said in an excited voice, 'you are the noblest of men . . . But,' he added, drawing back and pressing his hands together, 'are you sure you do not stand to lose anything yourself?'

'I? Don't forget I am a tradesman . . .'

'A tradesman! Come now,' exclaimed Tomasz, 'thanks to you I have learned that the word "tradesman" is today a synonym for greatness of soul, tact, heroism . . . You are a fine man!'

And he embraced him, almost weeping.

Wokulski made him sit down again for the third time, and at this moment someone knocked: 'Come in . . .'

In came Henryk Szlangbaum, pale, with glittering eyes. He stopped in front of Tomasz, bowed to him and said: 'Sir – I am Szlangbaum, son of the same "wretched usurer" you insulted in the shop in the presence of my colleagues and customers.'

'Sir . . . I didn't know . . . I am prepared to render you any satisfaction . . . first of all, I apologise . . . I was very angry,' said Tomasz, agitated.

Szlangbaum calmed down: 'Instead of giving me satisfaction,' he replied, 'please listen to me. Why did my father buy your house? Never mind that for today. But he did not cheat you – I'll give you decisive proof of that. My father will at once let you have that house for ninety thousand – I'll go further: the purchaser will let you have it for seventy thousand . . .'

'Henryk!' Wokulski interposed.

'I have finished. Good-day,' said Szlangbaum, and he left the room with a low bow to Tomasz.

'What a disagreeable thing,' Tomasz exclaimed after a moment, 'I'm afraid I did utter a few bitter words about old Szlangbaum in the shop, but I didn't know his son was there, upon my word . . . He will let me have the house back for seventy thousand after paying ninety thousand? Odd! What have you to say to that, Stanisław ?'

'Perhaps the house is really only worth ninety thousand,' Wokulski replied non-committally.

Tomasz began buttoning his clothes and tie. 'Thank you, Stanisław,' he said, 'both for your help and for concerning yourself with my business affairs. But – Bela wants you to dinner tomorrow . . . Get the money from the Prince's lawyer, and as to the percentage which you will be kind enough . . .'

'I'll pay it at once, six months in advance.'

'I am most grateful,' Tomasz went on. embracing him, 'so – au revoir till tomorrow. Don't forget the dinner . . .'

Wokulski conducted him across the yard to the gate, where the carriage was already waiting. 'This heat is frightful,' said Tomasz, getting into the carriage with some difficulty and assisted by Wokulski, 'What a disagreeable thing about those Jews . . . He gave ninety thousand and is prepared to let it go for seventy . . . Fancy! Upon my word . . .'

The horses moved off in the direction of Aleje Ujazdowskie.

On the way home, Tomasz sat bemused. He did not feel the heat, only a general weakness and roaring in the ears. Sometimes it seemed to him that he saw differently out of each eye, or that both saw worse. He leaned back in the corner of the carriage, rocking as if drunk with each jolt. His thoughts and feelings mingled in a strange way. Sometimes he imagined he was surrounded by a net of intrigues, from which only Wokulski could extricate him. Then that he was seriously ill and only Wokulski knew how to tend him. Then again that he was a dying, leaving behind an impoverished daughter deserted by everyone, whom only Wokulski would look after. And finally he thought it must be pleasant to own a carriage as light as this in which he was riding, and that if he asked

Wokulski for it, the latter would make him a present of it.

'Fearful heat!' Tomasz muttered.

The horses stopped in front of the house, Tomasz got out and went upstairs without even nodding to the driver. He could hardly move his heavy legs and when he reached his study he fell into a chair with his hat on, and sat thus for a few minutes much to the amazement of the servant, who saw fit to call his mistress.

'The business must have gone well,' he said to Izabela, 'for His Excellency is . . . sort of . . .'

Despite her apparent lack of interest, Izabela had been awaiting her father's return and the result of the auction with the utmost impatience, and she went to his study as quickly as was appropriate to good manners. For she always bore in mind that a young lady with her surname was not supposed to betray her feelings, even in the face of bankruptcy. Yet for all her self-control Mikołaj saw (from the bright flush on her cheeks) that she was excited and added once again in an undertone: 'Oh, the business must have gone well, because His Excellency . . . him . . .'

Izabela wrinkled up her beautiful brows and slammed the study door behind her. Her father was still sitting there with his hat on: 'What's the matter, father?' she asked with a touch of distaste, looking at his bloodshot eyes.

'Misfortune . . . ruin . . .' Tomasz replied, taking off his hat with some difficulty, 'I have lost thirty thousand roubles.'

Izabela went white and sat down on the leather *chaise-longue*.

'A wretched Jew, a usurer, frightened away competition, bribed my lawyer, and . . .'

'So we have nothing?' she murmured.

'How so, nothing? We still have thirty thousand, and ten thousand a year interest on it. That excellent Wokulski! I had no idea that such nobility existed . . . And you should have seen how he took care of me today.'

'Took care of you? Why?'

'I had a slight attack due to the heat and my vexation . . .'

'What sort of attack?'

'The blood ran to my head . . . but it is better now. Wretched Jew . . . but Wokulski – it was something quite unusual, I assure you.' He burst into tears.

'Papa, what's wrong? I'll send for the doctor,' Izabela exclaimed, kneeling down by his chair.

'No, it's nothing . . . calm yourself . . . But it crossed my mind that if I were to die, Wokulski is the only man you would be able to trust . . .'

'I don't understand you.'

'You mean you don't recognise me, isn't that it? You're surprised I could entrust your fate to a tradesman. But d'you see . . . when some people have plotted against us in our misfortune, others have deserted us, he hastened to assist and perhaps even saved my life . . . We apoplectics sometimes pass very close to death . . . so when it got me, I asked myself who would look after you. Joanna wouldn't, nor Hortensia, no one . . . Only wealthy orphans can find guardians.'

Seeing that her father was slowly regaining his strength and self-control, Izabela rose from her knees and sat down on the *chaise-longue*: 'What part do you intend this gentleman to play?' she inquired coldly.

'Part?' he echoed, eyeing her attentively, 'the part . . . of an adviser . . . a friend of the family, a guardian. The guardian of the small estate that will be left to you.'

'Oh, I have already long since estimated his value in that respect. He is an energetic man and attached to us. But less of that,' she added after a moment, 'how did you finish off the business of the house?'

'I'll tell you. A scoundrel of a Jew paid ninety thousand, so we have thirty thousand left. But since honest Wokulski is going to pay me ten thousand a year on this sum . . . Thirty-three per cent, imagine that!'

'Thirty-three, how so?' Izabela interrupted, 'ten thousand is ten per cent . . .'

'Not at all! Ten out of thirty means thirty-three per cent, for every hundred, d'you see?'

'I don't understand,' Izabela replied, shaking her head, ' I see that ten means ten: but if ten in tradesman's language means thirty-three, so be it . . .'

'You must realise that you don't understand. I'd explain it but I'm so tired I'll take a nap . . .'

'Should I send for the doctor?' asked Izabela, rising.

'God forbid!' exclaimed Tomasz with a gesture, 'once I get into the doctors' hands, I shan't survive . . .'

Izabela insisted no longer: she kissed her father's hand and brow, and went to her boudoir, deep in thought.

The uneasiness that had been haunting her for several days as to how the auction sale would end had left her without trace. So they still had ten thousand roubles a year, and thirty thousand in cash? So they could go to the Paris Exhibition, then perhaps to Switzerland, and back to Paris for the winter. Or no – for the winter they would come back to Warsaw and open their house again. And if some wealthy man, not old and ugly (as the Baron or marshal were – ugh!) should be found, not a parvenu and not stupid . . . (well, he might be stupid: in their world only Ochocki was clever, and he was an eccentric!). If such a suitor were to be found, Izabela would finally make up her mind . . .

'Father is capital with that Wokulski of his!' she thought, walking to and fro in her boudoir. 'Wokulski my guardian! Wokulski might make a very good adviser, a plenipotentiary, even the trustee of my estate . . . But the title of guardian can only belong to the Prince, who is our cousin and old friend of the family . . .'

She continued walking to and fro with her arms crossed on her bosom and it suddenly occurred to her to ask why her father had grown so affectionate towards Wokulski this day? That man, by some magical power, having won over all her environment, had gained the last position – her father! Her father, Mr Tomasz Łęcki, had wept . . . He, from whose eyes not a single tear had flowed since the death of her mother . . .

'I must admit, all the same, that he is a very good man,' she told herself. 'Rossi would not have been so pleased with Warsaw had it not been for Wokulski's concern. Well, but he will never be my guardian, not even in the event of a misfortune . . . As for the estate, well certainly . . . he might control it, but my guardian! Father must be terribly enfeebled even to conceive such a notion . . .'

Towards six that evening, Izabela was in the drawing-room when the bell rang and she heard Mikołaj's impatient voice: 'I told you to come back tomorrow, my master is poorly today.'

'What am I supposed to do when your master has money but is poorly, and when he's well he has no money?' replied another voice, lisping slightly like a Jew's.

At this moment the rustle of a woman's dress was heard in the vestibule, and Flora hastened in, saying: 'Be quiet! Quiet, for goodness sake . . . Come back tomorrow, Mr Spigelman . . . Surely you know the money will be here . . .'

'That's just why I have come today, and for the third time too. Tomorrow other people will come, and I'll be made to wait again.'

The blood went to Izabela's head and without realising what she did, she suddenly went into the vestibule: 'What is it?' she asked Flora. Mikołaj shrugged and tip-toed back into the kitchen.

'It's me, your ladyship . . . David Spigelman,' replied a little man with black beard and dark spectacles, 'I've come to see His Excellency on a little matter of business . . .'

'Bela, dear,' Flora exclaimed, trying to draw her cousin away. But Izabela freed herself and seeing that her father's study was unoccupied, she told Spigelman to go in.

'Think, Bela – what are you at?' Flora protested.

'I want to find out the truth once and for all,' said Izabela. She shut the study door, sat down and looking into Spigelman's dark glasses, she asked: 'What business have you to discuss with my father?'

'My apologies, your ladyship,' said the visitor, bowing, 'it is a very small matter. I only want my money back.'

'How much is it?'

'Altogether about eight hundred roubles.'

'You will get it tomorrow . . .'

'My apologies, your ladyship, but . . . for six months I've been getting that "tomorrow" week after week and don't see neither interest nor capital . . .'

Izabela felt breathless and there was a pain in her heart. However, she mastered herself: 'You know my father is to get thirty thousand roubles. . . Apart from that (she said this without thinking) we shall be getting ten thousand a year. Your small sum will not disappear – surely you understand that?'

'How ten thousand?' the Jew asked, and raised his head impudently.

'What do you mean – "how"?' she replied indignantly, 'interest on our fortune. . .'

'From thirty thousand?' the Jew interrupted a smile, thinking she wanted to trick him.

'Yes.'

'My apologies, miss,' Spigelman replied ironically, 'I have been making money a long time but I never heard of no such interest. On thirty thousand His Excellency may get three thousand, even then on a very dubious mortgage. But what's it to me? My business is to get my money back. For when the rest come tomorrow, they will be better than David Spigelman, and when His Excellency pays off the rest at interest, I'll have to wait a year . . .'

Izabela rose: 'I assure you you will get your money tomorrow,' she exclaimed, eyeing him contemptuously.

'Word of honour?' asked the Jew, relishing her beauty.

'On my word, you will all be paid off tomorrow. All of you, down to the last penny.'

The Jew bowed low and retreated backwards as he left the study: 'I'll see if your ladyship keeps her word,' he said as he left. Old Mikołaj was in the hall again and opened the door for Spigelman with such grace that the latter shouted at him from the stairs: 'What are you falling over yourself for, Mr Butler?'

Pale with fury, Izabela hurried to her father's bedroom. Flora stopped her. 'Leave him alone, Bela,' she said imploringly, 'your father is so ill . . .'

'I assured that man all our debts will be paid and they must be. Even if it prevents us from going to Paris . . .'

Tomasz, in slippers and without his frock-coat, was just walking about in his bedroom when his daughter entered. She observed that her father looked very poorly, his shoulders were bowed, his grey whiskers drooping, even his eyelids bowed, and he was as bent as an old man, but these observations only prevented her from an outburst of anger, not from settling the matter.

'I apologise, Bela, for being in this undress . . . What has happened?'

'Nothing, father,' she replied, controlling herself, 'some Jew was here . . .'

'It must have been Spigelman . . . He's as troublesome as a mosquito . . .' Tomasz exclaimed, clutching his forehead, 'let him come back tomorrow . . .'

'That is precisely what he is going to do – he and the other . . .'

'Good . . . very good . . . I have long been thinking of settling with them. Well, thank Heaven it has cooled off somewhat . . .'

Izabela was astounded by her father's tranquillity and wretched appearance. It was as though he had gained several years in age since that afternoon. She sat and looking around the bedroom asked, as if reluctantly: 'Do you owe them a great deal, papa?'

'Not much . . . a trifle . . . a few thousand roubles.'

'Are these the promissory notes which my aunt mentioned that someone had bought up last March?'

Mr Łęcki stopped in the middle of the room, cracked his fingers and exclaimed: 'O goodness! I had quite forgotten them!'

'So we have debts of more than a few thousand?'

'Yes, yes . . . a little more. I think it must be from five to six thousand. I'll ask that honest fellow Wokulski, he'll see to it for me . . .'

Despite herself, Izabela was shocked: 'Spigelman says,' she went on after a moment, 'that it is impossible to get ten thousand interest on our fortune. Three thousand at the most, and then on a dubious mortgage . . .'

'He's right – on a mortgage, but commerce is not mortgages. Commerce can provide thirty per cent . . . But how does Spigelman know about our interest rate?' Tomasz asked, wondering a little.

'I told him without meaning to,' Izabela explained, blushing.

'That was a pity . . . a great pity . . . it is better not to mention such matters.'

'Is it anything bad?' she whispered.

'Bad? Well, nothing bad, goodness me . . . But it is always better if people don't know the source of one's income . . . The Baron, or even the marshal himself, wouldn't have the reputations of millionaires and philanthropists if all their secrets were known . . .'

'Why is that, father?'

'You are still a child,' said Tomasz, somewhat embarrassed, 'you are an idealist, so . . . it might set you against them. But you have common sense, after all. The Baron, d'you see, is in some company with usurers and the marshal's fortune came mainly from lucky fires . . . and trading in beef during the Crimean war.'

'So that is what my suitors are like?' Izabela murmured.

'It means nothing, Bela. They have money and plenty of credit, and that is the main thing,' Tomasz assured her.

Izabela shook her head as if to dispel disagreeable thoughts: 'So, papa, we shall not be going to Paris?'

'Why not, my child, why not?'

'If you are going to pay five or six thousand to those Jews . . .'

'Oh, don't worry about that. I'll ask Wokulski to get me that amount at six or seven per cent, and we will pay it off at four hundred a year. After all, we have ten thousand.'

Izabela hung her head, softly drummed on the table and pondered: 'Aren't you afraid, papa – of Wokulski?' she asked, after thinking.

'I?' Tomasz cried, and struck himself on the chest, 'I'm afraid of Joanna, Hortensja, even of our Prince and all of them together, but not of Wokulski. If you'd seen how he bathed my head with eau de cologne today . . . And with what alarm he looked at me! He is the noblest man I ever met . . . He cares nothing for money, cannot profit from me but cares for my friendship . . . God has sent me him and at a time when . . . I am beginning to feel my age and perhaps . . . death.'

With this, Tomasz began blinking his eyes, from which a few tears oozed.

'Papa, you are ill!' Izabela cried, alarmed.

'No, no – it is the heat, the vexation and above all – my grievances. Just think: did anyone call on us today? No one, because they think we have already lost everything . . . Joanna is afraid I may borrow money from her for tomorrow's dinner . . . The same goes for the Baron and the Prince . . . When the Baron learns we have thirty thousand left, he will come here – for you. Just think that even if he married you with a dowry, he would not have to spend any money on me . . . But calm yourself; when they hear we have ten thousand a year, they will all come back again and you will reign in your drawing-room as before. My God, how vexed I am!' said Tomasz, wiping his tearful eyes.

'Am I to send for the doctor, papa?'

Her father considered: 'Tomorrow, tomorrow will do . . . by tomorrow it may have passed of its own accord.'

At this moment a knock came at the door: 'Who is it? Who's there?' asked Tomasz.

'The Countess has come,' said Flora's voice from the corridor.

'Joanna?' Tomasz exclaimed with joyful surprise, 'go to her, Bela . . . I must collect my wits somewhat . . . Well, just fancy! I wager she has found out about the thirty thousand . . . Go to her, Bela! Mikołaj!'

And he began fidgeting around the bedroom looking for various parts of his attire, while Izabela went to her aunt, who was already awaiting her in the drawing-room. Seeing Izabela, the Countess embraced her: 'So God is good, after all,' she exclaimed, 'to send you so much happiness! Well, I hear Tomasz got ninety thousand for the house and your dowry is safe. I'd never have supposed . . .'

'Aunt, my father expected more, but some Jew, the new purchaser, frightened off other bidders,' said Izabela, rather offended.

'Oh, my child – haven't you found out about your father's impractical ways? He may have imagined the house was worth millions, while in fact it was worth seventy thousand or so at the most. After all, houses are auctioned every day, everyone knows what they are like and what is paid for them. Anyhow, there is nothing more to be said; let your father imagine he was cheated, but you, Bela, do pray for the health of that Jew who paid ninety thousand . . . By the way, did you know Kazio Starski is back?'

A powerful flush appeared on Izabela's face: 'When? Where from?' she asked, confused.

'Straight from England, whence he'd gone from China. As handsome as ever, and now he's going to his grandmama's – she, apparently, is to leave him her fortune.'

'Doesn't she live in your neighbourhood?'

'That is precisely what I want to talk to you about. He asked a great deal about you, and I, being sure you have been cured of some of your whims, have advised him to call on you tomorrow.'

'Oh, delightful!' Izabela exclaimed, gratified.

'There, you see,' said the Countess, kissing her, 'your aunt is always thinking of you. He is an excellent match for you, and it will be all the easier to bring it off now that Tomasz has some capital, which ought to suffice him, and Kazio has heard something of Aunt Hortensja's will in your favour. Well, I daresay Starski is somewhat in debt. But in any case, what will be left him of his grandmother's fortune plus what you may get from Hortensja, ought to suffice you both for some time. Later – we will see. He still has an uncle; you have me, so your children will not be poor.'

Izabela kissed her aunt's hands in silence. At this moment she was so beautiful that the Countess, embracing her, drew her to a mirror and said, with a smile: 'Well, mind you look like this tomorrow and you'll see that the wounds in Kazio's heart will re-open . . . Though it is a pity you turned him down that time . . . You would have had a hundred or a hundred and fifty thousand roubles more today . . . I imagine that the poor boy must have spent a great deal of money in his despair . . . But . . .' the Countess added, 'is it true that you and your father want to go to Paris?'

'We intend to.'

'Please, Bela,' her aunt begged, 'do not go. I particularly want to suggest that you spend the rest of the summer with me. And you must, even if only for Starski's sake. You know, the young fellow will be bored in the country, he'll dream . . . You can meet every day and under such circumstances it will be the easiest thing in the world to attach him to you, even obligate him . . .'

Izabela blushed more than before and bowed her beautiful head: 'Aunt!' she whispered.

'Come, my child, don't play the diplomatist with me. A young lady of your age ought to marry – and whatever you do, avoid repeating your past mistakes. Kazio is a splendid *parti*; you won't tire of him quickly, and if he . . . if he does, then at least he will be your husband and will have to be tolerant about many things, just as you will. Where's your father?'

'My father is rather unwell . . .'

'Good Heavens! I daresay his unexpected good fortune has upset him . . .'

'He was ill with rage at that Jew . . .'

'Him and his illusions!' the Countess replied, rising, 'I'll drop in on him for a moment to talk about your holiday. As for you, Bela, I expect you will be able to take advantage of the time.'

After half an hour's intimate talk with Tomasz, the Countess said goodbye to her niece, reminding her once again of Starski.

At about nine, Tomasz, quite contrary to his habits, went to bed, while Izabela summoned her cousin Flora to her room for a talk: 'You know, Flora,' she said, reclining in the *chaise-longue,* 'that Kazio Starski is back and is to call on us tomorrow . . .'

'Ah . . .' Flora breathed, as if this event were already known to her, 'so he is not angry?' she asked, emphasising the last word.

'Surely not . . . At least, I don't know,' Izabela smiled, 'aunt says he is very handsome . . .'

'And in debt. But there is no harm in that. Who isn't nowadays?'

'What would you say, Flora, if I were to . . .'

'Marry him? I'd congratulate you both, of course. But what would the Baron say, not to mention the marshal, Ochocki and above all – Wokulski?'

Izabela rose hastily: 'My dear, what on earth puts Wokulski into your head?'

'Nothing . . .' Flora replied, plucking at the tape of her bodice, 'only I recall that in April you told me . . . that that man had been pursuing you with looks for a twelve-month, that he was surrounding you on all sides . . .'

Izabela burst out laughing: 'Ah, I remember! Of course, that was how it seemed . . . But today, now that I know him better, I can see he does not belong to the category of men one needs to fear. He adores me on the quiet, that's so: but he will adore me just the same, even if I were to . . . get married. A look, a pressure of the hand suffices admirers of Wokulski's sort . . .'

'Are you certain?'

'Completely. In any case, I've found that what seemed to me like snares on his part was nothing but business. Father is lending him thirty thousand roubles and who knows but what all his devices weren't for that purpose?'

'Suppose it were otherwise?' Flora asked, continuing to play with the fringe of her bodice.

'My dear, for goodness sake!' Izabela protested, 'why are you trying to vex me?'

'You yourself said that such people can wait patiently, set their snares, even risk everything and smash . . .'

'Not Wokulski, though.'

'Recollect the Baron . . .'

'The Baron insulted him in public.'

'But he apologised to you.'

'Oh Flora, don't tease me,' Izabela burst out, 'you are intent on making a demon out of this tradesman, perhaps because we lost so much on the sale of the house . . . because father is ill . . . and because Starski is back.'

Flora made a gesture as if to say more, but stopped: 'Goodnight, Bela,' she said, 'perhaps you are right, now.'

And she went out.

All night long Izabela dreamed of Starski as her husband, Rossi as her Platonic lover number one, Ochocki as number two and Wokulski as the trustee of their fortune. Not until ten next morning was she awakened by Flora who reported that Spigelman and another Jew had come: 'Spigelman? Oh yes . . . I had forgotten . . . Tell him to come back later. Is papa up?'

'He's been up an hour. I was just speaking to him about the Jews and he would like you to write a letter to Wokulski.'

'What for?'

'To ask him to be kind enough to call this afternoon and settle the bills of these Jews.'

'Wokulski has our money, certainly,' said Izabela, 'but it would not do for me to write to him on this matter. You write, Flora, on father's behalf. Here is paper, on my desk . . .'

Flora wrote the letter and meanwhile Izabela began dressing. The arrival of the Jews was like a dash of cold water, and the thought of Wokulski troubled her: 'So we really cannot do without this man?' she said to herself, 'well, if he has our money, then of course he must pay off our debts.'

'Please ask him,' she said to Flora, 'to come as soon as possible. For if Starski finds this vile Jew here . . .'

'He has known them longer than we have,' Flora murmured.

'All the same, it would be awful. You don't know the tone of voice that . . . that . . . used to me yesterday.'

'Spigelman,' Flora put in, 'yes, he is impertinent.'

She sealed the letter and took it into the hall, meaning to send away the Jews who were waiting there. Izabela knelt in front of an alabaster statue of the Virgin Mary, imploring her that the messenger would find Wokulski at home and that Starski would not meet the Jews in the house.

The alabaster Virgin Mary heard Izabela's prayers: within an hour, at breakfast, Mikołaj handed her three letters. One was from the Countess, her aunt. In it, she informed Izabela that the doctor would call on her father for a consultation between two and three o'clock, that Kazio Starski was leaving town before that evening and might call at any moment.

'Remember, dear Bela,' her aunt concluded, 'to behave so that the boy thinks of you on his journey and while in the country, to which you and your father must come within a few days. I have already arranged things so that he will not see any young ladies in Warsaw or in the country (apart from you, my angel). Except, of course, for his good old grandmother, the Duchess, and her uninteresting granddaughters.'

Izabela made a slight grimace: she did not care for this emphasis: 'My aunt is fussing over me,' she said to Flora, 'as if I had already lost all hope . . . I don't like that.'

And the picture within her of the handsome Kazio Starski darkened somewhat.

The second letter was from Wokulski, announcing he would be at their service at one o'clock: 'What time did you tell the Jews to come, Flora?' Izabela inquired.

'At one o'clock.'

'Thank goodness! If only Starski doesn't call just then,' said Izabela, picking up the third letter: 'This hand is somehow familiar,' she added 'whose is it, Flora?'

'Don't you recognise it?' Miss Flora replied, with a glance at the envelope, 'Baroness Krzeszowska's . . .'

A flush of anger mounted into Izabela's face: 'Ah, so it is,' she exclaimed, throwing the letter down on the table, 'please send it back, Flora, and write on the envelope 'Not Read' – what does she want, hateful woman . . . ?'

'You can easily find out,' Flora murmured.

'No, no, no! I don't want any letters from that insufferable creature. Some new chicanery, no doubt, for she writes nothing else . . . Still, see what she says. This is the last time I accept her scrawls . . .'

Flora opened the envelope slowly and began reading. Gradually her curiosity gave way to amazement, then to embarrassment: 'I ought not to read this,' she murmured, handing the letter to Izabela.

Dear Izabela, (wrote the Baroness)

I admit my behaviour hitherto may have earned your dislike and brought down upon me the rage of Merciful God, who looks after you so carefully. So I withdraw every thing, humble myself before you, dear Madam, and beg your forgiveness. For is it not proof of Heaven's favour to you that you have been sent Wokulski? A man as mortal as any has become the instrument of the Supreme Hand to punish me and reward you. Not only did he wound my husband in a duel (may God forgive all the wickedness he has committed towards me) but he has also purchased the house in which my beloved child passed away, and is probably demanding huge rents. You are a witness not only of my defeat, but you have also made twenty thousand roubles more than the house was worth.

In return for my repentance, dear Madam, pray persuade Mr Wokulski (who is angry with me, I know not why) to renew my lease and not to drive me out (by exaggerated demands) from the house where my only daughter expired. But this must be cautiously done, since Mr Wokulski does not wish – for reasons unknown to me – that anyone should speak of his purchase. For instead of buying the house himself (like an honest man) he put up the usurer Szlangbaum and also – in order to pay twenty thousand roubles above my offer – brought false bidders to the auction. Why did he behave in this mysterious fashion? You, my dear, must know that better than I, since it is you who are supposed to have invested your small capital with him. It is small, but with God's help (which is so clearly watching over you) and the well-known resourcefulness of Mr Wokulski, it will certainly bring in interest to compensate you for the bitterness of your position hitherto.

Recommending myself to your kindness, dear Izabela, and our mutual relations to the sure justice of Heaven, I remain, yours truly, though despised, and your humble servant, Krzeszowska.

As she read, Izabela went as pale as the paper. She rose from the table, crumpled the letter and raised her hand as if to hurl it into someone's face. Suddenly, seized by fear, she wanted to flee away or to call someone; but at that moment she recollected herself and went to her father.

Mr Łęcki was lying on the sofa in his slippers and dressing-gown, reading the *Courier*. He greeted his daughter very affectionately, and when she had sat down, looked at her in an attentive manner and said: 'Is the light bad in this room, or does it seem to me that my child is out of humour?'

'I am somewhat agitated.'

'So I observe, but it is from the heat. And today you ought,' he added, threatening her with a smile, 'today you must look nice, you mischievous thing, for young Kazio, so your aunt told me yesterday, is to visit . . .'

Izabela said nothing, her father went on: 'It's true that the lad is rather spoiled with everlasting gadding about the world, somewhat in debt too – but he's young, handsome, healthy and wild about you. Joanna hopes the Duchess will keep him in the country a few weeks, and the rest is up to you. And it might not be a bad thing, you know. A good name . . . his fortune will somehow be put together from various sources . . . And in addition he's a man of the world, well-bred, even a kind of hero, if it's true that he's been all around the world.'

'I had a letter from Krzeszowska,' Izabela interrupted.

'Ah? And what does the silly woman say?'

'She says our house was not bought by Szlangbaum, but by Wokulski, and that with the help of false bidders he gave twenty thousand more than it was worth.'

Speaking in a stifled voice, she looked in alarm at her father, fearing an outburst. But Tomasz merely sat up on the sofa, cracked his fingers and exclaimed: 'One moment! One moment! You know, it may be true.'

'How can it be?' Izabela rose hastily, 'he dares present us with twenty thousand roubles – and you can speak of it calmly?'

'I speak calmly because, had I delayed the sale, I should not have got ninety but a hundred and twenty thousand . . .'

'But we could not wait, as the house was up for auction.'

'And because we could not, we have lost and Wokulski will gain, because he can.'

After this remark, Izabela became somewhat calmer: 'So you do not consider it charity on his part? For yesterday you spoke of Wokulski as if you felt you had been trapped by him . . .'

'Ha ha ha!' Tomasz laughed, 'that's capital – simply capital! Yesterday I was somewhat agitated, even very much so, and something . . . something began to dawn upon me . . . But today! Ha ha ha! Let Wokulski overpay for the house. He's a tradesman and ought to know how much and what he is paying for. He loses on one and gains on another. I for one can't resent the fact that he took part in the auction of my house. Although I'd have the right to suspect some shady business in his putting up Szlangbaum, for instance.'

Izabela embraced her father cordially: 'Yes,' she said, 'you are right, papa. I didn't realise to the full what it all meant. This putting up of Jews at the sale clearly proves that this man, while playing at friendship, is doing business.'

'Of course!' Tomasz agreed, 'surely you have the sense to under-stand such a simple thing? Perhaps he isn't a bad man, but he's a tradesman always, a tradesman . . .'

A loud ringing came from the vestibule: 'That must be he. I'll go, papa, and leave the two of you together.'

She left her father's bedroom, but instead of Wokulski in the vestibule she saw a total of three Jews, loudly arguing with Mikołaj and Flora. She rushed from the vestibule and the phrase: 'My God! Why doesn't he come?' passed through her mind.

A storm of emotion was boiling in her heart. While agreeing with her father's views, Izabela had nevertheless guessed it was not true what he said. Wokulski had made no profit from the house, but had lost, merely in order to extricate them from a most fatal situation.

But while admitting this, she hated him: 'Scoundrel! Scoundrel!' she whispered, 'how dare he?'

Meanwhile, the Jews in the vestibule had started an angry scene with Flora. They declared they would not go until they got their money, that the young lady had given her word the previous day . . . And when Mikołaj opened the front door, they began abusing him: 'This is robbery! This is cheating! You know how to get money and then you say "My dear David . . ." but when the time comes . . .'

'What is the meaning of this?' said a new voice at that moment.

The Jews fell silent: 'What is the meaning of this? What are you doing here, Mr Spigelman?'

Izabela recognized Wokulski's voice.

'Me? Nothing . . . My respects, honoured sir . . . We are here on business, to see His Excellency . . .' Spigelman explained in a tone completely different from his previous noisy one.

'The gentleman told us to come for our money today . . .' put in another Jew, 'the young lady gave her word yesterday that we should all be paid off today, to the last penny . . .'

'And so you shall,' Wokulski interrupted, 'I am Mr Łęcki's plenipotentiary and will deal with your accounts in my office at six today.'

'No hurry . . . Why in such a hurry, honoured sir?' Spigelman replied.

'Pray come to my office at six, and you, Mikołaj, do not admit anyone on business while your master is ill.'

'Very good, sir! My master is waiting in his bedroom,' Mikołaj replied.

But when Wokulski had gone in, he pushed and tumbled the Jews out, with 'Begone, Yids! Begone!'

'Ah! Ah! Why so angry, sir?' the Jews muttered, very embarrassed. Tomasz greeted Wokulski with emotion; his hands were trembling slightly, so was his head. 'Well, look here,' he said, 'what these Jews get up to! They besiege our house . . . they alarm my daughter . . .'

'I have told them to come to my office at six and, with your permission, will then settle their bills. Is it a large sum?' Wokulski asked.

'Almost nothing . . . a matter of some five or six thousand roubles . . .'

'Five or six thousand?' Wokulski echoed, 'do you owe so much to those three?'

'No. I owe them some two thousand, perhaps a trifle more. But I must tell you, Stanisław (for this is the whole point) that last March someone bought my promissory notes. Who was it? That I don't know: however, I should like to be ready for all eventualities.'

Wokulski's face brightened: 'Pay off your debts,' he replied, 'as the creditors apply to you. Today we will dispose of those who have promissory notes dated later. So it amounts to two or three thousand?'

'Yes, yes . . . but, Stanisław, what confounded bad luck! You are to pay me five thousand for six months . . . Were you good enough to bring the money?'

'Of course.'

'I am indeed grateful. But what confounded bad luck that just now, when Bela and I and . . . and you . . . were to go to Paris, the Jews should seize two thousand from me. Of course Paris is out of the question?'

'How so?' Wokulski said, 'I'll pay what is owing and you need not touch your interest. You may go to Paris without hesitation.'

'Splendid of you,' Tomasz exclaimed, embracing him, 'for you see, my dear fellow,' he added, calming down, 'I was just wondering whether you couldn't obtain a loan for me somewhere, for paying off the Jewish debts at – say – seven or perhaps six per cent?'

Wokulski smiled at the financial naiveté of Tomasz: 'Of course,' he said, unable to control his good humour, 'you will get the loan. We'll repay some three thousand to the Jews and you'll pay the interest. How much would you like to pay?'

'Seven per cent – perhaps six . . .'

'Very well,' said Wokulski, 'you will pay a hundred and eight roubles interest and the capital will remain untouched.'

Tomasz, for the hundredth time at least, began blinking and tears appeared again: 'Noble soul! Noble!' he said, embracing Wokulski, 'God has sent you . . .'

'Do you think I could do otherwise?' Wokulski murmured.

There was a knock. Mikołaj entered and announced the physicians: 'Ah,' Tomasz exclaimed, 'my sister sent them. My God, I have never yet been doctored, but today . . . Please, Stanisław, go to Bela now. Mikołaj, announce Mr Wokulski to your mistress.'

'This is my reward . . . my life!' Wokulski thought, following

Mikołaj. In the vestibule he met the doctors, both known to him, and warmly recommended Tomasz to their care.

Izabela awaited him in the drawing-room. She was a trifle pale, but all the more beautiful. He greeted her and said cheerfully: 'I was very pleased that you liked the wreath for Rossi . . .'

He stopped. He was struck by the peculiar expression on Izabela's face, as she looked at him with some slight surprise as though she had never seen him before.

For a moment both were silent, then Izabela flicked a particle of dust from her ash-coloured gown and asked: 'So it was you who bought our house?'

Wokulski was so taken aback that for the first few moments he could not utter a word. It was as though his mind had stopped working. He turned pale, then reddened, and finally regained enough sense to reply in a stifled voice: 'Yes, I did.'

'Why did you put up a Jew to outbid?'

'Why?' Wokulski echoed, gazing at her like a frightened child, 'why? I am a tradesman, you see . . . and locking up capital may damage my credit . . .'

'You have been interesting yourself in our affairs for a long time. It seems to me that in April . . . you acquired our dinner-service?' Izabela said in the same tone.

This tone sobered Wokulski, he looked up and replied drily: 'Your dinner-service is at your disposal at any time.'

Now Izabela looked down. Wokulski noticed this and was embarrassed again. 'Why did you do it?' she asked quietly, 'why are you . . . persecuting us?'

It looked as though she was going to burst into tears. Wokulski lost all his self-control: 'I persecute you?' he exclaimed in an altered voice, 'could you find a more faithful servant . . . a more devoted dog . . . than me? For two years I have thought of only one thing – how to remove every obstacle from your path.'

At this moment the door-bell rang. Izabela started. Wokulski fell silent.

Mikołaj opened the drawing-room door and said: 'Mr Starski.'

At the same moment a man of medium height appeared on the threshold, graceful and slender, with a small moustache and an almost imperceptible bald spot. His expression was half merry, half mocking, and he at once exclaimed: 'I am delighted to see you again, cousin!'

Izabela gave him her hand in silence: a warm flush covered her face and languor glowed in her eyes.

Wokulski retired to a side table. Izabela introduced the gentlemen: 'Mr . . . Mr Wokulski . . . Mr Starski.'

Wokulski's name was uttered in such a manner that Starski, after bowing, sat down a few paces away, turned sideways from him. In reply, Wokulski sat down at the small table by the wall and began looking at an album.

'So you are back from China, cousin?' Izabela asked.

'From London – and I keep thinking I am still on board ship,' Starski replied, in quite noticeably halting Polish.

Izabela began speaking English: 'I expect you will be staying in this country for some time?'

'That depends,' Starski replied, also in English, 'who's that?' he added, glancing at Wokulski.

'My father's agent. What does it depend upon?'

'I think you have no need to ask, cousin,' said the young man, with a smile, 'it depends upon the generosity of my grandmother.'

'Very nice! And I was expecting a compliment . . .'

'Travellers don't pay compliments, for they know that compliments discredit a man in the eyes of a woman in no matter what latitude.'

'Did you make that discovery in China?'

'In China and Japan, but mainly in Europe.'

'And you expect to apply this principle in Poland, cousin?'

'I'll try and in your company, if you'll allow me. For it seems we are to spend the summer together. Is it not so?'

'That is what my aunt and father want, at least. However, it doesn't amuse me to hear that you intend checking your ethnographical observations . . .'

'That would be revenge on my part.'

'Ah – it's to be a battle, then?' Izabela asked.

'The paying off of old scores often leads to agreement.'

Wokulski was looking through the album with such attention that the veins stood out on his forehead.

'But revenge doesn't,' Izabela replied.

'Not revenge – but the recollection that I am your creditor, cousin.'

'So I am to pay off old scores?' Izabela smiled, 'you have not been wasting your time on your travels, cousin.'

'I prefer not to waste time on holidays,' said Starski, looking significantly into her eyes.

'That depends on the revenge.' Izabela replied, and she blushed again.

'The master is expecting you,' said Mikołaj, appearing in the drawing-room door.

The conversation broke off. Wokulski put down the album, rose, bowed to Izabela and Starski, then slowly followed the butler.

'Doesn't that man understand English, then? Won't he mind us not talking to him?' asked Starski.

'Oh no,' Izabela replied.

'So much the better: for I had the impression he did not care for our company.'

'And he has left us,' Izabela concluded carelessly.

'Bring me my hat from the drawing-room,' said Wokulski to Mikołaj, in the next room. Mikołaj brought the hat and took it to Tomasz's bedroom. In the vestibule he heard Wokulski whispering 'My God!' and clutching his head with both hands.

When Wokulski entered Tomasz's room, the doctors had gone. 'Well now, just think,' Mr Łęcki exclaimed, 'what confounded bad luck! The doctors have forbidden me to go to Paris, and I am to go to the country instead, on pain of death. Upon my word, I don't know where to take refuge from this heat. But it has affected you, you're changed . . . This is a hot apartment, is it not?'

'Yes. Allow me,' Wokulski said, taking a thick packet from his pocket, 'to hand you the money.'

'Well, really . . .'

'Here are five thousand roubles interest till mid-January. Please count it. And here is the receipt.'

Mr Łęcki counted the bundle of new hundred-rouble notes several times, then signed. As he put the pen down he said: 'Good, that is one thing over. And now for the debts . . .'

'The amount of two or three thousand, which you owe the Jews, will be paid today . . .'

'But, my dear Stanisław I don't want it for nothing . . . Pray deduct your interest very precisely . . .'

'A hundred and twenty to a hundred and eighty roubles a year . . .'

'Yes, yes . . .' Tomasz agreed, 'but supposing I were to need a small sum, then could I send someone to you . . . ?'

'You will receive the other half of the interest in mid-January,' Wokulski replied.

'I know. But, Stanisław, supposing I were to require a part of my capital? Not for nothing, of course . . . I would gladly pay interest.'

'Six per cent,' Wokulski interposed.

'Yes, six or . . . seven per cent.'

'No, sir. Your capital will bring in thirty-three per cent annually, so I cannot lend it at seven per cent.'

'Very well. In that case, do not dispose of my capital, but . . . you see, something may occur to . . .'

'You can withdraw your capital in mid-January, next year . . .'

'God forbid! I won't withdraw my capital from you, not even for ten years.'

'But I have taken your capital for only a year.'

'How is that? Why?' Tomasz asked, opening his eyes wider and wider.

'Because I can't tell what will happen a year from today. Such opportunities do not occur every year.'

'By the way,' said Tomasz, after a moment of disagreeable consideration, 'what on earth is this they're saying in town – that you, Mr Wokulski, have bought my house?'

'Yes, sir, it was I who bought your house. But I can sell it back to you on favourable terms within six months.'

Mr Łęcki felt himself flush. Not wishing, however, to relinquish his game, he asked in a lordly manner: 'And how much would you ask for selling it back, Mr Wokulski?'

'Nothing. I'll resell it for ninety thousand or even . . . less, perhaps.'

Tomasz withdrew, folded his arms, then sank into his great armchair and again some tears flowed down his face: 'Really, Stanisław,' he sobbed slightly, 'I see that the finest relations can be spoiled by . . . money. Am I vexed with you for buying the house? Have I complained? Yet you speak to me as though you were offended.'

'Excuse me,' Wokulski interrupted, 'but as a matter of fact I am somewhat irritable . . . The heat, no doubt.'

'Of course,' Tomasz exclaimed, rising and pressing his hand, 'so – let us forgive one another these sharp words . . . I am not angry with you, for I know . . . it is the heat.'

Wokulski bade him goodbye and stepped into the drawing-room. Starski had already left, Izabela was sitting there alone. Seeing him, she rose. Her face was more serene: 'Are you leaving?'

'I wanted to say goodbye.'

'And you won't forget Rossi?' she said with a faint smile.

'No. I will see that the wreath be given him.'

'Will you not hand it to him yourself? Why not?'

'I am leaving for Paris tonight,' Wokulski replied.

He bowed and went out.

For a moment Izabela stood amazed, then she hurried into her father's room: 'What does this mean, papa? Mr Wokulski said goodbye to me very coldly and says that – tonight he is leaving for Paris!'

'What? What? What?' Tomasz exclaimed, clutching his head with both hands, 'he must have taken offence . . .'

'Ah, of course . . . I mentioned to him the purchase of our house . . .'

'Good God! It was you . . . All is lost! Now I understand . . . Of course he was offended. Well,' he added after a moment, 'who'd have thought him so touchy? Such a commonplace tradesman . . .'

XX

The Journal of the Old Clerk

SO HE HAS left! Stanisław Wokulski – great organiser of a transport company, great director of a firm which has a turnover of some four millions a year – has left for Paris like any postilion for Miłosna . . . One day he says (to me in person) that he doesn't know when he'll be leaving, and next day – bang! – he's off.

He ate an elegant dinner at the Łęckis, drank his coffee, brushed his teeth – and was off. Well, well . . . after all, Mr Wokulski isn't a common-or-garden clerk who has to obtain leave from his master for a holiday once every few years. Mr Wokulski is a capitalist, he has some sixty thousand roubles a year, is on familiar terms with counts and princes, fights duels with barons and can leave when he chooses. And you, my salaried clerks, look after the business! That is why you have wages and bonuses.

But is he supposed to be a tradesman? It's tomfoolery, I'd say – not trade.

Still, there's no reason why a man shouldn't go to Paris, and on a mad impulse too – but not at times like these. Here we have the Berlin congress fuming, England claiming Cyprus, Austria after Bosnia . . . The Italians are shouting their heads off: 'Give us Trieste, or else . . .' I hear blood is flowing in Bosnia and (as soon as the harvest is in) war will break out sure as fate. And here he is setting out for Paris!

Hm! Now, why has he suddenly left for Paris? For the Exhibition? What concern is it of his? Is it perhaps in connection with the business he was to put through with Suzin? What sort of business can it be, I wonder, in which he'll make fifty thousand roubles as if it were handed him on a plate? They mentioned oil-drilling equipment or railway machinery, or was it a sugar factory? Well, my dear angels, you aren't by any chance going there to buy ordinary cannons rather than these fancy machines? France is on the point of a set-to with Germany . . . Young Napoleon is said to be staying in London, but after all Paris is nearer to London than Warsaw to Zamość . . .

Come, Ignacy, don't be precipitous in your judgements of your master Mr W. (in such cases it is advisable not to use his full name), do not condemn him, for you'll make a laughing-stock of yourself. Some important affair is underway here: that Mr Łęcki, who used to stay with Napoleon III, that alleged actor Rossi, an Italian (the Italians are forcibly reminding the rest of the world of Trieste!), and that dinner at the Łęckis immediately before his departure, and that purchase of the house . . .

Certainly Miss Łęcka is beautiful, but she is only a woman and Staś would not commit so many follies for her alone. All this has something to do with p—— (in such cases it is advisable to use abbreviations). There are big p—— involved in this.

It is already some two weeks since the poor fellow left, perhaps for ever . . . He writes dry, brief letters, says nothing about himself and sometimes makes me so miserable that I don't know what to do (not on his account, surely – merely from habit). I remember his departure. We had just shut up the shop and I was drinking tea at this very table (Ir is still poorly), when suddenly Staś's butler rushed in: 'The master wants you!' he roared and rushed out again. (What an impudent rascal he is, and how idle! You should have seen his expression when he appeared in the door and cried: 'Your master wants you!' Brute!) I wanted to admonish him: 'You fool! Your master is your master,' but he had rushed headlong away.

I hastily finished my tea, gave Ir some milk in a saucer and went to Staś. In the gateway I saw his butler flirting with three girls like young does. Well, I thought to myself, a loafer like you could cope with four of them, I daresay . . . (The devil himself can't come to terms with these women, though. There's Jadwiga, for instance, slender as could be, small and ethereal, but now her third husband has developed consumption.)

I went upstairs. The door to the apartment was open, and Staś himself was packing his suitcase by lamp-light. Something touched me: 'What does this mean?' I asked

'I'm leaving for Paris tonight,' he replied.

'But yesterday you said you wouldn't be leaving so soon . . .'

'That was yesterday . . .' he replied. He moved away from the suitcase and reflected for a moment. Then he added in a peculiar tone: 'Only yesterday . . . I was mistaken . . .'

These words took me aback in a disagreeable way. I looked at Staś attentively and amazement overwhelmed me. I'd never have believed that a man apparently so healthy or at least not wounded, could change so in the course of a few hours. He was pale, his eyes sunken, almost wild . . .

'How come this sudden change . . . of plans?' I asked, feeling that I was not asking what I wanted to know.

'My dear fellow,' he replied, 'don't you know that sometimes a single word will change a plan, even a person . . . Not to mention what a whole conversation can do . . .' he added in a whisper.

He continued packing and gathering together various articles, then went into the drawing-room. A minute passed – he did not return: two minutes – still no sign . . . I glanced through the open door and saw him leaning against the arm of a chair and absently staring out of the window. 'Staś . . .'

He jumped, and returned to his packing, asking: 'What is it?'

'Something is the matter . . .'

'No, nothing . . .'

'I haven't seen you like this for a long time . . .'

He smiled: 'No doubt since the time when the dentist extracted a tooth that happened to be sound,' he replied.

'Your setting out like this looks strange,' I said, 'isn't there anything you want to tell me?'

'To tell you? Yes, of course . . . We have about a hundred and twenty thousand roubles in the bank, so you won't be short of money . . . What else?' he asked himself, 'oh yes . . . Don't keep it a secret any longer that I bought the Łęcki house. In fact, go there and fix the rents according to the previous terms. You can raise Baroness Krzeszowska's by ten roubles or so, let her be vexed: but don't be hard on the poorer tenants . . . A tailor lives there, and some students: take what they pay, providing they pay regularly.'

He glanced at his watch, and seeing he still had time, lay down in silence on the *chaise-longue*, his hands over his head, eyes closed. This sight was inexpressibly painful. I sat down at his feet and said: 'Is anything the matter, Staś? Tell me what it is. I know I can't help, but d'you see . . . Sorrow is like poison – it does you good to spit it out.'

Staś smiled again (I don't like those half-smiles of his) and replied after a moment: 'I remember – how long ago it was! – sitting in a room with some fellow who was strangely frank. He told me incredible things about his family, contacts, his great deeds and then – he listened very attentively to my own story. And later took advantage of it.'

'What do you mean?' I asked.

'I mean, old man, that because I don't want to extract any confidences from you, I don't need to make them to you.'

'How so?' I exclaimed, 'is this how you regard confidences to a friend?'

'Never mind,' he said, getting up, 'it's all very well for school-girls . . . In any case, I have nothing to confide, not even in you. How tired I am,' he muttered, stretching.

Not until this moment did that scoundrel of a butler come in; he took Staś's suitcase and informed us the horses were waiting. Staś and I got into the carriage, but did not exchange a single word all the way to the railroad station. He eyed the stars and whistled softly, while I thought I must surely be on the way to a funeral.

At Vienna Station, Dr Szuman caught up with us: 'You are going to Paris, then?' he asked Staś.

'How do you know?'

'Oh, I know everything. I even know that Mr Starski is travelling by the same train . . .'

Staś recoiled. 'What sort of man is he?' he asked the doctor.

'An idler, a bankrupt – like all of them,' Szuman replied, 'and a former suitor into the bargain . . .'

'I don't care.'

Szuman said nothing, only eyed him obliquely.

They began ringing bells and blowing whistles. Travellers crowded into the carriages. Staś shook us by the hand.

'When will you be back?' the doctor asked him.

'Never – if I had my way,' Staś replied, and he got into an empty first-class compartment.

The train moved away. Pondering, the doctor watched its lights disappear, while I . . . almost burst into tears.

When the guards began closing the platform, I persuaded the doctor to take a walk along Aleje Jerozolimskie. The night was warm, the sky clear: I don't recall ever having seen so many stars before. And because Staś had told me that he often used to look at the stars while he was in Bulgaria (amusing idea!) I decided to look at the sky myself every evening. (And perhaps our gaze will meet on one of those twinkling lights, and he won't feel as lonely as he did then.)

Suddenly (goodness knows why) I began suspecting that Staś's unexpected departure was connected with politics. I therefore decided to cross-examine Szuman and, wishing to catch him out, said: 'It looks to me as if Wokulski is . . . in love, as it were.'

The doctor stopped dead on the pavement and, leaning on his stick, began laughing in a way that attracted the attention of the (fortunately) few passers-by: 'Ha ha! Have you only just made that monumental discovery? Ha ha! This old fellow pleases me . . .'

It was a ridiculous joke. However, I bit my lip and retorted. 'It was easy to make that discovery, even for someone . . . less skilled than I am (I think I caught him there!). But I prefer being cautious even in supposing things, Mr Szuman . . . In any case, I never dreamed that such an ordinary thing as love could bring about such havoc in a man.'

'You are mistaken, old man,' the doctor replied with a gesture. 'Love is an ordinary thing in nature and even to God, if you like.

But your stupid civilisation, based on Roman views long since dead and buried, on the interests of the papacy, troubadours, asceticism, the caste system and such-like rubbish has turned a natural feeling into – guess what? – a disease of the nervous system! Your supposedly chivalrous and romantic love is nothing more than a hideous commerce based on dishonesty, which is very properly punished by the lifelong imprisonment known as marriage . . . Woe to those who bring their hearts to such a market-place! How much talent, even life it devours . . . I know this very well,' he went on, breathless with rage, 'for although I'm a Jew and will remain one till the day I die, I was nevertheless brought up among your people and was even engaged to marry a Christian girl . . . Well, and they forced us to make so many compromises in our plans, they watched over us so tenderly in the name of religion, morality, tradition and goodness knows what else – that she died and I tried to poison myself . . . A man as clever as I am, and as bald.'

He stopped again on the sidewalk. 'Believe me, Ignacy,' he concluded in a hoarse voice, 'you will not find anything as vile as human beings, not even among the animals. In Nature, the male belongs to the female who pleases him and whom he pleases. So there are no idiots among the animals. But among us! I am a Jew, so am not allowed to love a Christian woman . . . He is in trade, so he has no right to a well-born lady . . . And you, who have no money, have no right at all to any woman whatsoever. Your civilisation is rotten! I'd gladly perish, provided its ruins came down on top of me . . .'

We walked on to the corner. A damp wind had been blowing up for some minutes, and was driving straight at us: the stars began to disappear in the west, veiled in clouds. There were fewer street-lamps. From time to time a carriage drove along the Boulevard, bespattering us with invisible dust: late passers-by were hurrying home.

'It's going to rain . . . Staś will be nearly at Grodzisk by now,' I thought. The doctor had pulled his hat down over his eyes and was walking along, brooding crossly. I felt more and more wretched, perhaps on account of the growing darkness. I'd never tell anyone this, but sometimes it seemed to me that Staś . . . no longer cared about politics, because he was quite at the beck and call of that young lady. I once mentioned something of this to him and his reply by no means decreased my suspicions.

'Is it possible,' I exclaimed, 'that Wokulski should have forgotten general matters, politics, Europe?'

'Not to mention Portugal,' the doctor interposed.

This cynicism outraged me: 'You mock,' I said, 'but you cannot deny that Staś could be something better than an unhappy admirer of Miss Łęcka. He might be a social agitator, not some wretched sighing lover . . .'

'You are right,' the doctor agreed, 'but what of it? A steam-engine is not a coffee-grinder, you know, but a huge machine: but when its wheels break, it becomes a useless object and is even dangerous. In your Wokulski, there is such a wheel, that is rusting and breaking down . . .'

The wind blew more and more strongly; my eyes were full of dust. 'Why should such a misfortune happen to him, of all people?' I asked (but in a casual tone, so that Szuman would not think I was asking for information).

'It is due both to Staś's nature and the relationships civilisation forms,' the doctor replied.

'His nature? He was never amorous.'

'And that has destroyed him,' Szuman went on, 'a thousand tons of snow, divided into flakes, merely scatter over the earth without harming the smallest blade of grass; but a hundred tons of snow, crammed into an avalanche, will smash houses and kill people. Had Wokulski been in love with a different woman every week of his life, he'd look fresh, he'd have his mind at rest and could do much good in the world. But, like a miser, he has hoarded his heart's capital and now we see the results of this economy. Love is beautiful when it has the charm of a butterfly; but when it awakens like a tiger after a long lethargy, then there's nothing amusing in it! A man with a healthy appetite is different from a man whose innards are rended with famine . . .'

The clouds were rising still higher: almost at the city gates we turned back. I thought that Staś must by this time be almost at Ruda Guzowska.

The doctor went on talking, more feverishly, waving his walking-stick still more fiercely: 'There are rules of hygiene for dwellings and clothes, for food and work, which the lower classes do not observe, and that is the cause of their high mortality rate, their short lives and their debility. But there are also rules of hygiene for love, which the intelligentsia fail to observe and even violate, and that is one of the causes for their downfall. Hygiene tells a man to eat when he is hungry, but for all that a thousand rules will trip you up, protesting: "Forbidden!" You will eat when we authorise you to, when you fulfil this, that and the other condi-tions laid down by morality, tradition, fashion . . . You must admit that in this respect the most backward states are in advance of the progressive societies, or at least of their intelligentsia.

'Just look, Ignacy, how well the nursery, the drawing-room, poetry, novels and plays work together to stupefy people. They urge you to seek ideals, be an ideal ascetic yourself and not only obey but even create some artificial condition or other. What's the result? A man, usually less trained in these matters, becomes the prey of a woman who is trained for nothing but that purpose. So women really rule civilisation!'

'What's wrong with that?' I asked.

'Confound it,' the doctor exclaimed, 'haven't you noticed, Ignacy, that if a man is spiritually a fly, a woman is still more so, for she has no wings or feet? Education, tradition, perhaps even inheritance make a monstrous thing of her with the pretence of making her a higher being. And this idle monstrosity, with its crooked feet, compressed trunk, empty brain – nevertheless has the task of bringing up future generations of mankind. So what does she instil in them? Does she teach her children to work for their living? No, they learn how to hold a knife and fork nicely. Do they learn how to understand the people among whom they will have to live? No, they learn to please by putting on grimaces and bowing. Do they learn real facts which determine our happiness or unhappiness? No, they learn to close their eyes to the facts and to dream about ideals. Our softness in life, our impracticality, laziness, flunkeyism and those terrible bonds of stupidity which have been weighing down mankind for centuries are the result of pedagogy as applied by women. And our women, in turn, are the product of a clerical, feudal and poetical theory of love, which is offensive to hygiene and to common sense . . .'

My head was whirling with the doctor's statements and he pressed on along the street like a madman. Fortunately lightning flashed, the first drops of rain fell and the excited speaker suddenly cooled down, jumped into a droshky and told the driver to take him home.

Staś was nearly at Rogow now, surely. Was he aware that we talked of nothing but him? And what did the poor devil feel, with one storm overhead and another, perhaps worse, in his heart?

Goodness, what a downpour, what a cannonade of thunderclaps! Ir, wrapped up into a bundle, barked at it in a stifled voice in his sleep and I went to bed under only a sheet. The night was oppressive. Oh Lord, I thought, watch over those who are fleeing abroad from unhappiness this night!

Sometimes a small incident is enough to make things, ancient as human sins, appear to us in a completely new light. For instance, I have known the Old Town since my childhood and it always seemed crowded and dirty to me. Not until I was shown, as a curiosity, a drawing of one of the old houses (in the *Illustrated Weekly*, with a caption) did I suddenly notice that the Old Town is beautiful. From that time on I have been going there at least once a week, and I discover new beauties there, and am also amazed that I never noticed them before.

So it is with Wokulski. I have known him twenty years, and

keep thinking he is a politician, body and soul. I'd have given my
life that Staś concerned himself with nothing but politics. Not until
that duel with the Baron and the ovation for Rossi did suspicions
that he might be in love awaken within me. I no longer doubt this
now, particularly after my talk with Szuman.

But that's nothing, for a politician can be in love too. Napoleon
I fell in love right and left, yet even so he shook Europe to its
foundations. Napoleon III also had a number of mistresses, and I
hear that his son is following in his father's footsteps, and has
already found himself some English girl or other. So if a weakness
for the ladies did not embarrass the Bonapartes, why should it
enfranchise Wokulski?

Just as I pondered thus, a small incident occurred which
reminded me of things long since dead and buried, which
presented Staś himself in another light. No, he is no politician; he is
something entirely different, which I do not even understand very
well.

Sometimes he seems to me a man injured by society. But hush!
Society never injures anyone. If we stopped believing that,
goodness knows what claims might not arise. Perhaps no one
would concern himself with politics, but would think of nothing
but settling accounts with his nearest and dearest. So it is better not
to open such questions. (How talkative I have become in my old
age, and none of it about what I meant to say when I started!)

Thus, as I was drinking tea in my room one evening (Ir is still
moody), the door opened and someone entered. I looked up − a
stout figure, red face, red nose, grey hair. I sniffed and caught the
smell of something like wine and mould in the room: 'This
gentleman,' thought I, 'is either a corpse or a cellarman. For no one
else would smell so of mould . . .'

'Well, I never!' the visitor exclaimed, 'you are become so proud
that you don't recognise a fellow?'

I rubbed my eyes. And it was none other than Machalski, the
cellarman from Hopfer's . . . We were in Hungary together and
later here in Warsaw; but we had not met for fifteen years, since he
moved to Galicia and remained a cellarman. Of course we
embraced like long-lost brothers, once, twice and a third time . . .

'When did you get here?' I asked.

'This morning,' said he.

'And where have you been until now?'

'I went to the Dziekanka, but I was so depressed that I went to
the Lesisz wine cellars . . . There are cellars for you, my dear sir!'

'And what did you do there?'

'I helped the old man a little and sat about. I'm not such a fool as
to walk around the town when there's a cellar like that to sit in.'

He was a real cellarman of the olden days. Not a dandy like those of today, who prefer going to dances rather than sitting in a wine-cellar. And who even wear patent leather shoes in the cellar! Poland will perish through such wretched tradesmen.

So we sat and talked until one in the morning. Machalski stayed the night with me, and at six the next morning he hurried off to Lesisz. 'What will you do after dinner?' I asked him.

'After dinner I'll drop in at Fukier's cellars, then I'll come back for the night,' he replied.

He stayed a week in Warsaw. Nights he spent at my place, and the days in wine-cellars. 'I'd hang myself,' he said, 'if I had to wander about outdoors for a week or more. The crowds, the heat, the dust . . . Maybe pigs can bear it, but not people.'

He seemed to me to be exaggerating. For although I, too, prefer the shop to Krakowskie Przedmieście, yet the shop is not a wine-cellar. The fellow must have grown eccentric in his wine-cellaring.

Of course, what did Machalski and I talk of, if not old times and Staś? In this manner, the story of Staś's youth came before me as if it were yesterday.

I recollect (it was in 1857 or '58) that I walked once into Hopfer's, where Machalski was working. 'Where's Jan?' I asked the lad.

'In the cellar.' So I went down into the cellar. Behold, there was Jan by the light of a tallow candle, siphoning wine from a barrel into bottles, and in the recess I saw two shadows lurking; a grey-haired old man and a young lad with cropped hair and the counte-nance of a brigand. They were Staś Wokulski and his father.

I sat down quietly (Machalski didn't like to be interrupted when drawing wine) and the grey-haired old man in a sand-coloured frock-coat was going on in a querulous voice to the lad: 'Why spend your money on books? Give it to me, because if I have to drop the law-suit, then everything will be wasted. Books won't extricate you from the humiliation you are now in, only the law-suit can do that. When I win and when we get back our estate, which grandfather left us, then people will remember that the Wokulskis are old-established gentlefolk and relatives will turn up . . . Last month you spent twenty zloty on books, yet that was just the amount I needed for a lawyer . . . Books, nothing but books! As long as you work in a shop they will spurn you, even if you are as wise as Solomon and although you are a gentleman and your grandfather on your mother's side was a chancellor. But when I win that law-suit, when we move into the country . . .'

'Let's go away,' the lad muttered, glancing sideways at me.

Obedient as a child, the old man wrapped his papers up in a red kerchief and went out with his son, who had to help him up the stairs.

'Who were those simpletons?' I asked Machalski, who had just finished his work and sat down on a stool: ' Ah,' he made a gesture, 'the old man isn't all there in the head, but the lad is bright. His name is Stanisław Wokulski. A bright rascal!'

'What can he do?' I asked.

Machalski snuffed the candle, poured me a glass of wine and said: 'He's been with us four years. Not much use in the shop or cellar, though . . . But as a mechanic! He constructed a sort of machine that pumps water, and then pours it on a wheel which works the pump. A machine like that could go on pumping until Judgement Day, but something went wrong, so it only worked fifteen minutes. It was up there in the dining-room and attracted customers for Hopfer: but six months ago it broke.'

'So that's the kind of lad he is,' said I.

'Well, not quite,' Machalski replied, 'there was a professor from the Technical College here, he had a look at the pump and said it was good for nothing, but that the lad was bright and ought to study. From that day on we've had pandemonium in the place. Wokulski has grown conceited, mumbles at customers, by day he looks half asleep but for all that he studies nights and buys books. On the other hand his father would sooner spend the money on a law-suit over some estate or other left by their grandfather. You heard what he said . . .'

'What does he hope to achieve by this studying?' I said.

'He says he'll go to Kiev, to the University. Ha, let him!' Machalski declared, 'perhaps for once it will make a man of a shop-clerk. I don't interfere with him, I don't make him work: when he's in the cellar, he can read if he likes. But upstairs the other clerks and customers plague him.'

'What does Hopfer think of it?'

'Nothing,' Machalski went on, putting another candle into the iron holder, 'Hopfer doesn't want to turn him away, for Kasia Hopfer dotes on Wokulski and maybe the lad will get his grand-father's estate back after all.'

'Does he dote on Kasia?' I inquired.

'He never so much as looks at her, ungovernable young rascal that he is,' Machalski replied.

I at once guessed that a lad with such a brain, who bought books and cared nothing for girls might do well as a politician, so I made the acquaintance of Staś that very day and from then on we have got on well together . . .

Staś was at Hopfer's three more years and during that time he made many acquaintances among the students and young officials who outdid one another in providing him with books so that he might take the university entrance exam. Among these young men was a certain Mr Leon, a lad still (he wasn't twenty yet), handsome and clever – but an enthusiast! He was, as it were, my assistant in

Wokulski's political education; for when I talked about Napoleon and the great mission of the Bonapartes, Mr Leon would talk about Mazzini, Garibaldi and other eminent persons. And how well he could inspire the soul!

'Work hard,' he sometimes said to Staś, 'and have faith, because faith can stop the sun in its course, not to mention improving the lot of mankind.'

'Maybe it will send me to the university?' Staś asked.

'I'm positive,' replied Leon, his eyes flashing, 'that if you have the faith the first apostles had, even for a while, you'd be at the university already.'

'Or in a lunatic asylum . . .' Wokulski muttered.

Leon began striding about the room, waving his arms. 'How despicable,' he exclaimed, 'if even a man like you has no faith. Just remember what you have already achieved in such a short time: you know so much that you might sit for the examination today . . .'

'But what shall I do there?' Staś sighed.

'Not much – by yourself. But some dozen, some hundreds like you and me . . . do you know what we might do?'

His voice broke off at this point. Leon went into convulsions. We could hardly calm him.

On another occasion, Leon reproached us for lacking the spirit of sacrifice. 'Don't you know,' he said, 'that Christ alone saved mankind through the power of sacrifice? How much better the world would be, if there had always been individuals prepared to sacrifice their lives . . .'

'Am I to sacrifice my life for customers who treat me like a dog, or for those lads and clerks who plague me?' Wokulski asked.

'Don't try to wriggle out of it!' Leon cried, 'Christ died for the sake of his executioners. But there is no spirit in you. Your spirit is rotting away . . . Listen to what Tyrteus said: "Sparta, perish! Ere the Messenine hammer crumble the monument of your greatness, and the tombs of your ancestors and scatter their revered bones as prey to the dogs and banish the shades of your forefathers from the gates . . . Oh ye people, ere the enemy claps you in fetters, smash your fathers' weapons on the threshold of your home and hurl yourselves into the abyss. Let not the world know what swords were yours, but that your hearts were wanting." Hearts!' Leon repeated.

Even then, Staś was very cautious in accepting Leon's theories; but the lad could influence people as well as any Demosthenes. I remember a crowded meeting one evening, when we all – young and old alike – burst into tears when Leon spoke to us of a perfect world in which stupidity, poverty and injustice would disappear: 'From that time on,' he said in great excitement, 'there will be no differences between people. Gentry and bourgeois, peasants and Jews – all will be brothers.'

'And clerks?' Wokulski asked from his corner.

But this interruption did not upset Leon. He suddenly turned to Wokulski, enumerated all the unpleasantness which Staś had been subjected to in the shop, the obstacles put to his studies, and wound up: 'So that you believe like a brother, so that you can cast out anger from your heart – here I kneel to you, and beg your forgiveness in the name of mankind.'

And he actually knelt down before Staś and kissed his hand. The people present grew still more moved, lifted Staś and Leon up and vowed that each would give his life for such men as they.

Today, when I remember those goings-on, it sometimes seems like a dream. Certainly I never met such an enthusiast as Leon before or after.

Early in 1861, Staś resigned from Hopfer's. He lived with me (in my room with a barred window and green curtains), dropped trade and at once began attending academic lectures as an auditor. His farewell to the shop was strange: I remember it because I was there myself. He embraced Hopfer, then went into the cellars to embrace Machalski, where he stayed a few minutes. Sitting in the dining-room, I heard a noise, the laughter of the customers and shop lads, but didn't suspect a joke.

Suddenly (the opening leading into the cellar was in the same room) I beheld a pair of red hands emerging from the cellar. These hands clutched at the floor and were immediately followed by Staś's head which appeared once and then again. The customers and lads were laughing.

'Aha!' one waiter exclaimed, 'see how difficult it is to get out of a cellar without the steps? And here you are hoping to jump out of the shop and into the university at one go! If you are so clever, come on out!'

Staś extended his arms from below again, grabbed the edge of the opening and pulled himself half-way up. I thought he would burst a blood vessel.

'Here he comes! Just look at him . . . He's doing it!' a second waiter cried.

Staś got one leg to the floor and in a moment was in the room. He was not angry, but he refused to shake hands with any of his colleagues, merely took his bag and went to the door.

'Come now, aren't you saying goodbye to the customers, Herr Doktor?' Hopfer's waiters shouted after him.

We walked along the street without uttering a word. Staś was biting his lips and it occurred to me that getting out of the cellar like that was a symbol of his life, which had led him to tearing up his roots from Hopfer's shop and setting out into a wider world. A prophetic incident! For to this very day Staś always comes out on top. And God knows what such a man mightn't do for his country if only the ladder were not moved away at every step he takes, and if he did not have to waste time and energy uprooting himself every time.

After moving into my room, he worked entire nights and days until sometimes I was quite cross with him. He rose before six and read. At ten he hurried to a lecture, then started reading again. At four he went out tutoring in various houses (mostly Jewish, where Szuman introduced him), and on coming home again he read and read until he went to bed, dead with fatigue, well after midnight.

He would have had a reasonable income from these lessons, had it not been for his father, who visited him from time to time, and only altered in that he wore a snuff-coloured frock-coat instead of the sand-coloured one, and wrapped his documents up in a blue handkerchief. Otherwise he remained the same as when I first met him. He would sit at his son's table and put his papers on his knees and say in a low querulous voice: 'Books . . . nothing but books! Here you are, wasting money on study, while I haven't enough for the law-suit. Even if you graduate from two universities, you won't get out of your present wretchedness until we get grandfather's estate back. Only then will people admit you're a gentleman, equal to others. And then relatives will turn up . . .'

Staś spent his spare time experimenting with balloons. He got a large demijohn and prepared some kind of gas in it, using vitriol (I don't remember what kind of gas it was) and filled a balloon – not a very large one, admittedly, but very artfully constructed. There was a machine with a propeller under it . . . And it actually flew up to the ceiling, then burst by hitting the wall. Thereupon Staś tinkered with it, repaired it, filled the demijohn with all sorts of messes, and tried again, interminably. Once the demijohn burst and the vitriol nearly burned out his eye. But that didn't matter to him, since he hoped the balloon would at least help him 'extricate' himself from his wretched position.

From the day when Wokulski moved into my room, our shop gained a new customer in Kasia Hopfer. I don't know what it was she liked about us – whether it was my beard, or Jan Mincel's stoutness. For though the girl had a dozen haberdashery shops nearer home, she came to ours several times a week: 'A ball of wool, please . . . A reel of silk, please . . . Ten groszy worth of needles . . .' She would run a mile in rain or shine for such things as these, and after buying a packet of pins for a few pennies, would sit half an hour in the shop talking to me: 'Why don't you gentlemen ever come to see us? . . . Along with Stanisław?' said she, blushing, 'my father is ever so fond of you both – we all are.'

At first I was surprised by old Hopfer's unexpected affection, and suggested to Kasia that I didn't know her father well enough to pay him visits. But she insisted: 'Stanisław must be angry with us, I can't think why, because at least papa . . . and all of us . . . are very fond of him. Stanisław surely can't complain that he has been unfairly treated by us . . . Stanisław . . .'

And while talking thus about Stanisław, she would buy silk thread instead of wool, or needles instead of a pair of scissors.

The worst of it was that the poor thing was pining away week by week. Every time she came to the shop for her little purchases, she seemed to be looking a little better. But as soon as the blush of momentary excitement had gone from her face, I could see she was even paler than before, her eyes unhappier and deeper set. And the way she used to inquire: 'Doesn't Stanisław ever come into the shop?' And she would look at the door leading to the passage and my apartment, where, at a few yards distance, Wokulski sat frowning over his books, never guessing that here he was so sought after.

I was sorry for the poor girl, so once, when drinking tea with Wokulski in the evening, I remarked: 'Don't be childish – call on Hopfer. The old man has plenty of money.'

'Why should I?' he replied, 'haven't I had enough of that place?' As he spoke, he shuddered.

'You ought to go, because Kasia dotes on you,' said I.

'Don't mention Kasia to me,' he interrupted, 'she's a very good girl, sometimes she would secretly sew on a coat-button for me, or throw a flower through the window, but she's not for me, nor I for her.'

'She's a positive dove of a child,' I put in.

'So much the worse, for I'm no dove. The only kind of woman who could attract me would be one like myself. And I've never met such a one.' (He met one sixteen years later, but God knows he has no reason to be glad of it!)

Kasia gradually ceased coming to the shop, and instead old Hopfer paid a visit to Mr and Mrs Jan Mincel. He must have mentioned Staś to them, for the next day Mrs Mincel hurried downstairs and began scolding me: 'What sort of a lodger have you, Ignacy, that young ladies dote on him so? Who's this Wokulski? Jan,' she turned to her husband, 'why hasn't the gentleman called on us? We must marry him off. Tell him to come upstairs this minute . . .'

'Oh, let him go upstairs,' Jan Mincel replied, 'but as for marrying him off, that I won't. I'm an honest shopkeeper and don't want to go in for match-making.'

Mrs Mincel kissed his sweaty face as if they were still on their honeymoon, but he pushed her aside mildly and wiped his face with his cravat: 'Devil take these women!' he said, 'they can't resist making people unhappy. Go on with your match-making, do! Hopfer, Wokulski, anyone – but remember I'm not going to pay for it!'

From that time on, whenever Jan Mincel went out of an evening for beer or to the club, Mrs Mincel would invite Wokulski and me in. Staś would drink his tea quickly, without even looking at her: then, with his hands in his pockets, would think about his balloons and sit like a block of stone, while our hostess urged him to fall in love: 'Is it possible, Mr Wokulski, that you've never been in love?' said she, 'as far as I know, you are twenty-eight years old, almost as old as I am . . . and I've long since regarded myself as an old woman, while you're still an innocent . . .'

Wokulski crossed one leg over the other, but still said nothing.

'Kasia is a delicious morsel,' said our hostess, 'fine eyes – though she seems to have a cast in one of 'em; a reasonable enough figure, although she must have one shoulder higher than the other (but that only adds to her charms). Her nose isn't quite to my liking, I admit, and her mouth is a little too big, but what a good girl she is! If she only had a little more sense . . . Well, but women don't acquire sense, Mr Wokulski, until they are thirty. When I was Kasia's age, I was as silly as a canary-bird . . . I fell in love with my present husband!'

On the third visit, Mrs Mincel welcomed us wearing a peignoir (it was a very fine peignoir, embroidered with lace), but I wasn't even invited the fourth time. I have no idea what they talked about. One thing was certain – Staś used to come home more and more bored, complaining that the silly woman was wasting his time, while Mrs Mincel told her husband that Wokulski was very stupid and would have to improve a great deal before she would marry him off.

'Work on him, my dear,' her husband would encourage her, 'for it is a shame about the girl and Wokulski too. It is awful to think that such a decent fellow, who has been a clerk so long, and who might inherit Hopfer's business, should want to waste himself at the university. Tfu!'

Confirmed in her good intentions, Mrs Mincel not only invited Wokulski to tea in the evenings (he usually didn't go), but sometimes popped anxiously into my room herself, inquiring whether Staś was sick and wondering why he had not yet fallen in love – he, almost older than she was (I think she was a little older than he was). At the same time, she began having hysterical fits, would scold her husband who left home for whole days at a time, and protest to me I was a scoundrel who didn't understand life, and took in doubtful persons as lodgers . . .

In a word, as such scenes began to occur in the house Jan Mincel grew thin, despite the fact that he drank more and more beer, while I thought I would either resign from my job with Mincel, or give Staś notice to leave.

How in the world did Mrs Mincel learn of my troubles? I have no idea. Suffice it to say that she popped into my room one evening, told me I was her enemy and must be a great scoundrel, since I was giving notice to quit a man as energetic as Wokulski . . . Then she added that her husband was a wretch, that all men were wretches and finally had hysterics on my sofa.

Scenes like this went on for several days, and I don't know what the outcome would have been, had it not been that one of the most extraordinary incidents I ever saw took place.

Once Machalski invited Wokulski and me to his place for the evening. We went there after nine, and in his favourite cellar, by the light of three tallow candles I saw several dozen people, including Mr Leon. I am sure I shall never forget that crowd of predominantly young faces against the background of the black walls of the cellar, looking out from behind barrels or half lost in the gloom.

As the hospitable Machalski greeted us on the stairs with huge glasses of wine (and very good wine too) and took me into his especial care, I must at once admit that my head began spinning and a few minutes later I was quite tipsy. So I sat down at a distance from the proceedings, in a deep alcove, and dozed, half-awake, half-asleep, as I watched the feasters.

I am not quite sure what happened down there, for the most fantastic notions whirled through my head. I dreamed that Mr Leon was speaking, as usual about the power of faith, lack of spirit and the need for sacrifice, which all those present loudly encored. The unanimous voices died down, however, when Leon started declaring that it was time to put these words into action. I must have been quite tipsy, for Leon seemed to be suggesting that one of us should jump from the Nowy Zjazd bridge down to the pavement below, and on this, everyone fell silent to a man, while several concealed themselves behind barrels.

'So no one can make up his mind to try?' Leon cried, wringing his hands. Silence. The cellar grew emptier.

'Nobody? Nobody?'

'I will,' said a voice I hardly recognised. I looked around. By a flickering tallow candle stood Wokulski. But Machalski's wine had been so strong that at this moment I passed out.*

After the banquet in the wine-cellar, Staś did not show himself at my dwelling for several days. Finally he entered − wearing someone else's clothes, thinner, but with his head high. Then for the first time I heard a sort of harsh note in his voice, which still makes a very disagreeable impression on me to this day.

From that time on, he entirely changed his way of life. He threw the balloon and propeller into a corner, where they soon began collecting spider-webs; he gave the demijohn to the caretaker for a water-jug, and never even glanced at his books. So that treasury of human wisdom lay about on shelves or the table, closed or open, while he . . .

Sometimes he would not be at home for several days together, not even for the night: then again he would drop in of an evening and throw himself on his bed, fully dressed. Sometimes, several gentlemen unknown to me would come instead of him, and spend the night on the sofa or in Staś's bed, without even thanking me or telling me their names or profession. Then again sometimes Staś would reappear and sit in the room for a few days, doing nothing, irritable, always on the alert, like a lover come to a tryst with a married lady and afraid of meeting her husband.

I do not suppose that this married lady was Małgosia Mincel, for she now looked as if a gadfly had bitten her. Mornings, the woman rushed around three or so churches, evidently wishing to pester merciful Heaven from several vantage points. Immediately after dinner she went to meetings of ladies who deserted their husbands and children to busy themselves with gossip in the expectation of great events. In the evenings, gentlemen would call on her: but they used to pack her off into the kitchen without even speaking to her.

It is hardly surprising that with such chaos at home I too began to grow confused. Warsaw seemed more crowded, everyone bemused. Every hour I expected some indefinable surprise, but nevertheless we were all in a good temper and our heads full of plans.

Jan Mincel, meanwhile, worried by his spouse at home, went out for beer early in the morning and did not come home till late. He even thought up a saying: 'What does it matter? Death only stings once . . .' which he used to repeat till his dying day.

Finally, Staś Wokulski entirely disappeared from my sight. Not until two years later did he write to me from Irkutsk, asking me to send his books.

In autumn 1870 (I had just come home from Jan Mincel's, he was ill in bed) I had just sat down to my evening tea in my room, when suddenly someone knocked: '*Herein*!' said I.

The door squeaked . . . I looked up, and there on the threshold was a bearded figure in a sealskin overcoat, fur outwards: 'Well,' said I, 'may the devil take me if it isn't Wokulski . . .'

'In person,' said the individual in sealskin.

'For goodness sake,' said I, 'you're joking to be sure . . . Or are you lost? Where in the world do you come from? Are you his spirit?'

'No, I'm alive,' said he, 'and hungry into the bargain.'

So he took off his cap, got out of his fur-coat, sat down by the candle. He really was Wokulski. He'd grown a beard like a brigand, had a countenance like Longinus (who put a spear into Christ our Lord), but of course it really was Wokulski.

'So you're back,' said I, 'have you just arrived?'

'Yes, and back for good.'

'What was that country like?'

'Not bad.'

'Hm . . . And the people?'

'Not bad.'

'Hm . . . And what did you live on?'

'I gave lessons,' said he, 'and I've brought six hundred roubles back with me.'

'Well, well . . . And what do you plan on doing now?'

'Well, I shan't go back to Hopfer's,' he replied, thumping the table-top, 'you probably don't know I'm a scholar now. I've even acquired several diplomas from scientific societies in St Petersburg.'

'So a waiter from Hopfer's has become a scholar! Staś Wokulski has diplomas from scientific societies in St Petersburg . . . Unheard of,' thought I.

What more is there to say? The lad found himself a place somewhere in the Old Town and lived on his savings for six months, buying plenty of books but little to eat. When his money was spent, he began looking for work, and a strange thing happened. Tradesmen wouldn't employ him because he was a scholar, but scholars wouldn't either, because he was an ex-waiter. So he was stuck, like Twardowski,* half-way between Heaven and earth. He might have blown his brains out on the Nowy Zjazd, had I not helped him out from time to time.

It is painful to think how hard life was. He grew thin, gloomy, morose . . . But he did not complain. Only once, when he was told there was no work for the likes of him, he whispered: 'I've been cheated . . .'

Just then Jan Mincel died. His widow buried him in a Christian manner, remained shut up in her room for a week, then summoned me in for a talk. I thought we should discuss the shop, the more so as I noticed a bottle of good wine on the table. But Mrs Mincel did not mention the fate of the shop. She burst into tears at the sight of me, as if I reminded her of her late husband, already buried a week, and poured me a generous glass of the wine, saying in a tearful voice: 'When my poor dear angel passed away, I thought only I was unhappy . . .'

'Angel?' I asked suddenly, 'Jan Mincel, perhaps? Excuse me, madam – although I was a true friend of your late husband, I wouldn't think of referring to a person who weighed two hundred pounds as an angel . . .'

'He weighed three hundred when he was alive,' the inconsolable widow interposed. Then she again veiled her face with a handkerchief and sobbed: 'Oh, will you never learn to be tactful,

Mr Rzecki? What a blow it was! It's quite true that my late lamented was never an angel, to be precise, particularly of late, but I have always been terribly unfortunate . . . Oh, lamentable, irreplaceable . . .'

'Of course, for the last six months . . .'

'Six months, what are you saying?' she cried, 'poor Jan was sick three years and for eight or more he . . . Alas, Mr Rzecki, what a source of misery that hateful beer is in marriage! It is eight years, sir, since I had a proper husband . . . But what a man he was, Mr Rzecki! Only now do I feel the whole weight of my misfortune . . .'

'Worse things can happen,' I ventured to interpose. 'Oh yes,' the poor widow sighed, 'you are perfectly right, worse things can happen. For example, there's Wokulski, who is supposed to be back now . . . Is it true he still has not found a post?'

'Nothing at all.'

'Where does he eat? And live?'

'Where does he eat? I don't even know that he does. And for where he lives – nowhere.'

'Terrible,' Mrs Mincel burst into tears. 'It seems to me,' she added after a moment, 'that I should be carrying out the last wish of the late lamented if I ask you to . . .'

'At your service, madam . . .'

'To give him lodgings in your apartment, and I'll send you down two dinners and two breakfasts . . .'

'Wokulski would not accept that,' I remarked. On this, Mrs Mincel burst into tears again. From despair at her husband's death, she was transformed into such a ferocious rage that she called me a scoundrel three times, a man ignorant of life, a monster . . . Finally she told me to be off, and she would manage the shop herself. Then she apologised and vowed on all that was holy that I must not be vexed by words dictated by her sorrow.

From that day on I often met our lady proprietor. Then, six months later, Staś told me . . . he was going to marry Mrs Mincel.

I stared at him . . . He shrugged: 'I know,' he said, 'that I'm a swine. But . . . even so, less than many of those who enjoy public esteem here.'

After a riotous wedding which many of Wokulski's friends attended (I don't know where they came from, but how the wretches ate . . . and drank the health of the happy couple – from tankards!), Staś moved upstairs to his wife's apartments. To the best of my recollection, all his possessions consisted of four parcels of books and scientific instruments, and as for furniture – a bubble-pipe and hat-box.

The clerks laughed (in corners, of course) at their new boss: I, however, was sorry he had broken with his heroic past and poverty

so abruptly. For human nature is odd: the less we tend to
martyrdom ourselves, the more we require it of our neighbours.

'He's sold himself to that old woman,' his acquaintances said,
'that would-be Brutus! . . . He studied, got into trouble and now –
flop!'

Two of his severest critics had been fervent suitors of Mrs
Mincel.

But Staś very quickly shut people's mouths, for he set to work at
once. About a week after the wedding he came into the store at
eight in the morning, sat down at the desk in the late Mr Mincel's
chair and served customers, made out bills, gave change, as if he
were only a paid clerk.

He did even more, for in his second year he started trading with
Moscow merchants, which proved very advantageous for business.
I may say that our turnover tripled under his rule.

I sighed with relief when I saw Wokulski did not intend to eat
his bread free; even the clerks stopped laughing at him, realising
that Staś worked harder in the shop than they did, and that he also
had more than a few duties to carry out upstairs. We at least rested
during holidays: whereas he, poor devil, had to take his wife by the
arm and march about the town – mornings to church, afternoons
paying calls and evenings to the theatre.

Her new husband put new life into Małgosia. She bought herself
a piano and began taking music lessons from an aged teacher so as
(she said) 'not to make Staś jealous'. She spent the hours free from
piano lessons at conferences with tailors, modistes, hairdressers and
dentists, making herself prettier every day. And how affectionate
she was towards her husband! Sometimes she would sit for hours at
a time in the shop, merely to gaze upon Staś. When she noticed
that some of the customers were pretty, she removed Staś from the
front of the shop to behind a cupboard, and told him to set his
office up there, within which he sat like a caged animal and did the
shop's accounts.

One day I heard a terrible crash inside this structure. I rushed in,
followed by the clerks. What a sight met our eyes! Małgosia was
lying on the floor, soaked in ink, the chair broken, having brought
the desk down on top of her, Staś was furious and embarrassed . . .
We lifted up the weeping lady, and from her incoherent
mumblings learned that she herself had been the author of all this
mess, by unexpectedly sitting down on her husband's lap. The
fragile chair had collapsed under their combined weight, and her
ladyship, in trying to avoid the catastrophe, had grabbed hold of the
desk and brought the whole thing down on herself.

Staś accepted these noisy proofs of connubial tenderness with the
utmost tranquillity, seeking consolation by burying himself in bills
and commercial correspondence. But instead of cooling off, her

ladyship became more and more fervent: when her husband, tired of sitting still, or in order to transact business, would sometimes go out into the town, she would hasten after him . . . to watch lest he go to a rendezvous!

Staś would sometimes disappear for a week at a time, especially in winter, to stay with a forester he knew, where he would hunt and wander about in the forests. But on the third day his wife would set off after her beloved truant, walk about in the thickets behind him and fetch him back to Warsaw as a result.

Wokulski kept silent for the first two years of this rigorous life. During the third year he began coming to my room every evening, and talking about politics. Sometimes, as we were chatting about old times, he would look around the room, suddenly break off the topic to begin another: 'Listen to me, Ignacy . . .'

At that moment, as if deliberately, the maid would rush downstairs, crying: 'The missus wants you! The missus is poorly!'

And he, poor devil, would shrug and go to her ladyship, without even beginning what it was he wanted to tell me.

After three years of such a life which, however, was irreproachable, I saw that this man of iron was beginning to wilt in the silken embraces of her ladyship. He grew pale and wan, stooping, threw aside his learned books and took to reading the newspaper, spending all his spare time talking to me about politics. Sometimes he left the shop before eight, and took his wife to the theatre or to pay a call, then finally started giving evening parties, where ladies old as sin, gentlemen in retirement and whist-players would gather.

Staś did not play; he only walked about between the card-tables and watched.

'Staś,' I sometimes said, 'take care! You're forty-three . . . At that age Bismarck had barely started his career.'

This, or similar remarks, roused him momentarily. Then he would throw himself into a chair and brood, with his head resting on his hand. Thereupon Małgosia would hurry in, crying: 'Staś, ducky! You're brooding again, we can't have that . . . And the gentlemen have drunk their wine . . .' So Staś rose, brought another bottle from the sideboard, poured wine into eight glasses and walked around the tables watching the gentlemen playing whist.

In this manner the lion was slowly but surely being transformed into a tame bull. When I saw him in his Turkish dressing-gown, slippers embroidered with beads and a silk night-cap, I could not believe that this was the same Wokulski who, fourteen years earlier in Machalski's cellar, had exclaimed: 'I will!'

When Kochanowski wrote: 'And thou shalt sit upon a fierce lion without fear, and ride on a huge dragon,'* he certainly had a woman in mind! For they are the riders and conquerors of the male sex!

Then, in the fifth year of marriage, Małgosia suddenly took to cosmetics . . . At first discreetly, then more energetically, and to all kinds . . . Hearing of a certain fluid which was said to return freshness and the charms of youth to ladies of a certain age, she anointed herself with it from top to toe one evening, with such effect that the doctors called in that very night to help could do nothing for her. And she died, poor thing, of blood-poisoning, only recovering consciousness sufficiently to call her lawyer and bequeath her entire estate to her dear Staś.

Staś said nothing after this misfortune either, but grew more mopish than ever. As he had an income of several thousand roubles a year, he stopped concerning himself with trade, broke off with his acquaintances and buried himself in learned books. I sometimes told him: 'Go out and meet people, enjoy yourself, after all, you're still young and could marry again . . .'

All in vain . . .

One day (six months after the death of Małgosia), seeing the lad growing old before my very eyes, I suggested: 'Staś, be off with you to the theatre. Today *Traviata* is playing; you saw it with your wife last time . . .'

He jumped up from the sofa, where he had been reading, and said: 'You know, you're quite right. I'll see what it's like this evening . . .'

He went to the theatre and . . . next day I hardly recognised him: my Staś Wokulski had awoken in the old man. He straightened up, his eyes regained their fire, his voice its strength. . .

From that time on he went to all the performances, concerts and lectures. Soon afterwards he left for Bulgaria, where he made his huge fortune, and a few months after his return an old gossip (Mrs Meliton) told me Staś was in love . . .

I laughed at this chatter, for no one who is in love goes off to a war. Not until now, alas, have I begun to suspect that the old woman was right.

And yet one never knows with Staś Wokulski. Just supposing . . . If it were so, how I'd laugh at Dr Szuman, who mocks politics so!

XXI

The Journal of the Old Clerk

THE POLITICAL situation is so uncertain that I should not be surprised if a war broke out in December. People still seem to think that wars can only break out in the spring; evidently they forget that the Franco-Prussian war started in summer. I do not share this prejudice against winter campaigns. In winter, the barns are full and the roads smooth; whereas in spring the peasants have no grain left and the roads are like cake: should a battery pass, you could take a bath there.

Winter nights, on the other hand, continue ten hours or more, warm clothes are needed, quarters for the troops, typhus . . . I sometimes thank God he did not make a Moltke* of me: he must be worried to death, poor devil. The Austrians, or rather the Hungarians, have marched into Bosnia and Herzegovina for good, but have been received very inhospitably. Even some Hadji Loja or other has turned up, said to be an excellant partisan, who has caused them much trouble. I am sorry for the Hungarian infantry, but even so, today's Hungarians are worth nothing. When the Huns suppressed them in 1849, they protested that every nation has the right to defend its own freedom. But today? They themselves are pushing their way into Bosnia, uninvited, and they call the Bosnians, who are defending themselves 'criminals and brigands'.

Upon my word, I understand politics less and less! And who knows but what Staś Wokulski wasn't right to lose interest in it (if he has?). But why am I going on about politics, when a great change has come about in my own life? Who would believe that for a week already I have not been concerned with the store? Temporarily, of course, otherwise I would surely go mad with boredom.

What happened was that Staś wrote to me from Paris (he also asked me to write to him) instructing me to look after the apartment house he bought from the Łęckis. 'As if I didn't have enough to do as it is,' thought I, but what could I do? I left the store in the charge of Lisiecki and Szlangbaum, and set off for Aleje Jerozolimskie to gather information about the house. Before I went, I asked Klein (who lives in the house) to tell me what was going on there. Instead of replying, he made a significant gesture.

'Is there a caretaker in the house?' I asked.

'Yes,' said Klein, with a grimace, 'he lives on the third floor, front.'

'That's enough,' I said, 'enough, Mr Klein!' (For I don't care to hear other people's opinions without seeing for myself. In any case Klein, a mere lad, might easily grow presumptuous if his elders start asking him for information.)

Hm, it can't be helped . . . So I sent my hat to be cleaned, paid two zloty for it, took a pocket pistol with me just in case, and set off for behind Alexander's Church.

There I beheld a yellow house with three storeys, its number coincided . . . and I even found Staś Wokulski's name on the plate (old Szlangbaum must have had it put up). I went into the yard: oh my! It stank like a chemical factory. The garbage was piled up to the second floor, while all the gutters were overflowing with soapy water. Only now did I notice that there was a 'Parisian Laundry' on the first floor in the yard, with enormous girls like two-humped camels. This encouraged me to go on.

So I called out: 'Caretaker!' For a while no one was to be seen; finally a stout woman appeared, so sooty I could not for the life of me imagine how so much dirt could be found in the vicinity of a laundry, and a Parisian one, too.

'Where's the caretaker?' said I, raising my hat.

'What do you want to know for?' the old woman muttered.

'I'm here on behalf of the landlord.'

'The caretaker is in jail,' said the old creature.

'Whatever for?'

'Oh, wouldn't you like to know?' she cried, 'because the landlord doesn't pay his wages, that's why!'

A nice thing to hear as introduction! Of course I went from the caretaker to the agent, on the third floor. Already on the stairs I could hear children howling, banging and the voice of a woman exclaiming: 'You rascal! You idler! Take that! and that!'

The door was open, in it a female in a less than white wrap was beating three children with a leather strap until it whistled.

'Excuse me,' I said, 'am I interrupting?'

Catching sight of me, the children vanished into the depths of the apartment and the female in a wrap, concealing the strap, asked in some confusion: 'Are you the landlord, sir?'

'No, but I have come on his behalf to see your husband, madam. I am Rzecki.'

The female looked at me incredulously for a moment, then said:

'Wicek, run to the warehouse for your father . . . Sir, pray step into the parlour.' A ragged lad tore between me and the door, gained the stairs and began sliding down the banisters. Embarrassed, I went into the parlour, the main ornament of which was a sofa with the stuffing coming out.

'This is what it means to be an agent,' said the female, showing me into an equally shabby chair, 'my husband works for gentlemen who are said to be rich, but if he didn't work in the coal warehouse as well, and take in copying for lawyers, we should not have a morsel to eat. And this is our apartment, just look at it,' she said, 'for these three black holes we pay a hundred and eighty roubles a year . . .'

Suddenly an alarming hissing sound reached us from the kitchen. The female in a wrap rushed out, whispering on the way: 'Kasia, go in and watch that gentleman!' And a very wretched little girl in a brown dress and dirty stockings came into the room. She sat down on a chair by the door and watched me with a gaze as suspicious as it was mournful. I would never have believed that people would take me for a thief in my old age . . . We sat in silence like this for some five minutes, observing one another, when suddenly a shriek was audible, and a banging on the stairs, and at this moment the ragged boy called Wicek ran in from the passage, with someone angrily shouting after him: 'Oh, you rascal! I'll give it to you yet . . .'

I divined that Wicek was lively by nature and that the person scolding him was his father. Then the gentleman himself appeared, wearing a stained frock-coat and trousers frayed around the cuffs. He also had a thick grizzled beard and red eyes. He came in, bowed civilly to me and asked: 'Have I the honour of speaking to Mr Wokulski?'

'No, sir. I am only the friend and manager of Mr Wokulski . . .'

'Aha,' he interrupted, shaking me by the hand, 'I have had the pleasure of noticing you in the store. A fine store, that!' he sighed, 'such stores lead to apartment houses, to landed property . . . that sort of thing.'

'Did you ever own a property?' I inquired.

'Bah! Why mention it? I expect you will want to see the accounts of the house,' the agent replied, 'I'll be brief: we have two kinds of tenants – some have not paid rent for six months, and the others pay fines to the magistrates, or tax arrears for the landlord. Furthermore, the caretaker gets no wages, the roof leaks, the police keep telling us to remove the garbage, one tenant has started a law-suit over the cellar rights, and two more are going to court over an incident on account of the attic – as for the ninety roubles I owe to the respected Mr Wokulski . . .'

'Pray do not worry,' I interrupted, 'Staś – that is, Mr Wokulski –

will certainly cancel your debt until October, and will then make a
new contract with you.'

The poor former landowner shook me cordially by the hand. An
agent like this, who had once owned his own property, seemed a
very interesting individual to me; but even more interesting was
the house, which produced no income!

I am bashful by nature: I am shy talking to people I don't know
and afraid of going into other people's houses (Good Heavens!
How long is it since I was in someone else's house?) But this time
the devil got into me, and I asked to meet the tenants of this
strange house. Back in 1849 things were sometimes hot, yet a man
still got ahead!

'Sir,' I said to the agent, 'would you very kindly introduce me to
some of the tenants? Staś – that's to say, Mr Wokulski – asked me
to look after his interests till he gets back from Paris . . .'

'Paris! . . .' the agent sighed, 'I remember Paris in 1859 . . . I
remember how they welcomed the Emperor back from the Italian
campaign . . .'

'Sir!' I cried, 'you saw Napoleon's triumphal return to Paris?'

He gave me his hand and replied: 'I saw something better, sir. I
was in Italy during the campaign and saw how the Italians
welcomed the French on the eve of the battle of Magenta . . .'

'Magenta? In 1859?' I asked.

'At Magenta, sir . . .'

The former landowner, who could not afford to have the stains
cleaned off his frock-coat, and I looked at one another. We gazed
into each other's eyes . . . Magenta! . . . 1859! Dear me . . .

'Tell me, sir,' said I, 'how the Italians welcomed you on the eve
of the battle of Magenta?'

'In 1859, Mr Rzecki – I have the honour of addressing Mr
Rzecki?'

'Yes, sir – I am Rzecki, former lieutenant, sir, of the Hungarian
infantry, sir . . .'

We gazed at one another. Goodness me!

'In 1859,' the former landowner went on, 'I was nineteen years
younger than I am today, and had some ten thousand roubles a year
. . . Those were the days, Mr Rzecki . . . It's true I used to spend
the interest and even some of the capital . . . So when the expro-
priations came . . .'

'Well,' I said, 'peasants are human beings too, sir, Mr . . .'

'Wirski,' the agent put in.

'Mr Wirski,' said I, 'the peasants . . .'

'It makes no difference to me,' he interrupted, 'what the peasants
are . . . Suffice it to say that in 1859 I had some ten thousand a year
income (plus loans), and was in Italy. I was curious about the
country which was driving out the Huns . . . And as I had no wife

or children, I had no reason to economise either, so I went as a volunteer with the front-line French troops . . . We reached Magenta, Mr Rzecki, without knowing where we were, nor which of us would see the next day's sunrise . . . You know that feeling, sir, when a man uncertain of tomorrow is in the company of men equally uncertain of their tomorrow?'

'Do I! Go on, Mr Wirski . . .'

'May the devil take me,' said the former landowner, 'if such days aren't the finest in a man's life . . . You're young, cheerful, healthy, you have no wife or children around your neck, you drink and sing and every now and then you look at the dark wall behind which tomorrow is hidden. Ha, you cry, more wine there, for I don't know what's behind that wall . . . Wine, there! Even kisses . . . ! Mr Rzecki,' the agent muttered, leaning towards me.

'So when you were with the front-line troops at Magenta . . . ?' I persisted.

'I marched with the cuirassiers,' said the agent. 'Do you know the cuirassiers at all, Mr Rzecki? There's only one sun in the sky, but a squadron of cuirassiers is like a hundred suns . . .'

'They're heavy troops,' I interposed, 'the infantry can crack them like a nut-cracker cracking nuts . . .'

'So we were drawing nearer, Mr Rzecki, to some little Italian town, when the local peasants told us the Austrian corps was not far off. We sent them into the town with the order, or rather – request – that when the population caught sight of us, they should make no sign . . .'

'Certainly not,' said I, 'with the enemy in the vicinity.'

'Within a half-hour,' the agent went on, 'we were inside the town . . . A narrow street, crowds on both sides, we could hardly pass through in marching order, women in the windows and on balconies. . . . And such women, Mr Rzecki! Each one with a bunch of roses in her hand. Those in the street didn't utter a word, for the Austrians were close by . . . But the women on the balconies plucked their bouquets to pieces and showered the sweating, dusty cuirassiers with rose-petals thick as snow . . . Oh, Mr Rzecki, if you'd seen that now: crimson, pink, white – and their hands, those Italian women . . . The lieutenant blew kisses right and left . . . Meanwhile, a snowstorm of pink petals scattered over the golden helmets, breastplates and snorting horses . . . To crown it all, an old Italian with a crooked stick and flowing grey hair stepped up to the lieutenant. He seized the neck of his horse, embraced it, and with a cry of "Evviva l'Italia!" dropped dead on the spot! That was our evening before Magenta.'

Thus spoke the former landowner, and tears flowed from his eyes down to his stained frock-coat.

'May the devil take me, Mr Wirski,' I cried, 'if Staś doesn't let you have this apartment for nothing!'

'We pay a hundred and eighty roubles a year,' the agent sobbed. We both dabbed our eyes.

'Sir,' I said, 'Magenta was Magenta, but business is business. You may care to introduce me to some of the tenants.'

'Come along,' said the agent, jumping up from his shabby chair, 'come along, I'll show you the oddest of them . . .'

He hurried out of the parlour and, sticking his head through the door into what appeared to be the kitchen, cried: 'Manya, I'm going out. As for Wicek, I'll attend to you this evening . . .'

'I'm not the landlord, papa, that you should settle your accounts with me,' replied a childish voice.

'Forgive him,' I murmured to the agent.

'I should think so, indeed!' he replied, 'he wouldn't go to sleep if he didn't have a good hiding first. He's a good boy,' he said, 'a lively boy, but a scamp.'

We left the apartment and stopped at a door on the staircase. The agent knocked cautiously while the blood ran from my head to my heart, and from my heart down into my boots. It might even have leaked out of my boots and away down the stairs to the gate, had not someone inside replied: 'Come in . . .'

We entered. Three beds. A young man with a black beard in student's garb was lying on one, with a book in his hand and his feet on the bed-rail. The clothes on the other beds looked as if a hurricane had swept through the room and turned everything upside down. I also saw a trunk, an empty valise and many books on shelves, on the trunk and on the floor also. Finally there were a few bent chairs and ordinary unpolished tables where, on looking more closely, I observed a painted chess-board and overturned chess-men.

Then I felt quite faint: for, next to the chess-men I saw two human skulls: in one was tobacco, and the other held sugar.

'What's this?' asked the bearded young man without getting up.

'This is Mr Rzecki, the landlord's plenipotentiary,' said the agent, indicating me.

The young man got up on one elbow, eyed me sharply and said: 'The landlord's . . . ? At this moment I am landlord here, and do not recollect appointing this gentleman . . .'

This reply was so strikingly simple that Wirski and I were dumbfounded. Meanwhile, the young man rose lazily from the bed and began buttoning up his trousers and waistcoat without the slightest haste. Despite the systematic manner with which he followed this occupation, I am certain that at least half the buttons on his garments remained unbuttoned.

'Aaaah!' he yawned. 'Pray sit down, gentlemen,' he said, gesticulating in such a manner that I did not know whether he was asking us to be seated on the valise or on the floor. 'Warm, Mr Wirski,' he added, 'ain't it? Aaaah!'

'As a matter of fact, your neighbour opposite has been complaining about you young gentlemen,' the agent replied with a smile.

'What the deuce?'

'That you wander naked about the room . . .'

The young man at once flew into a temper: 'Has the old fool gone off his head? Does he expect us to wear fur coats in a heatwave like this? The impudence of the man, upon my word . . .'

'Well, please don't forget he has a grown-up daughter . . .'

'What's that to me? I'm not her father. The old booby! Upon my word, he's lying, we don't go about naked.'

'I've seen you with my own eyes,' the agent interrupted.

'That's a lie, upon my word,' the young man exclaimed, flushing with anger, 'it's true that Maleski goes about without his shirt on, and Patkiewicz goes about without underpants, but in a shirt. So Miss Leokadia sees an entire costume . . .'

'Yes, and she has to draw all the curtains,' the agent replied.

'It's the old man who draws them, not her,' the student replied with a gesture, 'she peeps through the chinks in the curtains. Anyway, my dear sir, if Miss Leokadia is allowed to vex the whole yard, then surely Maleski and Patkiewicz have the right to walk about as they choose in their room?'

As he spoke, the young man strode up and down. Whenever his back was turned, the agent winked at me and made grimaces denoting great desperation. After a pause he said: 'You gentlemen owe us four months' rent.'

'Oh, you're back to that again!' the young man cried, putting his hands in his pockets, 'how often must I tell you not to talk to me of this nonsense, but to Patkiewicz or Maleski? After all, it's easy enough to remember – Maleski pays for even months, February, April, June – while Patkiewicz pays for the odd, March, May, July . . .'

'But none of you ever pays!' the agent exclaimed impatiently.

'Whose fault is it if you don't come at the proper time?' the young man roared, clapping his hands together, 'you've been told a hundred times to come to Maleski in even months, to Patkiewicz in odd . . .'

'What about you?'

'Me? Not at all,' the young man exclaimed, threatening us, 'I don't pay rent on principle. Whom am I to pay? And what for? Ha ha! Serve you right.'

He began walking still more rapidly about the room, laughing and scowling by turns. Finally he began whistling and looking out of the window, impudently turning his back to us . . . I lost my temper: 'Allow me to remark,' I exclaimed, 'that this disregard of an agreement is more than somewhat strange . . . A person supplies you with a dwelling, but you see fit not to pay for it.'

'Who gives me a dwelling?' cried the young man, sitting on the window sill and swinging himself about as if he intended throwing himself down from the third floor. 'I took this apartment and will stay here till they throw me out. Agreement, indeed! They make me laugh with their talk of agreements . . . If society wants me to pay for a place to live, society should pay me enough for the lessons I give to suffice for rent. It's laughable! For three hours teaching a day I get fifteen roubles a month; they take away nine for food, three for laundry and services – and what about my clothes, and fees! Yet they still want me to pay rent . . . Throw me out into the street,' he said angrily, 'let the dog-catcher shoot me . . . You have a right to that, but not to make comments and complain . . .'

'I fail to understand your excitement,' said I, calmly.

'I have good reason to be excited,' the young man replied, swinging more and more in the direction of the yard, 'as society didn't kill me at birth, as it wants me to study and pass dozens of exams, it has put itself under an obligation to give me work that will ensure my survival . . . Yet it either refuses me work, or cheats me out of payment for it . . . And if society does not keep its agreement with me, why should it expect me to keep mine to it? But what's the use of talking, I don't pay rent as a matter of principle, and *basta*! The more so because the present owner of the house didn't build it: he didn't bake the bricks, nor make the lime, lay the walls, risk breaking his neck. He came with money, possibly stolen, and paid someone else, who had perhaps robbed another person, and on that principle he wants to make me his slave. Such reasoning makes me laugh!'

'Mr Wokulski never robbed anyone,' I said, rising, 'he made his fortune by hard work and saving.'

'Be quiet,' the young man interrupted, 'my father was a competent doctor, he worked night and day and made what you might call good pay, and he saved . . . three hundred roubles a year! As your house cost ninety thousand roubles, my father would have had to live and write prescriptions for three hundred years. I don't believe the new landlord worked for three hundred years . . .'

My head began spinning with these arguments: but the young man went on, 'You can turn us out, of course. Then you'll see what you've lost. All the laundry-girls, all the cooks in the house will lose their tempers, and Madame Krzeszowska will begin to torment her neighbours unchallenged, to count each visitor who calls and every spoonful of flour they use . . . By all means throw us out! Then Miss Leokadia will start singing her scales and vocalises in a soprano voice mornings and contralto in the evenings . . . And the devil will take this house where we're the only ones to keep order.'

We made to leave: 'So you definitely will not pay the rent?' I asked.

'Certainly not!'

'Perhaps you would at least start paying from next October?'

'No, sir. I have not much longer to live, so I hope to introduce at least one principle – if society wants individuals to respect agreements, then let society carry out its agreements with individuals. If I have to pay rent to anyone, then let others pay me as much for lessons to suffice for that rent. D'you understand me, sir?'

'Not entirely, sir,' I replied.

'That is not surprising,' said the young man, 'in old age the brain withers away and is incapable of accepting new ideas.'

We bowed to one another, and the agent and I went out. The young man shut the door behind us, but after a moment he ran out to the stairs and shouted: 'And tell the agent to bring two policemen with him, for they will have to eject me by force!'

When the unusual young man had finally gone back to his apartment and locked the door on us in a manner which made it plain he regarded his conference with us as over, I stopped halfway down the stairs and said to the agent: 'I see you have coloured window-panes, here?'

'Oh, certainly . . .'

'But they need cleaning.'

'Yes, so they do,' said the agent.

'And I think,' I added, 'that this young man will keep his word regarding not paying rent?'

'Sir, that's nothing,' the agent exclaimed, 'he says he won't pay, and he doesn't; but the other two don't say anything and don't pay either. They're extraordinary tenants, Mr Rzecki . . . But they never let me down.'

I shook my head involuntarily, though I felt that if I were the landlord of such a house, I'd be shaking my head all day long. 'So no one here pays, or at least not regularly?' I asked the former landowner.

'That's not surprising,' Mr Wirski replied, 'in a house where the rent has been collected for so many years by creditors, the most honest tenant grows spoiled. Nevertheless, we have some regular ones, such as Baroness Krzeszowska, for instance.'

'Who?' I exclaimed, 'ah, yes the Baroness lives here . . . She even wanted to buy the house.'

'And she will,' the agent whispered, 'unless you gentlemen hold fast. She'll buy it even if it costs her entire fortune. And it's a good-sized fortune, though the Baron has demolished it greatly.'

I was still standing halfway down the stairs, under a window with red, green and blue panes. I was recollecting the Baroness, whom I had only seen a few times in my life, and who had always struck me as a very eccentric person. She knew how to be pious and stubborn, humble and vulgar, at one and the same time . . .

'What sort of person is she, Mr Wirski?' I asked.

'She's an unusual person, sir . . . Like all hysterical females,' the former landowner muttered, 'she lost her daughter, her husband left her . . . Nothing but angry scenes.'

'Let us call on her, sir,' I said, going down to the second floor. I felt so bold that the idea of the Baroness did not alarm me, but almost attracted me. But when we stopped at her door and the agent rang, I felt a cramp in my calves. I was rooted to the spot, and that was the only reason why I didn't bolt. In a moment my courage left me, and I recalled the scenes at the auction.

A key turned, the latch clattered and the face of a young girl, wearing a white cap, appeared in the half-open door: 'Who is it?' the girl asked.

'Me, the agent.'

'What do you want?'

'I'm here with the owner's representative.'

'And what does *he* want?'

'He's the representative . . .'

'Who am I to say, then?'

'Tell your mistress,' said the agent, by now rather irritated, 'that we have come to discuss the apartment.'

'Aha . . .'

She closed the door and went away. Some two or three minutes passed before she came back and, after unlocking several locks, showed us into an empty drawing-room.

This drawing-room had a strange appearance. The furniture was draped with ash-coloured coverings, so was the piano and the chandelier suspended from the ceiling: even the columns in corners, holding statues, wore the same ash-coloured garments. All in all, it gave the impression of a room whose owner had gone away, leaving behind only servants who were most meticulous about tidiness.

Beyond the door a conversation between a woman's and a man's voice was audible. The woman's voice was that of the Baroness: I recognised that of the man, but could not place it.

'I could swear,' said the Baroness, 'he maintains relations with her. The other day he sent her a bouquet by special messenger . . .'

'Hm . . . hm . . .' the other man's voice interposed.

'A bouquet which that detestable coquette has thrown out of the window, on purpose to deceive me . . .'

'Yet the Baron is in the country, far from Warsaw,' the man replied.

'But he has friends here,' the Baroness cried, 'and if I didn't know you, I'd suspect that you were the go-between for these shameful acts.'

'But, madam . . .' the man's voice protested, and at this moment the sound of two kisses were heard, on the hand, I believe.

'Come, Mr Maruszewicz, none of your sentimentality! I know your kind! You smother a woman in caresses until she trusts you, then you squander away her fortune and ask for a divorce . . .'

So it is Maruszewicz, I thought: a fine pair!

'Not at all,' said the man's voice behind the door, more quietly, and again two kisses were heard, certainly on the lady's hand.

I glanced at the former landowner. He lifted his gaze to the ceiling, and his shoulders went up almost to his ears: 'Scoundrel!' he whispered, indicating the door.

'You know him?'

'Hm . . .'

'So,' said the Baroness in the other room, 'take these three roubles to the Holy Cross Church and pay for three votive masses, so that God may bring him back to his senses . . . Or, no,' she added, in a somewhat different tone, 'pay one votive mass for him, and two for the soul of my poor little girl . . .'

Suppressed sobbing interrupted her words: 'Pray calm yourself,' urged Maruszewicz, mildly.

'Go, please go now,' she replied.

Suddenly the drawing-room door opened and Maruszewicz halted on the threshold as though turned to stone, while behind him I saw the yellowish face and bloodshot eyes of Madame the Baroness. The agent and I rose. Maruszewicz withdrew into the depths of the other room and evidently left by another door, while the Baroness exclaimed crossly: 'Marysia! Marysia!'

In ran the girl in white cap, black dress and white apron. This get-up would have made her look like a nurse, if her eyes had not sparkled so mischievously.

'How could you bring these gentlemen in here?' the Baroness asked.

'You told me to . . .'

'Blockhead! Off with you,' the Baroness hissed. Then she turned to us: 'What do you want, Mr Wirski?'

'Mr Rzecki here is the representative of the landlord,' the agent replied.

'I see. Very well,' said the Baroness, coming into the drawing-room slowly without asking us to be seated. This is what she looked like: a black dress, yellowish face, livid lips, eyes red from weeping and hair tightly combed back. She folded her arms like Napoleon, looked at me and said: 'I see. So you're the representative of . . . let me see – Mr Wokulski, isn't it? Pray tell him from

me, sir, that either I leave this apartment, for which I pay him
seven hundred roubles very regularly, – do I not, Mr Wirski?'

The agent bowed. 'Or,' the Baroness went on, 'Mr Wokulski
rids his house of all this dirt and immorality . . .'

'Immorality?' I inquired.

'Yes, sir,' the Baroness insisted, nodding, 'those laundry-girls
who sing vile songs all day long in the yard, and laugh upstairs in
the evenings with those . . . students. Those criminals, who throw
cigarettes down at me, or pour dirty water . . . And finally that Mrs
Stawska, who is goodness knows what – a widow, a divorcée, who
lives on goodness knows what . . . That woman seduces the
husbands of virtuous, terribly unfortunate wives . . .'

She began blinking, then burst into tears: 'It's monstrous,' she
sobbed, 'to be chained to such a hateful house by the memory of a
child which will never be erased from my heart. She used to run
through these very rooms . . . She used to play down there in the
yard . . . And she looked out of the windows which I, her bereaved
mother, am not allowed to look out of . . . They want to drive me
away . . . They all want to drive me out . . . I am in everybody's
way . . . Yet I cannot move from here, for each plank on the floor
bears traces of her little feet . . . Her tears and her laughter are
associated with every wall . . .'

She sank onto the sofa and burst into sobs: 'Ah!' she wept, 'men
are worse than beasts. They want to drive me away from this place
where my little girl breathed her last . . . Her little bed and all her
toys are still in their place. I dust her room myself, so that not the
smallest thing is moved. I have been over every inch of the floor on
my knees, I have kissed every trace of my little girl, yet they want
to drive me out. You will drive out my suffering, my longing, my
despair sooner!'

She covered her face and sobbed in a heart-rending manner. I
noticed that the agent's nose was turning red and could feel tears in
my own eyes. The Baroness's grief for her dead child so disarmed
me that I had not the courage to mention raising the rent. Her
weeping unnerved me so that, had it not been the second floor, I
would surely have jumped out of the window.

So, in my anxiety to console the sobbing woman at any price, I
remarked with the utmost mildness: 'Madam, pray calm yourself.
What would you have us do? Can we help at all?'

There was so much sympathy in my voice that the agent's nose
turned even redder. One of the Baroness's eyes dried up, though
the other continued weeping, as a sign that she did not consider her
argument closed, nor me defeated.

'I demand . . . I demand . . .' said she, sighing, 'I demand that I
am not driven from the place where my child died . . . where
everything reminds me of her . . . I cannot, no, I cannot tear myself

away from her room . . . I cannot move her things and her toys . . . It is vile to exploit misfortune in this way.'

'Who is exploiting misfortune?' I inquired.

'Everyone, starting with the landlord, who makes me pay seven hundred roubles . . .'

'Pardon me, madam,' the agent exclaimed, 'seven fine rooms, two kitchens the size of drawing-rooms, two closets . . . Why don't you let someone else have three of the rooms? There are two front doors, after all.'

'I will not let anyone else have them,' she replied firmly, 'because I am convinced my wandering husband will come to his senses any day now, and come back to me . . .'

'In that case, you must go on paying seven hundred roubles . . .'

'If not more,' I murmured.

The Baroness looked at me as though she wanted to shrivel me up into a cinder and drown me in her tears. Oh, what a very grand woman, to be sure . . . It makes my flesh creep to think of her.

'Never mind about the rent,' she said.

'Very sensible,' Wirski praised her, bowing.

'Never mind about the landlord's demands . . . But I cannot pay seven hundred roubles for an apartment in a house like this.'

'What do you expect?' I inquired.

'This house is a disgrace to respectable people,' she exclaimed with a gesture, 'it is not for myself, but for decency's sake that I beg . . .'

'What?'

'That those students who live upstairs be removed . . . They won't let me look out of the windows and demoralise everyone . . .' Suddenly she jumped up from the sofa: 'There, do you hear that?' she cried pointing to the door which led to the room overlooking the yard. In fact, I heard the voice of the eccentric dark-haired young student, who was shouting from the third floor: 'Marysia! Marysia, come up here . . .'

'Marysia!' the Baroness cried.

'Here, madam . . . What is it?' the girl answered, rather red in the face. 'Don't stir from this apartment! There you are, sir,' said the Baroness, 'it is like this for days at a time. And in the evenings the laundry-girls go up there . . . Sir!' she exclaimed, pressing her hands together piously, 'drive those nihilists out, they are a source of depravity and danger to the whole house. They keep tea and sugar in human skulls . . . They poke the samovar with human bones! They want to bring a whole corpse into the house . . .'

She began crying again so that I thought she would have hysterics: 'Those gentlemen,' I said, 'do not pay their rent, so it is very possible that . . .'

The Baroness dried her eyes: 'But of course,' she interrupted, 'you must get rid of them . . . But sir,' she exclaimed, 'although they are wicked and depraved, that . . . that Stawska female is even worse . . .'

I was amazed to see the flame of hatred which glittered in the eyes of madame the Baroness, at the mention of the name 'Stawska'.

'Mrs Stawska lives here?' I asked involuntarily, 'that pretty . . .'

'Ah, another of her victims!' the Baroness cried, pointing at me, and she began speaking in a deep voice, her eyes flashing: 'Grey-haired old man, mind what you are at! For she is a woman whose husband, accused of murder, has run away abroad . . . So how does she live? How does she manage to dress so well?'

'She works like a Trojan,' the agent whispered.

'You too!' the Baroness exclaimed, 'my husband – I am convinced it is he – sends her bouquets from the country. The agent of this house is in love with her, and collects her rent at the end of the month . . .'

'But, madam . . .' the former landowner protested, and his face grew as red as his nose.

'Even that good-for-nothing Maruszewicz,' the Baroness went on, 'even he watches her through the window for days at a time . . .'

The Baroness's dramatic voice went into sobs again: 'And to think,' she groaned, 'that a woman like that has a daughter, a daughter she is bringing up for hellfire, while I . . . I believe in justice and heavenly mercy, but I cannot understand – no, I cannot understand the justice which has deprived me and yet leaves her child to that . . . that . . . Sir!' she exclaimed at the top of her voice, 'you may leave those nihilists if you will, but she . . . you must get rid of her! Let her apartment remain empty, I will pay for it, providing she has no roof over her head . . .'

I found this detestable. I made a sign to the agent that we should take our leave and said coldly, with a bow: 'You must allow the landlord, Mr Wokulski, to decide this for himself.'

The Baroness crossed her arms like a person shot in the heart: 'Ah! So that's how it is?' she hissed, 'already you and that . . . that Wokulski are in league with her! Ha! I will, therefore await God's judgement . . .'

We left, not being detained any longer; on the stairs I staggered like a drunk man.

'What do you know of this Mrs Stawska?' I asked Wirski.

'She's the most honest woman in the world,' he replied, 'young, pretty, keeps the whole household . . . Her mother's pension is barely enough for the rent.'

'So she has a mother?'

'Yes. She is a good woman, too.'

'And how much rent do they pay?'

'Three hundred roubles,' the agent replied, 'it's like taking money from orphans . . .'

'Let us call on these ladies,' said I.

'Very gladly,' he exclaimed, 'and as for what that crazy woman says about them – why, pay no attention. She hates Stawska, though I can't think why. Perhaps because she's pretty and has a little daughter just like an angel.'

'Where do they live?'

'In the front wing, on the second floor.'

I don't remember coming down the main stairs, nor crossing the yard, nor yet going up to the second floor of the wing. Before me stood Mrs Stawska and Wokulski . . . My goodness, what a fine pair they would make; but what of it, since she has a husband already? These are matters in which I have not the slightest desire to meddle. To me it seems one thing, to them it would seem another, and to fate something different again . . .

Fate, fate! It draws people together strangely. Had I not gone into Hopfer's wine-cellars years ago, to see Machalski, I would not have met Wokulski. Again, had I not urged him to go to the theatre, perhaps he would not have met Miss Łęcka. I have unwittingly stirred up trouble for him, and do not want to do so again. Let the Lord God do it . . .

When we stopped at the door of Mrs Stawska's apartment, the agent smiled mischievously and whispered: 'Mind now . . . First we must find out if the young lady is at home. She is well worth seeing, my dear sir!'

'I know it, I know it . . .'

The agent did not ring, but knocked once, then again. Suddenly the door opened quite violently, and there was a fat, dumpy servant-girl with her sleeves rolled up and soapy hands an athlete might have envied: 'Oh, it's the agent,' she exclaimed, 'I thought it was him again . . .'

'What, has someone been making a nuisance of himself ?' Wirski asked, in an outraged tone of voice.

'No, nobody ain't,' the girl said in peasant speech, 'only someone sent a bouquet today. They say it's that Maruszewicz from over the way.'

'Scoundrel!' the agent hissed.

'Men are all alike. If they take a fancy to a girl, they're after her like moths around a candle.'

'Are both the ladies at home?' Wirski asked.

The fat servant-girl looked at me suspiciously: 'Are you with that gentleman?' she asked him.

'Yes, he is the landlord's plenipotentiary.'

'Is he young or old?' she inquired further, gazing at me like a judge eyeing a prisoner.

'He's old – can't you see for yourself?' the agent replied.

'Middle-aged,' I interrupted. (For goodness sake, they will be calling fifteen-year-old boys 'old' next!)

'Both the ladies are at home,' said the servant-girl, 'but a young girl just came to the young mistress for a lesson. But the old lady is in her room.'

'Hm . . .' the agent muttered, 'well, announce us to the old lady.'

We went into the kitchen, where a pail filled with soap suds and children's underclothing stood. A child's drawers, blouses and stockings were hanging up to dry on a line near the hearth. (It is always obvious when there's a child in the house.)

We heard the voice of an elderly lady through the half-open door: 'With the agent? . . . Some gentleman?' said the invisible lady, 'perhaps it is Ludwik, for I was just dreaming . . .'

'Come in, if you please,' said the servant, opening the door to a little drawing-room.

It was a small, pearly-coloured room, with emerald-green furniture, a piano, both windows full of pink and white flowers, prizes of the Fine Arts Society on the walls, a lamp with tulip-shaped glass on the table. After the tomb-like drawing-room of the Baroness Krzeszowska with its furniture done up in dark covering, it seemed more cheerful here. The room looked as if a guest was expected. But the chairs, too symmetrically placed around the table, showed that the guest had not yet arrived.

After a moment, a lady advanced in years came in, wearing an ash-coloured dress. I was struck by the almost white colour of her hair around a thin face which was not, however, too old, and very regular. The lady's features were somehow familiar.

Meanwhile, the agent had undone two buttons on his stained frock-coat and, having bowed with the elegance of a true gentleman, said: 'May I present Mr Rzecki, the plenipotentiary of our landlord, and my colleague . . .'

We glanced at each other. I admit I was somewhat startled by our suddenly being 'colleagues'. Wirski noticed this and added, with a smile: 'I say "colleague" because we have both been abroad and seen interesting things . . .'

'So you have been abroad? Fancy that!' the old lady exclaimed.

'In 1849, and somewhat later,' I interposed.

'And did you ever come across Ludwik Stawski, by any chance?'

'Come, madam,' Wirski exclaimed, smiling and bowing, 'Mr Rzecki was abroad thirty years ago, and your son-in-law left only four years ago . . .'

The old lady made a gesture as if to chase away a fly: 'That's so,' she said, 'whatever am I talking about? But I keep on thinking about Ludwik. . . . Pray be seated.'

We did so, while the former landowner bowed again to the imposing old lady, and she to him. Not until now did I observe that the ash-coloured dress was darned in many places, and a strange melancholy came upon me at the sight of these two people, one in a stained frock-coat, the other in a darned dress, behaving like princes. The levelling plough of time had passed over them both . . .

'I expect you know about our trouble,' said the imposing lady, turning to me, 'my son-in-law was involved in a very terrible matter four years ago . . . Most unjustly . . . Some dreadful woman was murdered . . . Oh, dear, I don't like to speak of it . . . Enough that someone close warned him he was suspected. Most unjustly, Mr . . .'

'Rzecki,' the former landowner put in.

'Most unjustly, Mr Rzecki . . . Well, and the poor fellow fled abroad. Last year the real murderer was found out, Ludwik's innocence established, but what of that, when he hasn't written to us for two years?'

Here she leaned towards me and whispered: 'Helena, my daughter, Mr . . .'

'Rzecki,' the agent exclaimed.

'My daughter, Mr Rzecki, is being ruined . . . frankly, she is ruining herself by advertising in foreign newspapers, but nothing ever comes of it . . . She's still a young woman, Mr . . .'

'Rzecki,' Wirski prompted.

'A young woman, Mr Rzecki, not at all plain . . .'

'Perfectly lovely,' the agent interrupted warmly.

'I was quite like her,' the elderly lady went on with a sigh, nodding to the former landowner, 'here's my daughter, sir, not at all plain, still young, with a little child . . . and perhaps longing for others. Although, Mr Wirski, I vow I have never heard a word of complaint from her . . . She suffers in silence, but I understand how she suffers . . . I too was thirty when . . .'

'Which of us wasn't, once?' the agent sighed deeply.

The door squeaked and in ran a little girl with knitting-needles in her hand: 'Please, grandma,' she cried, 'I shall never finish this dress for my dolly . . .'

'Helena,' the old lady exclaimed sternly, 'you have not said good-day.'

The little girl made two curtsies, to which I replied clumsily, and Mr Wirski like a prince, and she went on showing her grandma the needles from which a little black woollen square was dangling: 'Please grandma, the winter is coming, and my dolly won't have anything to wear in the street. Please grandma, I have dropped another stitch . . .'

(A perfectly lovely child . . . Goodness me, why isn't Staś her father? Perhaps he would not behave so foolishly?)

Her grandma apologised to me, took the wool and the needles, and at this moment in came Mrs Stawska.

I must confess that at the sight of her I behaved with dignity: but Wirski quite lost his head. He jumped up like a student, fastened a button on his frock-coat, then blushed and began stammering: 'May I present Mr Rzecki, our landlord's plenipotentiary . . .'

'How do you do?' said Mrs Stawska, bowing, her eyes lowered. But a powerful blush and traces of alarm on her face suggested I was not a welcome visitor.

'Just wait,' thought I. And I imagined Wokulski in my place in the room: 'Just wait, I'll prove to you you have nothing to fear . . .'

Meanwhile, Mrs Stawska, having sat down, was so embarrassed that she began fidgeting with her daughter's dress. Her mother lost her good humour too, and the agent became quite sheepish.

'Just wait, all of you,' thought I and, adopting a very stern expression, asked: 'How long have you been living in this apartment, ladies?'

'Five years,' Mrs Stawska replied, blushing still more. Her mother quivered where she sat.

'And how much do you pay?'

'Twenty-five roubles a month,' the younger lady whispered. At the same moment she went pale, began rubbing her dress and, certainly without realising it, cast such an imploring look at Wirski that . . . had I been in his place, I would have proposed to her at once.

'We still owe,' she added, still more softly, 'for July . . .'

I scowled like Lucifer, and drawing in as much breath as there was air in the apartment, declared: 'You ladies owe us nothing . . . until October. The fact is that Staś – I mean, Mr Wokulski – has written to me that it is sheer robbery to take three hundred roubles for three rooms on this street. Mr Wokulski cannot permit such extortion, and told me to inform you that from October this apartment will be rented at two hundred roubles. If you do not wish . . .'

The agent almost fell out of his chair. The old lady clasped her hands, and Mrs Stawska gazed at me with wide-open eyes. Such eyes! And how she could use them! I vow that if I were Wokulski, I'd have proposed to her on the spot. Obviously there is nothing doing with her husband, if he hasn't written for two years. Besides, what are divorces for? Why has Staś such a fortune?

Again the door creaked, and a girl about twelve years old appeared, with a school hat on, and a bundle of school books in her hand. She was a child with a round, red face, not betraying much intelligence. She curtsied to us, to Mrs Stawska and to her mother, kissed little Helena on both cheeks, and went out, obviously going home. Then she came back from the kitchen and, blushing to the roots of her hair, asked Mrs Stawska: 'Can I come the day after tomorrow?'

'Yes, dear . . . come at four o'clock,' Mrs Stawska replied, also embarrassed.

When the little girl had finally left, Mrs Stawska's mother said in a displeased tone: 'And that is called a lesson, for goodness sake . . . Helena has been working with her for an hour and a half, and gets forty groszy a lesson . . .'

'Mother!' Mrs Stawska interrupted, looking at her imploringly.

(Were I Wokulski, I'd already have come back from the wedding. What a woman! What features! What expressive looks! I never saw anything like it in my life . . . And her little hands, her figure, her height, her movements and those eyes!)

After a moment of embarrassing silence, the younger lady spoke again: 'We are very grateful to Mr Wokulski for the terms on which he rents the apartment . . . Surely this is the only time a landlord has ever been known to lower the rent of his own accord. But I do not know . . . whether we ought to take advantage of his kindness.'

'It is not kindness, madam, but the honesty of a true gentleman,' the agent put in. 'Mr Wokulski has lowered my rent too, and I accepted . . . The street, after all, is third-rate, little traffic . . .'

'Yet it's easy to find tenants,' Mrs Stawska interposed.

'We prefer ones known to us for quietness and respectability,' I replied.

'You are quite right,' the old lady assured me, 'respectability in the house is our guiding principle . . . Even though little Helena sometimes throws pieces of paper in the yard, Franusia immediately clears them away . . .'

'But, grandma, I was only cutting out envelopes, for I wrote letters to papa to come back,' the little girl protested.

The shadow of sorrow and weariness flitted across Mrs Stawska's face. 'No news?' the agent inquired. The young lady shook her head slowly: I am not sure that she didn't sigh, though softly.

'What a fate for a young and pretty woman!' the older lady cried, 'neither maid nor wife . . .'

'Mother . . . !'

'Neither widow nor divorcée, in a word – and no one knows why or how. You can say what you like, Helena, but I tell you Ludwik is dead . . .'

'Mother! Mother!'

'Yes,' said her mother, loftily, 'here we are, all awaiting him every day, every hour, but it's all for nothing. He's either denied or renounced you, so you are under no obligation to wait for him.'

Tears came into the eyes of both ladies: the mother's of anger, and the daughter's . . . I don't know . . . Perhaps of grief for a ruined life.

Suddenly a thought went through my brain which (had it not been mine) I would have considered a stroke of genius. But less of that. Suffice it to say there was something in my face and attitude that, when I straightened myself in the chair, crossed my legs and coughed, made them all gaze at me, even little Helena.

'Our acquaintance,' said I, 'is too brief for me to venture . . .'

'Never mind,' Mr Wirski interrupted, 'good deeds can be accepted even from strangers . . .'

'Our acquaintance,' I repeated, silencing him with a look, 'is really very short. Allow me, however, to suggest that Mr Wokulski might use his influence to find your husband . . .'

'Ah!' the older lady groaned, in a way I could not but regard as manifesting joy.

'Mother! . . .' Mrs Stawska interrupted.

'Helena,' said her grandmother firmly, 'go and play with your doll and make her the dress. I have picked up the stitch for you, now run along . . .'

The little girl was somewhat startled, perhaps even intrigued, but she kissed her grandma and her mother's hands and went out with her knitting.

'Pray, sir,' the old lady continued, 'if we are to speak frankly, then I am not so much concerned . . . That is, I do not believe Ludwik is still alive. Anyone who doesn't write for two years . . .'

'Mother, that's enough . . .'

'Not at all,' her mother interrupted, 'if you still don't feel your position, then I do. It is impossible to go on living with this eternal hope – or threat . . .'

'Mother dear, I alone have the right, when my happiness and duty . . .'

'Don't mention happiness to me!' her mother exclaimed, 'it ended on the day when your husband fled from the police, who found out some sinister relations with that money-lender. I know he was innocent, I was ready to swear it. But neither you nor I understand why he used to go to her . . .'

'Mother, these gentlemen are strangers,' Mrs Stawska cried in desperation.

'Me a stranger?' the agent asked reproachfully, but he rose from his chair and bowed.

'You're not a stranger, nor is that gentleman,' the old lady went on, indicating me, 'surely he is an honest man . . .'

It was my turn to bow.

'So I tell you, sir,' the old lady continued with a sharp look at me, 'we are living in continual uncertainty about my son-in-law, and this uncertainty is ruining our peace of mind. But I confess I fear his return more than anything.'

Mrs Stawska covered her face with a handkerchief and ran to her room.

'Weep, then – weep!' said the old lady, crossly, shaking a finger after her. 'Such tears, though painful, are at least better than the tears you weep every day . . . Sir,' she turned to me, 'I accept everything God sends, but I feel that if this man came back, he would finish off my child's happiness. I vow,' she added more quietly, 'that she no longer loves him, though she herself doesn't realise it. Yet I am certain . . . she would go to him, if he called . . .'

Stifled sobbing interrupted her words. Wirski and I looked at one another and said goodbye to the elderly lady.

'Madam,' I said, leaving, 'before the year is out, I will bring news of your son-in-law. And perhaps,' I murmured, with an involuntary smile, 'matters will work out so that . . . we shall all be pleased . . . All of us, even some who are not present . . .'

The old lady looked at me inquiringly, but I said nothing. I bade goodbye to her once more, and went out with the agent, not inquiring about Mrs Stawska.

'Drop in and see us any evening you like,' the elderly lady called when we were already in the kitchen. Of course I will! But will my trick with Staś work out? Heaven knows. Calculations do not work when the heart is at stake. But I will at least try to unfasten that woman's hands, and that will be something.

On leaving the apartment of Mrs Stawska and her mother, I quitted the agent, in mutual pleasure. But when I returned home I pondered over the results of my survey of the tenants until my head was spinning.

I was supposed to settle the finances of the house, and here I have done so in such a manner that the income will certainly decrease by three hundred roubles a year. Hm! Perhaps Staś will reconsider and sell his acquisition, which was not in the least necessary, after all.

Ir is still poorly.

Politics are still much the same: continual uncertainty.

XXII

Grey Days and Baneful Hours

WITHIN fifteen minutes of leaving Warsaw by the
Bydgoszcz railroad, Wokulski felt two peculiar, though
completely different sensations: he was enveloped in
fresh air, while he himself fell into a strange lethargy. He could
move about freely, was sober; he thought clearly and rapidly, but
nothing concerned him – neither his fellow travellers nor his destination. This apathy grew as the distance from Warsaw increased.
Beyond Pruszków, he almost relished the drops of rain entering
through the open window into the compartment; later, he was
somewhat stirred by a violent thunderstorm on the far side of
Grodzisk: he even longed for a thunderbolt to strike him dead. But,
when the storm had passed, he sank into apathy again and did not
concern himself with anything, not even with the fact that the
neighbour on his right had gone to sleep against his shoulder, nor
that the passenger opposite had taken off his boots and was resting
his feet almost on Wokulski's knees, in socks that were at least
clean.

Around midnight, something like a dream descended upon him,
or perhaps it was merely a still more profound apathy. He drew a
curtain over the compartment lamp, shut his eyes and thought that
this peculiar apathy would pass with the sunrise. But it did not;
indeed, it intensified towards morning, and continued to increase.
It made him feel neither good nor wretched: only indifferent.

Then his passport was collected, he had breakfast, bought
another ticket, had his luggage moved to another train, and they
travelled on. Another railroad station, another change of trains,
another departure . . . The compartment rattled and shook; the
engine whistled now and again, kept stopping . . . People speaking
German began getting into the compartment in twos and threes . . .
Then the Polish-speaking people disappeared altogether, and the
compartment filled entirely with Germans.

The landscape changed too. Woods surrounded by dikes

appeared, consisting of trees standing equidistant from one another, like soldiers. The wooden huts thatched with straw disappeared, and more two-storey houses with tiled roofs and gardens began coming into view. Another stop, another meal . . . An enormous city . . . Berlin, probably . . . Another departure . . . German-speaking people kept getting in and out of the train, but now they spoke with a slightly different accent. Then night and sleep . . . No, not sleep: merely apathy.

Two Frenchmen appeared in the compartment. The landscape was again entirely different: wide horizons, mountains, vineyards. Here and there a large, two-storey house, old and solid, screened by trees, enveloped in ivy. Another Customs inspection. A change of trains, two Frenchman and a Frenchwoman got in and made enough noise for ten. They were evidently well-bred people: nevertheless, they laughed, changed places several times and apologised to Wokulski, though he didn't know why.

At one station, Wokulski wrote a note to Suzin: 'Paris, Grand Hotel', and gave it with a banknote to the conductor, not caring how much he gave him, nor even whether the telegram arrived. At the next stop, someone thrust a whole bundle of banknotes into his hand, and they travelled on. Wokulski observed it was night again, and again fell into a state which might have been a dream, or was perhaps only lassitude. His eyes were closed; yet he thought he was asleep and that this strange state of indifference would leave him in Paris. 'Paris . . . Paris . . .' he said, still asleep, 'I've been looking forward to Paris for so long . . . This will pass . . . Everything will pass.'

Ten o'clock in the morning and another station. The train had stopped under a roof: noise, shouting, people running about. Wokulski was surrounded by three Frenchmen offering their services. Suddenly someone caught his arm: 'Well, Stanisław Piotrowicz, I'm glad to see you.'

Wokulski stared for a moment at a giant with a red face and flaxen beard, then said: 'Ah, Suzin . . .' They embraced. Suzin was accompanied by two more Frenchmen, one of whom took Wokulski's baggage check.

'Glad you are here,' said Suzin, embracing him again, 'I thought I would hang myself here in Paris without you . . .'

'Paris . . .' Wokulski thought.

'But never mind me,' Suzin went on, 'you've become so stuck-up among those miserable gentlefolks of yours that you don't care about me any more. But it would have been a pity if you'd let the money slip. You'd have lost some fifty thousand roubles.'

The two Frenchmen accompanying Suzin reappeared and told them everything was ready. Suzin took Wokulski by the arm and led him out to a square containing many omnibuses and one- and two-horse carriages, with drivers sitting up in front or behind. After a few dozen paces they came to a two-horse carriage with a footman. They got in and drove off. 'Look,' said Suzin, 'this is the rue La Fayette, and that the Boulevard Magenta. We'll drive all the way down the rue La Fayette to our hotel near the Opéra. Paris is more a miracle than a city, I assure you. Wait till you see the Champs-Elysées and the Seine and the Rivoli . . . Oh, it's a marvel, I assure you. Perhaps the women are a trifle too forward here. But tastes differ. In any case, I'm delighted you're here: fifty thousand roubles aren't to be sneezed at . . . Ah, there's the Opéra and the Capucines, and this is our abode . . .'

Wokulski caught sight of a huge, five-storey building, wedge-shaped, with an iron balcony encircling the second floor, standing in a street planted with young trees and packed with omnibuses, carriages, people on horseback and on foot. The traffic was as thick as if at least half of Warsaw had gathered to stare at an accident; the roadway was as smooth as the pavement. He realised he was in the very heart of Paris, but felt no emotion, no curiosity. Nothing mattered.

The carriage drove through an imposing gate; the footman opened the carriage door; they stepped out. Suzin took Wokulski by the arm and conducted him into a small room which, after a moment, began ascending. 'This is an elevator,' Suzin said. 'I have two apartments here, one on the first floor at a hundred francs a day, the other on the third at ten. I took one for you at ten francs. It can't be helped – the Exhibition, you see.'

They emerged from the elevator into a corridor and a moment later were in an elegant drawing-room with mahogany furniture, a large bed under a canopy and a wardrobe with a huge mirror in place of the door. 'Sit down, Stanisław Piotrowicz. Do you want something to eat and drink, here or in the restaurant? Well, the fifty thousand are yours . . . I am delighted.'

'Tell me,' Wokulski spoke for the first time, 'what am I to get the fifty thousand for?'

'Perhaps more than that . . .'

'Very well, but what's it for?'

Suzin threw himself into an armchair, clasped his hands over his belly and burst out laughing: 'Well, merely for asking for it . . . Another man wouldn't have asked . . . But, being you, you must know why you're making so much money. You idiot!'

'That's no answer.'

'Then – I'll tell you,' said Suzin, 'first because you taught me sense in Irkutsk for four years. Had it not been for you, I wouldn't be the Suzin I am. Well, Stanisław Piotrowicz, I am not one of your people, I do return a favour for a favour.'

'That's not a reply either,' Wokulski interposed.

Suzin shrugged. 'Please don't ask me for an explanation here; you'll understand when we go downstairs. Perhaps I'll buy some Parisian haberdashery, or a dozen or so merchant ships. I don't know a word of French or German, so I'll need a man like you.'

'I know nothing of ships . . .'

'No matter. We can find railroad, mercantile and military experts here . . . I'm not concerned with them, but with a man who can talk on my behalf . . . for me . . . In any case, keep your eyes open when we go downstairs, and your lips sealed, and when we leave you will not recall a word of what has passed. You are capable of that, Stanisław Piotrowicz, so ask me no more. I'll make my ten per cent, I'll pay you ten per cent of my profits, and the matter ends. But do not ask why, nor against whom . . .'

Wokulski was silent.

'American and French industrialists are coming to see me at four o'clock. Will you join us?' Suzin asked.

'Very well.'

'And now for a stroll around the town.'

'No, I'll go to sleep now.'

'Very well. Let's go to your apartment.'

They left Suzin's room and went into a completely identical apartment a dozen yards away. Wokulski threw himself on the bed, Suzin went out on tip-toe and closed the door. After Suzin's exit, Wokulski closed his eyes and tried to fall asleep. Not so much to fall asleep, perhaps, as to dispel some insistent thought on account of which he had fled from Warsaw. For a time it seemed to him to have been dispelled, or that it had stayed behind and was now anxiously in search of him, wandering from Krakowskie Przedmieście to Aleje Ujazdowskie: 'Where is he? Where is he?' the spectre was whispering.

'Suppose it follows me here?' Wokulski asked himself. 'Well, surely it won't find me here in this huge city, in such a vast hotel.' But then he thought: 'Maybe it's already looking for me here?'

He closed his eyes still tighter and began swaying on the mattress which seemed unusually wide and exceptionally springy. Outside his door in the hotel passage people were talking and hurrying about as though something had just happened; outside the window there was an ill-defined noise consisting of the rattle of countless carriages, bells ringing, human voices, trumpets, revolver shots and goodness knows what else, but all stifled and distant. Then he imagined a shape was looking in at him through the window, and later that someone was going from door to door in the passage, knocking and asking: 'Isn't he here?'

In fact, someone came up and knocked and even banged on his door, but getting no answer they went away again. 'It won't find me, it won't . . .' Wokulski thought. Then he opened his eyes, and his hair stood on end. Facing him he saw a room exactly like his own, the same bed with a canopy, with himself on the bed. It was one of the most profound shocks he ever experienced in his life, to see with his own eyes that here, where he believed himself entirely alone, he was nevertheless accompanied by an inseparable companion – himself.

'An ingenious system of espionage, to be sure,' he muttered, 'these wardrobes fitted with mirrors are ridiculous.' He jumped off the bed, his double did the same, just as quickly. He ran to the window, so did the other. He feverishly opened his valise to change, and the other began changing too, clearly with the intention of going into the town. Wokulski felt he must flee from this room. The spectre from which he had fled Warsaw was already here; it was standing on the threshold.

He washed, put on clean linen, changed. It was barely twelve-thirty. 'Three hours and a half,' he thought, 'I must do something to fill them . . .'

Hardly had he opened the door when a servant said: 'Monsieur?' Wokulski asked him the way to the stairs, gave the man a franc and hurried down from the third floor like a man pursued. He went out of the gate and stopped on the pavement.

It was a wide street, lined with trees. Just then, half a dozen carriages and a yellow omnibus, weighed down with passengers above and below, flew past him. On the right, far off somewhere, a square could be seen; on the left – at the foot of the hotel – a small awning, under which a throng of men and women sat at small round tables, practically on the pavement, drinking coffee. The men, as though *décolleté*, wore flowers or ribbons in their button-holes and crossed one leg over the other precisely as high as was appropriate in the vicinity of five-storey houses; the women were slender, slight and dusky, with fiery glances, yet modestly dressed.

Wokulski turned to the left and saw, around the corner of the hotel – that very same hotel! – another awning, another throng of people drinking something alongside the pavement. Here there must have been a hundred people, if not more; the gentlemen wore insolent expressions, the ladies were vivacious, friendly and quite unaffected. One- and two-horse carriages continued to roll by, a constant stream of pedestrians hurried past in both directions, a yellow and green omnibus passed through, its route frequently intersected by that of brown omnibuses, all full up inside, their roofs all loaded down with passengers above.

Wokulski found himself in the middle of a square from which seven streets led off. He counted them once, twice – seven streets . . . Where was he to go? . . . In the direction of the trees, perhaps . . . Two of the streets intersecting at a right angle were thus lined . . .

'I will follow the hotel wall,' thought Wokulski. He made a half turn to the left and stopped, amazed.

In the distance to the left a formidable edifice was visible. On the ground floor, a series of arcades and statues; on the first, huge stone columns and slightly smaller marble ones with gilded capitals. In the corners at the level of the roof were eagles and gilded statues, poised above the gilded forms of capering horses. The roof was smooth at the near end, farther off was a cupola culminating in a crown, and farther still, a three-cornered roof, also bearing a group of figures on its pinnacle. Everywhere marble, bronze, and gold; columns, statues, medallions everywhere . . .

'The Opéra? . . .' thought Wokulski. 'But there is more marble and bronze here than in the whole of Warsaw? . . .' Recalling his shop, the pride of the city, he coloured, and walked on. He felt that Paris had overwhelmed him at the very first step and – he was content.

The traffic of omnibuses and pedestrians grew at an alarming rate. Every few paces found verandahs, little round tables, people sitting by the pavement. A carriage, with a footman behind, was followed by a cart pulled by a dog, an omnibus overtook him, then two people with handbarrows, then a larger cart with two wheels, then a lady and gentlemen on horseback and again an endless stream of carriages. Closer, by the pavement, stood a cart with flowers, another with fruit; opposite was a pieman, a news vendor, a junk dealer, a knife grinder, a bookseller . . .

'M'rchand d'habits . . .'

'Figaro! . . .'

'Exposition! . . .'

'Guide Parisien! . . . trois francs! . . . trois francs! . . .'

Someone thrust a book into Wokulski's hand. He paid three francs and crossed the street. He walked quickly, but despite this he could see that everything was overtaking him: carriages and dogs. Why, this was some great race; and so he quickened his pace, and though he still overtook no one, he was now attracting attention. He was solicited above all by the vendors of books and newspapers; women looked at him, the men laughed at him in a mocking manner. He felt that he, Wokulski, who made such a stir in Warsaw, was here as overawed as a child and – he liked it . . . Ah, how he longed to be a child once more, back in the days when his father was seeking the advice of his friends: should he send him to a merchant, or to school?

Here the street curved somewhat to the right. For the first time, Wokulski noticed a three-storey house and a kind of melancholy overcame him. A three-storey house among the five-storeyed! . . . What a pleasant surprise . . .

Suddenly a carriage with a groom on the box passed by, with

two women inside. One was unknown, the other . . . 'Can it be?'
Wokulski whispered, 'no, impossible . . .' Nevertheless, he felt his
energies ebb away. Fortunately there was a café alongside. He
threw himself into a chair close to the pavement, a waiter appeared,
asked something and then brought iced coffee and cognac. At the
same time a flower-girl pinned a rose in his button-hole, and a
newspaper vendor laid *Figaro* in front of him. He tossed her ten
francs, gave him a franc, drank the coffee and began reading: 'Her
Majesty Queen Izabela . . .'

He crumpled the newspaper, thrust it into his pocket, paid for
the coffee without finishing it, and rose. The waiter was eyeing
him surreptitiously; two customers, twirling light canes, crossed
their legs still higher and one of them stared insolently at him
through a monocle. 'Suppose I were to hit that nincompoop on
the jaw?' Wokulski thought, 'tomorrow a duel, perhaps he'd kill
me . . . But if I killed him?' He walked past the nincompoop and
stared into his face. The nincompoop's monocle fell down his
waistcoat and he lost his inclination to scoff.

Wokulski walked on and looked attentively at the buildings.
What splendid shops! Even the most paltry looked better than his,
although it was the finest in Warsaw. Stone houses: almost each
floor had great balconies or balustrades along the entire façade.
'This Paris looks as though all the inhabitants must feel the need of
constant communication, either in the cafés or on their balconies,'
Wokulski thought. The roofs were impressive too, high, loaded
with chimney-stacks, prickly with chimney-pots and spires. A tree
or lamp or kiosk or column mounted with a globe rose every few
paces along the streets. Life was effervescent here, so powerfully
that it was unable to use up its energies in the neverending traffic,
in the swift rush of people, in the erection of five-storey houses, so
it had also burst out of walls in the forms of statues or bas-reliefs,
and out of the streets in the shape of innumerable kiosks.

Wokulski felt he had been extricated from stagnant water and
suddenly plunged into boiling water which 'storms and roars and
foams'. He, a grown man, energetic in his own climate, felt like a
sensitive child here, impressed by everything and everyone.
Meanwhile, all around him, the city 'seethed and boiled and
roared and foamed'. Unable to see any end to the crowds,
carriages, trees or dazzling store windows, or even of the street
itself, Wokulski was gradually overcome with stupefaction. He
stopped hearing the passers-by chattering, then grew deaf to the
cries of the street traders, finally to the rattle of the wheels. Then it
seemed to him he had seen such houses, traffic, cafés before: still
later, he thought that it wasn't so impressive after all, and finally
his critical faculties awoke and he told himself that although more
French was to be heard in the streets of Paris than in Warsaw, yet

the local accent here was worse, the pronunciation less clear.

Pondering thus, he slowed down and ceased stepping aside for people. And when he thought that the French would now surely begin pointing him out, to his surprise he saw that he attracted less attention. After an hour in the streets he had become an ordinary drop in the ocean of Paris. 'So much the better,' he muttered.

Hitherto, houses had risen to his right and left at every few dozen paces, then a side-street would appear. But now a monotonous wall of houses continued ahead for several hundred yards. Uneasily he quickened his step and, to his great satisfaction, finally gained a side-street: he turned to the right slightly and read: rue St-Fiacre. He smiled, recollecting a novel by Paul de Kock. Then he reached another side-street and read rue du Sentier. 'Never heard of it,' he thought. A few dozen yards further on, he saw rue Poissonnière, which reminded him of a criminal case, then a whole series of short streets emerging opposite the Gymnase theatre.

'What's that?' he wondered, catching sight of a huge building to his right, unlike anything he had seen before. It was a vast stone block with a semi-circular arched gateway. It was a gate of course, which stood at the intersection of two streets. There was a little booth to one side where omnibuses stopped; a café almost exactly opposite and a pavement separated from the centre of the street by a short iron railing.

A couple of hundred paces further, another similar gate, and between them a wide street, extending to the right and to the left. The traffic suddenly grew more dense; at least three different types of omnibus and tram ran here.

Wokulski looked right and saw two rows of street lamps, two lines of kiosks, two lines of trees and two lines of five-storey houses reaching the length of Krakowskie Przedmieście and Nowy Świat avenue together. The end was out of sight; only somewhere in the distance the street rose towards the sky; the roofs descended to the ground, and everything disappeared. 'I'll go that way, even if I get lost and am late for the meeting,' he thought. Then, at a corner, a young woman passed him, her figure and movements making a powerful impression on Wokulski: 'Can it be? . . . No . . . First, she stayed behind in Warsaw and then, I've already met another like her . . . Illusions.'

But his strength, even his memory were ebbing. Now he had stopped at the junction of two streets planted with trees, with no idea whatsoever of how he had come there. Panic fear, known to people lost in a forest, gripped him; fortunately a one-horse carriage drove by, whose driver grinned at him in a very friendly manner: 'The Grand Hotel,' said Wokulski, getting in.

The driver touched his cap and cried: 'Gee up, Lisette! I daresay this noble foreign gentleman will treat you to a quart of beer for

your trouble . . .' Then, turning sideways to Wokulski, he said:
'Either of two things, citizen – you've just arrived, or you've
lunched well . . .'

'I arrived today,' Wokulski replied, soothed by the sight of his
round, red, clean-shaven face.

'And you've had a drop to drink, that's clear,' the driver
remarked, 'do you know the fare?'

'Never mind that . . .'

'Gee up, Lisette. I like this foreign gentleman and think that only
fares like this should turn up at our stand. Are you sure, citizen,
that it's the Grand Hotel you want?' He turned to Wokulski.

'Quite sure'.

'Gee up, Lisette. This foreign gentleman is beginning to interest
me. Are you from Berlin, citizen?'

'No.'

The driver eyed him a moment, then said, 'So much the better
for you. True, I've nothing against the Prussians, although they
took Alsace from us and a large piece of Lotharingia too, but I
never like having a German at the back of me . . . Where are you
from, citizen?'

'Warsaw.'

'Ah, ça! A fine country, a rich country . . . Gee up, Lisette! So
you're a Pole. I know the Poles . . . Here's Opéra Square, citizen,
and there's the Grand Hotel.'

Wokulski tossed the driver three francs, hurried through the gate
and up to the third floor. Hardly had he stopped at his door when a
smiling servant appeared and handed him a note from Suzin with a
packet of letters: 'Many visitors – many lady visitors too,' said the
servant, looking at him cheerfully.

'Where are they all?'

'In the reception room and the waiting room and the dining
room. Mr Jumart is growing impatient.'

'And who might Mr Jumart be?' asked Wokulski.

'Your secretary and Mr Suzin's . . . A very efficient man, who
could be of great service if he were certain . . . of a thousand-franc
tip,' said the servant mischievously.

'Where is he now?'

'In your reception room on the first floor. Mr Jumart is a very
talented person, but I too might be of use to your excellencies,
although my name is Miller. The truth is I'm an Alsatian, and would
pay you ten francs a day, upon my word, instead of taking them
from you, if we could finish off the Prussians once and for all.'

Wokulski went into his room: 'In the first place,' Miller persisted,
'you gentlemen should beware of that Baroness . . . who is already
waiting in the library, though she wasn't supposed to come until
three. I swear she's a German . . . Me, I'm an Alsatian, after all.'

Miller said the last phrase in an undertone and retreated down the corridor. Wokulski opened Suzin's note and read: 'Meeting postponed until eight – you have plenty of time, so pray deal with the visitors, especially the women. I am too old to cope with them, God knows.' Wokulski began glancing through the letters. Most were advertisements from tradesmen, hairdressers, dentists, requests for assistance, offers to reveal various secrets, an appeal from the Salvation Army. Out of all these letters, Wokulski was most struck by this: 'A young person, elegant and attractive, seeks to visit Paris with you, sharing expenses. Leave reply with the hotel porter.'

'A strange city,' Wokulski muttered. A second, still more interesting letter was from the Baroness who was waiting in the library for an interview at three o'clock. 'Half an hour yet . . .'

He rang and ordered lunch. A few minutes later he was served with ham, eggs, steak, an unidentifiable fish, several bottles of various beverages, and black coffee. He ate ravenously, drank liberally, finally told Miller to take him to the reception room. The servant walked along the corridor with him, touched a bell, said something into a speaking-tube, then conducted Wokulski to the elevator. A minute later Wokulski was on the first floor and as soon as he emerged from the elevator he was stopped by a distinguished gentleman with a small moustache, in a frock-coat and white tie. 'Jumart . . .' said this gentleman, with a bow.

They went several yards down a corridor and Jumart opened the door of a splendid drawing-room. Wokulski almost drew back on seeing the gilded furniture, huge mirrors and the walls adorned with bas-reliefs. In the centre was a huge table covered with a costly cloth and heaped with papers. 'May I announce the visitors?' Jumart asked. 'They are not dangerous, I think . . . But may I venture to draw your attention to the Baroness? She's in the library.' He bowed and went solemnly into another drawing-room, which seemed to be a waiting room.

'For goodness sake, have I got myself involved in an imbroglio?' Wokulski wondered.

Hardly had he sat down in an armchair and started looking through the papers when a servant in a blue frock-coat with gilt epaulettes entered and handed him a visiting-card on a tray. It was engraved: 'Colonel . . .' and a name which conveyed nothing to Wokulski.

'Ask him in . . .'

A moment later there appeared a man of imposing stature with a grey imperial, similar whiskers and a red ribbon in his button-hole. 'I know your time is precious,' said the visitor, bowing slightly, 'my business is brief. Paris is a splendid city in every respect: whether for amusement or for study . . . but it needs an experienced guide. Since I know all the museums, galleries, theatres,

clubs, monuments, government and private institutions, in a word
– everything – if you wish, sir . . .'

'Pray leave your address,' Wokulski replied.

'I speak four languages, I have a wide acquaintance in the artistic,
literary, scientific and industrial worlds . . .'

'I cannot give you an answer just now,' Wokulski interposed.

'Shall I call again, or await your summons?' the visitor asked.

'Yes, I'll reply by letter . . .'

'Pray bear me in mind,' said the visitor. He rose, bowed and left.

The servant brought in another visiting-card and soon another
visitor appeared. He was a plump, red-faced man who looked like
the proprietor of a textile emporium. He kept bowing as he crossed
from the door to the table: 'What can I do for you?' Wokulski
asked.

'My dear sir, have you not guessed, from the name Escabeau?
Hannibale Escabeau?' the visitor was surprised, 'the Escabeau rifle
fires seventeen rounds a minute: but the one I shall have the
honour to show you fires thirty . . .'

Wokulski's expression was so astounded that Hannibale
Escabeau, himself, began wondering: 'Surely I have not made a
mistake?' the visitor asked.

'You have,' said Wokulski, 'I'm a haberdashery merchant, and
rifles do not concern me at all.'

'But I was told – in confidence . . .' said Escabeau significantly,
'that you gentlemen . . .'

'You were misinformed . . .'

'Ah, so? In that case, my apologies . . . It must be another room,'
said the visitor, bowing as he retired.

The blue frock-coat and white trousers reappeared with another
visitor: this time he was a small, lean, dark man with restless eyes.
He almost ran up to the table, dropped into a chair, peered around
at the door, then moved closer to Wokulski and began in a low
voice: 'Very likely this will surprise you, sir . . . But the matter is
urgent   . . . too urgent . . . In the past few days I have made a
tremendous discovery in roulette . . . All it requires is to double the
stake six or seven times . . .'

'Forgive me, sir, but I am not interested,' Wokulski interrupted.

'You don't trust me? Naturally . . . But I have a roulette wheel
here, we might try . . .'

'Excuse me, sir, I haven't time now.'

'Three minutes, sir . . . One minute . . .'

'Not even half a minute.'

'So when am I to come back?' asked the visitor, with a very
desperate look.

'Not soon, at any rate.'

'Sir, at least lend me a hundred francs to make an official test . . .'

'I can spare you five,' Wokulski replied, putting a hand into his pocket.

'Oh no, sir – thank you . . . I am no trickster . . . But perhaps . . . Please give me it . . . I'll repay you tomorrow. You may change your mind in the meantime.'

The next visitor, an impressively stout individual, wearing a row of miniature medals, offered Wokulski the diploma of a Doctor of Philosophy, or a title of nobility, and seemed very surprised when his offer was declined. He left without even saying good-bye.

A short interval followed. Wokulski seemed to catch the rustle of a woman's gown in the waiting-room. He listened intently. At this moment the footman announced the Baroness.

Another long pause, then a woman appeared in the drawing-room, so beautiful and distinguished that Wokulski involuntarily rose to his feet. She might have been about forty: of imposing stature, with very regular features and the attitude of a great lady. He showed her a chair in silence. But as she sat down, he noticed she was agitated and clutching at a lace handkerchief. Looking suddenly into his eyes, she asked: 'Do you recognise me?'

'No, madam.'

'Have you never even seen any of my portraits?'

'No.'

'Then you can never have been to Berlin or Vienna?'

'No, never.'

The woman sighed deeply. 'So much the better,' she said, 'I'll be bolder . . . I am not a Baroness at all . . . I am someone entirely different. But less of that. I find myself temporarily in an embarrassment. I need twenty thousand francs . . . But as I don't want to pawn my jewellery, so . . . Do you understand me?'

'No, madam.'

'Well . . . I have an important secret to dispose of . . .'

'I have no right to acquire secrets,' Wokulski replied, already embarrassed.

The woman shifted in her chair: 'No right, sir? Then why are you here?' she said, with a slight smile.

'I haven't the right, all the same . . .'

The lady rose. 'This,' she said, excitedly, 'is an address where you can contact me within twenty-four hours, and here is a note which may give you cause to think . . . Good-bye.'

She went out with a rustle of her gown. Wokulski glanced at the note and found it contained those details of himself and Suzin which are usually shown in passports. 'Hm,' he thought, 'Miller and she read my passport and made a note of its contents, not without mistakes, either – Wokulsky, indeed! Confound it! Do they take me for a child?'

As no more visitors appeared, Wokulski summoned Jumart:

'Your wish, sir?' asked the elegant secretary.

'I want to talk to you . . .'

'In confidence? In that case, allow me to take a seat . . . The performance is over; the costumes have gone back to the wardrobe; the actors have become equals . . .'

He said this in a somewhat ironical tone and behaved as befitted a very well-educated man. Wokulski grew increasingly surprised by him: 'Tell me,' he said, 'what sort of people were those?'

'Your callers?' Jumart inquired, 'people – like any others: guides, inventors, go-betweens . . . Each works as best he may, and tries to do as best he can from his work. And, since they like making a profit if it's to be had for more than it's worth – well, that's a trait of the French.'

'You aren't a Frenchman?'

'I? . . . I was born in Vienna, educated in Switzerland and Germany, I have lived a long time in Italy, England, Norway, America . . . My surname best defines my nationality: I belong to the herd I happen to be living in – a bull with bulls, a horse with horses. But, since I know the source of my income and what I spend it on, people know me – so nothing concerns me.'

Wokulski eyed him intently: 'I do not understand you,' he said.

'You see, sir,' said Jumart, drumming on the table, 'I have observed too much of the world to care about a man's nationality. Only four kinds of man exist for me – not counting languages. The first are those whose source of income I know, and how they spend it; the second are those whose source of income I know, though I don't know how they spend it. The third's expenses are known, while his source of income is unknown, and the fourth kind are those whose sources of income and expenditures I don't know. I know that Mr Escabeau gets his income from a knitting factory, and he spends it on making some devilish weapons, so I respect him. As for the Baroness – I don't know where she gets her money, nor how she spends it, so I don't trust her.'

'I am a tradesman, Mr Jumart,' Wokulski remarked, disagreeably impressed by the exposition of the above theory.

'I know. And you are also a friend of Mr Suzin, which gives you interest. But my remarks didn't refer to you, sir; I merely offered them as a lecture which, I trust, may be of some profit to me.'

'You are a philosopher,' Wokulski muttered.

'Indeed, I am a Doctor of Philosophy of two universities,' Jumart replied.

'Yet you play the role of . . . ?'

'A servant, you were going to say?' Jumart interposed, smiling. 'I work, sir, in order to live and assure myself an income when I grow old. I care nothing for titles; I have had so many already . . . The world is like an amateur theatre, where it is not done to insist on leading parts but reject minor roles. In any case, all roles are good, providing they are well played and not taken too seriously.'

Wokulski stirred. Jumart rose, bowed elegantly and said: 'I recommend my services to you, sir.' Then he went out of the drawing-room.

'Do I have a fever, or what?' Wokulski whispered, clutching his head with both hands, 'I knew Paris was strange, but not quite so strange . . .' It was only three-thirty when Wokulski glanced at his watch: 'Four hours and more till the meeting,' he thought, unnerved by not knowing what to do with the time. He had seen so many new things, talked to so many new people, yet it was only three-thirty! He was seized by an undefinable alarm, and felt the lack of something . . . 'Shall I have another meal? No . . . Or read? No . . . Or talk? I've had enough conversation.'

People disgusted him; perhaps the least detestable were those infected with inventor's mania and Jumart, with his classification of the human species. He lacked the courage to go back to his hotel room, with its huge mirror; so what else was left him but to inspect the sights of Paris? He asked to be shown the dining-room of the Grand Hotel. Everything in it was splendid and immense, from the walls, ceiling and windows down to the number and dimensions of the tables. But Wokulski hardly looked at it; instead, he fixed his gaze on one of the huge, gilded chandeliers and thought: 'When she reaches the age of the Baroness . . . accustomed as she is to spending tens of thousands of roubles a year, who knows she won't go the same way as the Baroness? After all, that woman was once young too, and some madman like myself may have been insane about her, and she never asked where the money was coming from . . . Today she knows – from trading in secrets! Accursed sphere, which breeds such beautiful women who are so . . .'

He felt oppressed in the dining-room, so he hurried out of the hotel to plunge into the noise of the streets: 'The first time I went to the left,' he thought, 'I'll go to the right now.'

Blindly wandering through an immeasurable city was the only thing that possessed a sort of bitter fascination for him: 'If only I could lose myself in these crowds . . .' he thought. So he turned to the right. He crossed a small square and entered a very large one, copiously planted with trees. In its centre was a square building surrounded by columns, like a Greek temple: it had great bronze doors covered with bas-reliefs and another bas-relief on the façade, apparently depicting the Day of Judgement. Wokulski walked around the building and thought of Warsaw. What effort they needed to erect small, transient and trivial buildings there! Here, however, human force erected monsters as if for diversion, and was so little weary of the labour involved that it covered them with ornamentation.

He noticed a small street opposite, and a huge square beyond, in

which a slender column stood. He walked in that direction. As he
approached, the column grew taller and the square expanded. Large
fountains were playing both in front of and behind the column;
yellowing clumps of trees, like gardens, stretched to right and left;
in the background was a river, above which the smoke of a swiftly
passing steamboat streamed along. Relatively few carriages were
moving around the square, but there were many children with
their mothers and nursemaids. Soldiers of various regiments were
walking about, and a band was playing somewhere.

Wokulski approached the obelisque and was amazed. He found
himself in the centre of an area two miles long and half a mile
wide. Behind was a garden, in front a very long drive. On both
sides were squares and palaces, and a huge arch stood far off on a
hill. Wokulski felt that epithets and superlatives failed him.

'This is the Place de la Concorde; that's an obelisk from Luxor
(genuine, sir!); behind us are the Tuileries, in front the Champs-
Elysées and there, at the end, the Arc de Triomphe . . .' Wokulski
glanced around: beside him was hovering a gentleman in dark
spectacles and rather shabby gloves. 'We might go that way – a
divine stroll! Look at the traffic!' said the stranger. All at once he
broke off, walked rapidly away and disappeared between two
passing carriages.

Meanwhile a uniformed man in a short cape approached. He
gazed at Wokulski a moment and said, with a smile: 'You are a
foreigner? Pray beware of casual acquaintances in Paris . . .'

Wokulski instinctively touched the side pocket of his top-coat
and realised his silver cigarette-case was gone. He flushed, politely
thanked the officer in the cape, but did not admit his loss. Jumart's
definition crossed his mind, and he told himself that he knew the
source of income of the man in shabby gloves, though he knew
nothing of his outgoings: 'Jumart is right,' he thought, 'criminals
are less suspect than people who acquire their money Heaven
knows where,' and he recalled many such in Warsaw. 'Perhaps
that's why there are no buildings, no Arcs de Triomphe there . . .'

He walked along the Champs-Elysées and was stunned by the
unending stream of carriages and carts, amidst which rode men and
women on horseback. As he walked, he tried to dispel the dismal
thoughts which encircled him like a flock of bats. He walked on
and was afraid to look back: in this street, effervescent with splendour and gaiety, he seemed like a crushed worm dragging its
entrails behind it.

He reached the Arc de Triomphe, and turned back slowly.
When he reached the Place de la Concorde again, he saw – behind
the Tuileries – a huge black balloon which rose rapidly into the air,
remained there a while, then slowly sank down: 'The Giffard
balloon,' he thought, 'a pity I haven't time today . . .'

He turned from the square into some street, where a garden stretched to the right, separated by iron railings and posts on which vases stood, and to the left was a series of apartment houses with semicircular roofs, a forest of chimneys large and small, and neverending balustrades . . . He walked slowly and thought with alarm that after a visit of barely eight hours, Paris had begun to bore him . . .

'Bah!' he muttered. 'But the Exhibition, the museums, the balloon? . . .'

Continuing along the rue de Rivoli, at around seven o'clock he reached the square on which, solitary as a finger, rose a gothic tower surrounded by trees and a low fence of iron bars. More streets again branched off from here.

Feeling tired, Wokulski beckoned to a horse-drawn cab and within half an hour was back in his hotel, having passed the already familiar Porte St-Denis on the way.

The meeting with ship-builders and engineers lasted until midnight, accompanied by many bottles of champagne. Wokulski, who had to substitute for Suzin in the talks and to take copious notes, did not feel at ease until he had this work. Refreshed, he hurried to his room and, instead of tormenting himself with the mirror, took a plan of Paris to bed with him. 'Nothing to it,' he thought, 'some hundred square miles in area, two million inhabitants, thousands of streets, ten thousand public conveyances . . .' Then he read a long list of the most celebrated buildings in Paris and thought with shame that he would never find his way around this city. 'The Exhibition . . . Notre-Dame . . . Les Halles . . . the Bastille . . . the Madeleine . . . the sewers . . . goodness!' he said.

He turned out the light. The street was quiet; a grey glow of light, probably reflected from the clouds, entered at the window. But there was a roaring and a ringing in Wokulski's ears, and before his eyes stretched streets as smooth as floors, trees surrounded by iron fences, buildings of hewn stone, throngs of people and carriages coming and going Heaven knows where. He fell asleep watching this crowd of sights, and thought, that come what may, he would remember his first day in Paris for the rest of his life.

Then he dreamed that the ocean of houses and forests of statues and endless lines of trees were falling in upon him, and that he himself was asleep in a profound tomb, alone, tranquil, almost happy. He was asleep, thinking of nothing, forgetful of everyone, and would sleep thus for ever were it not, alas, for a drop of grief that lay within or alongside him, so minute that the human eye could not perceive it, yet so bitter that it could poison the whole world.

From the day when he first plunged into Paris, a life that was almost mystical started for Wokulski. Apart from a few hours devoted to advising Suzin with the ship-builders, Wokulski was entirely free, and he spent the time in perfectly disorganised visits to the city. He would choose a neighbourhood from the index in his Guide, and would go there in an open carriage without even looking at the street-plan. He climbed steps, walked around buildings, hurried through halls, stopped at interesting sights, and drove on again according to the alphabetical index, in the same carriage, which he hired for the day. But, since what he most feared was the lack of something to do, he spent his evenings looking at the city plan, crossing out the places he had visited and making notes.

Sometimes Jumart accompanied him on these excursions and took him to places the guidebooks did not mention: to merchant stores, to factory workshops, to the homes of craftsmen, to student quarters, to the cafés and restaurants along the streets of the fourth quarter. It was here at last that Wokulski became acquainted with the real life of Paris.

In the course of these trips he climbed towers: St-Jacques, Notre-Dame and the Panthéon; he went up the Trocadéro in a lift, descended into the Parisian sewers and to the catacombs decorated with human skulls; he visited the world exhibition, the Louvre, and Cluny, the Bois de Boulogne, and cemeteries, the cafés de la Rotonde, du Grand Balcon, and fountains, schools and hospitals, the Sorbonne and the fencing halls, the Conservatory and musical halls, animal fights and theatres, the Stock Exchange, the July Column and temple interiors. All these sights created chaos around him, corresponding to the chaos reigning in his own soul.

Sometimes, running over the objects seen in his mind – from the Palace of Exhibitions, two kilometres in circumference, to the pearl in the Bourbon crown, no bigger than a pea – he asked: what is it that I want? And it emerged that he wanted nothing. Nothing gripped his attention, nothing quickened the beating of his heart, or prompted him to action. If, for the price of a walking trip from the cemetery of Montmartre to that of Montparnasse, he was offered the whole of Paris with the condition that it should absorb and stimulate him, he would not have gone those five kilometres. But he walked tens of them daily, only in order to deaden his memories.

Sometimes it seemed to him he was a being which had been born by a strange chapter of accidents, a few days ago, here on the pavements of Paris, and that everything which came into his mind was only an illusion, a dream from some earlier existence which had never really existed. Then he told himself that he was perfectly happy; he rode from one end of Paris to the other and scattered handfuls of louis d'or like a madman. 'It's all the same to me,' he muttered. If only it weren't for that particle of grief, so minute yet so bitter!

Sometimes, against the background of grey days, when it seemed to him that the whole world of palaces, fountains, sculptures, pictures and machinery was collapsing about him, an incident occurred to remind him he was not an illusion, but a real man, sick of a cancer in his soul. He was once in the Théâtre de Varietés, in the rue Montmartre, a few hundred yards from his hotel. Three farces were to be performed, with an operetta as entr'acte. He went there to stun himself with buffoonery, but almost as soon as the curtain rose, he heard a phrase from the stage, uttered in a tearful voice: 'A lover can forgive his mistress anything, except another lover . . .'

'Sometimes a man has to forgive three or four!' cried a Frenchman sitting next to him, laughing.

Wokulski felt stifled; the earth seemed to be giving way, the ceiling coming down upon him. He could not stay in the theatre. He rose from his seat which, unfortunately, was in the centre of a row, and drenched in a cold sweat, treading on his neighbours' toes, he fled from the performance.

He hastened in the direction of the hotel, then went into the first pavement café. He did not recall what he was asked, nor what he replied. All he knew was that he was served with coffee and a carafe of brandy marked with little lines which indicated the contents of a glass. Wokulski drank and thought: 'Starski is the second lover, Ochocki the third . . . And Rossi? Rossi, for whom I arranged the claque, and to whom I took that present at the theatre. What was he? You fool – she's Messalina, if not physically, then morally . . . And I? I am supposed to be insane about her . . . I!'

He felt his own rage steadying him: when it was time for the bill, he realised the carafe was empty. 'All the same, brandy helps . . .' he thought. From then on, whenever he was reminded of Warsaw or met a woman with something special in her gestures, dress or looks, he would go into a café and drink a carafe of brandy. Only then did he venture to recall Izabela, and would feel surprised that a man like him should love a woman like that. 'Yet surely I deserve to be the first and the last,' he thought. The brandy carafe emptied, he leaned his head in his hand and dozed, to the great amusement of the waiters and customers.

Then he would again visit the Exhibition, the museums, the artesian wells, schools and theatres, for days at a time, not to learn anything, but to deaden his memories.

Slowly, against the background of dull and ill-defined sufferings, a question began to take hold of him: was there some kind of order in the construction of Paris? Was there one object with which it could be compared, a system according to which it could be regulated?

Seen from the Panthéon and from the Trocadéro, Paris appeared the same: a sea of houses, criss-crossed by a thousand streets, the irregular roofs looked like waves, the chimneys like spray, and the towers and columns like larger waves.

'Chaos!' said Wokulski. 'But how could it be otherwise in a place where a million endeavours converge. A great city is a cloud of dust; it has contingent contours, but can have no logic. If it did, the fact would have been discovered long ago by the authors of guides; for is that not their role? . . .'

And he examined a plan of the city, mocking his own efforts. 'Only one man, and a genius at that, can create a style, a plan,' he thought. 'But that a million people, working across several centuries and ignorant of each other, should create some kind of a logical whole, it is simply impossible.'

Slowly, however, to his great surprise, he perceived that this Paris, built over several centuries, by a million people, ignorant of each other and with no plan in mind, did, nevertheless, have a plan, it constituted a whole, even a very logical one.

He was first struck by the fact that Paris was like a great bowl, nine kilometres wide from north to south and eleven kilometres long from east to west. To the south, this bowl was cracked and divided by the Seine, which cut it in a bow running from the north-east corner through the centre of the city and turning to the south-west corner. An eight-year-old child could have outlined such a plan.

'All right,' thought Wokulski, 'but where is the order in the positioning of individual buildings . . . Notre-Dame in one direction, the Trocadéro in another, and the Louvre, the Exchange, the Sorbonne! . . . Nothing but chaos . . .'

But when he began to examine the plan of Paris more closely, he noticed something that not only native Parisians had failed to perceive (which was less strange), but even K. Baedeker, who claimed the right to know his way about the whole of Europe.

Despite an apparent chaos, Paris did have a plan, a logic, even though it had been built over several centuries by millions of people ignorant of each other and giving no thought at all to logic or style.

Paris possessed what could be called a backbone, the city's crystal axis.

The Vincennes forest lay in the south-east, and the edge of the Bois de Boulogne on the north-west side of Paris. So – this crystal axis of the city was like a great caterpillar (almost six kilometres in length) which, bored with the Bois de Vincennes, had gone for a walk to the Bois de Boulogne.

Its tail leaned against the Place de la Bastille, its head on the Etoile, its body cleaved almost to the Seine. The Champs-Elysées were the neck, the Tuileries and Louvre its corset, and its tail was the Hôtel de Ville, Notre-Dame and, finally, the July Column on the Place de la Bastille.

This caterpillar possessed many long and short legs. From the head, the first pair leaned to the left: the Champ de Mars, the Trocadéro Palace and Exhibition; to the right they reached as far as the Montmartre cemetery. The second pair (of shorter legs) reached the Military School on the left, the Hotel des Invalides, and the Chamber of Deputies; to the right the Madeleine church and the Opéra. Then (ever on towards the tail), to the left the School of Fine Arts, to the right the Palais Royal, the bank and Stock Exchange; to the left the Institut de France and mint, to the right Les Halles; to the left the Palais du Luxembourg, the Cluny museum and Medical School, to the right the Place de la République, with the Prince Eugène barracks.

Aside from the crystal axis and the regularities in the general contours of the city, Wokulski also became convinced (something the guides pointed out anyway) that in Paris there existed whole divisions of human labour and some order in their arrangement. Between the Place de la Bastille and the Place de la République were grouped mainly trade and craftsmen; opposite them, on the other bank of the Seine, was the 'Latin Quarter', a nest of students and scholars. Between the Opéra, the Place de la République and the Seine was export trade and finance; between Notre-Dame, the Institut de France and the Montparnasse cemetery clustered the remains of the country's aristocracy. From the Opéra to the Etoile stretched the neighbourhood of the wealthy parvenus, and opposite them, on the left bank of the Seine, opposite the Hotel des Invalides and the Military School, was the seat of military affairs and World Exhibitions.

These observations woke new currents in Wokulski's soul, of which he had not thought before, or only imprecisely. And so the great city, like a plant or beast, had its own anatomy and physiology. And so the work of millions of people who proclaimed their free will so loudly produced the same results as bees building regular honeycombs, ants raising rounded mounds, or chemical compounds forming regular crystals.

Thus there was nothing accidental in society, but an inflexible law which, as if in irony at human pride, manifested itself so clearly in the life of the most capricious of nations, the French! It had been ruled by Merovingians and Carolingians, Bourbons and Bonapartes; there had been three republics and a couple of anarchies, the Inquisition and atheism; rulers and ministers followed one upon the other like the cut of gowns or the clouds in the sky . . . But despite so many apparently fundamental changes, Paris took on ever more precisely the form of a dish torn by the Seine; the crystal axis was delineated ever more clearly running from the Place de la Bastille to the Etoile; ever more clearly did the districts define themselves: the learned and the industrial, the ancestral and the industrial, the military and the parvenu.

Wokulski perceived this same fatalism in the history of a dozen of the more prominent Parisian families. The grandfather, as a humble craftsman, worked at the rue du Temple, sixteen hours a day; his son, plunging into the Latin quarter, set up a larger workshop in the rue St-Antoine. His grandson, even more submerged in the scholarly district, moved as a great tradesman to the Boulevard Poissonnier, and his grandson, as a millionaire, set up house in the neighbourhood of the Champs-Elysées so that . . . his daughters could suffer from nervous dispositions at the Boulevard St-Germain. Thus a race exhausted with work and enriched near the Bastille, worn out alongside the Tuileries, expired in the vicinity of Notre-Dame. The city's topography reflected this history of its inhabitants.

Pondering this strange regularity of facts, recognised as irregular, Wokulski sensed that if anything was to cure his apathy, it would be analysis of this kind.

'I am a strange man,' he said to himself, 'and so have gone mad, but civilisation will rescue me.'

Every day in Paris brought him new ideas or clarified the secrets of his own soul. Once, drinking iced coffee in a café, a street singer drew near the verandah and, to the accompaniment of a harp, sang:

> Au printemps, la feuille repousse,
> Et la fleur embellit les prés,
> Mignonette, en foulant la mousse,
> Suivons les papillons diapres.
> Vois les se poser sur les roses;
> Comme eux aussi, je veux poser,
> Ma lèvre sur tes lèvres closes,
> Et te ravir un doux baiser!

And at once several customers echoed the last passage: 'Fools!' Wokulski thought, 'they've nothing better to do than repeat such rubbish.' He rose, scowling, and with a pain in his heart, walked through a crowd of people as lively, noisy, chattering and singing as children let out of school: 'Fools! Fools!' he repeated.

But suddenly he wondered whether it was not he, rather, who was the fool? 'If all these people were like me,' he told himself, 'Paris would be a hospital for the melancholy mad. Everyone would be haunted by memories, the streets would turn into puddles, the houses into ruins. Yet they take life as it is, they pursue practical aims, are happy and create masterpieces. And what am I pursuing? First it was perpetual motion and guided balloons, then a position to which my own allies refused to admit me, then a woman I'm hardly allowed to approach. But I have always either sacrificed myself or submitted to ideas created by those classes which want to make me their servant, their slave . . .'

And he imagined how it would have been if he'd been born in Paris instead of Warsaw. In the first place, he would have been enabled to learn more as a child because of the many schools and colleges. Then, even if he had gone into trade, he would have experienced less unpleasantness and more help in his studies. Further, he wouldn't have worked on a perpetual motion machine, for he'd have known that many similar machines which never worked were to be found in the museums here. Had he tried to construct guided balloons, he would have found models, a whole crowd of dreamers like himself, and even help if his ideas were practical.

And, had he finally made a fortune for himself and fallen in love with an aristocratic young lady, he would not have encountered so many obstacles in approaching her. He might have made her acquaintance and either recovered or won her hand. Under no circumstances would he have been treated like a Negro in America. Besides, was it possible in Paris to fall in love as he had done – to the point of insanity? Here lovers did not despair, but danced, sang and lived a gay life. If they could not have an official marriage, they created a free union: if they could not keep their children, they put them out to nurse. Here love would surely never lead a sensible man into madness.

'The last two years of my existence,' thought Wokulski, 'have been passed in the pursuit of a woman I might even have rejected if I'd known her better. All my energies, studies, talents and huge fortune are absorbed into a single emotion because I am in trade and she an aristocrat. Perhaps society, by harming me harms itself?'

Here Wokulski reached the apex of his self-criticism: he saw how preposterous his situation was, and resolved to extricate himself: 'What am I to do, though? What am I to do?' he thought. 'Why, the same as everyone else, to be sure!' And what did they do? . . . Above all they worked extraordinarily hard, up to sixteen hours a day, regardless of Sundays and holidays, thanks to a selection process here in which only the strongest had the right to survive. A sickly man would perish before the year was out, an incompetent one within a matter of years, and only the strongest and cleverest were left.

These, thanks to the work of whole generations of strivers like themselves, found here the satisfaction of all their needs. Huge sewers protected them from disease, wide streets facilitated the flow of air; the Halles Centrales provided food, a thousand factories – clothing and furniture. When a Parisian wanted to see nature, he travelled beyond the city or to the Bois; if he wanted art to gladden his eyes, he went to the Louvre; and when he desired knowledge, he had museums and scientific collections.

To strive for happiness in all domains – this was the substance of Parisian life. Here, a thousand carriages were introduced to counter tiredness; to counter boredom, hundreds of theatres and shows; to counter ignorance, hundreds of museums, libraries, and lectures. Here, not only man met with concern, but even the horse, for whom a smooth road was provided. Here, care was lavished even on the trees, which were transported in special carts to their new places of abode, protected with iron baskets from all who might harm them, ensured moist conditions, nurtured in the event of disease.

Thanks to a solicitude towards all things, objects finding themselves in Paris possessed a variety of advantages. Houses, furniture and utensils were not only useful, but beautiful; they pleased not only the sinews, but also the mind. And vice versa – works of art were not only beautiful, but useful. At the side of triumphant arches and church steeples were steps, facilitating one's ascent to look at the town from a height. Statues and paintings were accessible not only to their devotees, but to artists and sculptors who were permitted to make copies in the galleries.

A Frenchman, when he created something, first took care that the work should meet its aim, and only then that it should be beautiful. And, not content with that, he strove also for permanence and purity. Wokulski ascertained this truth at every step and with every object, beginning with the carts carrying away rubbish, to the Venus de Milo surrounded by a barrier. He guessed also the consequences of such economy, that work was not wasted here: each generation gave its successors the finest works of its forefathers, supplementing them with its own output.

In this way, Paris was an ark in which were housed the trophies of a dozen centuries, if not whole millenniums, of civilisation. There was everything here, from monstrous Assyrian statues and Egyptian mummies, to the latest discoveries of mechanics and electrotechnology, from jars in which Egyptian women had carried their water 4000 years ago, to the great hydraulic wheels of St-Maur.

'The men who created these marvels,' thought Wokulski, 'or who collected them together in one place, they were not crazed idlers like myself . . .'

And thus saying to himself, he felt overcome by shame.

And, after dealing with Suzin's business for a few hours, he would wander around Paris. He strolled down unknown streets, immersed himself in a crowd of thousands, plunged into the apparent chaos of things and events, and at the bottom of it all he found order and law. Then again he would drink brandy for a change, play cards or roulette, or give way to dissipation. It seemed to him that he was going to encounter something extraordinary in this volcanic centre of civilisation, and that a new epoch in his life would start here. At the same time he felt that his hitherto scattered fragments of knowledge and his opinions would merge into a sort of unity or philosophical system, which might explain to him many of the world's mysteries and the meaning of his own existence.

'What am I?' he asked himself sometimes, and gradually he formulated his own reply: 'I am a man who has gone to waste. I had great talents and energy, but have done nothing for civilisation. The eminent people I meet here don't have even half my powers, yet they leave behind them machines, buildings, works of art, new ideas. But what shall I leave behind? My store, perhaps – but that would have gone to wrack and ruin if Rzecki were not looking after it . . . Yet I haven't been idle: I struggled for three men, and had I not been helped by chance I wouldn't even have the fortune I now possess.'

Then it occurred to him to ask what he had squandered his powers and his life on? 'On struggling with an environment into which I didn't fit. When I wanted to study, I could not, because in my country scholars aren't needed – only peasants and store clerks. When I wanted to serve society by sacrificing my own life if need be, fantastic dreams were put forward instead of a practical programme and then – were forgotten. When I sought work, I was not given any, but shown an easy way to marry an old woman for her money. When I finally fell in love, and wanted to become the legal father of a family, the pastor of a domestic circle, the holiness of which everyone acclaimed, then I was placed in a situation from which there was no way out. So much so, that I don't know whether the woman I was crazy about was an ordinary flirt whose head had been turned, or perhaps a lost soul like myself, who had not found her proper way. Judging by her behaviour, she is an eligible young lady looking for the best possible husband: when one looks into her eyes, she is an angelic spirit, whose wings have been clipped by human conventions. If I'd had some tens of thousands of roubles a year, and a passion for whist, I'd have been the happiest man in Warsaw,' he said to himself, 'but because in addition to a stomach I have a soul which is greedy for knowledge and love, I would have had to perish there. That is a region where certain kinds of plants cannot grow, nor certain kinds of people either . . .'

And at this moment, for the first time, the idea of not returning to Poland appeared clearly to him: 'I'll sell the shop,' he thought, 'withdraw my capital and settle in Paris. I won't get in the way of people who don't want me . . . I'll visit the museums, perhaps take to some special studies, and life will pass, if not happily, then at least painlessly.'

Only one incident, one person could bring him back to Poland and keep him there . . . But this incident hadn't happened, and indeed, others had occurred to detach him more and more from Warsaw and attach him increasingly to Paris.

XXIII

An Apparition

ONE DAY he was conducting business as usual with clients in the reception room. He had just dismissed an individual who offered to fight duels on his behalf, another who was a ventriloquist and wanted to take part in diplomacy, and a third, who promised to reveal to him the treasures buried by Napoleon's general staff at Berezina, when a footman in a blue frock-coat announced: 'Professor Geist!'

'Geist?' Wokulski repeated, and he experienced a peculiar sensation. It occurred to him that iron, in the vicinity of a magnet, must feel such sensations: 'Ask him in.'

A moment later in came a very small and skinny man, with a face as yellow as wax. He had not a single grey hair on his head.

'How old might he be?' thought Wokulski. Meanwhile, the visitor was eyeing him sharply, and they sat thus for a minute or perhaps two, appraising one another. Wokulski was seeking to estimate the age of the newcomer. Geist appeared to be examining him.

'Your orders, sir?' Wokulski finally exclaimed.

Geist shifted in his seat: 'What can I order?' he replied with a shrug, 'I have come here to beg, not to give orders.'

'What can I do for you?' inquired Wokulski, for his visitor's face seemed strangely likeable to him.

His guest rubbed his head: 'I came here with one thing,' he said, but I'm going to talk of something else. I wanted to sell you a new explosive . . .'

'I won't buy it,' Wokulski interrupted.

'Won't you?' asked Geist, 'and yet I was told you gentlemen are seeking something of the sort for the navy. But never mind . . . I have something else for you . . .'

'For me?' asked Wokulski, surprised not so much by Geist's words as by his looks.

'Did you not at one time fly a captive balloon?' said his guest.

'Yes, I did.'

'You are wealthy and an expert in natural sciences.'

'Yes,' Wokulski replied.

'And there was a time when you meant to jump off a bridge?' asked Geist. Wokulski pushed his chair back.

'Do not be surprised,' said his visitor. 'In my life I have seen some thousand natural scientists, while I have had four suicides in my laboratory, so I am an expert in this type of person. You have glanced at the barometer too often for me not to have recognised a natural scientist, while even schoolgirls recognise a man thinking of suicide.'

'What can I do for you?' Wokulski asked again, wiping the sweat from his face.

'I won't say much,' Geist declared. 'Do you know what organic chemistry is?'

'It's the chemistry of carbon compounds . . .'

'And what do you think of the chemistry of hydrogen compounds?'

'There is no such thing.'

'There is,' Geist replied, 'but instead of volatiles, fats, aromatic bodies, it gives new products . . . New products, Monsieur Suzin, with very interesting properties. . . .'

'What does that have to do with me,' said Wokulski dully, 'I'm a tradesman.'

'You are not a tradesman, sir, but a desperado,' Geist replied. 'Tradesmen don't think of jumping out of a balloon . . . As soon as I saw you, I thought, "This is the man for me." But you vanished from my sight as soon as you left the porch . . . Today chance has brought us together again . . . Mr Suzin, we must discuss the hydrogen compounds, and if you are wealthy . . .'

'In the first place, I am not Suzin.'

'No matter, since all I need is a wealthy desperado,' said Geist.

Wokulski gazed at Geist almost fearfully. Questions flashed through his mind: is he a conjuror or secret agent, a madman or perhaps he's really a spirit? Who knows that Satan is only a myth and doesn't appear to people at certain times? The fact is, however, that this old man of indeterminate age had tracked down the most secret thought of Wokulski who had recently been dreaming about suicide, but so timidly that he had lacked the courage even to formulate the plan to himself.

His visitor continued gazing at him and smiled with tranquil irony: but when Wokulski opened his mouth to ask him something, he interrupted: 'Don't trouble yourself, sir. I have already spoken with so many people regarding their own characters and my inventions that I can tell in advance what you wish to know. I'm Professor Geist, an old madman, as they say in all the cafés around the university and polytechnic. Once I was called a great chemist, until . . . until I went beyond the boundary of scientific knowledge in force, today. I reported articles, I produced inventions in my own name or in the names of my collaborators, who even shared the profits with me conscientiously. But since the time when I discovered phenomena not to be found in the annals of the Academy, I have been denounced not only as a madman but as a heretic and traitor . . .'

'Here, in Paris?' Wokulski whispered.

'Aha!' Geist laughed, 'here, in Paris. In Altdorf or Neustadt, a heretic and traitor is the man who doesn't believe in the clergy, Bismarck, the ten commandments and the Prussian constitution. Here one may mock Bismarck and the constitution, but you run the risk of apostasy if you don't believe in the multiplication table, the theory of wave movement, the consistency of specific gravities and so forth. Show me, sir, one city in which men's brains are not cramped by some dogma or other, and I'll make it the capital of the world and the cradle of a new race of men . . .'

Wokulski cooled down: he was certain he was dealing with a maniac. Geist gazed at him and went on smiling: 'I'm ending, Mr Suzin,' he said. 'I've made great discoveries in chemistry, I have created a new science, I have found new industrial products which people scarcely dared even to dream of before. But . . . I still need a few extremely important facts, and I have no more money. I've sunk four fortunes in my research, and used up a dozen or more men: so now I need another fortune and new men . . .'

'Why this confidence in me?' asked Wokulski, calm now.

'That's simple,' replied Geist. 'Thoughts of suicide come to a madman, a scoundrel or to a man of high worth, for whom the world is too small.'

'But how do you know I am not a scoundrel?'

'And how do you know that a horse isn't a cow?' Geist replied. 'During my enforced vacations, which have lasted for several years, alas, I have been occupying myself with zoology and making a special study of the species, Man. In this single species, with its two hands, I discovered dozens of animal types ranging from oysters and earthworms to owls and tigers. What is more, I have discovered blends of these types: tigers with wings, serpents with the heads of dogs, falcons with the shells of tortoises, which of course the imagination of poetic geniuses had already divined. And amidst all this menagerie of beasts and monsters, here and there I have found a real man, a being with sense, heart and energy. You, Mr Suzin, have the unmistakable traits of a man and that is why I have spoken so frankly to you: you are one in ten, perhaps in a hundred thousand.'

Wokulski frowned. Geist burst out: 'What? Perhaps you think I am flattering you to gain a few francs? I'll call on you again tomorrow and you'll see how unfair you are just now, and stupid.'

He jumped up, but Wokulski stopped him: 'Don't be angry, professor,' he said, 'I didn't want to offend you. But here I am visited almost every day by various kinds of tricksters.'

'Tomorrow I'll convince you I am neither a trickster nor a madman,' Geist replied. 'I'll show you something seen by only six or seven men who . . . are dead now. Ah, if only they were still alive!' he sighed.

'Why not until tomorrow?'

'Because I live some distance away, and have no money for a horse-drawn cab.'

Wokulski pressed his hand: 'You won't be offended, professor?' he asked, 'if . . .'

'If you give me the fare? No. After all, I told you to start with that I'm here to beg and am perhaps the most wretched beggar in Paris.'

Wokulski gave him a hundred francs. 'For goodness sake,' Geist smiled, 'ten would do. Who knows but what you won't be giving me a hundred thousand tomorrow . . . Do you have a large fortune?'

'Around one million francs.'

'A million!' Geist repeated, clutching his head. 'I'll be back in two hours. God grant that I become as necessary to you, as you are to me.'

'In that case, be so kind, professor, as to come to my room on the third floor. This is a public room.'

'I prefer the third floor . . . I'll be back in two hours,' replied Geist, and he quickly hurried out of the room. A moment later Jumart appeared: 'The old fellow bored you,' he said to Wokulski, 'eh?'

'What sort of man is he?' Wokulski asked casually.

Jumart stuck out his lower lip. 'He's a madman,' he replied, 'but when I was still a student, he was a great chemist. Well, then he produced some invention or other, he's said to have some strange objects to display, but . . .' He tapped his forehead with one finger.

'Why do you call him a madman?'

'What other epithet can you give to a man', replied Jumart, 'who believes he has succeeded in decreasing the specific gravity of bodies, or is it of metals – I don't recall?'

Wokulski bade him good-bye and went to his room: 'What a strange city,' he thought, 'where there are to be found treasure-seekers, hired defenders of a man's honour, distinguished ladies who trade in secrets, waiters who discuss chemistry and chemists who want to decrease the specific gravity of bodies . . .'

Towards five, Geist appeared in his room: he was somehow

agitated and locked the door behind him. 'Mr Suzin,' he said, 'it is
very important to me that we should understand one another. Tell
me – do you have obligations: a wife, children? Although it doesn't
seem to me . . .'

'I have no one.'

'But you have a fortune? A million . . .'

'Very nearly.'

'And tell me,' said Geist, 'why you are thinking of killing
yourself?'

Wokulski shuddered. 'That was temporary,' he said, 'I felt giddy
in the balloon.'

Geist shook his head. 'You have a fortune,' he muttered, 'you
are not striving for fame, or at least not yet . . . There must be a
woman in it,' he cried.

'Possibly,' replied Wokulski, highly embarrassed.

'It's a woman!' said Geist. 'That's bad. One can never know
what she will do and what she will lead to. In any case, listen,' he
added, looking into his eyes, 'if you ever again feel the need to try
. . . Do you understand? Don't kill yourself, but come to me.'

'Perhaps I'll come right away,' said Wokulski, looking down.

'Not right away!' Geist replied vivaciously. 'Women never
destroy men right away. Have you already settled your accounts
with that individual?'

'It seems to me . . .'

'Aha, it only seems so. That's bad. In any case, bear my advice in
mind. It is very easy to destroy yourself in my laboratory, I assure
you!'

'What have you brought, professor?' Wokulski asked him.

'That's bad, that's bad!' Geist muttered. 'I have to find a buyer
for my explosive material. But I thought we would combine . . .'

'First, sir, show me what you've brought,' Wokulski interrupted.

'You are right,' replied Geist, and he brought a medium-sized
box out of his pocket. 'Look,' he said, 'this is why people call me
mad!'

The box was of metal, shut in a singular manner. Geist in turn
touched pins fixed in various places, casting feverish and suspicious
glances at Wokulski from time to time. Once he even hesitated and
made a gesture as if to put the box away: but he collected himself,
touched a few pins and the lid shot up.

At this moment he was seized by another attack of suspicion.
The old man sank to the couch, hid the box behind his back and
fearfully gazed around the room, then at Wokulski. 'I'm committing a folly!' he muttered. 'What madness to risk everything for the
first person I happen upon.'

'Don't you trust me, sir?' asked Wokulski, no less moved.

'I trust no one,' said the old man viciously, 'for what assurance can anyone give me? A promise or his word of honour? I'm too old to believe in promises. Only mutual profit can insure against the vilest treachery, and even that not always . . .'

Wokulski shrugged and sat down. 'I'm not forcing you, sir,' he said, 'to share your troubles with me. I have enough of my own.'

Geist did not remove his gaze from him, but he gradually calmed down. Finally he exclaimed: 'Come over here, to the table. Look, what is this?'

He showed him a metal ball of dark colour.

'It looks to me like printer's metal.'

'Pick it up.'

Wokulski took the ball and was amazed to find it so heavy.

'This is platinum,' he said.

'Platinum?' Geist echoed with a mocking smile. 'Here's platinum for you.'

And he handed him a platinum ball of the same size. Wokulski weighed both in his hands: his amazement grew.

'Surely this is almost twice the weight of platinum?' he whispered.

'Yes . . . yes,' Geist laughed. 'One of my academic friends even called it "compromised platinum". A neat phrase, isn't it? To indicate a metal whose specific gravity is 30.7. They always do that. Whenever they succeed in finding a name for a new thing, they at once say they have explained it on the basis of established laws of nature. Conceited asses – the wisest of all, such as so-called humanity abounds with. Do you recognise this?' he added.

'Well, it is a glass bar,' replied Wokulski.

'Ha ha!' Geist laughed. 'Pick it up, examine it. Curious glass, is it not? Heavier than iron, with a granulated cross-section, an excellent conductor of heat and electricity, which can be cut. Do you see how well this glass passes for metal? Perhaps you would like to heat it, or try it with a hammer?'

Wokulski rubbed his eyes. There was no doubt in his mind that such glass had never yet been seen in this world.

'And this?' asked Geist, showing him another bar of metal.

'That must be steel.'

'Not sodium or potassium?' asked Geist.

'No.'

'Pick up this steel.'

Now Wokulski's amazement became something like alarm: the supposed steel was as light as a scrap of paper.

'Surely it is hollow?'

'Cut it through, or if you haven't anything to do so with, then come to my place. You will see there far more similar curiosities and will be able to submit them to any tests you choose.'

Wokulski gazed in turn at the metal heavier than platinum, at the transparent metal, at the metal lighter than fluff. As long as he was holding them, they seemed to him the most natural things under the sun: for what is more natural than an object which acts upon the mind? But when he gave the samples back to Geist, amazement overcame him as well as incredulity, wonder and alarm. So he inspected them again, shook his head, believed and doubted by turns.

'Well, then?' asked Geist.

'Have you shown these to chemists?'

'I have . . .'

'And what have they to say?'

'They inspected them, shook their heads and declared it's all tricks and deceit, with which serious science cannot be concerned.'

'How so! Didn't they even make tests?' asked Wokulski.

'No. Some of them even said outright that if they had to choose between violating the laws of nature and delusions of their own minds, they prefer not to believe their own minds. And they added that to make serious experiments on such tricks might overturn a man's common sense, and they finally declined.'

'Are you not announcing the discoveries?'

'Not for a moment. Indeed, their intellectual impotence gives me the best guarantee of preserving the secrets of my inventions. Were it otherwise, they'd have been seized upon, sooner or later the processes would have been discovered and they'd have found that which I do not want to give them.'

'In other words?' Wokulski interposed.

'They'd have discovered a metal lighter than air,' replied Geist calmly.

Wokulski threw himself into a chair. For a moment both were silent: 'Why are you keeping this transcendental metal secret from mankind?' Wokulski finally asked.

'For many reasons,' replied Geist. 'In what is called mankind, barely one genuine man is to be found in ten thousand bulls, sheep, tigers and serpents. This has always been so, even in the Stone Age. Various inventions have been bestowed on this humanity in the course of centuries. Bronze, iron, gun-powder, the magnetic needle, printing, steam-engines and electric telegraphs came willy-nilly into the hands of geniuses and idiots, noble people and criminals. And the result? By acquiring increasingly powerful weapons, stupidity and depravity have increased and multiplied instead of gradually dying out. I,' Geist continued, 'don't intend to repeat that error, and if I finally discover a metal lighter than air I will pass it on only to genuine men. Let them once and for all equip themselves with a weapon for their exclusive use: let their race multiply and gain power, while the animals and monsters in human form gradually die out.'

'He is very eccentric, to be sure,' thought Wokulski. Then he added aloud: 'What prevents you from carrying out these plans?'

'The lack of money and assistants. For the final discovery eight thousand tests or so must be made, which – roughly speaking – would take one man twenty years. But four men would do them in five or six years.'

Wokulski rose from his chair and began walking about the room, pondering. Geist continued to watch him. 'Let us suppose,' Wokulski exclaimed, 'that I could provide you with the money and even one or two assistants. But where is the proof that your metals aren't some weird trick, and your hopes illusions?'

'Come to my place, you'll see, you can carry out some experiments of your own, and you'll be convinced, I see no other way,' Geist replied.

'When could I come?'

'When you choose. Give me ten francs or so to buy the necessary chemicals. And here's my address,' Geist concluded, giving him a grubby note.

Wokulski handed him three hundred francs. The old man packed his samples, closed the box and, as he left, said: 'Write to me the day before you come. I am at home nearly all the time, dusting my retorts.'

When Geist had gone, Wokulski felt bemused. He looked at the door through which the chemist had disappeared, then at the table where he had just been shown natural objects, then again he touched his own hands or head, and walked about stamping his feet to convince himself he was not dreaming. 'Yet it's a fact,' he thought, 'that this man showed me two elements of some kind: one heavier than platinum, the other lighter than sodium. He even told me he's looking for a metal lighter than air.'

'Providing there is no incomprehensible fraud behind all this,' he said aloud, 'I'd have an idea it would be worthwhile sentencing myself to years of imprisonment for. Not only would I find absorbing work and the fulfilment of the wildest dreams of my youth, but I'd also see an aim before me, higher than any other to which the human soul has ever aspired. The question of flying ships would be solved, man would acquire wings.'

Then he again shrugged, folded his arms and muttered: 'No, it's impossible.'

The burden of these new natural laws or new illusions oppressed him so much that he felt the need of sharing it with someone, if only partially. So he hurried down to the elaborate reception room on the first floor and summoned Jumart. As he was wondering how to initiate this strange conversation, Jumart himself facilitated it. No sooner did he appear in the room, than he said with a tactful smile: 'Old Geist went away very excitedly.

Did he convince you, or was he defeated?'

'Well, talk never convinces anyone, only facts,' replied Wokulski.

'So there were facts too?'

'Only the promise of them, as yet. But, tell me, sir,' Wokulski went on, 'what would you think if Geist showed you a metal similar in every respect to steel, but two or three times lighter than water? Supposing you saw such material with your own eyes, and touched it with your own hands?'

Jumart's smile became an ironic grimace: 'What could I say, my God, except that Professor Palmieri exhibits still greater curiosities for five francs a person.'

'Who is Palmieri?' Wokulski asked in surprise.

'A professor of hypnotism,' Jumart replied, 'a celebrated individual. He is living in the hotel, and three times a day he exhibits his hypnotic arts in a hall which, unfortunately, only holds sixty people. It is eight o'clock now, so the evening performance is just beginning . . . If you wish, we might go there, sir – I am admitted free.'

Such a powerful flush mounted into Wokulski's face that it covered his forehead and even neck. 'Let us go,' he said, 'to this Professor Palmieri.' Privately he added: 'So this great thinker Geist is a charlatan, and I a fool, who paid three hundred francs for a display worth five . . . How he caught me!'

They went up to the second floor and into a drawing-room furnished as richly as the others in this hotel. A greater part was already filled with old and young spectators, men and women elegantly dressed and all very intent upon Professor Palmieri, who had just concluded a short speech on hypnotism. He was a man of middle age. A faded and dark man with an unkempt beard and expressive eyes. He was surrounded by a few pretty women and some young men with thin and apathetic faces.

'Those are the mediums,' Jumart whispered, 'Palmieri exercises his art on them.'

The spectacle, of about two hours' duration, showed Palmieri sending his mediums to sleep by the use of his gaze, but in such a manner that they were still able to walk, answer questions and perform various acts. The persons sent to sleep by the hypnotist also displayed unusual muscular strength in obeying his commands, and even more unusual lack of sensitivity, or hyper-sensitivity of the senses.

As Wokulski was seeing these phenomena for the first time in his life, and did not conceal his incredulity in the least, Palmieri invited him into the front row. Here, after some experiments, Wokulski realised that the phenomena he was witnessing were not conjuring tricks, but derived from some unknown properties of the nervous system. But he was most interested and even alarmed by two demonstrations which had a certain relevance to his own life. In them, the medium was persuaded of non-existent things. Palmieri gave one of the sleepers the stopper of a carafe, declaring it to be a rose. At once the medium began sniffing the stopper, displaying great enjoyment as he did so.

'What are you at, sir?' Palmieri cried to the medium, 'that is asaphoetida.'

And the medium instantly threw the stopper away in disgust, rubbed his hands and complained that they stank.

To another, he gave a handkerchief and, when he told him the handkerchief weighed a hundred pounds, the medium began slumping, trembling and sweating under its weight. On seeing this, Wokulski sweated too: 'I understand Geist's secret now,' he thought, 'he hypnotised me.'

But he experienced the most painful feeling of all when Palmieri put to sleep a frail young man, then wrapped a coal shovel in a towel and persuaded his medium it was a young and beautiful woman he must love. The medium embraced and kissed the shovel, kneeled before it and uttered the most affectionate expressions. When it was put underneath a sofa, he crawled in after it on all fours, like a dog, and drove away by force four men who tried to hold him back. When Palmieri hid it and announced she had died, the young man lapsed into such despair that he writhed on the floor and beat his head against the wall. At that moment Palmieri puffed into his eyes and the young man woke up with tears streaming down his cheeks, much to the applause and laughter of the audience.

Terribly agitated, Wokulski quit the hall: 'So it is all a lie! The alleged inventions of Geist and his intellect, my insane love and even *she* . . . She herself is nothing but an illusion of my bewitched thoughts. . . . The only reality which never deceives and which does not lie is surely – death.'

He hastened into the street, rushed into a café and ordered cognac. This time he drank a carafe and a half, and as he drank he thought that this Paris, in which he had found the apex of intellect, the greatest illusions and total disillusion, would surely be his tomb: 'What am I waiting for? What have I to find out? If Geist is a common trickster, and if a man can fall in love with a coal shovel, what is left to me?'

Dazed with the cognac, he went back to his hotel and fell asleep with his clothes on. And when he awoke at eight next morning, his first thought was: 'There is no doubt that Geist, by hypnotism, cheated me over his metals. But – who hypnotised me when I was insane about that woman?'

Suddenly he resolved to obtain information from Palmieri. So he dressed hastily and went down to the second floor. The master of the mysterious art was awaiting clients: but as there were none yet, he received Wokulski at once, taking twenty francs in advance for his fee.

'Can you', Wokulski asked, 'persuade anyone that a coal shovel is a woman, and that a handkerchief weighs a hundred pounds?'

'Anyone who lets himself be put to sleep.'

'Then kindly put me to sleep and repeat the trick with the handkerchief on me.'

Palmieri began his rites: he stared into Wokulski's eyes, touched his brow, rubbed his hands from wrists to palm . . . Finally he drew back, reluctant: 'You, sir, are not a medium,' he declared.

'But supposing I had an incident in my life like that person with the handkerchief?' Wokulski asked.

'That's impossible; you can't be put to sleep. Even if you were, and underwent the illusion that the handkerchief weighed a hundred pounds, you still wouldn't remember it on waking up.'

'Don't you think, sir, that someone might hypnotise me more skilfully?'

Palmieri took offence at this: 'There is no more skilled hypnotist than I,' he exclaimed. 'I, too, could put you to sleep, but it would require several months' work . . . It would cost two thousand francs. . . . I have no intention of wasting my fluid for nothing . . .'

Wokulski, not at all displeased, left the hypnotist. He still did not doubt that Miss Izabela could have bewitched him: she had had plenty of time, after all. But then Geist could not have put him to sleep in the course of a few minutes. Besides, Palmieri had declared that those put to sleep did not remember their visions: whereas he recalled every detail of the old chemist's visit.

So if Geist had not put him to sleep, he was not a trickster. Therefore his metals existed . . . and the discovery of a metal lighter than air was possible! 'This is a city', he thought, 'in which I've experienced more during one hour than in my whole life in Warsaw. What a city!'

For several days Wokulski was very busy. In the first place, Suzin left after purchasing a dozen or so ships. The completely legal profit from this transaction was huge – so huge that the share due to Wokulski covered all the expenses he had incurred during his recent months in Warsaw. A few hours before bidding farewell to Suzin, Wokulski lunched with him in his lavish hotel room, and they of course discussed their profits. 'You have miraculous good luck,' Wokulski exclaimed.

Suzin took a mouthful of champagne and, laying his hands, adorned with rings, on his belly, said: 'It is not good luck, Stanisław Piotrowicz, but millions. You can cut down an osier with a knife, but an oak needs an axe. A man who has kopeks does business in kopeks, and profits in kopeks: but a man who has millions can't help making profits in millions. A rouble, Stanisław Piotrovich, is an overworked nag – you have to wait several years for it to give birth to another rouble: but a million is as fertile as a rabbit: it produces several litters every year. In two or three years, Stanisław Piotrowicz, you, too, will have a tidy little million or so, and then you'll see how other money runs after it. Though in your case . . .'

Suzin sighed, frowned and drank more champagne.

'What about me?' asked Wokulski.

'Well . . .' Suzin replied, 'you, instead of doing business for yourself, in your own trade in this city, you do nothing. You wander around with your head up or down, not looking at anything, or even (as a Christian I'm ashamed to say it!) flying in the air in a balloon. Are you thinking of becoming a fairground jumper, then? And let me tell you, Stanisław Piotrowicz, you have offended a very distinguished lady, that Baroness. Yet you might have visited her, played cards, met charming women and found out about all sorts of things. I'd advise you to let her make something out of you before you leave: if you don't give a lawyer a rouble, he'll find ways to extract a hundred. Oh, my dear fellow . . .'

Wokulski listened attentively, Suzin sighed again and went on: 'And you confer with magicians (faugh! the powers of darkness . . .) though there, I assure you, you won't make a penny-piece, and may offend the Almighty . . . It's not decent! The worst of it is you think no one else knows what is troubling you. Yet everyone knows you are undergoing some kind of moral crisis – except that one person thinks you're trying to acquire forged currency, and another suspects you'd gladly go into bankruptcy, if you haven't already.'

'Do you think this?' asked Wokulski.

'Ah! Stanisław Piotrowicz, it is not right of you to call me a fool. You think I don't know that you're preoccupied with a woman . . . Well, a woman can be a tasty dish, and sometimes it so happens that a woman can turn the head of some quite solid man. Enjoy yourself, therefore, when you have money. But I'll tell you one thing, Stanisław Piotrowicz – shall I?'

'Please do.'

'He who asks for a shave must not be angry if he gets scratched. Let me tell you a parable, you idiot. There is some miraculous water in France that cures all sicknesses (I forget its name). So listen – some people go there on hands and knees and hardly dare look: but others unceremoniously drink the water and clean their teeth in it. Ah, Stanisław Piotrovich, you don't know how those who coarsely drink mock the ones who pray. Consider, therefore, whether you are not one of them, and if you are – then spit on everything. But what's the matter? Does it hurt? Of course . . . Well, try more wine.'

'Have you heard anything about her?' Wokulski asked dully.

'I swear I have heard nothing out of the ordinary,' Suzin replied, striking himself on the chest. 'A tradesman needs clerks, and a woman needs men to kneel before her, if only to conceal the bold man who refuses to kneel. It's very natural. But don't you, Stanisław Piotrowicz, go against the herd – or, if you must, then hold your head high. Half a million roubles capital is not to be sneezed at: people ought not to laugh at such a man.'

Wokulski rose and stretched himself like a man on whom an operation with red-hot irons had just been performed. 'It may be so, or it may not . . .' he thought, 'but if it is, then I'd give a part of my fortune to any happy admirer for curing me.'

He went back to his room and began for the first time to run over in his mind, quite calmly, all Izabela's admirers whom he had seen with her, or even heard of. He recollected significant conversations, melting looks, strange implications, all Mrs Meliton's reports, all the gossip about Izabela circulating amidst her admiring public. Finally he sighed deeply: it seemed to him he had found a thread to lead him out of the labyrinth. 'It will lead me into Geist's workshop, surely,' he thought, feeling that the first seeds of contempt had fallen into his heart.

'She has the right, she has every right! . . .' he muttered, laughing. 'But what a choice, or perhaps even choices . . . Ah, what a vile creature I am; and Geist considers me a human being . . .'

After Suzin's departure, Wokulski reread a letter from Rzecki, handed him that day. The old clerk wrote little about business, but a great deal about Mrs Stawska, the unhappy but beautiful woman whose husband had disappeared. 'I will be for ever in your debt,' wrote Rzecki, 'if you can provide definitive evidence whether Ludwik Stawski is dead or alive.' There followed a list of dates and localities in which the missing man had been seen since leaving Warsaw.

'Stawska? . . . Stawska? . . .' Wokulski thought, 'ah, yes, I know . . . She's that pretty woman with the little girl, who lives in my apartment house. What a strange coincidence: perhaps I bought the Łęcki house in order to make the acquaintance of this other woman? She means nothing to me as long as I stay here, but why not help her, since Rzecki asks me to? Excellent! Now I'll have a reason for giving the Baroness a present, as Suzin so firmly suggested . . .'

He took the Baroness's address and drove to Saint-Germain. In the wing of the house she lived in was an old curiosity shop. Talking to the porter, Wokulski involuntarily glanced at some books and caught sight, with joyful surprise, of a copy of

Mickiewicz's poetry, the very same edition he had read while still a clerk at Hopfer's. The sight of the worn covers and musty paper brought his entire youth before his eyes. He at once bought the book, and could have kissed it like a relic.

The doorman, whose heart Wokulski had won with a franc, took him to the door of the Baroness's apartment, wishing him (with a smile) an agreeable time. Wokulski rang, and at once saw a footman in pink livery. 'Hm . . .' he muttered.

In the drawing-room, naturally enough, there were gilded articles of furniture, pictures, carpets, flowers. A moment later the Baroness appeared, with the look of an offended person who, nevertheless, is willing to forgive. In fact she forgave him. During a brief conversation, Wokulski mentioned the purpose of his visit, wrote down Stawski's name and the locations where he had been, and urged the Baroness to provide him with accurate news of the missing man through her numerous contacts.

'It is possible,' said the great lady, 'but . . . will not the expense discourage you? We must appeal to the German police, the English, the American . . .'

'Well? . . .'

'So you are prepared to spend some three thousand francs?'

'Here's four thousand,' said Wokulski, giving her a cheque for the appropriate sum, 'and when may I expect a reply?'

'I cannot say,' replied the Baroness, 'perhaps within a month, perhaps not for a year. I think, however,' she added severely, 'that you have no doubt my search will be genuine?'

'So much so, that I'm leaving an order for another two thousand francs, payable at Rothschild's on receipt of news about this man.'

'Are you leaving soon?'

'Oh no. I shall stay here for a while yet.'

'Ah, so Paris has charmed you,' said the Baroness with a smile. 'You will like it still better from the windows of my drawing-room. I am at home every evening.'

They parted with mutual gratification: the Baroness at her client's wealth, and Wokulski because he had been able to take Suzin's advice and to fulfil Rzecki's request at one blow.

Now Wokulski was left entirely isolated in Paris, with nothing to do. Once again he visited the Exhibition, the theatres, unknown streets, forgotten halls in museums. Once again he admired the vast potential of France, the regularity in the erection and life of this city, with its population of a million, the influence of the mild climate on the expeditious development of civilisation . . . Again he drank cognac, ate costly dishes or played cards in the Baroness's drawing-room, where he always lost . . .

This way of spending time tired him out well enough, but gave not a drop of joy. The hours dragged by like days, the days were interminable, and the nights did not bring tranquil sleep. For, although he slept fast, without unpleasant or agreeable dreams, and although he lost consciousness, he could not rid himself of a sensation of unfathomed bitterness in which his soul was drowning, seeking in vain either the abyss or the shore. 'Give me an aim . . . or death,' he sometimes said, looking at Heaven. Then a moment later he would smile and think: 'To whom am I speaking? Who will listen to me in this machinery of blind forces I've become the plaything of? What a cruel destiny it is not to be attached to anything, not to wish for anything, yet to understand so much . . .'

It seemed to him he could see an immense factory, from which emerged new suns, new planets, new species, new nations – but in which there were people and hearts which the Furies were tearing apart – love, hope and pain. Which is the worst of these? Not pain, for it at least never lies: but hope, which hurls a man the deeper, the higher it has elevated him . . . And love, that butterfly with one wing called uncertainty, the other – deception.

'It is all the same to me,' he muttered. 'If we must stupefy ourselves with something, then let us do so with no matter what . . . With what, though?'

Then, in the depths of obscurity called Nature, two stars seemed to appear to him. One was pallid but fixed – this was Geist and his metals; the other, sparkling as the sun or suddenly dying out – was *she*. 'Which am I to choose?' he thought, 'if one is doubtful and the other inaccessible and uncertain? Even if I were to attain her, should I ever trust her? Could I ever trust her?'

All this made him feel that the moment for a decisive battle between intellect and heart was approaching. His intellect attracted him to Geist, his heart to Warsaw. He felt that some day soon he would have to choose: either hard work which would lead to extraordinary fame, or a flaming passion which surely threatened to reduce him to ashes.

'But what if both are illusions, like that coal shovel and the handkerchief that weighed a hundred pounds?'

He visited the hypnotist Palmieri again, and after paying the twenty francs for an interview, began questioning him: 'So you say, sir, that it is impossible to hypnotise me?'

'What do you mean – impossible?' said Palmieri, vexed. 'It is not possible immediately, since you are not a medium, sir. But I could make you one, if not within a few months, then within a few years.'

'So Geist did not delude me,' Wokulski thought. He added, aloud: 'And could a woman hypnotise a man, Mr Palmieri?'

'Not only a woman could, but so could a piece of wood, a doorknob, water – in a word, anything in which the hypnotist places his force. I can hypnotise my mediums with a pin: I can say to them 'I am pouring my fluid into this pin, and you will fall asleep when you look at it.' So much the easier, therefore, to transfer my power to a woman. Providing, of course, that the person hypnotised be a medium.'

'And then I'd be as attached to this woman as your medium was to the coal-shovel?' asked Wokulski.

'Why, naturally,' Palmieri replied, glancing at his watch.

Wokulski left him, and as he wandered about the streets, he thought: 'As for Geist, I almost have proof he wasn't deceiving me with hypnotism: there wasn't time. But what of her? – I am not sure but that she didn't bewitch me in this way. There was time, but – who made me her medium?'

The more he compared his love for Izabela with the feelings of most men for most women, the more unnatural it all seemed to him. How is it possible to fall in love with someone at first sight? Or how is it possible to be insane about a woman seen once in several months, and then only to perceive that she cares nothing for you?

'Bah!' he muttered, 'infrequent meetings are precisely what gave her the nature of an ideal. Who knows but what I wouldn't have been completely disillusioned if I'd known her better?'

He was surprised to have no news of Geist. 'Can the learned chemist have made off with three hundred francs and won't show himself again?' he wondered. Then he was ashamed of such suspicions: 'Perhaps he's ill?' he murmured. He took a horse-drawn cab and went to the address in the Charenton district, far outside the city walls. The road stopped by a walled fence: beyond it were visible the roof and upper windows of a house. Wokulski got out and approached an iron gate in the wall, fitted with a knocker. After knocking several times, the gate suddenly opened and Wokulski went into the yard. The house had one storey, and was very old: this was attested by its moss-covered walls, dusty windows, broken in places. In the centre of the façade was a door to which led some stone steps, very dilapidated. As the gate had already closed with a dull thud, and there was no doorman to be seen, Wokulski halted in the middle of the yard, surprised and troubled. Suddenly a head in a red cap appeared at the window of the first and only floor, and a familiar voice cried: 'Is it you, Mr Suzin? Good-day!'

The head disappeared but the open window proved it had not been an illusion. Several minutes later, the centre door squeaked open and there stood Geist. He wore shabby blue trousers, wooden sabots and a grubby flannel shirt.

'Congratulate me, Mr Suzin!' said Geist, 'I have sold the rights to my explosive to an Anglo-American firm, and appear to have done rather well. A hundred and fifty thousand francs cash, and twenty-five centimes for every kilogram sold.'

'Well, under the circumstances you'll surely abandon your metals,' said Wokulski, smiling.

Geist eyed him with good-natured contempt. 'These conditions,' he replied, 'have altered my situation so much that I need not concern myself for the next few years with a wealthy partner. But as for the metals, I am just now working on them, look . . .'

He opened a door to the right of the wing. Wokulski saw a large square room, very cold. In the centre stood a huge cylinder, like a barrel: its metal sides were a yard thick and held in four places by powerful hoops. Various pieces of apparatus were attached to the bottom: one looked like a safety valve through which a small cloud of steam emerged from time to time and quickly evaporated, the other was reminiscent of a manometer with its hand moving.

'A steam boiler?' Wokulski asked. 'Why such thick sides?'

'Touch it,' said Geist.

Wokulski did so, and exclaimed with pain. Blisters rose on his fingers, but they were from cold, not heat. The vat was terribly cold, and the cold could be felt throughout the room.

'Six hundred atmospheres of internal pressure,' Geist added, not noticing Wokulski's mishap.

The latter started on hearing this figure. 'A volcano!' he murmured.

'That is why I urged you to work here,' Geist replied, 'As you can see, an accident is easily come by . . . Let us go upstairs.'

'You leave the vat unattended?' Wokulski asked.

'Oh, a nurse-maid isn't required for this work: everything functions by itself and there can be no surprises.'

Upstairs they found themselves in a large room with four windows. Its furniture consisted mainly of tables scattered with retorts, bowls and pipes of glass, porcelain and even lead or brass. A dozen or so artillery shells lay on the floor and in corners, including several exploded ones. Stone or brass bowls full of coloured liquids stood by the windows: a bench along one wall carried a huge electric pile. Not until he turned around did Wokulski notice an iron safe bricked into the wall near the door, a bed covered with a worn quilt from which dirty padding was emerging, a desk with papers by a window and an armchair, leather-covered but torn and shabby, by it.

Wokulski looked at the old man, like the poorest of labourers in his wooden sabots, then at the equipment, from which poverty stared out, and he thought that nevertheless this man might acquire millions for his inventions. But he had renounced them for the good of some future, better humankind . . . Geist at this moment reminded him of Moses leading an unborn generation into the Promised Land.

But the old chemist did not guess Wokulski's thoughts this time: he gazed gloomily at him and said, 'Well, Mr Suzin, a sombre place, sombre labour. I have been living forty years like this. Several millions have already gone into these pieces of apparatus, and perhaps that is why their owner does not enjoy himself, has no servants and sometimes nothing to eat . . . It is no occupation for you,' he added with a gesture.

'You are wrong, professor,' Wokulski replied, 'and besides, the grave is certainly no more cheerful.'

'What do you mean – "the grave"? . . . Rubbish, sentimental rubbish,' Geist muttered. 'There are neither graves nor death in Nature; there are various forms of existence, some of which enable us to be chemists, others only chemical substances. Intellect consists of taking advantage of opportunities which arise, not of wasting time on nonsense, but in doing something.'

'I understand that,' Wokulski replied, 'but . . . forgive me, sir, your discoveries are so novel.'

'I understand, too,' Geist interrupted, 'my discoveries are so novel that . . . you regard them as trickery! In this respect the members of the Academy are no wiser than you, so you're in good company . . . Aha! Would you like to see my metals again, to test them? Very well . . .'

He hurried to the iron safe, opened it in a very complicated way and began bringing out, one after another, the blocks of metal heavier than platinum, lighter than water, and transparent . . . Wokulski examined them, weighed, heated, hit them, let electric currents pass through them, cut them with a knife. These tests took several hours: in the end, however, he decided that, physically at least, he was dealing with genuine metals.

When he had finished the tests, Wokulski sat down wearily in the armchair; Geist put away his specimens, closed the safe and asked, smiling: 'Well, now – fact or illusion?'

'I don't understand at all,' Wokulski murmured, clutching his head with both hands, 'my head is reeling! A metal three times lighter than water . . . incomprehensible!'

'Or a metal around 10 per cent lighter than air, what? . . .' laughed Geist. 'Specific gravity refuted . . . The laws of nature undermined, what? Ha! Ha! . . . Not at all. The laws of Nature, in so far as they are known to us, will remain intact, even in the face of my metals. Only our ideas about the properties of bodies and their internal structures will be extended, as will the limits of human technology, of course.'

'And specific gravity?' asked Wokulski.

'Listen to me,' Geist interrupted, 'and you will soon understand wherein the essence of my discoveries lies, although, I hasten to add, you will be unable to copy them. There are no miracles here, and no trickery; these are things so simple that an elementary school pupil could understand them.'

He took a steel cube from the table and handing it to Wokulski said: 'Here is a ten-centimetre cube, solid, cast in steel; take it in your hand, how much does it weigh?'

'Around eight kilograms . . .'

He handed over another cube of the same size, also steel, asking: 'And this one?'

'This one weighs around half a kilogram . . . But it is hollow . . .' replied Wokulski.

'Excellent! And how much does this cubic frame of steel wire weigh?' asked Geist, handing it to Wokulski.

'It weighs a dozen or so grams . . .'

'So you see,' Geist interposed, 'we have three cubes of the same size and the same substance, but which differ in weight. Why? Because the solid cube has most steel particles, the hollow one fewer, and the wire the least of all. Imagine, then, that instead of using *complete particles* I succeeded in constructing something made of the *frames of particles*, and you will understand the secret of the discovery. It depends on a change in the internal structure of materials, which is no novelty even for contemporary chemistry. So, what do you think? . . .'

'When I see the specimens, I believe you,' replied Wokulski, 'but when I leave this place . . .' He made a gesture of despair.

Geist reopened the safe, looked in and produced a small fragment of metal reminiscent of bronze, which he handed to Wokulski: 'Take this as an amulet against doubting my reason or veracity. This metal is some five times lighter than water, and it will remind you of our meeting. Moreover,' he added with a smile, 'it has one great property: it need fear no chemical reactions . . . It will vanish sooner than betray my secret . . . And now, be off, Mr Suzin, rest and ponder what you are going to do with yourself.'

'I'll come here,' Wokulski murmured.

'No, no – not yet,' Geist replied, 'you have not yet settled your accounts with the world; and, as I have money for the next few years, I don't insist . . . Come back when nothing remains of your earlier illusions.'

He shook him impatiently by the hand, and led him to the door. On the stairs he said goodbye once more and returned to the laboratory. When Wokulski emerged into the yard, the gate was already open, and when he passed through and stood opposite his horse-drawn cab, it slammed shut.

Returning to town, Wokulski first of all bought a golden medallion, placed the fragment of new metal inside it and suspended it around his neck like a scapula. He wanted to go for a stroll, but noticed that the traffic tired him: so he went to his room. 'Why have I come back here?' he thought, 'why don't I go to Geist's?'

He sat down in an armchair and lost himself in memories. He saw the Hopfer establishment, the dining-room and the customers who jeered at him: he saw his perpetual motion machine, and the model balloon he tried to steer. He saw Kasia Hopfer who had wasted away for love of him . . . 'To work! Why don't I set to work?' His gaze mechanically fell on the table, where lay his recently purchased book of Mickiewicz's poetry: 'How often I used to read this,' he sighed, picking it up. The book opened of its own accord, and Wokulski read: 'I start up, I learn by heart phrases with which to curse your cruelty, learned and forgotten for the millionth time . . . But when I see you, I cannot understand why I am once again so calm, colder than clay, only to burn again, be silent as before . . .'

'I know, now, by whom I am bewitched.'

He felt tears in his eyes, but controlled himself and they did not fall: 'All of you poets have wasted my life . . . You have poisoned two generations,' he whispered, 'these are the results of sentimental views on love . . .'

He closed the book and hurled it into a corner, so that the pages fell apart. It bounced back from the wall, fell into the wash-stand then slithered with a mournful rustling to the floor. 'Serves you right! That's the place for you,' Wokulski thought, 'for who but you presented love to me as a holy mystery? Who taught me to despise ordinary women, and seek an unattainable ideal? Love is the joy of the world, the sun of life, a cheerful melody in the wilderness, but what did you make of it? A mournful altar, in front of which obsequies are sung over trampled human hearts!'

Then the question struck him: 'If poetry has poisoned your life, who poisoned poetry? And why did Mickiewicz only yearn and despair, instead of laughing and rejoicing like the French street singers?

'Because he, like I, loved a high-born lady who was to be the prize not of reason, labour, devotion and sacrifice even of genius but . . . of money and a title.

'Poor martyr,' Wokulski thought, 'you gave of your finest to the nation, but what fault is it of yours that, in pouring out your own soul, you also poured out the sufferings with which it impregnated you? It is they who are guilty of your, my and our unhappiness.'

He rose and reverently picked up the scattered pages: 'It is not enough that you were tortured by them, but are you to answer for their crimes as well? It is they who are guilty that your heart, instead of singing, groaned like a cracked bell.'

He lay down on the sofa and again thought: 'What a strange country mine is, in which two entirely different races have for so long been living side by side: the aristocrats and the commoners. One claims to be a noble plant which has the right to drain dry the clay and manure, and the other either accedes to such claims, or else lacks the strength to protest against the injustice.

'How did this all work out for the perpetuation of one class and the strangling in the embryo of every other! They believed so strongly in noble birth, that even the sons of artisans and dealers either bought coats of arms or pretended to be impoverished noble countrymen. No one had the courage to declare himself the child of his merits, and even I, fool that I am, spent several hundred roubles on the purchase of a noble patent.

'Am I to go back there? What for? Here at least I have a nation living by all the talents with which man is endowed. Here the foremost places in society are not occupied by the mildew of dubious antiquity, but by essential forces which strive onwards – labour, intellect, will-power, creativity, knowledge, skill and beauty, and even sincere feelings. There, on the other hand, labour stands in the pillory, and depravity triumphs! He who makes a fortune is called a miser, a skinflint, a parvenu; he who wastes money is called generous, disinterested, open-handed . . . There, simplicity is eccentric, economy is shameful, artistry symbolised by shabby elbows. There, in seeking to acquire the denomination of a man, one must either have a title and money, or a talent for squeezing into drawing-rooms. Am I to go back there?'

He began to pace the room and count: 'Geist is one, I am a second, Ochocki a third . . . We will find at least another two such, and after four or five years we will have exhausted the eight thousand experiments necessary to discover a metal lighter than air. And then what? . . . What will happen to today's world at the sight of the first flying machine, without wings, without complicated mechanisms, and durable as an armoured ship?'

It seemed to him that the hum of the street outside his windows was growing and spreading, engulfing the whole of Paris, France, and Europe. And that all human voices melted into a great cry: 'Glory! . . . Glory! . . . Glory! . . .'

'Have I gone mad?' he muttered. Hastily he undid his waistcoat, brought out the golden medallion from beneath his shirt and opened it. The scrap of metal, like brass and as light as a feather, was in its place. Geist had not deceived him; the door to the great invention was open. 'I'll stay,' he whispered. 'Neither God nor man would forgive me for neglecting this cause.'

Dusk was falling. Wokulski lit the gas lamp over the table, brought out paper and pen, and began writing: 'Dear Ignacy, I want to discuss very serious matters with you, but as I am not coming back to Warsaw, please . . .'

Suddenly he thrust the pen aside: fear overcame him at the sight of the words he had written – 'as I am not coming back to Warsaw . . .'

'Why not go back?' he whispered. 'Yet – why should I? To meet Izabela again, to lose myself again?

'I must settle these stupid accounts once and for all.'

He walked about, thinking: 'There are two ways open: one leads to incalculable reforms for humanity, the other to pleasing and perhaps even winning the hand of a woman. Which shall I choose? For it is a fact that every new and important material, every new force has meant a new stage in civilisation. Bronze created classical civilisation, iron the Middle Ages; gunpowder completed the Middle Ages, and coal began the nineteenth century. Why hesitate: Geist's metal could initiate a civilisation previously only dreamed of, and who knows whether it might not actually ennoble the human species . . .

'And, on the other hand, what do I have? . . . A woman, who would not hesitate to bathe in the presence of a parvenu such as I. What am I in her eyes beside those *élégants*, for whom empty conversation, a happy idea, and a compliment constitute the most important things in life? What would that pack, not excluding herself, say at the sight of the ragged Geist and his immense discoveries? They are so ignorant, it would not even surprise them.

'Let us suppose, in the end, that I married her, what then? . . . The salon of the parvenu would immediately be inundated with all open and secret admirers, cousins of varying degrees, and I don't know who else! . . . And once again, I would have to close my eyes to their glances, deafen myself to their compliments, discreetly move away from their confidential conversations – about what? . . . About my shame or stupidity? . . .

'A year of such existence would debase me to the point of lowering myself to suffer jealousy of such individuals . . .

'Ah, would I not prefer to throw my heart to a hungry dog than to give it to a woman who cannot even guess at the difference between them and me.

'*Basta*! . . .'

He sat down at the table once again and began a letter to Geist. Suddenly, he stopped: 'I'm ridiculous,' he said aloud, 'I want to commit myself without settling my affairs . . .'

'Times have changed,' he thought. 'Earlier, a man like Geist would have been the symbol for Satan, with whom an angel in the form of a woman was struggling for a human soul . . . But today – which is Satan, which the angel?'

Someone knocked. A servant entered and gave Wokulski a long letter: 'From Warsaw,' he murmured, 'Rzecki? Is he writing me another letter? No, it's from the Duchess . . . Perhaps to inform me of Izabela's marriage?'

He tore open the envelope, but hesitated a moment before reading. His heart began beating faster. 'What difference does it make to me?' he muttered, and began:

Dear Stanisław, Evidently you are enjoying yourself in Paris, since you have apparently forgotten your friends. And the grave of your poor late 'uncle is still waiting for the headstone you promised, and also I should like your advice on building a sugar factory, which people are persuading me to undertake in my old age. Shame on you, Stanisław, and in the first place you should be sorry you do not see the blush on the face of Izabela, who is now with me and is quite excited to hear I am writing to you. Dear girl! She is staying with her aunt in the neighbourhood and often visits me. I suspect you caused her some great mortification; so do not delay in apologising, and come as fast as you can, straight to me. Bela will be staying here a few days longer, and perhaps I shall succeed in begging forgiveness for you . . .

Wokulski jumped up from the table and, opening the window, stood at it to reread the Duchess's letter; his eyes glittered, a flush broke out on his cheeks. He rang once, again, a third time . . . Finally he ran into the corridor, shouting: '*Garçon*! Hey, *garçon*!'

'Sir . . . ?'

'My bill!'

'What bill?'

'For the past five days. The total, d'you understand?'

'At once, sir?' the servant was surprised.

'At once and . . . a carriage to the Gare du Nord. At once!'

XXIV

A Man Happy in Love

O N HIS return to Warsaw from Paris, Wokulski found another letter from the Duchess. The old lady entreated him to come at once, and stay a few weeks at her house: 'Do not think,' she concluded, 'that I am inviting you on account of your recent successes, or showing off because I am acquainted with you. This sometimes happens, though not with me. I only want you to rest after your long labours, and perhaps relax at my house, where in addition to your tedious old hostess, you will also find the company of young and pretty women.'

'What do young and pretty women concern me!' Wokulski muttered. The next moment, however, he wondered what successes the Duchess was referring to? Could it be that his profits were known even in the provinces, though he had not mentioned them to anyone?

However, the Duchess's words soon ceased surprising him when he surveyed his business interests. Since his departure for Paris, the turnover in trade had again increased and went on increasing every week. A dozen or more new merchants had started business dealings with him, and only one of his previous customers had withdrawn, writing to him a sharp letter declaring that as he did not run an arsenal, but an ordinary textile store, he saw no purpose in maintaining further relations with the firm of Mr Wokulski, with which he would settle all accounts by the New Year. The traffic in merchandise was so great that Ignacy, on his own responsibility, had rented a new warehouse, and taken on an eighth clerk and two despatchers.

When Wokulski looked through the ledgers (at Rzecki's urgent request he set about them a few hours after returning home from the railway station), Ignacy opened the fireproof safe and, with a ceremonious expression, took out from it a letter from Suzin.

'Why this formality?' Wokulski asked with a smile.

'Letters from Suzin must have particular attention,' Rzecki

answered emphatically. Wokulski shrugged and read it. Suzin proposed a new deal for the winter months, almost as important as the Parisian one.

'What would you say to this?' he asked Ignacy, having explained what it was about.

'Staś,' said the old clerk, looking down, 'I trust you so implicitly that even if you burned down the city, I'd still feel sure you had done it with a noble aim in mind.'

'You are an incurable dreamer, old fellow!' Wokulski sighed, and broke off the conversation. He did not doubt that Ignacy again suspected him of some political machinations.

Rzecki was not the only one to think this. Going home, Wokulski found a whole pile of visiting-cards and letters. During his absence, some hundred influential people, titled and wealthy, had called on him, at least half of whom he did not know. The letters were still more remarkable. They were either requests for assistance, or for recommendations to various civil and military authorities, or else anonymous letters, mostly insulting. One called him a traitor, another a flunkey who had acquired so much skill in servility at Hopfer's that today he voluntarily put on livery for the aristocracy, if not worse. Another anonymous letter accused him of protecting a woman of bad reputation; yet another reported that Mrs Stawska was a coquette and adventuress and Rzecki a cheat, who was stealing the rent of the newly acquired apartment house and sharing it with the agent, a certain Wirski.

'Some fine rumours are circulating about me, to be sure,' thought Wokulski, looking at the heap of papers.

In the street, too, whenever he had time to notice, he realised he was the object of general interest. Many persons bowed to him; sometimes complete strangers pointed to him as he passed; but there were also some who turned away their heads with obvious dislike. Among them he noticed two acquaintances from Irkutsk, which impressed him in a disagreeable manner.

'What are they up to?' he thought, 'have they gone crazy?'

On the day after his return to Warsaw, he replied to Suzin that he accepted the offer, and would go to Moscow in mid-October. Late that evening he left for the Duchess's estate, which lay a few miles from the recently constructed railroad.

He noticed at the railroad station that here, too, his person attracted attention. The station master introduced himself and ordered a separate compartment for him; the chief conductor, showing him to his seat, said that he intended to find him a comfortable place where he might sleep, work or talk without interruption.

After a long delay, the train slowly moved off. It was already deep night, no moon and no clouds, and there were more stars in the sky than usual. Wokulski opened the window and eyed the constellations. Siberian nights came to his mind, when the sky was usually almost pitch black, strewn with stars like a snowstorm, where the Little Bear moved almost overhead, while Pegasus, Hercules and the Heavenly Twins shone lower on the horizon than in his country. 'Could I, a clerk in Hopfer's, have known anything of astronomy,' he thought bitterly, 'if I had not been there? And should I have heard anything of Geist's discoveries if Suzin had not forced me to go to Paris?'

And he saw with his inner eye his own long and unusual life, which seemed to extend from the far east to the far west: 'Everything I know, everything I have, everything I can still achieve, does not come from here. Here I have found only humiliation, envy or applause of dubious value when I was successful: if I had not been successful, those who bow to me today would have trampled me underfoot.'

'I will leave here,' he whispered, 'I'll go away! Unless she prevents me . . . For what will my fortune give me, if I cannot use it to suit myself? What is the value of a life spent decaying between the club, my store and drawing-rooms where one has to play whist to avoid gossip, or gossip to avoid playing whist?

'I wonder,' he said to himself after a moment, 'why the Duchess invited me so pointedly? Perhaps it was on Izabela's account?' He felt hot and slowly sensed a change take place in his soul. He recalled his father and uncle, Kasia Hopfer, who so loved him, Rzecki, Leon, Szuman, the prince, and many many others, who had shown him proof of undoubted goodwill. What was all his education and wealth worth if he were not surrounded by kindly hearts; what use would Geist's greatest discovery be if it were not to prove a weapon which would ensure the final victory to a better and nobler race? . . .

'There is much for us to do,' he whispered. 'There are people among us whom it would be worth helping or strengthening . . . I am too old to make epoch-making discoveries, let the Ochockis of this world occupy themselves with that . . . I prefer to augment others' happiness and to find happiness myself . . .'

He closed his eyes, and seemed to see Izabela looking at him in that strange way which was hers alone, approving his intentions with a tranquil smile.

Someone knocked at the compartment door, and the chief conductor appeared, saying: 'Baron Dalski is wondering whether he might join you. He is travelling in this carriage.'

'The Baron?' Wokulski asked, in surprise, 'of course, ask him to step this way . . .'

The conductor withdrew and closed the door. Wokulski recalled that the Baron belonged to the trading company with the East and that he was one of the now rather few suitors of Izabela. 'What can he want with me?' Wokulski thought, 'perhaps he too is going to visit the Duchess in order to make a definite proposal to Izabela in the open air? Providing Starski has not got there first . . .'

Footsteps and voices were heard in the corridor, the door opened again and the conductor reappeared accompanied by a very lean gentleman with a tiny, pointed and grizzled moustache, an almost grey and even smaller beard, and very grey hair.

'This can't be he,' Wokulski thought, 'he used to be quite dark . . .'

'My profoundest apologies for disturbing you,' said the Baron, swaying with the train's motion, '. . . profoundest . . . I would not venture to intrude on your solitude, were it not that I wanted to inquire whether you are going to visit our respected Duchess, who has been expecting you all week?'

'That is precisely where I am bound for. How are you, Baron? Pray be seated.'

'Capital,' the Baron exclaimed, 'I am going there too. I've been staying at the Duchess's nearly two months. That's to say, sir, not so much staying as continually visiting. Either from my own house which is being done up, or from Warsaw . . . I am now on my way back from Vienna, where I was buying furniture, but I'll be staying at the Duchess's only a few days, for I have to alter all the tapestries at the palace, put up only two weeks ago. But there's no help for it . . . They weren't liked, so we must take them down, no help for it!'

He smiled and blinked, and Wokulski felt cold. 'Who is the furniture for? Who didn't like the tapestry?' he asked himself in alarm.

'My dear sir,' the Baron went on, 'you have just completed your mission. My congratulations!' he added, pressing his hand, 'from the first moment, sir, I felt respect and liking for you, and this is now changing into genuine admiration. Yes indeed, sir. Our tendency to avoid political life has done us great harm. You were the first to break with the absurd principle of abstinence from it, and for that, sir, I admire you . . . After all, we must concern ourselves with the matters of the state in which our properties are, where our future lies . . .'

'I don't understand you, Baron,' Wokulski suddenly interrupted.

The Baron grew so confused that he sat for a moment without a word or movement. Finally he stammered: 'I apologise . . . Indeed, I had no intention of . . . But I think my friendship for the venerable Duchess who, sir, so . . .'

'Let us have done with explanations,' said Wokulski with a smile, pressing his hand, 'are you pleased with your purchases in Vienna?'

'Very much so, sir . . . very much. Will you believe me, though when I say there was a moment when I intended to disturb you in Paris, on the advice of the venerable Duchess . . .'

'I would gladly have been of service. What was the matter?'

'I wanted to have a diamond set there,' said the Baron, but as I came across some splendid sapphires in Vienna . . . I have them with me, and if you permit . . . Are you an expert in jewels?'

'Who are these sapphires for?' Wokulski thought. He wanted to straighten his back, but felt he could neither raise his arms nor move his legs. Meanwhile, the Baron had produced four velvet boxes from various pockets, placed them on the seat and began opening them. 'This is a bracelet,' he said, 'modest, is it not? One stone . . . The brooch and earrings are more ornate: I even ordered them to change the setting . . . This is the necklace . . . Simple but tasteful, and perhaps that is why it is beautiful . . . Fiery, sir, are they not?'

As he spoke, he moved the sapphires before Wokulski's eyes, in the flickering light of the lamp. 'Don't you like them?' the Baron suddenly asked, seeing that his companion did not answer.

'Of course, very fine. To whom are you bringing this gift?'

'To my fiancée,' the Baron replied, in a tone of surprise, 'I thought the Duchess would have mentioned our family happiness to you?'

'Not a word.'

'It is just five weeks today that I proposed and was accepted.'

'To whom did you propose? . . . The Duchess?' said Wokulski in an altered voice.

'No, no . . .' the Baron exclaimed, recoiling, 'I proposed to Ewelina Janocka, the Duchess's grand-daughter. Don't you remember her? She was at the Countess's for the blessing that year, didn't you notice her?'

A long moment passed before Wokulski realised that Ewelina was not Izabela Łęcka, that the Baron had not proposed to Izabela and was not bringing the sapphires for her.

'Excuse me,' he exclaimed to the uneasy Baron, 'but I am so agitated I simply don't know what I'm saying.'

The Baron jumped up and hastily began putting away the boxes. 'What inattention on my part!' he cried, 'I noticed from your looks that you were tired, but despite that I dared interrupt your sleep . . .'

'No, sir, I have no intention of sleeping, and it will be agreeable to pass the remainder of the journey in your company. That was a momentary weakness, which has already passed.'

To begin with, the Baron made a fuss, and wished to leave; but on seeing that Wokulski was, in fact, better, he sat down again, assuring him he would only stay a few minutes. He felt the urge to tell someone of his happiness. 'What a woman,' said the Baron expansively, 'when I met her, she seemed cold as a statue, only interested in clothes. Like every woman, she adores dressing, but what intellect too! I wouldn't say this to anyone else, sir, but I'll tell you, Mr Wokulski. I began to go grey very young, and from time to time I'd touch up my moustache with pomade. Well, but who'd have thought it? Hardly had she noticed than she forbade me once and for all to dye: she said she had a particular liking for grey hair, and that as far as she's concerned, only a grey-haired man is really handsome. So I asked her "What do you think of a grizzled man?" "They are the most interesting," said she. And how she spoke! . . . Am I boring you, Mr Wokulski?'

'Oh, my dear sir! It is always a pleasure to meet a happy man.'

'I really am happy, and in a way which surprises me,' the Baron continued, 'for I have often thought of getting married, and my doctors have suggested I should for several years past. So I planned to take a pretty woman, well-educated, with a good name and presence, though without demanding any kind of romantic love from her. But there you are, sir! Love has crossed my path, and lit a fire in my heart with a single glance . . . Indeed, Mr Wokulski, I am in love . . . no, I am insane . . . I would not say this to anyone but yourself, for whom I felt an almost fraternal liking from the start . . . I am insane! I think only of her – when I sleep I dream about her, when I don't see her I am literally ill, sir. No appetite, depressing thoughts, a kind of ceaseless agitation . . .

'But I beg you will not repeat what I am telling you, even to yourself, Mr Wokulski. I wanted to put her to the test; that was despicable of me, was it not? Yet, never mind, a man doesn't easily believe in happiness. So, wishing to put her to the test (but not a word about this to anyone, sir!), I had a settlement drawn up, according to which – if the marriage came to nothing through anyone's fault (d'you understand me?) – I am to pay the lady fifty thousand roubles for her disappointment. My heart sank within me for fear lest . . . she spurn me. But what d'you think? When the Duchess mentioned this plan to the young lady, she burst into tears . . . "What's this?" says she, "does he think I will renounce him for some fifty thousand roubles? For, if he suspects me of being interested, and doesn't admit of any more elevated motives in a woman's heart, then he ought to understand that I wouldn't give a million roubles for fifty thousand . . ."

'When the Duchess told me this, I hastened to Ewelina's room and fell at her feet without a word . . . Now, in Warsaw, I've made my will, and in it I name her the one and only heiress, even if I die before our wedding. All my family in all my life has not given me as much joy as this child in the course of a few weeks. And what will it be like later? What later, Mr Wokulski? I wouldn't put such a question to anyone else,' the Baron concluded, warmly shaking him by the hand. 'Well, goodnight . . .'

'An amusing story, upon my word,' Wokulski muttered, when the Baron had gone, 'that old man is really up to his neck in it.'

And he could not dispel the figure of the Baron, who had looked like a shadow against the amaranthine background of the carriage seat. So he observed the lean face, on which brick-red flushes glowed, his hair which seemed to be powdered with flour, his large sunken eyes in which an unhealthy gleam flickered. His outburst of passion had made a droll yet mournful impression in a man who kept covering up his throat, checking that the window was tightly shut and continually changed his seat in the compartment for fear of draughts.

'He's in a fine state,' thought Wokulski. 'Is it possible that a young woman could fall in love with such a mummy? He's certainly ten years older than I, and how incompetent and naive into the bargain!

'Very well, but supposing this young woman does really love him. For it is hard to suppose she is deceiving him. In general, women are nobler than men: not only do they commit fewer sins, but they sacrifice themselves far more often than we do. So, if such a vile man were by chance found, who lied from morning to night for money, could a woman be suspected of anything similar, especially a young lady brought up in a respectable family? Of course, something must have got into her head, and she must be bemused, if not by his personal charms, then by his position. Otherwise she couldn't help betraying that she is playing a comedy, and the Baron would have noticed, for love looks through a microscope.

'Yet, if a young girl can fall in love with such an old fool, why shouldn't she fall in love with me?'

'I keep coming back to myself,' he whispered. 'This notion has already become a kind of monomania.'

He opened the window which the Baron had closed and, to dispel his obsessive thoughts, began looking at the sky again. Pegasus was already fading to the west, and to the east rose Sagittarius, Orion, Canis Minor and Gemini. He eyed the manifold stars that were scattered in this section of the sky, and into his mind came that strange, invisible power of attraction, which binds distant worlds in one unity more strongly than material chains.

'Attraction . . . attachment . . . They are one and the same, ultimately; a power so strong that it engulfs everything, so fertile that all lives comes from it. If we deprive the earth of its attachment to the sun, it would fly off into space and in a few years would be a block of ice. If we pushed some wandering star into the solar system, who knows that life mightn't awaken on it? So why is the Baron to break down under the law of attachment, which pervades all nature? And is there a greater abyss between him and Ewelina than between earth and sun? What is surprising in human madness, since the world is equally mad.'

Meanwhile the train went more slowly and stopped for long periods in stations. The air grew cold, in the east the stars turned pale. Wokulski closed the window and lay down on the sofa. 'If,' he thought, 'a young woman can fall in love with the Baron, why should not I . . . ? For, after all, she is not deceiving him . . . In general women are nobler than we are . . . They lie less.'

'If you please, sir, this is your station . . . The Baron is already taking tea . . .'

Wokulski roused himself: the conductor was standing over him, and had awakened him in the most respectful manner.

'Morning already?' he asked in surprise.

'It is nine o'clock, we have been standing in the station half an hour. I didn't wake you, for the Baron said not to, sir, but as the train is leaving now . . .'

Wokulski got out quickly. The station was new, not yet finished. Nevertheless, they provided him with water for washing, and brushed his clothes. He came to himself entirely and went into a small buffet, where the beaming Baron was at his third glass of tea. 'Good morning!' the Baron cried in a familiar way, shaking Wokulski's hand. 'Landlord, tea for the gentleman . . . A beautiful day, is it not, perfect for a horse-back ride. But they have played a nice trick on us!'

'What has happened?'

'We must wait for the horses,' the Baron went on, 'fortunately I sent a telegram at two o'clock in the morning, to announce your arrival. The day before yesterday I sent the Duchess a telegram from Warsaw, but the station master tells me I made an error and ordered the horses for tomorrow. Luckily, I sent a telegram today on route. They dispatched a courier with it at three, the Duchess will get the telegram by six, and at eight at the latest the horses will be here. Let us wait another hour, and in the meanwhile you must become acquainted with the neighbourhood. A very pretty place, sir.'

After breakfast they went on to the platform. The district looked flat and almost bare from here: a clump of trees was visible here and there, and brick buildings among them.

'Are those manors?' asked Wokulski.

'Ah yes . . . there are many nobles in these parts. The land is wonderfully cultivated; you have lupin here, clover . . .'

'I see no village,' broke in Wokulski.

'Because these are manorial lands, and you know the saying, sir: "Many ricks on the manor's field; on the peasant's — many people."'

'I have heard,' said Wokulski suddenly, 'that the Duchess has a large number of guests.'

'Ah, my dear sir,' cried the Baron, 'on a fine Sunday it's like being at a ball at one's club: dozens of people drive over. Even today we ought to find a crowd of permanent guests. Well, in the first place, my fiancée is staying here. Then there is Mrs Wąsowska, a charming little widow, about thirty, with a great fortune. It seems to me that Starski is interested in her. Do you know Starski, sir? A disagreeable person, arrogant, rude . . . I'm surprised that a lady with intellect and taste, like Mrs Wąsowska, can take any pleasure in the company of such a frivolous creature . . .'

'Who else?' asked Wokulski.

'There is also Fela Janocka, the cousin of my young lady: a very sweet child, she is about eighteen. And Ochocki . . .'

'What is he doing here?'

'When I left, he was spending entire days fishing. But as his tastes change so frequently, I am not at all sure that I shan't see him next as a hunter . . . But what a noble young man, what knowledge! Well, and he has achieved a great deal: he has already produced several inventions.'

'Yes, an unusual man,' said Wokulski. 'Who else is visiting with the Duchess?'

'No one else, though Mr Łęcki and his daughter very often come down for a few days, or a week. A most distinguished person,' the Baron went on, 'full of rare qualities. Surely you know them? Happy is the man to whom she will give her hand and heart. What charm, sir – what intellect: indeed one can only respect her as a goddess! Don't you think so, sir?'

Wokulski surveyed the landscape, unable to reply. Fortunately a servant ran up at this moment to tell the Baron the carriage had come. 'Excellent!' the Baron cried, and gave the man a few coins, 'take our things, my good man, and let us, sir, be off. In two hours you'll be making the acquaintance of my fiancée.'

XXV

Rural Diversions

FIFTEEN minutes passed before their things were packed into the carriage. Finally Wokulski and the Baron got in, the driver in yellow livery waved his whip in the air and the pair of fine grey horses set off at a steady canter.

'Oh, I recommend Mrs Wąsowska to you,' said the Baron, 'she's a jewel, not a woman, and so witty! She has no thoughts of marrying again, but loves being surrounded by admirers. It is hard, sir, not to adore her, but adoration is perilous. She is paying Starski back for all his frivolity. D'you know Starski, sir?'

'I met him, once . . .'

'A distinguished man, but disagreeable,' said the Baron. 'My fiancée has quite an antipathy for him. He affects her nerves so that the poor girl quite loses her good humour in his company. I am not surprised, for they are diametrically opposed characters: she is serious, he trivial – she full of feeling, even sentimental, he a cynic.'

As he listened to the Baron's chatter, Wokulski surveyed the countryside which was slowly changing its looks. Half an hour from the station, woods appeared on the horizon, with hills nearer: the road wound among them, ran across their summits, or down into valleys. On one such elevation, the driver turned to them, pointed ahead with his whip and said, 'See, the ladies and gentlemen are coming along in the brake.'

'Where? Who?' cried the Baron, almost climbing on to the box. 'Ah yes, it is they . . . A yellow brake with piebald foursome . . . I wonder who it can be? Just look, sir.'

'It seems to me I can see something red,' Wokulski replied.

'That's Mrs Wąsowska. I wonder if my fiancée is with her?' added the Baron in a lower voice.

'There are several ladies,' said Wokulski, who was thinking at this moment of Izabela. 'If she is with them, that will be a good omen,' he thought.

Both carriages approached one another rapidly. There was a

violent cracking of a whip, cries and the waving of handkerchiefs
from the brake: while in the other carriage, the Baron was leaning
still further out and trembling with excitement. The carriage
stopped, but the brake passed it headlong in a storm of laughter and
cries, and stopped a dozen yards away. Clearly something was being
discussed in a noisy manner, and must have been decided, for all
the company got out and the brake drove on.

'Good morning, Mr Wokulski!' someone cried from the box,
waving a long whip. Wokulski recognised Ochocki. The Baron ran
towards the company. A lady in a white scarf, carrying a white lace
parasol, came slowly towards him, her hands outstretched, the wide
sleeves falling away. The Baron took off his hat at a distance and,
on reaching his fiancée, almost buried himself in her sleeve. After
an outburst of emotion which, though to him was short, seemed
very long to the spectators, the Baron suddenly recollected himself
and said: 'Madam, allow me to introduce Mr Wokulski, my best
friend . . . As he will be staying here some time, I hereby call upon
him to take my place at your side when I am away.'

He again implanted several kisses in the depths of the sleeve,
from which a beautiful hand stretched towards Wokulski. He
pressed it, and felt an icy chill: he looked at the lady in the white
scarf and saw a pale face with huge eyes, in which sorrow and fear
were apparent.

'An unusual fiancée,' he thought.

'Mr Wokulski,' cried the Baron, turning to two ladies and a man
who had by now approached: 'Mr Starski . . .' he added.

'I've already had the pleasure,' said Starski, taking his hat off.

'I too,' Wokulski replied.

'How shall we fit in now?' asked the Baron, seeing that the brake
had driven up.

'Let us all ride together,' cried a young blonde girl whom
Wokulski guessed to be Felicja Janocka.

'There are two seats in our carriage,' observed the Baron,
sweetly.

'I understand, but none of that,' exclaimed a lady in a red dress,
with a beautiful contralto voice, 'the engaged couple will come
with us, and Mr Ochocki and Mr Starski can go in the carriage, if
they like.'

'Why me?' asked Ochocki from the box.

'Or I?' added Starski.

'Because Mr Ochocki drives atrociously, and Mr Starski is
impossible,' said the widow firmly.

Now Wokulski noticed that this lady had superb chestnut hair
and black eyes, and her entire countenance was lively and
energetic.

'So you dismiss me already?' Starski sighed in a droll manner.

'You know I always dismiss admirers who bore me. Now, let us get in, ladies and gentlemen. The engaged couple first. Fela next to Ewelina.'

'Oh no,' the blonde girl protested, 'I shall get in last, for grandmama does not let me sit next to the engaged couple.'

The Baron, with more elegance than skill, handed in his fiancée, and sat down opposite her. Then the widow took the seat next to the Baron, Starski next to the fiancée, and Felicja next to him.

'If you please . . .' the widow cried to Wokulski, drawing in the folds of her red dress, which had spread over half the seat. Wokulski sat down opposite Felicja, and noticed that the young lady was looking at him with admiration and surprise, blushing now and then.

'Couldn't we ask Mr Ochocki to give the reins back to the driver?' asked the widow.

'My dear lady, why are you everlastingly squabbling with me?' Ochocki said, vexed, 'I am going to drive . . .'

'I give you my word I shall kill you if you have an upset.'

'That remains to be seen,' Ochocki replied.

'Ladies and gentlemen, did you hear that?' the widow cried, 'is there no one to take my part?'

'I'll be revenged for you,' put in Starski in rather faulty Polish, 'let the two of us move into the carriage.'

The pretty widow shrugged, the Baron again kissed his fiancée's hands, and Felicja blushed. Wokulski glanced at the fiancée. She noticed him, replied with a glance of scorn and suddenly changed from profound misery to childish merriment. She gave the Baron her hand for more kissing, and even touched him accidently with her foot. Her admirer was so excited that he turned pale and his lips grew livid.

'But you have no idea of how to drive!' the widow cried, trying to poke Ochocki with the tip of her parasol. At this moment Wokulski jumped out. At the same time, the first pair of horses turned into the middle of the road, the other pair after them, and the brake tilted violently to the left. Wokulski held it up and the horses, reined in by a courier, stopped.

'Didn't I tell you that monster would upset us?' the widow cried. 'What next, Mr Starski?'

Wokulski looked into the brake, and saw this momentary scene: Felicja was shaking with laughter, Starski had fallen face downwards on the pretty widow's lap, the Baron was clutching the courier and his fiancée, pale with fright, had seized hold of the box with one hand and Starski's arm with the other.

The brake righted itself in the twinkling of an eye, and everything went back to its proper place. Only Felicja was still shrieking with laughter.

'I don't understand, Fela, how you can laugh at a moment like this,' exclaimed the fiancée.

'Why not? Nothing terrible could happen. After all, Mr Wokulski is riding with us,' said the young lady. However, she recollected herself and, blushing still more, first hid her face in both hands, then peeped at Wokulski as much as to say she was very offended.

'As for me, I am prepared to subscribe to several accidents like that,' Starski cried, looking significantly at the widow.

'On condition I am protected from proofs of your feelings,' replied the widow, frowning and taking the place opposite Wokulski.

'Come now, you yourself said today that widows are permitted everything.'

'But widows do not permit everything. No, Mr Starski, you must unlearn those Japanese customs.'

'They are universal customs,' Starski replied.

'Not of the half of the world I am used to,' the widow interrupted, grimacing and looking at the road.

Silence fell in the brake. The Baron was twirling his grizzled moustache with relish, and his fiancée became miserable again. Felicja, having taken the widow's seat next to Wokulski, almost turned her back on him, casting scornful and melancholy glances at him from time to time. Why? He did not know.

'I expect you ride well,' Mrs Wąsowska said to Wokulski.

'What makes you think so?'

'Oh come – please answer my question.'

'Not very well, but I ride.'

'I am sure you ride well, for you instantly divined what the horses would do in the hands of such a master as Julian. We'll ride together . . . Mr Ochocki, from today I excuse you from riding with me.'

'I am very pleased to hear it,' Ochocki retorted.

'Oh, what a charming way to answer a lady!' cried Felicja.

'I'd sooner answer them than ride out with them. When Mrs Wąsowska and I last went riding, I fell off my horse six times in two hours, and wasn't easy for five minutes together. Let Mr Wokulski try now.'

'Fela, tell that person I am not speaking to him,' exclaimed the widow, pointing to Ochocki.

'Young man,' said Fela, 'this lady refuses to speak to you. She says you are common.'

'What! Now you yearn for the company of men with nice manners?' asked Starski, 'pray try, perhaps I'll let myself be induced to apologise.'

'When did you leave Paris?' the widow asked Wokulski.

'A week tomorrow.'

'And to think I haven't been there for four months . . . It's my favourite city.'

'Zasławek!' Ochocki announced, and raised his whip to execute a tremendous crack which, however, did not come off, because the whip, clumsily thrown back, caught amidst the ladies' parasols and the gentlemen's hats.

'Really, ladies and gentlemen,' cried the widow, 'if you want me to come riding with you, you must tie that man up. Quite frankly, he's dangerous.'

An uproar started in the brake again, because Ochocki was supported by Felicja: she insisted that he drove well for a beginner, and accidents will happen to even the most careful drivers. 'Fela, my dear,' replied the widow, 'you're at the age when anyone with fine eyes is a good driver.'

'Today my appetite will be really good,' said the Baron to his fiancée, but, on realising he had spoken too loudly, he began whispering again.

They had already reached the Duchess's estate, and Wokulski could see the residence. On a fairly high though gentle hill stood a one-storey palace with two wings. Behind it were the ancient and green trees of a park; in front stretched what looked like a broad meadow, cut by paths, adorned here and there with a clump of trees, a statue or a summer-house. At the foot of the hill a wide expanse of water gleamed, evidently a pond, on which boats and swans were rocking. Against its green background, the palace – bright yellow in colour, with white pillars – looked both imposing and inviting. Brick outbuildings were to be seen among the trees to right and left.

To the whip-cracking which Ochocki succeeded in producing this time, the brake drove across a marble bridge in front of the palace – with only one wheel going over the lawn. The travellers descended, though Ochocki did not hand over the reins and drove the carriage around to the stable. 'Remember, lunch is at one o'clock,' Felicja called.

An old servant in a black frock-coat approached the Baron: 'Her ladyship,' he said, 'is in the pantry. Perhaps the gentlemen will go to their rooms?' After ushering them into the left wing, he showed Wokulski into a large room, its open windows overlooking the park. A moment later, a lad in livery hurried in, bringing water, and set about unpacking the valise.

Wokulski looked out of the window. In front stretched a lawn adorned with clumps of old spruce, birch and linden trees, beyond which wooded hills were visible. Immediately by the windows was a clump of lilacs, with a nest in it, to which sparrows were flying. The warm September breeze entered the room from time to time, bringing indefinable scents.

The guest gazed at the clouds, which seemed to touch the tree-tops, at the shafts of light which fell between the dark branches of the spruces, and was content. He did not think of Izabela. Her image, burning within his soul, had dissolved in the face of the simple pleasures of nature: his sick heart fell silent, and for the first time in a long while, tranquillity and calm enveloped him.

But, recollecting he was here on a visit, he hastily began dressing. Hardly had he finished, than there came a light tap and the old servant entered: 'Her ladyship invites you to table.'

Wokulski followed him. They entered a corridor and soon were in a large dining-room, its walls panelled half-way up with dark wood. Felicja was talking to Ochocki in a window, while the Duchess was seated in a chair with high arms, between Mrs Wąsowska and the Baron. Seeing her guest, she rose and took a few steps forward: 'Welcome, Stanisław,' she said, 'thank you for taking my advice.' But when Wokulski bowed over her hand, she kissed him on the brow, which made a certain impression on those present.

'Sit here, by Kazia. And do you, pray, take care of him,' she said.

'Mr Wokulski deserves it,' the widow replied, 'had it not been for his presence of mind, Mr Ochocki would have broken our bones for us.'

'Whatever next!'

'He can't even drive a pair of horses, yet he tried his hand on a foursome. I preferred him when he spent his time fishing.'

'Good God!' Ochocki groaned, greeting Wokulski cordially, 'thank goodness I'm not going to marry that woman!'

'My good man . . . if you're proposing yourself to me as a husband, you had better remain a coachman,' cried Mrs Wąsowska.

'They're always squabbling,' said the Duchess with a smile.

Ewelina Janocka entered, and a few minutes later Starski came in by another door. They greeted the Duchess, who responded cordially, though gravely. Lunch was served.

'In my house, Stanisław,' said the Duchess, 'the custom is that we are only obliged to meet at table. Apart from that, everyone does as he chooses. I recommend, therefore, that if you are afraid of boredom, you dance attendance on Kazia Wąsowska.'

'I'm taking Mr Wokulski into my charge at once,' the widow replied.

'Aha!' the Duchess murmured, glancing fleetingly at her guest.

Felicja blushed for goodness knows how many times that day, and asked Ochocki for wine. 'No, no . . . water, please,' she corrected herself. Ochocki obeyed, shaking his head as he did so, and making a very desperate gesture.

After luncheon, during which Ewelina spoke to no one but the Baron and Starski flirted with the black-eyed widow, the guests bade goodbye to their hostess and separated. Ochocki went up to the attic of the palace where, in a small room especially arranged for the purpose, he had established a meteorological observatory, the Baron and fiancée went into the park and the Duchess detained Wokulski.

'Tell me,' she said, 'since first impressions are often correct – how do you like Mrs Wąsowska?'

'She seems a lively and vivacious woman.'

'You are right. And the Baron?'

'I hardly know him. He's an old man.'

'Oh, dear, yes, very old,' the Duchess sighed, 'but nevertheless he wants to get married. And what have you to say of his fiancée?'

'I don't know her at all, though it surprises me that she should care for the Baron who may, of course, be the most excellent of men.'

'Yes, she's a strange girl,' said the Duchess, 'and I may tell you I'm starting to lose my heart to her. I'm not going to interfere in her marriage, since more than one girl envies her, and everyone says she's made a good match. But what she was to have received after my death will go to others. Anyone who has the Baron's millions doesn't need my twenty thousand.' Vexation was to be heard in the old lady's voice.

Soon she dismissed Wokulski and advised him to walk in the park. He went into the yard, and walked around the left wing where the kitchens were, and into the park. Later on, the two first observations he made in Zasławek often came into his mind. In the first place he noted a kennel not far from the kitchens, and in front of it a dog on a chain, which, on seeing a stranger, began barking, howling and leaping up as if it had rabies. But as the dog had a cheerful look and was wagging its tail, Wokulski patted it, which brought about such an influx of good humour in the fierce beast that it would not let the guest go. He howled, snapped at his clothes, lay down on the ground as if to demand a caress or at least the sight of a human face. 'A strange watch-dog,' Wokulski thought.

At this moment another strange sight emerged from the kitchen: a fat old farm labourer. Wokulski, who had never before seen a fat peasant, entered into a conversation with him: 'Why do you keep this dog on a chain?'

'To make him ferocious and prevent thieves coming into the house,' said the peasant with a smile.

'But why not take on a vicious dog?'

'Her ladyship wouldn't keep a nasty-tempered dog. Here even the dogs must be good-natured.'

'As for you, old fellow, what do you do?'

'I'm the bee-keeper, but before that I was the steward. When a bull smashed my ribs, her ladyship set me bee-keeping.'

'Are you happy?'

'At first, without work, I was sick – but later I got used to it, and now I am.'

Saying goodbye to the peasant, Wokulski turned into the park and walked about for a long time in a linden grove, not thinking. He seemed to have come here surfeited and poisoned by the uproar of Paris, the noise of Warsaw, the rattle of railroad trains and all the uneasiness and pain he had lived through, all of which were now evaporating. Had he been asked 'What is the countryside?' he would have replied: 'It is peace.'

Then he heard someone running after him. Ochocki caught up with him, carrying two fishing-rods. 'Wasn't Felicja here?' he asked, 'she was to have come fishing with me at two-thirty . . . But there's a woman's idea of punctuality for you! Perhaps you'll come with us? But you'd rather not . . . Perhaps you'd sooner play piquet with Starski? He's already ready for that, except when he can find partners for whist.'

'What is Mr Starski doing here?'

'What do you think? He's living with his grandmother, who is also his godmother – the Duchess Zasławska, and now he's worrying that he certainly won't inherit her fortune. A fine penny, too – some three hundred thousand roubles! But the Duchess prefers to support foundlings rather than the casino at Monaco! Poor devil!'

'What's wrong?'

'Hm! He'll get nothing from his grandmother, and has broken with Kazia – so he may as well shoot himself. You must know, sir,' Ochocki went on, fidgeting with the rod, 'that at one time the present Mrs Wąsowska, while still unmarried, had a weakness for Starski. Kazio and Kazia – a well-chosen pair, eh? Apparently Mrs Kazia came here three weeks ago still influenced by this idea (she has a nice little fortune from her late husband – possibly as much as the Duchess, even!) They got on well for a few days, and Kazio even realised a new bill of exchange with a Jew on account of the dowry, but then – something went wrong. Mrs Wąsowska simply laughs at Kazio, while he pretends to put a good face on things. In a word, it's bad! He'll have to give up his travelling, and settle down on some sandy farm until his uncle dies – in fact, he's been ill for a long time with a stone.'

'But what has Mr Starski been doing up to now?'

'Getting into debt, mainly. He gambled a little, travelled a little (mainly, though, in the bars of Paris and London, as I really can't believe in that China of his), and specialising in turning the heads of young married women. He's a past master at that, and has such a reputation that married women can't resist him, while unmarried girls believe that anyone Starski begins flirting with will immediately find a husband. It's as good a pastime as any!'

'Certainly,' Wokulski murmured, already somewhat easier in mind regarding his rival: 'He won't turn the head of Izabela.'

They came to the end of the park, beyond the railings of which a row of brick buildings was to be seen. 'Oh, just look, what an unusual woman the Duchess is!' said Ochocki, pointing, 'do you see those palaces? They're farm cottages for labourers. And the house over there is a refuge for farm children: there are some thirty of them, all washed and cared for like little princes . . . And that villa is a shelter for old people, of whom there are four: they have a pleasant time cleaning hair for mattresses for the guests' rooms. I've wandered about various parts of this country, and I've seen farm-labourers living everywhere like pigs, their children playing in the mud like piglets. When I came here for the first time I could hardly believe my eyes. I seemed to be in Utopia, or in the pages of a boring but virtuous novel, in which the author describes what the gentry should be like, but never are . . . The old lady has impressed me. If you want to know what sort of library she has, what she reads . . . I was taken aback when she once asked me to explain a point of Darwinism, which she dislikes only because it sees the struggle for existence as a fundamental law of nature.'

Felicja appeared at the end of the alley: 'Well, Julian, shall we go?' she asked Ochocki.

'Mr Wokulski is coming with us.'

'Oh?' asked the young lady, in surprise.

'You prefer not?' Wokulski inquired.

'Not at all . . . But I thought you would be better off in the company of Mrs Wąsowska.'

'Felicja!' cried Ochocki, 'don't play at sarcasm, if you please. It doesn't come off.'

Offended, the young lady walked ahead in the direction of the pond, the two men after her. They fished through the heat of the day until five o'clock. Ochocki caught a two-ounce gudgeon, and Miss Felicja tore the lace on her sleeve. Consequently, a squabble broke out between them to the effect that young ladies had no idea how to hold a fishing-rod, and that men can't sit still for a moment without talking.

The dinner-bell finally reconciled them. After dinner, the Baron went to his room (at this time of day he always had migraine), while the rest of the company planned to meet in a summer-house in the park, where fruit was usually eaten.

Wokulski went there half an hour later. He thought he would be first, but he found all the ladies there, and Starski addressing them. He sat stretched out in a cane chair and was speaking with a bored expression on his face, tapping his boot with a riding-crop: 'If marriages have ever played a part in history, then it wasn't marriage

for love, but those of self-interest. What would we know today of
Jadwiga or Maria Leszczyńska if those ladies had not known how to
make a judicious choice? Who would Stefan Batory or Napoleon I
have been if they had not married women of influence? Marriage is
too important an event to enter into on the strength of feelings
alone. It isn't a poetical union between two souls, but an important
event for many people and interests. If I were to marry a chambermaid or governess, I should be lost to my world tomorrow. No
one will ask me what the temperature of my feelings was, but what
income I have for keeping up a household, and who is the woman
I am introducing into my family.'

'Political marriages are one thing, and those entered into for
money, to a person one doesn't love, are another,' said the
Duchess, looking at the ground and tapping the table with her
fingers. 'That is violence done to the most sacred feelings.'

'Oh, grandmama, dear!' Starski replied, with a sigh, 'it's easy to
talk of feelings when one has twenty thousand a year. Everyone
says "Vile money! Detestable money!" But why does everyone,
from a farm-labourer to a minister of government, use up their
spare time with work? Why do miners and sailors risk their lives?
Simply for this vile money – because vile money gives them
freedom for at least a few hours a day, or a few months in the year,
or a few years in a man's life. Everyone mistakenly despises money,
but each one of us knows that it's the manure in which personal
freedom, science, art, even ideal love, all grow. Where did courtly
love and the love of troubadours grow? Not, certainly, amidst
tailors and smiths, not even among doctors and lawyers. It was
cultivated by the wealthy classes which created women with
delicate skin and white hands, and produced men with enough
time to adore women.

'We have here with us a representative of the men of action in
Mr Wokulski who, as you yourself said, grandmama, has more than
once given proof of his heroism. What attracted him to danger?
Money, of course, which today is a power in his hands.'

The room grew quiet, all the ladies looked at Wokulski. After a
moment of silence, he replied: 'Yes, you are right, I made a fortune
amidst difficult adventures, but do you know why I did so?'

'Excuse me,' Starski interrupted, 'I'm not reproaching you, on
the contrary – I regard it as a praiseworthy example for everyone.
But how do you know, sir, whether a person who marries for
money doesn't have noble aims in view too? My parents are
supposed to have married for love, but they weren't happy and as
for me, the fruit of their feelings, it's useless to talk . . . Meanwhile,
my admirable grandmama here married against her own feelings
but today she is the benefactor of the entire neighbourhood. Better
still,' he added, kissing the Duchess's hand, 'she is correcting my

parents' errors – they were so taken up with love that they forgot
to provide a fortune for me. And we have another example in the
person of charming Mrs Wąsowska.'

'Come, sir,' said the widow, blushing, 'you speak as if you were
the prosecuting attorney at the Last Judgement. I'll reply like Mr
Wokulski: do you know why I did it?'

'Yet you did it, and so did grandmama, and we all do the same,'
said Starski with ironical coldness, 'except, of course, for Mr
Wokulski, who has enough money to cultivate his feelings.'

'I did the same,' Wokulski exclaimed in a stifled voice.

'You married for money?' asked the widow, opening her eyes
wide.

'Not for money, but to obtain work and not starve to death. I
know well that law of which Mr Starski speaks.'

'And so?' put in Starski, looking at his grandmother.

'And because I know it, I pity those who must comply with it,'
concluded Wokulski. 'It must be the greatest unhappiness in life.'

'You are right,' said the Duchess.

'You begin to interest me, Mr Wokulski,' added Mrs Wąsowska,
stretching out her hand to him.

During the entire conversation, Ewelina had been concentrating
on her embroidery. At this moment she raised her eyes and glanced
at Starski with such a look of despair that Wokulski was startled . . .
But Starski continued tapping his boot with the riding-crop, biting
a cigar and smiling half-mockingly, half-sadly.

The voice of Ochocki was heard behind the summer-house:
'Look, I told that Mrs . . .'

'Well, that's in the summer-house, not in the undergrowth,'
replied a young girl with a basket in her hand.

'You're absurd,' Ochocki muttered, entering and looking
uneasily at the ladies.

'Aha, the conquering hero comes,' said the widow.

'I give you my word, I came through the undergrowth merely to
get here more quickly,' Ochocki explained.

'You drove off the road, just as you did with us, today . . .'

'On my word . . .'

'Better take me back, instead of explaining,' the Duchess interrupted.

Ochocki gave her his arm, but his expression was so embarrassed
and his hat so awry that Mrs Wąsowska could not control her
merriment, which brought another series of blushes to Felicja's
face, and made Ochocki dart several angry looks at the widow.

The entire company moved to the left down a side alley to the
farm. First went the Duchess and Ochocki, then the girl with the
basket, then the widow and Felicja, followed by Ewelina and
Starski. At the gate, the noise in front increased, but at this moment

Wokulski seemed to hear a quiet conversation behind him:
'Sometimes I'd sooner be dead . . .' whispered Miss Ewelina.

'Be brave . . . be brave,' Starski replied in the same way.

Only now did Wokulski understand the purpose of the walk to
the farm, as a whole crowd of hens ran across the yard to the
Duchess and she threw grain to them from the basket. Old
Mateuszowa, their keeper, appeared behind the hens to tell her
mistress all was well, although a falcon had been flying over the
yard since morning, and one of the hens had choked on a pebble
that afternoon, but recovered.

After a survey of the poultry, the Duchess inspected the barns
and stables, where the labourers – mostly elderly people – made
their reports to her. An accident almost occurred. Suddenly, a large
colt ran out of the stable and jumped up at the Duchess, like a dog
standing on its hind legs. Fortunately Ochocki stopped the mischievous animal, and the Duchess gave the colt its usual portion of
sugar.

'It will do you an injury one day, grandmama,' said Starski,
displeased, 'who ever heard of caressing colts which will be horses
one day?'

'You always talk too sensibly,' the Duchess replied, stroking the
colt, which put its head on her shoulder and later ran after her, so
the labourers had to take it back to the stable. Even some cows
recognised their mistress, and greeted her with a stifled mooing, not
unlike muttering.

'A strange woman,' Wokulski thought, looking at the old lady
who knew how to arouse affection in animals, and even in human
beings.

After supper, the Duchess went to bed, and Mrs Wąsowska
proposed a stroll in the park. The Baron agreed, though reluctantly:
he put on a thick top-coat, wrapped a scarf around his neck, and
walked ahead with his fiancée, taking her by the arm. No one
knew what they were talking about, but they saw she was very
pale, and he had livid patches on his cheeks.

Towards eleven, all separated and the Baron, coughing, accompanied Wokulski to his room: 'Well, sir, have you taken a good
look at my fiancée? How beautiful she is! A positive Vestal, is she
not? And when that strange look of melancholy appears on her
sweet face – have you observed – then she's so charming that . . .
I'd give my life for her! I wouldn't tell this to anyone except you,
sir, but she produces such an effect on me that I don't know
whether I shall ever dare caress her . . . I only want to pray to her.
I'd kneel at her feet, sir, and look into her eyes, and be happy if she
would let me kiss the edge of her dress. Am I boring you?'

He coughed so hard that his eyes became bloodshot. After a rest,
he went on: 'I don't often cough, but today I've caught a slight

cold. . . . I'm not prone to catching a cold, except in autumn and New Year. Well, it will pass, for just yesterday I had Chalubinski and Baranowski in for a consultation, and they told me that if I take care of myself, I shall keep well . . . I also asked them (this is between you and me) what they thought of my marriage. But they said that marriage is such a personal thing . . . I pointed out to them that Berlin doctors told me long ago to marry. This made them think, and one of them immediately said: "It's a pity you didn't carry out their advice at once." So I may tell you, sir, that I've now decided to do it before Advent.'

He had another fit of coughing. He rested, then suddenly asked Wokulski, in altered voice: 'Do you believe in a future life?'

'Why?'

'You see, sir, faith in that protects a man from despair. I, for instance, understand that I myself shall not be as happy I might once have been, nor can I give her complete happiness. The only consolation I have is the thought that we shall meet in another, better world, where we shall both be young. For she,' he added, thoughtfully, 'will belong to me there too, since Holy Writ teaches us that what binds two people on earth will bind them in Heaven. Perhaps you, like Ochocki, don't believe this? But you must admit that . . . sometimes you do, and you won't give your word that it won't be so.'

A clock in the next room struck midnight: the Baron jumped up in agitation, and bade Wokulski goodnight. A few minutes later his mounting cough could be heard at the far end of the wing. Wokulski opened the window. Calcutta hens were loudly crowing near the kitchen, in the park an owl hooted: one star broke from the sky and fell somewhere behind the tree. The Baron went on coughing.

'Is everyone in love as blind as he?' Wokulski thought, 'for it's clear to me, and probably to everyone else, that this young woman doesn't love him at all. Perhaps she's in love with Starski . . . I don't understand the situation,' he went on, 'but mostly probably it is like this: that young woman is marrying for money, and Starski is encouraging her in this with his theories. Perhaps he's in love with her himself? Not likely . . . Rather, he's already bored by her, and is forcing her into the marriage . . . Unless – but no, that would be monstrous. Only street women have lovers who trade in them. What a stupid notion! Starski may well be her friend, and is advising her what he himself believes. After all, he openly says that he himself will only marry a rich woman. That principle is as good as any other, as Ochocki would say. The Duchess rightly said that today's young people have strong heads and cold hearts. Our example has put them off sentimentality, so they believe in the power of money, which, moreover, is proof of sound sense. No,

Starski is witty, perhaps something of a spendthrift, an idler, but he doesn't lack spirit.

'Though I wonder why Mrs Wąsowska is so set against him? She may have a weakness for him, and since she also has money, they'll end by marrying. But what concern is it of mine?

'I wonder why the Duchess didn't mention Izabela today? Well, I won't inquire. They'd immediately start talking about us.'

He fell asleep, and dreamed he was the Baron in love, with Starski playing the part of the friend of the family. He woke up, and smiled. 'That would cure me at once,' he murmured.

In the morning he went fishing again with Felicja and Ochocki. When everyone gathered for lunch at one o'clock, Mrs Wąsowska exclaimed: 'Will you have them saddle two horses for us? For Mr Wokulski and me?' Then, turning to Wokulski, she added: 'We leave in half an hour. From now, you begin your service with me.'

'Just the two of you?' inquired Felicja, blushing.

'Would you like to ride with Julian?'

'Oh, I say! Please don't dispose of my person for me,' Ochocki protested.

'Fela will remain with me,' the Duchess interposed.

Blood and tears flowed into the eyes of Felicja. She glanced at Wokulski, first with anger then with contempt, and finally ran out of the room on the pretext of getting a handkerchief. When she returned, she looked like Mary, Queen of Scots in the act of forgiving her executioners, and her nose was red.

Punctually at two, a couple of fine mounts were brought around. Wokulski already waited at one, and a few minutes later Mrs Wąsowska appeared. She had on a close-fitting riding-habit, as shapely as Juno, with her chestnut hair done in a bun. She placed one foot in the groom's hand and sprang nimbly into the saddle. The riding-crop quivered in her hand.

Meanwhile, Wokulski was coolly adjusting the reins. 'Hurry, sir, hurry!' she cried, drawing the reins on her horse so that it performed a circle and rose on its haunches: 'Once outside the gates, we will gallop . . . *Avanti Savoia!*'

Wokulski finally mounted, Mrs Wąsowska impatiently cut her horse with the crop and they rode out of the yard. The road followed a linden alley a mile long. Flat fields lay on both sides, here and there were haystacks big as huts. The sky was clear, the sun cheerful, from afar could be heard the clatter of a threshing machine. They cantered for several minutes. Then Mrs Wąsowska put the handle of her crop to her lips, leaned forward and flew off at a gallop. The veil of her hat fluttered behind her like ash-coloured wings: '*Avanti! Avanti! . . .*'

They galloped several minutes. Suddenly the lady brought her horse to a halt: she was flushed and breathless. 'Enough,' she said, 'let's ride more slowly now.' She rose in her saddle and gazed attentively towards blue woods visible in the east. The alley came to an end: they rode on across fields where pear trees and hay-ricks stood green. 'Tell me, sir,' she said, 'is it a great pleasure to make a fortune?'

'No,' said Wokulski, after a moment's reflection.

'But spending it?'

'I don't know.'

'You don't know? Yet people say great things of your fortune. They say you have sixty thousand a year.'

'I have a good deal more today, but I spend very little.'

'How much?'

'Some ten thousand.'

'That's a shame. I decided to spend a great deal of money last year. My plenipotentiary and accountant assure me I spent twenty-seven thousand . . . I overdid things, but I didn't dispel my ennui. Today I thought I would ask you the effect of spending sixty thousand a year. But you don't spend so much . . . That's a pity. Do you know what? Spend sixty thousand – or no, a hundred thousand a year – then tell me whether it has any effect, and what kind. Will you?'

'I can tell you in advance that it won't.'

'No? Then – what is money for? If a hundred thousand a year doesn't bring happiness, what does?'

'You could have it on a thousand a year. Everyone carries happiness within himself.'

'Or can get it for himself?'

'No, madam.'

'Do you say that, you unusual man?'

'Even if I were unusual, it's from suffering, not happiness. And still less through spending money.'

A dust-cloud appeared near the wood, Mrs Wąsowska watched it a moment, then suddenly cut at her horse and turned to the right, into the fields and off the road: '*Avanti! Avanti! . . .*' They rode ten minutes, then Wokulski drew rein. He had stopped on a hill, above a meadow as beautiful as a dream. What was there in it that was beautiful? The greenness of the grass, the curving flow of the stream, or the trees leaning over it, or the clear sky? Wokulski did not know.

But Mrs Wąsowska was not interested. She was riding headlong uphill, as if seeking to impress her companion by her courage. When Wokulski rode slowly after her, she turned her horse and impatiently exclaimed: 'Come, sir – are you always so tedious? I didn't bring you for a ride in order to yawn, after all. Pray entertain me, immediately!'

'Immediately? Very well. Mr Starski is a very interesting man.'

She leaned backwards as though about to fall off, and kept looking into Wokulski's eyes: 'Ah!' she cried with a laugh, 'I didn't expect to hear such a banal remark from you . . . Mr Starski interesting? To whom? To such geese as Ewelina, perhaps, but to me, for example, he has ceased to be.'

'And yet. . . .'

'No "And yets". . . . He was at one time, when I intended to become the victim of marriage. Fortunately, my husband was civil enough to die early, and Mr Starski is so uncomplicated that with my experience, I saw through him within a week. He always wears that beard à la Archduke Rudolph, and has the same manner of seducing women. His glances, his hints, his mysteries are as familiar to me as the cut of his jacket. He always avoids girls without dowries, is cynical with married ladies, and sighs to eligible young women who are about to get married. Good God, how many such have I met in my life! Today I need something new.'

'In that case, Mr Ochocki . . .'

'Oh yes, Ochocki is interesting, and might even be dangerous – but for that to happen, I'd need to be born again. He's a man not of this world, while I belong to it heart and soul. How naive he is, and how splendid! He believes in ideal love, he'd shut himself up in his laboratory and be certain it would never betray him. No, he's not for me.'

Suddenly she exclaimed: 'What is wrong with this saddle? The girth has come unfastened . . . Pray look.'

Wokulski jumped off his horse: 'Will you dismount?' he asked.

'Certainly not. Please look at it.'

He went around to the right side – the girth was tightly fastened: 'Not there! Here! Something is wrong, near the stirrup.'

He hesitated, then drew aside her riding-habit and put his hand under the saddle. Suddenly the blood rushed to his head: the widow had moved her leg in such a way that her knee touched Wokulski's face: 'Well?' she asked impatiently, 'what is it?'

'Nothing,' he replied, 'the girth is tight.'

'Sir, you kissed my leg!' she exclaimed.

'No!'

She struck her horse with the crop and flew off at a gallop, exclaiming: 'A fool – or a stone!'

Wokulski remounted slowly. Inexpressible remorse seized his heart when he thought: 'Does Izabela go riding? And who adjusts her saddle?'

When he caught up with Mrs Wąsowska, she burst out laughing: 'Ha ha ha! You are priceless!' Then she began speaking in a low, metallic voice: 'A fine day has been written in the history of my life – I played the role of Potiphar's wife, and found a Joseph . . . Ha ha ha! Only one thing alarms me: that you don't appreciate how I can turn a man's head. At a moment like that, a hundred other men in your place would have protested they couldn't live without me, that I have robbed them of their peace of mind, and so forth . . . But he says "No" brusquely . . . For that one "No" you ought to gain a seat in the kingdom of Heaven among the innocents. A high chair, with a bar in front! Ha ha ha!'

She rocked to and fro on her saddle, laughing.

'But what would you have done, had I replied like the rest?'

'I'd have had one more triumph.'

'And what would that have meant to you?'

'I am filling up the emptiness of my life. Out of ten men who propose to me, I choose the one who seems most interesting, I play with him, dream of him . . .'

'And then?'

'I consider the next ten, and choose one.'

'How often?'

'Once a month. What would you?' she added with a shrug, 'this is love in the age of steam and electricity.'

'I see. This even reminds me of the railroad.'

'Because it rushes along like a storm, and gives off sparks?'

'No. It travels fast, and picks up as many passengers as it can.'

'Mr Wokulski!'

'I did not wish to offend you, madam: I only said what I heard.'

Mrs Wąsowska bit her lip. They rode in silence for a time. After a while, Mrs Wąsowska spoke: 'I have placed you, sir: you're a pedant. Every evening – I don't know when, but certainly before ten o'clock – you do your accounts, then you go to bed, but before going to sleep, you say your prayers and repeat aloud: "Thou shalt not covet thy neighbour's wife." Isn't it so?'

'Pray continue, madam.'

'I'll say no more, for talking to you bores me. Ah, this world brings nothing but disappointment! When we put on our first long dress, when we go to our first ball, when we first fall in love – then it seems to us that here is something new. But after a while we realise that it has already happened before, or is nothing. I remember last year, in the Crimea, a party of us were travelling along a very wild road, along which bandits once lurked. And just as we were talking about it, two Tatars came out from behind a cliff . . . Good God! I thought, will they kill us, for their expressions were terrible, though they were handsome men. And do you know, sir, what they proposed? . . . They wanted to sell us some grapes! . . . Grapes, sir! They were selling us grapes, and I was thinking about bandits. I wanted to knock them down in my anger, truly. Well, today you reminded me of those Tatars, sir. . . The Duchess told me a few weeks ago that you're a very unusual man, quite different from the rest, but now I see you're the most ordinary of pedants. Aren't you?'

'Yes.'

'You see, I know men. Perhaps we might gallop again? Or – no, I don't feel like it, I'm tired. Oh, if only I could meet a really new man once in my life!'

'What would happen?'

'He'd have a new way of behaving, he'd say new things to me, sometimes vex me to distraction, then take mortal offence and of course have to apologise. Oh, he'd love me to distraction! I'd impress myself so on his heart and mind that he wouldn't be able to forget me, not even in his grave . . . Well – I understand that kind of love.'

'And what would you give him in exchange?' asked Wokulski, who was growing increasingly depressed and unhappy.

'I don't know! Perhaps I'd decide on some folly or other.'

'Now I'll tell you, madam, what this new man would obtain from you,' said Wokulski, spleen mounting within him. 'First he would acquire a long list of your former admirers, then another list of the admirers to come after him, and in the entr'acte he'd have the opportunity of checking . . . whether your saddle is firm.'

'That's vile!' cried Mrs Wąsowska, gripping her riding-crop.

'It's merely a repetition of what I heard from you, madam. If I speak too frankly, however, on such short acquaintance . . .'

'Not at all, please go on. Perhaps your impertinence will be more diverting than the frigid civility I know by heart. Of course a man like you despises women such as I. Well, speak up!'

'By your leave . . . In the first place, let's not use strong words which aren't suited to a horseback ride. There is no question of feelings between us, only of points of view. In my opinion, your view of love implies differences which can't be reconciled.'

'Oh?' the widow was surprised, 'but what you call differences, I can quite perfectly accord with life.'

'You mentioned frequent changes of lovers.'

'Call them admirers, please.'

'Then you want to find some unusual man or other who wouldn't forget you even in his grave. To my mind that can never be attained. With your extravagant views, you will never become economical, nor will an unusual man wish to fit in with several ordinary ones.'

'He may not be aware of them,' the widow interrupted.

'Ah, so we have deception, too – but it can only succeed if your hero is blind and stupid. Even if he were, would you have the courage to deceive a man who loved you so much?'

'Very well, so I would tell him everything, and add: "Remember Christ forgave Mary Magdalene, than whom I, after all, am less sinful, though I have hair as fine as hers. . ."'

'And that would suffice?'

'I think so.'

'But what if it didn't?'

'I'd leave him in peace and go on my way.'

'But first you'd impress yourself in his heart and mind so that he couldn't forget you, even in the grave!' Wokulski burst out. 'That's a fine world of yours . . . And how charming are women who, when a man surrenders his own soul to them in the best of faith, must glance at their watch so that he doesn't meet his predecessors, or interrupt those to come! Madam, even dough takes a long time to rise: is it possible to cultivate great feelings so hastily, and in such a market? Madam, pray be done with talk of great feelings: they'll prevent you from sleeping, and spoil your appetite. Why poison a man's life when you don't even know him? Why upset your own good temper? Better stick to your programme of rapid and frequent triumphs, which don't harm other people and fill your life for you somehow.'

'Is that all, Mr Wokulski?'

'I suppose so.'

'Now let me tell you something. All of you are scoundrels . . .'

'Another strong word . . .'

'Yours were stronger, sir. You are all wretches. When a woman, at a certain stage in her life, dreams of an ideal love, you mock her illusions and demand a flirtation, without which a girl is boring, and a married woman stupid. Not until she – thanks to your collective efforts – allows banal proposals to be made, glances at you fondly, presses your hand – only then does some medieval moralist in a cowl emerge from a dark corner and solemnly curse her, created though she is in the form and likeness of a daughter of Eve: "You are not allowed to love, you will never be truly loved, because you had the misfortune to be put up for market, and because you have no illusions left!" Yet who stole her illusions, if not you and your brothers? What sort of world is this, in which illusions are first stripped off and the naked body then sentenced to death?'

Mrs Wąsowska brought a handkerchief out of her pocket and began biting it. A tear sparkled on her eyelashes, and fell on to the horse's mane. 'Please ride on,' she cried, 'you are exasperatingly shallow. Be off . . . and send Starski to me: his impudence is more amusing than your priestly solemnity.'

Wokulski bowed and rode ahead. He was irritated and embarrassed.

'Where are you going, sir? Not that way . . . Ah, you are going to get lost, then tell everyone at dinner that I took you off the right road. Follow me, please.'

Riding a few paces behind Mrs Wąsowska, Wokulski thought:

'So that's the sort of world it is? Some women sell themselves to decrepit men, others treat human hearts as though they were veal. But she's a strange woman . . . For she is not wicked, and even has noble impulses.'

Half an hour later, they were riding across the hill from which the Duchess's manor was visible. Mrs Wąsowska suddenly turned her horse, glanced sharply at Wokulski and asked: 'Is it to be peace between us, or war?'

'May I be frank?'

'Pray do.'

'I am profoundly grateful to you. I've learned more in an hour from you than ever before in my whole life.'

'From me? You merely think so. I have a few drops of Hungarian blood in my veins, so when I'm on horseback I go mad, and talk nonsense. Mind, though – I don't withdraw a word of what I said, but you are wrong if you think you understand me. Now, kiss my hand; you really are interesting.'

She stretched out her hand, which Wokulski kissed, opening his eyes wide in amazement.

XXVI

Under the Same Roof

WHILE Wokulski and Mrs Wąsowska were squabbling or riding through the fields, Izabela arrived at Zasławek from the Countess's estate. The day before, she had received a letter by special messenger, and now, at the express wish of her aunt, she had arrived, though reluctantly. She was certain she would find Wokulski already at Zasławek, powerfully supported by the Duchess, so the sudden journey had seemed improper to her: 'Even if I am to marry him, some day,' she told herself, 'that is no reason why I should hasten to welcome him.'

But because her things were packed, the carriage ordered, and her personal maid already waiting on the front seat, Izabela decided to go. Farewells with her relatives were full of significance. Mr Łęcki, constantly agitated, dabbed his eyes; the Countess, slipping a velvet purse into her hand, kissed her on the brow and said: 'I shall neither advise nor dissuade you. You're a sensible girl, you know your position, so you must decide for yourself, and accept the consequences.'

What should she decide? What consequences was she to accept? The Countess did not explain.

This year's stay in the country was profoundly modifying some of Izabela's opinions: this was not brought about by the fresh air, however, nor the beautiful landscapes, but by events and the opportunity to ponder over them tranquilly. She had come here at the express request of her aunt, for the sake of Starski, who people said would inherit the Duchess's fortune. But after considering her grandson, the Duchess had declared that she would leave him at most, a thousand a year, which would certainly be useful to him in his old age. She decided to leave her entire fortune to illegitimate children and their unfortunate mothers.

Starski instantly lost all value in the Countess's eyes. He lost it in Izabela's by declaring he would not propose to a 'penniless girl', but preferred a Chinese or Japanese girl, providing she had some tens of thousands a year: 'It isn't worth risking one's future for anything less,' said he.

As he said this, Izabela stopped regarding him as a serious suitor. But because he sighed softly and glanced fleetingly at her as he said it, Izabela thought that handsome Kazio must have some romantic secret and that he was making a sacrifice in seeking a rich wife. For whom? Perhaps for her? Poor boy, but there was no help for it. Perhaps she would find a way to sweeten his sufferings one day, but now she must hold him at a distance. This was all the easier because Starski began to insinuate himself very strongly into the favours of wealthy Mrs Wąsowska, and to lurk at a distance around Ewelina Janocka, no doubt to erase the traces that he had once been in love with Izabela: 'Poor boy, but there's no help for it. Life has its duties, which we must carry out even though they are hard.'

In this manner Starski, perhaps the most suitable suitor for Izabela, was crossed off her list. He could not marry a poor woman, but had to seek a rich wife: these were two impassable abysses between them.

Her second suitor, the Baron, crossed himself off by becoming engaged to Ewelina. Izabela had felt a horror of the Baron as long as he had been trying to get into her good graces, but when he abandoned her so abruptly, she grew almost alarmed. Could it be that there were women in the world for whose favours it was possible to renounce her? Could it be that a time might come when even such aged admirers would abandon Izabela?

The ground seemed to be giving way underfoot and, influenced by the undefined alarms besieging her, Izabela spoke about Wokulski to the Duchess in quite benevolent terms. Who knows that she mightn't even have said: 'What is Mr Wokulski doing? I'm very sorry he may have taken offence on my account. Sometimes I reproach myself for not behaving towards him as he deserved.'

She cast down her eyes and blushed so that the Duchess thought it essential to invite Wokulski to stay: 'Let them meet in the fresh air,' thought the old lady, 'and God will dispose. He's a jewel among men, and she's a good girl, so perhaps they will reach an understanding. For I'd wager he has a weakness for her.'

Some days later, Izabela's disagreeable feelings had begun to wear off, and she started to regret her remarks to the Duchess about Wokulski. 'He'll think me ready to marry him,' she said to herself.

Meanwhile, the Duchess had confided in Mrs Wąsowska, who was also staying with her, that Wokulski was coming to Zasławek, that he was a very rich widower, a man of the most unusual sort, who wanted to marry and who, perhaps, might fall in love with Izabela. Mrs Wąsowska listened to the remarks about Wokulski's fortune, widowed state and matrimonial qualifications in a very indifferent manner. But when the Duchess called him an unusual man, she grew curious: learning, however, that he might fall in love with Izabela, she recoiled like a pedigreed horse carelessly touched by a spur.

Mrs Wąsowska was the best of women, she had no thought of marrying again, and still less of stealing suitors from other women. But as long as she had her place in society, she could not allow a man to fall in love with any other woman except herself. They had the right to marry for money: Mrs Wąsowska was even prepared to help them do so – but as for adoration, that was her prerogative. Not because she considered herself very beautiful, but because she had a weakness in that respect.

Learning Izabela was to arrive that day, Mrs Wąsowska forced Wokulski to come riding. When she saw a dust-cloud on the high-road near the woods, raised by her rival's carriage, she turned aside into the fields and there made a great scene over her saddle, which failed.

Meanwhile, Izabela drove up to the palace. All the guests received her on the porch, and greeted her in almost identical terms: 'You know,' the Duchess whispered, 'Wokulski is here.'

'All we wanted was you,' cried the Baron, 'for Zasławek to be a perfect paradise. For we already have a very agreeable companion and eminent guest . . .'

Felicja Janocka took Izabela aside and, with tears in her voice, began: 'You know, Wokulski is here. Ah, if only you knew what sort of man he is . . . But I'd sooner say nothing, or you too will think I'm interested in him . . . Well, just fancy, Mrs Wąsowska told him to go riding with her, just the two of them . . . If you'd seen how the poor man blushed! So did I. For I went fishing with him too, though only as far as the pond, and Julian was with us. As for going out riding with him! Not for anything in the world! I'd sooner die . . .'

Having evaded these greetings, Izabela went to the room appointed her. 'That Wokulski aggravates me,' she murmured.

It was not really aggravation, but something else. On the way here, Izabela had felt dislike towards the Duchess for her urgent invitation, towards her aunt for ordering her to leave at once, and above all towards Wokulski. 'So do they really want to give me to this parvenu?' she asked herself. 'Ah, he will see what comes of this!'

She had been certain that the first person to welcome her would be Wokulski, and had decided to treat him with the utmost scorn. Yet Wokulski did not hasten to greet her, but had instead gone riding with Mrs Wąsowska. This affected Izabela in a disagreeable way, and she thought: 'She's still a flirt, even though she's thirty.'

When the Baron called Wokulski an eminent guest, Izabela felt something like pride, but it was very fleeting. When Felicja, in a pointed way, betrayed she was jealous of Wokulski, something like alarm seized Izabela, though only for a moment. 'Fela is a simpleton,' she told herself.

In a word: the contempt she had planned throughout her journey to demonstrate for Wokulski disappeared entirely in the face of such mixed feelings as slight anger, slight satisfaction and slight alarm. At this moment, Wokulski seemed to Izabela to be different from hitherto. He was not merely a haberdashery merchant, but a man who had just come back from Paris, who had a huge fortune and social contacts, whom the Baron admired and with whom Mrs Wąsowska flirted.

Hardly had Izabela time to change when the Duchess entered her room. 'Bela, my dear,' said the old lady, after kissing her again, 'why doesn't Joanna come to see me?'

'Papa is poorly, she doesn't want to leave him.'

'Pray don't say that. She won't come because she doesn't want to meet Wokulski, that's the secret,' said the Duchess, in some agitation. 'She likes him when he pours out money for her orphanages . . . I must tell you, Bela, that your aunt will never have any sense.'

Her former spleen arose in Izabela. 'Perhaps my aunt doesn't think it the thing to show such consideration for a tradesman,' she said, blushing.

'A tradesman! . . . A tradesman!' cried the Duchess, 'the Wokulskis are as genteel as the Starskis, or even the Zasławskis. As for being in trade . . . Bela, Wokulski has never sold what your aunt's grandfather sold . . . You can tell her so, when the opportunity arises. I prefer an honest tradesman to a dozen Austrian counts. I know perfectly well what their titles are worth.'

'But you will grant that birth . . .'

The Duchess smiled ironically: 'Believe me, Bela, birth is the last attribute of people who are born. As for purity of blood . . . Oh, Heavens, it is very fortunate that we don't concern ourselves overly much with checking such things. I may tell you that birth isn't worth mentioning to anyone as old as I. Such people usually remember grandfathers and fathers, and sometimes wonder why a grandson resembles a footman instead of his father. Much can be explained by looking closely.'

'Yet you are very fond of Mr Wokulski,' Izabela murmured.

'Yes, indeed,' the old lady replied firmly, 'I loved his uncle, all my life I have been unhappy simply because they took me away from him, and for the very same reasons as your aunt has for wanting to despise Wokulski today. But he won't let himself be trampled underfoot, indeed no!' said the Duchess. 'Anyone who can raise himself out of such poverty, who can make himself a fortune without a shadow of reproach, and can educate himself as he has done, need not care a jot for the opinions of drawing-room society. I am sure you know the part he is playing today, and the reason why he went to Paris. I assure you he won't go to the drawing-rooms, but that they will come to him, and the first will be your aunt, if she wants something. I know the drawing-rooms better than you, my child, and believe me, they will very soon find themselves in Wokulski's vestibule. He's no idler like Starski, no dreamer like the Prince, no half-wit like Krzeszowski. He's a man of action . . . The woman he chooses for his wife will be happy. Unfortunately, our young ladies are more demanding than they have experience or hearts. Not all, though . . . But forgive me if I have said anything unkind. Lunch will be ready at once.'

After this, the Duchess went out, leaving Izabela plunged in deep meditation. 'He could certainly take the Baron's place,' Miss Izabela told herself, 'the Baron is worn out and ridiculous, while people at least respect Wokulski. Kasia Wąsowska knew what she was about when she took him for that ride. Ha, we shall see whether Mr Wokulski can be faithful. He set a fine example of it by going riding with another woman! Very courtly of him!'

Almost at this moment, Wokulski came back from his ride with Mrs Wąsowska, and in the yard he saw the carriage with the horses being taken out. He was touched by some ill-defined premonition, but dared not ask: he even pretended not to see the carriage. He gave his horse to a lad in front of the house, and told another to bring water to his room. Just as he was about to inquire who had arrived, something stuck in his throat, and he could not utter a word. 'What folly,' he thought, 'even if it's she, what of that? She's a woman like Mrs Wąsowska, Felicja, Ewelina . . . And I am not like the Baron.'

But, thinking this, he felt that to him she was different from other women, and that if she were to ask him to, he would lay his fortune, even his life, at her feet. 'Folly! Folly!' he whispered, walking about his room, 'after all, here's her admirer Starski, with whom she agreed to spend a gay holiday. I recall those glances . . .'

Anger seethed inside him. 'Let us see, Izabela, what you are, and what you're worth! Now I'll be your judge,' he thought.

Someone knocked, an old footman came in. He glanced around the room and said, in a subdued voice: 'Her Grace told me to say Miss Łęcka is here, and that if you are ready, luncheon is served.'

'Tell Her Grace I am coming at once,' Wokulski replied.

When the servant had gone, he stood a moment at the window, looking into the park illuminated by slanting sun-rays, and at a lilac tree, on which birds were cheerfully chirruping. He gazed, but a dull fear imbued his heart as he wondered how he would greet Izabela: 'What shall I say, how will I look?' It seemed to him that all eyes would be upon them both, and that he would compromise himself by some tactless act: 'Didn't I tell her I'm the faithful servant of them both . . . like a dog! But I must go down . . .'

He left the room, returned, then once more entered the corridor. He approached the door slowly, step by step, feeling all his energy ebbing away, that he was a simpleton about to appear before a king. He took hold of the doorknob, then paused . . . Women's laughter resounded in the dining-room. There was a blackness before his eyes, he wanted to run away and have the servant tell them he was ill. Suddenly, he heard footsteps behind him, so pushed the door open.

He saw the entire company in the depths of the room, and first of all, Izabela talking to Starski. She was gazing at him in the same way, and he had the same ironical smile as that time in Warsaw . . . All at once, Wokulski regained his energy: a wave of anger struck his brain. He entered with head back, greeted the Duchess and bowed to Izabela, who blushed and gave him her hand: 'How are you? How is Mr Łęcki?'

'Papa has recovered somewhat . . . He sends you his regards.'

'I am much obliged for the kind thought. And the Countess?'

'My aunt is very well.'

The Duchess sat down in her chair: the others began taking their places at the table.

'Mr Wokulski, here, by me,' cried Mrs Wąsowska.

'With the greatest pleasure, if a soldier has the right to sit down in the presence of his commanding officer.'

'Has she already taken command over you, Stanisław?' asked the Duchess, with a smile.

'Yes, indeed. Such drilling doesn't often take place . . .'

'He is taking his revenge because I led him off the straight and narrow path,' Mrs Wąsowska interposed.

'I was sure it would be so, but never supposed it would happen so soon,' explained the Baron, displaying a fine set of false teeth.

'Pray pass the salt, cousin,' said Izabela to Starski.

'Of course . . . There, I've upset it, we shall quarrel.'

'Surely there's no risk of that,' Izabela replied, with diverting gravity.

'Have you two undertaken not to quarrel?' Mrs Wąsowska asked.

'We don't intend ever to apologise,' Izabela replied.

'Charming!' said Mrs Wąsowska, 'in your place, Kazio, I'd lose all hope at once.'

'Was I ever allowed to have any?' Starski sighed.

'Real happiness for both of us . . .' Izabela whispered.

Wokulski listened and watched. Izabela was speaking naturally, in a very tranquil manner, joking with Starski, who did not look at all mortified on that account. But he glanced sideways from time to time at Ewelina Janocka, who was whispering to the Baron, and who turned pale, then pink.

Wokulski felt a great weight lifted from his heart. 'Of course,' he thought, 'if Starski is interested in anyone here, it's Ewelina, and she in him.' At this moment joy and great cordiality towards the deceived Baron awoke within him. 'I'm not going to warn him,' he told himself. Then he added: 'Such pleasure at anyone else's misfortune is a very despicable feeling.'

Dinner ended, Izabela came to Wokulski. 'You know, sir,' she said, 'what my feelings were upon seeing you here? Remorse . . . I recalled that we were to have gone to Paris, the three of us – I, my father and you, and that of the three, fortune was only kind to you. At least you enjoyed yourself? For all three of us? You must surrender to me one-third of your experiences.'

'Suppose they were not happy?'

'Why not?'

'If only because you were not there, when we were to have been together.'

'But, to my certain knowledge, you know how to enjoy yourself without me,' Izabela retorted, and moved away.

'Mr Wokulski!' cried Mrs Wąsowska. But after a glance at him and Izabela, she said in a reluctant tone: 'But no – it doesn't matter. I'll let you off today. Ladies and gentlemen, let's walk in the park. Mr Ochocki . . .'

'Mr Ochocki is going to teach me meteorology today,' declared Felicja.

'Meteorology?' Mrs Wąsowska repeated.

'Yes . . . We are going up to his observatory now.'

'Do you intend to learn nothing but meteorology?' Mrs Wąsowska asked. 'In any event, I advise you to ask your grandmama what she thinks of this meteorology.'

'You are always making difficulties,' said Ochocki, crossly. 'You are permitted to go riding with me on impassable roads, but Felicja isn't even allowed to peep into the observatory.'

'Run along and peep, my dears – but let's be off to the park. Baron! Bela . . .'

They went out. First came Mrs Wąsowska with Izabela, then Wokulski, then the Baron and his fiancée, and finally Felicja and Ochocki, who gesticulated and exclaimed: 'You will never learn anything new, except a new and eccentric fashion in hats, or the seventh figure of a contre-danse, when some half-wit invents one. Nothing, ever!' he added, dramatically, 'because there will always be some creature . . .'

'Fie, Julian, how can you speak so?'

'Yes, some insufferable creature who considers it improper of you to come into the observatory with me.'

'But perhaps it really is wrong?'

'Wrong! To display your bosom is all right, to take singing-lessons from an Italian with dirty fingernails . . .'

'But, sir . . . If young ladies were continually alone with young men, they might fall in love.'

'What of it? Let them! Is it better that she shouldn't fall in love, and be stupid? You're a silly creature, Felicja.'

'Oh, sir . . .'

'Come, don't turn my head with your exclamations. Either you want to learn meteorology, and in that case let's go upstairs! . . .'

'But with Ewelina, or Mrs Wąsowska . . .'

'Oh, all right. Let's stop this comedy,' Ochocki concluded, thrusting his hands angrily into his pockets.

The young couple talked so loudly that they could be heard all over the park, much to the gratification of Mrs Wąsowska, who burst out laughing. When they fell silent, the whispering of the Baron and Ewelina came to Wokulski's ears.

'Isn't it true,' asked the Baron, 'that Starski is losing ground? Every day, madam, he loses ground. Mrs Wąsowska laughs at him, Izabela treats him with the utmost contempt, and even Felicja isn't interested in him. Haven't you noticed?'

'Yes,' his fiancée whispered softly.

'He is one of those young men whose entire adornment consists of the hopes of a large inheritance. Am I not right?'

'Yes . . .'

'But when his hope of a bequest from the Duchess fell through, Starski stopped being interesting. Isn't it so?'

'Yes,' replied Ewelina, with a deep sigh, 'I'm going to sit down here,' she said, in a louder voice, 'perhaps you would bring me my shawl . . . Forgive me . . .'

Wokulski glanced around. Ewelina had sunk to a bench, pale and tired, with the Baron fussing over her. 'I'll bring it directly,' he said. 'Mr Wokulski,' he added, noticing him, 'pray be kind enough to take my place. I'll hurry, and will be back in a moment.'

He kissed his fiancée's hand, and went off towards the palace. Not until now did Wokulski notice that the Baron had very thin legs, and did not control them very well.

'Have you known the Baron long?' asked Ewelina, 'let us walk a little, toward the summer-house . . .'

'I have only just had the pleasure . . .'

'He admires you greatly . . . He says it's the first time he has met a man so agreeable to talk to . . .'

Wokulski smiled. 'No doubt,' he said, 'because he talks all the time about you.'

Ewelina blushed a great deal: 'Yes, he is a very worthy man, he loves me very much. There's a difference of age between us, that's true – but what's wrong with that? Experienced women claim that the older a husband, the more faithful he is, and, after all, for a woman, her husband's attachment is everything – isn't it so? Each of us seeks love in life, and who could promise that I'll meet another man like him? There are younger men than he, better looking, perhaps even more talented; yet not one of them has ever told me with such sincere feeling that the ultimate happiness of his life is in my hands. Pray tell me – can one resist that, even though acceptance on my side requires some sacrifice?' She stopped in the alley, and looked into his eyes, uneasily awaiting a reply.

'I don't know, madam. It's a question of personal feeling,' he replied.

'I'm sorry you should answer me so. Grandmama says you are a man of great character: hitherto I never met a man of great character, and my own is very weak. I don't know how to resist anything, I'm afraid to refuse . . . Perhaps I'm doing wrong, or at least, certain people have given me to understand I'm doing wrong in marrying the Baron. Do you think so, too? Could you reject a person who said he loved you more than his own soul, or that without your love the brief remainder of his life would be passed in solitude and despair? If someone were falling into an abyss in your presence, and was shouting for help – wouldn't you give him your hand, and hold on until help came?'

'I'm not a woman, and have never been asked to restrict my life for someone else's sake, so I don't know what I'd do,' said Wokulski, indignantly. 'All I know is that, as a man, I wouldn't beg – not even for love. And I must also tell you,' he added to the woman who was watching him with parted lips, 'that not only I wouldn't ask, but I wouldn't even accept a sacrifice begged from someone's heart. Such gifts are only temporary, as a rule.'

Starski hurried up to them by a side path, very preoccupied. 'Mr Wokulski, the ladies are looking for you in the linden alley. My grandmama, Mrs Wąsowska . . .'

Wokulski hesitated what to do at this moment.

'Oh, pray don't concern yourself with me,' said Ewelina, pinker than ever, 'the Baron will be back directly, and the three of us will catch up with you.'

Wokulski bade them goodbye and walked away: 'A fine thing!' he thought, 'Ewelina is going to marry the Baron out of pity, and is flirting with Starski . . . I can understand a woman marrying for money, though it's a stupid way of earning a living. I can even understand a married woman who, after a happy life, suddenly falls in love and deceives her husband. Sometimes she's forced into it by the fear of scandal, her children, a thousand other things . . . But a young woman deceiving her fiancée is an entirely new spectacle.'

'Ewelina! . . . Ewelina!' cried the Baron, coming in Wokulski's direction. The latter suddenly turned and walked away in between the flower-beds: 'I wonder,' he murmured, 'what I'll say to him if he finds me? Why the devil did I step into this mud?'

'Ewelina! . . . Ewelina! . . .' the Baron cried, already much further away.

'A nightingale calling its mate,' Wokulski thought. 'And yet can one entirely condemn this woman? She herself admits she has no character and, in a lower voice, that she needs money which she hasn't got, but without which she, like a fish out of water, can't live. The unhappy creature marries a rich man. But at the same time her heart calls out within her, an admirer persuades her to get married, and both think that the old man's caresses won't spoil their own taste, so they think up a new invention – deception before marriage – and don't even try to patent it. After all, they may be virtuous enough to have agreed not to deceive him until after the wedding . . . Charming people! Society sometimes comes up with very odd products . . . And to think that such a thing might happen to any of us! Truly, one should mistrust poets when they praise love as the greatest happiness.'

'Ewelina! . . . Ewelina! . . .' cried the Baron, groaning.

'What a vile performance,' Wokulski thought, 'I'd sooner put a bullet through my head than marry such an idiot.'

In an alley near the farmhouse he met the ladies, including the Duchess and a chambermaid, carrying her basket. 'Ah, here you are,' said the old lady to Wokulski, 'that's good. Wait here, all of you, for Ewelina and the Baron, who will surely find her in the end,' she added, frowning slightly, 'and Kazia will visit the horses.'

'Mr Wokulski might also treat his horse to some sugar, as it bore him so well today,' interrupted Mrs Wąsowska, rather sulkily.

'Don't tease,' said the Duchess, 'men like riding, not coddling themselves.'

'Ungrateful things,' Mrs Wąsowska murmured, giving the Duchess her hand. They walked off, and soon disappeared through a gate. Mrs Wąsowska glanced back, but on seeing that Wokulski was watching her, she quickly turned away her head.

'Shall we look for the engaged pair?' asked Izabela.

'As you choose,' Wokulski replied.

'But perhaps it will be better to leave them alone? They say that happy people don't care for witnesses.'

'Were you never happy?'

'Me? . . . Of course. But not in the same way as Ewelina and the Baron.'

Wokulski looked at her attentively. She was pondering, as tranquil as the statue of a Greek goddess. 'No, this woman will not deceive me,' Wokulski thought.

They walked for some time in silence towards the wilder side of the park. From time to time, a window of the palace appeared between the old trees, gleaming with red flames of sunset.

'Was it your first visit to Paris?' Izabela asked.

'Yes . . .'

'It's a marvellous city, isn't it?' she exclaimed, suddenly looking into his eyes. 'Let people say what they choose, but Paris – even conquered – is still the centre of the world. Did it give you that impression?'

'It was very impressive. After a few weeks there I seemed to gain strength and energy. Not until I went to Paris did I really learn to be proud of the fact that I work for a living.'

'Pray explain . . .'

'It's very simple. Here, human labour produces poor results: we're a poor and neglected country. But there, work illuminates like the sun. The buildings, covered from roof to pavement in ornaments like valuable caskets . . . And those forests of pictures and statues, whole regions of machinery, and that chaos of factory and craftsmen's products! In Paris I realised that man only seems to be a frail, weak being. In reality, man is a creature of genius and an immortal giant, who can erect cliffs with as much ease as he creates from them something more delicate than lace.'

'Yes,' Izabela replied, 'the French aristocracy had the opportunity and the time to create masterpieces.'

'The aristocracy?' asked Wokulski.

Izabela came to a halt in the alley: 'Surely you don't want to claim that the galleries of the Louvre were created by the Convention or by manufacturers of Parisian haberdashery?'

'Of course not, but the magnates didn't create them either. They're the collective work of French builders, bricklayers, painters and sculptors from all over the world, who have nothing in common with the aristocracy. To crown idlers with the benefits and work of men of genius, or even only working men – that's capital!'

'Idlers and aristocracy?' cried Izabela. 'I think that phrase is more forceful than just.'

'May I ask you a question?' Wokulski inquired.

'Pray do . . .'

'First, I withdraw the word "idlers", if it offends you, but then . . . Pray show me a man in the sphere we are speaking of who has done something? I know some two hundred of these men, and they're acquaintances of yours too. And what do they all do, from the Prince – the most excellent person in the world – though in his case, it may be explained by his age, down to . . . well, even Mr Starski, who can't justify his everlasting holidays by possessing a fortune.'

'My young cousin? He has surely never tried to serve as an

example of anything. Besides, we aren't talking about our aristocracy, but about the French.'

'And what do they do?'

'Oh, Mr Wokulski, they have done a great deal. In the first
place, they created France, they were her knights, her leaders,
ministers and priests. Finally, they collected the art treasures you
admire so.'

'Please tell me, now – they gave a great many orders, and spent a
great deal of money, but someone else created both France and the
art. They were created by poorly paid soldiers and sailors, by
farmers and craftsmen burdened by taxation, and finally by artists
and scholars. I'm an experienced man, I assure you it's easier to
plan than to execute, and easier to spend money than to make it.'

'You're an irreconcilable foe of the aristocracy.'

'No, madam, I cannot be an enemy of those who do me no
harm. But I think they occupy privileged places without earning the
right to them, and that they preach contempt for work in society,
and admiration for idle extravagance to maintain their own places.'

'You're prejudiced, since even this idle aristocracy – as you call it
– plays an important part in the world. What you call extravagance
is really comfort, pleasure and polish, which the lower orders learn
from the aristocracy, and so grow civilised themselves. I have heard
from very liberal people that there must be classes in society that
cultivate science, art and refined manners – first, so that others may
take living examples from them, and then to provide encouragement for noble actions. So in England and France more than one
man, even of low birth, providing he acquires a fortune, will first of
all establish a house for himself in order to invite persons of good
society, and then he tries to behave so that he himself is accepted.'

A powerful flush appeared on Wokulski's face. Izabela noticed
this without looking, and went on: 'Finally, what you call the
aristocracy, and what I call the upper class, is a good race. Perhaps a
certain part of it idles too much: but when anyone of that class sets
about doing something, he is at once marked by energy, good sense
and nobility. Excuse me for quoting what the Prince has often said
to me about you: "If Wokulski were not a fine gentleman, he
wouldn't be what he is today."'

'The Prince is mistaken,' Wokulski replied drily. 'What I have,
and what I know weren't given to me by genteel birth, but by hard
work. I've done more, so I own more than others.'

'But could you have done more if you'd been born someone
else?' Izabela asked. 'My cousin Ochocki is a scientist and democrat
like you, and despite that he believes there are good and bad races
of men, as does the Prince. He quotes you as proof of inheritance:
"Wokulski," he says, "has won success from destiny, but his tough-
ness of spirit comes from his breeding."'

'I am very grateful to all those who do me the honour of including me in some privileged race,' said Wokulski, 'but I shall never believe in privilege without work, and shall always set the benefits to society of the low-born higher than any well-bred pretensions.'

'Don't you think there is benefit to society in the cultivation of refined feelings and elegant manners?'

'Of course, but that role in society is played by women. Nature gave them more sensitive hearts, more lively imaginations, more subtle minds – it is they, not the aristocracy, who preserve elegance, kindliness in manners in everyday life, and can arouse the most elevated feelings in us. Woman is the lamp whose light gilds the road of civilisation. She is the unseen source of actions requiring unusual effort or strength.'

Now Izabela blushed. They walked on for a time in silence. The sun had already set, and the moon's scythe was gleaming in the west, between the trees. Wokulski, lost in thought, was comparing the two conversations of the day, one with Mrs Wąsowska, the other with Izabela: 'How different these two women are! . . . And was I not right to attach myself to this one?'

'May I ask you a question that troubles me?' asked Izabela suddenly, in a soft voice.

'Pray do . . .'

'Is it not true that when you left for Paris you were very offended with me?'

He wanted to reply that it had been worse than offence, for it had been the suspicion of deceit, but said nothing.

'I feel guilty towards you . . . I suspected you . . .' she began.

'Of malversions in acquiring your father's house through money-lenders?' Wokulski asked, smiling.

'Oh no!' she replied vivaciously, 'on the contrary, I suspected you of a very Christian action, which I couldn't have forgiven in anyone else. For a time I thought you had bought our house . . . and paid too dearly for it.'

'Surely your mind is at rest now?'

'Yes. I know that the Baroness Krzeszowska wants to pay ninety thousand for it.'

'Really? She has said nothing to me, though I can foresee what will happen.'

'I am so pleased you lost nothing, for . . . now I can thank you with my whole heart,' said Izabela, giving him her hand. 'I understand the significance of what you did. My father would have been abused or cheated by the Baroness, but you saved him from ruin, perhaps from death. One doesn't forget such things.'

Wokulski kissed her hand.

'It's dark already,' she said awkwardly. 'Let us go back to the palace. Surely everyone else has left the park.'

'If she isn't an angel, then I'm a swine,' Wokulski thought.

Everyone was already in the palace, where supper was soon served. The evening passed gaily. Towards eleven, Ochocki took Wokulski to his apartment. 'Well?' Ochocki said, 'I hear that you and my cousin Izabela have been talking about the aristocracy. Did you convince her, sir, that they are *canaille*?'

'No. Izabela defends her opinions very well. How splendidly she talks!' Wokulski replied, trying to conceal his confusion.

'No doubt she told you that the aristocracy cultivate the sciences and arts, that they are the guardians of refined manners and that their attitude is the aim towards which our democrats are striving and are ennobled . . . I keep hearing these arguments: I've had enough of them.'

'At the same time, you yourself believe in good breeding,' said Wokulski, painfully touched.

'Naturally . . . But this good breeding must be continually renewed, otherwise it soon goes bad,' Ochocki replied. 'Well, goodnight, sir. I must see what the barometer reads, for the Baron's bones ache, and tomorrow we may have rain.'

Scarcely had Ochocki left him than the Baron appeared in Wokulski's room, coughing, feverish, but all smiles. 'Ah, very nice,' he said, and his eyelids twitched nervously, 'very nice . . . You betrayed me, sir. You left my fiancée all alone in the park . . . I'm joking, joking,' he added, pressing Wokulski by the hand, 'all the same, I could rightly be vexed with you, were it not that I came back quite soon and . . . just then met Mr Starski, who was coming in our direction from the other end of the alley.'

Wokulski flushed like a boy for the second time that evening. 'Why did I get involved in this net of intrigue and deceptions?' he thought, still irritated by Ochocki's words.

The Baron coughed and, after a rest, went on in a lower voice: 'Pray do not suppose, sir, that I am jealous of my fiancée. That would be despicable . . . She's not a woman, but an angel, for whom I would at any moment sacrifice my entire fortune, my life . . . What am I saying? I'd place my eternal life in her hands, just as confidently as I believe the sun will rise tomorrow. I may not see it, for each of us is mortal, goodness knows. But of her I have no fear, not a shadow of fear, I give you my word of that, Mr Wokulski. I wouldn't believe my own eyes, not to mention any suspicions or hints,' he included, more loudly.

'But,' he began again after a few moments, 'that Starski is a horrible person. I wouldn't say this to anyone else, but do you know how he behaves with women? Do you think he sighs, flirts, begs for a kind word, for a touch of the hand? No, sir: he treats them like females in the most brutal manner. He acts on their nerves by his talk, his looks . . .'

The Baron broke off, his eyes bloodshot. Wokulski suddenly said, sharply: 'Who knows, Baron, but that Starski isn't right? We're taught to regard women as angels, and we treat them so. But if they are primarily females, then we look even more stupid and feeble in their eyes than we are, and Starski must triumph. He's the master of the cashbox who also possesses the real key to the lock, Baron!' he concluded with a laugh.

'You say this, Mr Wokulski?'

'I do, sir, and sometimes I wonder whether we don't adore women too much, whether we don't treat them too seriously: more seriously, more ceremoniously than we should.'

'Ewelina is one of the exceptions!' cried the Baron.

'I don't deny that there are exceptions, but who knows whether a man like Starski hasn't discovered a general law?'

'Perhaps,' said the Baron, irritated, 'but the law doesn't apply to Ewelina. If I defend her – or rather, don't wish her to know Starski, since she can defend herself, it's merely because a man like that shouldn't spoil her pure mind with his phrases . . . Well, you're bored. Excuse me for the visit, at such an unsuitable time.'

The Baron went out, closing the door quietly. Wokulski remained alone, plunged in melancholy thoughts: 'What was it Ochocki said about having had enough of Izabela's arguments? So what she said wasn't an outburst of feeling, but a lesson studied long ago? Her arguments, her excitement, even her emotions are only means by which well-bred young ladies bewitch fools like me?

'But perhaps he's in love with her and wishes to discredit her in my eyes? Well, if he loves her, why should he discredit her? Let him speak up, and let her choose . . . Of course, Ochocki's chances are better than mine: I haven't lost my senses to the point of not appreciating that . . . Young, handsome, talented – ha! Let him choose: fame, or Izabela . . .

'Besides,' he went on to himself, 'what's it to me if Izabela always uses the same arguments? She isn't the Holy Ghost, to think up new ones every time, nor am I so unusual that it would be worth her while to strive for originality. Let her say what she likes . . . What's more important is the fact that general laws about women don't apply to her. Mrs Wąsowska is first and foremost a pretty female of the species, but not her . . .

'Didn't the Baron say the same thing of his Ewelina?'

The lamp went out. Wokulski quenched it, and threw himself into bed.

For the next two days it rained, and the guests at Zasławek did not go out. Ochocki took to his books and hardly ever showed himself; Ewelina suffered from migraine; Izabela and Felicja read French magazines, and the rest of the company, led by the

Duchess, played whist. On one occasion, Wokulski noticed that Mrs Wąsowska, instead of indulging in a flirtation with him, for which opportunities kept arising, behaved very indifferently. He was struck, however, that when Starski tried to kiss her hand, she hastily drew it away, and told him, crossly, never to dare to do it again. Her anger was so sincere that Starski himself was surprised, and embarrassed, while the Baron, though his cards were not going well, was in an excellent humour. 'Would you allow me to kiss your hand?' he asked, some time after this incident.

'You – of course,' she replied, giving him her hand. The Baron kissed it as though it were a relic, glancing triumphantly at Wokulski, who thought that his titled friend really had little reason for over-much satisfaction.

Starski was gazing at his cards so intently that he appeared not to notice what had happened.

On the third day it cleared up, and the fourth was so fine and dry that Felicja proposed a drive to pick mushrooms. That day the Duchess ordered lunch earlier and dinner later. Towards twelve-thirty, the brake drove up in front of the palace, and Mrs Wąsowska gave the signal to get in. 'Let's make haste and not waste time . . . Where's your shawl, Ewelina? Let the servants get into the brake and take the baskets. And now,' she added, glancing fleetingly at Wokulski, 'let each gentleman choose his lady . . .'

Felicja wanted to protest, but at this moment the Baron leaped to Ewelina, and Starski to Mrs Wąsowska, who bit her lip, said: 'I never thought you would choose me again . . .' and gave Wokulski a withering look.

'We, cousin, shall keep together,' Ochocki cried to Izabela, 'but you will have to sit on the box, for I'm going to drive.'

'Mrs Wąsowska won't let you, for you will overturn us,' exclaimed Felicja, to whom Fate had ordained Wokulski.

'Oh, let him drive, let him overturn us,' said Mrs Wąsowska, 'today I wouldn't care if we all got our legs broken . . . I pity the mushroom that gets into my hands.'

'I'm the first of them,' exclaimed Starski, 'if it comes to being devoured . . .'

'Very well, if you agree to have your head cut off first,' Mrs Wąsowska replied.

'I lost it long ago . . .'

'Not before I noticed . . . But let us be off . . .'

XXVII

Woods, Ruins, Enchantments

THEY set off. The Baron, as usual, was whispering to his fiancée, Starski flirting outrageously with Mrs Wąsowska, who accepted it cordially enough, to Wokulski's surprise, and Ochocki drove the four-in-hand. This time, however, his enthusiasm was restrained by the vicinity of Izabela, to whom he kept turning.

'That Ochocki is a merry young fellow,' thought Wokulski, 'he says he's had quite enough of Izabela's arguments, but now he's talking to her and nobody else . . . Of course, he wants to prejudice me against her . . .' And he fell into a very dismal frame of mind, for he was certain that Ochocki was in love with Izabela, and that there was really no point in struggling against such a rival. 'Young, handsome, talented,' he told himself. 'She'd have neither eyes nor sense if, in choosing between us, she didn't give him priority. But even if she did, I'd have to admit she has a noble nature to prefer Ochocki to Starski. Poor Baron, and his even more wretched fiancée, who is so obviously pining for Starski. She must have a very empty head and heart . . .'

He contemplated the autumn sunshine, the grey stubble and the ploughs slowly moving across the fallow earth and, with profound grief in his soul, he imagined for a moment that he had entirely lost hope and resigned his place by Izabela to Ochocki: 'What's to be done? What shall I do if she chooses him? It was my misfortune ever to have met her . . .'

They rose on to a hilltop where a distant landscape lay before them, consisting of several villages, woods, a river, and a small town, with a church. The brake swayed from side to side: 'Oh, what a splendid view!' cried Mrs Wąsowska.

'Like looking down from a balloon steered by Mr Ochocki,' added Starski, clutching the rail.

'Have you ever been in a balloon?' asked Felicja.

'Ochocki's balloon?'

'No, a real one . . .'

'Alas, never,' Starski sighed, 'though I can imagine at this moment that I'm flying in a very paltry one.'

'Mr Wokulski certainly has,' said Miss Felicja in a tone of the utmost conviction.

'Come, Felicja, what will you accuse Mr Wokulski of next?' Mrs Wąsowska scolded her.

'As a matter of fact, I have . . .' said Wokulski in surprise.

'You have? Oh, splendid,' cried Felicja, 'pray tell us all about it.'

'You have?' exclaimed Ochocki from the box, 'hey there, wait a moment, I'll join you.'

He tossed the reins to the groom, although they were driving downhill, jumped off the box and sat down in the brake opposite Wokulski. 'So you've flown in a balloon?' he repeated, 'where was it? When?'

'In Paris, but it was a captive balloon. Half a mile up, hardly any distance,' replied Wokulski, somewhat embarrassed.

'Pray go on . . . You must have had an enormous view. What did you feel?' said Ochocki. He was strangely altered: his eyes widened, a flush appeared on his face. Looking at him it was hard to doubt that at this moment he had forgotten Izabela. 'It must be a stupendous thrill . . . Go on, sir,' he insisted, pressing Wokulski's knee.

'The view really was magnificent,' Wokulski replied, 'because the horizon was many miles wide, and the whole of Paris and its surroundings looked like a relief map. But the trip wasn't agreeable: perhaps only the first time.'

'What were your impressions?'

'Odd . . . One thinks one is rising, then suddenly sees that one isn't moving oneself, but that the ground is falling rapidly away. It's such an unexpected and disappointing sight that . . . one feels like jumping out.'

Ochocki pondered and gazed before him at goodness knows what. Several times he seemed to want to jump out of the brake, and his companions, who were silent, apparently irritated him.

They drove into a field, followed by two servant-girls in a carriage. The ladies took baskets. 'And now, each lady, with her cavalier, is to go in a different direction,' commanded Mrs Wąsowska. 'Mr Starski, I warn you that today I'm in an excellent humour, and what that means – Mr Wokulski already knows,' she added, laughing excitedly, 'Mr Ochocki, Bela – into the woods, pray, and don't reappear until . . . you have picked a whole basket of mushrooms. Felicja!'

'I am going with Michalina and Joanna,' replied Miss Felicja hastily, glancing at Wokulski as though he were an enemy against whom she had to protect herself with the two servant-girls.

'Let us be off, cousin,' said Izabela to Ochocki, seeing that the company had already gone into the woods, 'but pray take my basket and fill it yourself, for I must admit it doesn't amuse me.'

Ochocki took the basket and threw it into the carriage. 'What are mushrooms to me?' he muttered sulkily, 'I've wasted two months fishing, picking mushrooms, entertaining ladies and such-like nonsense. Other men have been up in balloons. I was going to Paris, but the Duchess insisted I should have my holiday here. A fine holiday I've had! I've grown utterly stupid. I can't even think straight. I've lost my talents . . . Ah, confound the mushrooms! I'm so cross . . .'

He made a gesture, then put both hands into his pockets and walked off into the wood, head bent, muttering.

'A charming companion,' Izabela exclaimed to Wokulski with a smile. 'He'll be like this until the end of the holiday. I knew he'd be upset as soon as Starski mentioned balloons.'

'Thank Heaven for those balloons,' Wokulski thought, 'a rival like this for Izabela isn't dangerous.' And at this moment he felt very fond of Ochocki.

'I'm sure,' he said to Izabela, 'that your cousin will produce some great invention one day. Who knows – perhaps he will be an epoch in the history of mankind,' he added, thinking of Geist's projects.

'You think so?' Izabela replied, quite indifferently, 'perhaps . . . Yet my cousin is sometimes impertinent, which occasionally suits him, but then again he can be a bore, which doesn't suit even an inventor. When I look at him, an anecdote about Newton comes into my mind. He's supposed to have been a great man, isn't he? But what of it, when he was sitting with a young lady one day, took hold of her hand – would you believe it! – and began cleaning his pipe with her little finger! If a genius does that, I wouldn't thank you for a husband who was one . . . Let's walk a little into the woods, shall we?'

Each of Izabela's words fell into Wokulski's heart like a drop of sweetness: 'So she likes Ochocki – who doesn't – but won't marry him . . .'

They walked along a narrow path which formed the limit of two woods: to the right oaks and beeches grew, to the left were pinetrees. Mrs Wąsowska's red bodice gleamed between the pines from time to time, or the white veil of Ewelina could be seen. At one point the path forked, and Wokulski wished to turn aside, but Izabela prevented him: 'No, no,' she said, 'don't let's go that way, for we shall lose sight of the others, and the woods are only attractive to me when there are other people about. At this moment, for instance, I can understand them . . . Just look . . . Isn't that part like a huge church? The rows of pines are columns, there's a side nave, and there the great altar. Just look! Now the sun between the boughs looks like a Gothic window. What an extraordinary variety of sights! There you have a lady's boudoir, and those low bushes are her dressing-table. There's even a mirror, which yesterday's rain left behind. And this is a street, isn't it? Rather crooked, but a street all the same . . . And yonder is a market-place or square. Do you see it all?'

'I do, when you point it out,' Wokulski replied with a smile, 'but one needs a very poetic imagination to see the resemblances.'

'Really? Yet I've always thought myself the embodiment of prose.'

'Perhaps because you haven't yet had an opportunity to discover all your capabilities,' Wokulski replied, displeased because Felicja was approaching.

'What's this, aren't you picking mushrooms?' Felicja cried, 'they're marvellous: there are so many we haven't enough baskets and must empty them into the carriage. Shall I get you a basket, Bela?'

'No, thank you.'

'Or you, sir?'

'I don't think I could tell a mushroom from a toadstool,' Wokulski replied.

'Capital!' cried Felicja, 'I never expected such a retort from you . . . I'll tell grandmama, and shall ask her not to let any of the gentlemen eat mushrooms, or at least not the ones I pick.'

She nodded and walked off.

'You've vexed her,' said Izabela, 'that wasn't nice. She is well disposed towards you.'

'Felicja takes pleasure in picking mushrooms, I in listening to you talking about the woods.'

'That is very flattering,' said Izabela, blushing a little, 'but I'm sure my lectures will soon bore you. The woods aren't always beautiful in my eyes, sometimes they are terrible. If I were alone here, I should certainly not see any streets, churches or boudoirs. When I'm alone, the woods alarm me. They stop being a stage setting, and begin to be something I don't understand, and which I fear. The birds' voices are so wild, sometimes I hear a sudden cry of pain, or sometimes mockery, because I have come among monsters. Then each tree seems a living thing, which wants to enfold me in its branches and strangle me: each bush trips me up in a treacherous manner to prevent me getting away. And all this is the fault of my cousin Ochocki, who told me Nature wasn't created for the benefit of mankind. According to his theories, everything is alive, and is alive for its own sake.'

'He was right,' Wokulski murmured.

'How so? Do you believe that too? So you think this wood isn't meant for the use of people, but has some business of its own, no worse than ours?'

'I've seen immense forests, in which man only appears once in a generation, yet they flourished more than ours . . .'

'Don't say that! You degrade human values, and it's not in accord with Holy Writ. God gave man the earth to dwell on, and vegetation and animals for his food.'

'In a word, you think Nature should serve people, and people should serve the privileged and titled classes. No, madam. Both Nature and man live for themselves alone, and only those who possess more strength and who work more have the right to rule. Strength and work are the only privileges in this world.'

Izabela was vexed: 'You can say what you like, sir,' she declared, 'and here I believe you, for I see your allies all around us.'

'Will they never be your allies?'

'I don't know . . . Perhaps . . . I hear of them so often, nowadays, that, some day, I may come to believe in their power.'

They emerged into a field enclosed by hills, on which grew drooping pines. Izabela sat down on the stump of a felled tree, and Wokulski on the ground near her. At this moment Mrs Wąsowska appeared with Starski on the edge of the field. 'Bela,' she cried, 'won't you relieve me of this cavalier?'

'I protest,' Starski exclaimed, 'Izabela is quite content with her companion, and I with mine.'

'Are you, Bela?'

'Yes, she is,' Starski cried.

'So be it,' Izabela said, trifling with her parasol and gazing at the earth. Mrs Wąsowska and Starski disappeared over the hill, Izabela trifled more and more impatiently with her parasol. Wokulski's pulses were ringing like bells in his head. As the silence was lasting a little too long, Izabela broke it: 'Almost a year ago, I was at a September picnic, here. There were some thirty people from the neighbourhood. They lit a bonfire over there . . .'

'Did you enjoy yourself more than today?'

'No. I was sitting on this same tree-trunk . . . Something was missing . . . And, though this rarely happens to me, I was wondering what would happen in a year's time.'

'How strange,' Wokulski murmured, 'I, too, was living in a forest camp, more or less a year ago, though it was in Bulgaria. I was wondering whether I'd still be alive in a year's time.'

'And what else? What were you thinking of?'

'Of you.'

Izabela shifted uneasily, and turned pale. 'Me?' she asked, 'did you know me?'

'Yes. I've known you for several years, though sometimes it seems to me I've known you for centuries. Time expands enormously when we continually think of a person, awake and asleep . . .'

She rose from the tree-trunk as though to flee. Wokulski rose too: 'Pray forgive me if I have caused you any pain. Perhaps in your eyes, a man such as I hasn't any right to think of you. In your world, such a prohibition is possible. But I belong to a different world. In my world, the fern and the moss have as much right to look at the sun as the pines have, or . . . the mushrooms. So pray tell me outright, madam, whether I may or may not think about you? Today I shall ask nothing more.'

'I scarcely know you,' whispered Izabela, evidently confused.

'I ask nothing of you today. I'm only inquiring whether you regard it as offensive that I think of you – nothing more. I know the views of the class in which you were brought up towards men such as I, and I know that what I am saying at this moment might be called impertinence. So pray tell me frankly, and if there is such a great difference between us, then I will no longer strive for your favour . . . I'll leave today or tomorrow, without shade of resentment, indeed – completely cured.'

'Every man has the right to think . . .' Izabela replied, in still greater confusion.

'Thank you, madam. By that phrase you have shown me that, in your eyes, I stand no lower than the Messrs Starski, the marshals and such-like . . . I understand that even under these conditions, I still may never win your affection . . . That is still far off . . . But at least I know I have human rights, and from now on, you will judge me by my actions, not by titles I don't possess.'

'You are a gentleman, and the Duchess says you are as good as the Starskis, even the Zasławskis.'

'Indeed I am, even more so than many of the people I meet in the drawing-rooms. My misfortune is that, in your eyes, I'm also a tradesman.'

'Well, you don't have to be, that depends on you,' said Izabela, more boldly.

Wokulski considered this. At that moment the others began calling and hallooing in the wood, and within a few minutes all the company, with servants, baskets and mushrooms, appeared in the meadow.

'Let's go back,' said Mrs Wąsowska, 'mushrooms bore me, and it's time for luncheon.'

The next few days passed in a strange manner for Wokulski: had he been asked what they meant to him, he would surely have replied they were a dream of happiness, one of those periods in life for which, perhaps, nature brought man into the world.

An indifferent observer might have thought the days monotonous, even boring. Ochocki sulked from morning to night, glued together and launched ingenious forms of gliders. Mrs Wąsowska and Felicja read, or worked on an altar cloth for the local priest. Starski played cards with the Duchess and Baron.

So Wokulski and Izabela were entirely isolated, and even had to be together continually. They walked in the park or in the meadows, they sat under an ancient linden tree in the courtyard, but mostly they boated on the lake. He rowed, she from time to time threw a crust to swans which swam silently after them. More than one passer-by paused on the highroad and gazed in wonder at the unusual group formed by the white boat, with two people seated in it, and the two white swans with their wings raised like sails.

Later, Wokulski could not even recollect what they talked about at such moments. Mostly they were silent. Once, she asked him how snails could move under the surface of the water: then again – why do clouds have different colours? He explained, and it seemed to him he was gathering all nature from earth to sky in his arms and placing it at her feet.

One day it occurred to him that if she were to order him to plunge into the water, and perish, he would have died blessing her.

During these excursions on the lake and also during their walks in the park, and whenever they were together, he felt an immeasurable peace within him, and the whole world from east to west was full of tranquillity, in which even the rattle of carriages, barking dogs or rustling leaves were wonderfully beautiful melodies. He seemed no longer to be walking, but floating across an ocean of mystical bemusement, he was no longer thinking or feeling or desiring – only loving. The hours disappeared like lightning flashes that blaze and perish on a distant horizon. No sooner was it morning, than it was already afternoon, then evening – and a night, full of restlessness and sighs. Sometimes he thought the day had been divided into two unequal parts: a day briefer than the twinkling of an eye, and a night longer than the eternity of damned souls.

One day the Duchess summoned him: 'Be seated, Stanisław,' she said, 'well, are you enjoying yourself here?'

He shuddered like a man suddenly aroused. 'Me?' he asked.

'Are you bored?'

'I'd give my life for a year of such – boredom.'

The old lady shook her head. 'Sometimes one thinks so,' she replied. 'I don't know who it was that said man is happiest when he sees around him that which he carries within himself. But never mind asking why one is happy, providing one is. Forgive me if I awaken you.'

'Pray continue, madam,' he replied, involuntarily turning pale.

The Duchess was still gazing at him, shaking her head slightly:

'Well, you needn't think I shall awaken you with bad news. I'll do it in the ordinary way. Have you considered the sugar-factory they want me to build here?'

'Not yet.'

'Well, no hurry. But you've completely forgotten your uncle. And he, poor soul, lies not far from here, three miles away, at Zasław. Perhaps you might go there tomorrow? It's a pretty district, and there are the castle ruins. You might spend some time very pleasantly, and do something about the memorial stone. You know,' the old lady added, sighing, 'I've changed my mind. There's no need to demolish the stone near the castle. Leave it where it is, and arrange to have these words engraved on it: "In every spot, and at every moment . . ." You know them?'

'Yes, of course.'

'More people visit the castle than the cemetery, they will read it, and perhaps think of the final limits of everything in this world, even of love . . .'

Wokulski left the Duchess in great agitation: 'What did that conversation mean?' he wondered. Fortunately he met Izabela walking toward the lake, and forgot everything else.

Next day, the whole company went to Zasław. They passed woods, green hillocks, valleys with yellow paths. The region was pretty, the weather even better, but Wokulski, lost in unhappy thoughts, paid no attention to anything. He was no longer alone with Izabela as he had been the day before: he was not even sitting near her in the brake, but opposite to Felicja, and above all . . . But this was merely an illusion, he even smiled inwardly at his own premonitions. Starski seemed to be glancing at Izabela in a strange way, so that she blushed.

'Oh nonsense,' he told himself, 'why should she deceive me. I'm not even her fiancé . . .'

He roused himself, and was only slightly displeased that Starski was sitting next to Izabela. But only slightly . . . 'Well, after all, I can't prevent her,' he thought, 'from sitting with whom she chooses. And I won't degrade myself by jealousy which in any case is a vile feeling, and most often founded merely on appearances. Besides, if she and Starski wanted to exchange melting looks, they wouldn't behave so obviously. I'm a madman.'

A few hours later, they arrived. Zasław, formerly a small town but now only an insignificant settlement, stands in a valley surrounded by marsh-land. All the buildings are one-storeyed, wooden and old, apart from the church and former town hall. In the middle of the market-place, or rather square, filled with booths and taverns, stands a great pile of rubbish and a well, its ramshackle roof supported on four rotting posts. As it was the sabbath, the market was empty and all the booths shut. A mile outside the town, to the south, lay a group of hills. On one stood the ruins of the castle, consisting of two hexagonal towers from whose tops and windows was hanging copious vegetation: a group of old oak trees grew on another.

When the travellers halted in the market-place, Wokulski got out in order to call on the priest, while Starski took command. 'So we,' he said, 'shall go in the brake to those oaks, and eat what God provides and the cooks prepare. Then the brake can come back for Mr Wokulski.'

'No, thank you,' replied Wokulski, 'I don't know how long I'll be, and prefer to walk. In any case, I must visit the ruins too.'

'I'll come with you,' Izabela exclaimed, 'I want to see the Duchess's favourite stone,' she added in a lower voice, 'so please let me know how long you'll be.'

The brake moved off, Wokulski entered the presbytery and finished his business within fifteen minutes. The priest told him that no one in the town would object if an inscription were made on the castle stone, providing it was not indecent or impious . . . On learning it concerned a memorial for the late captain Wokulski, whom he had known personally, the priest offered to help facilitate the matter. 'We have here,' he said, 'a certain Węgiełek, a lively young scamp, partly a smith and partly a joiner, so perhaps he will be able to engrave on the stone. I'll send for him.'

Soon Węgiełek appeared, a fellow in his twenties, with a cheerful and intelligent face. On learning from the priest's servant that he might be able to earn some money, he had put on a grey top-coat with flaps and tails down to the ground, and had rubbed his hair copiously with grease.

As Wokulski was in a hurry, he bade goodbye to the priest and walked towards the ruins with Węgiełek. When they reached the settlement boundary, Wokulski asked the young man: 'Can you write well, my good man?'

'Indeed I can, sir. They've sometimes given me copying from the magistrate's court, though I haven't a light hand. And those verses the agent at Otrocz used to write to the forester's daughter were all my own work. He only bought the paper, and he still hasn't paid me forty groszy for my writing. And he also wanted curlicues . . .'

'Could you write on stone?'

'Concave, not convex? Why not? I'd undertake to write on iron, or even glass, and in any kind of letters you like – script, printed, Gothic, Hebrew . . . For it was I, without boasting, who painted all the shop boards in town.'

'And that Cracovian, hanging above the inn?'

'Of course.'

'And where did you see such a Cracovian?'

'Mr Zwolski has a carter who's from those parts, so I took a look at him.'

'And did you see that he had two left feet?'

'I beg pardon, sir, it's not feet people from the provinces take notice of but the bottle. When they see the bottle and the glass, then they'll reach Szmul's place and no mistake.'

Wokulski liked the enterprising lad more and more: 'Aren't you married yet?' he asked.

'No. I won't marry them that wear kerchiefs, and the ones that wear hats don't fancy me.'

'What do you do when there are no shop signs to paint?'

'Well, sir – a little bit of this, and a little bit of that, and sometimes nothing. Before, I went in for carpentry, and had more work than I could handle. In a few years I'd saved a thousand roubles. Then my place burned down, and I still haven't got over it. All the wood, the workshop, everything was reduced to ashes, and I can tell you, sir, that the hardest of my files melted just like pitch. When I looked at the heap of ashes, I was really angry, but today I'm sorry about it.'

'Did you rebuild? Do you have a workshop now?'

'Ah, sir . . . I've built a shed in the garden, so my mother has a place to cook, but the workshop . . . For that, sir, I'd need five hundred roubles cash, honest to God I would . . . Look how many years my late father had to slave before he could set up house and collect tools.'

They approached the ruins. Wokulski was meditating. 'Listen,' he said suddenly, 'I like you, Węgiełek. I'll be in this neighbourhood,' he added with a sigh, 'for another week or so. If you make a good job of the engraving, I'll take you to Warsaw for a time. There I'll see how good you are, and maybe something can be done about the workshop.'

The young fellow turned his head to left and right, eyeing Wokulski. Suddenly it occurred to him that this must be a very wealthy gentleman, perhaps even one of those gentlemen God sometimes sends to look after poor people, and he took off his cap.

'What is it? Put your cap on,' said Wokulski.

'My apologies, sir. Maybe I said something I shouldn't have said. People say that in the olden days . . . But now, sir, there are no such gentlemen. My late father said that he himself knew of a gentleman who took an orphan from Zasław, and made a great lady of her, and left so much money to the people that they built a new bell-tower.'

Wokulski smiled as he saw the lad's embarrassed expression, and he thought with a strange feeling that with his own annual income he might make a hundred more such as he happy: 'Money really is a great power, only one must know how to use it.'

They were already at the castle hill when Felicja's voice called; 'Mr Wokulski, here we are!'

Wokulski looked up and saw a cheerful fire among the oak trees, around which the company from Zasławek were sitting. A footman and chambermaid had set up the samovar a few paces away.

'Wait, I'll join you,' cried Izabela, rising from the carpet. Starski leaped to help: 'I'll come with you,' he said.

'No, thank you, I'll go down myself,' replied Izabela, withdrawing. Then she began to descend the steep path with as much grace and ease as though it were an alley in the park.

'My suspicions are vile,' Wokulski muttered. At this moment, a mysterious voice seemed to be ordering him to choose between the thousands like Węgiełek, who needed help, and this one woman coming down the hillside: 'But I've already made my choice,' Wokulski thought.

'I can't get up to the castle by myself, you will have to give me your hand,' said Izabela, stopping beside Wokulski.

'Perhaps the lady and gentleman will deign to take an easier path?' Węgiełek exclaimed.

'Lead the way!'

They encircled the hill and began climbing to its summit up the bed of a dried stream.

'What a strange colour these stones are,' cried Izabela, looking at pieces of limestone stained brown.

'Crude ore,' Wokulski replied.

'Oh no,' Węgiełek put in, 'that's not ore – but blood.'

Izabela drew back. 'Blood?' she echoed.

They halted on the hill-top, screened from the rest of the company by a broken-down wall. From here, they could see the castle courtyard, overgrown with thorns and barberries. Under one of the towers a huge block of granite was leaning against the wall.

'That's the stone,' said Wokulski.

'That stone? I wonder how they got it here? My good man, what were you saying about blood?' Izabela asked Węgiełek.

'It's an old story,' Węgiełek replied, 'my grandfather told it to me, and everyone around knows it.'

'Tell it to us,' Izabela insisted, 'I like hearing legends told in ruins. The castles of the Rhine are full of them.'

Węgiełek was not in the least put out by this request. Indeed, he smiled and began: 'In the olden days, when my grandfather used to go bird-catching in the oak-trees, water used to run over those stones we came up by. Now water only comes in the spring, or after heavy rain, but when my grandfather was young, it ran all year round. There was a stream here.

'And when grandfather was a boy, a big stone lay at the bottom of the stream, as if someone had used it to block a hole. And really there was a hole, which was a window into some vaults, where great treasures are hidden, the likes of which can't be found anywhere else in the whole world. Among these treasures slept a young lady, maybe a princess, on a bed of pure gold, very pretty and richly dressed. And the reason why she sleeps is that someone drove a gold pin into her head, out of malice or hatred perhaps: goodness knows. So she sleeps and will never wake up until someone draws the pin out of her head and marries her. But that's hard to do, and even dangerous, for monsters guard the treasures and the young lady too. I know well what they're like, because until my house burned down I had a tooth as big as my fist, which my grandfather found in this very spot – that's the truth, I'm not telling a lie. And if one tooth alone was as big as my fist (I saw it myself, and often held it in my hand), then the head must be big as a stove, and the whole person the size of a barn.

'People had long known,' Węgiełek went on, 'of the young lady and her treasures: because twice a year, at Easter and at St John's Eve, the stone on the bottom of the stream would move, and if anyone were standing over it, he might see down into the pit, and the wonderful things there.

'One Easter (my grandfather was not even born yet), a young smith came here from Zasław. He stood by the stream and wondered 'Why shouldn't I see the treasures? I'd get at them immediately, through the smallest of holes. I'd load my pockets, and wouldn't have to puff my bellows any more.' No sooner had he thought this that all at once the stone moved aside, and the smith saw heaps of money, pure gold dishes and splendid clothing, just like you see at a fair . . .

'But when he set eyes on the sleeping lady, who was so beautiful, the smith froze in amazement. She was fast asleep, but tears were streaming from her eyes, and each one that fell, whether on her nightdress or bed or floor changed at once into a jewel. She was asleep and sighing with pain from that pin: whenever she sighed, the leaves on the trees over the stream rustled in sympathy.

'The smith wanted to go down into the vault: but because the time had passed, the stone closed again, so that the stream flowed over it. From that day on, my smith couldn't settle down at all. His work flagged. Wherever he looked, he saw nothing but the glassy stream and the young lady within it, shedding tears. Soon he pined away, for something was continually gripping his heart in burning tongs. It bemused him. When at last he could bear his longing no more, he went to a woman who knew about herbs, gave her a silver rouble and asked for help.

'"Well now," said the woman, "there's nothing else for it, but you must wait for St John's Eve, and when the stone moves again, you must climb into the pit. If you take the pin from her head, she will wake, you will marry her, and you'll be a great gentleman such as the world has never seen. But don't forget me then, that I advised you well. And remember this: when the monsters surround you and you take fright, cross yourself at once and in God's name . . . It's all a question of your not taking fright; evil cannot fasten on a man who's not afraid."

"'And tell me," said the smith, "how does it show that a man is seized with fright? . . ."

"'Like that, are you?" said the woman. "Well, off with you to the pit, and when you return, remember me."

'The smith went to the stream every day for two months, and didn't stir from it for a week before St John's Eve. Then the time came. At midday the stone moved, and my smith jumped into the pit with his axe in hand. My grandfather used to say that what happened to him then would make anyone's hair stand on end. Monsters surrounded him, and another man would have died just for looking at them. There were bats big as dogs, which flapped their great wings at him. Then a toad big as a rock stood in his path, then a snake caught him by the legs, and when the smith hit it, the snake started weeping like a human being. There were wolves so fierce that when foam dropped from their muzzles, it burst into flames and holes burned in the rocks.

'All these monsters jumped on him, seized him by the jacket and sleeves, but not one dared harm him. For they saw that the smith was not afraid, and evil disappears like a shadow before a man who isn't afeard. "Smith, you will perish here!" cried the monsters, but he only gripped his axe and spoke to them – excuse me, but in such a way as would be shameful to repeat to a lady and gentleman.

'At last my smith reached the golden bed to which the monsters had no access, but only stood all around gnashing their teeth. At once he saw the golden pin in the young lady's temple, seized it and pulled it half-way out. The blood spurted . . . And the young lady seized his coat in her hand and cried out: "Why are you hurting me?"

'Not until now did the smith take fright. He shuddered and let his hands drop. This was just what the monsters wanted. The one with the biggest muzzle jumped at the smith and shook him so that blood spurted out through the opening and stained the rocks, which you saw with your own eyes. But at the same time, the smith broke off a tooth big as a man's fist, which my grandfather found in the stream, later on.

'Then the stone closed over the window into the pit, and no one has been able to find it since. The stream dried, and the young lady was left down there, half-awakened. She cries so loudly that sometimes shepherds in the fields hear her, and she will weep for ever and ever.'

Węgiełek ceased. Izabela lowered her head and traced some marks on the gravel with the tip of her parasol. Wokulski dared not look at her. After a long silence he said to Węgiełek: 'That was an interesting story . . . But tell me, now – how will you set about engraving the stone?'

'I don't know what it is I'm to engrave, sir.'

'To be sure . . .'

Wokulski brought out notebook and pencil, and when he had written, gave it to the young man: 'Only four lines, sir?' Węgiełek said, 'it will be ready in three days. On that stone the letters could surely be an inch high. Ah, I forgot a string for measuring. I'll go down to the driver, sir – perhaps he will have one. I'll be back immediately.'

Węgiełek ran off down the hill-side. Izabela glanced at Wokulski. She was pale and moved. 'What are the verses?' she asked, stretching out her hand. Wokulski handed her the page: she began reading in an undertone: 'In every place, every hour, where I wept with you, played with you – I shall be with you always and everywhere, for I left there part of my soul.'

Her voice dropped to a whisper. Her lips quivered, tears came into her eyes. For a moment she crumpled the sheet, then slowly turned away her head and the page fell to the ground. Wokulski knelt to recover it. Then he touched Izabela's dress, and no longer aware of what he was doing, he seized her by the hand: 'You will awaken, my princess . . .' he said.

'I don't know . . . Perhaps . . .' she replied.

'Hey there!' Starski called from below, 'come along, lunch will get cold.'

Izabela dabbed her eyes, and hastily left the ruin. Wokulski went after her.

'What were you doing so long?' Starski asked with a smile, giving his hand to Izabela, who quickly took it.

'We were listening to an unusual story,' Izabela replied, 'really, I never knew that such legends could exist in this country, and that simple people could tell them in such an interesting manner. What are you giving us for lunch, cousin? Ah, that young fellow was inimitable. Ask him to tell you . . .'

Wokulski was no longer vexed because Izabela was walking with Starski, leaning on his arm and even flirting with him. The emotion he had witnessed, and her one insignificant phrase had dispelled all his fears. He was immersed in a tranquil meditation, where not only Starski but the entire company had disappeared from before his eyes.

Later, he recalled going up the hill to the oak tree, eating hungrily, being merry, talkative and even flirting with Felicja. But what they said, and what he replied – he never knew.

The sun was setting and clouds had appeared in the sky when Starski told the servants to clear away the cutlery, baskets and carpet, and proposed going home. They got into the brake in the same order as before. After wrapping Ewelina in her shawls, the Baron leaned over to Wokulski and murmured with a smile: 'If you continue in your present mood for one day more, you'll turn all the ladies' heads.'

'Oh, well . . .' replied Wokulski, with a shrug.

He sat at the end of the brake, opposite Felicja. Ochocki took his place by the coachman, and they drove off. The sky clouded over, darkness was falling fast. Yet it was very gay inside the brake, thanks to a squabble between Mrs Wąsowska and Ochocki, who forgot his balloons and, dangling his legs over the edge of the box, turned to the company. Suddenly, wishing to light a cigarette, he struck a match and illuminated the entire interior, Starski most of all.

At this moment, Wokulski recoiled violently: something had flashed before his eyes. 'Nonsense,' he thought, 'I've drunk too much . . .'

Mrs Wąsowska burst into a brief laugh, but at once controlled herself and began speaking: 'What a very original way of sitting, Mr Ochocki . . . Fie, tomorrow you'll have to kneel. Ah, unworthy creature, he'll be putting his feet on someone's knees next. Turn around at once, sir, or I'll tell the coachman to leave you by the wayside.'

Cold sweat broke out on Wokulski's forehead, but he shrugged and thought: 'Premonitions – premonitions! What nonsense . . .'

And he dispelled them with a superhuman effort of will . . . He regained his good humour, and began talking to Mrs Wąsowska very gaily.

But when they returned to Zasławek late at night, he slept like a log, and even had an amusing dream. Next morning, when Wokulski went for a stroll before breakfast, the first person he met in the yard was Izabela's chambermaid: she was carrying several gowns, and a boy dragging a trunk came after her.

'What's this?' he thought, 'today is Sunday, surely she isn't leaving . . . She can't leave on a Sunday. Besides, she or the Duchess would have mentioned it to me.'

He walked to the lake, hurried around the park as if seeking to dispel his forebodings. The thought that Izabela might be leaving nagged him. He suppressed it so much that it was no longer clear, only an insignificant vexation somewhere in the depths of his heart.

At breakfast, the Duchess seemed to greet him more affectionately than usual, everyone seemed to be behaving more ceremoniously,

Felicja seemed to be gazing at him insistently, as if reproachfully. Then again, after breakfast, it seemed to him that the Duchess made some kind of signal to Mrs Wąsowska. 'I must be ill,' he thought.

But he at once recovered, for Miss Izabela declared she wanted to stroll in the park: 'Does anyone want to accompany me?' she asked.

Wokulski leapt to his feet, the others remained seated. So he found himself alone in the garden with Izabela, and again the tranquillity he always felt in her presence returned to him. Halfway down an alley, Izabela said: 'I am very sorry to be leaving Zasławek . . .' 'Sorry?' Wokulski thought, but she went on quickly, 'I must leave. My aunt wrote on Wednesday for me to go back, but the Duchess didn't show me the letter, she kept me here. It wasn't until a special messenger arrived yesterday . . .'

'Are you leaving tomorrow?' Wokulski asked.

'Today, after lunch,' she replied, lowering her gaze.

'Today!' he repeated.

They were just passing a fence behind which, in the farm-yard, stood the carriage in which Izabela had come. The coachman was arranging reins around the box. But this time, neither the news nor the preparations for departure made any impression on Wokulski. 'Well, what of it?' he thought, 'anyone who comes, must also leave. It is very natural.'

This calmness surprised even him.

They walked a few more paces under the overhanging branches, then all at once, a terrible despair seized him. He felt that if the carriage for Izabela had driven up at this moment, he would have thrown himself under its wheels to prevent her from leaving. Let the carriage run over him and stop his sufferings once and for all!

Then another wave of calmness descended, and Wokulski wondered where such adolescent thoughts had come from. After all, Miss Izabela had the right to leave when she chose, to go where she chose, and with whom she pleased.

'Will you be staying with your aunt much longer?' he asked.

'A month at most.'

'A month!' he repeated, 'will I at least be permitted to call on you later?'

'Oh yes, please do,' she replied, 'my father is a great friend of yours.'

'And you?'

She blushed and was silent.

'You don't reply,' said Wokulski, 'you don't even guess how dear each of your words is to me, when I hear them so rarely. And now you are leaving without giving me even a shadow of hope.'

'Perhaps time will help,' she murmured.

'If only it would! But in any case, allow me to tell you something, madam. You see, in life, one can find people more amusing than I am, more elegant, with titles, even with larger fortunes. But you will surely not find another attachment like mine. For if love is measured by suffering, then love such as mine has perhaps never before been seen in this world. I haven't the right to complain to anyone for that. It's destiny. By what strange paths it has led me to you! How many disasters had to occur before I, a poor lad, was able to acquire an education which lets me speak to you today? What accident drove me to the theatre where I saw you for the first time? And didn't a series of miracles found the fortune I now possess?

'When I think of these things, it seems to me I was destined even before birth to meet you. If my poor uncle hadn't fallen in love as a young man, I wouldn't be here today. And is it not strange that I myself, instead of amusing myself with women as other men do, have hitherto avoided them and also deliberately waited for one, for you . . .'

Izabela imperceptibly wiped away a tear. Wokulski, without looking at her, said: 'Not long ago, when I was in Paris, I had two choices before me. One led to a great invention which might change the history of the world – the other to you. I renounced the first, for an invisible chain binds me here – the hope that you will love me. If that is possible, then I'd prefer happiness with you to the greatest fame without you: fame is but a counter for which we sacrifice our own happiness for others. But if I am deluding myself, only you can take the spell off me. Tell me you have not, and never will have any feeling for me . . . and I'll go back, where I should perhaps have remained from the first.'

'Is it to be so?' he asked, taking her hand.

She did not utter a word.

'Then I will stay,' he said after a moment, 'I'll be patient, and you yourself will give me the signal that my hopes have been fulfilled.'

They went back to the palace. Izabela was somewhat altered, but she talked gaily to everyone. Tranquillity came back to Wokulski. He was no longer desperate because Izabela was leaving, he told himself he would see her in a month, and that sufficed for him at present. After luncheon, the carriage drove up: the departures began. In the porch Izabela whispered to Mrs Wąsowska: 'Perhaps, Kazia, you won't tease that poor man?'

'Whom do you mean?'

'Your namesake.'

'Ah, Starski . . . We'll see.'

Izabela gave Wokulski her hand. 'Until we meet again,' she murmured, with emphasis.

She drove away. The entire company stood in the porch watching the carriage which moved off around the lake, disappeared behind a hillock and reappeared, until finally only a cloud of yellow dust was left.

'A very fine day,' said Wokulski.

'Yes, indeed,' Starski replied.

Mrs Wąsowska was eyeing Wokulski with lowered lashes.

They all separated slowly. Wokulski remained alone. He went to his room, but it seemed very empty: then he wanted to stroll in the park, but something kept him away . . . He thought Izabela must be still in the house, and could not for the life of him grasp that she had left, that she was already a mile away from Zasławek, and that each second was taking her further away from him. 'She has gone, after all,' he thought, 'she has gone – but what of it?'

He went to the lake and gazed at the white boat around which the water was gleaming, until his eyes ached. Suddenly one of the swans swimming along the opposite bank caught sight of him, and flew with a fluttering of wings to the punt. And at this moment Wokulski was seized with such vast, limitless unhappiness, as though he were on the point of quitting life itself . . .

Plunged in his own bitter thoughts, Wokulski hardly noticed what was going on around him. Nevertheless, towards evening, he observed that the whole company at Zasławek, after coming in from the park, was peevish. Felicja shut herself up with Ewelina in her room, the Baron was irritable and Starski ironical and impudent.

After dinner the Duchess summoned Wokulski. Signs of vexation were also apparent in the old lady, though she tried to hide them. 'Have you been thinking at all, Mr Stanisław, of the sugar-factory?' she asked, sniffing a little flask – always a sign of emotion. 'Think of it, pray, and talk to me, for all this gossip has upset me.'

'Are you worried?' asked Wokulski.

She made a gesture: 'Ah, worry . . . All I want is for this marriage between Ewelina and the Baron to take place, or be broken off. Either let them both go away, or Starski . . . It's all the same.'

Wokulski lowered his gaze and was silent, guessing that Starski's flirtation with the Baron's fiancée must have taken on a still more obvious form. But what concern was that to him?

'These young girls are silly creatures,' the Duchess began after a moment, 'they think that when one of them catches a rich husband and a handsome lover as well, then she will fill up her life. Silly creatures! They don't realise that soon the old husband and the empty lover will grow hateful, and that sooner or later she'll want to meet a genuine man. And if one comes along, to her misfortune, what can she give him? The charms she's sold, or a heart defiled by such as Starski?

'And to think that almost every one of them must go through such a school before she gets to understand people! Earlier, even if she meets the noblest of men, she can't appreciate him. She'll choose a rich old man or impudent scoundrel, will waste her life in their company, and not until some future time will she wish to be born again. . . . Usually too late, and in vain.

'What surprises me most,' she went on, 'is the fact that men don't understand these dolls. It's no secret to any woman, from Mrs Wąsowska to my chambermaid, that neither heart nor sense has yet awoken in Ewelina: it's all asleep in her . . . Yet the Baron regards her as a divinity, and deludes himself, poor wretch, that she loves him.'

'Why not warn him?' Wokulski asked in a stifled voice.

'For goodness sake, that would be useless . . . Did I ever once give him to understand that Ewelina is still only a spoiled child and a doll? Perhaps something will come of her one day, but not at present! Starski is just right for her. And what,' she added, after a pause, 'have you thought about the sugar-factory? Have a horse saddled tomorrow, ride out in the fields by yourself or – better still – with Wąsowska. She's a worthy woman, I may tell you . . .'

When Wokulski left the Duchess, he was in a state of alarm. 'What was she saying,' he thought, 'about the Baron and Ewelina? Wasn't she quite simply warning me? For Starski flirts with others as well as Ewelina. What happened in the brake? I'd sooner shoot myself . . .'

But then he recollected himself. 'In the brake,' he thought, 'it was either an illusion, in which case I'm doing an innocent woman an injustice, or if it was a fact . . . Well, I'm certainly not going to be the rival of that operetta libertine, and sacrifice my life for a depraved woman. She has the right to flirt with whom she pleases, but not to deceive a man whose only crime is that he loves her. I must get away from this Capua, and set to work. I'll fulfil my life better in Geist's laboratory than in any drawing-room.'

Towards ten o'clock the Baron came into his room, terribly changed. At first he smiled and joked, then sank breathlessly into a chair and said, after a moment: 'You know, my dear Mr Wokulski, I sometimes think – not in my own experience, for my fiancée is the noblest of girls – but sometimes I think women deceive us . . .'

'Yes, sometimes . . .'

'Perhaps it isn't their fault,' said the Baron, 'but one must admit that sometimes they let themselves be trifled with by intriguers.'

'Yes, indeed they do.'

The Baron was shivering so much that his teeth chattered. 'Don't you think, sir,' he asked, after pondering, 'that such things should be prevented?'

'In what way?'

'By removing a woman from contact with the intriguers, at least.'

Wokulski laughed aloud: 'It's possible to free a woman from intriguers, but is it possible to free her from her own instincts? What would you advise if the man whom you consider a trifler or intriguer is to her a male of the same species as herself?'

Gradually a feeling of rage began dominating him. He walked about the room, and said: 'How can one struggle against a law of nature by which a bitch, even of the best breed, will couple – not with a lion – but with a dog? Show her a whole menagerie of the noblest animals, but she'll renounce them all for a few dogs. Yet it is hardly surprising, for they are her species.'

'So in your opinion there's no help for it?' asked the Baron.

'Not at present, but at some future time there will be sincerity in human relations, and freedom of choice. When a woman won't need to pretend to love or flirt with every man, then at once she will discard those she doesn't care for, and will go to the man who suits her taste. Then there won't be any deceived lovers or deceivers, relationships will be formed in a natural manner.'

When the Baron left, Wokulski went to bed. He did not sleep all night, but he regained equanimity. 'What sort of complaint can I have against Izabela?' he thought, 'after all, she didn't say she loved me; all she did was to give me barely a shadow of hope that it may happen at some time. She's right, for she hardly knows me. What sort of illusions are these? . . . Starski? . . . But she wants to match him with Mrs Wąsowska, so surely it hasn't occurred to her to flirt with him. The Duchess? . . . The Duchess likes Izabela, she told me so, and besides, she invited me here . . . I have time. I'll get to know her better, and if she falls in love with me, I'll be happy and can be at rest. If not – I'll go back to Geist. In any case, I'll sell the apartment house and the store, but will stay in the trading company with Russia. That will bring me in a hundred thousand roubles or so within a few years, and won't lay her open to the charge of being a tradesman's wife.'

After breakfast next morning, he ordered a horse and rode out on the pretext of surveying the district. Without thinking, he turned along the road by which Izabela's carriage had driven away the day before, and where he believed traces of wheels were still visible. Then, almost mechanically, he rode towards the wood where they had so recently gone for mushrooms. At this spot she had laughed, here she had talked to him, here she surveyed the view . . .

Suspicion, anger, everything, died away within him. In their place, an unhappiness as fine as tears, yet burning like everlasting fire, began flowing into his heart. Entering the wood, he dismounted and led the horse. This was the path along which they had both walked, but it seemed somehow different. This part of the wood was supposed to resemble a church – today there was no trace of a likeness. All around was grey and quiet. Only the croaking of crows which were at this moment flying over the wood, and the bark of a squirrel as it climbed a tree could be heard.

Wokulski reached the clearing where he and Izabela had talked: he even found the tree-stump she had sat on. Everything was as it had been: only she was absent . . . Already the undergrowth was turning yellow, and sorrow drooped from the pine trees like spider-webs. So impalpable, yet it entangled him!

'It's madness,' he thought, 'to make oneself too dependent on another human being. I worked for her alone, I think of her, I live for her. The worst is that I rejected Geist for her sake . . . Well, but what more would I have got from Geist? I'd be as dependent as I am today, except that my master would be an old German instead of a beautiful woman. And I'd work the same, even harder, except that today I'm working for my own happiness, and there it would be for the happiness of others, who in any case would have a good time, and fall in love at my expense.

'Besides, what right have I to complain? A year ago I hardly dared dream about Izabela, and today I know her, I'm even trying to win her affection . . . But do I know her? She's a conventional aristocrat, yes – but she still hasn't looked around the world. She has a poetic spirit, or perhaps merely presents one. She's a flirt, but that will change if she falls in love with me . . . In a word, it isn't bad, and within a year . . .'

At this moment his horse raised its head and neighed: neighing and the sound of hoofs echoed in the depths of the wood. Soon a woman on horseback appeared at the end of the drive, and Wokulski recognised Mrs Wąsowska. 'Hop, hop!' she cried, laughing. She jumped off her horse, and gave the reins to Wokulski. 'Tie him up, sir,' she said, 'ah, how well I know you! An hour ago I asked the Duchess where you were. "He's gone out looking for a site for the sugar-factory." "Just so," thought I, "he's gone into the woods to dream." I ordered a horse and here I find you, sitting on a tree-stump in a state of exaltation. Ha ha ha!'

'Do I look so comical?'

'No! You do not look at all comical to me, but – how shall I word it? – unexpected. I imagined you very differently. When they told me you were a tradesman who had also made a fortune, I thought: "A tradesman? So he's come into the country either to woo a rich young woman, or to obtain money from the Duchess for some business." In any case, I thought you a cold man, calculating, a man who estimates the values of the trees as he walks in a wood, and who doesn't look at the sky because it doesn't pay interest. But what do I find? A dreamer, a medieval troubadour who disappears into the wood to sigh and gaze upon last week's traces of *her* feet! A faithful knight, who loves one woman through life and death, and is impudent to the others. Oh, Mr Wokulski, how amusing this is – and how old-fashioned!'

'Have you quite finished?' Wokulski asked coldly.

'Yes . . . Have you something to add?'

'No, madam. I suggest we go back to the house.'

Mrs Wąsowska blushed scarlet. 'I trust,' she said, taking the horse's bridle, 'that you don't think I speak of your love in this manner so as to catch you for myself? . . . You say nothing. So let's be serious. There was a moment when I liked you: there was, but it passed. Even if it hadn't, even if I were dying for love of you, which will certainly not happen, for I haven't yet lost any sleep or appetite – I wouldn't surrender to you, do you hear me? – not even if you came crawling at my feet. I couldn't live with a man who loves another woman as you do. I am too proud. Do you believe me?'

'Yes!'

'I thought so. If I vexed you with my remarks, it was simply out of benevolence. Your madness impresses me, I hope you will be happy and that's why I say – throw off the medieval troubadour, for this is the nineteenth century, women are different from what you imagine, as even twenty-year-old youths know.'

'What are they really like?'

'Pretty, agreeable, they like twisting you around their little fingers, and will fall in love only enough to enjoy it. No woman will accept a dramatic love, or at least not all women . . . First she must grow tired of flirtations, and then she will find herself a dramatic lover . . .'

'In a word, you are insinuating that Izabela . . .'

'Oh, I insinuate nothing about Izabela,' Mrs Wąsowska protested vivaciously, 'in her there is material for a fine woman, and the man she falls in love with will be happy. But before she falls in love . . . Pray help me mount.'

Wokulski did so, then mounted his own horse. Mrs Wąsowska was agitated. She rode ahead in silence for a while: suddenly she turned back to him and said: 'My last word. I know people better than you may suppose . . . I am afraid you may be disillusioned. If that ever happens, remember my advice: don't act under the influence of passion, but wait. Things often look worse than they really are.'

'Satan!' Wokulski muttered. The whole world began revolving around him and seemed infused with blood.

They rode on without speaking. At Zasławek, Wokulski went to the Duchess. 'I'm leaving tomorrow,' he said, 'and as for the sugar-factory, don't build one.'

'Tomorrow?' the old lady echoed, 'and what will happen about the stone?'

'If you permit, I'll go to Zasław, I'll inspect the stone, and I have other business there, too.'

'Then God be with you . . . There is nothing for you to do here. And call on me in Warsaw. I shall be going back at the same time as the Countess and the Łęckis.'

That evening Ochocki came to his room. 'Confound it!' he cried, 'I had so many things to discuss with you . . . But there, you were with the ladies all the time, and now you're leaving.'

'Don't you care for the ladies?' asked Wokulski with a smile, 'perhaps you are right!'

'It isn't that I don't care for them. But since I found out that great ladies are no different than chambermaids, I prefer the latter. These women,' he went on, 'are all geese, even the cleverest of them. Yesterday, for instance, I spent a half-hour explaining to Wąsowska the advantages of steering a balloon, I told her frontiers would disappear, nations be brothers, civilisation progress . . . She gazed into my eyes so that I'd have sworn she understood. Then, when I'd finished, she asked: "Mr Ochocki, why don't you get married?" Did you ever hear anything like it! Of course, it took me another half hour to explain that I had no thought of marrying, that I wouldn't marry Felicja, or Izabela, or even her . . . Good God, I don't know a single woman in whose constant company I wouldn't turn stupid in six months.' He stopped, and began taking his leave.

'One moment,' said Wokulski, 'when you come back to Warsaw, pray call on me. Perhaps I shall be able to give you news of an invention which admittedly will take half a lifetime, but – you'll like it.'

'Balloons?' asked Ochocki with a fiery look.

'Something better. Goodnight.'

Next day, towards noon, Wokulski bade goodbye to the Duchess's household. A few hours later he was in Zasław. He called on the priest, and told Węgiełek to be ready to set off for Warsaw. Having done this, he went to the castle ruins.

The four lines were already engraved on the stone. Wokulski read them several times, and his gaze rested on the words: '. . . always, everywhere I shall be with you . . .'

'And if not?' he murmured.

Despair gripped him at this thought. Just then he only had one longing – that the earth might give way and swallow him up, along with these ruins, this stone and this inscription.

When he went back to the village, the horses had been fed, Węgiełek was standing by the carriage with his green trunk. 'Do you know when you'll be coming back?' Wokulski asked.

'In God's good time, sir,' Węgiełek replied.

'Get up.'

He threw himself upon the cushions and they moved off. An old woman made a sign of the Cross to them from a distance. Węgiełek caught sight of her and took off his cap: 'Take care of yourself, mama!' he called from the box.

XXVIII

The Journal of the Old Clerk

S O HERE we are in 1879. If I were superstitious, or didn't know that bad times are followed by better, I'd be afraid of this year 1879. For whereas its predecessor ended badly, it has started off even worse. For example – England went to war with Afghanistan at the end of last year, and in December things went badly for her. Austria had a great deal of trouble with Bosnia, and an insurrection broke out in Macedonia. In October and November, there were attempts on the lives of King Alfonso of Spain and King Umberto of Italy. Both escaped unharmed. Also in October, Prince Jósef Zamoyski, a great friend of Wokulski's, died. I think his death interfered in more than one way with Wokulski's plans.

Scarcely has 1879 started than – may the devil take it! – the English, still not yet disentangled from Afghanistan, have a war in Africa, down in the Cape of Good Hope, against some Zulus or other. Here in Europe we have nothing less than an outbreak of typhus in the Astrakhan district, and it may reach us any day.

What a lot of trouble this typhus creates! Everyone I meet says: 'Well now, serve you right for importing calico from Moscow. You'll see, you'll bring the plague with it!' And the anonymous letters, roundly cursing us! I fancy, however, that their writers are mostly our rivals, or Lodz manufacturers of calico. The latter would be only too glad to see us break our necks, even if there were no plague. Of course, I don't repeat even a hundredth part of these insults to Wokulski: but I think he hears and reads them more than I.

Strictly speaking, I intended to set down in these pages the story of an amazing court case, a criminal case, which Baroness Krzeszowska has brought against none other than the pretty, virtuous, adorable Mrs Helena Stawska. But such rage overcomes me that I cannot collect my thoughts. So to distract my attention, I write about other things . . .

She brought a criminal case against Mrs Stawska for theft! Theft! Her! . . . Of course we emerged victorious from the mud. But at what a cost . . . I, for instance, couldn't sleep for well nigh two months. And if today I go out for a beer in the evenings, a thing I never used to do, and even sit in saloons till midnight, I do so from sheer mortification. To bring a charge of theft against that divine creature! Goodness knows, only a half-crazy woman like the Baroness would do such a thing.

Because of it, the ferocious harpy paid us ten thousand roubles . . . Ah, if it depended on me, I'd have squeezed out a hundred thousand. Let her weep, let her have spasms, let her die even. Vile woman! But let's think of something other than human iniquities.

Strictly speaking, who knows whether honest Staś wasn't the involuntary cause of Mrs Stawska's misfortunes: or perhaps not so much he, as I myself . . . I introduced him to her by force, I advised Staś not to call on that monster, the Baroness, and finally I wrote to Wokulski, when he was in Paris, that he should try to obtain news of Ludwik Stawski. In a word, it was I who vexed that serpent Krzeszowska. I paid for it for two months! But there's no help for it. Good God, if you exist, have mercy on my soul, if I have a soul – as a soldier of the French Revolution once said. (Ah, how old I'm growing, how old I'm growing! Instead of getting to the point at once I prattle, I repeat myself, I ramble . . . Although, upon my word, I believe I'd have a fit if I began to write at once about that monstrous, that shameful court case . . .)

Now, let me collect my thoughts. Staś was in the country during September, at the Duchess's. I cannot imagine why he went there, nor what he did. But I could see, from the few letters he wrote me, that it didn't go very well. What the devil took Izabela Łęcka there? Surely he isn't interested in her any more? I'll be damned if I don't make a match of it between him and Mrs Stawska. I'll make a match of it, I'll lead them to the altar, I'll make sure he makes the vows properly, and then . . . Maybe I'll blow out my brains, I don't know? . . . (Old fool! . . . Is it for you to think of such an angel! . . . Besides, I don't think of her at all, particularly since I became convinced that she loves Wokulski. Let her love him, providing both are happy. And I? Come, Katz, my old friend, would you have been any bolder than I?

In November, on the very day that the house in Wspólna Street collapsed, Wokulski returned from Moscow. Again, I don't know what he was doing there: suffice it that he made some seventy thousand roubles . . . These profits are beyond my grasp, but I am sure that any business in which Staś was involved must have been honest.

A few days after his return, a respectable merchant comes up to me and says: 'My dear Mr Rzecki, I am not in the habit of interfering in other people's business, but – pray warn Wokulski, not from me, but from you, that his partner Suzin is a great scoundrel and will certainly go bankrupt very soon. Warn him, sir, for I pity him . . . Wokulski, even though he has got on to the wrong road, always deserves sympathy.'

'What do you mean by a "wrong road"?' I asked.

'Well, now, Mr Rzecki,' said he, 'anyone who goes to Paris and buys ships when England is involved in an incident and so forth – he, Mr Rzecki, is not marked by a citizen's virtues.'

'My dear sir,' said I, 'how does the buying of ships differ from the buying of hops? Bigger profits, no doubt . . .'

'Well,' said he, 'let's not make an issue of it, Mr Rzecki. I'd have nothing against anyone else doing it, but not Wokulski . . . After all, we both know his past, and I perhaps better than you, for sometimes the late lamented Hopfer placed orders with me through him . . .'

'My dear sir,' said I to this merchant, 'are you casting aspersions on Wokulski?'

'No, sir,' said he to this, 'I'm simply repeating what the whole town is saying. I don't want to harm Wokulski in the least, especially in your eyes, as you are his friend (and very properly, for you knew him when he was different from today), but . . . You must admit, sir, that this man is damaging trade. I don't judge his patriotism, Mr Rzecki, but I'll tell you frankly (for I must be frank with you) that those Muscovite calicos . . . Do you understand me, sir?'

I was furious. For although I am a lieutenant of Hungarian infantry, I couldn't comprehend in what way German calico is better than Muscovite calico. But there was no talking to my merchant. The brute raised his eyebrows, shrugged and waved his hands about so that in the end I thought he must be a fine patriot, and I a dummy, although when he was filling his pockets with roubles and imperials, hundreds of bullets were flying past my head . . .

Of course, I told Staś all this, and he replied with a sigh: 'Calm yourself, my dear fellow. These very people who are warning me Suzin is a scoundrel, were writing to Suzin a month ago to say that I'm a bankrupt, a robber, an ex-rebel.'

After my talk with the honest merchant, whose name I won't even mention, and after all the anonymous letters I received, I decided to make a note of the various views expressed by respectable people about Wokulski. Here's the first: Staś is a bad patriot because his cheap calicos have spoiled the Lodz manufacturers' business a little. Very well! What's next?

In October, about the time when Matejko* finished painting his *Battle of Grünwald* (a large and showy picture, which should not be

exhibited to soldiers who took part in real battles), Maruszewicz –
that friend of Baroness Krzeszowska – rushed into the shop. What a
change – he's gone up in the world! He'd a golden charm on his
chest or rather on the place where people have stomachs, so thick
and long that he might have used it for a dog-collar. A diamond
pin in his tie, new gloves, new shoes, and his body (a wretched
enough body, goodness knows!) dressed in a new suit. In addition,
he looked as though he hadn't a penny in debts, but paid cash for
everything. Klein, who lives in the same house, later explained to
me that Maruszewicz plays cards regularly, and has been lucky for
some time past.

So in rushed my dandy, with his hat on and an ebony walking-
stick in his hand, and after looking around uneasily (he has a rather
furtive look), he asked: 'Is Mr Wokulski here? Ah, Mr Rzecki . . .
A word, I beg.'

We went behind a cupboard. 'I'm here with excellent news,' he
said, pressing my hand affectionately, 'you can sell your apartment
house, the one the Łęckis used to own . . . Baroness Krzeszowska
will buy it. She has regained her capital by a law-suit against her
husband, and (if you want to drive a bargain) she'll pay ninety
thousand roubles, and even something extra to help you leave.'

He must have seen the gratification on my face (the purchase of
that house was never to my taste), for he pressed my hand still more
fervently – if a live corpse can do anything fervently – and, smiling at
me sweetly (I felt nauseated by his sweetness), he began murmuring:
'I can be of service to you gentlemen . . . an important service . . .
The Baroness depends very much on my advice, and if . . .'

Here he was taken with a slight fit of coughing: 'I understand,'
said I, guessing who I was dealing with, 'and Mr Wokulski won't
make any difficulties about a bonus . . .'

'Come, sir,' he exclaimed, 'whatever do you mean? The more so
as the Baroness's attorney will come to you gentlemen with a
definite offer. In any case, I'm not concerned. What I have is quite
adequate . . . But I have some poor relatives, to whom you
gentlemen may want, on my recommendation, to . . .'

'If you please, sir,' I interrupted, 'we prefer to place a sum
directly into your hands, providing of course that the business goes
through.'

'Oh, it will – I can give you my word,' Mr Maruszewicz assured
me.

But because I didn't promise him an honorarium, he lurked
about the shop for a while, then left, whistling.

Towards evening, I told Staś this: but he defeated me by silence,
which made me think. So next day I hurried to our attorney (who
is also the Prince's attorney), and communicated Maruszewicz's
news to him.

'So she'll pay ninety thousand?' said the attorney in surprise (he is a very eminent person), 'but, my dear Mr Rzecki, apartment houses are going up, and next year they're going to build some two hundred new ones. In these conditions, my dear Rzecki, we'd be doing her a favour if we sold the house for a hundred thousand. The Baroness is very interested in this apartment house (if one may use that word in connection with such a distinguished lady), and we might get a much larger sum from her, my dear Mr Rzecki.'

I bade farewell to the eminent attorney, and went back to the store, firmly resolved not to interfere in the sale of the apartment house. Not until then did it occur to me that Maruszewicz is a great scoundrel.

Now that I've calmed down sufficiently to collect my wits, I'll describe the repulsive law-suit the Baroness brought against that angel, that perfect lady, Mrs Stawska. If I don't write it all down, in a year or two I won't be able to credit my memory that such a monstrous thing could happen.

Please note that firstly, Baroness Krzeszowska has long detested Mrs Stawska, because she thought everyone was in love with her, and secondly, that this very same Baroness wanted to buy the apartment house from Wokulski as cheaply as possible. These are two important facts, whose significance I'm only just beginning to understand (I'm getting old, my goodness, that I am . . .)

I have visited Mrs Stawska often since meeting her. Not every day. Sometimes once in a few days, though sometimes twice on the same day. After all, I was responsible for the house, that's one thing. Then I had to tell Mrs Stawska I'd written to Wokulski with regard to finding her husband. Furthermore, I had to call on her with the news that Wokulski hadn't found out anything definite. Then I visited her to study Maruszewicz's habits through the windows of her apartment, as he lodges in the opposite wing. Then too, I was concerned with investigating Baroness Krzeszowska and her relations with the students who live upstairs, and whom she was everlastingly complaining of.

An outsider might think I visited Mrs Stawska too often. However, after mature consideration, I decided I didn't visit her often enough. After all, I had an excellent post in her apartment for observing the entire building, and in addition I was cordially made welcome. Whenever I called, Mrs Misiewicz (the respectable mother of Mrs Helena) would greet me with open arms, little Helena would climb into my lap and Mrs Stawska herself livened up, and said that during the hours I spent in their apartment, she forgot her troubles. So how could I help visiting them often since they welcomed me so? Upon my word, I did not visit them enough, I think, and had I greater chivalrous leanings I should have sat there from morning till night. Even if Mrs Stawska were to dress in my presence. What harm would it have done?

During these visits I made several important observations. First, those students on the third-floor front were really restless spirits. They sang and they shouted until two in the morning, sometimes they even howled and, all in all, tried to use the most inhuman sounds possible. During the day, if only one was home – and there was always someone – whenever Baroness Krzeszowska put her head out of the window (she did so a dozen or more times a day), someone would always try to pour slops down on her.

I must even say that a sort of game developed between her and the students overhead, which consisted of her peeping out of the window, then trying to draw her head back in again as quick as she could, while they tried to pour slops down as often and as copiously as possible.

Then, in the evenings, these young men who had no one overhead to soak them with slops, would call the washerwomen and servant-girls of the entire building into their room. Shrieks and spasms of weeping could be heard in the Baroness's apartment.

My second observation related to Maruszewicz, who lived almost *vis-à-vis* Mrs Stawska. This man followed a very peculiar way of life, marked by unusual regularity. He failed to pay his rent regularly, regularly every few weeks they removed a quantity of objects from his apartment: statues, mirrors, carpets, clocks. But what was more interesting – just as regularly they brought in new mirrors, new carpets, new clocks and statues to his apartment . . . After each removal, Mr Maruszewicz would appear for the next few days at one of his windows. He shaved at it, combed his hair, waxed his moustache, even dressed in it, casting very ambiguous looks in the direction of Mrs Stawska's windows. But when his apartment filled again with new articles of luxury and comfort, then Mr Maruszewicz drew the blinds again. Then (incredible though it sounds!) lights burned day and night in his apartment, and the voices of many men, and sometimes even of women, could be heard. But what concern of mine is another man's business?

One day early in November, Staś said to me: 'Apparently you're visiting Mrs Stawska?'

I grew quite warm. 'I beg your pardon,' I exclaimed, 'what do you mean?'

'Nothing at all,' he replied, 'I don't suppose you call on her by the window, but in the regular way. In any case, do as you please, but pray tell the ladies at your earliest opportunity that I've had a letter from Paris . . .'

'In connection with Ludwik Stawski?' I asked.

'Yes.'

'Have they finally found him?'

'Not yet, but they're on his track, and expect soon to solve the problem of his whereabouts.'

'Maybe the poor devil is dead,' I cried, pressing Wokulski's hand, 'please, Staś,' I added, after cooling off somewhat, 'do me a favour, visit these ladies and tell them the news yourself.'

'I'm not an undertaker, to give people this kind of gratification,' Wokulski said indignantly.

But when I began telling how respectable the ladies were, how often they inquired whether he would visit them one day . . . and when I also mentioned it would be worth while to take a look at the apartment house, he began to yield. 'I care little for the house,' he said, shrugging his shoulders, 'I'm going to sell it any day now.'

In the end he let himself be persuaded, and we went there around one o'clock that afternoon. In the yard, I noticed the blinds drawn fast in Maruszewicz's apartment. Obviously he had acquired a new set of furniture.

Staś glanced carelessly around at the windows of the house and listened to my report on the improvements without paying the slightest attention. We had laid a new floor in the gateway, mended roofs, painted walls, and had the stairs washed once a week. In a word, we have made a thoroughly presentable house out of a neglected one. Everything was in order, not excluding the yard and the drains: everything – except the rents.

'In any case,' I concluded, 'your manager Mr Wirski will give you more detailed information. I'll send the caretaker for him at once.'

'Oh, never mind the rents and the manager,' Staś muttered, 'let's call on this Mrs Stawska, then get back to the store.'

We entered the first floor of the left wing, where there was a strong smell of boiling cauliflower: Staś frowned and I knocked on the kitchen door. 'Are the ladies home?' I asked the plump cook.

'As if they wasn't, whenever you come,' she replied, winking.

'You see how they welcome us,' I whispered to Staś in German. He nodded in reply, and thrust out his lower lip.

In the little sitting-room Mrs Stawska's mother was, as usual, knitting a stocking: she rose from her chair and stared in surprise on seeing Wokulski. Little Helena peeped in from the other room: 'Mama,' she whispered so loudly that she must have been audible in the yard, 'Mr Rzecki and some other gentleman have come.'

At this moment Mrs Stawska joined us. Seeing both ladies, I exclaimed: 'Our landlord, Mr Wokulski, has come to pay his respects and give you news . . .'

'Of Ludwik?' Mrs Misiewicz caught on, 'is he alive?'

Mrs Stawska turned pale, then blushed just as quickly. At that moment she was so pretty that even Wokulski gazed at her, if not with admiration, then at least with cordiality. I am certain he would have fallen in love with her on the spot, had it not been for that confounded smell of cauliflower wafting in from the kitchen.

We sat down. Wokulski asked the ladies whether they were content with their apartment, then told them that Ludwik Stawski had been in New York two years earlier and moved to London under an assumed name. He mentioned in passing that Stawski had been ill at that time, and he was expecting definite news within a few weeks. On hearing this Mrs Misiewicz referred several times to her handkerchief for help. Mrs Stawska was calmer, only a few tears trickled down her cheeks. To hide her emotion, she turned with a smile to her little daughter and said in a low voice: 'Say thank you, Helena, to the gentleman for bringing us news of papa.'

Again her tears sparkled, but she controlled herself. Meanwhile, Helena made a curtsy to Wokulski and then, after gazing at him with wide-open eyes, suddenly put her arms around his neck and kissed him on the mouth. I will never forget the change which Staś's countenance underwent at this unexpected embrace. To my knowledge, no child had ever kissed him before, and at first he drew back in surprise: then he put his arms around little Helena, gazed at her tenderly, and kissed her on the brow. I'd have sworn he was about to rise and say to Mrs Stawska: 'Allow me, madam, to take the place of this dear little girl's father . . .'

But – he didn't; he lowered his head and fell into his usual brooding. I'd have given half my annual wages to know what he was thinking about then just. Of Miss Łęcka, perhaps? Ah, my age is telling again . . . What of Miss Łęcka? She can't hold a candle to Stawska!

After a few minutes' silence, Wokulski asked: 'Do you ladies like your neighbours?'

'Depends which ones you mean,' Mrs Misiewicz said.

'Of course we do, very much,' Mrs Stawska interposed. As she spoke, she glanced at Wokulski and blushed.

'Is Baroness Krzeszowska a pleasant neighbour?' Wokulski asked.

'Oh, sir! . . .' Mrs Misiewicz cried, raising a finger.

'She's an unfortunate woman,' Mrs Stawska interposed, 'she has lost her daughter . . .'

Saying this, she twisted a corner of her handkerchief and tried to glance from beneath those magnificent eyelashes – not at me at all. But her eyelids must have been heavy as lead, for she blushed still more and became increasingly serious, as though one of us had vexed her.

'And who might that Mr Maruszewicz be?' Wokulski went on, as though not thinking of the two ladies present at all.

'A ne'er-do-well, a scamp,' Mrs Misiewicz replied hastily.

'No, mama, he's only eccentric in his ways,' her daughter

corrected her. At this moment her eyes were wide open, and their pupils enlarged as never before.

'Those students are said to be very ill-behaved,' said Wokulski, staring at the piano.

'Like all young men,' Mrs Misiewicz replied, blowing her nose loudly.

'Mind, Helena, your bow has come undone again,' said Mrs Stawska, leaning forward to her little daughter, perhaps to hide her embarrassment at the mere mention of the students' misbehaviour.

By this time, Wokulski had irritated me with his conversation. A man must be either a half-wit or badly brought up to ask such a pretty woman about the other tenants! So I stopped listening to him, and began looking around the yard mechanically. And this is what I saw: in one of Maruszewicz's windows, the blind had been moved aside, and through the gap someone was looking in our direction: 'The confounded man is spying on us,' thought I. I turned my gaze to the second-floor front. Goodness me! In the furthest room of the Baroness Krzeszowska's apartment, both windows were open and in the depths could be seen . . . she herself in person, gazing at Mrs Stawska's apartment through opera-glasses.

'May God have mercy on the serpent!' said I to myself, certain that scandal would result from all this peeping.

I did not pray in vain. Heavenly punishment was already suspended over the meddler's head, in the shape of a herring dangling from a window on the third floor. A mysterious hand, attired in a navy-blue sleeve with a silver band, was holding the herring: beyond it, a thin face wearing a malicious smile kept appearing every few moments. My insight wasn't needed to guess that this was one of the non-paying students, waiting for the Baroness to appear in her window so he could drop the herring on her. But the Baroness was more cautious, and the student grew bored. He shifted the providential herring from one hand to the other, and, no doubt to kill time, made very unpleasant grimaces at the girls in the Parisian laundry.

Just as I was deciding that the attack on the Baroness would come to nothing, Wokulski rose and began bidding the ladies goodbye.

'Are you gentlemen leaving so soon?' Mrs Stawska murmured, and at that moment she grew exceedingly embarrassed.

'Perhaps you gentlemen will call more often . . .' Mrs Misiewicz added. But that milksop, Staś, instead of asking the ladies to let him call every day or to let him board there (which I would certainly have done in his place), this . . . this eccentric asked if they needed any repairs done in the apartment!

'Oh, everything necessary has been done by kind Mr Rzecki,' Mrs Misiewicz replied, turning to me with an agreeable smile (to

be frank, I don't care for such smiles from persons of a certain age).
Staś paused a moment in the kitchen, and the smell of cauliflower
clearly irritated him, for he said to me: 'A ventilator or something
must be installed here.'

On the stairs I couldn't control myself any longer, and cried: 'If
you were to come here more often, you'd have seen for yourself
what improvements are needed in the house. But what's the house
to you, or even such a pretty woman!'

Wokulski stopped in the passage and muttered, gazing at a
gutter: 'Hm! If I'd met her earlier, perhaps I'd have married her.'

Hearing this, I had a strange feeling: I was pleased, but it was also
as though someone had stuck a pin in my heart: 'So you're not
going to get married, then?' I asked.

'Who knows?' he replied, 'maybe I will . . . But not to her.'

Hearing this, I experienced an even stranger feeling: I was sorry
Mrs Stawska wouldn't get Staś as her husband, but at the same
time, a burden seemed to have been lifted from my chest.

Hardly had we entered the yard when I looked up, and there
was the Baroness, leaning out of her window and calling to us:
'You, sir! . . . I beg . . .'

Suddenly she shrieked in a heartrending voice: 'Ah! Nihilists!'
and retreated into the depths of her room. At that moment, a
herring fell into the yard a few feet from us, whereupon the
caretaker hurled himself upon it with such voracity that he didn't
even notice me.

'Won't you call on the Baroness?' I asked Staś, 'she seems
anxious to see you about something.'

'Why doesn't she leave me alone, for goodness sake,' he replied
with a shrug. In the street he hailed a droshky and we went back to
the store without speaking, but I am positive he was thinking of
Mrs Stawska, and if it hadn't been for those confounded cauli-
flowers . . .

I was so on edge, so vexed, that on closing the store I went out
for a beer. There I met Councillor Węgrowicz, who was still busy
tearing Wokulski's reputation to shreds, but who has very happy
political notions . . . and I argued with him until midnight.

Well, now – what did I set out to write about? Ah! Three or
perhaps four days after our visit to Mrs Stawska, Staś comes into the
store and hands me a letter addressed to himself: 'Just read this,' said
he, with a smile. I opened it and read:

'Mr Wokulski! Forgive me not addressing you as Dear sir, but I
cannot bring myself to use such a form to a man from whom
everyone is turning away in disgust. Unfortunate man! You have
not yet rehabilitated yourself from your earlier misdeeds, but you
are already disgracing yourself by new ones. Today the whole town
is talking of nothing but your visits to a woman of bad reputation,

Stawska. You have rendezvous with her in Town, you creep into her apartment nights, which might suggest you have not entirely lost all sense of shame, but you even visit her by broad daylight, in the presence of servants, young men and the respectable lodgers in that ill-famed apartment house.

'Do not deceive yourself, wretched man, that you are alone in carrying on an intrigue with her. You are being helped by your manager, that wretch Wirski, and by your plenipotentiary, Rzecki, who has turned grey with dissipation.

'I must add that not only is Rzecki deceiving you with your mistress, but is also robbing you of income from the house, for he had lowered the rents of certain tenants, firstly that Stawska. As a result, your house is worthless, you stand on the brink of ruin and, indeed, a noble benefactor would do you a great favour by buying that ruin of the Łęckis at a small loss to yourself.

'If, therefore, such a benefactor could be found, then dispose of your burden, take what you can get, be grateful and flee the country before human justice chains you and throws you into a dungeon. Be on your guard! Beware! And take the advice of a well-wisher.'

'Quite a woman, what?' asked Wokulski, seeing I had finished.

'May the devil take her!' I exclaimed, guessing he meant the author of the letter. 'So I have turned grey with dissipation, have I? I steal! I flirt! Damned serpent!'

'Well, well . . . calm down, here is her lawyer,' said Staś.

At this moment into the store came a little man in an old fur coat, a faded top-hat and huge galoshes. He entered, gazed around like a police spy, asked Klein when Wokulski would be there, suddenly pretended he had only just caught sight of us, approached Staś and whispered: 'Mr Wokulski, is it not? May I have a few words with you, in private?'

Staś winked at me, and the three of us went into my apartment. The visitor removed his coat, whereat I noticed his trousers were still more frayed and his hair still more moth-eaten than his fur coat. 'Allow me to introduce myself,' said he, stretching his right hand to Wokulski and his left to me, 'I am lawyer – '

Here he mentioned his name and – stood thus with his hands in the air. By a strange coincidence, neither Staś nor I felt any desire to take them. He realised this, but was not abashed. Indeed, with the best face in the world, he wiped his hands together and said, with a smile: 'You gentlemen don't even ask what business brings me here?'

'We suppose you will tell us yourself,' Wokulski replied.

'Right you are!' the visitor cried. 'I'll be brief. There is here in town a certain rich though very miserly Lithuanian (the Lithuanians are very miserly people!), who has asked me to recommend some apartment house to him for purchase. I have some fifteen on my books, but out of respect for you, Mr Wokulski, for I know the good you are doing our country, I recommended your house, the one that used to be Łęcki's, and after two weeks' work on him, I achieved so much that he is now ready to pay . . . Guess how much, gentlemen? Eighty thousand roubles! A splendid offer, isn't it, now?'

Wokulski flushed with anger, and for a moment I thought he was going to throw the visitor out of the house. However, he controlled himself and replied in that tone he has, that sharp and disagreeable tone: 'I know this Lithuanian. His name is Baroness Krzeszowska.'

'What's that?' cried the attorney in amazement.

'That miserly Lithuanian won't pay eighty thousand, but ninety thousand for my house, while you, sir, propose a lower price as so to make more profit for yourself.'

'Ho ho ho!' the attorney began chuckling, 'who would do otherwise, my dear Mr Wokulski?'

'Pray tell your Lithuanian, sir,' Staś interrupted, 'that I'll sell the house, but for a hundred thousand. And that until New Year. After New Year, I'll raise the price.'

'But what you're saying is inhuman,' the visitor burst out. 'You want to tear her last penny away from that wretched woman . . . What will the world say to this, pray consider!'

'I don't care what the world says,' Wokulski declared, 'and if the world wants to moralise to me as you do, sir, I'll show it the door. Come, sir – there's the door, d'you see!'

'I'll give ninety-two thousand, but not a penny more,' the attorney replied.

'Put your overcoat on, you will catch cold in the yard . . .'

'Ninety-five th – ' the attorney interposed, and began putting on his coat hastily.

'Well, goodbye to you, sir,' said Wokulski, opening the door.

The lawyer bowed low and went out, adding sweetly from the threshold: 'I'll be back in a day or two. Perhaps you'll be better disposed, sir . . .'

Staś shut the door in his face. After the horrible attorney's visit, I knew what to expect. The Baroness was certainly going to buy Staś's house, but would first use all manner of means to bargain for it. I know those means! One was the anonymous letter in which she blackened Mrs Stawska's reputation and said I'd turned grey with dissipation. But as soon as she buys the house, she will drive out the students first of all, and certainly poor Mrs Helena too. If only her hatred would stop there!

Now I can narrate all the events that followed, post-haste. After the attorney's visit, I felt an evil premonition. I decided to call on

Mrs Stawska that very day, and warn her of the Baroness. Above all, though, I would tell them to sit at the windows as rarely as possible. For the ladies, apart from the virtues that adorn them, have the disastrous habit of sitting all day at the window. Mrs Misiewicz does it, so does Mrs Stawska, little Helena, and even the cook, Marianna. Not only do they sit there all day, but they sit there evenings too, by lamplight, and never think to pull down the blinds, except on going to bed. So everything that happens in their apartment can be seen as if they were inside a lantern.

To respectable neighbours, this way of passing the time would be the finest proof of their respectability: they demonstrate in every way that they've nothing to hide. But when I recalled that the ladies were constantly being spied on by Maruszewicz and the Baroness, and when I also thought that the Baroness hates Mrs Stawska – then I was seized by the worst forebodings. That very evening, I wanted to hasten to my noble friends and urge them by all I hold sacred not to sit all the time in their windows, and not expose themselves to the Baroness's spying. However, at nine-thirty precisely I felt thirsty, and went for a beer instead of going to the ladies.

Councillor Węgrowicz was there, as well as Szprott the commercial traveller. They were just saying something about the house that collapsed in Wspolna Street, when suddenly Węgrowicz clinked his tankard against mine and said: 'More than one other house will collapse before New Year!'

Szprott winked. I didn't care for that wink, as I have never liked winking, so I asked: 'What, pray, are those grimaces supposed to mean?'

He laughed foolishly, and said: 'You know better than we do. Wokulski's selling his store . . .'

Good God! . . . I'm surprised I didn't hit him over the head with my tankard. Fortunately I restrained my first impulse, drank two tankards of beer in rapid succession, and asked in an outwardly calm voice: 'Why should Wokulski sell his store – and who to?'

'Who to, indeed!' Węgrowicz cried, 'as if there weren't enough Jews in Warsaw! Three or more of them will get together, and make Krakowskie Przedmieście horrible, thanks to Mr Wokulski, who keeps his own carriage and goes to visit the aristocracy in their country houses. Good God! I remember how the poor devil used to serve my beef cutlet at Hopfer's . . . There's nothing left now but to go to the wars and ransack the Turks.'

'Why should he sell the store?' I asked, pinching my knee to prevent my anger breaking out at the old wretch.

'He'll do well to sell it,' Węgrowicz replied, taking up yet another tankard of beer, 'what's he doing among tradespeople, a gentleman like him, a diplomat, an innovator – who imports new merchandise? . . .'

'I fancy there's another reason,' Szprott interrupted. 'Wokulski is wooing Miss Łęcka, and although he's been turned down, he keeps on calling, so he must have hopes . . . But Miss Łęcka wouldn't marry a haberdashery merchant, not even if he is a diplomat and innovator.'

Sparks flew before my eyes. I banged my tankard on the table, and shouted: 'You're lying, sir, it's all lies, Mr Szprott! And there's my card,' I added, casting my visiting-card on the table.

'What are you giving me your card for?' Szprott replied, 'are you inviting me to a party, or what?'

'I demand satisfaction, sir,' I cried, still banging on the table.

'Hoity-toity,' said Szprott, wagging a finger at me. 'It's all right for you to demand satisfaction, for you're a Hungarian officer. Murdering a man or two and having yourself chopped up into the bargain is bread and meat to you . . . But I, sir, am a commercial traveller, I have my wife, children and business to attend to.'

'I'll make you fight a duel!'

'Make me? Will you get me there under police escort? If you was to say anything of the sort when you're sober, I'd go to the police myself, and they'd show you what's what.'

'You've no pride, sir!' I cried.

Now he began banging on the table too: 'No pride? Who are you speaking to? Don't I pay my bills, do I sell bad goods, have I ever gone bankrupt? We'll see who has pride – in Court!'

'Calm down,' Councillor Węgrowicz implored, 'duels were fashionable long ago, not now . . . Shake hands.'

I rose from the table, which was by now flooded with beer, paid my bill at the counter and left. I will never again set foot in that detestable hole.

Of course, after all the excitement I couldn't go to Mrs Stawska's. At first I thought I wouldn't sleep a wink all night. But somehow I dropped off. And when Staś came into the store next day, I asked him: 'Do you know what people are saying? That you're selling the store!'

'Suppose I am – what would be wrong in that?'

(True enough! What would be wrong in it? Just fancy – such a simple thought never struck me!) 'But, d'you know,' I whispered, 'they also say you're going to marry Miss Łęcka.'

'Suppose I were?' he replied.

(He's right! What, isn't he allowed to marry anyone he chooses, even Mrs Stawska? Fancy me not realising it, and squabbling unnecessarily with Szprott on that account!)

Of course I had to go out again that evening, not so much for the beer, as to be reconciled with the unjustly offended Szprott, so again I didn't call on Mrs Stawska, and didn't warn her not to sit at the windows. So it wasn't without sorrow that I learned dislike for

Wokulski was increasing among tradespeople, that our store was to be sold and Staś will marry Miss Łęcka. I say 'will', for if he were not certain he wouldn't have expressed himself so decisively to me.

Now I know for sure whom he was yearning for in Bulgaria, whom he acquired a fortune for by tooth and claw . . . God's will be done . . . Just look, though, how far I've wandered from my topic . . . But now I'll really set about describing the episode of Mrs Stawska, and will narrate it quick as a flash.

XXIX

The Journal of the Old Clerk

JUST AFTER eight I went to visit the ladies. As usual, Mrs Stawska was giving lessons to some young ladies in the other room, and Mrs Misiewicz and little Helena were sitting at the window – as usual. I don't know what they could see at night, but certainly everyone could see them. I'd have sworn that the Baroness, in one of her unlit windows, was sitting with opera-glasses, staring into the ground floor, for her blinds were not drawn.

I retired behind the curtain so that the monster should not see me, at least, and immediately asked Mrs Misiewicz: 'My dear madam, no offence meant, but why do you ladies sit at the windows all the time? It isn't nice . . .'

'I'm not afraid of draughts,' said the respectable matron, 'and I take great pleasure in it. How can we help looking out of the window, when it's our only entertainment? Do we go anywhere? Do we see anyone? Since Ludwik went away, our relations with other people have been broken off. For some, we're too poor, for others – suspect . . .' She wiped her eyes, then pursued: 'Oh, poor Ludwik did wrong to run away: even if they'd sent him to prison, his innocence would have come to light, and we'd all be together again. But God alone knows where he is, and Helena . . . You tell us not to look out! Yet she, poor thing, keeps waiting, listening and watching for Ludwik to come back, or at least for a letter from him. If anyone runs across the yard, she rushes to the window at once, thinking it's the postman. Or if the postman comes to our door (we, Mr Rzecki, very rarely get letters), then if you were to see Helena . . . She changes, turns pale, trembles . . .'

I dared not open my mouth, and after a pause the old lady went on: 'I, too, like sitting in the window, especially if it's a fine day and the sky is bright, for then my late lamented husband comes to mind, as if he were still alive.'

'Yes,' I murmured, 'the sky reminds you of him because he now dwells there.'

'Not in that respect, Mr Rzecki,' she interrupted, 'I know he's in Heaven, for where else should such a good-natured man be? But when I look at the sky and at the walls of this house, the happy day of our wedding comes into my mind at once. The late lamented Klemens was wearing a blue frock-coat and yellow nankeen trousers, the very same colour as our house. Oh, Mr Rzecki,' the old lady sobbed, 'believe me when I say that for the likes of us, a window sometimes is as good as the theatre, a concert and friends. What else do we have to look at?'

I cannot describe how sad I felt to hear such a dramatic account of merely looking out of windows . . . The pupils of Mrs Stawska, having finished their lessons, were setting off home, and their charming teacher made me happy with her appearance. When I greeted her, she had cold hands and an expression of weariness and sorrow on her heavenly face. On seeing me, however, she deigned to smile (dear angel! It was as though she guessed that her sweet smile illuminates for me the darkness of life for an entire week).

'Mama, did you tell Mr Rzecki,' said Mrs Stawska, 'of the honour we had today?'

'Ah no, I forgot,' Mrs Misiewicz interposed.

Meanwhile, the two young ladies had gone, after curtsying, and we remained alone, so it was quite like a family circle. 'Just think,' said Mrs Stawska, 'we had a visit from the Baroness today! At first I was almost frightened because she, poor thing, hasn't a very attractive look, so pale, always in black, and she has a sort of expression, too . . . But she disarmed me in a moment when, on seeing Helena, she burst into tears and fell on her knees before me, crying: "My poor little child was just like her, and now's she's dead!" . . .'

I turned cold all over on hearing this. However, not wanting to alarm Mrs Stawska perhaps for no reason, I dared not speak to her of my forebodings. I merely asked: 'What did she want?'

'She came to ask me to help her set in order her linen, dresses, lace – in a word, all her household goods. She expects her husband to return to her soon, and she wants to freshen up some little trifles, and to buy others. And as she says she has no taste, she asked me to help, and promised to pay me two roubles for three hours a day.'

'What did you say to that?'

'Goodness, what could I say? Of course I accepted gratefully. Admittedly, it is only temporary work, but very convenient, for only yesterday (I don't know why), I lost one music lesson, at five złoty an hour . . .'

I sighed, guessing that the cause of the loss might be an anonymous letter, in the writing of which Baroness Krzeszowska had great fluency. But – I said nothing. For how could I advise Mrs Stawska to decline two roubles a day?

Oh dear, Staś, Staś! Why shouldn't you marry her? Miss Łęcka has got into your head. I only hope you don't regret it.

From then on, whenever I called on my respected lady friends, Mrs Stawska would tell me in the greatest detail the story of her relations with Baroness Krzeszowska, whose apartment she frequented every day, and naturally worked six hours instead of three, for the same two roubles. Mrs Stawska is a very mild-tempered lady, nevertheless, as I could see from her implied expressions both the Baroness's apartment and her entire environment astounded and appalled Mrs Stawska. First, the Baroness makes no use of her large apartment. The drawing-room, boudoir, bedroom, dining room, the Baron's room – all are empty. The furniture and mirrors are covered up; the plants which once bloomed are only dusty sticks today, or vases full of dried earth; dust on the costly tapestries. God knows what she eats, sometimes she doesn't take a bite of anything hot for days on end, and she only keeps one servant in that great apartment, and treats her like a wanton and a criminal. When Mrs Stawska asked her whether she wasn't unhappy living in that emptiness, she replied: 'What am I to do, bereaved orphan and almost widow that I am? Unless the good Lord inspires my wicked husband to repent his wicked deeds and come back to me, only then will my hermit-like existence change. But as far as I can make out from the dreams and premonitions which Heaven sends me during my fervent prayers, my husband ought to return any day, for he has no money and no credit, that unfortunate, unhappy madman . . .'

Hearing this, Mrs Stawska made the private comment that the Baron's fate, after repentance, might not be enviable.

The persons who call on the Baroness did not arouse Mrs Stawska's confidence, either. Often, old ladies of disagreeable aspect visit her, with whom she talks of her husband in an undertone in the vestibule. Sometimes Maruszewicz comes, or an attorney in an old fur coat. The Baroness would take these gentlemen into the dining room, and when she talked to them, she would weep and complain so loudly that she was audible all over the apartment.

To Mrs Stawska's timid inquiry as to why she didn't live with her relatives, the Baroness replied: 'Whom with, my dear lady? I have none, and even if I had, I wouldn't receive such greedy and vulgar people in my house. My husband's family won't have anything to do with me, because I am not genteel: though this has not prevented them, all the same, from squeezing two hundred thousand roubles out of me. They were civil enough as long as I kept lending them money on permanent loan: but when I grew sick of it, they broke off relations, and they even persuaded my unhappy husband to place my estate under constraint. Oh, what I went through on account of those people . . .' she added, weeping.

The only room (says Mrs Stawska) in which the Baroness spends the whole day, is the little room of her late daughter. This must be a very mournful and strange corner, for everything has been left as it was when the little girl died. So there's her bed, on which the linen is changed every few days, a closet with her clothes, which are also brushed and cleaned in the drawing-room, for the Baroness won't let these sacred relics be taken into the yard. There's a little table, with books and an exercise book open at the page on which the poor little child wrote for the last time: 'Holy Virgin, form . . .' And, last of all, there's a little shelf, full of large and small dolls, little beds and dolls' garments.

In this room, Mrs Stawska darns laces or silks, of which the Baroness has a great deal. Mrs Stawska cannot divine whether she is ever likely to wear them again.

One day, the Baroness asked Mrs Stawska if she knew Wokulski. But, although she got the answer that Mrs Stawska hardly knows him, she began: 'You'd be doing me a great favour, dear madam, a real charity, if you'd go and see that gentleman regarding a matter of great importance to me. I want to buy this house and will pay him ninety-five thousand roubles, but he, out of sheer obstinacy and nothing more, is asking a hundred thousand. That man wants to ruin me . . . Pray tell him he's killing me . . . That he will draw down Heavenly punishment on himself for such greed!' the Baroness shrieked and cried.

Mrs Stawska, very embarrassed, told the Baroness she couldn't possibly speak to Wokulski of this: 'I don't know him . . . He's only called on us once . . . Besides, would it be proper for me to interfere in such matters?'

'Oh, you can make him do anything you choose,' the Baroness retorted, 'but if you don't want to save me from death . . . God's will be done. Pray do your Christian duty at least, and tell that man I am well disposed towards you.'

Hearing this, Mrs Stawska rose to leave. But the Baroness hastily embraced her, and begged her forgiveness, so that tears flowed from the excellent Mrs Stawska's eyes and she stayed.

When she had told me all this, Mrs Stawska ended with a question that had the tone of a request: 'So Mr Wokulski doesn't want to sell this house?'

'Of course he does,' I replied, vexed, 'he's selling the house, the store, everything . . .'

A bright blush spread over Mrs Stawska's face: she turned her chair back to the lamp, and quietly asked: 'Why?'

'As if I knew!' I said, feeling that terrible pleasure caused by tormenting our dear ones, 'as if I knew! They say he wants to get married'

'Aha,' Mrs Misiewicz interposed, 'people are saying it's Miss Łęcka.'

'Is this true?' Mrs Stawska whispered. Suddenly she pressed one hand to her bosom as if breathless, and went into the other room.

'Here's a fine to-do,' thought I, 'she sets eyes on him once, and here she is swooning away . . .'

'I don't know why he should get married,' I told Mrs Misiewicz, 'because he isn't even lucky with women.'

'Get along with you, Mr Rzecki,' the old lady cried, 'he not lucky with the ladies?'

'After all, he isn't handsome.'

'He? . . . But he's a perfectly handsome man! What a build, what a noble countenance, and what eyes! You, Mr Rzecki, surely don't know anything about it. But I must confess (at my age, after all!) that although I have seen many handsome men (Ludwik was very handsome too), this is the first time I've seen anyone like Wokulski. He'd attract notice in a thousand.'

I was privately amazed at this flattery. For although I know Staś is very handsome, yet all the same, he's not as handsome as all that . . . Still, I'm not a woman!

When I bade my ladies goodnight at ten, Mrs Stawska was altered and mournful, and complained that her head ached. Oh, that donkey, Staś! The woman has fallen in love with him at first sight, and he, the madman, is running after Miss Łęcka. Is there order in this world? If I were the Lord God . . . But why chatter on in vain?

People are talking about laying drains in Warsaw. The Prince even called on us, and invited Staś to a meeting on the subject. When he finished his conversation about drains, he questioned him about the apartment house. I was present, and well remember every word: 'Is it true (forgive me for asking about such matters) – is it true, Mr Wokulski, that you're asking a hundred and twenty thousand from the Baroness Krzeszowska for your house?'

'No, it isn't,' Staś replied, 'I am asking a hundred thousand, and not a penny less will I take.'

'The Baroness is eccentric, hysterical but . . . she's also an unhappy woman,' said the Prince. 'She wants to buy that house because her beloved daughter died there, and also in order to protect the rest of her savings from her husband, who loves squandering money . . . Perhaps you, sir, will make her some concessions? It's a fine thing to do good to unhappy people,' the Prince concluded with a sigh.

I admit that although I am only a shop-assistant, this charity at someone else's expense surprised me. Staś felt this even more strongly, for he replied in a firm manner: 'Am I to lose several thousand roubles just because the Baron squanders money and his wife would like to have my house? Why, pray?'

'Well, don't be offended, my dear sir,' said the Prince, pressing

Wokulski's hand, 'you know we all live with people: they help us attain our ends, so we too have certain obligations.'

'No one helps me, indeed – many interfere,' Staś replied. They parted very coldly. I noticed that the Prince was displeased.

What extraordinary people! Not only did Wokulski form a trading company with the Empire and give them the opportunity to make fifteen per cent on their capital, but now they want him to bestow several thousand roubles on the Baroness, at their request! What a mischief-maker she is, though, and there's nowhere she won't worm her way into . . . For there was even some priest came to see Staś, with a religious exhortation that he should sell his house to the Baroness for ninety-five thousand. And because Staś declined, we shall soon hear, no doubt, that he is an atheist.

Now comes the main incident, which I shall relate post-haste.

When I called again one evening on Mrs Stawska (the day when the Emperor Wilhelm took power after the incident with Nobiling),* my goddess, that excellent woman, was in splendid fettle and full of admiration for – the Baroness!

'Just think,' said she, 'what an excellent woman the Baroness Krzeszowska is, despite her eccentricities. She noticed I was unhappy without little Helena, and she asked me outright to take Helena with me to her apartment for the few hours.'

'Those six hours for two roubles?' I interrupted.

'Not six – four, at most . . . Helena plays there very nicely, although she is not allowed to touch anything, but all the same, how she gazes at the late child's dolls!'

'Are they such pretty toys?' I asked, privately making a certain plan.

'Perfectly lovely!' said Mrs Stawska, animatedly, 'especially one enormous doll with dark hair, and when you press her . . . here, under the bodice,' she added, blushing.

'Don't you mean on the stomach? . . . forgive me, madam,' I inquired.

'Yes,' she said hastily, 'then the doll moves its eyes and cries "Mama!" How charming it is, I'd like to own it myself. Its name is Mimi. When Helena saw it the first time, she pressed her hands together and was quite turned to stone. And when Baroness Krzeszowska touched it, and the doll started talking, Helena cried: "Oh mama, how pretty she is, how clever . . . Can I give her a kiss?" And she kissed the tip of its enamelled shoe. Since then, she's been talking about the doll in her sleep: as soon as she wakes, she wants to go to the Baroness's apartment, and when she's there, she's perfectly happy to spend the whole day gazing at the doll, with hands pressed together as though she were praying. Indeed,' Mrs Stawska concluded in an undertone (Helena was playing in the other room), 'I'd be very happy if I could buy her a doll like that.'

'It must certainly be a very expensive toy,' Mrs Misiewicz remarked.

'That's not the point, mama. Who knows whether I shall ever be able to bring her as much happiness as I might today, by one doll,' Mrs Stawska replied.

'I think,' said I, 'that we have just such a doll in the store. If you would deign to call . . .'

I dared not make her a present, realising it would be more agreeable if she herself helped make the child happy. Although we were talking in lowered voices, Helena evidently overheard us speaking of the doll, and she ran in from the other room with sparkling eyes. To turn her attention elsewhere, I asked, 'Well now, Helena, so you like the Baroness?'

'Quite well,' the child replied, leaning against my knees and looking at her mother. (Oh Lord, why aren't I her father?)

'And does she talk to you?'

'Not very much. Once she asked me if Mr Wokulski kisses me a lot.'

'Did she, now! And what did you say to that?'

'I said I didn't know who Wokulski is. And then the Baroness said . . . Oh, how loudly your watch ticks. Show me!'

I took out my watch and gave it to Helena: 'And what did the Baroness say?' I asked.

'The Baroness said: "How is it that you don't know who Mr Wokulski is? Why, he's the man who visits you with that deb . . . debchee, Rzecki." Ha ha ha! You're a chee! Show me the inside of your watch.'

I glanced at Mrs Stawska. She was so taken aback, that she even forgot to scold Helena. After tea and dry rolls (for, as the servant girl said, there was no butter to be had that day), I bade the excellent ladies farewell, vowing to myself that if I were in Staś's shoes, I wouldn't let the Baroness have the apartment house for less than two hundred thousand roubles.

Meanwhile, after exhausting various influential people and fearing lest Wokulski either put up the price or sell the house to someone else, that serpent finally decided to buy it for a hundred thousand. She's supposed to have been furious for several days, to have gone into hysterics, beat the servant girl, insulted her attorney in the surveyor's office, but she finally signed the deed of acquisition. For the next few days after the purchase of our house there was peace.

Peace, that's to say, in that we heard nothing of the Baroness, though her lodgers called on us with complaints. First came the tailor, the one on the third-floor back, whining that the new owner was raising his rent by thirty roubles a year. When I explained to him for a half hour that this was nothing to do with us, he wiped his eyes, scowled and bade me goodbye with the words: 'Obviously Mr Wokulski doesn't have God in his heart, if he can sell the house to a person who injures other people.'

Did you ever hear the like? Next day the owner of the Parisian laundry appeared. She wore a velvet salope, had much dignity in her gestures and even more firmness in her expression. She sat down on a chair in the store and looked around as though she fully intended to purchase several Japanese vases, then began: 'Well, thank you, sir! You have behaved very well to me, to be sure . . . You bought that house in July and sold it in December, just like a tradesman, without warning anyone.'

She grew red in the face and went on: 'Today that trollop sent some booby to me, with notice to leave. I don't know what's got into her, after all I pay regular . . . And here she turns me out of the house, the hussy, and even casts aspersions on my establishment . . . She says my young ladies make eyes at the students, which is a lie, and she thinks . . . she imagines I'll find another place in the middle of winter . . . that I'll move out of the house my customers have got used to. But I stand to lose thousands of roubles by this, and who will compensate me?'

I grew hot and cold by turns as I listened to this speech, uttered in a powerful contralto voice in the presence of several customers. I hardly had time to pull the female into my room, and implore her to start proceedings against us for damage and loss.

A few hours after this female – lo and behold, in comes a student, the one with a beard who didn't pay rent on principle: 'Ah, how are you?' says he, 'is it true that the devilish Krzeszowska has bought the house from you?'

'It is,' said I, privately certain he'd start to strike me.

'Confound it!' said the bearded student, 'but that Wokulski was a fine landlord (N.B. Staś hasn't had a penny piece out of them for their apartment), and now he's sold the house. So Krzeszowska can turn us out of that hole?'

'Hm . . . Hm . . .' I replied.

'And she will, too,' he added, sighing, 'we've already had some German with the demand that we move out. But I'll go to the devil before they get rid of us without court proceedings, or if they do . . . We'll give the whole house something to talk about! Good-day, sir.'

'Well,' thought I, 'that one at least has no complaints against us. Evidently they're really prepared to give the Baroness something to think about . . .'

Finally, next day, Wirski rushes in: 'You know what, colleague?' he said, indignantly, 'the old girl has sacked me, and ordered me to move out by New Year.'

'Wokulski has already made provision for you,' I replied, 'you'll get a post in the trading company.'

By thus listening to some, calming others and comforting yet others, I survived the main attack, somehow. I also understood that the Baroness was sowing disaster amidst the tenants like Tamerlaine, and I felt an instinctive uneasiness regarding the pretty and virtuous Mrs Stawska.

During the second half of December, I looked up one day – the door opened, and in came Mrs Stawska. As pretty as ever (she is always pretty when unhappy and when she looks worried). She gazed at me out of her charming eyes and said quietly: 'Would you be kind enough to show me the doll?'

The doll (and three similar ones) had long been ready, but I was so embarrassed that I couldn't find them for a few minutes. Klein is absurd with those grimaces of his: he's ready to think I'm in love with Mrs Stawska. Finally I extricated the boxes – there were three large dolls, a brunette, a blonde and one with chestnut hair. Each had real hair, each blinked its eyes when pressed in the tummy, and uttered a sound which Mrs Stawska took to be 'Mama', Klein to be 'Papa', and I to be 'Uhu'.

'Lovely,' said Mrs Stawska, 'but they must be very expensive.'

'Madam,' said I, 'these are goods we want to dispose of, so we can let them go very cheaply. I'll see my boss . . .'

Staś was working behind the cupboards, but when I told him Mrs Stawska had come and what she wanted, he dropped his accounts and hurried into the store in an affable mood. I even noticed that he gazed at Mrs Stawska as cordially as though she had made a powerful impression on him. Well, finally! Thank goodness!

'A bargain's a bargain,' we told Mrs Stawska, adding that the dolls were damaged goods for which there was no demand, so we could dispose of them for three roubles.

'I'll take this one,' she replied, choosing the chestnut, 'because it is exactly like the Baroness's. Helena will be delighted.'

When it came to paying, Mrs Stawska was again seized by scruples: she thought such a doll must be worth at least fifteen roubles, and only the combined efforts of Wokulski, Klein and me succeeded in convincing her that we still had a profit on three roubles.

Wokulski went back to his business, and I asked Mrs Stawska the news from the house, and what her relations with the Baroness were like?

'I have none,' she replied, blushing, 'Baroness Krzeszowska made such a scene because she had to pay a hundred thousand for the house on account of my not interceding with Mr Wokulski on her behalf, and so forth . . . that I said goodbye to her, and won't go there any more. Of course, she's given us notice to quit by New Year.'

'Did she pay you what she owed?'

'Oh . . .' Mrs Stawska sighed, dropping her muff, which Klein instantly retrieved.

'So – she didn't?'

'No . . . She said she hadn't any money just then, and wasn't sure if my bill was right.'

Mrs Stawska and I smiled at the Baroness's eccentricities, then said goodbye hopefully. As she was going out, Klein opened the door for her so gallantly that either he regards her as our boss's future wife – or is in love with her himself! He also lives in the Baroness's house, and sometimes visits Mrs Stawska: but during his visits he sits there so dejectedly that little Helena once asked her grandma: 'Didn't Mr Klein take his castor oil today?' He's a dreamer! But who wouldn't dream of such a woman?

Now I will describe the tragedy, the mere recollection of which stifles me with rage.

On the day before Christmas Eve in the year 1878, I was in the store when I got a letter from Mrs Stawska, asking me to go there that evening. The letter impressed me as being marked by emotion, so I thought perhaps she had had news of her husband. 'He'll certainly come back,' I thought, 'may the devil take lost husbands who find themselves after a few years.'

Towards evening, in rushes Wirski, breathless and confused: he dragged me into my room, shut the door, threw himself into the armchair without taking his coat off, and said: 'Do you know why Krzeszowska stayed in Maruszewicz's apartment till midnight yesterday?'

'Till midnight – in Maruszewicz's apartment?'

'Yes, and with that scoundrel, her attorney, too. The blackguard Maruszewicz looked out of his window and saw Mrs Stawska dressing a doll, and the Baroness went into his apartment with her opera-glasses to check.'

'What then?' I asked.

'Why, a doll belonging to the Baroness's late daughter disappeared from her apartment a few days ago, and today that madwoman is accusing Mrs Stawska of . . .'

'Of what?'

'Of stealing the doll!'

I crossed myself. 'Think no more of it,' I said, 'that doll was bought in our store.'

'I know,' he said, 'but at nine o'clock this morning the Baroness rushed into Mrs Stawska's apartment with a policeman, ordered him to seize the doll and write out a charge. The charge has already gone to court . . .'

'Are you mad, Mr Wirski? After all, the doll was bought here!'

'I know, I know – but what does that signify when there's already a scandal?' said Wirski. 'The worst of it is (I know this from the policeman) that, because Mrs Stawska didn't want Helena to find out about the doll, she didn't want to show it at first, begged them to speak quietly, burst into tears . . . The policeman says he was embarrassed, because in the first place he didn't know why the Baroness had brought him into Mrs Stawska's apartment. But when the serpent began shrieking: "She robbed me! The doll disappeared on the very day when Stawska was in my apartment for the last time . . . Arrest her, for I will answer with my entire fortune that the charge is just!" – so then my policeman took the doll to the police station, and asked Mrs Stawska to go with him . . . A scandal, a dreadful scandal!'

'And what did you do then?' I asked, furious with rage.

'I wasn't home at the time. Mrs Stawska's servant made matters worse by calling the policeman names in the street, for which she is now sitting in the jail herself . . . While that owner of the Parisian laundry, hoping to curry favour with the Baroness, called Mrs Stawska names . . . The only satisfaction we have is that the honest students poured something so nasty on the Baroness's head that it can't be washed out . . .'

'But the court! What about justice?' I cried.

'The court will find Mrs Stawska not guilty,' he said, 'that is obvious. But as for the scandal, well . . . The poor lady is ruined: today she dismissed her pupils, and didn't go to any lessons. She and her mother sat weeping.'

Of course, I hastened to Mrs Stawska without waiting for the store to close (this is happening ever more often nowadays), and I even took a droshky. On the way, I was struck by the happiest of thoughts – to inform Wokulski of the matter. So I called on him, uncertain whether he would be home, for he spends more and more time dancing attendance on Miss Łęcka.

Wokulski was in, but somehow absent-minded: his courting is obviously not doing him any good. However, when I told him my tale of Mrs Stawska, the Baroness and the doll, the young fellow livened up, raised his head and his eyes flashed (I have sometimes noticed that the best cure for our own troubles are those of someone else).

He heard me out attentively (his mournful thoughts took flight), and said: 'The Baroness is a damned nuisance . . . But Mrs Stawska needn't worry: her case is as clear as daylight. Is she the only person that human baseness strikes?'

'It's all very well for you to talk,' I replied, 'for you're a man and, above all, have plenty of money. She, on the other hand, has lost all her lessons, poor thing, as a result of this incident or rather – she's declined them herself. So, what is she going to live on?'

'Oh!' Wokulski cried, striking his forehead, 'I hadn't thought of that.'

He walked up and down the room several times (frowning hard), stumbled against a chair, drummed on the window-pane and suddenly halted in front of me. 'Very well,' he said, 'go to the ladies, and I'll be there within the hour. I have an idea we'll do some good business with Mrs Miller.'

I looked at him with admiration. Mrs Miller recently lost her husband, who had been a haberdashery merchant like us; all her store, property and credit depended on Wokulski. So I almost guessed what Staś was going to do for Mrs Stawska.

I galloped along the street in a droshky, going like three steam-engines, and rushed like a positive sky-rocket to the beautiful, noble, unhappy, abandoned Mrs Stawska. I had my lungs full of cheerful exclamations, and on opening the door felt like shouting with a laugh: 'Think nothing of it, ladies!'

Then I went in – and all my good humour stayed outside the door.

Just imagine what I found. Marianna in the kitchen with her head wrapped up, and a swollen face – certain proof she had been in a police cell all day. The stove had gone out, the dinner dishes were unwashed, the samovar not ready, while around the poor swollen creature sat the janitor's wife, two servant girls and the milk-woman, all with funereal expressions.

A chill went down my spine, but I walked into the drawing-room. An almost identical sight met my eyes. In the middle was Mrs Misiewicz in her armchair, also with her head tied up and around her were Mr and Mrs Wirski, also the owner of the Parisian laundry who had quarrelled with the Baroness again, and several other ladies, who were talking in undertones but, for all that, blowing their noses a whole octave higher than usual. To crown it all, I noticed Mrs Stawska by the stove, sitting on a little stool, as pale as a sheet.

In a word – a tomb-like atmosphere, faces pale or greenish, eyes tear-stained and noses red. Only little Helena was surviving somehow. She was sitting at the piano, with her little old doll, hitting the keys with its hands from time to time and saying: 'Quiet, Zosia, quiet! Don't play the piano, mama's head aches.'

Pray add to this the dimmed lamplight which was smoking a little and . . . the blinds up – and anyone will understand the feelings that seized me. On seeing me, Mrs Misiewicz began pouring out what must have been all that was left of her tears: 'Ah, so you've come, noble Mr Rzecki! Aren't you ashamed of poor women overcome with disgrace? No, don't kiss my hand . . . Our wretched family! Ludwik sentenced, now it's our turn . . . We shall have to move to the world's end. I've a sister near Częstochowa, we will go there to end our broken lives . . .'

I whispered to Wirski tactfully to invite the other guests to leave and drew nearer to Mrs Stawska. 'I wish I were dead,' she said to me, in greeting.

I must confess that after being there a few minutes I got the horrors. I'd have sworn that Mrs Stawska, her mother and even these friends of hers were really in disgrace and that there was nothing left for anyone of us but death. The desire for death did not, however, prevent me from turning down the smoking lamp, which had already started sprinkling the room with fine but very black soot.

'Well, ladies,' Mr Wirski exclaimed suddenly, 'let's be off, for Mr Rzecki has something to discuss with Mrs Stawska.'

The visiting ladies, whose sympathy had not lessened their curiosity, declared they would discuss it with us. But Wirski began giving them their wraps so vigorously that the poor embarrassed creatures, after kissing Mrs Stawska, Mrs Misiewicz, Helena, and Mrs Wirski (I thought they'd start kissing the chairs before they'd finished), finally removed themselves and took Mr and Mrs Wirski with them.

'A secret's a secret,' said the most determined of the ladies, 'and you're not needed here either.'

Another outburst of farewells, kisses, comfortings followed, and the whole crowd almost came to blows, fussing at the door and on the stairs. Sometimes I think the Lord created Eve to spoil Adam's stay in Paradise.

Finally we were left in the family circle, but the little drawing-room was so full of soot and sorrow that I lost all my vitality. In a querulous voice I asked Mrs Stawska to permit me to open the window, and in a tone of involuntary reproach advised her at least to draw the blind in the windows from now on. 'Don't you recollect, madam,' said I to Mrs Misiewicz, 'that I remarked on those blinds long ago? If they'd been down, Baroness Krzeszowska wouldn't have been able to spy on what was going on in your apartment.'

'That's true, but whoever would have expected it?' Mrs Misiewicz replied.

'It was just our misfortune,' Mrs Stawska whispered.

I sat down in an armchair, pressed my hands so that the bones cracked, and listened with calm desperation to Mrs Misiewicz's lamentations of the disgrace which came upon their family every few years, of death which was the limit of human sufferings, of the late Mr Misiewicz's nankeen trousers and sundry other things. Before an hour had passed, I was certain that the proceedings over the doll would terminate in wholesale suicide, during which I, expiring at Mrs Stawska's feet, would dare confess I loved her.

Then someone gave a loud ring at the kitchen door-bell. 'The police!' Mrs Misiewicz shrieked.

'Are the ladies in?' the newcomer asked Marianna in a voice so self-assured that I at once regained courage. 'It's Wokulski,' I told Mrs Stawska, and twirled my whiskers. A blush resembling the petals of a pale rose on snow appeared on Mrs Stawska's charming face. A heavenly creature! Oh, why am I not Wokulski? Then wouldn't I . . . ?

Staś entered. Mrs Stawska went to greet him. 'You don't despise us?' she asked in a stifled voice. Wokulski looked into her eyes with amazement . . . once, then again (believe me) he kissed her hand. The delicacy with which he did so is best attested by the fact that there was none of the lip-smacking which is usually heard on such occasions.

'So you have come, noble Mr Wokulski? You're not ashamed of poor women overcome with disgrace?' Mrs Misiewicz began her speech of welcome for I don't know how many times.

'Allow me,' Wokulski interrupted, 'your situation is certainly disagreeable, ladies, but I see no reason for despair. The matter will be cleared up in a few weeks: only then will despair be possible – but not for any of you ladies, only for the crazy Baroness. How are you, Helena?' he added, kissing the little girl.

His voice was so tranquil and firm, and his manner so entirely unaffected, that Mrs Misiewicz stopped lamenting and Mrs Stawska looked somewhat more cheerful.

'So what are we to do, noble Mr Wokulski, who isn't ashamed to . . . ?' Mrs Misiewicz began.

'We must wait for the trial,' Wokulski interposed, 'to inform the Baroness in court that she is lying, to start a case against her for defamation of character, and not to forgive her a moment of it, even if she goes to jail. A month or two in a cell will do her a great deal of good. In any case, I've spoken to my lawyer, who will come to see you tomorrow, ladies.'

'God has sent you to us, Mr Wokulski,' cried Mrs Misiewicz in a voice that was already quite natural, pulling the kerchief off her head.

'I've come here on a more important matter,' said Staś to Mrs Stawska (obviously he was in a hurry to say goodbye to her, the donkey!), 'have you given up your lessons?'

'Yes.'

'Then give them up for good and all. It's wretched work, and doesn't pay. Go into trade.'

'Me?'

'Yes, madam, you. Do you know accounting?'

'I studied it . . .' Mrs Stawska murmured. She was so upset that she sat down.

'Excellent. Because the responsibility for yet another store and its owner, a widow, has fallen on me. Because almost all the capital is mine, I must have someone I can trust in the business. Will you therefore accept the post of cashier, with wages . . . of seventy-five roubles a month, to start with?'

'Do you hear that, Helena?' Mrs Misiewicz turned to her daughter, making a grimace of the utmost surprise as she did so.

'So you, sir, would entrust your cash-office to me, against whom a law-suit . . . ?' Mrs Stawska began, and burst into tears.

However, both ladies soon calmed down, and half an hour later we were all drinking tea, not only talking, but even laughing. Wokulski was the cause! There's no one in the world like him! How is it possible not to love him? True enough, I may have an equally kind heart, but I still need a little something more – in a word, the half million roubles my dear Staś possesses.

Soon after Christmas, I installed Mrs Stawska in the store of Mrs Miller, and the latter welcomed the new cashier very cordially, spending half an hour to explain to me how noble, wise and handsome Wokulski is . . . That he'd saved the store from bankruptcy, and her and her children from poverty, and how good it would be if such a man were to marry. A charming creature, for all her thirty-five years! Scarcely has she taken one husband to the Powazki cemetery than right away (upon my soul!) she'd like to get married again, to Wokulski of course. I can't reckon up how many of these women there are chasing Wokulski (or his thousands of roubles?).

For her part, Mrs Stawska is delighted with everything: the job, which brings her in a better wage than she ever had before, and a new apartment which Wirski found for her. It is not a bad apartment at all: they have a vestibule, a little kitchen with a sink and water laid on, three very nice little rooms and above all, a garden. For the time being it contains three dried-up sticks and a pile of bricks, but Mrs Stawska is convinced that in summer she'll make a paradise of it. A paradise no bigger than a handkerchief!

The year 1879 began with a victory in Afghanistan for the British, who entered Kabul under General Roberts. No doubt Kabul sauce will get dearer! But Roberts is a gallant fellow: he has only one hand, but for all that he hit the Afghans till their feathers flew . . . Although it's not hard to defeat savages: I'd like to see how you'd perform, Mr Roberts, if you had Hungarian infantry to deal with!

Wokulski also had a battle just after New Year, with that trading company he established. I think that one more session would suffice for him to dispel all his partners to the four winds. Strange folk, though they're all intelligentsia: industrialists, merchants, gentlefolk, princes! He established a company for them, but they regard him as an enemy of this company, and claim that they're the only ones who are making any contribution. He pays them seven per cent half-yearly, but they still grimace and would like to lower the wages of their workers.

As for these dear workers, on whose behalf Wokulski is protesting! What don't they say of him! Don't they call him an exploiter (N.B. in our line of business, he pays the biggest wages and bonuses), and some set traps for others . . .

I have been unhappy to observe that for some time now, habits hitherto unknown have begun blossoming among our people: such as working little, complaining very loudly, quietly spinning intrigues and starting rumours. But what are other people's affairs to me?

I will now finish off, with the utmost expedition, my account of a tragedy which ought to cause every noble heart to quake.

I'd almost forgotten the shameful law-suit brought by Baroness Krzeszowska against pure, innocent, wonderful Mrs Stawska, when – towards the end of January – two thunderbolts fell on us: the news that plague had broken out in Vietlanka, and a summons to court for Wokulski and me on the next day. My feet were hurting and the pain went from heels to knees, then to my stomach, aiming of course towards my heart. I thought to myself: 'Is it plague or paralysis?' But as Wokulski accepted his summons quite indifferently, I too took courage.

In the evening I went confidently to the ladies in their new apartment, and on the way I heard in the street 'Clink-clink, clink-clink!' Oh goodness, can they be taking away prisoners? What a terrible omen. . . . Dear me, what sad thoughts overcome me: what if the court doesn't believe us? (mistakes are possible, after all), and suppose they should hurl that most noble of women in prison, for a week, even for a day! What then? She'd never survive, nor would I . . . Or if I did, then it would only be so that poor little Helena should have a guardian . . .

Yes! I must live. But what sort of life would it be?

I went into the house. Another tableau! Mrs Stawska sitting pale on a little stool, and Mrs Misiewicz with a kerchief soaked in cooling water over her head. The old lady smelled of camphor from two yards away and spoke in a mournful voice: 'Oh, noble Mr Rzecki, who isn't ashamed of unhappy humiliated women . . . Just fancy the misfortune: Helena's court case tomorrow . . . Just think what will happen if the court makes a mistake, and condemns this unhappy woman to the hulks? But calm yourself, Helena, be brave, perhaps God will avert it . . . Though last night I had a terrible dream . . .'

(She had a dream, and I met prisoners . . . It won't pass without a disaster!)

'But,' say I, 'for goodness sake! Our case is proved, we'll win it . . . Besides, what is this compared to the terrible matter of the plague?' I added, to turn Mrs Misiewicz's attention another way.

And I managed beautifully! For didn't she shriek out: 'The plague? Here in Warsaw? There now, Helena, didn't I tell you? Ah, we're all done for! During the plague everyone shuts themselves up indoors . . . They pass food to you on poles . . . They pull the dead bodies out on hooks!'

Ugh . . . I saw I'd upset the worthy old thing, so in order to stop her dwelling on the plague, I mentioned the trial again, whereupon the dear lady replied with a long exposition on the disgrace pursuing her family, on the possible imprisonment of Mrs Stawska, on the way the samovar was leaking . . . In a word, the last evening before the court case, when energy was most needed, that last evening passed for us between plague and death, disgrace and prison. My mind grew so muddled that when I found myself outside in the street I didn't know whether to turn right or left.

Next morning (the case was to be heard at ten o'clock), I went by eight in a carriage to my ladies, but found no one home. They had all gone to confession: mother, daughter, granddaughter and cook, and they united themselves with God until nine-thirty while unfortunate I (after all, this was January) walked up and down in front of the gate in the frost, and thought: 'A fine business! They'll be late for court, if they aren't already, the court will give a verdict in absentia, they'll of course condemn Mrs Stawska, they'll think she has absconded and will send out a warrant for her arrest . . . It's always the way with these women!'

Finally all four of them arrived, with Wirski (can that pious man also have been to confession today?) and we went to court in two droshkies: I and Mrs Stawska and little Helena, Wirski with Mrs Misiewicz and the cook. Too bad they didn't take the frying-pans, samovar and oil-stove with them! In front of the court we saw Wokulski's carriage, in which he and his lawyer had driven up. They were waiting for us at the stairs, which looked as muddy as if a battalion of infantry had passed that way – and their expressions were perfectly calm. I would even wager they'd been talking about something entirely different, not about Mrs Stawska at all.

'Oh, my dear Mr Wokulski, who isn't ashamed of poor women covered in . . .' Mrs Misiewicz began. But Staś gave her his arm, the lawyer Mrs Stawska, Wirski took little Helena by the hand, and I assisted Marianna, and thus we went into the court-room.

It reminded me of a school: the judge was sitting on an elevation, like a professor at his desk, and facing him on two rows of benches were lodged the accused and witnesses. At this moment, my youthful years came so clearly to my mind, that I involuntarily glanced to the stove, certain I would see there a porter with his cane, and the bench on which we were whipped. I even wanted, in my absent-minded way, to cry out: 'I won't do it again, teacher!' but I recollected myself in time.

We began installing our ladies on the benches, and squabbling as we did so with the Jews who, as I later was informed, are the most patient of all audiences at court cases, especially those involving stealing or cheating. We even found a seat for honest Marianna, whose face, as she sat down, looked as though she wanted to cross herself and say a prayer.

Wokulski, our lawyer and I placed ourselves on the front bench, next to an individual in a torn overcoat with a black eye, at whom one of the policemen was looking in a nasty manner.

'Some other incident with the police, no doubt,' thought I.

Suddenly my mouth dropped open of its own accord for surprise: for I now perceived a whole crowd of persons known to me in front of the judge's bench. To the left of the table was Baroness Krzeszowska, her poor little thing of a lawyer and that scoundrel Maruszewicz, while to the right were the two students. One was marked by his very shabby overcoat and unusually fluent speech; the other by a still shabbier overcoat, a coloured scarf around his neck, and he looked, goodness me, as if he'd escaped from a morgue.

I looked more closely at him. Yes, it was he, the same skinny young man who, during Wokulski's first visit to Mrs Stawska, had dropped a herring on the Baroness's head. The dear fellow! But I never saw anyone so thin and yellow-looking.

At first, I thought a court case was going on between these charming young men and the Baroness in respect to that herring. Then, however, I realised that something else was the matter – namely, that Baroness Krzeszowska, now that she was the owner of the house, wanted to expel from it her most fervent enemies, who were at the same time her least profitable tenants. The case between the Baroness and the young men had reached its climax.

One of the students, a handsome lad with whiskers and side-burns, rising on tiptoe and falling back on his heels, was telling the judge something: meanwhile he was executing circular movements with his right hand, and with his left twirling his moustache, sticking out his little finger which was adorned by a ring without any jewels in it.

The second young man was gloomily silent, hiding himself behind his colleague. I noticed something odd in his attitude: he was pressing both hands to his chest, with his palms extended as though he were holding a book or picture.

'What are your names, gentlemen?' asked the judge.

'Maleski,' said the owner of the side-burns with a bow, 'and Patkiewicz,' he added, indicating his gloomy companion with a very distinguished gesture.

'But where is the third gentlemen?'

'He's poorly,' Mr Maleski replied airily, 'he is our sub-tenant, and in any case he very rarely stays in our apartment.'

'How so? Very rarely? Where does he go by day?'

'He's at the University, in the anatomical laboratory, sometimes having dinner.'

'But at night?'

'In that respect, I can only give you confidential information, your honour.'

'But where is he registered as living?'

'Oh, he's registered at our address, because he don't want to be subject to the authorities,' Mr Maleski explained in a lordly manner.

The judge turned to Baroness Krzeszowska: 'So you, madam, don't want to keep these gentlemen on?'

'Not at any price,' the Baroness lamented. 'All night long they roar, howl, stamp and whistle . . . There isn't a servant girl in the house they haven't inveigled into the apartment. Oh, Lord!' she cried, turning away her head.

The judge was startled by this exclamation, but not I . . . For I'd seen that Mr Patkiewicz, without removing his hands from his chest, had suddenly turned up his eyes and dropped his jaw so that he looked like a living corpse. His face and entire attitude would indeed have appalled even a healthy man.

'The most dreadful thing is that these gentlemen pour some liquid or other out of their windows . . .'

'On you, madam?' asked Mr Maleski, impudently.

The Baroness turned livid with rage, but was silent: she was ashamed to admit it.

'What more?' said the judge.

'The very worst of all (which has brought me into a nervous decline) is that these gentlemen knock on my windows several times a day with a human skull . . .'

'Do you indeed, gentlemen?' asked the judge.

'Allow me the privilege of explaining to your honour,' replied Maleski, with the attitude of a man about to dance a minuet, 'we are looked after by the caretaker of the house, who lives downstairs; so as not to waste time going up and down to the third floor, we have a long piece of string, and we tie to it whatever comes to hand (sometimes it may even be a human skull) . . . and we knock on his window with it,' he concluded, in such dulcet tones that no one could be alarmed by an equally delicate tapping.

'Oh Heavens!' cried the Baroness, tottering.

'A sick woman, evidently,' Maleski muttered.

'Not so,' the Baroness cried, 'pray hear me, your honour! I can't bear to see that other one . . . He keeps making faces like a dead body . . . I lost my daughter not long ago,' she concluded in tears.

'On my word of honour, the lady is seeing things,' said Maleski, 'who here looks like a dead body? Patkiewicz? A handsome young fellow like Patkiewicz?' he added, pushing forward his colleague who, at this very moment, was pretending for the fifth time to be a dead body.

Everyone burst out laughing: to preserve his gravity, the judge buried himself in documents and, after a long pause, decreed that laughing was not allowed and anyone disturbing the peace would be fined.

Taking advantage of the confusion, Patkiewicz tugged his colleague by the sleeve and gloomily whispered: 'What's this, you beast, are you making fun of me in public, Maleski?'

'Well, but you're handsome, Patkiewicz. Women go crazy over you.'

'Not on that account, though,' Patkiewicz muttered in a much more tranquil tone.

'Well, now – will you gentlemen pay the twelve roubles fifty kopeks for the month of January?' asked the judge.

This time, Mr Patkiewicz imitated a man who had a cataract and the left side of his face paralysed. Mr Maleski plunged meanwhile into deep meditation. 'If we could stay until the vacation,' he said after a moment, 'then . . . But no! Let the Baroness take away our furniture!'

'No, I don't want any more, I don't . . . Just move out, gentlemen! I won't claim any rent!' the Baroness cried.

'How that woman is compromising herself,' our lawyer whispered. 'Venturing into the law courts with a scoundrel like that adviser of hers!'

'But we have claims against you, madam, for damages and loss,' Maleski cried. 'Who ever heard of a person refusing lodgings to respectable people at this time of year? Even if we find lodgings, they'll be so wretched that two of us at least will die of consumption.'

Mr Patkiewicz, no doubt with a view to adding greater weight to the speaker's words, began moving his ears and the skin on the top of his head, which provoked a new attack of mirth in the court.

'I've never seen anything like it!' said our lawyer.

'Such a court case?' asked Wokulski.

'No – that fellow moving his ears. He's an artist!'

Meanwhile the judge entered sentences and announced that Messrs Maleski and Patkiewicz were to pay the twelve roubles and fifty kopeks rent and leave the apartment before February 8th. At this point an unusual incident occurred. On hearing the sentence, Mr Patkiewicz underwent such a powerful moral shock that his face turned green and he swooned away. Fortunately he fell into the embrace of Mr Maleski; otherwise the poor devil would have injured himself quite dreadfully.

Of course, voices of sympathy were raised in the court room, and Mrs Stawska's cook burst into tears. Embarrassed, the judge interrupted the sitting and, with a nod to Wokulski (how comes it they are acquainted?) went into his office, while two porters almost carried out the unfortunate young man, who this time really resembled a dead body.

Not until he was laid on a bench in the vestibule, and one of those present declared he should be sprinkled with water, did the sick man suddenly sit up and say, threateningly: 'Come, now! No silly jokes, if you please.'

With this he at once put on his coat, energetically pulled on his shabby galoshes and quit the court with a light step, much to the confusion of the porters, the accused and the witnesses.

At this moment, a court official approached our bench and whispered to Wokulski that the judge would be pleased to have him to lunch. Staś went out, but Mrs Misiewicz began calling to me with desperate signals: 'Oh dear me! Oh goodness!' said she, 'Do you know why the judge has summoned that most noble gentleman? He wants to tell him that Helena is lost! Oh, that wicked Baroness must have great friends in high places! She's already won one case, and no doubt it will be the same with Helena. Oh, woe is me! Do you happen to have any cordial drops, Mr Rzecki?'

'Are you poorly, madam?'

'Not yet, though there's such a smell in here . . . I'm terrible afraid for Helena's sake . . . If they sentence her, she will certainly swoon and perhaps die if we don't bring her around quickly. Don't you think it would be a good idea, Mr Rzecki, if I were to beg the judge on my knees to . . .'

'Quite unnecessary, madam. Our lawyer has just said that the Baroness may want to withdraw the charge, but it's too late.'

'But if we too yield?' cried the old lady.

'Come, not that, my dear madam,' I exclaimed, somewhat impatiently, 'either we leave the court completely cleared, or . . .'

'We shall perish! Is that what you were going to say?' the old lady interrupted. 'Oh, don't say so . . . You don't even know, sir, how disagreeable it is at my age to hear death mentioned.'

I retreated from the despairing old lady and went to Mrs Stawska: 'How do you feel?'

'Very well,' she replied energetically, 'though last night I was terribly frightened; but now, after confession, I breathe more easily, and since I've been here I've been quite calm.'

I pressed her hand long . . . long . . . in the way that only true lovers press hands and hurried to my place, for Wokulski, followed by the judge, had come back into court.

My heart was beating like a hammer. I looked around. Mrs

Misiewicz was evidently praying with her eyes shut, Mrs Stawska was very pale but firm, the Baroness was tugging at her wrap and our lawyer eyed the ceiling, stifling a yawn.

At this moment Wokulski too looked at Mrs Stawska, and – may the devil take me! – if I didn't see an expression of sentiment in his eyes rarely to be found there. After a few more trials like this, I'm sure he'll fall desperately in love with her.

The judge went on writing for a while, and when he had finished he informed those present that Krzeszowska's case against Mrs Stawska over the theft of a doll would be heard. He called both parties and their witnesses into the centre.

I took my stand by the benches, consequently I was able to overhear the conversation of two old biddies, of whom the younger and red-faced one was explaining to the elder: 'Now, just look: that pretty lady stole the other lady's doll.'

'Fancy coveting a doll!'

'Well, never mind that. Not everyone can steal a mangle.'

'It was you as stole the mangle,' said a coarse voice from behind them, 'him as takes his own property ain't no thief, but him as gives fifteen roubles deposit and thinks he already owns the property . . .'

The judge was still writing, and I was trying to recall the speech I'd composed the previous day in Mrs Stawska's defence and to shame the Baroness. But the words and phrases were so muddled in my head that I began looking around the court. Mrs Misiewicz was still quietly praying, and Marianna, next to her, was in tears. Baroness Krzeszowska's face was grey, her lips drawn, her eyes downcast: but fury could be seen in every fold of her dress. Next to her stood Maruszewicz, staring at the floor, and behind him was the Baroness's maidservant, as terrified as though they were about to lead her to the scaffold.

Our lawyer stifled his yawns. Wokulski clenched his fists, but Mrs Stawska was gazing at everyone in turn with such benign tranquillity that, had I been a sculptor, I would have taken her as a model for a statue of accused innocence.

Despite Marianna's efforts, little Helena ran into the courtroom and caught her mother by the hand, asking in an undertone: 'Mama, why has that gentleman told mama to come here? I'll whisper something to you: you have been naughty, mama, and now you'll have to stand in the corner.'

'Clever little creature,' said the red-faced biddy to the elder one.

'Pity you ain't as clever . . .' muttered the coarse voice behind her.

'Just you try being clever . . .' the biddy replied crossly.

'May you die in convulsions and do your mangling in Hell on the mangle o'mine,' her enemy retorted.

'Silence!' cried the judge. 'What has Baroness Krzeszowska to say in the case?'

'Hear me, Your Worship!' the Baroness began declaiming, placing one leg forward, 'of my late child was left to me, as my dearest souvenir, a doll, which that lady over yonder very much liked (she pointed at Mrs Stawska), and so her did daughter.'

'Was the accused ever in your apartment?'

'Yes, I hired her to do sewing . . .'

'And never paid her!' roared Wirski from the back of the court.

'Silence!' the judge thundered at him. 'Well, and what else?'

'On the day I dismissed that woman,' said the Baroness, 'the doll vanished. I thought I'd die of grief, and at once began suspecting her . . . I had good cause, for a few days later my friend Mr Maruszewicz saw through the window that this woman, who lives opposite him, had my doll in her apartment and was changing its dress so it wouldn't be recognised. I went into his apartment with my legal adviser, and looked through opera-glasses, and saw my doll really was in that woman's apartment. So next day I went and took away the doll, which I see there on the bench, and made a complaint.'

'Was Mr Maruszewicz certain that it was the same doll as the Baroness's?' the judge asked him.

'That's to say . . . properly speaking . . . I'm not certain.'

'Why did Mr Maruszewicz say that to the Baroness?'

'As a matter of fact . . . I didn't mean . . .'

'Don't lie, sir!' the Baroness cried, 'you came running to tell me, laughing, that Stawska had stolen the doll and that it was just like her . . .'

Maruszewicz began changing his expression, sweating and even shifting from one foot to the other, which is always proof of great contrition.

'Wretch!' muttered Wokulski, quite loudly. But I saw this comment didn't console Maruszewicz. Indeed, he seemed to grow still more confused. The judge turned to Krzeszowska's maid servant: 'Was this doll in the apartment?'

'I don't know which . . .' the witness murmured. The judge pushed the doll towards her, but the maidservant said not a word, only blinked and wrung her hands.

'Oh, it's Mimi!' exclaimed little Helena.

'There, your worship!' the Baroness cried, 'her own daughter is bearing witness against her!'

'Do you recognise this doll?' the judge asked little Helena.

'Oh, I do! One just like it was in that lady's room . . .'

'Is this the same one?'

'No, not this one . . . The other had a grey dress, and black shoes, but this one has brown shoes.'

'Well, now,' said the judge, putting the doll down, 'what has Mrs Stawska to say?'

'I bought this doll in Mr Wokulski's store.'

'And how much did you pay for it, madam, if you please?' the Baroness hissed.

'Three roubles.'

'Ha ha ha!' the Baroness laughed, 'this doll cost fifteen . . .'

'Who sold you the doll?' the judge asked Mrs Stawska.

'Mr Rzecki,' she replied, with a blush.

'What has Mr Rzecki to say?' asked the judge.

This was precisely the moment to utter my speech. So I began: 'Your worship . . . It is with painful surprise that I . . . I mean . . . I see before me evil triumphant, and so forth . . . this oppressed lady . . .'

Suddenly my mouth dried up, so I couldn't utter a word. Fortunately Wokulski spoke up: 'Rzecki was present at the sale, the doll was sold by me.'

'For three roubles?' asked the Baroness, her eyes glittering like those of a lizard.

'Yes, for three roubles. It was shop-soiled, we were disposing of it.'

'Would you sell me such a doll for three roubles?'

'No, madam. Nothing will ever be sold to you in my store!'

'What proof do you have, sir, that this doll was purchased in your store?' asked the judge.

'That's the point!' cried the Baroness, 'the proof!'

'Hush!' the judge threatened her.

'Where did you buy your doll, madam?' Wokulski asked the Baroness.

'At Lesser's.'

'So we have proof,' said Wokulski. 'I imported this kind of doll from abroad, in parts: heads and bodies separate. If you will unfasten the head, your honour, my name will be found inside.'

The Baroness started to grow uneasy. The judge picked up the doll which had caused so much chagrin and cut its waistcoat with his official scissors, then began very attentively unfastening the head from the torso. Helena, surprised at first, watched this operation then turned to her mother and said in a low voice: 'Mama, why is that gentlemen undressing Mimi? She will be shy . . .'

Suddenly realising what was going on, she burst into tears and, hiding her face in Mrs Stawska's dress, cried: 'Oh, mama – why is he cutting her? It hurts terribly . . . Mama, mama, I don't want them to cut Mimi up.'

'Don't cry, Helena, Mimi will get better and be still prettier,' Wokulski soothed her, no less moved than she. Meanwhile, Mimi's head had fallen amidst the papers. The judge looked inside and, handing the label to the Baroness, asked: 'Well, madam, pray read what is written there?'

The Baroness pressed her lips together, but said nothing.

'Then let Mr Maruszewicz read aloud what is written there.'

'Jan Mincel and Stanisław Wokulski,' groaned Maruszewicz.

'Not Lesser?'

'No.'

All this time, the Baroness's maid had been behaving in a very ambiguous manner: she blushed, turned pale, hid between the benches . . . The judge was watching her out of the corner of his eye: suddenly he said: 'Now, miss, pray tell us what happened to this doll? The truth, if you please, for you are under oath . . .'

The girl he addressed, clutched at her head with the utmost terror, fell on her knees at the bench, and replied: 'The doll got broken, your honour.'

'The doll of yours, Baroness Krzeszowska's doll?'

'The very same . . .'

'Well, but only her head would break, so where's the rest?'

'In the attic, your honour. Oh, what won't I get for this?'

'You won't get anything: it would be worse not to tell the truth. And you, madam, the accuser, do you hear this?'

The Baroness looked down and folded her arms over her bosom like a martyr. The judge began writing. A gentleman seated on the second bench (the mangler, of course) exclaimed to the red-faced lady: 'So now, did she steal it? Just look, madam, what comes of your chatter! Eh?'

'If a woman is pretty, she can get out of going to jail,' said the red-faced biddy to her neighbour.

'You won't, though!' the mangler muttered.

'You're a fool!'

'You're a bigger one!'

'Silence!' the judge exclaimed. Then we were told to rise, and heard a judgement exculpating Mrs Stawska entirely.

'Now,' the judge ended, 'you can enter a charge of slander.'

He came down into the court, shook Mrs Stawska by the hand and added: 'I am sorry to have charged you, and am very pleased to congratulate you.'

Baroness Krzeszowska had spasms, and the red-faced lady said to her neighbour: 'Even the judge is partial to a pretty face . . . But it won't be so on the Day of Judgement,' she sighed.

'Oh, how she blasphemes!' muttered the owner of the mangle.

We started leaving. Wokulski gave Mrs Stawska his arm and moved ahead, while I began carefully conducting Mrs Misiewicz down the grubby staircase.

'I said it would end this way,' the old lady assured me, 'but you didn't believe me.'

'I didn't believe you?'

'Yes, you were ever so dejected . . . Goodness, what's that?'

Her last words were directed towards the poor student who, along with his companion, was waiting at the door, obviously for Baroness Krzeszowska, and thinking it was she coming out, he'd done himself up like a dead body for the benefit of – Mrs Misiewicz. He at once saw his error, and was so ashamed that he ran a few steps forward. 'Patkiewicz! Stop! Here they come!' Maleski exclaimed.

'Devil take you,' Patkiewicz burst out, 'you always have to compromise me.'

On hearing a noise in the doorway, he turned and once again displayed the dead body – to Wirski. This finally brought about the collapse of the young men: so they went home, very vexed with each other, and on different sides of the street. But by the time we caught up with them in our carriages, they were together again, and bowed to us with the utmost civility.

XXX

The Journal of the Old Clerk

I KNOW WHY I wrote so much about Mrs Stawska's law-suit. This is why . . . There are many unbelievers in this world, and I too am sometimes an unbeliever and doubt Heavenly Providence. Sometimes, too, when political matters go badly, or when I see human misery and scoundrels triumphant (if one may use such a phrase), I sometimes think to myself: 'You old fool, Ignacy Rzecki! You imagine the Napoleons will regain their throne, that Wokulski will do something extraordinary because he has talent, and will be happy because he's honest. You think, you donkey, that although scoundrels prosper while honest people don't, that nevertheless the evil ones will be shamed, and the good covered with glory in the end. Is that what you imagine? If so, you are very foolish. There is neither order nor justice in the world; it's a battlefield. If the good conquer in the fight, it's all right – while if the bad do, then it's bad: but don't for a moment think there is a power which protects only the good . . . People are like leaves, blown by the wind: when it lands them in a flower-bed, they lie in a flower-bed: but when it throws them into mud – they lie in the mud.'

I have sometimes thought this to myself in moments of doubt; but Mrs Stawska's trial led me to a completely opposite conclusion, to the belief that sooner or later good people will obtain justice. For, just consider . . . Mrs Stawska is an excellent lady, so she ought to be happy; Staś is a man beyond all price, so he too should be happy. Yet Staś is always vexed and sad (so much that I feel like weeping when I see him), and Mrs Stawska is put on trial for stealing. So – where's the justice that rewards the good? You'll see in a moment, you man of little faith! To help you understand that there is order in this world, I will copy out the following prophecy. In the first place, Mrs Stawska will marry Staś and be happy with him. In the second, Wokulski will renounce that Miss Łęcka of his, and will marry Mrs Stawska, and be happy with her. In the third, young Lulu will become Emperor of France this year, under the name of Napoleon IV he will beat the Germans to a frazzle and will bring justice to the whole world, as my late father prophesied.

That Wokulski will marry Mrs Stawska, and do something out of the ordinary – of this I haven't the slightest doubt. Admittedly, he isn't engaged to her yet, hasn't even proposed, but . . . he himself doesn't realise. But I can see it. I can clearly see how things will go, and would suffer my head to be chopped off that it will be so – I have a political nose!

Just watch what happens!

On the day after the trial, Wokulski was at Mrs Stawska's in the evening, and stayed till eleven. Next day he was in Mrs Miller's store, inspected the ledgers, and greatly praised Mrs Stawska, which discomfited Mrs Miller somewhat. Next day, however . . . Well, I admit he was at Mrs Miller's not at Mrs Stawska's, but odd things happened to me. Before noon (somehow there were no customers in the store), who should unexpectedly come up to me but young Szlangbaum, that Israelite who works in the Russian linen department. I looked up, there he was, rubbing his hands, his moustache twirled up, head high . . . And I thought to myself 'Has he gone mad, or what?' But he bows, with his head high, and says these very words: 'I daresay, Mr Rzecki, that whatever happens, we'll still be friends . . .'

I think to myself: 'What the devil's this, can Staś have sacked him?' So I reply: 'You can rest assured, Mr Szlangbaum, of my cordiality, providing you haven't committed any fraud, Mr Szlangbaum.'

I emphasised the last words, for my Mr Szlangbaum looked as though he intended either to purchase our store, (which seems unlikely to me), or steal the cash-box . . . which, though he's honest, I wouldn't consider out of the question.

Evidently he noticed this, for he smiled slightly and went back to his department. A quarter of an hour later, I walked in there as though by chance, but found him at work as usual. Indeed, I'd even say he was working harder than usual; he trotted up ladders, pulled down rolls of reps and velvet, put them back in the cupboards and, in a word, was bustling about like a bee. 'No,' I thought, 'surely this fellow will never rob us.'

I noticed – and this also made me ponder – that Mr Zięba was being humbly civil to Szlangbaum, and was looking at me rather haughtily, though not very. 'Ha!' I thought, 'he wants to compensate Szlangbaum for his previous insults, and to preserve his personal honour as far as I, the most senior clerk, am concerned. Very decent of him, for we should always condescend a little to those above us, but be exaggeratedly civil to those beneath.'

That evening I went to the tavern for beer. Whom should I see but Mr Szprott and Councillor Węgrowicz! Ever since that contretemps which I've mentioned with Szprott, he and I have been on terms of mutual indifference, but I greeted the councillor cordially enough. And he says to me: 'Well, has it happened?'

'Excuse me,' I said, 'but I don't understand you (I thought he was alluding to Mrs Stawska's law-suit), I don't understand you at all, Councillor.'

'What don't you understand?' says he, 'not the fact that the store has been sold?'

'Cross yourself, Councillor,' say I, 'what store?'

The respectable old councillor had already got six bottles inside of him, so he began laughing and says: 'Pooh! I may cross myself if I choose, but they won't let you do so when you give over eating Christian bread and take to Jewish challah instead; there now, people say the Jews have bought that store of yours . . .'

I thought I would have an apoplectic stroke: 'Councillor,' say I, 'you're too serious a man not to tell me where you heard this news!'

'The whole town's talking,' replied the councillor, 'and besides, let Mr Szprott here explain.'

'Mr Szprott,' say I, with a bow, 'I didn't intend to speak to you, the more so that when I asked you for satisfaction you, like a scoundrel, refused it . . . Like a scoundrel, Mr Szprott . . . However, I must tell you that you're either repeating gossip, or making it up yourself.'

'What's that?' roared Szprott, banging the table with his fist as he had done the previous time, 'I refused because I'm not here to give satisfaction to you, nor to any man. Yet I'll repeat that the Jews are buying that store of yours.'

'What Jews?'

'Goodness knows – the Szlangbaums, Hundbaums – how should I know?'

I was so overcome with rage that I ordered beer, and Węgrowicz says: 'There'll be a nasty to-do one day with these Jews. They're pressing in on us, turning us out of jobs, buying us up – so it's hard to cope with 'em. We'll never get the better of them by cheating, that's for sure, but when it comes to bare fists, then we'll see who comes off best.'

'You are right, Councillor!' added Szprott. 'Those Jews will seize everything so that in the end it will have to be taken from them by force, to maintain stability. For just look, gentlemen, at what is happening, if only in the courts.'

'Well,' say I, 'if the Jews buy our store, I'll join in with the rest of you; my fist still carries some weight. But in the meantime, for goodness sake, don't spread rumours about Wokulski and don't agitate people against the Jews, because there's enough bitterness without that.'

I went home with a headache, furious with the whole world. I woke up several times in the night, and each time I dropped off again I dreamed that the Jews had really bought our store, and that I, so as not to starve to death, was going around the courtyards with a barrel-organ on which was written: 'Take pity on a poor old ex-Hungarian officer.'

Not until the morning did I hit upon one simple and sensible idea, to wit, discuss it firmly with Staś, and if in fact he was going to sell, then to try for another position.

A fine prospect after so many years of service! If I were a dog, at least they'd put a bullet through my head. But a man has to demean himself, uncertain to the end whether he won't end his days in the gutter.

Wokulski wasn't in the store that morning, so at about two I went off to see him. Could he be sick? I went into the gateway of the house he lives in, and ran across Dr Szuman. When I told him I wanted to see Staś, he replied: 'Don't go. He's irritable, and had better be left in peace. You'd better come with me for a glass of tea. Apropos, do I have a sample of your hair?'

'It seems to me,' I replied, 'that I'll soon be giving you my hair along with the rest of my skin.'

'Do you want to have yourself stuffed?'

'I ought to, for no one has yet seen anyone so stupid as I am.'

'Cheer up,' Szuman replied, 'there are stupider people. But what's the matter?'

'Never mind what's the matter with me, but I've heard that Staś is selling the store to the Jews . . . Well, and I won't work for the likes of them.'

'What's this, has anti-Semitism got into you, too?'

'No; but it's one thing not to be an anti-Semite, and another to work for the Jews.'

'So who will work for them, then? For although I'm a Jew, I don't wear their livery. In any case,' he added, 'how did such thoughts get into your head? If the store is sold, you'll have an excellent position in the company trading with Russia.'

'That company is uncertain,' I interposed.

'Very,' Szuman agreed, 'because there are so very few Jews in it, and too many magnates. But that's no concern of yours, for . . . don't give the secret away, though . . . but it's no concern of yours what happens to the store and the company, since Wokulski has left you twenty thousand roubles in his will.'

'Me? In his will? What does this mean?' I cried, in amazement.

We had just entered Szuman's apartment, and the doctor ordered the samovar. 'What does this bequest mean?' I asked, somewhat uneasy.

'Bequest! . . . Bequest! . . .' muttered Szuman, walking around the room and scratching the back of his head. 'What does it mean? I don't know, it's enough that Wokulski made it. Clearly he wants to be ready for any eventuality, like all sensible merchants.'

'Can it mean another duel?'

'Oh, for goodness sake . . . Wokulski has too much sense to commit the same folly twice. Only, my dear Mr Rzecki, anyone who is concerned with such a female must be prepared . . .'

'With what female? Mrs Stawska?' I asked.

'What has Mrs Stawska to do with it?' said the doctor, 'I'm thinking of more important game, of Miss Łęcka, whom that madman has fallen hopelessly in love with. He's beginning to see what sort of a bad egg she is, he's suffering and fretting, but he can't break with her. The worst thing is a late love affair, particularly when it hits a fellow like Wokulski.'

'Whatever can have happened? Only yesterday he was at a dance at the Town Hall.'

'Of course he was, because she was there, and I was there because the pair of them were. A fine business!' the doctor muttered.

'Couldn't you speak more plainly?' I asked impatiently.

'Why not, since everyone knows all about it?' said the doctor. 'Wokulski is insane about the young lady, she flirts with him very cleverly, while her other admirers . . . wait. It's a scandal,' Szuman went on, walking around the room again, and rubbing his head: 'While Izabela was penniless and had no suitors, then not even a dog would visit them. But when Wokulski turned up, rich, with a great reputation and contacts which people somewhat exaggerate, then such a flock gathered around Miss Łęcka of more or less stupid, spoiled and handsome bachelors that you can't get a sight of her. Each of them sighs, turns up his eyes, whispers tender phrases, presses her hand fondly as they dance . . .'

'And what does she have to say to this?'

'Wretched woman!' said the doctor, shrugging. 'Instead of despising the throng which has already deserted her several times, she revels in their society. Everyone sees that, and the worst is that – Wokulski sees it too.'

'Why in the devil's name doesn't he leave her? It's all very well for some, but surely he won't let himself be made a fool of ?'

The samovar was brought. Szuman dismissed the servant, and poured tea. 'You see,' he said, 'he would certainly quit her if he were able to evaluate things sensibly. There was a moment last night at the ball, when the lion awoke in Staś, and when he went to exchange a few words with Miss Łęcka, I'd have sworn he said to her: "Goodnight, madam, I've seen your cards and won't play with them!" The expression he had, as he went over to her! But what of it? The young lady gave him a look, whispered, pressed his hand, and my Staś was so happy all evening, so happy that . . . today he wants to put a bullet through his head – if it weren't that he's expecting another of those looks, another whisper and touch of the hand . . . The fool doesn't see that she distributes the very same favours to ten men, and in much bigger doses.'

'What sort of woman is she?'

'Like hundreds and thousands of others. Pretty, spoiled, but soulless. To her, Wokulski's value equals his money and importance: he's all right for a husband, of course – for want of a better. But for her lovers, she chooses men that suit her book. And yet he,' Szuman went on, 'in Hopfer's cellar and on the steppe, fed himself on the heroines of Romantic poetry and such-like chimeras, so that he sees a divinity in Miss Łęcka. He doesn't merely love her, he adores her, he worships her, would gladly fall on his knees before her . . . A bitter awakening awaits him! For, although he's a full-blooded Romantic, he isn't going to imitate Mickiewicz who forgave the woman who mocked him, even yearned for her after the betrayal, bah! then made her immortal. A fine lesson for our young ladies; if you want fame, betray your most fervent admirers! We Poles are condemned to act as fools even in a matter as simple as love.'

'Do you think, doctor, that Wokulski will be such a fool?' I asked, feeling the blood boil within me as it did at Vilagos.

Szuman almost jumped out of his chair. 'Oh, damnation!' he cried, 'nowadays a man can go crazy until he tells himself "Suppose she loves me, suppose she's what I think she is?" But if he doesn't notice that they're mocking him, I . . . I'd be the first, though a Jew, to spit in his face . . . Such a man may be unhappy, but he doesn't have the right to be abject.'

Not for long had I seen Szuman so irritated. He's a Jew from top to toe, but a true friend and a man with a sense of honour. 'Well,' said I, 'calm yourself, doctor. I have the cure for Staś.'

And I told him everything I knew about Mrs Stawska, adding, 'I'll die, I promise you that, doctor, if I don't marry Staś to Mrs Stawska. She's a woman with sense and feeling, and will repay love with love, and he needs just such a woman.'

Szuman shook his head and raised his eyebrows: 'Well, try it . . . The only cure for one woman is another. Though I'm afraid the cure is too late.'

'He's a man of iron,' I interposed.

'And therefore dangerous,' the doctor replied. 'It's hard to erase what has once been written in such a man's soul, and difficult to repair what is broken.'

'Mrs Stawska will do it.'

'God grant that she does.'

'And Staś will be happy.'

'Hm . . .'

I bade farewell to the doctor full of hope. I love Mrs Stawska, that I do, but I'd renounce her – for him. Providing it isn't too late! But no . . .

Next afternoon, Szuman dropped in at the store; from the way he grinned and bit his lips, I saw something was grieving him and put him into an ironic mood. 'Have you seen Staś?' I asked, 'today he's . . .'

He drew me behind the cupboards, and began speaking in an irritable voice: 'Just see what women can reduce even a man like Wokulski to! Do you know why he's agitated!?'

'Has he found out that Miss Łęcka has a lover?'

'If only he had . . . That might be a radical cure, but she's too sharp-witted to let such a naive admirer see what's going on behind the scenes. No, something else is the matter. It's comical, it's humiliating to talk of . . .' the doctor scowled. He struck his bald head, and went on in a lower voice: 'Tomorrow the Prince is giving a ball, at which Miss Łęcka will of course be present. And do you know, sir, that as yet the Prince hasn't invited Wokulski, although the invitations have been out two weeks? And would you credit that Staś is ill on this account?'

The doctor laughed shrilly, baring his decayed teeth, and I, goodness knows why, blushed for shame.

'Now do you understand what sort of decline our man may be in?' asked Szuman. 'He's been mortifying himself for two days because some prince or other hasn't asked him to a ball. Him, our dear friend, our admirable Staś!'

'Did he tell you this himself?'

'Bah!' the doctor muttered, 'that's the whole point, he didn't. If he had the courage to tell me, then he'd be able to refuse a very late invitation.'

'Do you think he'll be invited?'

'Hm! Not to invite him would cost fifteen per cent on the capital which the Prince has invested in the company. He'll invite him because Wokulski is still a force to be reckoned with, thank God! But, knowing his weakness for Miss Łęcka, the Prince is out to irritate him, to play with him, like a dog that meat is shown to, then taken away from, in order to teach him to walk on his hind-legs. Never fear, sir, they won't let him go, they're too smart for him: but they want to tame him so that he will serve them, fetch and carry and even bite people they don't like.'

He took his fur cap and left, with a brief nod. Always the eccentric.

The day passed wretchedly for me; I even made several errors in my accounts. Then, as I was thinking of closing the store, Staś appeared. He seemed to have grown thinner in the past few days.

He greeted the clerks indifferently and began turning over papers on his desk. 'Are you looking for something?' I asked.

'Wasn't there a letter from the Prince?' he asked, without looking me in the eye.

'I sent all the letters on to your apartment.'

'I know, but one might have been overlooked.'

I'd sooner have had a tooth out than hear this question. So Szuman was right. Staś mortified that the Prince hasn't invited him to the ball!

When the store was closed and the gentlemen gone, Staś said: 'What are you doing tonight? Won't you invite me in for tea?'

Of course I gladly did so, and recalled the good old days, when Staś used to spend nearly every evening at my place. How far off those times are! Today he was gloomy, I was embarrassed, and although we both had a great deal to say, neither looked the other in the eye. We even began talking about the weather, and it was not until a glass of tea in which there was a half glass of brandy, that my tongue grew slightly loose. 'They're still saying,' I remarked, 'that you're selling the store.'

'I've almost sold it,' replied Wokulski.

'To the Jews?'

He jumped up, and thrusting his hands into his pockets, began walking around the room: 'To whom else?' he asked. 'To those who don't buy the store when they have money, or to those who would buy it because they've got none? The store is worth some hundred and twenty thousand roubles – am I to throw it in the mud?'

'The Jews are ousting us all, something terrible . . .'

'Out of what? Positions we don't hold, or into positions we force them to take, beg them to take? None of our gentlemen will buy my store, but everyone will give a Jew money to buy it for him . . . and pay him a good percentage on the capital invested.'

'Is that so?'

'Of course it is, I know who is lending money to Szlangbaum . . .'

'Is Szlangbaum buying it?'

'Who else? Maybe Klein, Lisiecki or Zięba? They'd never get the credit or, if they did, would squander it.'

'There's going to be trouble with the Jews,' I muttered.

'There already has been a great deal, it's gone on for over eighteen centuries, and what's the outcome? Very noble individuals have perished in anti-Jewish persecutions, and the only ones to survive were those who could protect themselves from destruction. So now what sort of Jews do we have? Persistent, patient, sly, self-reliant, quick-witted, and commanding a mastery of the one weapon left to them – money. By wiping out everything that was good, we have produced an artificial selection and protected the worst.'

'Have you considered, though, that when your store gets into their hands, some dozen Jews will obtain well-paid work, and a dozen of our own people will lose it?'

'That's not my fault,' said Wokulski, irritated. 'It's not my fault if the people with whom I have social contacts insist on my selling the store. Society will lose, that's true, but that is what society wants.'

'And your obligations?'

'What obligations?' he exclaimed. 'Towards those who call me an exploiter, or to those who rob me? An obligation carried out ought to bring a man something, otherwise he's a victim, from whom no one has the right to demand anything. And I, what do I have to gain? Hatred and cheating on one hand, contempt on the other. Just tell me – is there any crime I haven't been accused of, and for what? For making a fortune, and giving subsistence to hundreds of people.'

'You find slanderers everywhere.'

'But nowhere to such an extent as here. Elsewhere, a parvenu like me would have enemies, but I'd also have recognition that would compensate for the injustices. But here . . .'

He made a gesture. I drank up another glass of tea and brandy in one gulp, to give myself courage. Staś, hearing footsteps in the passage, walked to the door. I guessed he was awaiting the Prince's invitation. My head was already whirling, so I asked: 'And do the people for whose sake you're selling the store appreciate you any better?'

'Suppose they do?' he asked, pondering.

'And will they love you more than the people you are deserting?'

He hastened to me and looked me swiftly in the eye. 'If they do?' he retorted.

'Are you certain?'

He cast himself into an armchair. 'How should I know?' he murmured, 'how should I know? What's certain in this world?'

'Has it never occurred to you,' I said with increasing boldness, 'that you may not only be exploited and cheated, but even laughed at and despised? Tell me, have you never thought of that? Anything can happen in the world, so one should take care to avoid, if not disappointment, then at least becoming a laughing-stock. The devil take it!' I concluded, banging the table with my glass, 'a man can make a sacrifice if he has the wherewithal, but he cannot let himself be misused.'

'Who is misusing me?' he cried, rising.

'All the people who don't respect you as you deserve.'

My own boldness appalled me, but Wokulski made no reply. He sat down on the sofa and clasped his hands behind his head, a sign of unusual emotion. Then he began talking about the store accounts in a completely calm voice. Towards nine, the door opened and Wokulski's butler came in. 'Here's a letter from the Prince,' he cried.

Staś bit his lip and stretched out one hand without rising. 'Give it to me,' he said, 'and go to bed.'

The servant went out. Staś opened the envelope slowly, read the note – and after tearing it into several pieces – threw it into the stove.

'What is it?' I asked.

'An invitation to the ball tomorrow,' he replied, drily.

'Aren't you going?'

'I wouldn't dream of it.'

I was dumbfounded. And suddenly the most brilliant idea in the world occurred to me. 'You know,' said I, 'maybe we might spend the evening at Mrs Stawska's tomorrow?'

He sat up and replied with a smile: 'Come, that wouldn't be a bad idea! A most agreeable woman, and I haven't been there for ages. We must take the opportunity to send a few toys for the little girl.'

The wall of ice which had formed between us now burst. We both regained our earlier frankness and talked of past times until midnight. On saying goodnight, Staś told me: 'A man sometimes makes a fool of himself, but sometimes he regains his common sense. May God reward you, my old friend!'

My dear, beloved Staś! I'll marry him to Stawska even if I burst in the attempt.

On the day of the Prince's ball neither Staś nor Szlangbaum were in the store. I guessed they must be arranging the sale of our business. At any other time, an incident like this would have spoiled my mood for the entire day. But this day I didn't think once of the disappearance of our firm, and its replacement by a Jewish name-plate. What did the store matter to me, as long as Staś was happy, or had at least got out of his miseries? I must marry him off, come what may . . .

That morning I sent Mrs Stawska a note announcing that Wokulski and I were coming for tea that day. I ventured to add a box of toys for Helena. It included a forest with animals, a set of dolls' furniture, a little tea-set and a brass samovar. Total: 13 roubles, 60 kopeks, with packing.

I still have to think how to get around Mrs Misiewicz. Then I'll make a pair of pliers out of Grandma and the little daughter, and will so squeeze the pretty mother by the heart that she'll have to surrender before Midsummer Day. (Oh, confound it! And that husband abroad? Well, what of him, let him look after himself . . . Besides, for some ten thousand roubles we'll get a divorce for desertion and very likely he's dead.)

When the store closed, I went to Staś. The footman, holding a
starched shirt in one hand, opened the door. Passing the bedroom,
I saw a tail-coat over a chair, a waistcoat . . . Could it be that our
visit would come to nothing?

Staś was reading an English book in his study (God alone knows
what he wants with studying English! A man can marry even if he's
deaf and dumb, after all.) He greeted me cordially, though not
without a certain hesitation. 'I must seize the bull by the horns,'
thought I, and without putting down my cap, I said: 'Well, come,
there's no point in lingering. Let's be off, else the ladies will be
going to bed.'

Wokulski laid aside the book, and pondered. 'A nasty evening,'
he said, 'it's snowing.'

'That won't prevent other people from going to the ball, so why
should it spoil our evening?' I replied, as though I didn't know
what he meant. It was as though I'd stung him. He jumped up, and
ordered his great-coat. The servant, as he helped him into it, said:
'Mind and be back right away, sir, for it's time to dress, and the
barber is coming.'

'No need,' Staś replied.

'Surely you won't go dancing without combing your hair?'

'I'm not going to the ball.'

The servant threw up his hands in surprise, and struck an attitude.
'Whatever are you thinking of today!' he cried, 'you behave as if
you was wrong in the head . . . Mr Łęcki begged you so . . .'

Wokulski left the room hastily and slammed the door in the face
of his impudent servant. 'Aha,' thought I, 'so the Prince realises
Staś may not come, and sent, as it were, his father-in-law with an
invitation! Szuman is right to say they won't want to let go of him,
but even so, we'll get him away from you all!'

A quarter of an hour later, we were at Mrs Stawska's. The
delight with which we were received! Marianna had spread clean
sand in the kitchen, Mrs Misiewicz had on a silk, snuff-coloured
dress, and Mrs Stawska had such fine eyes, a blush and lips that a
man could have kissed such a pretty woman to death. I don't want
to exaggerate, but goodness me! Staś gazed at her with great attention all evening. He didn't even have time to notice that little
Helena was wearing a new scarf.

What an evening it was! How Mrs Stawska thanked us for the
toys, how she sweetened Wokulski's tea for him, how she brushed
him with the edge of her sleeve several times! Even today, I am
sure that Staś will come here as often as possible, at first with me,
then later – without.

In the middle of supper, a good or perhaps bad spirit directed
Mrs Misiewicz's eyes to the *Courier*. 'Just look, Helena,' she said to
her daughter, 'there's a ball tonight at the Prince's.'

Wokulski grew sombre and instead of gazing into Mrs Stawska's eyes, began staring at his plate. Taking courage, I remarked, not without irony: 'Just think of all the fine company to be at such a one's as the Prince's! Costumes, refinement . . .'

'Not as fine as you might suppose,' the old lady replied. 'Often the dresses aren't paid for, and as for refinement! One thing is certain – it'll be one thing in the drawing-room with the counts and princes, but another in the cloakroom, with the poor people.'

How very apt the old lady was, with her criticism. 'Just listen to her, Staś,' I thought, and I went on to inquire: 'So great ladies aren't very refined in the way they treat working girls?'

'My dear sir!' replied Mrs Misiewicz, with a wave of the hand, 'we know one shop-girl those ladies give work to, for she is very clever and cheap. Sometimes she's in floods of tears when she comes back from them. How often she has to wait to fit a dress, to make improvements, for the bill! And their tone of voice in conversation, such rudeness, such bargaining . . . This shop-girl says (upon my word!) that she'd sooner deal with four Jewish women than with one great lady. Though no doubt nowadays the Jewesses have become spoiled too: when one of 'em gets rich, she starts talking nothing but French, bargaining, complaining . . .'

I wanted to ask if Miss Łęcka dressed with this shop-girl. But I was sorry for Staś. His face had changed so, poor devil.

After tea, Helena began setting up the toys she'd just received on the carpet, exclaiming with joy; Mrs Misiewicz and I sat by the windows (the old lady just can't keep away from those windows!), while Wokulski and Mrs Stawska installed themselves on the couch: she had some sewing, he a cigarette.

As the dear old lady began telling me with the utmost enthusiasm what an excellent county prefect her late husband had been, I didn't hear very much of what Mrs Stawska and Wokulski were saying. But it must have been interesting, for they said in low voices: 'I saw you, madam, at the Carmelites, at the graves.'

'And I recall you best, sir, when you came to the apartment house where we were living, last summer. And I don't know why, but it seemed to me . . .'

'And the trouble there was with the passports! . . . Goodness knows who collected them, who he gave them back to, whose names he wrote in them . . .' Mrs Misiewicz was telling me.

'Of course, as often as you please,' said Mrs Stawska, blushing.

'And I won't be intruding?'

'A charming couple,' I said in an undertone to Mrs Misiewicz.

She glanced at them and replied, sighing: 'What of it, even supposing poor Ludwik is dead?'

'Let's trust in God . . .'

'That he's alive?' asked the old lady, not betraying any delight at all.

'No, I don't mean that . . .'

'Mama, I want to go to bed now,' Helena exclaimed.

Wokulski rose from the sofa and bade goodbye to both ladies. 'Who knows,' thought I, 'if the fish hasn't taken the bait?'

Outdoors snow was still falling: Staś accompanied me home and waited in the sledge until I'd entered the gate, I don't know why. I walked in, then paused in the passage. And only then, when the door-man had shut the gate, did I hear the bells of the departing sledge in the street. 'So that's it, is it?' I thought. 'Let's see where you're off to now.'

I dropped in at my room, put on my old greatcoat and top-hat and thus disguised went out half an hour later into the streets. Staś's apartment was in darkness, so he wasn't home. Where might he be? I hailed a passing sledge and got out a few minutes later not far from the Prince's house. Several carriages were standing in the street, others still driving up; already the first floor was lit up, music playing, and in the windows, dancing shadows fluttered past from time to time. 'Miss Łęcka is there,' thought I, and somehow my heart ached.

I looked around. Goodness, what clouds of snow! I could barely see the gas-lights flickering in the wind. Bed-time.

Wanting to hail a sledge, I crossed the street, and . . . almost bumped into Wokulski . . . standing under a tree, covered with snow, staring into the windows: 'So that's it! Even if it's the death of me, my friend, you're to marry Mrs Stawska!'

Faced with this peril, I decided to act energetically. Next morning I went to Szuman, and said: 'Do you know, doctor, what has happened to Staś?'

'What, did he break a leg?'

'Worse. Despite being invited twice, he wasn't at the Prince's ball but around midnight he disappeared from his house, and there, standing out in the snow, he watched the windows. Do you understand me?'

'I do. No need to be a psychiatrist, for that.'

'So,' I went on, 'I have decided irrevocably to marry off Staś this year, even before Midsummer Day.'

'To Miss Łęcka?' the doctor caught me up. 'I'd advise you not to get involved in that.'

'Not to Miss Łęcka, but to Mrs Stawska.'

The doctor began tapping his head: 'It's a madhouse,' he cried. 'Everyone included . . . You obviously have water on the brain, Mr Rzecki,' he added, a moment later.

'You insult me, sir!' I cried impatiently.

He stopped, seized my lapels and said crossly: 'Listen to me, sirrah . . . I'll use a simile you ought to understand. If you have a drawer full of wallets, for example, could you put ties in the same drawer? You couldn't. So, if Wokulski has his heart full of Miss Łęcka, how can you push Mrs Stawska in?'

I disentangled his hands from my lapels, and replied: 'I'd take out the wallets and put the ties in, d'you see, learned sir?'

And I left at once, for his arrogance vexed me. He thinks he has a monopoly of common sense. From the doctor I went to Mrs Misiewicz. Mrs Stawska was at her store, I sent Helena into the other room to her toys, sat myself down with the old lady and began without more ado: 'Dear madam! Do you think that Wokulski is an honourable man?'

'Oh, my dear Mr Rzecki, how can you ask such a thing? He lowered the rent in his own house for us, saved Helena from disgrace, gave her a position at seventy-five roubles, sent little Helena ever so many toys . . .'

'Very well,' I interrupted, 'if you agree, madam, that he is a fine man, you must also admit, in the utmost secrecy, that he is very unfortunate.'

'For goodness sake!' the old lady crossed herself, 'he unfortunate, who has such a store, a company, a huge fortune? He who recently sold his apartment house! Unless he has debts I know nothing of.'

'Not a penny,' I said, 'and, after settling his business affairs, he has some six hundred thousand roubles, although two years ago he only had thirty thousand, plus the store of course. But, madam, money isn't everything, for a man has a heart as well as a pocketbook.'

'Yet I hear he's getting married, to a pretty young lady, a Miss Łęcka.'

'That is his misfortune: Wokulski cannot, must not marry her.'

'Is there something the matter with him? Such a healthy man . . .'

'He must not marry Miss Łęcka, she is no match for him. He needs a wife like . . .'

'Like my Helena!' Mrs Misiewicz interposed promptly.

'That's it!' I cried, 'and not only like her, but her in person. Her very self, Mrs Helena Stawska is what we need for his wife.'

The old lady burst into tears: 'Do you know, my dear Mr Rzecki, that this is my fondest wish? For I'll give my word that good Ludwik is dead . . . I've dreamed of him so often, and every time he was either naked, or somehow different from what he used to be . . .'

'Besides,' said I, 'even if he isn't dead, we'll get a divorce.'

'That's it! Everything can be got for money.'

'Just so! The whole point is that Mrs Stawska mustn't be obstinate.'

'Worthy Mr Rzecki!' cried the dear old lady, 'she, I promise you, is in love, poor little thing, with Wokulski. Her good humour is gone, she doesn't sleep nights, only sighs, the poor little woman's growing thin, and when you both were here yesterday, something happened to her . . . I, her own mother, didn't recognise her.'

'So! *Basta!*' I interrupted, 'my hand on it that Wokulski will be here as often as possible, and you . . . Pray make Mrs Stawska well disposed to him. We'll tear Staś out of the hands of that Miss Łęcka, and . . . surely, by midsummer, the wedding . . .'

'For goodness sake – but what about poor Ludwik?'

'He's dead, he's dead,' said I, 'I give my word he is.'

'Hm, in that case, God's will be done . . .'

'Only pray keep it a secret. There's a great deal at stake.'

'What do you take me for, Mr Rzecki,' said the old lady, offended. 'Here,' she added, tapping her bosom, 'here all secrets are buried as though they were in a tomb. And especially the secret of my own child and that noble man.'

Both of us were deeply moved. 'Well, now,' said I after a moment, getting ready to take my leave, 'could anyone have supposed that such a small thing as a doll might help make two people happy?'

'A doll? How so?'

'How so? Why, if Mrs Stawska hadn't bought the doll in our store, there'd have been no court case, Staś wouldn't have worried about Mrs Stawska's fate, Mrs Stawska wouldn't have fallen in love with him, so they wouldn't have got married . . . For, strictly speaking, if any warm feeling has been aroused in Staś for Mrs Stawska, it's only since the court case.'

'Aroused, you say?'

'Hm! Didn't you see how they were whispering yesterday, on that couch? Wokulski hasn't been so lively for a long time, nor so excited as yesterday.'

'Heaven has sent you, my dear Mr Rzecki!' cried the old lady, and on bidding her farewell, she kissed my brow.

Today I'm really pleased with myself and even if I didn't want to, would have to admit I have the brains of Metternich. How I came upon the notion of Staś falling in love with Mrs Stawska, how I arranged everything so as not to be interrupted . . . Today I haven't the slightest doubt that both Mrs Stawska and Wokulski have fallen into the trap. She has been growing thin for several weeks (but is still prettier, the mischievous thing!) and he's quite lost his head. Providing he isn't at the Łęckis in the evening, which rarely happens in any case, for that young lady is everlastingly at balls, then the young fellow goes over to Mrs Stawska's, and stays there up to midnight. And how lively they are, as he tells her tales of Siberia, Moscow, Paris . . . I know this because Mrs Misiewicz tells me everything next day, as the greatest secret, of course.

Only one thing I didn't like. On learning that Wirski sometimes visits our ladies to let off steam, I set off to warn him. I was just leaving home, when I met Wirski in the passage. Of course I turned back, lit the lamp, we talked a little about politics . . . Then I changed the subject, and began formally: 'I have to inform you, confidentially . . .'

'I know what you mean!' he said, laughing.

'What do you know?'

'Why, that Wokulski is in love with Mrs Stawska!'

'Good God,' I cried, 'whoever told you?'

'First of all, don't be afraid of betraying a secret,' he said, gravely, 'because in our house, the secret is as good as buried in a well.'

'But who told you?'

'Well, my wife did, after she heard it from Mrs Kolerowa.'

'And where did she get it from?'

'Mrs Radzińska told Mrs Kolerowa, and Mrs Radzińska was told the secret under a most solemn oath by Mrs Denowa, you know, Mrs Misiewicz's friend.'

'How careless of Mrs Misiewicz!'

'Come, now!' says Wirski, 'what was the poor old lady to do, when Mrs Denowa reproached her because Wokulski sits in their apartment till all hours, because there's something improper going on . . . Of course, the old lady got agitated and told her there was no question of anything like that, but of marriage, and that probably they'll get married by midsummer.'

It made my head ache, but what was to be done? Oh, these old ladies!

'What's the latest in town?' I asked Wirski, to put an end to this worrying conversation.

'Scandalous things,' says he, 'with the Baroness! But give me a cigar, sir, for it's two long stories.'

I gave him the cigar, and he told me things which finally convinced me that sooner or later the wicked must be punished, the good rewarded, and that there is a spark of conscience in the stoniest of hearts. 'When did you last visit our ladies?' Wirski begins.

'Four . . . five days ago,' I replied, 'you'll understand, sir, that I don't want to interrupt Wokulski, and I advise you not to, either. A young lady and a gentleman reach an understanding faster than we old folks.'

'If you please, sir!' Wirski interrupted, 'a man of fifty ain't old: he's ripe.'

'Like an apple falling off a tree.'

'You're right, sir: a man of fifty is very prone to falling. If it weren't for his wife and children . . . Mr Ignacy! Devil take me, if I wouldn't like to compete with the young fellows! But, sir, a man

who's married is a cripple: women don't look at him, although . . .
Mr Ignacy!'

At this point his eyes sparkled, and he performed such a
pantomime that if he's truly pious, he'll go to confession
tomorrow.

I've already noticed, generally speaking, that the gentry are such
that they've no head for scholarship, nor yet for business, you never
get them to work, but they're always ready for the bottle, for
fighting and chasing women, even if they get to them in a coffin.
Profligate creatures!

'That's all very well,' say I, 'but what were you going to tell me,
Mr Wirski?'

'Aha, what was I thinking of ?' says he, his cigar smoking like a
barrel of tar, 'well, now – you remember those students in our
apartment house, who lived above the Baroness?'

'Maleski, Patkiewicz and the third one. How can I help remembering such young devils? Jolly fellows!'

'Oh, very,' Wirski agreed, 'may God be my witness if we could
keep a young cook more than eight months, not with those rascals
in the house. Mr Rzecki! I may tell that the three of them would
populate all the orphanages . . . Evidently that's what they teach
'em at the University. In my time, in the country, if a father with a
young son gave away three or four cows every year . . . Tut-tut!
Even the priest was vexed then, for they depraved his flock. As for
them, sir . . .'

'You were about to tell me of the Baroness,' I interposed, for I
don't like it when nonsense occupies a grizzled pate.

'Just so. Well, now . . . The worst scoundrel was that
Patkiewicz, who pretended to be a dead body. When evening
came, and that monster got out on the stairs, then I may tell you,
there was such squealing you'd think a whole pack of rats was
passing by.'

'But the Baroness . . .'

'Just so, indeed . . . Well, now, my dear sir . . . Well, and
Maleski was there too! Now, as you know, sir, the Baroness got a
court order for the lads to move out by the 8th. But they don't
budge . . . The 8th, 9th, 10th . . . There they still are, and the
Baroness's spleen quite swelled up with vexation. In the end, after
taking advice from her so-called lawyer and Maruszewicz, on
February 15th she brings in a bailiff, with the police.

'So up this bailiff goes to the third floor – bang, bang! The lads'
door is locked, but they ask "Who's there?" from inside.

'"Open in the name of the law," says the bailiff.

'"The law is all very well," say they, inside, "but we don't have
the key. Someone has locked us in, the Baroness no doubt."

'"You gentlemen are making fun of the police," says the bailiff, "but you know you ought to move out."

"'Certainly,'" they say, inside, "but after all, we can't get out through the keyhole. Not unless . . .'"

'So of course the bailiff sends the janitor for a carpenter, and waits on the stairs with the police. In about a half hour, along comes the carpenter; he opens the regular lock with a pick-lock, but can't do anything about the English snap-latch. He twists and turns, but in vain . . . So off he goes for tools, which takes him another half hour, and in the meantime there's running and banging in the yard, and the Baroness on the second floor gets a most terrible attack of the spasms.

'The bailiff is still waiting on the stairs, when Maruszewicz rushes up: "Sir!" he shouts, "just take a look at what they're up to!" So the bailiff runs out into the yard, and sees this: the third-floor window was open (and this, mark you, in February!), and out of that window into the yard came flying pillows, quilts, books, human skulls and such-like. Shortly afterwards, out comes a trunk on a rope and after it – a bed.

'"Well, and what have you to say to this?" cries Maruszewicz.

'"I must file a report," says the bailiff, "besides, they're moving out, so maybe it isn't worth interrupting 'em." Then – another spectacle. A chair appears in the open window on the third floor, with Patkiewicz sitting on it, his two colleagues give him a push and – young Patkiewicz comes riding down in the chair on ropes! At this point, the bailiff came over faint, and one of the policemen crossed himself.

'"He'll break his neck!" cry the women, "goodness gracious, may Heaven protect him!" Maruszewicz, being a nervous man, took refuge with the Baroness, and meanwhile the chair and Patkiewicz stop at the second floor, at the Baroness's window.

'"Enough of these larks, young gents!" cries the bailiff to Patkiewicz's two colleagues, who were lowering him.

'"Can't be done! The ropes are giving way!" they cry.

'"Watch out, Patkiewicz," shouts Maleski, up above. There's a terrible scene in the yard. The women (more than one being extremely interested in Patkiewicz's health) start shrieking, the policemen froze stiff, and the bailiff loses his head entirely: "Climb on the parapet! Break the window!" he shouts to Patkiewicz.

'Your Patkiewicz didn't have to be told twice. So he begins knocking on the Baroness's window in such a way that Maruszewicz not only opened the ventilator, but dragged the lad into the room himself. Even the Baroness runs up in alarm, and says to Patkiewicz: "Good God! Why did you have to play such a prank?" "Otherwise I wouldn't have had the pleasure of bidding farewell to you, dear lady," Patkiewicz replied, and – so I hear – he displays to her such a dead body, that the old girl tumbled over on the floor, crying out: "Will no one defend me? Are there no men? I need a man! . . . A man! . . ."

'She shrieked so loud that she could be heard all over the yard, and the bailiff misconstrued her cries, for he said to the policemen: "Oh, that poor lady has been took badly . . . Poor thing, she's been separated two years from her husband."

'Patkiewicz, being a medical man, felt the Baroness's pulse, prescribed valerian drops and left, calm as you please. Meanwhile, the carpenter had set about breaking down the English latch. When he'd finished and quite ruined the door, Maleski suddenly recollected that both keys to the lock and the latch were in his own pocket.

'Hardly had the Baroness come to her senses, than the lawyer began trying to persuade her to start a case against Patkiewicz and Maleski. But the old girl was already so disgusted with court cases that she merely berated her adviser, and vowed that from then on she would never rent an apartment to students, not even if it had to stand empty for ages.

'Then, so they told me, she began, with a great deal of crying, to implore Maruszewicz to persuade the Baron to beg for her forgiveness and move into the apartment again: "I know he hasn't a penny," she sobbed, "he's not paying his rent, and is living on credit along with that footman of his. Nevertheless, I will forgive all and pay his debts, providing he changes his ways and comes home. I can't cope with a house like this without a man . . . I'll die within a year . . ."

'I see God's punishment in this,' Wirski concluded, puffing out cigar smoke, 'and the instrument of punishment will be the Baron.'

'And the second tale?' I inquired.

'The second is shorter, but more interesting. Just imagine sir, the Baroness Krzeszowska paid a visit to Mrs Stawska yesterday.'

'Oh, confound it!' I murmured, 'that's a bad sign.'

'Not at all,' said Wirski. 'The Baroness went to Mrs Stawska's, burst into tears, had an attack of hysteria and asked both the ladies, almost on her knees, to forget the trial over that doll, for otherwise she'd have no peace to the end of her days.'

'So they promised to forget it?'

'Not only that, but they kissed her and even promised to reconcile her with Wokulski, of whom the Baroness speaks very highly.'

'Oh, damnation!' I exclaimed, 'why ever did they talk to her about Wokulski? That's asking for trouble.'

'Come, what are you saying?' Wirski reproached me, 'she's repentant, she regrets her sins and will certainly improve.'

'It was already midnight, so he left, I didn't stop him as he'd already vexed me somewhat with his belief in the Baroness's repentance. Still, who knows, maybe she really has repented?

Postscript. I was certain MacMahon would succeed in carrying out a *coup d'état* on behalf of young Napoleon. But today I've learned that MacMahon has fallen, and that Citizen Grévy has become President of the Republic, while young Napoleon has gone off to war in some Natal or other, in Africa. No help for it – let the lad learn how to fight battles. In six months or so he'll return, covered in glory, so that the French themselves will want him back and we, meanwhile, will marry Staś to Mrs Stawska. For when I set about anything, I have Metternich's ways, and understand the natural course of events. So – long live France under the Napoleons, and Wokulski with Mrs Stawska!

XXXI

Ladies and Women

FORTUNE looked with a kindly eye for the third or fourth time on the house of Mr Łęcki during Carnival and Lent. His drawing-room was full of visitors, and visiting cards fell into his vestibule like snow. Once again Tomasz found himself in the fortunate position of having visitors to receive, and even of being able to choose between them. 'I shall certainly die soon,' he sometimes told his daughter, 'but at least I've had the gratification of people knowing my true worth beforehand.'

Izabela heard this with a smile. She did not want to dispel her father's illusions, but was certain that the swarms of guests were paying tribute to her – not to her father.

After all, Mr Niwiński, the most elegant go-between, danced most frequently with her, not her father. Mr Malborg, the paragon of elegance and arbiter of fashion, talked to her, not to her father, while Mr Szatalski, a friend of both the aforesaid, felt unhappy and inconsolable on her account, not her father's. Mr Szatalski made this clear to her, and even though he was neither as elegant a dancer as Mr Niwiński, nor an arbiter of fashion like Mr Malborg, nonetheless he was the friend of both. He lived near them, ate with them, ordered English or French suits when they did, and ladies of mature judgement, unable to see any other virtues in him, called him – poetical.

Then a tiny incident occurred, a single phrase, which forced Izabela to seek the secret of her triumphs elsewhere. During a call, she said to Miss Pantarkiewicz: 'I've never enjoyed myself in Warsaw as I have this year.'

'That is because you are quite charming,' Miss Pantarkiewicz replied briefly, covering her face with a fan as though to conceal an involuntary yawn.

'Unmarried girls of a certain age know how to be quite charming,' said Mrs de Gins Upadalska loudly to Mrs de Fertalski Wywrotnicka.

The movement of Miss Pantarkiewicz's fan and the phrase of Mrs de Gins Upadalska gave Izabela food for thought. She had too much good sense not to understand the situation, especially one so clearly stated. 'What is that "certain age"?' she wondered. 'Twenty-five isn't a certain age . . . What are they talking about?'

She glanced aside, and caught Wokulski's eyes upon her. As she had to choose between attributing her triumphs to 'a certain age' and Wokulski – she began to reflect upon the latter. Who knew but that he was the involuntary creator of the flattery which surrounded her on all sides?

She began recalling things. First, Mr Niwiński's father had money invested in Wokulski's firm (even Miss Izabela knew this), which brought him in great profits. Then Mr Malborg, who had once graduated from some technical school or other (though he never betrayed the fact) had, through Wokulski's good offices (which he kept very secret) tried to obtain a position on the railways. In fact, he succeeded, though it had the great drawback of providing less than three thousand roubles a year. Mr Malborg even held this against Wokulski, but, out of regard for the conventions, he limited himself to uttering his name with an ironical grimace.

Mr Szatalski had no money invested in the firm, nor did he have a position on the railways. But since his two friends Messrs Niwiński and Malborg resented Wokulski, he too resented him, and expressed his resentment when he sighed to Izabela: 'There are lucky people, who . . .'

What these lucky people looked like was something Izabela never found out. The only thing was that at the word 'who . . .' Wokulski came into her mind. Then she would clench her tiny fists, and say to herself: 'Despot . . . Tyrant . . .'

Yet Wokulski never revealed the slightest tendency to despotise or tyrannise. He just kept gazing at her, and wondering: 'Are you she . . . Or aren't you?'

Sometimes, catching sight of young and elderly dandies besieging Izabela, whose eyes glittered like diamonds or stars in the sky, a cloud would float across the firmament of his admiration and cast a shadow of ill-defined doubts on his soul. But Wokulski refused to look at the shadow. Izabela was his life, his happiness, his sun – which no fleeting clouds could eclipse, not even imaginary ones.

Sometimes he thought of Geist, the eccentric sage, with his tremendous inventions, who had shown him a purpose in life other than Izabela. Then one glance from Izabela sufficed to bring Wokulski back from his fantasies: 'What's humanity to me?' he said, with a shrug. 'I wouldn't give away one of her kisses for all humanity, for all the world's future, for my own eternal life . . .'

And at the thought of this kiss, something strange happened to him. His will-power weakened, he felt he was losing his senses and that to regain them, he must see Izabela again, in the company of dandies. Only when he heard her clear laughter and decisive phrases, only when he saw the fiery glances she bestowed on Messrs Niwiński, Malborg and Szatalski, did it seem to him for a moment that a curtain had risen for him, beyond which he could see another world, and a different Izabela. Then, goodness knows why, his own youth, full of titanic efforts, blazed forth before him. He saw his own labours at extricating himself from poverty, heard the whistle of bullets that had flown past his head, saw Geist's laboratory where tremendous things were being created, and, looking at Messrs Niwiński, Malborg and Szatalski, he thought: 'What am I doing here? How comes it that I am worshipping at the same altar as they?'

He wanted to burst out laughing, then again he fell a prey to illusion, and it seemed to him that a life such as his was worth placing at the feet of a woman like Izabela.

Be this as it may, a change began coming about within Izabela in favour of Wokulski, under the influence of Mrs de Gins Upadalska's incautious *mot*. She eavesdropped attentively on the conversation of gentlemen who visited her father and saw, in consequence, that each of them had a little capital he wanted to invest with Wokulski 'at fifteen per cent, let's hope', or a cousin for whom he wanted a position, or that he sought to make Wokulski's acquaintance for some other purpose. As for the ladies, they too either wanted to push someone, or had eligible daughters and did not conceal that they wanted to get Wokulski away from Izabela or even, if they were not too mature, would be glad to make him happy themselves.

'To be the wife of such a man!' said Mrs de Fertalski Wywrotnicka. 'And not necessarily his wife, either!' replied with a smile Baroness von Ples, whose husband had been paralysed for five years.

'Tyrant . . . despot . . .' Izabela kept repeating, feeling that the merchant she despised was attracting many glances, much hope and much jealousy.

Despite the vestiges of contempt and loathing which lurked within her, she had to admit that this brusque and gloomy man meant more, and looked better, than either the marshal or Baron Dalski, or even Messrs Niwiński, Malborg and Szatalski.

But the greatest effect on her attitude was made by the Prince.

The Prince, whose invitation to offer Baroness Krzeszowska ten thousand roubles Wokulski had declined in December, and in January and February had not given a penny to the poor people he patronised – the Prince had lost his affection for Wokulski. Wokulski had deeply disappointed the Prince. The Prince had thought and believed that a man like Wokulski, once he'd obtained princely favour, ought to renounce all his own taste and interests, and even his fortune and his person into the bargain. He ought to like what the Prince liked, hate what the Prince hated, serve only the Prince's ends, and humour only his whims. Yet this parvenu (though, no doubt, he was of genteel origin) would not consider being the Prince's servant, and even dared to be independent; sometimes he argued with the Prince, or – worse still – refused his requests point-blank.

'A coarse man . . . a businessman . . . an egoist,' thought the Prince – but he was increasingly surprised by the impudence of the parvenu.

Chance had it that Mr Łęcki, unable to cover up the fact that Wokulski was courting Izabela, asked the Prince for his opinion of Wokulski, and for advice. Now, despite his manifold weaknesses, the Prince was basically honest. In stating an opinion about other people, he did not depend on his own views alone, but obtained others. So he asked Mr Łęcki for a few weeks' delay 'to form my own opinion', and, since he had many social contacts and a sort of police force of his own, he found out various things. First, he observed that the gentry, though they sneered at Wokulski as a parvenu and a democrat, boasted of him on the quiet: 'Plainly he's one of us, even though he went into trade.'

Moreover, whenever the question arose of putting up someone against the Jewish bankers, the most obdurate gentry chose Wokulski. Tradesmen, and manufacturers above all, hated Wokulski, but the most serious complaints they could make against him were 'He's a gentleman . . . a great gentleman . . . a diplomat,' which the Prince could in no way hold against him.

But the most interesting information was supplied to the Prince by nuns. There was a coachman in Warsaw, and his brother, a railroad man on the Warsaw–Vienna line, who both blessed Wokulski. There were students, who announced that Wokulski was paying them stipends; there were craftsman who owed him their workshops, and pedlars whom Wokulski had helped establish stores.

There was also (as the sisters declared, with pious horror and blushes), there was also a fallen woman, whom Wokulski had saved from destitution, handed over to the Magdalenes, and finally made an honest woman of, as far (so the nuns said) as such an individual could ever be an honest woman.

These accounts surprised and also alarmed the Prince. And at once Wokulski grew more powerful in his estimation. Here, after all, was a man with his own programme, who was even practising politics on his own account, and who had a great deal of importance amidst common folk. So, when the Prince came to Mr Łęcki at the appointed time, he did not fail to visit Izabela too. He pressed her hand in a significant manner, and said these enigmatic words: 'My dear cousin, you have an unusual bird in hand. Hold him, pet him, so he will grow up to be of use to our unhappy country . . .'

Izabela blushed a great deal: she guessed that this unusual bird was Wokulski.

'Tyrant . . . despot . . .' she thought, Nevertheless, the first ice had been broken in Wokulski's relations with Izabela. She was already making up her mind to marry him.

One day, when Mr Łęcki was poorly and Izabela reading in her boudoir, she was told that Mrs Wąsowska was waiting in the drawing-room. Izabela at once hastened thither and found, as well as Mrs Wąsowska, her cousin Ochocki, who was very sullen. Both ladies kissed with demonstrative affection, but Ochocki, who could see without looking, noticed that either one of them or both was vexed with the other, though not very much. 'Can it be on my account?' he thought, 'one should never get too involved.'

'You here, too, cousin!' said Izabela, giving him her hand, 'why so sad?'

'He ought to be cheerful,' Mrs Wąsowska interrupted, 'for he has been flirting with me all the way from the bank, and to very good purpose. On the corner of the Boulevard I let him undo two buttons on my glove, and kiss my hand. If you knew, Bela, how little he knows about kissing . . .'

'Is that so?' exclaimed Ochocki, blushing to the roots of his hair, 'very well! From now on, I will never kiss your hand again. I swear it!'

'You will kiss them both before this day is over,' Mrs Wąsowska retorted.

'May I pay my respects to Mr Łęcki?' Ochocki asked formally, and without waiting for Izabela to reply he walked out of the room.

'You embarrassed him,' said Izabela.

'He shouldn't flirt if he doesn't know how. In such things, clumsiness is a mortal sin. Isn't it?'

'When did you get back?'

'Yesterday morning,' Mrs Wąsowska replied, 'but I had to go to the bank twice, and to the stores, and to set things right at home. Meanwhile, Ochocki is helping me until I find someone more diverting. If you can surrender someone more interesting . . .' she added pointedly.

'What rumours are these!' said Izabela, blushing.

'They even reached me in the country. Starski was telling me, not without envy, that this year as always you, of course, are the queen. Apparently Szatalski has quite lost his head.'

'And both his boring friends, too,' Izabela put in, with a smile.

'All three fall in love with me each evening, each has proposed to me at a time which wouldn't interfere with the others, and later all three confided their sorrows in one another. These gentlemen do everything in company.'

'And what did you have to say?'

Izabela shrugged. 'Do you really want me to tell you?' she asked.

'I also heard,' Mrs Wąsowska said, 'that Wokulski has proposed.'

Izabela began toying with the fringe of her gown: 'Well, he proposed! He proposes to me whenever he sees me: whether he's looking at me, or not – speaking or not . . . like all men.'

'And you?'

'For the time being, I am proceeding with my campaign.'

'May one know what it is?'

'Of course, I don't want it to be a secret. First, while I was still at the Duchess's . . . how is she?'

'Very poorly,' Mrs Wąsowska replied, 'Starski hardly leaves her room now, and the notary comes every day, but apparently in vain . . . So, what of the campaign?'

'While I was at Zasławek,' Izabela went on, 'I mentioned disposing of his store (here a blush came over her) and now it's to be sold by June at the latest.'

'Capital! What next?'

'I'm having trouble with that trading company. He would jettison it immediately, of course, but I am in two minds. With the company, his income is about ninety thousand roubles and only thirty thousand without it, so you can understand my hesitation is natural.'

'I see you're becoming an expert in figures.'

Izabela made a contemptuous gesture: 'Oh, I'm sure I'll never understand them. But he explains it to . . . father too, and aunt.'

'Do you speak so openly to him?'

'Well, no . . . But because we aren't allowed to ask so many things, we have to guide conversations so that everything is told us. Surely you know that?'

'Of course. And what next?' Mrs Wąsowska asked, not without a trace of impatience.

'The last condition concerns a purely moral aspect. I have learned that he has no family, which is his greatest virtue, and I have reserved the right to keep all my friends.'

'And he agreed without protesting?'

Izabela gazed rather scornfully at her friend. 'Can you doubt it?' she said.

'Not for a moment. So – Starski, Szatalski . . .'

'Yes, Starski, Szatalski, the Prince, Malborg . . . In a word, all the men it pleases me to choose today and in future, all of them must be guests in my home. Can it be otherwise?'

'Quite right. But don't you fear jealous scenes?'

Izabela laughed: 'Me in scenes! . . . Jealousy and Wokulski! . . . ha ha ha! There is no man in the world would dare make a scene to me, least of all he. You have no idea of his adoration, his surrender . . . And his limitless trust, even his yielding of his own individuality – really disarm me. Who knows whether they alone are not attaching me to him?'

Mrs Wąsowska imperceptibly bit her lip. 'You'll both be very happy, or at least . . . you will,' she said, controlling a sigh. 'Although . . .'

'Do you see an "although?"' Izabela asked, with unfeigned surprise.

'Let me tell you something,' Mrs Wąsowska went on, in a tone of calmness unusual for her, 'the Duchess is very fond of Wokulski, it seems to me she knows him very well, though I don't know how, and she has often talked of him to me. Do you know what she once said?'

'You intrigue me,' replied Izabela, increasingly surprised.

'She said, "I'm afraid Bela doesn't understand Wokulski at all. I think she's playing with him, but he is not a man to be played with. Also, it seems to me that she will appreciate him – but too late."'

'The Duchess said that?' asked Izabela coolly.

'Yes! Anyway, I'll tell you it all. She ended her remarks with a phrase that moved me strangely: "Mark my words, Kazia, that it will be so, for people who are dying can see clearly."'

'Is she so ill?'

'She is certainly very poorly,' Mrs Wąsowska ended drily, feeling that the conversation was beginning to terminate.

A moment of silence followed, fortunately interrupted by Ochocki's reappearance. Once again Mrs Wąsowska very cordially said goodbye to Izabela, and, with a fiery glance at her companion, said: 'Now let's go home for lunch.'

Ochocki made a great face, meant to indicate he would do no such thing. But, after scowling some more, he took his hat and they left. When they were in the carriage, he turned aside from Mrs Wąsowska to gaze into the street, and began: 'If only Bela would finish one way or the other with Wokulski . . .'

'You, of course, would prefer it to finish this way, rather than the other, so as to become one of the family friends. But there's nothing doing,' said Mrs Wąsowska.

'If you please, madam,' he replied indignantly, 'that isn't my game . . . I leave it to Starski and his like . . .'

'Why does it concern you, then, that Bela should finish?'

'A great deal. I'd give my right arm that Wokulski knows some important scientific secret, but I'm certain he won't come out with it while he's in this state of fever. Ah, these women, with their sickening coquetry.'

'Is yours any better?' asked Mrs Wąsowska.

'We are allowed . . .'

'You are? Proud fellow!' she was indignant, 'so speaks a progressive man in the age of emancipation!'

'May the devil take emancipation!' Ochocki replied. 'Emancipation, indeed! You women would like to have all the privileges of men, but no obligations. Open the door for them, vacate the places man has paid for, fall in love with 'em, and they . . .'

'That's because we are your happiness,' Mrs Wąsowska replied mockingly.

'What sort of happiness is it? There are a hundred and five women to every hundred men, so why should we worry?'

'No doubt your admirers, the cloakroom girls, won't.'

'Of course not! The most insufferable women are the great ladies, and waitresses in restaurants. The demands they make, and how they turn up their noses!'

'You forget yourself,' said Mrs Wąsowska, haughtily.

'Let me kiss your hand, then,' he replied, instantly carrying out his intention.

'Not that hand, if you please.'

'This one, then . . .'

'There now, didn't I say you'd kiss both my hands before the day was out?'

'Upon my soul! . . . I don't intend to lunch with you . . . I'll get out.'

'Stop the carriage!'

'Why?'

'Well, if you want to get out?'

'Not just here . . . Oh, how unfortunate I am with such a wretched disposition as mine!'

Wokulski came to the Łęckis' every few days, and usually only found Mr Tomasz, who greeted him with paternal affection, and then would talk for several hours about his ailments or business interests, gently giving him to understand he considered him a member of the family already.

As a rule, Izabela wasn't home: she was at her aunt's, or with the Countess or friends, or out shopping. But if Wokulski was lucky, they spoke briefly together about unimportant matters, since Izabela was always on the point of going somewhere, or expecting visitors.

A few days after Mrs Wąsowska's visit, Wokulski found Izabela at home. Giving him her hand which, as usual, he kissed with pious veneration, she said: 'Do you know, sir, that the Duchess is very poorly?'

Wokulski was taken aback: 'Poor, worthy old lady . . . If I were sure my arrival wouldn't alarm her, I'd go . . . Does she have people to look after her?'

'Oh, yes,' Izabela replied. 'Baron Dalski is there, with his wife,' she smiled, 'for Ewelina has already married the Baron. Fela Janocka is there, and . . . Starski.'

A slight blush appeared on her face, and she fell silent.

'Such are the consequences of my tactlessness,' thought Wokulski. 'She has noticed that Starski is odious to me, and now grows embarrassed at any mention of his name. How vile of me!'

He wanted to say something cordial about Starski, but nothing came. To break the awkward silence, he said: 'Where are you going for the summer?'

'Goodness knows. Aunt Hortensja is rather sickly, so perhaps we shall go to see her in Cracow. I must admit I'd prefer Switzerland, if it depended on me.'

'On who else?'

'On my father . . . Besides, goodness knows what may happen,' she replied, blushing and glancing at Wokulski in a manner all her own.

'Let us suppose that everything goes as you wish,' he said, 'would you, then, accept me as a companion?'

'If you deserve it . . .'

She said this in such a tone of voice that Wokulski lost control of himself, for the umpteenth time this year. 'How can I earn your kindness?' he asked, taking her hand. 'Pity? No, not pity. That is a feeling as disagreeable for the giver as for the taker. I don't want pity. But pray consider, what shall I do without seeing you for so long? It's true that even now we meet very rarely; you can't begin to guess how time drags for those who are waiting . . . But as long as you're in Warsaw, I tell myself "I'll see her again tomorrow . . . the day after tomorrow . . . "Besides, if not you yourself, at least I can see your father, Mikołaj, this house . . . Ah, you could do a merciful act and terminate – I don't know . . . my sufferings, my premonitions – with a single word. After all, you know the saying that the worst certainty is better than any uncertainty.'

'And if the certainty be not the worst?' asked Izabela, without looking into his eyes.

The bell rang in the hall and after a moment Mikołaj presented the visiting cards of Messrs Rydzewski and Pieczarkowski.

'Ask them in,' said Izabela.

Two very elegant men entered the drawing-room, one being characterised by narrow shoulders and a quite marked bald spot, the other by caressing glances and a subtle manner of speaking. They

entered side by side, holding their hats at precisely the same elevation. They bowed in an identical manner, sat down in an identical
manner, and crossed their legs in an identical manner, after which
Mr Rydzewski began trying to keep his shoulders straight, and Mr
Pieczarkowski to speak without drawing breath.

He said that at present the Christian world was celebrating Lent
with parties, that before Lent there had been the Carnival, during
which everyone enjoyed themselves no end, and that the worst
time would come after Lent, when no one would know what to
do. He then informed Izabela that during Lent, as well as parties,
there were lectures, at which one could pass the time very agreeably if one were sitting next to ladies of one's acquaintance, and
that the most elegant receptions during Lent were at the
Rzezuchowskis. 'Quite delightful, quite original, I assure you,' he
said. 'The supper, of course, is the usual thing – oysters, lobster,
fish, meat – but to finish, for those who like it – guess what?
Genuine porridge . . . what kind was it?'

'Bordeaux,' interrupted Mr Rydzewski, for the first and last time.

'Not Bordeaux – buckwheat. Quite marvellous, quite heavenly!
Each grain looked as if it had been cooked separately. We really set
to – I, Prince Kiełbik, Count Sledziński . . . Quite fabulous! It was
served in the ordinary way, in silver bowls . . .'

Izabela was gazing at the speaker with such interest, emphasising
his every word with a movement, smile or glance in such a way
that everything began swimming before Wokulski's eyes. So he
rose, bade the company goodbye and hastened out into the street:
'I don't understand this woman,' he thought. 'When is she herself,
for whom is she herself?'

But after walking a few hundred yards in the frost, he cooled
down. 'After all,' he thought, 'what's extraordinary about it? She
must live among the people she is used to; and if she lives among
them, she must listen to their foolish talk. Is it her fault that she is as
beautiful as a goddess, and indeed is one, to everyone? Although . . .
a taste for such company . . . Oh, how vile I am, always vile, vile!'

Whenever such doubts beset him like troublesome flies after a
visit to Izabela, he hastened back to work. He checked accounts,
learned English phrases, read new books. But when these didn't
help, he walked to Mrs Stawska's, spent the whole evening in her
apartment and, strangely enough, found, if not complete tranquillity then at least relief, in her company.

They talked of the most everyday things. Usually, she told him
how business in the Miller store was steadily improving because
people had learned that the store belonged mainly to Wokulski.
Then she said that Helena was growing more and more well-
mannered, and if she was ever naughty, then Grandmama frightened her by saying she'd tell Mr Wokulski, and the child stopped

misbehaving at once. Then again she would mention Mr Rzecki, who sometimes called and was much liked by granny, because he told her many things about Mr Wokulski's life. And that granny also liked Mr Wirski, who quite simply adored Mr Wokulski.

Wokulski looked at her in surprise. To begin with, it occurred to him that this was flattery, and he felt disagreeably. But Mrs Stawska said these things with so much innocent simplicity that he slowly began to divine in her the best of friends who, though she overestimated him, was nevertheless speaking without a trace of deception.

He also noticed that Mrs Stawska was never concerned about herself. When she finished in the store, she would think about Helena, or help her mother, or worry about the servant's problems and those of many other people, mostly poor and unable to show their gratitude by anything. And when these were lacking, she would peep into the canary's cage, to change its water or sprinkle grain.

'The heart of an angel!' thought Wokulski. One evening he said to her: 'Do you know what strikes me when I look at you?'

She glanced at him in alarm.

'That if you were to touch a badly hurt person, not only would the pain leave them, but surely their wounds would heal.'

'You think me a witch?' she asked, very troubled.

'No, madam. I think the saints must have looked like you.'

'Mr Wokulski is right,' affirmed Mrs Misiewicz.

Mrs Stawska began laughing. 'Oh, the saints – and me!' she replied. 'If anyone could look into my heart, he'd realise how much I deserve condemnation . . . But now it is all the same to me,' she added, with despair in her voice.

Mrs Misiewicz imperceptibly crossed herself, but Wokulski did not notice. He was thinking of another woman.

Mrs Stawska could not describe her feelings for Wokulski. She had known him by sight for several years, he had even impressed her as a handsome man, but he never concerned her. Then Wokulski vanished from Warsaw, the news spread that he had gone to Bulgaria, and later that he had made a great fortune. He was much talked of, and Mrs Stawska began to grow interested in him as an object of public curiosity. When one of her acquaintance said of Wokulski: 'That's a man with diabolical energy,' Mrs Stawska liked the phrase 'diabolical energy', and she made up her mind to observe Wokulski more closely.

With this purpose in mind she sometimes called at the store. A few times she did not find Wokulski there at all, once she saw him, but from the side, and once she exchanged a few words with him. Then he made a peculiar impression on her. She was struck by the contrast between the phrase 'diabolical energy' and his manner: he did not look in the least diabolical, rather he was calm and sorrowful. And she noticed one other thing: he had large, dreamy eyes, so very dreamy . . .

'A handsome man,' she thought.

One summer day she had met him in the gateway of the house she lived in. Wokulski looked at her with interest, and she was overcome with such embarrassment that she blushed to the roots of her hair. She was vexed with herself for this embarrassment and blushing, and had been cross with Wokulski for a long time because he looked at her so curiously.

From that time on, she had been unable to conceal her embarrassment whenever his name was mentioned in her presence: she felt a sort of compunction, but did not know whether it was for him or for herself. But it was rather for herself, for she never felt compunction for other people; and in the end – what fault was it of his that she should be so absurd and embarrassed without any cause?

When Wokulski bought the house she was living in, and when Rzecki lowered the rent with his approval, Mrs Stawska (although they explained to her that a rich landlord could, and was even obliged, to lower the rents) felt grateful to Wokulski. Gradually, gratitude changed into admiration, when Rzecki began calling on them and telling her many things out of the life of his Staś.

'He's an extraordinary man,' Mrs Misiewicz would tell her, sometimes. Mrs Stawska listened in silence, but gradually decided that Wokulski was the most extraordinary man who existed in this world.

After Wokulski's return from Paris, the old clerk visited Mrs Stawska more often, and made ever greater confidences in her. He said – as a very great secret, of course – that Wokulski was in love with Miss Łęcka and that he, Rzecki, didn't approve at all.

Dislike for Miss Łęcka and sympathy for Wokulski began increasing within Mrs Stawska. Already at that time it occurred to her, though only for a moment, that Wokulski must be terribly unhappy, and that anyone who extricated him from the wiles of the coquette would be most deserving.

Later, two great catastrophes befell Mrs Stawska: the trial over the doll, and the loss of her earnings. Not only did Wokulski continue his acquaintance with her, which after all he need not have done; but he even exonerated her in court, and offered her a well-paid post in the store. Then Mrs Stawska admitted to herself that this man concerned her, and that he was as dear to her as Helena and her mother.

From that time on, a strange life began for her. Everyone who visited them spoke to her of Wokulski, either directly or by implication. Mrs Denowa, Mrs Kolerowa and Mrs Radzińska explained to her that Wokulski was the best match in Warsaw; her mother insisted that Ludwik was dead and, even if he weren't, then he didn't deserve to have her remember him. Finally Rzecki, whenever he called, told her that his Staś was unhappy, that he must be saved and that the only person who could save him was herself.

'How?' she asked, not understanding properly what she was saying.

'Love him, and a way will be found,' Rzecki replied.

She did not reply, but privately reproached herself bitterly because she could not love Wokulski, although she wanted to. Her heart had dried up: she wasn't even sure whether she still had one. Admittedly, she thought continuously of Wokulski during her work in the store, or at home; she looked forward to his visits, and was irritable and sad when he didn't come. She often dreamed about him, but that, after all, is not love; she was not capable of love. To tell the truth, she had even stopped loving her husband. It seemed to her that memories of the absent are like a tree in autumn, from which leaves fall in drifts, leaving only a black skeleton.

'What has love to do with me?' she thought, 'all passion is spent in me.'

Meanwhile, Rzecki was still carrying on his sly plans. First he told her that Miss Łęcka would ruin Wokulski, then that only another woman could bring him to his senses; then he confided that Wokulski was much more tranquil in her company and finally (though he said this in the form of an implication) that Wokulski was beginning to love her.

Influenced by these confidences, Mrs Stawska grew thinner, looked poorly, even began to be afraid. For she was dominated by one thought: what would she say if Wokulski were to confess that he loved her? Admittedly her heart had long since died, but would she have the courage to reject him, and admit that nothing concerned her any more? Could she not be concerned by a man such as he, not because she owed him something, but because he was unhappy, and loved her? 'What woman,' she thought, 'could not but take pity on a heart so deeply wounded, and so silent in its pain?'

Plunged in this inner conflict, which she could not confide in anyone, Mrs Stawska failed to notice the changes in Mrs Miller's attitude, her smiles and insinuations.

'How's Mr Wokulski?' the shop woman would sometimes ask. 'Today you look wretched . . . Mr Wokulski ought not to let you work so . . .'

One day, about the middle of March, Mrs Stawska came home to find her mother in tears. 'What is it, mama? . . . What has happened?' she inquired.

'Nothing, nothing, my child. Am I to poison your life with gossip? Good God, how detestable people are!'

'You must have had an anonymous letter. I keep getting anonymous letters every few days, which call me Wokulski's mistress, but what of it? I guess it is the work of Baroness Krzeszowska, and throw the letters into the fire.'

'No, no, my child . . . If it were only an anonymous letter . . . But that worthy Mrs Denowa and Mrs Radzińska were here today . . . But why should I poison your life? They say (apparently it's to be heard all over town) that instead of going to the shop, you visit Wokulski . . .'

For the first time in her life, a lioness awoke in Mrs Stawska. She raised her head high, her eyes flashed and she replied firmly: 'Even if it were so, what then?'

'For goodness sake, what are you saying!' her mother groaned, pressing her hands together.

'What if it were so?' Mrs Stawska insisted.

'And your husband?'

'Where is he? Anyway, let him kill me . . .'

'But your daughter? . . . Little Helena?' the old lady whispered.

'Let's not talk of her, but of me . . .'

'Helena . . . my child . . . But you aren't . . . ?'

'His mistress? No, I'm not, because he hasn't asked me. What do I care for Mrs Denowa or Mrs Radzińska, or my husband who has deserted me? I don't know what has come over me . . . I only feel that this man has taken away my soul.'

'Be sensible, at least . . . Besides . . .'

'I am, as far as I can be. But I care nothing for a world that condemns two people to torture, simply because they love one another. Hatred is allowed,' she added, with a bitter smile, 'stealing, killing – everything is allowed, except love. Ah, mama, if I am not right, then why did not Christ say to people "Be sensible" instead of "Love one another"?'

Mrs Misiewicz fell silent, alarmed by this unexpected outburst. She felt that the heavens were falling when such phrases came from the lips of this dove, the like of which she had never heard, never read, which had never occurred to her, not even when she had had typhus.

Next day Rzecki called: he entered with a troubled expression, and when she told him everything, he left, broken. Because that very day, an incident had occurred: who had come to the store to see Szlangbaum but Maruszewicz, and they'd talked for nearly an hour. The other clerks, on hearing that Szlangbaum was buying the store, had grown meek before him at once. But Ignacy stiffened, and when Maruszewicz left, he immediately inquired: 'What business do you have with that scoundrel, Henryk?'

But Szlangbaum had already stiffened too, so he replied to Mr Rzecki, thrusting out his lower lip: 'Maruszewicz wants to borrow money for the Baron and obtain a position for himself, for they're already saying in town that Wokulski is handing his company over to me. He promises me in return that the Baron and Baroness will call on me, at home.'

'And will you receive such a viper?' asked Rzecki.

'Why ever not? The Baron will be for me, and the Baroness for my wife. In my soul, I'm a democrat, but what am I to do, if foolish people think a drawing-room looks better with barons and counts in it than it does without 'em? A lot is done for the sake of social contacts, Mr Rzecki.'

'I congratulate you.'

'Well, well . . .' Szlangbaum added. 'Maruszewicz also told me it's going about town — that Staś has started keeping that . . . that Stawska. Is it true, Mr Rzecki?'

The old clerk spat at his feet and went back to his desk.

Towards evening he called on Mrs Misiewicz to take council with her, and he learned from her own mother that Mrs Stawska was not Wokulski's mistress simply because he hadn't asked her.

He left Mrs Misiewicz in despair: 'Let her be his mistress,' he said to himself. 'Oh, goodness . . . How many well-known ladies are the mistresses of the vilest fellows . . . But the worst is that Wokulski doesn't think about her at all. Here's a fine to-do! Ha, something will have to be done.'

But as he couldn't think of anything, he went to Dr Szuman.

XXXII

How Eyes Begin to Open

THE DOCTOR was sitting by a lamp, with a green lampshade, industriously looking through a heap of papers.

'What's this?' Rzecki inquired, 'are you working on human hair again? Goodness, what a quantity of figures . . . Like a store ledger.'

'That's because they are the accounts of your stores and your company,' Szuman replied.

'Where did you get them?'

'I've had enough, Szlangbaum is trying to persuade me to entrust my capital to him. As I prefer having six thousand a year to four thousand, I'm prepared to listen to his suggestions. But as I don't like acting in the dark, I asked for figures. Well, as I see, we shall do business.'

Rzecki was surprised. 'I never thought,' he said, 'that you would concern yourself with such matters.'

'That's because I've been stupid,' the doctor replied with a shrug. 'Wokulski has made a fortune before my very eyes, Szlangbaum is making one, and here I sit like a stone on my few pennies. He who doesn't go ahead, retreats.'

'But making money isn't your concern!'

'Why isn't it? Not everyone can be a poet or a hero, but everyone needs money,' said Szuman. 'Money is the larder of the noblest force in nature – human labour. It's the "open sesame" at which all doors fly open, it's the table-cloth on which one can always find a dinner, it's the Aladdin's lamp, by rubbing which everything one wants is to be had. Magic gardens, splendid palaces, beautiful princesses, faithful servants, friends ready to make sacrifices – all these are to be had with money.'

Rzecki bit his lip: 'You were not always of this opinion,' he said.

'*Tempora mutantur et nos mutamur in illis*,' the doctor replied, calmly. 'I've wasted ten years studying hair, I spent a thousand roubles publishing a brochure a hundred pages long and . . . not even a dog remembers it, or me. I will try to devote the next ten years to financial operations, and am convinced in advance that people will love and admire me. Providing I open a drawing-room, and keep a carriage.'

For a moment they were silent, and did not look at one another. Szuman was moody and Rzecki almost ashamed. Finally he remarked: 'I would like to talk to you about Staś.'

The doctor impatiently pushed the papers aside: 'What can I do to help him?' he muttered, 'he's an incurable dreamer who will never regain his senses. He is moving disastrously towards material and spiritual ruin, like all of you, and your entire system.'

'What system?'

'Your Polish system.'

'And what would you replace it with, doctor?'

'Our Jewish one . . .'

Rzecki almost jumped off his chair: 'Only a month ago, you were calling the Jews "kikes".'

'So they are. But they have a great system; it will triumph, whereas yours is leading to bankruptcy.'

'And where is this new system to be found?'

'In the minds that have emerged from the Jewish masses, and which have ascended to the peaks of civilisation. Take Heine, Borne, Lassal, Marx, Rothschild, Bleichroder, and you'll discover the new ways of the world. It's the Jews who have established them: despised, persecuted, but patient and full of genius.'

Rzecki rubbed his eyes; he felt he was dreaming, though awake. After a moment he said: 'Forgive me, doctor, but . . . are you making fun of me? Six months ago I heard something entirely different from you . . .'

'Six months ago,' replied Szuman, irritated, 'you heard me protest against the old order, but today you are hearing a new programme. A man isn't an oyster which grows so close to its rock that one needs a knife to pull it off. A man looks around him, he thinks, makes judgements and consequently rejects his former illusions, when he realises that they are illusions. But neither you nor Wokulski can grasp this. You're all going bankrupt, all of you . . . Fortunately your places will be taken by new powers.'

'I fail to understand you.'

'You will in a moment,' the doctor declared, growing more excited. 'Take the Łęcki family – what have they done? They squandered a fortune; it was squandered by the grandfather, father and the son, who was left with thirty thousand saved by Wokulski – and a beautiful daughter, to serve as security. But what have the Szlangbaums been doing in the meanwhile? Making money. The grandfather made money, so did the father, so is the son today, although until recently he was but a modest clerk, but within a year he'll give our commerce a shake-up. And they know this, for old Szlangbaum wrote a charade last January: "The first in German stands for serpent, the second a plant: together – they climb," and he told me the answer was "Szlangbaum". A poor charade, but a good piece of work,' the doctor added, smiling.

Rzecki looked away. Szuman went on: 'Take the Prince, what's he doing? He sighs over "this unhappy country", and that's all. Or Baron Krzeszowski. He thinks of acquiring money from his wife. Or Baron Dalski. He is withering away for fear his wife deceives him. Mr Maruszewicz hunts for loans, and when he can't get them, he sneers; while Mr Starski sits by his dying grandmama, to get her to sign a will drawn up in his favour.'

'Other gentlemen, both high and low, who have a premonition that all Wokulski's business is going to pass into Szlangbaum's hands are already paying calls on the latter. They don't know, poor devils, that he will lower their incomes by at least five per cent . . . The cleverest of them, Ochocki, on the other hand, dreams of flying machines instead of exploiting the electric lamp he has invented. Bah! It seems to me he has been asking Wokulski's advice about them for some days past. Birds of a feather: dreamers both . . .'

'Surely you don't reproach Staś for anything, doctor?' Rzecki interrupted impatiently.

'No, except that he has never cultivated his profession, but has always chased after illusions. As a clerk, he wanted to be a scholar, but once he started studying, he decided he wanted to be a hero. He made a fortune, not because he was a tradesman, but because he was insane about Miss Łęcka; and now that he's gaining her – though that is still very uncertain – he's already begin to take council with Ochocki. . . . Upon my word, I don't understand it; what can a financier have to talk about with a man like Ochocki? . . . Lunatics!'

Rzecki pinched himself so as not to quarrel with the doctor: 'Pray notice,' he remarked after a moment, 'I came to see you, not only about Wokulski, but about a woman . . . A woman, Mr Szuman, against whom even you won't find anything to say.'

'Your women are worth precisely as much as your men. In ten years, Wokulski might be a millionaire and a power to be reckoned with in this country, but because he has involved his destiny with Miss Łęcka, he's selling a profitable store, abandoning a trading company no worse than the store, and will proceed to squander his fortune. Or Ochocki . . . Anyone else, in his shoes, would be working on electric lighting, since his invention has succeeded. Meanwhile, he gads around Warsaw with that pretty Mrs Wąsowska, to whom a good dancer means more than the greatest inventor. A Jew would act differently. If he were an electrical engineer, he'd find himself a woman who would either sit in his workshop with him, or who could sell electricity. If he were a financier like Wokulski, he wouldn't fall blindly in love, but would choose a rich wife. Or he might marry a poor and pretty one, but then her charms would have to pay interest. She would open a drawing-room for him, attract visitors, smile at the rich, flirt with the richest – in a word, would support the interests of the firm in all ways, instead of wrecking it.'

'Here too, you were of a different mind six months ago,' Rzecki interposed.

'Not six months but ten years ago. Bah! I took poison after my fiancée died, but that is just another argument against your system. Today it almost sickens me to think I might have died, God knows why, or have married a woman who would have squandered my money.'

Rzecki rose: 'So now your ideal is Szlangbaum?' he said.

'He's not my ideal, but at least he's an active man.'

'Who has acquired the store accounts . . .'

'He has the right to them. After all, he will be its owner in July.'

'Meanwhile he's demoralising his colleagues, his future clerks.'

'He'll dismiss them.'

'And this "ideal" of yours, when he asked Staś for a position, was he thinking even then of taking over our store?'

'He's not taking it over, he's buying it!' the doctor cried. 'Perhaps you'd sooner the store went to rack and ruin without finding a buyer? . . . And which of you is the smarter? – you, who after decades of work, have nothing – or he, who in the course of a year will have conquered such a fortress without, mind you, doing anyone an injustice, and paying Wokulski cash into the bargain?'

'Maybe you're right, though it doesn't look that way to me,' muttered Rzecki, glancing at him.

'It doesn't look that way to you, because you are one of those people who must grow over with moss, like stones, without moving from where they are. For you the Szlangbaums must always be clerks, the Wokulskis masters, and the Łęckis "Your Excellency". No, sir! Society is like boiling water; what was below yesterday will come to the top tomorrow.'

'And fall back into the dregs again the next day,' Rzecki concluded. 'Goodnight to you, doctor.'

Szuman shook him by the hand: 'Are you angry?'

'No. But I don't believe in worshipping money.'

'It's a transitory phase.'

'Who would swear to you that the dreams of Wokulskis or Ochockis aren't transitory? A flying machine seems absurd, but only on the surface; I know something of it's worth, as Staś has been explaining it to me for years. But if, for instance, a man like Ochocki were to succeed in making one, then just think which would be more valuable to the world: Szlangbaum's ingenuity, or the dreams of Wokulski and Ochocki?'

'Fiddle-de-dee,' the doctor interrupted, 'I shan't be here to see it.'

'If you were, you would surely have to change your plans a third time.'

The doctor grew embarrassed: 'Well, that's as may be,' he said. 'What business did you have with me?'

'It concerned poor Mrs Stawska . . . She has really fallen in love with Wokulski.'

'Ach . . . You might at least not bother me with such matters,' the doctor rebuffed him. 'When some are growing in wealth and power and others going bankrupt, he pesters me with the romance of some Mrs Stawska or other. You shouldn't have played at Cupid.'

Rzecki left the doctor, so troubled that he did not even notice the brutality of the latter's final words. Not until he reached the street did he realise it, and he felt cross with Szuman. 'There's Jewish friendship for you,' he muttered.

Lent was not as boring as society had feared. First, Providence sent a flood of the Vistula, which gave rise to a public concert and several private musical evenings with recitations. Then a certain gentleman from Cracow, the hope of the aristocratic party, appeared in a series of lectures at the Agricultural Exhibition, attended by the best company. Next, Szegedyn was flooded, which again brought forth small collections but enormous traffic in the drawing-rooms. Amateur theatricals were held in the house of a countess, at which two plays were performed in French, and one in English.

Izabela took an active part in all these philanthropic activities. She attended concerts, busied herself with presenting a bouquet to the scholar from Cracow, appeared in *tableaux vivants* as the Angel of Mercy, and played in Musset's *On ne badine pas avec l'amour*. Messrs Niwiński, Malborg, Rydzewski and Pieczarkowski quite showered her with bouquets, while Mr Szatalski confided to several ladies that he would very likely have to do away with himself that same year.

When news of the intended suicide spread, Mr Szatalski became the hero of parties, and Izabela acquired the nickname 'the cruel'. When the gentlemen disappeared to play whist, ladies of a certain age found their greatest pleasure in bringing together Izabela and Szatalski by means of ingenious manoeuvres. They gazed with indescribable sympathy through their lorgnettes at the sufferings of the young man; it was almost as good as a concert. They grew angry with Izabela only when they saw that she appreciated her own privileged situation and seemed to say with each movement and glance: 'Look, he loves me – he's unhappy on my account.'

Wokulski sometimes found himself at these gatherings, he saw the ladies' lorgnettes directed at Szatalski and Izabela, he even heard the remarks which buzzed around his ears like wasps, but he understood nothing at all. No one bothered about him, since they knew he was a serious suitor.

'Unhappy love causes a great deal more interest,' Miss Rzezuchowska once whispered to Mrs Wąsowska.

'Who knows where unhappy even tragic love really is, here?' Mrs Wąsowska replied, looking at Wokulski.

Fifteen minutes later, Miss Rzezuchowska asked to have Wokulski introduced to her, and during the next quarter of an hour informed him (lowering her eyes as she did so) that in her opinion, the most beautiful role a woman can play is to cherish wounded hearts that are suffering in silence.

One day at the end of March, Wokulski called on Izabela, and found her in high spirits: 'Excellent news,' she exclaimed, greeting him with unusual cordiality, 'did you know that the famous violinist Molinari is here?'

'Molinari?' Wokulski echoed, 'ah yes, I saw him in Paris.'

'You speak so coldly of him?' Izabela was surprised, 'can it be you didn't care for his playing?'

'I confess, madam, that I didn't even notice how he played.'

'That is impossible . . . You can't have heard him. Mr Szatalski says (though he always exaggerates) that after hearing Molinari, he could die without regrets. Mrs Wywrotnicka is delighted with him, and Mrs Rzezuchowska plans on giving a party for him.'

'He strikes me as a rather second-rate violinist.'

'Come, sir . . . Mr Rydzewski and Mr Pieczarkowski were able to see his album, composed entirely of press-cuttings. Mr Pieczarkowski says that Molinari's admirers presented it to him. All the European critics call him a genius.'

Wokulski shook his head: 'I saw him in a concert-hall where the most expensive seat cost two francs.'

'That's impossible, it can't have been him . . . He got a decoration from the Holy Father, another from the Shah of Iran, he has a title . . . Second-rate violinists do not acquire such honours.'

Wokulski gazed in amazement at Izabela's flushed cheeks and sparkling eyes. These were such powerful arguments that he doubted his own memory, and replied: 'Possibly . . . possibly.'

But his indifference towards art affected Izabela in a disagreeable manner. She turned sulky and talked rather coolly to Wokulski for the rest of the visit.

'I'm a fool,' he thought on leaving. 'I always have to come out with something that displeases her. If she's so fond of music, she may regard my opinion of Molinari as sacrilege.' And all next day he bitterly reproached himself for his ignorance of art, his naiveté, lack of delicate feeling and even for lack of respect to Izabela. 'It's certain,' he told himself, 'that this violinist who has made such an impression on her is better than I care to own. A person must be stuck up to utter such decisive judgements as I did, the more so as I can't have known anything of his playing.'

Shame overwhelmed him. On the third day he received a brief note from Izabela. 'Sir,' she wrote, 'you must arrange for me to meet Molinari, it is essential, essential . . . I have promised my aunt to persuade him to play at her house for the Orphanage benefit; you will understand how much this means to me.'

At first, it seemed to Wokulski that to approach the violinist of genius would be one of the most difficult tasks he had ever been commanded to execute. Fortunately he recalled knowing a musician who had not only met Molinari, but was already following him everywhere, and accompanying him like a shadow. When he confided his problem in the musician, the latter opened his eyes very wide, then frowned, but finally, after long pondering, replied: 'Oh, this will be difficult, very difficult, but we'll see what can be done. But I must prepare him, make him well-disposed to you. Do you know what we'll do? Call at his hotel tomorrow, at one in the afternoon. I'll be there for lunch. Then you can discreetly summon me through a servant, and I'll arrange an audience for you.'

These precautions and the tone in which they were uttered affected Wokulski disagreeably; nevertheless he went to the hotel at the appointed time: 'Mr Molinari is in?' he asked the porter. The latter, who knew Wokulski, sent a page upstairs then began passing the time in conversation: 'You can't think, sir, how busy the hotel is with this Italian! People flock to see him as though he were a sacred image, but mostly they're ladies . . .'

'Is that so?'

'Yes, sir. One of them first of all sent him a letter, then a bouquet, then came in person, wearing a veil and thinking no one would recognise her . . . You can't think, sir, how the staff laughed! He doesn't see them all, though one of 'em gave his footman three roubles. But sometimes when he's in a good humour, he'll take two more rooms, one on either side of the corridor, and entertain a lady in both . . . He's a determined beast.'

Wokulski glanced at his watch. Some ten minutes had passed in waiting, so he said goodbye to the porter and went upstairs, feeling anger beginning to boil within him. 'Stupid fool!' he thought, 'and as for those light women of easy virtue . . .'

On the way he met the page, who was out of breath. 'Mr Molinari, sir,' he said, 'told me to ask you to wait a little longer.'

Wokulski felt like seizing the page by the scruff of the neck, but hesitated and – went downstairs again.

'Are you leaving, sir? What am I to say to Mr Molinari?'

'Tell him to . . . You understand me?'

'I'll tell him, sir, but he won't understand,' the page replied, pleased and, hurrying back to the porter, said: 'At least there's one gentleman here so has sized up that Italian scoundrel . . . The dog! He is all puffed up, but he looks at a penny three times before he'll give you it. Son of a bitch, monster . . . wretch . . . vagabond . . .skunk!'

There was a moment in which Wokulski felt resentful towards Izabela. How could she be so enthusiastic about a man that even the hotel staff made fun of? How could she join his long list of female admirers? And, after all, was it proper to make him seek acquaintance with such a humbug?

But he cooled down at once: the very correct idea occurred to him that as Izabela didn't know Molinari, she was simply letting herself be borne along on the current of his reputation. 'She'll get to know him and will cool down,' he thought, 'but I am not going to serve as a go-between.'

When Wokulski got home, he found Węgiełek, who had been waiting for him an hour. The lad looked more at home in the city, but was somewhat thin. 'You've lost colour, grown thin,' said Wokulski, contemplating him, 'have you been misbehaving?'

'No, sir, I've been ill for ten days. Something in my neck was so painful that the doctor operated. But I went back to work yesterday.'

'Do you need money?'

'No, sir. I only wanted to speak to you about going back to Zasławek.'

'So that's what is bothering you. Have you learned anything?'

'Indeed I have. I've done some carpentry and cabinet-making. I've learned how to make pretty baskets, and draw too. Even paint a bit, if it comes to that.' As he spoke, he bowed, blushed and squeezed his cap in one hand.

'Good,' said Wokulski after a moment, 'you'll get six hundred roubles for tools. Enough? When do you want to go home?'

The lad blushed still more, and kissed Wokulski's hand. 'Sir, begging your pardon, I'd like to get married . . . Only I don't know . . .' He scratched his head.

'To whom?' asked Wokulski.

'To Maria, who lives with the coachman Wysocki's family. I live there too, upstairs.'

'So he wants to marry my repentant?' Wokulski thought. He walked about the room, and said: 'Do you know Maria well enough?'

'Why not? After all, we meet three times a day, and sometimes I spend Sunday with her, or both of us do, with the Wysockis.'

'I see. But do you know what she was a year ago?'

'I do, sir. Hardly had I got there by your kindness, than Mrs Wysocka right away says to me: "Take care, young fellow, for she's of easy virtue . . ." So I knew from the very start what she was: she never pulled the wool over my eyes at all.'

'How did it come that you want to marry her?'

'Goodness knows, sir, one way or another. At first I used to laugh at her, and when anyone passed the window, I'd say: "A friend of Maria, no doubt, as you've eaten bread from more than one stove." But she didn't say anything, only looked down, turned her sewing-machine until it steamed, and reddened up to the eyes. Later on, I noticed someone was doing my laundry for me; so, at Christmas, I bought her an umbrella for ten złoty, and she bought me six linen handkerchiefs, with my name on them. But Mrs Wysocka said: "Don't be taken in, young fellow, she's after you!" But I never let it into my head – though if she'd not been a wicked woman, I'd have married her come Shrovetide.

'On Ash Wednesday, Wysocki told me how things stood with Maria. Some lady in velvet had agreed to take her into service, but what kind of service, for goodness sake! She kept wanting to run away, but they kept ahold of her, and said: "Either stay here, or we will send you to prison for theft." "What have I stolen, then?" says she. "Our incomes, you heathen," they shout. And she'd have stayed there until doomsday (so Wysocki said), if Mr Wokulski hadn't seen her in church. Then he bought her out, and saved her.'

'Go on, go on,' Wokulski exclaimed, seeing Węgiełek hesitate.

'It struck me at once,' Węgiełek continued, 'that it wasn't wickedness, but misfortune. And I asked Wysocki: "Would you marry Maria?" "One wife is more than enough," says he. "But if you was single?" "Well," says he, "how can I say, not having any interest in women?" Seeing the old man didn't want to talk, I swore at him, so that in the end he said: "I wouldn't marry her, because I wouldn't be sure that the old ways didn't come back to her. When a woman's good, she's good, but when she's wanton, she's no good."

'Meanwhile, at the beginning of Lent, the Good Lord afflicted me with such pains that I had to stay home and the doctor operated on me. And didn't Maria start coming to see me, to make the bed, bandage my wound . . . The doctor says that if it hadn't been for her, I'd have kept to my bed another week. Sometimes I'd be irritable, particularly when I felt badly, so one day I says: "What are you doing all this for, Maria? You think I'm going to marry you, but I'd be a fool to take a girl who has served ten . . ." But she didn't answer, only looked away and her tears came . . . "After all, I understand," she says, "that Mr Węgiełek won't marry me." Then I, beggin' your pardon, sir, came all over pitiful when I heard that. And I told Mrs Wysocka: "You know, I might marry Maria." And she says: "Don't be silly, for . . ." But I dare not say it . . .' Węgiełek suddenly stopped, and again he kissed Wokulski's hand.

'Go on.'

'Well, Mrs Wysocka told me – that if I marry Maria, I might offend Mr Wokulski, after his kindness to us all. Who knows but what Maria don't visit him? . . .'

Wokulski stopped in front of him. 'Is that what you're afraid of?' he asked. 'I give you my word of honour I never see this girl.'

Węgiełek sighed with relief: 'Thank God for that. For in the first place, I wouldn't dare get in your way, sir, after all your kindness, and then again . . .'

'Then again – what?'

'In the second place, sir, she went wrong through misfortune, wicked people misused her, and that wasn't her fault. But if she should have wept over me when I lay sick, and came to visit you too, sir – then she would be such a wicked woman, that she'd be like a mad dog that has to be killed lest it bite people.'

'And so?' asked Wokulski.

'Well, now I'll marry after the holiday,' Węgiełek replied. 'After all, she can't suffer for other people's sins. It wasn't her wish.'

'Do you have any other matters to discuss?'

'No, sir.'

'Then farewell, and call on me before your wedding. She will get five hundred roubles dowry, and whatever is necessary for linen and the household.'

Węgiełek left him, very moved.

'That is the logic of simple hearts,' Wokulski thought, 'contempt for crime, and pity for misfortune.'

The simple citizen became, in his eyes, an emissary of eternal justice, which brought tranquillity and forgiveness to a fallen woman.

At the end of March, a great party was given at the Rzezuchowskis' in honour of Molinari. Wokulski received an invitation addressed by the fair hand of Miss Rzezuchowska. He arrived quite late, just as the maestro had let himself be persuaded to make the audience happy by playing one of his own compositions. One of the local musicians sat down to accompany him at the piano; another brought the maestro his violin; a third turned over the accompanist's music; a fourth took his place behind the maestro with the intention of emphasising by his expressions and gesticulations the most beautiful or hardest passages. Someone asked those present for silence: the ladies sat down in a semi-circle; the men gathered behind their chairs. The performance began.

Wokulski looked at the violinist and was first struck by certain likenesses between him and Starski. Molinari had the same small moustache, the same little beard and the same expression of boredom which characterises men who are lucky with women. He played well, and looked respectable, but one could see that he had accepted the role of a benevolent demi-god to his followers. From time to time, the violin sounded louder, the man behind the maestro took on an expression of admiration, and a quiet, brief rustle went through the audience. Amidst the fashionably dressed men, and the listening, musing, dreamy or dozing ladies, Wokulski caught sight of women's faces marked with an unusual expression. There were heads thrown passionately back, flushed cheeks, burning eyes, parted and trembling lips, as though they were under a drug.

'Horrible,' thought Wokulski, 'what sick individuals are these, harnessed to the triumphal car of this man!'

Then he looked to one side, and was struck cold. He saw Miss Łęcka, still more excited and impassioned than the others. He could not believe his own eyes.

The maestro played some fifteen minutes, but Wokulski no longer heard a single note. Finally, a long burst of applause awoke him. Then again he forgot where he was, but for all that he very distinctly saw Molinari whisper into Mr Rzezuchowski's ear, Mr Rzezuchowski take him by the arm – and introduce him to Izabela.

She greeted him with a blush and look of indescribable admiration. And because all were now summoned to supper, the maestro gave her his arm and took her into the supper room. They passed right by him, Molinari even elbowed him, but they were so occupied with each other that Izabela didn't notice Wokulski. Then they sat down at a table for four – Mr Szatalski with Miss Rzezuchowska, Molinari with Izabela – and it was evident they were very pleased to be together.

Again it seemed to Wokulski that a veil had fallen from before his eyes, and he could see beyond it an entirely different world, and another Izabela. But at the same moment, he felt such chaos in his mind, pain in his chest, madness in his nerves, that he fled to the entrance hall and then into the street, afraid he was going to lose his mind. 'Merciful God!' he whispered, 'take this curse off me!'

A few paces from Molinari, Mrs Wąsowska was sitting at a microscopic table with Ochocki. 'My cousin begins to interest me more and more,' said Ochocki, looking at Izabela. 'Do you see her?'

'I've been watching for an hour,' Mrs Wąsowska replied, 'but it strikes me Wokulski has noticed something too, for he was very changed. I am sorry for him.'

'Oh, you can set your mind at rest regarding Wokulski. True he is crushed today, but he'll come around again. Such men aren't slain by a fan.'

'There may be a scene . . .'

'Not likely,' said Ochocki. 'People with strong feelings are only dangerous when they have no reserves left.'

'You mean that woman . . . what's her name? – Sta . . . Star . . .?'

'God forbid, there's nothing there, and never was. Besides, for a man in love, another woman doesn't provide a reserve.'

'What does?'

'Wokulski has a powerful mind, and knows of a wonderful invention which would really turn the world upside down.'

'Do you know of it?'

'I know the content, I've seen the proof; but not the details. I swear,' said Ochocki, growing excited, 'that a man could sacrifice ten mistresses for such a cause.'

'So you sacrifice me, ungrateful one?'

'Are you my mistress? I'm not a madman, after all.'

'But you are in love with me.'

'As Wokulski is with Izabela? Not on your life . . . Although I'm prepared at any moment to . . .'

'You're badly bred, anyway. But – so much the better if you're not in love with me.'

'I know why. You are sighing for Wokulski.'

A strong blush overcame Mrs Wąsowska; she grew so confused that she dropped her fan. Ochocki retrieved it. 'I don't want to play a game with you, monster,' she said after a moment. 'He concerns me, inasmuch as . . . I'm doing all I can for him to win Bela, because . . . that madman loves her.'

'I swear that of all the women I know, you are the only one worth anything! But enough of this. Ever since I found out that Wokulski loves Bela (and how he does!), my cousin has been making a strange impression on me. Earlier, I used to regard her as exceptional – today, she strikes me as ordinary; earlier, as exalted – today, shallow . . . But this is only at moments, and I see I may be wrong.'

Mrs Wąsowska smiled. 'It's said,' she remarked, 'that whenever a man looks at a woman, Satan puts rose-coloured spectacles on him.'

'Sometimes he takes them off.'

'Not without suffering for it,' Mrs Wąsowska replied. 'But do you know, sir,' she added, 'since we are almost cousins, let us be less formal with each other . . .'

'Thank you, I think not.'

'But why?'

'I have no intention of becoming your admirer, madam.'

'I am offering you friendship.'

'Precisely. It is a bridge over which . . .'

At this moment Izabela suddenly rose from her seat and came to them: she was indignant.

'Are you abandoning the maestro?' Mrs Wąsowska asked her.

'He is impertinent!' said Izabela, in a tone which contained anger.

'I'm very glad, cousin, that you've found out that clown so quickly,' said Ochocki. 'Won't you sit down?'

But Izabela gave him a thunderous look, began talking to Malborg, who had just come up, then went out of the room. On the threshold she glanced over her fan at Molinari, who was talking very gaily to Miss Rzezuchowska.

'It seems to me, Mr Ochocki,' said Mrs Wąsowska, 'that you will have to become another Copernicus before you learn caution. How could you call that man a clown in Izabela's presence?'

'But she called him impertinent!'

'Nevertheless she is interested in him.'

'Well, please don't joke with me. If she isn't interested in a man who adores her . . .'

'Then she will interest herself all the more in a man who despises her.'

'A taste for strong condiments is a sign of weak health,' Ochocki commented.

'Which of us women here is healthy!' said Mrs Wąsowska, embracing the company with a contemptuous glance. 'Give me your hand, and let's go into the drawing-room.'

In the hall they met the Prince, who greeted Mrs Wąsowska with great satisfaction.

'Well, Your Highness, and Molinari?' she asked.

'Beautiful tone . . . very . . .'

'And shall we receive him at home?'

'Oh yes – in the vestibule.'

Within a few minutes the Prince's witticism had gone all around the rooms. Mrs Rzezuchowska had to leave her guests because of a sudden migraine.

When Mrs Wąsowska, talking with friends on the way, went into the drawing-room with Ochocki, she saw Izabela already sitting there with Molinari. 'Which of us was right?' she asked, nudging Ochocki with her fan: 'Poor Wokulski!'

'I assure you he is less so than Izabela.'

'Why?'

'Because if women only love men who despise them, my cousin will soon have to be crazy about Wokulski.'

'Will you tell her that?' asked Mrs Wąsowska indignantly.

'Never! After all, I am his friend, and that alone places me under an obligation not to warn him. But I'm a man too, and God knows I feel it, when this sort of conflict arises between a man and a woman.'

'The man will lose it.'

'No, madam. The woman will lose, and completely. After all, that is why women everywhere are slaves – they attach themselves to those who despise them.'

'Don't commit sacrilege.'

As Molinari had started talking to Mrs Wywrotnicka, Mrs Wąsowska approached Izabela, took her arm and they began promenading about the drawing-room. 'So you've become reconciled to the impertinent?' Mrs Wąsowska inquired.

'He apologised,' Izabela replied.

'So quickly? And did he mend his ways?'

'It is my business to see that he need not.'

'Wokulski was here,' said Mrs Wąsowska, 'and left rather suddenly.'

'Long ago?'

'When you were sitting down to supper: he was standing right by the door.'

Izabela frowned. 'My dear Kazia,' she said, 'I know what you mean. Let me tell you once and for all, that I have no intention of renouncing my likings and pleasures for Wokulski's sake. Marriage isn't a prison, and I am less suited than anyone to being a prisoner.'

'You are right. Though is it proper to hurt such feelings for a whim?'

Izabela grew embarrassed: 'What am I supposed to do?'

'That depends on you. You are not engaged to him, yet.'

'Quite so. I understand now,' and Izabela smiled.

Mr Malborg and Mr Niwiński were standing by a window and watching both ladies through their eye-glasses. 'Beautiful creatures,' sighed Mr Malborg.

'Each in a different style,' Mr Niwiński added.

'Which do you prefer?'

'Both.'

'I – Izabela, then – Wąsowska.'

'How delightfully they embrace! . . . How they smile! It is all meant to tease us. Mischievous creatures?!'

'Underneath they may hate one another.'

'Well, not just now at least,' Mr Niwiński concluded.

Ochocki approached the ladies as they strolled. 'Are you in the conspiracy against me too, cousin?' Izabela inquired.

'A conspiracy? Never. I can be at only open war with a woman.'

'At open war with a woman! Whatever does this mean? Wars are carried out with a view to concluding an advantageous peace.'

'That isn't my system.'

'Really?' said Izabela with a smile. 'So let us make a wager that you will lay down your arms, for I consider the war has started.'

'You will lose it, cousin, even over the points on which you expect the greatest victory,' Ochocki replied solemnly.

Izabela turned sulky.

'Bela,' the Countess whispered to her, coming up at this moment, 'we are leaving.'

'And has Molinari promised?' Izabela asked in the same tone.

'I haven't mentioned it,' the Countess replied haughtily.

'Why not, aunt?'

'He has made a bad impression.'

If Izabela had been informed that Wokulski had died on Molinari's account, the great violinist would have lost nothing in her eyes. But to hear that he had made a bad impression affected her disagreeably. She bade goodbye to the musician coolly, almost haughtily.

Although their acquaintance had lasted only a few hours, Molinari greatly interested Izabela. When, on returning home late that night, she gazed at her Apollo, the marble god seemed to her to have something of the violinist's attitude and features. She blushed to recollect how very often the statue changed its features; for a short while it had even resembled Wokulski. However, she grew calmer at the thought that today's change was the last, that her predilections hitherto had been based on errors and that if Apollo symbolised anyone, that person could only be Molinari.

She could not fall asleep, the most contradictory feelings were at war in her heart: anger, fear, curiosity and a sort of tenderness. Sometimes even amazement arose, when she recalled the violinist's boldness. His first words had been that she was the most beautiful woman he knew: going in to supper, he had clasped her arm passionately, and declared he loved her. And at supper, despite the presence of Szatalski and Miss Rzezuchowska, he had sought her hand under the table so insistently that . . . what could she do?

She had never before encountered such violent feelings. Surely he must have fallen in love with her at first sight, madly, eternally. Had he not whispered to her in the end (which obliged her to leave the table) that he would not hesitate to give his life for a few days spent with her. 'What did he not risk by saying such a thing?' Izabela thought. It did not occur to her that at most he had risked her quitting his society before supper was over.

'What feelings . . . what passion . . .' she repeated inwardly.

For two days, Izabela did not go out, nor did she see callers. On the third day, Apollo, though still resembling Molinari, sometimes recalled Starski. That afternoon she received Messrs Rydzewski and Pieczarkowski, who declared that Molinari was already leaving Warsaw, that he had offended society, that his album of press-cuttings was a fraud, because unfavourable notices had been left out of it. Finally they added that only in Warsaw would such a second-rate violinist and common individual receive such an ovation.

Izabela was indignant, and reminded Mr Pieczarkowski that he and none other had praised the musician. Mr Pieczarkowski, in surprise, appealed to Mr Rydzewski, who was present and to Szatalski (who wasn't) to bear witness that he had mistrusted Molinari from the start.

For the next two days, Izabela regarded the great musician as the victim of jealousy. She kept telling herself that he alone deserved her sympathy and that she would never forget him. Meanwhile, Szatalski sent her a bouquet of violets, and Izabela noticed, not without some misgivings, that Apollo was beginning to look like Szatalski, and that Molinari was rapidly being erased from her memory.

Almost a week after the concert, when she was sitting in her boudoir in the dark, a long-forgotten vision appeared before her eyes. She seemed to be travelling in a carriage with her father down from a mountain into a valley full of clouds of smoke and steam. A huge hand emerged from the clouds, holding a card, at which Tomasz gazed with agitated curiosity. 'With whom is Papa playing?' she thought. At this moment, the wind blew and from the clouds appeared Wokulski's face, also huge.

'I had this same vision a year ago,' said Izabela to herself. 'What can it mean?'

Only now did she realise that Wokulski hadn't been to see them for a week.

After the Rzezuchowskis' party, Wokulski had gone home in an unusual state of mind. The attack of frenzy passed, and yielded to apathetic tranquillity. Wokulski did not sleep all night, but this did not strike him as disagreeable. He lay still, without thinking of anything, merely listening curiously for the hours. One . . . Two . . . Three . . .

Next day he rose late, and kept listening to the clock as he drank tea, until afternoon. Eleven . . . Twelve . . . One . . . How boring! He wanted something to read, but did not feel like going to the library for a book; so he lay down on the *chaise-longue*, and began thinking about Darwin's theory: what is natural selection? The result of a struggle for existence, in which beings that don't possess certain attributes perish, and talented ones survive. What is the most important attribute? Sexual attraction? No, the horror of death. If horror of death didn't put a brake on man, this wisest of animals would not drag the chain of life. There are traces in ancient Indian poetry that once a human race existed, with less horror of death than we have. And that race perished, and its descendants are either slaves or ascetics.

What is horror of death? A natural instinct based on illusion. There are people with a horror of mice, which are very innocent creatures, and even of strawberries, which are very delicious (when did I last eat strawberries? . . . Yes, at Zasławek, last September . . . What a charming place Zasławek is; I wonder if the Duchess is still alive, and whether she has a horror of death?).

For what, after all, is the horror of death? An illusion! To die means not to be anywhere, not to feel anything, and not to think of anything. How very many places I am *not* in, today; not in America, Paris, the moon, I'm not even in my store, and nothing troubles me. And how many things have I *not* thought of, and am not thinking of? I am thinking of one thing only, not millions of other things, I don't know of them, even, and nothing concerns me.

So what can be disagreeable in the fact that *not* being in millions of places, but in one particular place, and *not* thinking millions of things, only one particular thing – that I should stop being in this one place and thinking of one thing? Really, the fear of death is the most absurd illusion humanity has been subjected to for many centuries. Savages fear thunder, the noise of firearms, even mirrors: and we, allegedly civilised, fear death . . .

He rose, looked out of the window and smiled to see people hurrying somewhere, bowing to one another, assisting ladies. He watched their violent gestures, great interests, the unconscious gallantry of the men, the mechanical coquetry of the women, the indifferent expressions of the cab-drivers, the misery of their horses, and he could not resist the comment that all this life, full of agitation and torment, is but a capital folly.

He sat thus all day. Next day, Rzecki came and reminded him it was April 1st, and Łęcki must be paid two thousand five hundred roubles interest. 'That's so,' Wokulski replied, 'take it to him.'

'I thought you would go yourself.'

'I don't feel like it.'

Rzecki fidgeted around the room, snorted, finally said: 'Mrs Stawska is down in the dumps, somehow. Perhaps you'll pay her a visit?'

'True, I haven't been to see her for a long time. I'll go this evening.'

On gaining this response, Rzecki couldn't contain himself. He said goodbye very affectionately to Wokulski, rushed to the store for some money, then got into a droshky and told the driver to go to Mrs Misiewicz's address.

'I have dropped by for only a moment,' he exclaimed joyfully, 'as I have important business to transact. I may tell you, madam, that Staś will be here later today. I think (though this is in the utmost secrecy) that Wokulski has finally broken with the Łęckis.'

'Can it be?' cried Mrs Misiewicz, clasping her hands.

'I am almost certain, but . . . Good-day to you . . . Staś will be here this evening.'

In fact, Wokulski came that evening and, which is more important, began calling every evening. He came rather late, when little Helena was already in bed, and Mrs Misiewicz had gone to her room, and he would spend a few hours with Mrs Stawska. As a rule, he was silent and listened to her accounts of Mrs Miller's shop, or incidents in the streets. He rarely spoke, and when he did, it was in aphorisms which didn't have much relevance to what was said to him. Once, for no reason, he remarked: 'A man is like a moth: he hurls himself blindly into the flame, although it hurts and will consume him. He does this,' he added, after reflecting, 'until he recovers his senses. And this is how he differs from a moth.'

'He's referring to Miss Łęcka,' Mrs Stawska thought, and her heart beat faster.

On another occasion he told her a strange anecdote: 'I heard of two friends, one of whom lived in Odessa, the other in Tobolsk; they hadn't met for several years, and longed to see one another. Finally, the man in Tobolsk, unable to bear it any longer, decided to surprise his friend and he went to Odessa without advising him. But he didn't find him at home, because the man in Odessa, who also longed to see his friend, had left for Tobolsk. Business matters prevented them from meeting during the return trip. They didn't meet for some years, and do you know what happened?'

Mrs Stawska gazed at him.

'The two of them met in Moscow on the same day, in the same hotel, in adjacent rooms. Destiny sometimes plays jokes on people.'

'This does not happen very often in life,' Mrs Stawska murmured.

'Who knows? Who knows?' Wokulski responded. He kissed her hand and left, thoughtful.

'It will not be thus with us! . . .' she thought, deeply moved.

During the evenings he spent in Mrs Stawska's home, Wokulski was relatively lively, ate a little, and talked. But for the remainder of the day, he sank into apathy. He hardly ate, but drank a great deal of tea, did not concern himself with business, was not present at the quarterly meeting of the company, read nothing, and didn't even think. A power he could not name had hurled him outside the sphere of all matters, hopes, desires and his life, like a dead weight, was moving on in the midst of desolation.

'After all, I'm not going to shoot myself,' he thought. 'If I'd gone bankrupt, then perhaps . . . But like this? I'd despise myself if a woman's skirts were to remove me from this world . . . I should have stayed in Paris . . . Who knows but that today I might not possess a weapon which will sooner or later eradicate all monsters with human faces?'

Rzecki, guessing what was going on, called at various times of day, and tried to draw him into conversation. But neither the weather, nor trade, nor politics concerned Wokulski. Only once did he grow livelier, when Mr Ignacy commented that Mrs Miller was persecuting Mrs Stawska.

'What does she mean by it?'

'Jealousy, perhaps, because you visit Mrs Stawska and pay her a good salary.'

'Mrs Miller can set her mind at rest,' said Wokulski, 'when I hand the store over to Mrs Stawska and make her the cashier.'

'Don't say that, for goodness sake!' Rzecki exclaimed in alarm, 'you'd ruin Mrs Stawska if you did.'

Wokulski began walking about: 'You're right. But all the same, if the women are squabbling, they must be separated. Persuade Mrs Stawska to set up a store for herself, and we will provide the capital. I thought of that once before, but now I see it shouldn't be postponed any longer.'

Of course Ignacy instantly hastened to his lady friends and told them the great news. 'I don't know whether it would be proper to accept such a sacrifice,' said Mrs Misiewicz, uneasily.

'What sacrifice?' Rzecki exclaimed. 'You'll repay us in a few years, and *basta!* What do you think?' he asked Mrs Stawska.

'I'll do as Mr Wokulski wishes. If he tells me to open a store, I shall; if he tells me to stay with Mrs Miller, I shall.'

'But, Helena,' her mother reflected, 'just think what a risk you are running, to speak thus! Thank goodness no one can hear.'

Mrs Stawska fell silent, greatly to Mrs Misiewicz's mortification: she was alarmed by the determination of her hitherto mild and submissive daughter.

One day, as Wokulski was walking in the street, he met Mrs Wąsowska. He bowed, and walked aimlessly on; then a servant caught up with him: 'Madam wishes . . .'

'What has been happening to you?' exclaimed the beautiful widow, as Wokulski approached the carriage, 'pray get in, let us drive along the Boulevard.' He obeyed, they drove off.

'What does this mean?' Mrs Wąsowska continued, 'you look dreadful, you haven't been near Bela for ten days . . . Well, say something!'

'I have nothing to say. I'm not ill, and I don't think Izabela needs my visits.'

'What if she does?'

'I never had any such illusions; today less than ever.'

'Well, well . . . My dear man, let's speak frankly. You are jealous, which always lowers a man in a woman's estimation. You were vexed by Molinari.'

'You are wrong, madam. I am so little jealous that I am not

going to interfere in the least with Izabela choosing between Molinari and myself. I know, after all, that we both have equal rights.'

'My dear man, that is bitter!' Mrs Wąsowska scolded him. 'How now, is a poor woman not to speak to other men, should one of you deign to admire her? I didn't think a man like you would treat a woman in such a harem-like fashion. Besides, what concern is it of yours? Even if Bela flirted with Molinari, what of it? It lasted one evening and ended with such a contemptuous goodbye from Bela that it was quite disagreeable to see.'

His depression left Wokulski: 'Madam, don't let's pretend we don't understand one another. You know that a woman is as holy as an altar to a man who loves her. Right or wrong, that's how it is. Now, if the first adventurer to come along approaches this divinity as if she were a chair, and treats her as though she were, and the altar is delighted by such treatment, then . . . Do you understand me, madam? We begin suspecting that the altar really is a chair. Have I made myself clear?'

Mrs Wąsowska fidgeted on the cushions of her carriage: 'Oh, my dear man, only too clear! But what would you say if Bela's coquetry were merely an innocent revenge, or rather, a warning?'

'To whom?'

'You. After all, you're continually preoccupied with Mrs Stawska.'

'I? Who says so?'

'Suppose there are witnesses — Baroness Krzeszowska, Mr Maruszewicz . . .'

Wokulski put his hands to his head: 'And you believe that . . . ?'

'No, because Ochocki assured me there's nothing in it: but whether anyone could calm Bela in such a fashion, and whether she can put up with it, is another matter.'

Wokulski took her hand. 'Dear madam,' he murmured, 'I withdraw everything I've said on Molinari's account. I swear to you that I honour Izabela, and that my ill-judged words are my greatest misfortune . . . Only now do I realise what I permitted myself, by saying that . . .'

He was so upset that Mrs Wąsowska couldn't help being sorry for him. 'Come, now,' she said, 'pray calm yourself, and don't exaggerate. On my word of honour (though it's been said that women have no honour), I assure you that what we have been talking about will remain between ourselves. Besides, I'm certain that even Bela would forgive you that outburst. It was unworthy of you, but . . . a lover can be forgiven such things.'

Wokulski kissed both her hands, but she tore them away. 'Pray don't make up to me, because a man in love is an altar to a woman . . . And now, be off with you to Bela, and . . .'

'And what, madam?'

'And admit that I know how to keep my promises.'

Her voice trembled, but Wokulski did not notice. He jumped out of the carriage, and hastened to the apartment house occupied by Mr Łęcki, where they had just stopped. When Mikołaj opened the door, he asked to be announced to Miss Łęcka. She was alone, and at once asked him in, blushing and embarrassed. 'You haven't been to see us for so long,' she said, 'were you ill?'

'Worse, madam,' he replied, without taking a seat, 'I offended you deeply for no reason.'

'Me?'

'Yes, I offended you with my suspicions. I . . .' he said in a stifled voice, 'I was at the concert the Rzezuchowskis gave. I left without even bidding you goodnight . . . I can't say more . . . I only feel that you have the right to refuse to receive me, as a man who did not appreciate you . . . who dared to suspect . . .'

Izabela looked deeply into his eyes and, stretching out a hand, said: 'I forgive you. Pray be seated.'

'Do not be hasty with your forgiveness, it may raise my hopes.'

She reflected: 'Goodness, how can I help that? Pray have your hopes, if you are so eager to . . .'

'Can you say that, Izabela?'

'Evidently it was predestined,' she replied with a smile.

He kissed her hand passionately and she did not prevent him. Then he went to the window and took something from around his neck. 'Pray accept this from me,' he said, and gave her a golden medallion on a chain. Izabela began examining it with curiosity. 'A strange gift, is it not?' said Wokulski, opening the medallion. 'Do you see this metal, light as a spider-web? Yet it's a jewel such as no treasury possesses, the seed of a great invention which may change humanity. Who knows that airships may not be born from it? But no matter. In giving it to you, I am placing my future in your hands.'

'So it is a talisman?'

'Very nearly. It's something which might draw me away from this country, and engulf my fortune and the rest of my life in new work. Perhaps it would be a waste of time, lunacy, but in any case, the thought of it was your only rival. The only one . . .' he repeated with emphasis.

'Did you think of leaving us?'

'No longer ago than this morning. That's why I'm giving you the amulet. Henceforward, madam, I have no other happiness in the world; all that is left to me is you – or death.'

'If that be so, I take you into captivity,' said Izabela, and she suspended the medallion around her neck. But when she went to thrust it under her bodice, she looked down, and blushed.

'How vile I am,' thought Wokulski, 'to think I suspected such a woman . . . Wretch that I am . . .'

When he went home, and dropped in at the store, he was so radiant that Ignacy was not a little alarmed. 'What's the matter with you?' he asked.

'Congratulate me. I am engaged to Miss Łęcka.'

But instead of congratulating him, Rzecki turned very pale. 'I had a letter from Mraczewski,' he said after a moment, 'Suzin sent him to France in February, as you know.'

'Well?' Wokulski interrupted.

'So – he writes from Lyons that Ludwik Stawski is alive and living in Algiers, but under the alias of Ernest Walter. Apparently he's trading in wines. Someone saw him a year ago.'

'We will check this.' said Wokulski, and he calmly noted the address in his diary.

Henceforth he spent every afternoon at the Łęckis, and was asked to stay to dinner once in a while. A few days later, Rzecki came to him. 'Well, old man?' Wokulski exclaimed, 'how are things with your Prince Lulu? Are you still angry with Szlangbaum for buying the store?'

The old clerk shook his head: 'Mrs Stawska isn't with Mrs Miller any longer. She's rather poorly . . . She talks of leaving Warsaw . . . Maybe you'll drop by there?'

'True, I ought to,' he replied, rubbing his head. 'Did you mention the store to her?'

'Of course; I even lent her twelve hundred roubles.'

'Out of your own poor savings? Why shouldn't she borrow from me?'

Rzecki didn't answer.

Towards two o'clock, Wokulski drove to visit Mrs Stawska. She looked very worn; her charming eyes seemed even larger and unhappier than before. 'What's this? asked Wokulski, 'I hear you want to leave Warsaw?'

'Yes, sir. Perhaps my husband will come back,' she added in a stifled voice.

'Rzecki has told me, and permit me to see what I can do to confirm the news.'

Mrs Stawska burst into tears. 'You're so good to us,' she whispered, 'may you be happy . . .'

At the same time Mrs Wąsowska was visiting Izabela, and learned from her that she had accepted Wokulski. 'At last!' said Mrs Wąsowska, 'I thought you were never going to make up your mind.'

'So I have given you a pleasant surprise,' Izabela retorted. 'In any case, he's an ideal husband – rich, unusual, and above all, a man with the heart of a dove. Not only is he not jealous, but he even apologised for his suspicions. That finally disarmed me . . . True love is blindfold . . . You don't say anything?'

'I'm thinking . . .'

'What of?'

'That if he knows you as well as you know him, then neither of you knows the other . . .'

'Our honeymoon will be all the more agreeable.'

'Let me wish you . . .'

XXXIII

A Couple Reconciled

IN MID-APRIL, Baroness Krzeszowska suddenly changed her way of life. Hitherto her days had been passed in scolding Marysia, writing letters to the tenants to tell them the stairs were littered with garbage, asking the janitor whether anyone had torn down the 'To Rent' notice, if the girls from the Parisian laundry spent the night in the house, or if the police had asked to see her about anything. Nor did she omit to remind him that should anyone apply for the third-floor apartment, he was to study young persons especially, and if they were students, to tell them the apartment was already rented.

'Mind what I tell you, Kasper,' she concluded, 'for you will lose your position if any student creeps into my house. I've had enough of those nihilists, libertines, atheists who carry human skulls . . .'

After every such conference, the janitor would go back to his cubby-hole, throw down his cap and cry: 'I'll hang myself, that I will, if I have to stand this woman any longer! On Friday, it's market day – janitor, go to the drugstore twice a day, attend to the mangle, and God knows what else. She's already told me I'm to go with her to the cemetery to set a grave in order! Did anyone ever hear of such a thing? I'll quit on Midsummer day, even if I have to lose twenty roubles . . .'

But after mid-April, the Baroness grew milder. Several circumstances contributed. In the first place, she was visited one day by an unknown lawyer with a confidential inquiry whether she knew anything about the Baron's bank deposit. If there were such a thing in existence – though the lawyer doubted it – then it should be brought to light in order to liberate the Baron from his compromising situation. For his creditors were ready to adopt desperate measures.

The Baroness solemnly assured the lawyer that her husband the Baron, despite all the depravities and the torments to which he had subjected her, possessed no funds at all. At this point, she had an attack of the spasms, which induced the lawyer to beat a hasty retreat. However, when the high priest of justice had quit her apartment, she returned to her senses very swiftly, and, after calling Marysia, said to her in an unusual calm voice: 'It will be necessary, Marysia, to put up new curtains, for I have a feeling that our unfortunate master is coming back.'

A few days later, the Prince in person was at the Baroness's house. They were closeted together in the most distant room, and held a long conversation, during which the Baroness burst into tears several times and swooned away once. What could they have been talking of? Even Marysia didn't know. But when the Prince had gone, the Baroness at once ordered Maruszewicz to be summoned, and when he hastened in, she said in a strangely mild voice, interwoven with sighs: 'I have the idea, Mr Maruszewicz, that my errant husband has finally come to his senses. Pray be kind enough, therefore, to go into town and buy a man's robe and a pair of slippers. Buy them in your size, for the two of you, poor things, are both equally slender.'

Mr Maruszewicz's eyebrows went up, but he took the money and made the purchases. The Baroness thought that the price of forty roubles for a robe, and six roubles for slippers was rather high, but Mr Maruszewicz told her he didn't know anything about prices, and that he'd bought them in the best stores, so nothing further was said.

Then, a few days later, two Jews called at Baroness Krzeszowska's apartment to ask whether the Baron was at home . . . Instead of falling upon them with a shriek, as she usually did, the Baroness very calmly invited them to leave. Then, calling Kasper, she said: 'I have the idea, my dear Kasper, that our poor master will be moving in today or tomorrow. You must put a carpet on the stairs to the second floor. But mind, my child, that they don't steal the rods . . . And it must be beaten every few days.'

Henceforward she no longer scolded Marysia, wrote no letters, didn't torment the janitor . . . All she did was to walk about in the large apartment, arms folded, pale, quiet, agitated. At the sound of a droshky stopping in front of the house, she would rush to the window: at the sound of the door-bell, she would rush to the threshold and eavesdrop through the half-open door to know who was talking to Marysia. After a few days of this kind of life, she grew still paler and more agitated. She ran faster for shorter distances, often sank into a chair with her heart beating, and finally took to her bed.

'Tell them to take up the carpet on the stairs,' she said to Marysia in a hoarse voice, 'some scoundrel must have lent your master money again.'

Hardly had she said this, than there was a brisk ring at the door-bell. The Baroness sent Marysia first and she herself, touched by a premonition, began dressing despite her headache. Everything slithered through her fingers. Meanwhile, Marysia, opening the door on its chain, saw a very distinguished gentleman with a silk umbrella and valise on the landing. Behind the gentleman, who looked rather like a butler despite his carefully trimmed moustache and copious side-whiskers, were porters with trunks and bags.

'What is it?' the servant girl asked automatically.

'Open the door,' replied the gentleman with the valise, 'it's the Baron's things, and mine.' The door opened, the gentleman ordered the porters to put the trunks and bags in the vestibule, and inquired: 'Where's His Excellency's study?'

At this moment the Baroness hurried in, her robe undone, hair in disorder. 'What's this?' she cried, in an emotional voice. 'Oh, it's you, Leon. Where's your master?'

'At Stepek's café, I believe . . . I should like to put away the things, but I don't see either my master's study, nor a room for me.'

'Wait a moment,' cried the Baroness feverishly, 'Marysia will move out of the kitchen, and you can . . .'

'Me in the kitchen, madam?' asked the gentleman named Leon, 'surely madam is joking? According to my agreement with His Excellency, I am to have my own room.'

The Baroness became embarrassed. 'What am I saying?' she exclaimed, 'will you, Leon, move into the third floor for the time being, into the apartment that used to be the students.'

'Now I understand you,' Leon replied, 'if there are several rooms, I might even live with the chef.'

'What chef?'

'Surely Your Excellencies can't do without a chef? Take the things upstairs,' he turned to the porters.

'What are you doing?' the Baroness shrieked, seeing them collecting all the trunks and bags.

'They're taking my things. Carry on!' Leon commanded.

'And His Excellency's?'

'Oh, here you are,' the servant replied, handing Marysia the valise and umbrella.

'But the bed-linen? His clothes? His things?' the Baroness cried, wringing her hands.

'Pray don't create a scene in front of the servants, madam,' said Leon threateningly, 'His Excellency should have all those things at home.'

'That's so, that's so,' whispered the Baroness, mortified.

Once installed upstairs, whither they still had to bring a bed, table, some chairs and a wash-basin with a jug of water, Mr Leon put on his tail-coat, white tie, a clean shirt (a trifle too small for

him), went back to the Baroness and sat himself down gravely in
the hall. 'Within a half hour,' he told Marysia, looking at his gold
watch, 'His Excellency should be here, for he has a nap every day
between four and five o'clock. Well, now, miss – are you bored
here?' he added, 'if so, I'll liven you up . . .'

'Marysia, come here!' called the Baroness, from her room.

'Why are you rushing off, miss?' Leon inquired, 'will the old
girl's business vanish, then? Let her wait a bit.'

'I dare not, she's terrible when she's angry,' whispered Marysia,
breaking away from him.

'That's because you spoiled her. They'll bang nails into your
head if you let them. You'll find things easier with the Baron, he's
a connoisseur. But you'll have to dress different, not like a school
ma'am. We don't like nuns.'

'Marysia! Marysia!'

'Well, run along, but take it easy,' Leon advised.

Despite Leon's prediction, the Baron arrived at his wife's apartment nearer five than four. He wore a new frock-coat and fresh hat
and carried a cane with a silver horse-shoe in his hand. His expression was calm, but his faithful servant saw powerful emotion underneath. While still in the hall, the Baron's eye-glasses fell off twice
and his left cheek twitched a great deal more than it had done
before the duel, or when he'd been struck with a billiard cue:
'Announce me to Her Excellency,' he said in a somewhat stifled
voice. Leon opened the drawing-room door and almost threateningly cried: 'His Excellency!'

And when the Baron had gone in, he shut the door, sent away
Marysia, who had hurried out of the kitchen – and began eavesdropping.

The Baroness, seated on the sofa with a book, rose on seeing her
husband. When the Baron made a deep bow, she wanted to curtsy
back, but sank on the sofa instead. 'My husband . . .' she
whispered, covering her face. 'Oh! What have you been doing?'

'I am very sorry,' said the Baron, bowing a second time, 'to pay
my respects to you in such circumstances.'

'I am ready to forgive all, if . . .'

'That is very gratifying to us both,' the Baron interrupted, 'for I
too am ready to overlook everything concerning myself.
Unfortunately, you have deigned to take advantage of my good
name which, although not marked in the history of the world by
anything remarkable, yet deserves to be spared that.'

'Your name?' the Baroness repeated.

'Yes, madam,' replied the Baron, bowing for the third time, his
hat still in his hand. 'Forgive me for mentioning this painful matter,
but . . . for some time past, my name has been figuring in all the
law courts. At this moment, you apparently have, on hand, three

court cases: two with tenants, and one with your former lawyer, who is an out-and-out scoundrel and no mistake.'

'But, husband mine!' cried the Baroness, jumping up, 'recollect that you at this moment have eleven court cases on hand, respecting debts of thirty thousand roubles.'

'Pardon me! I have seventeen court cases respecting thirty-nine thousand roubles of debts, if my memory serves. But they are cases over debts. Not a single one have I brought against a respectable woman for stealing a doll . . . My sins do not include writing a single anonymous letter to blacken an innocent woman, nor has a single one of my creditors been obliged to run away from Warsaw, pursued by scandal, as has happened to a certain Mrs Stawska, thanks to the interference of Baroness Krzeszowska.'

'Stawska was your mistress.'

'Pardon me! I don't deny I sought her favours, but I declare on my honour that she is the noblest woman I ever met in my life. Pray do not be vexed by this superlative applied to another person, and pray deign to believe me when I say that Mrs Stawska left even my . . . my attempts unanswered. And because, madam, I have the honour of knowing the average woman . . . so my evidence means something.'

'What, therefore, is it that you want, my husband?' asked the Baroness, now in a firm voice.

'I want . . . to defend the name we both bear. I want . . . to enjoin respect for Baroness Krzeszowska in this house. I want to terminate the court cases, and give you protection. To do so, I am obliged to ask you for hospitality. But when I settle my accounts . . .'

'You will leave me?'

'Undoubtedly.'

'And your debts?'

The Baron rose. 'My debts are of no interest to you, madam,' he said, in a tone of profound conviction. 'If Mr Wokulski, an ordinary gentleman, can make several millions in the course of a few years, then a man with my name can pay off forty thousand in debts, and I too will demonstrate that I know how to work.'

'You are ill, husband mine,' replied the Baroness. 'You know very well that I come from a family which made its own fortune, and I can tell you that you will never be able to work, not even to support yourself . . . Not even to feed the poorest of men.'

'So you reject the protection I am offering you, madam, thanks to the persuasion of the Prince and concern for the honour of my name?'

'Not at all! Pray begin to look after me at last, for hitherto . . .'

'As far as I am concerned,' the Baron interrupted, with another bow, 'I shall try to forget the past.'

'You forgot it long ago . . . You haven't even visited our daughter's grave . . .'

Thus the Baron installed himself in his wife's abode. He broke off all the law-suits against the tenants, and told the Baroness's former lawyer that he would have him horse-whipped if he ever spoke disrespectfully of his client, wrote a letter of apology to Mrs Stawska and sent her (to Częstochowa) an enormous bouquet. Finally, he engaged a chef and paid visits with his spouse to various persons in society, having first of all told Maruszewicz, who spread it around town, that if any lady did not return the call, the Baron would require satisfaction from her husband.

Drawing-room society was much upset by the Baron's wild claims; however, everyone returned calls on the Baron and Baroness, and almost everyone entered into closer social relations with them. In return, the Baroness – and this was a sign of the utmost delicacy of feeling on her part – paid off her husband's debts without a word to anyone. She was haughty to some of the creditors, she wept with others, and deducted various amounts from nearly everyone on account of money-lender's interest. She grew agitated – but she paid.

She had several pounds of her husband's promissory notes in a separate drawer of her writing desk when the following incident occurred. Wokulski's store was to be taken over in July by Henryk Szlangbaum; and since the new owner did not want to take over the debts or claims of the previous owner, Mr Rzecki was obliged to settle accounts urgently. Among others, he sent a bill for several hundred roubles to Baron Krzeszowski, with the request for an early reply. The note, like all communications of this sort, fell into the hands of the Baroness who, instead of paying, sent Rzecki an insolent letter in which she did not hesitate to refer to swindles, the dishonest purchase of her mare, and so forth.

Within twenty-four hours of sending this letter, Rzecki appeared at the Baron's house, stating that he wished to see him. The Baron received him very cordially, although he did not conceal his surprise on seeing that the former second of his opponent was very irritated.

'I am visiting you because I have a claim to make,' the old clerk began. 'The day before yesterday I ventured to send you a bill . . .'

'Yes, of course . . . I owe you gentlemen something . . . How much is it?'

'Two hundred and thirty-six roubles, thirty kopeks.'

'I will endeavour to satisfy you tomorrow.'

'That is not all,' Rzecki interrupted, 'for yesterday I received this letter from your worthy spouse.'

The Baron read the piece of paper Rzecki handed him, pondered and replied: 'I am very sorry the Baroness used such uncivil language, but . . . as for that mare, she's right. Mr Wokulski (though I don't hold it against him) let me have the mare for six hundred, but took a receipt for eight hundred.'

Rzecki went livid with rage: 'Baron, I regret this incident, but . . . One of us has been the victim of a trick . . . A nasty trick, sir! And here's the proof.'

He produced two sheets of paper from his pocket and gave one to Krzeszowski. The Baron glanced at it, and exclaimed: 'So it was that scoundrel Maruszewicz! Upon my word, he gave me only six hundred roubles, and talked about the business-like attitude of Wokulski into the bargain . . .'

'And this?' asked Rzecki, handing him another sheet.

The Baron looked over the document from top to bottom. His lips whitened. 'Now I understand it all,' he said, 'this receipt is forged, forged by Maruszewicz. I never borrowed any money from Wokulski.'

'Yet the Baroness has called us swindlers.'

The Baron rose. 'Forgive me, sir,' he said, 'in my wife's name I solemnly beg your pardon, and apart from any satisfaction you gentlemen may require, I will do all I can to redress the wrong done to Mr Wokulski . . . Yes, sir. I will pay visits to all my friends and tell them that Mr Wokulski is a gentleman, that he paid eight hundred for the mare, and that we have both been the victims of the intrigues of that scoundrel Maruszewicz. The Krzeszowskis, sir . . . Mr – ?'

'Rzecki.'

'My dear Mr Rzecki, the Krzeszowskis never blackened anyone's reputation. They may have erred, but in good faith, Mr – ?'

'Rzecki.'

'My dear Mr Rzecki . . .'

On this, the conversation ended; for the old clerk, despite the Baron's insistence, did not want and indeed refused to listen to any excuses, or even to see the Baroness. After showing Rzecki to the door, the Baron, unable to restrain himself, exclaimed to Leon: 'Those tradesmen are honest folk, all the same . . .'

'They have the cash, Your Excellency, and the credit,' Leon replied.

'You fool! . . . Don't we have honour, because we've no credit?'

'We do, Your Excellency, but of a different sort.'

'Not a tradesman's sort, I hope.'

And he ordered his going-out clothes.

Rzecki went straight to Wokulski from the Baron and told him of Maruszewicz's machinations, of the Baron's contrition and finally handed him the forged papers, advising him to start a law-suit. Wokulski listened gravely, even nodded his head, but was looking goodness knows where and thinking goodness knows what. The old clerk, noticing there was nothing to detain him, said goodbye to his Staś and remarked as he left: 'I see you are infernally busy, so you'll do best if you put the matter in the hands of your lawyer at once.'

'Very well . . . very well . . .' Wokulski replied, not realising what Ignacy had said. At this precise moment, he was thinking of the castle ruins at Zasław, where he had seen tears in Izabela's eyes for the first time: 'How noble she is! . . . What delicacy of feeling! It will be long before I can get to know all the treasures of that beautiful soul.'

He called on Mr Łęcki twice a day, or at least went into society where he was likely to find Izabela, to gaze at her and exchange a few words. At present this sufficed him, but he dared not think of the future. 'It seems to me I'll die at her feet,' he told himself, 'well, and what of it? I'll die gazing at her, and will perhaps be able to see her for all eternity. Who knows whether the life to come doesn't close in a man's last feeling?' And he recited Mickiewicz:

> And after many days or many years,
> When I am summoned to abandon my tomb,
> You will remember your sleeping friend
> And journey down from heaven to revive him.
>
> Once more will I be drawn to your white breast,
> Once more will your dear arm encircle me;
> I will awake – as from a moment's sleep,
> Kissing your cheeks, gazing into your eyes.

A few days later, Baron Krzeszowski called on him. 'I've been here twice,' he cried, fidgeting with his eye-glasses which were apparently his only care in life.

'Have you?' asked Wokulski. Suddenly he recollected Rzecki's tale, and that he'd found two of the Baron's visiting cards on the table only the day before.

'Can you guess why I'm here, sir?' said the Baron. 'Mr Wokulski, am I to apologise to you for an involuntary injustice?'

'Say no more, Baron,' Wokulski interrupted, embracing him, 'it's nothing. In any case, even if I made two hundred roubles by bargaining over your mare, would I need to hide the fact?'

'That's so!' replied the Baron, clutching his forehead, 'fancy my not thinking of that earlier . . . Apropos profit, couldn't you show me some way to get rich fast? I urgently need a hundred thousand roubles within a year.'

Wokulski smiled.

'You smile, cousin (I suppose I may begin to call you that?) – you smile, yet you yourself have made millions in the course of two years, and honestly too.'

'Not quite so much,' Wokulski added, 'but in any case, that fortune was not worked for – it was won. I won a dozen or more times by doubling my stakes each time like a card-player, and my only virtue was that I played with unmarked cards.'

'Luck again!' cried the Baron, plucking off his eye-glasses. 'I, cousin, don't have a pennyworth of luck. I gambled away half my fortune, ladies of easy virtue devoured the other half – there's nothing left but to put a bullet through my brains. No, I definitely have no luck! Look, now . . . I thought Maruszewicz would seduce the Baroness. Then I might have had some peace and quiet at home. How tolerant she would be towards my own little misdemeanours! But what happened? The Baroness wouldn't dream of deceiving me, while a prison cell awaits that fool. Pray ensure that he's locked up, for his rascally ways are beginning to bore even me. So,' he concluded, 'we're in agreement. I'd only add that I have visited all my acquaintances whom those incautious remarks of mine about the mare may have reached, and have explained the matter in the utmost detail . . . Let Maruszewicz go to prison; it's the most appropriate place for him, and his absence will mean a few thousand roubles a year to me . . . I also visited Mr Tomasz and Miss Izabela, and explained our misunderstanding to them. It's dreadful, the way that scoundrel could squeeze money out of me! Although I haven't had a penny for a year, he was always borrowing from me. A scoundrel with genius! I feel that if they don't put him to hard labour, I'll never rid myself of him. Au revoir, cousin!'

Less than ten minutes had elapsed after the Baron's departure when the servant announced to Wokulski some gentleman who wished urgently to see him, but refused to give his name. 'Can it be Maruszewicz?' Wokulski thought.

In fact Maruszewicz entered, pale, with glittering eyes. 'Sir!' he said in a gloomy voice, closing the study door, 'you see before you a man who has made up his mind . . .'

'What have you decided?'

'To end it all. This is a difficult moment, but there's no help for it. My honour . . .' he paused, then went on indignantly, 'I could kill you first, of course, as you are the cause of my misfortunes.'

'Well, don't stand on ceremony,' said Wokulski.

'You joke, but I really do have a gun, and am prepared . . .'

'Show your preparedness, then.'

'Sir! This is not the way to speak to a man on the brink of the grave. If I came here, it was only to prove to you that despite the error of my ways, I have a noble heart.'

'And why are you standing on the brink of the grave, pray?'

'To preserve my honour, which you wish to strip me of?'

'Come, preserve that valuable treasure,' replied Wokulski, and he produced the fatal documents from his desk. 'Are these the papers you're worried about?'

'How can you ask? You are making mock of my despair.'

'Look here, Mr Maruszewicz,' said Wokulski, glancing over the papers, 'I might at this moment tell you a few home truths, or leave you in uncertainty for a while. But as we are both grown men . . .'

He ripped up the papers and handed the pieces to Maruszewicz: 'Keep these as a souvenir.'

Maruszewicz fell on his knees before him. 'Sir!' he cried, 'you have saved my life . . . My gratitude . . .'

'Don't be silly,' Wokulski interrupted, 'I was perfectly at rest regarding your life, just as I am certain that sooner or later you'll end up in prison. The point is that I don't want to facilitate that journey for you.'

'Sir, you are merciless,' Maruszewicz replied, mechanically dusting down his trousers. 'A single cordial word, a single affectionate handclasp might have set me on a new path. But you can't bring yourself to do it.'

'Well, good-day, Mr Maruszewicz. All I ask is that you don't hit on the idea of signing my name, for if you do . . .'

Maruszewicz left in a huff.

'It was for you, my dearest, that one prisoner has been spared. It's a terrible thing to imprison anyone, even a criminal and fraud,' Wokulski thought. For a while, a struggle went on within him. First he reproached himself because, having been in a position to rid the world of a scoundrel, he had failed to do so; then again he wondered what would happen to him, if he himself were imprisoned, torn away from Izabela for months, perhaps years: 'How dreadful never to see her again! Who knows that mercy isn't the best justice? . . . How sentimental I'm becoming!'

XXXIV

Tempus Fugit, Aeternitas Manet

A LTHOUGH the business with Maruszewicz had been settled in
private, news of it spread. Wokulski told Rzecki, and asked
him to cancel the Baron's supposed debt from the ledgers.
Maruszewicz told the Baron, adding that the Baron ought not to be
angry with him, since the debt had been cancelled and he,
Maruszewicz, intended to turn over a new leaf. 'I feel,' he said with
a sigh, 'that I'd be another man, if only I had three thousand a year.
Vile world, in which men such as I have to be wasted . . .'

'Come now, calm yourself,' the Baron pacified him, 'I like you,
but everyone knows very well that you're a scoundrel.'

'Have you looked into my heart, Baron? Do you know what
feelings are there? Oh, if only there were some tribunal that could
read a man's soul, you'd all see which of us is the better: I – or
those who judge and condemn me.'

As a result, both Rzecki and the Baron, as well as the Prince and
several counts, learned of Maruszewicz's 'latest prank'. All admitted
that Wokulski had behaved nobly, though not like a man. 'It was a
very beautiful deed,' said the Prince, 'but not in Wokulski's style.
He looked to me like one of those men who constitute a force in
society for creating good and punishing scoundrels. Any priest
would have behaved the way Wokulski did with Maruszewicz . . .
I'm afraid the man is losing his energy.'

As a matter of fact, Wokulski was not losing his energy, though
he had changed in many respects. He did not, for instance, work at
the store, even felt a dislike of it, because the name of a haberdashery tradesman lowered him in Izabela's eyes. On the other
hand, he began working more earnestly with the company for trade
with the Empire, because it was bringing in enormous profits, and
this increased the fortune he hoped to offer Izabela.

Ever since the time when he had proposed and been accepted,
he had been dominated by a strange wistfulness and sympathy. It
seemed to him that he couldn't have done anyone any harm, and

even that he couldn't have protected himself from injustice, providing it didn't affect Izabela. He felt an ungovernable need to do good to others. In addition to a bequest for Rzecki, he intended to give his former clerks Lisiecki and Klein four thousand roubles apiece, as compensation for the harm he had done them by selling the store to Szlangbaum. He also set aside some twelve thousand roubles as bonuses for the employees, janitors, labourers and drivers. He not only saw to it that Węgiełek had a riotous wedding, but added several hundred roubles to the sum promised the young couple. Because a daughter was born at this time to the carrier Wysocki, he stood as her godfather; and when the crafty father gave the child the name Izabela, Wokulski put away five hundred roubles for a dowry.

This name was very dear to him. Sometimes, when he was sitting alone, he took paper and pencil, and would write endlessly: 'Izabela . . . Iza . . . Bela . . .' and then burn it, lest the name of his beloved fall into someone else's hands. He meant to buy a small estate outside Warsaw, to build a villa and call it 'Izabelino'. He remembered how, during his travels in the Urals, a certain scholar who had discovered a new mineral sought his advice: how to name it? And he reproached himself that, though he had then not yet made Izabela's acquaintance, still it had not occurred to him to call it 'izabelite'. Finally, reading in the newspapers of the discovery of a new planetoid, the naming of which was also the cause of some concern to its discoverer, he wanted to put up a huge prize for the astronomer who would discover a new heavenly body and call it: Izabela.

His overwhelming attachment to one woman did not, however, exclude thoughts of another. Sometimes he recalled Mrs Stawska who, as he knew, had been prepared to sacrifice everything for his sake, and he felt a sort of pang of conscience. 'Well, what could I do?' he said. 'Is it my fault I love one, while the other . . . If only she could forget me, and be happy.' In any case, he decided to ensure her future, and find out about her husband: 'Let her not have to worry about tomorrow, at least. Let her have a dowry for the child.'

Every few days he saw Izabela in society, surrounded by young, middle-aged and old men. But he was no longer irritated by the men flirting, nor by her glances and smiles. 'It's her nature,' he thought, 'she can't look or smile differently. She's like a flower, or the sun, which involuntarily makes everyone happy, is beautiful in everyone's eyes.'

One day he received a telegram from Zasławek, summoning him to the Duchess's funeral. 'She's dead, then . . .' he murmured, 'what a pity about that fine woman. . . Why wasn't I present when she died?'

He was sorry, grew sad – but didn't go to the funeral of the old lady who had shown him so much kindness. He dared not part from Izabela even for a few days.

He knew very well, now, that he didn't belong to himself, that all his thoughts, feelings and longings, all his plans and hopes were anchored in this one woman. If she were to die, he would not need to do away with himself; his soul would fly after her of its own accord, like a bird that rests only a moment on a branch. Besides, he did not even speak to her of love, any more than we speak of the weight of our bodies, or of the air that surrounds and fills a man. If, during the course of a day, he happened to think of anything except her, then he would shake his head in amazement, like a man who has miraculously discovered himself to be in some unknown region. This wasn't love, it was ecstasy.

One day in May, Mr Łęcki summoned him. 'Imagine,' he said to Wokulski, 'we have to go to Cracow. Hortensja is poorly, she wants to see Bela (I've an idea it's to do with her will), and she would certainly be pleased to make your acquaintance. Can you accompany us?'

'At any time,' Wokulski replied. 'When is it to be?'

'We ought to leave today, but tomorrow will do.'

Wokulski promised to be ready on the morrow. When he said goodbye to Mr Tomasz and looked in on Izabela, he learned that Starski was in Warsaw . . .

'Poor fellow,' she said, laughing, 'the Duchess only left him two thousand a year, and ten thousand in cash. I advised him to make a good he prefers to go to Vienna, and thence very likely to Monte Carlo . . . I told him to travel with us. It will be gayer, don't you think?'

'Of course,' Wokulski replied, 'especially as we shall have a private compartment.'

'Until tomorrow, then!'

Wokulski settled his most urgent business, reserved a drawing-room compartment to Cracow, and at about eight in the evening, having sent on his things, called at the Łęckis. The three of them had tea together, and set off for the railroad station just before ten.

'Where can Mr Starski be?' Wokulski inquired.

'Goodness knows,' Izabela replied, 'perhaps he won't come at all. . . . He's so changeable.'

They got into the carriage, but Starski was still not there. Izabela bit her lip, glancing out of the window now and then. Finally, when the second bell had rung, Starski appeared on the platform. 'Here we are!' cried Izabela. But as the young man didn't hear her, Wokulski hurried out and brought him into the compartment. 'I thought you were never coming!' said Izabela.

'I very nearly didn't,' Starski replied, greeting Tomasz, 'I was at

Krzeszowski's, and just think, *ma cousine*, that we played cards from noon to nine.'

'You lost, of course.'

'Of course . . . Good luck deserts such as I,' he added, glancing at her. Izabela blushed slightly.

The train started to move. Starski sat down at Izabela's left, and began talking to her, half in Polish, half in English, gradually more and more in English. Wokulski sat to the right of Izabela, but as he didn't want to interrupt the conversation he rose and sat down by Tomasz.

Mr Łęcki, rather poorly, put on a plaid overcoat and pulled a blanket over his knees. He ordered all the windows to be shut, and the lamps, which bothered him, shaded. He promised himself he would go to sleep, and even felt sleep coming upon him. In the meanwhile, he entered into conversation with Wokulski, and began expatiating on his sister Hortensja who had been so attached to him when young, on the court of Napoleon III who had spoken to him several times, on the politeness and the love affairs of Victor Emmanuel, and innumerable other topics.

Wokulski listened attentively as far as Pruszków. After Pruszków, the weary and monotonous voice of Tomasz began to tire him. On the other hand, Izabela's conversation in English with Starski kept coming to his ears with increasing clarity. He even caught a few sentences which interested him and he asked himself if he should not warn them that he understood English?

He was just about to rise from his seat, when he happened to glance at the window at the opposite side of the carriage and in it saw, as if in a mirror, the faint reflection of Izabela and Starski. They were sitting very close together, both were flushed, although they were talking in a light manner, as though of insignificant things. But Wokulski noticed that the indifferent tone did not correspond to the content of their talk: he even sensed that they wanted to deceive someone by this light tone. And at this moment, for the first time since he'd known Izabela, the terrible word 'Cheat! . . . Cheat! . . .' flew through his mind. He leaned back against the wall of the compartment, looked in the glass – and listened. It seemed to him that each word Starski and Izabela uttered was falling like drops of leaden rain upon his face, head and chest. He had no thought of warning them that he could understand what they were saying, just listened – and listened.

The train was passing through Radziwiłłów, and the first phrase which caught Wokulski's attention was: 'You may reproach him with anything,' Izabela was saying, in English, 'he's not young or distinguished; he's far too sentimental, and sometimes a bore – but avaricious? Suffice it to say that even papa calls him over-generous.'

'And that business with Mr K.?' Starski interposed.

'About the race-horse? One can see you're just up from the provinces. The Baron called on us lately, and said that if ever the person we are referring to behaved like a gentleman, it was in this matter.'

'No gentleman would let a forger go, if he hadn't had some dealings with him behind the scenes,' Starski replied with a smile.

'How often has the Baron forgiven him?'

'Just so – the Baron has all sorts of little sins which Mr M. knows of. You don't protect your protégé very well, *ma cousine*,' said Starski, mockingly.

Wokulski leaned hard against the wall so as not to jump up and strike Starski. But he controlled himself. 'Everyone has the right to judge others,' he thought. 'Besides, let's see what comes next.'

For some moments he heard only the rattle of the wheels, and noticed that the carriage was swaying. 'I never felt a carriage sway so before,' he told himself.

'And that medallion?' Starski mocked, 'was that your only premarital gift? Not a very generous fiancé; he loves you like a troubadour, but . . .'

'I assure you,' Izabela interrupted, 'that he'd give me his entire fortune.'

'Take it, cousin, and lend me a hundred thousand . . . By the way, have you found this miraculous piece of tin?'

'No, I haven't, and I'm so vexed. God, if he were to find out . . .'

'That you lost his metal – or that we looked for it together?' Starski whispered, pressing close to her arm.

A mist veiled Wokulski's eyes. 'Am I losing consciousness?' he thought, grasping the strap by the window. It seemed to him the carriage was beginning to rock and that it would be derailed at any moment.

'You're insolent, you know!' said Izabela in a stifled voice.

'That is precisely my strength,' Starski replied.

'For heaven's sake . . . He may notice . . . I hate you!'

'You'll be crazy about me, for no one could hate me. Women love devils.'

Izabela moved closer to her father. Wokulski stared into the opposite window, and listened.

'I must tell you,' she said, vexed, 'that you won't cross the threshold of our house. If you dare . . . I'll tell him everything.'

Starski laughed: 'I won't come, cousin, until you send for me, but I am sure that will happen very soon. In a week, this adoring husband will bore you and you'll want more amusing society. You'll remember your scoundrel of a cousin, who has never been serious in his life, always witty, always ready to adore you, never jealous, who can yield place to others, respect your whims . . .'

'Taking your reward in other ways,' Izabela interrupted.

'Just so! If I didn't you'd have no cause to forgive me, and could fear my reproaches.'

Without changing position he encircled her with his right arm, and pressed her hand with his left, under her cloak. 'Yes, little cousin,' he said, 'a woman like you isn't going to be satisfied with the daily bread of respect, or the cake of adoration . . . You need champagne, someone must bewilder you with cynicism . . .'

'It's easy to be a cynic.'

'But not everyone dares to be. Ask this gentleman whether it ever occurred to him that his tender prayers are worth less than my sacrilege?'

Wokulski was no longer listening to the conversation; his attention had been absorbed by another fact – the change which had suddenly started to occur within himself. If yesterday he had been told that he would be the speechless auditor of any such conversation, he wouldn't have believed it; he'd have thought that each word would kill him or drive him to frenzy. But now that it had happened, he was forced to admit that there's something worse than betrayal, disillusion and humiliation.

But – what was it? Yes: travelling by train! How the carriage was shuddering . . . how it was rushing along! The shuddering of the train made itself felt in his legs, lungs, heart, brain; everything inside him was shuddering, every bone, every fibre of nerve . . .

And this rushing onwards through limitless fields, under the enormous vault of sky! And he had to travel on, God only knows how much further . . . Five, perhaps even ten minutes . . .

What was Starski, or even Izabela? One was as bad as the other . . . But this railroad, this railroad . . . and this shuddering. He felt he would burst into tears, begin screaming, smash the window and jump out . . . Or worse: he felt he was going to implore Starski to save him . . . From what? There was a moment when he wanted to hide himself under the seat, beg the others to sit on it, and travel like that to the next station . . .

He shut his eyes, clenched his teeth, gripped the edge of the seat with both hands; sweat burst out on his forehead and streamed down his face, and the train shuddered and rushed along . . . Finally a whistle was heard, then another, and the train stopped in a station. 'I'm saved,' Wokulski thought.

At the same moment Mr Łęcki woke up. 'What station is this?' he asked Wokulski.

'Skierniewice,' Izabela replied.

The conductor opened the door. Wokulski leaped up. He knocked against Tomasz, staggered against the opposite seat, tripped on the step and rushed into the buffet. 'Vodka!' he exclaimed.

Surprised, the waitress handed him a glass. He lifted it to his lips, but felt a pressure in his throat and nausea, so put down the glass untouched.

Starski was talking to Izabela in their compartment: 'Well, I must say, cousin,' he said, 'that one doesn't jump out of a compartment quite so hastily, in front of ladies.'

'Perhaps he's ill?' Izabela replied, feeling some uneasiness.

'Not an illness, surely, that won't brook delay . . . Would you like me to order something?'

'Soda water . . .'

Starski went into the buffet: Izabela looked out of the window. Her ill-defined uneasiness was increasing. 'There's something the matter,' she thought, 'how strange he looked . . .'

Wokulski went from the buffet to the end of the platform. He took several deep breaths, drank some water from a barrel by which a poor woman and some Jews were waiting. Slowly he came to, and on seeing the chief conductor, said: 'My good man, find a piece of paper . . .'

'What's the matter, sir?'

'Nothing. Get a piece of paper from your office, and say at my compartment that there's a telegram for Wokulski.'

'For you, sir?'

'Yes.'

The conductor was extremely surprised, but went to the telegraph office. A few minutes later he emerged and, approaching the compartment in which Mr Łęcki and his daughter were seated, cried: 'Telegram for Mr Wokulski!'

'What's this? Show me!' exclaimed Tomasz, anxiously.

But at this moment Wokulski stopped by the conductor, took the paper, calmly opened it and pretended to read it, although it was quite dark at that spot. 'What kind of telegram is it?' Tomasz asked him.

'From Warsaw,' Wokulski replied, 'I must go back.'

'Go back?' Izabela cried, 'is it some misfortune?'

'No, madam. My partner has sent for me.'

'Profit – or loss?' Tomasz whispered, leaning out of the window.

'Huge profits,' Wokulski replied in the same manner.

'In that case – go back,' Tomasz advised.

'But why wait here?' Izabela cried. 'You must wait for a train, and you'd do better to travel on with us until we meet it. We can have a few more hours together.'

'Bela's advice is excellent,' Mr. Tomasz interposed.

'No, sir,' Wokulski replied, 'I prefer travelling back on an engine rather than waste a few hours.'

Izabela gazed at him, wide-eyed. At this moment she saw something entirely novel about him, and he interested her. 'What a profound character,' she thought.

In the course of a few moments Wokulski had, for no reason, grown powerful in her eyes, while Starski seemed small and ludicrous. 'Why is he staying? Where did that telegram come from?' she wondered, and the ill-defined uneasiness gave place to terror.

Wokulski went back to the buffet for a porter to get his things out, and met Starski.

'What's wrong?' Starski exclaimed, staring at him in the light from the waiting-room. Wokulski seized his arm and dragged him along the platform. 'Don't be angry at what I say, Mr Starski,' he said in a dull voice. 'You are mistaken about yourself . . . There's as much of the devil in you, as there is poison in a match-head . . . And you have none of the qualities of champagne . . . Your attributes are closer to those of overripe cheese which stimulates poor digestions which a plain flavour might cause to vomit . . . Excuse me.'

Starski listened, dumbfounded. He didn't understand a word, yet he seemed to understand something. He began supposing he had a madman on his hands.

The second bell rang, a crowd of travellers hurried out of the buffet to the carriages. 'And let me give you a piece of advice, Mr Starski. In taking advantages of the affections of the fair sex, traditional caution is better than more or less devilish impudence. Your boldness unmasks women. But, as women don't like being unmasked, you may lose credit with them, which would be a misfortune for both you and your pupils.'

Starski still didn't understand what this was all about. 'If I have offended you in some way,' he said, 'I'm ready to give you satisfaction.'

The third bell rang: 'Gentlemen, all aboard!' cried the conductors.

'No, sir,' said Wokulski, escorting him back to the Łęckis' compartment, 'if I wanted satisfaction from you, you'd be dead already, without any extra formalities. It is you, rather, who have the right to demand satisfaction from me, for daring to enter the garden where you cultivate your flowers . . . In any case, I shall be at your disposal . . . You know my address?'

They drew near the carriage, by which the conductor was already standing. Wokulski forced Starski to mount the step, thrust him into the compartment, and the conductor slammed the door. 'What's this, aren't you going to say goodbye, Stanisław?' asked Tomasz in surprise.

'A pleasant journey,' he replied, bowing.

Izabela stood in the window. The station-master blew his whistle, the locomotive responded. 'Farewell, Iza, farewell,' Wokulski cried, in English.

The train moved off. Izabela threw herself into the seat opposite her father. Starski went to the other corner of the compartment.

'Well, well,' Wokulski muttered to himself, 'the pair of you will come together again before you reach Piotrkow.'

He watched the train moving away and laughed.

He stood alone on the platform and listened to the roar of the departing train; sometimes the roaring decreased, sometimes it fell silent, then again grew stronger, until it finally stopped. Then he heard the footsteps of the station staff going home, the moving of little tables in the buffet; the lights began going out inside the buffet and a yawning waiter locked the glass door, which squeaked expressively.

'They lost my metal while looking for the medallion!' Wokulski thought. 'I'm sentimental, and a bore . . . She must have champagne as well as the daily bread of respect and the cake of adoration . . . The cake of adoration, that's witty! But what sort of champagne does she like? Ah, the champagne of cynicism . . . That's witty too. Well, learning English has paid off, at any rate.'

Wandering aimlessly on, he walked between two rows of goods wagons. For a moment he didn't know which way to go – and suddenly he had a hallucination. He seemed to be standing inside a huge tower which was silently collapsing. It did not kill him, but was surrounding him on all sides with a wall of ruins, from which he could not extricate himself. There was no way out!

He shuddered, and the vision disappeared. 'Obviously sleep is overcoming me,' he thought. 'Properly speaking, nothing that has happened has been a surprise; it could have been foretold, I even foresaw it all . . . What was she interested in? Balls, parties, concerts, clothes. . . . What did she love? Herself. It seemed to her that the whole world existed for her sake, and she herself in order to have a good time. She flirted . . . yes, that's the word – she flirted in the most shameless manner with all men; she fought with all the women for beauty, tribute, toilettes . . . What did she do? Nothing. She adorned drawing-rooms. The only thing by which she could acquire a material existence was her love – false merchandise! And that Starski! . . . What's he? A parasite, like she is. He was merely an incident in her life, which has been full of such incidents. I can't hold it against him; like called to like. Yes, she's a Messalina of the imagination! Any man who wanted to, could embrace her and seek for the medallion, even that Starski, poor wretch, who had to become a seducer for lack of anything better to do: 'I used to believe that here on earth, are angels with bright wings . . .' Fine angels, indeed! Bright wings! Mr Molinari, Mr Starski and God knows how many more of them. This is the result of knowing women through poetry.

'I should have learned about women, not through the spectacles of Mickiewicz or Krasiński or Słowacki's poetry, but through statistics, which teach us that every angel is one-tenth a prostitute; well, and if I'd been disillusioned, at least it would have been pleasant . . .'

At this moment, there was a roaring noise of some sort; water was being poured into a boiler or tank. Wokulski stopped. It seemed to him that in this long-drawn and melancholy sound he could hear an entire orchestra, playing the Invocation from *Robert le Diable*: 'You who repose beneath the cold clay . . .' Laughter, weeping, sorrow, squeaks and weird cries all resounded together, and above them rose a powerful voice full of hopeless grief.

He could have sworn he heard an orchestra, and again he had a hallucination. He seemed to be in a cemetery, among open graves from which hideous shadows were flitting out. After a moment, each shadow became a beautiful woman, among whom Izabela cautiously moved, beckoning to him with her hand and gaze . . . He was overwhelmed with such terror that he crossed himself, and the phantoms disappeared. 'Enough,' he thought, 'I shall go out of my mind here . . .'

And he decided to forget Izabela.

It was already two at night. A lamp with a green shade was burning in the telegraph office, and the tapping of the apparatus could be heard. A man was walking past the station, he touched his cap: 'When does the train leave for Warsaw?' Wokulski asked him.

'At five o'clock, sir,' the man replied, making as if to kiss his hand. 'If you please, sir, I'm . . .'

'Not until five!' Wokulski echoed. 'Horses, perhaps . . . What time does the next train from Warsaw get in?'

'In forty-five minutes. If you please, sir . . .'

'Three-quarters of an hour . . .' Wokulski murmured. 'Quarters. . . . Quarters . . .' he repeated, sensing that he was not articulating the letter 'r' properly. He turned away from the unknown man and walked by the flower-beds, in the direction of Warsaw. The man watched him, shook his head and disappeared into the darkness.

'Quarters . . . Quarters . . .' Wokulski muttered. 'Is my tongue refusing to function? What an extraordinary muddle; I studied how to win Izabela, but have learned how to lose her. Or Geist. He produced a great invention, and entrusted me with a sacred deposit, so that Mr Starski might have one more reason for researches . . . She has deprived me of everything, even my last hope . . . If I were asked at this moment whether I really knew Geist, or saw his strange metal, I wouldn't be able to reply, and I don't even know whether it wasn't all an illusion. Oh, if only I could stop thinking about her . . . For a few minutes . . .

'Well, I won't think about her . . .'

The night was starry, the fields dark, signal lamps glowed at great distances along the track. Walking along in a ditch, Wokulski tripped over a large stone and at that moment there stood before his eyes the ruins of the castle at Zasław, the stone on which Izabela had been seated, and her tears. But this time a look of deceit gleamed behind her tears.

'I won't think about her . . . I'll go to Geist, I'll work from six in the morning to eleven at night, I shall have to observe every change of pressure, temperature, current . . . It won't leave me a spare moment.'

He had the impression that someone was coming after him. He turned around, but saw nothing. However, he noticed that his left eye saw less well than the right, and this began to irritate him immeasurably. He wanted to go back to people, but felt he wouldn't be able to endure the sight of them. Merely thinking was a torture, painful. 'I never knew how much a man's own soul can weigh,' he muttered. 'Ah, if only I could stop thinking . . .'

Far away in the east, a glimmer showed and the thin sickle of the moon appeared, enveloping the landscape in an indescribably sombre light. And suddenly another vision appeared to Wokulski. He was in a silent and deserted forest; the pine trunks were slanting in a peculiar manner, not a bird uttered, the wind did not stir the smallest twig. There was no light, only a mournful dusk. Wokulski felt that this dusk, sorrow and grief were flowing from his heart, and that it would all end surely with death, if it ever did . . .

Wherever he looked among the pines, scraps of grey sky peered in, each of which changed into the vibrating window of the train, and in which could be seen the pallid reflection of Izabela in Starski's embrace.

Wokulski could no longer withstand the visions; they dominated him, devoured his will-power, distorted his thoughts and poisoned his heart. His soul lost all its independence; any impression dominated him, reflected in thousands of increasingly sombre and painful forms, like echoes in a deserted building.

He stumbled over another stone, and this insignificant fact awoke horrifying thoughts in him; it seemed to him that he himself had once, once . . . been a cold, blind, senseless stone. But as he had lain proud in his deadness, which the greatest of earthly cataclysms had not been able to disturb, a voice spoke within or above him, asking: 'Dost wish to become a man?'

'What is a man?' the stone had asked.

'Dost wish to see, hear, feel?'

'What is feeling?'

'Dost wish something entirely new? Dost wish an existence which in one moment can experience more than all stones through millions of ages?'

'I do not understand,' the stone replied, 'it is all the same to me.'

'But if,' the supernatural voice had asked, 'if, after this new existence, you are left with eternal sorrow?'

'What is sorrow? It is all the same to me.'

'Become a man, then,' had been the reply.

And he had become a man. He lived a few dozen years, and in the course of them he longed and desired more than the dead world could know in all eternity. Rushing in pursuit of one desire, he encountered thousands of others; in fleeing from one suffering, he plunged into an ocean of suffering, and felt, pondered and absorbed so many unconscious forces that in the end he awoke all Nature against him. 'Enough!' voices began calling on all sides, 'enough! Make way for others at the spectacle! Enough . . . Enough,' the stones call, with the trees, wind, earth and sky: 'Make way for others . . . Let them experience this new existence.'

Enough! . . . So once more, he was to become nothing, and this at the very moment when his higher existence, like a last souvenir, was giving him nothing but despair for what he had lost, and grief for what he had not attained . . .

'If only the sun would rise,' Wokulski whispered, 'I'll go back to Warsaw . . . I'll set myself to work at something or other and put a stop to all these stupidities which are shattering my nerves. Does she want Starski? Let her have Starski! Have I lost my bet on her? Very well! For all that, I won on other things . . . A man can't have everything.'

For some moments he had been aware of a clammy moisture on his moustache. 'Blood?' he thought. He wiped his mouth, and by the light of a match saw froth on his handkerchief: 'Am I going insane, or what?'

Then, in the distance, he saw two lights slowly approaching him: behind them loomed a dark mass, above which was flying a thick cloud of sparks. 'A train?' he said to himself, and it seemed to him this was the same train in which Izabela was travelling. Once again he saw the drawing-room car illuminated by a lamp screened with blue silk, and in the corner he caught sight of Izabela in Starski's embrace.

'I love her so . . . I love her so . . .' he whispered, 'and I can't forget . . .'

At this moment he was overwhelmed with an anguish which human language cannot express. His exhausted thoughts, his painful feelings, his shattered will, his entire being tormented him. And suddenly he no longer felt any desire, only a hunger and thirst for death.

The train was steadily drawing nearer. Without realising what he was doing, Wokulski fell across the track. He was shuddering, his teeth chattered, he gripped the sleepers with both hands, his mouth was full of froth . . . The lamplight fell across the track which began quietly drumming under the approaching locomotive. 'God be merciful . . .' he whispered, and he closed his eyes.

Suddenly he felt a hasty and violent pull which dragged him off the track . . . The train thundered past a few inches from his head, scattering him with steam and hot ashes. For a moment, he lost consciousness and when he came to he found a man sitting on his chest and holding him by the hands.

'What in heaven's name are you doing, sir?' said the man. 'Whoever heard of such a thing? After all, God . . .'

He did not finish, Wokulski thrust him off, seized him by the collar and with a single movement hurled him to the ground. 'What do you want of me, wretch?' he cried.

'Sir . . . Respected sir . . . I'm Wysocki . . .'

'Wysocki? Wysocki?' Wokulski repeated. 'You're lying. Wysocki is in Warsaw.'

'But I'm his brother, the railroad man. It was you, sir, who found me my job last year, after Easter. How could I stand by and watch such a thing happen? Besides, sir, people aren't allowed to throw themselves under the train.'

Wokulski reflected and let him go. 'Everything turns against me, whatever I do,' he whispered. He was very weary, so he sat down on the ground by a wild pear tree no bigger than a child, growing in this spot. Just then a wind blew and moved the leaves of the tree, making a sound which for some unknown reason reminded Wokulski of old times. 'Where's my happiness?' he thought.

He felt a pressure in his chest, which gradually mounted into his throat. He wanted to draw a deep breath, but could not; he thought he would suffocate, and seized the tree with both hands as it went on rustling. 'I'm dying . . .' he exclaimed. It seemed to him his blood was boiling, his chest exploding, he writhed in pain and suddenly burst into tears. 'Merciful God! Merciful God!' he kept repeating, amidst sobs.

The railroad man crouched over him and cautiously put one hand under his head. 'Weep, sir,' he said, leaning down, 'weep, sir, and call upon God . . . You will not call on Him in vain. He who puts himself into God's hands and sincerely trusts in Him, no terrible fear shall fall upon him . . . He will save you from the devil's traps . . . What's wealth, or the greatest treasure? Everything betrays a man, only God will not desert him.'

Wokulski pressed his face to the earth. It seemed to him that with every tear, a little pain, disappointment and despair fell from his heart. His disordered mind began finding its way back to equilibrium. He already realised what he had been doing, and he understood that in a time of misery, when everything else had betrayed him – the earth, a simple man and God remained faithful to him.

Gradually he grew calmer, sobs tore his chest less often, he felt weak all over and fell into a deep sleep.

When he woke, day was dawning; he sat up, rubbed his eyes, saw Wysocki beside him and remembered everything. 'Did I sleep long?' he asked.

'Fifteen minutes . . . Maybe a half hour,' the railroad man answered.

Wokulski brought out his wallet, produced several hundred-rouble notes, and giving them to Wysocki, said: 'Mind . . . yesterday I was drunk. Tell no one what happened here. Take this . . . For your children . . .'

The railroad man kissed his hand. 'I thought you had lost everything, sir, and that was why . . .' he said.

'You are right,' Wokulski replied thoughtfully, 'I've lost everything . . . except my fortune. I won't forget you, although . . . I'd rather be dead.'

'I thought right away, sir, that a gentleman like you wouldn't go looking for trouble, even if you lost all your money. Human wickedness was the cause. . . . But an end will come to that, too . . . God works slow, but He is just, you will see, sir.'

Wokulski got up from the ground and began walking to the station. Suddenly he turned back to Wysocki. 'When you are in Warsaw,' he said, 'come to me . . . But not a word of what happened here.'

'I won't say a word, so help me God,' Wysocki replied, and he took off his cap.

'But a second time,' Wokulski added, putting a hand on his arm, 'a second time . . . If you meet another man . . . You understand me? If you meet another man, don't save him . . . When a man wishes to stand before God's judgement with his injuries, don't stop him! Don't!'

XXXV

The Journal of the Old Clerk

THE POLITICAL situation grows increasingly serious. Now we have two coalitions. Russia and Turkey on one side, Germany, Austria and England on the other. And if this is so, then it means that a war may break out at any moment, during which important, very important questions will be resolved.

But will there really be a war? For we always like to delude ourselves. This time yes, without fail. Lisiecki tells me that I predict war each year and have never been right. Pardon me, but he's a fool . . . It was one thing in those years, another today.

I read in the papers, for example, that in Italy Garibaldi is agitating against Austria. Why is he agitating? Because he expects a great war. And that's not all, for a few days later I heard that General Turr is entreating Garibaldi, calling Heaven to witness, not to make trouble for the Italians . . .

What does it mean? . . . It means, translated into common parlance: 'You, Italians, make no move, for if Austria wins she will in any case give you Trieste. But if she loses by your fault, you will get nothing . . .'

These are grave omens, this campaigning of Joe Garibaldi's and these reassurances of Turr's. Joe is campaigning, for he sees war around the corner, and Turr appeases for he sees further profit.

But will war break out so soon? At the end of June or in July? . . . An inexperienced politician might think so, but not I. For the Germans would not start a war without securing themselves against France.

And how, then, will they secure themselves? . . . Szprott says there is no way to do it, but I see that there is, and a very simple way at that. Oh, Bismarck's a wily bird, I'm beginning to like him! . . . For why did Germany and Austria drag England into their alliance? . . . Obviously to entice France and persuade her into an alliance. This will be done in the following way:

The young Napoleon, Lulu, serves in the English army and is

fighting the Zulus in Africa like his grandfather, Napoleon the Great. When the English end the war, they will make little Napoleon a general and will address the French thus:

My dear people! Here you have Bonaparte who fought in Africa and there covered himself in eternal glory like his grandfather. Make him then your emperor, like his grandfather, and we will negotiate Alsace and Lorraine away from the Germans. You'll have to pay them a few billions, but that's better than waging another war which will cost ten billion and which would be precarious for you . . .

The French will, naturally, make Lulu their emperor, take back their land, pay, enter into an alliance with Germany, and then Bismarck, having all that money, will perform his tricks! . . .

Oh, Bismarck's a clever devil and if someone's to do it, only he can pull off such a plan. I felt ages ago that here was a real old fox, and I had a weakness for him, though I masked it . . . A proper rogue! . . . He's wed to a Puttkamerow; and it's well known that the Puttkamerows are related to Mickiewicz. What's more, apparently he's passionately fond of the Poles, and even advised the son of the heir to the throne to learn Polish . . .

Well, if there is no war this year . . . then I will have a story to tell Lisiecki about hot air! He, poor fool, thinks that political intelligence depends on believing in nothing. Rubbish! . . . Politics depends on the combinations which emerge from the state of affairs.

So, long live Napoleon IV! . . . For though no one thinks of him today, I am still sure that in this hurly-burly he will play the main role. And if he is able to get down to business, then he will not only regain Alsace and Lorraine for free, but will even push the borders of France to the Rhine with complete success. As long as Bismarck doesn't realise too soon and become aware that using a Bonaparte is the same thing as harnessing a lion to a barrow. It even seems to me that in this one question Bismarck will miscalculate. And, to tell the truth, I'll not grieve for him, for I never trusted him.

Somehow, my health isn't what it should be. I won't say that anything ails me, but there it is . . . I can't do much walking, I've no appetite, I don't even feel very much like writing.

In the store, I have hardly anything to do, for Szlangbaum rules there, and I remain only to deal with Staś's affairs. By October Szlangbaum will have paid us off entirely. I shall not be poor, for honest Staś assured me fifteen hundred a year for life; but when a man thinks that soon he will not mean anything in the store, that he won't have the rights to anything . . .

Life isn't worth living . . . If it weren't for Staś and young Napoleon, this earth is sometimes so painful to me that I could do

away with myself . . . Who knows, my old colleague Katz, that you
didn't act for the best? True, you have no hopes, but you don't fear
disappointments either. I won't say that I do, for after all, neither
Wokulski nor Bonaparte . . . But, all the same . . .

How tired I am; already it's hard for me even to write. I'd gladly
travel somewhere . . . Good God, for twenty years I haven't been
beyond the Warsaw toll-gates! And sometimes I have a great
yearning to visit Hungary once more before I die . . . Perhaps I'd
find the bones of my comrades on those former battlefields. Ah,
Katz! Do you remember the smoke, the bullets, the signals? How
green the grass was, and how the sun shone!

No help for it, I must take a journey, see mountains and forests,
bathe in the sun and in the air of the wide plains, and begin a new
life. Perhaps I'll even move to some place in the provinces near
Mrs Stawska, for what else is left to a retired clerk?

This Szlangbaum is an odd fellow; I'd never have thought, when I
knew him poor, that he'd turn up his nose so. Already, I see, he has
made the acquaintance – through Maruszewicz – of barons, through
the barons – of counts, though he hasn't yet been able to reach the
Prince, who is polite to the Jews, but keeps them at a distance.

And when the likes of Szlangbaum turns up his nose, there's an
outcry in town against the Jews. Whenever I drop in for a beer,
someone always catches hold of me and scolds me because Staś sold
the store to Jews. The councillor complains that the Jews are
depriving him of a third of his pension; Szprott affirms the Jews
have wrecked his business; Lisiecki weeps, because Szlangbaum has
given him notice as of midsummer, but Klein keeps silent.

Already they're beginning to write against the Jews in the
newspapers, but what is still odder is that even Dr Szuman,
although himself a Jew, lately had the following conversation with
me: 'You'll see, sir, that in a few years there will be trouble with
the Jews.'

'Allow me,' say I, 'but you yourself praised them recently.'

'I did, because they're a race of genius, but with vile characters.
Imagine, sir, that the Szlangbaums, old and young, wanted to cheat
me, so . . .'

'Hm,' I thought to myself, 'you're beginning to turn against 'em,
now they've defrauded you.' And, to tell the truth, I quite lost my
liking for Szuman.

And what don't they say about Wokulski! A dreamer, an idealist,
a romantic . . . Perhaps because he never did anything mean.

When I told Klein of my conversation with Szuman, my skinny
colleague replied: 'He says there will be trouble with the Jews in a
few years? Set his mind at ease, sir, it will come sooner.'

'Good God!' say I, 'why?'

'Because we know them well, even though they are flirting with us,' Klein replied. 'They're sly! But they have miscalculated. We know what they are capable of, if they had the strength.'

I regarded Klein as a very progressive man, perhaps even too much so, but now I think he's a great reactionary. Besides, what does that 'we' and 'us' mean?

Yet this is supposed to be the age which followed the eighteenth century, which inscribed on its banners: Freedom, Equality, Fraternity! What did I fight against the Austrians for, in the devil's name? What did my comrades die for? Jokes! Premonitions! The Emperor Napoleon IV will remake everything. Then Szlangbaum will stop being arrogant, and Szuman stop boasting he's a Jew, and Klein won't threaten them.

These times are not far off, for even Staś Wokulski . . . Oh, how tired I am . . . I must go away somewhere.

I'm not so old as to have to think of death; but, my God, when they take fish out of water, even the youngest and healthiest must die, since it lacks its own element . . . Goodness knows whether I haven't become just such a fish out of water; Szlangbaum has already acquired power in the store, and, in order to demonstrate his authority, has sacked the porter and accountant simply because they didn't show him enough respect. When I spoke up for the poor devils, he replied angrily: 'Look how they treat me, sir – and how they treat Wokulski! They used not to bow so low to him, but every movement, every look made it obvious they'd have jumped into the fire for him.'

'So you, Mr Szlangbaum, would like them to jump into the fire for you?'

'Of course. After all, they eat my bread, they profit by me; I pay their wages.'

I thought that Lisiecki, who had turned livid on hearing this nonsense, would box his ears for him. However, he controlled himself and merely asked: 'And do you know, sir, why we'd jump into the fire for Wokulski?'

'Because he has more money,' Szlangbaum replied.

'No, sir. Because he has something you haven't got, and never will have,' said Lisiecki, striking himself on the chest.

Szlangbaum went as red as a vampire. 'What is it?' he cried. 'What haven't I got? We cannot work together, Mr Lisiecki . . . You insult my religion!'

I seized Lisiecki by the arm and drew him behind the cupboards. All the gentlemen were laughing at the sight of Szlangbaum . . . Only Zięba (he alone is staying on in the store) flared up and cried: 'The boss is right! One shouldn't make fun of a man's religion, for that is a sacred thing. Where's freedom of conscience? Where's progress? Civilisation? Emancipation?'

'Obsequious little man,' Klein muttered, then said into my ear: 'Isn't Szuman right to say they are asking for trouble? You saw what he was like when he first came here, sir, and what he's like today?'

Of course, I scolded Klein, for what right has he to alarm his fellow citizens? However, I cannot conceal from myself that Szlangbaum has changed greatly within the course of a year. Previously he was mild, today he's arrogant and contemptuous; previously he kept silent when an injury was done him, today he quarrels for no reason. Previously he called himself a Pole, today he flaunts his Jewishness. Previously he even believed in nobility and disinterestedness, but now he talks of nothing but money and social contacts. It's bad!

For all this, he is humble to the customers and the counts, and would even lick the barons' boots. But he is a real hippopotamus toward his subordinates; he keeps flaring up and treading on people's toes. It isn't nice . . . All the same, the councillor, Szprott, Klein and Lisiecki have no right to threaten him with trouble.

So what do I now signify in the store, alongside a dragon like this? When I want to do the accounts, he watches me over my shoulder; if I give an order, he at once repeats it in a loud voice. I am being increasingly edged out of the shop. To customers he keeps saying: 'My friend Wokulski . . . My friend Baron Krzeszowski . . . My clerk Rzecki . . .' though when we are alone, he calls me 'Dear old Rzecki'.

I have a few times given him to understand, in the most delicate manner, that these affectionate terms give me no pleasure. But he, poor devil, didn't even realise it; however, I am in the habit of waiting a long time before I insult anyone. Lisiecki does it on the spot, so Szlangbaum respects him.

In his own way, Szuman was right when he saw that we and our ancestors only thought of how to squander money, while they and theirs of how to make it. In this respect, they would already be in the vanguard of mankind, if human values were only based on money . . . But what's all this to me?

As I haven't much to do in the store, I think more and more often of a trip to Hungary. Not to have seen a cornfield or forest in twenty years . . . Terrible! I began applying for a passport; I thought it would take a month. Meanwhile, Wirski set about it and – hey presto! – he got my passport in four days. I was almost alarmed.

No help for it, I must leave for a few weeks at least. I thought that preparations for a trip would take me some time, but not at all . . . Wirski interfered again, one day he bought me a travelling trunk, on the next he packed my things, and said: 'Be off with you!'

I almost grew angry. Why the devil do they want to get rid of me? Out of spite, I ordered to have my things unpacked, and covered the trunk with a carpet, for it vexes me. Yet, all the same, I'd like to go somewhere . . . somewhere . . .

First, though, I must regain my strength. I still have no appetite, I'm growing thin, sleep badly, although all day long I am drowsy. I have dizzy spells, my heart beats so . . . Ah well, it will all pass.

Klein is beginning to neglect himself too. He comes to work late, carries pamphlets, goes to meetings with goodness knows whom . . . But, worse still, he has already taken a thousand roubles of the money intended for him by Wokulski, and spent them in one day. What on?

Despite this, he is a good lad. And the best test of his honesty is the fact that even Baroness Krzeszowska hasn't thrown him out of her house, where he lives on the third floor, as he used to, always quiet, never disturbing people.

If only he would extricate himself from those unnecessary social contacts: for though there may not be trouble with the Jews, yet with them it's a different story . . . May the Lord bless and protect him!

Klein has told me an amusing and instructive tale. I laughed till the tears came, and at the same time I gained still more evidence of God's justice, though in a small way. 'Brief is the triumph of the ungodly,' says the Bible, or some Father of the Church. Whoever said it, sentence has come to pass on both the Baroness and Maruszewicz, for sure.

Everyone knows that once the Baroness had rid herself of Maleski and Patkiewicz, she told the janitor not under any circumstances to rent the apartment on the third floor to students, even if it had to stand empty. In fact, the students' rooms were not rented for several months, but at least the Baroness was pleased.

In the meantime, her husband the Baron went back to her and he, of course, took over control of the apartment house. And since the Baron continually needs money, he was strongly tempted by that empty apartment despite the Baroness's prohibition, which lessened their income by a hundred and twenty roubles a year. Above all, however, it was Maruszewicz (they have already been reconciled!), who is continually borrowing money from Krzeszowski, who egged him on: 'Why, Baron,' he sometimes asked him, 'should you check whether an applicant for the apartment is, or is not, a student? Why all this fuss? Providing he don't come in uniform, then he's not a student; and if he pays a month in advance, then take it, and be quits!'

The Baron took this advice very much to heart; he even told the janitor that if a tenant were to show up, to send him in without asking questions. Of course the janitor told his wife this, and his wife told Klein, who felt like acquiring neighbours best suited to his own taste.

So, a few days after these orders were given, an elegant young man appeared at the Baron's, with a strange countenance, and still more strangely dressed; his trousers didn't match his waistcoat, his waistcoat didn't match his coat, and his tie didn't match anything.

'There's a room in your house for rent to a single gent, Baron,' said the dandy, 'at ten roubles a month?'

'Yes, there is,' says the Baron, 'you may look at it.'

'Oh, that isn't necessary. I am certain that Your Excellency wouldn't rent a bad apartment. May I pay a deposit?'

'Pray do,' says the Baron, 'and, because you take my word for it, I won't ask you for any references.'

'As Your Excellency wishes . . .'

'Mutual confidence is enough between well-bred people,' replied the Baron, 'I hope, therefore, that neither my wife nor I – but especially my wife – will have cause to complain about you gentlemen.'

The young man pressed his hand fervently. 'I give you my word,' he said, 'that we shall never cause any bother to your wife who, perhaps unjustly, has been prejudiced . . .'

'Enough, enough!' the Baron interrupted. He took the deposit and gave a receipt.

When the young man had gone, the Baron summoned Maruszewicz. 'I don't know,' said the Baron anxiously, 'whether we haven't committed a folly . . . I have a tenant now, but judging from the description, I'm afraid he is one of the young men my wife drove out.'

'Never mind,' Maruszewicz replied, 'providing they've paid in advance.'

Next morning three young men moved into the apartment, but so quietly that no one saw them. No one even noticed that they held sessions with Klein in the evenings. However a few days later, Maruszewicz – very vexed – rushed to the Baron, exclaiming: 'Do you know, Baron, that they are precisely those scoundrels the Baroness threw out? Maleski, Patkiewicz . . .'

'Never mind,' replies the Baron, 'they won't vex my wife, providing they've paid in advance.'

'But they're vexing me!' Maruszewicz burst out. 'If I open a window, one of them shoots peas at me through a pea-shooter, which isn't at all agreeable. And when a few people visit me, or one of the ladies (he added more quietly) they drum on the windows with peas, so it's impossible to sit there . . . They interfere with me . . . They compromise me . . . I shall go to the police station, and complain!'

Naturally the Baron told his lodgers this, and begged them not to shoot peas at Maruszewicz's windows. They ceased, but for all that, whenever Maruszewicz received any lady in his apartment, which happened rather often, one of the lads at once leant out of the window, and bawled: 'Janitor! Janitor! Do you know who the lady is, who went to see Mr Maruszewicz?'

Of course, the janitor doesn't even know that a woman went there, but after such questions the entire apartment house is informed of the fact. Maruszewicz is furious with them, the more so as the Baron's reply to his complaints was: 'You yourself advised me not to keep the apartment empty.'

And the Baroness is grown humble, because on the one hand she fears her husband, and on the other – the students. In this way, the Baroness and Maruszewicz are being punished for her malice and spite, and for his intrigues, by one and the same instrument, while honest Klein has the company he wanted.

Yes, there is justice in the world!

That Maruszewicz is shameless, upon my word! Today he hurried to Szlangbaum with a complaint about Klein. 'Sir,' he said, 'one of your clerks, who lives in Baroness Krzeszowska's house, is quite simply compromising me.'

'How is he compromising you, sir?' asked Szlangbaum, opening his eyes wide.

'He visits with those students whose windows look out on the yard. And, sir, they stare into my windows, shoot peas at me, and if several persons gather, they shout that there's a card-sharping school in my apartment.'

'Mr Klein will not be working for me after July,' replied Szlangbaum, 'you'd better speak to Mr Rzecki, they've known one another longest.'

Maruszewicz called on me in turn, and again told his story of the students who call him a card-sharp or compromise ladies visiting him. 'Fine ladies!' thought I, while I replied aloud, 'Mr Klein is in the store all day, so he cannot be responsible for his friends.'

'Yes, but Mr Klein has some secret understanding with them; he persuaded them to move back into the house; he visits them and receives them in his apartment.'

'A young man,' I replied, 'naturally prefers to keep company with other young men.'

'But I don't want to suffer on that account! Let him keep them quiet . . . Or I'll start a court case against them all.'

What a hope – that Klein should pacify the students, or unite them in sympathy for Maruszewicz! However, I warned Klein and added that it would be very unpleasant if he, a clerk of Wokulski's, were to have a court case involving students' antics. Klein heard me out, then shrugged. 'What's it to do with me?' he replied, 'I might hang such a scoundrel, but I don't shoot peas at his windows, or call him a card-sharp. What are his card parties to me?'

He was right. So I didn't say another word.

I must be off . . . away! If only Klein doesn't get mixed up in some foolishness. It's terrible how childish they are; they'd like to rebuild the world, but at the same time they perform such silly antics.

Either I am quite mistaken, or we are on the eve of extraordinary events. One day in May, Wokulski travelled with Mr and Miss Łęcki to Cracow, and told me clearly that he didn't know when he would be back – perhaps not for a month.

Yet he returned, not within a month, but on the very next day, so wretched-looking that he was pitiful to see. It was terrible to see what had come over this man in the course of twenty-four hours. When I asked him what had happened, and why he'd come back, he first of all hesitated, then said he'd received a telegram from Suzin and was leaving for Moscow. But within the next twenty-four hours he changed his mind and declared he wasn't going.

'But if it's important business?' I asked.

'May the devil take business,' he muttered and shrugged.

Now he doesn't leave his house for whole days at a time, and for the most part he lies down. I visited him, but he received me irritably; I learned from the butler that he refuses to see anyone. I sent Szuman to him, but Staś wouldn't even talk to Szuman, and merely told him he needed no doctors. This didn't satisfy Szuman; as he is something of a busybody he began inquiries on his own account, and learned strange things.

He said that Wokulski had left the train around midnight, at Skierniewice, pretending he'd received a telegram, that afterwards he'd disappeared from the station and didn't return until dawn, covered with mud, apparently tipsy. At the station, they think he got drunk and spent the night in a field. This explanation didn't convince either Szuman or me. The doctor declares that Staś must have broken with Miss Łęcka, and perhaps even attempted something preposterous . . . But I think he really did have a telegram from Suzin. In any case, I must travel for my health's sake. I am not yet an invalid, and cannot renounce my future on account of a temporary enfeeblement.

Mraczewski is here and is staying with me. The lad looks like a Bernardine Father, has grown manly, sunburnt, plump. And how much of the world he's seen in the last few months! He went to Paris, then Lyons; from Lyons he went to Częstochowa, to Mrs Stawska, and they came to Warsaw together. Then he took her back to Częstochowa, stayed a week and apparently helped her arrange the store. Then he went to Moscow, from where he returned to Częstochowa and Mrs Stawska, stayed a while and at present is with me.

Mraczewski declares that Suzin did not telegraph to Wokulski, and in addition he is certain that Wokulski has broken with Miss Łęcka. He must even have said something to Mrs Stawska, since that angelic woman, while in Warsaw a few weeks ago, was kind enough to visit me and inquire very sincerely about Staś: 'Is he well? Is he very changed and sad? Will he never recover from his despair?'

Despair? Even if he's broken with Miss Łęcka, thank God there are still plenty of other women, and if he wants to, Staś could marry Mrs Stawska. A priceless little woman, how she loved him – and who knows whether she still does? Good God, I'd be delighted if Staś were to go back to her. So pretty, so noble, so much devotion . . . If there is still any order in the world (which I sometimes doubt), then Wokulski ought to marry Mrs Stawska. But he must make haste, for unless I am very much mistaken, Mraczewski is starting to think of her. 'Sir,' he sometimes says to me, wringing his hands, 'what a woman, what a woman! If it weren't for her unfortunate husband, I'd have proposed to her already.'

'But would she accept you?'

'I don't know . . .' he sighed.

He sank into a chair so that it trembled, and said: 'When I met her the first time after her departure from Warsaw, it was as though I'd been struck by lightning, I liked her so . . .'

'Well, and she made an impression on you even earlier.'

'But not of this sort. After travelling from Paris to Częstochowa, I was drowsy, but she looked so pale, with such sad eyes, that I immediately thought: suppose I succeed? So I tried flirting with her. But she rejected me after the first words, and when I fell on my knees to her and swore I loved her – she burst into tears! Ah, Ignacy, those tears . . . I lost my head entirely . . . If the devil would take her husband once and for all, or if I had the money for a divorce . . . Ignacy! After a week of living with this woman, I'd either die or take to my bed. Yes, sir . . . Only today do I feel how much I love her.'

'But suppose she is in love with somebody else?' I asked.

'With whom? Wokulski, may be? Ha! Ha! . . . Who would fall in love with that gruff old bear? . . . A woman needs to be shown feelings, passions, to be spoken to of love, to have her hands pressed, and if possible, also . . . But could that lump of clay do anything of the kind? He made up to Izabela like a pointer to a duck, because he thought he would enter into contact with the aristocracy and that the young lady had a dowry. But when he saw how things were, he ran away from her at Skierniewice. Oh sir, one can't treat women so!'

I admit I don't care for Mraczewski's raptures. When he starts hurling himself at her feet, whining, sobbing, then in the end he'll turn Mrs Stawska's head. And Wokulski may regret it, because – on my word of honour as an ex-officer – she was the only woman for him.

But let us wait, and in the meantime – be off!

Brr! So I left. I bought a ticket to Cracow, got into the train at the Warsaw–Vienna railroad station and then, after the third departure bell had rung, I jumped out again. I can't leave Warsaw and the store even for a little while. I got my luggage back from the railroad on the next day, it had gone as far as Piotrków. If all my plans go like this, I must congratulate myself.

XXXVI

A Soul in Lethargy

LYING or sitting in his room, Wokulski mechanically recalled his return from Skierniewice to Warsaw. Around five that morning, he had bought a first-class ticket at the railroad station, though he was uncertain whether he had asked for it or whether it had been given to him without his asking. Then he got into a second-class compartment, and there he found a priest, who looked out of the window for the entire journey, also a red-haired German who took off his spats and slept like a log, with his feet (in dirty socks) on the opposite seat. Finally, facing him, had been an old lady, who had such a bad toothache that she didn't even object to the behaviour of her neighbour in the socks.

Wokulski wanted to calculate the number of persons travelling in the compartment, and with great difficulty he noticed that, without him there were three, and with him – four. Then he began wondering why three persons plus one person makes four altogether – and he fell asleep.

In Warsaw, he didn't come to himself until he was riding in a droshky in Aleje Jerozolimskie. But who had carried his valise for him, and how had he got himself into the droshky? This he did not know, and it didn't even matter to him.

He got into his apartment after ringing for half an hour, though it was already nearly eight in the morning. A sleepy servant opened the door, undressed, alarmed by his sudden return. On entering the bedroom, Wokulski realised that the faithful servant had been sleeping in his own bed. He did not reproach him, merely ordered tea.

The servant, wide-awake but also embarrassed, hastily changed the bed linen and pillow-cases, and when he saw the newly made bed Wokulski did not drink the tea, but undressed and lay down to sleep. He slept until five that afternoon and then, after washing and dressing to go out, he sat down involuntarily in an armchair in the drawing-room and dozed until evening. When the street lamps were lit, he ordered a lamp and a steak from a restaurant. He ate it greedily, drank wine and went to bed again around midnight.

Next day Rzecki visited him, but he didn't recall how long he stayed, or what they talked about. Not until the following night, when he woke up for a moment, did he seem to see Rzecki with a very worried expression. Then he lost count of time entirely, did not notice any difference between day and night, did not consider whether the hours were passing too fast or too slow. In general he didn't concern himself with time, which – as it were – did not exist for him. He only felt an emptiness within himself and around him, and was not certain whether his apartment hadn't grown larger.

Once, he envisioned himself lying on a high catafalque, and he began thinking about death. It seemed to him he must inescapably die of paralysis of the heart; but this neither alarmed nor consoled him. Sometimes his legs hurt from the constant sitting in the armchair, and then he thought that death was coming and he calculated with indifferent wonder how fast the pain would reach his heart. These observations gave him a sort of temporary pleasure, but they soon dissolved into apathy again.

He told the servant not to let anyone in; nevertheless, Dr Szuman visited him a few times. During the first visit, he took his pulse and told him to show his tongue.

'In English?' asked Wokulski, but at once recollected himself and took his hand away. Szuman gazed sharply into his eyes. 'You are unwell,' he said, 'what ails you?'

'Nothing. Have you gone back to practising medicine?'

'I should say so!' Szuman exclaimed, 'and the first cure I made was myself; I healed myself of dreaming.'

'Very nice,' Wokulski replied. 'Rzecki mentioned something of your cure to me.'

'Rzecki is an imbecile . . . an old Romantic. That's a dying breed! Anyone who wants to live must look at the world soberly. Pay attention, and close each eye in turn . . . When I tell you . . . the left . . . the right . . . Cross your legs.'

'What are you doing, my dear fellow?' Wokulski inquired.

'Examining you.'

'Oh? And you hope to find something?'

'I expect so.'

'And then?'

'I shall cure you.'

'Of dreaming?'

'No, of neurasthenia.'

Wokulski smiled and said after a moment: 'Can you take out a man's brain and provide him with another in its place?'

'Not yet.'

'Well, in that case let me alone.'

'I can give you other desires.'

'I already have them. I should like to sleep under the earth, as deep as . . . the well in the Zasław castle. And also I'd like them to heap me with ruins, me and my fortune, and even any trace of the fact that I ever existed. These are my desires, the fruit of all the ones that went before.'

'Romanticism!' exclaimed Szuman, patting him on the shoulder, 'but that too will pass.'

Wokulski made no reply. He was angry with himself for his own last phrase, and was surprised: whence had that sudden frankness come? Why had he said that? Why had he exposed his own wounds, like some shameless beggar?

After the doctor had gone, he observed that something within him had changed; against the background of his previous apathy, some sort of feeling had appeared. It was at first a nameless ache, very small, but which rapidly increased and reached its medium. To begin with, it might have been compared to the delicate pricking of a pin, but later to a sort of obstruction in the heart, no bigger than a hazelnut. He already regretted the apathy, when Feuchtersleben's phrase crossed his mind: 'I was glad of my pain, for it seemed to me I could see within myself that fruitful struggle which created and still creates everything in this world, where infinite forces are everlastingly in conflict.'

'All the same, what can it be?' he asked himself, feeling that in his soul the place of apathy was being taken by dull pain. At once he replied: 'Yes, it is the awakening of consciousness.'

Slowly, in his mind, an image which seemed hitherto to have been veiled in mist began to appear. Wokulski watched it curiously, and saw – the shape of a woman in a man's embraces. This image at first had the pale gleam of phosphorescence, then it grew pink – yellow – greenish – finally as black as velvet. Then it disappeared for a few moments and again began appearing by turn in all the colours, starting with phosphorescence and ending in black. At the same time the pain intensified. 'I suffer, therefore I am,' thought Wokulski, and he smiled.

Thus several days passed in watching that image change colour and in pain which varied in intensity. Sometimes it disappeared altogether, reappeared as minute as an atom, grew, filled his heart, his whole being, the entire world . . . And at the moment when it exceeded all bounds, it again faded and yielded to absolute tranquillity and amazement.

Slowly something new began to be born in his soul; the desire to rid himself of these pains and the image. This was like a spark glowing in the night. A sort of feeble consolation gleamed for Wokulski. 'Am I still capable of thinking?' he asked himself. In order to check this, he began recalling the multiplication tables, then multiplying two figures by one, and two figures by two. Not believing himself, he wrote down the results of his sums and checked them . . . The multiplication on paper agreed with those in his head, and he sighed with relief. 'I haven't yet gone out of my mind,' he thought joyfully.

He began imagining to himself the arrangement of his own apartment, the streets of Warsaw, of Paris . . . His spirits revived, for he saw that not only could he remember precisely but that these exercises brought him a certain kind of relief. The more he thought of Paris, the more clearly he could see the traffic, buildings, markets, museums and the more firmly that image of the woman in the man's embraces was obscured.

He began walking about his apartment and his glance fell on a pile of illustrated books. There were books from the Dresden and Munich art galleries, *Don Quixote* illustrated by Doré, Hogarth engravings . . . He recalled that men condemned to the guillotine spent their time most tolerably in looking at pictures . . . And from then on, he passed whole days looking at drawings. Finishing one book, he set about another, a third . . . then he came back to the first again.

The pain grew numb; the spectres appeared less frequently, his spirits revived . . . Most often he looked at *Don Quixote*, which made a powerful impression on him. He recalled the strange story of a man living for years in the sphere of poetry – just as he had done, who had hurled himself at windmills – like him, who was shattered – like him, who had wasted his life pursuing an ideal woman – like him, and found a dirty cow-girl instead of a princess – as he had done!

'All the same, Don Quixote was happier than I,' he thought. 'He didn't begin to awaken from his illusions until the brink of the grave. But I?'

The longer he looked at the engravings, the more familiar he grew with them – the less they absorbed his attention. Behind Don Quixote, Sancho Panza and Doré's windmills, behind Hogarth's *Cock-fight* and *Drunkenness*, there began to appear to him the interior of the compartment, the vibrating window-pane and, in it, the indistinct image of Starski and Izabela. Then he threw aside the engravings and began reading books he had known in his childhood, or in Hopfer's cellar. With deep emotion he revived in his memory the *Life of St Genevieve*, the *Rose of Tannenburg*, *Rinaldini*, *Robinson Crusoe* and, finally, *The Thousand and One Nights*. Once again it seemed to him that neither time nor reality existed any longer, and that his wounded soul had escaped from the earth to wander in magic lands where only noble hearts beat, where vice did not dress up in the mask of deceit, where eternal justice ruled, curing pain and rewarding injustices.

And here one strange point impressed him. Whereas he had drawn the illusions which had terminated in the dissolution of his own soul from Polish literature, he found solace and peace only in foreign literatures. 'Are we really a nation of dreamers?' he wondered in alarm, 'and will the angel who touched the pool at Bethesda, surrounded by sick people, never descend upon us?'

One day he was brought a thick letter. 'From Paris?' he thought, 'yes, from Paris. I wonder what it can be?' But his curiosity was not strong enough for him to open and read it: 'Such a thick letter! Who the devil writes so much nowadays?'

He threw the packet on his desk, and took to reading the *Thousand and One Nights* again. What a delight they were to his weary mind, those palaces of precious stones, trees whose fruit was jewels! The magic words, at which walls gave way, magic lamps by which enemies could be confounded or a man could move hundreds of miles in the twinkling of an eye! And the powerful magicians! What a shame that such power fell into the hands of wicked and vile people!

He put down the book and, smiling at himself, dreamed he was a magician who possessed two trifles: power over the forces of Nature, and the power to make himself invisible. 'I believe,' he thought, 'that after a few years of my rule, the world would look different . . . The greatest scoundrels would change into Socrates and Plato.'

Then he noticed the letter from Paris and recalled Geist's words: 'Humanity consists of reptiles and tigers, amidst which barely one in the whole crowd is a human being. Today's misfortunes spring from the fact that great inventions fell into the hands of men and monsters indifferently . . . I shall not commit that error, and if I finally discover a metal lighter than air, I will pass it on only to real men. Let them equip themselves with arms for their own eyes: let their number multiply, and grow in power . . .'

'It would undoubtedly be better,' he muttered, 'if men like Ochocki and Rzecki were strong, not the Starskis and Maruszewiczes. There's a purpose for you!' he went on thinking, 'if I were younger . . . Although . . . Well, even here there are people and there's a great deal to be done.'

Again he began reading a tale in the *Thousand and One Nights*, but noticed that it no longer absorbed him. The earlier pain had begun to fret his heart, and before his eyes the image of Izabela and Starski was sketched with increasing clarity. He recalled Geist in his wooden sandals, and his strange house surrounded by its wall. And suddenly it seemed to him that the house was the first step of a huge staircase, at the top of which stood a statue disappearing into the clouds. It represented a woman, whose head and bosom were out of sight, only the brass folds of her robe could be seen. It seemed to him that there was an inscription 'Unchangeable and pure' on the step which her feet touched. He did not understand what this was, but felt that from the statue's feet there flowed into his heart some greatness full of tranquillity. And he was surprised that he, being capable of experiencing this feeling, should be in love or angry with Izabela, or jealous of Starski.

Shame struck him in the face, though there was no one in the room. The vision disappeared, Wokulski came to. Once again, he was only a man in pain, and feeble; but in his soul a powerful voice resounded, like the echo of an April storm, predicting resurrection and spring with its thunderclaps.

On June 1st, Szlangbaum visited him. He came with some embarrassment, but regained his spirits after surveying Wokulski. 'I didn't visit you before,' he began, 'because I knew you were unwell and didn't want to see anyone. Well, but now, thank God, everything has passed.'

He fidgeted in his chair and threw a furtive glance around the room; perhaps he had expected to find it in greater disorder.

'Have you some business to discuss?' Wokulski asked him.

'Not so much business, as a proposal . . . Just when I heard you were ill it occurred to me . . . You see, you need a long rest, respite from all business, so it occurred to me you might invest that hundred and twenty thousand roubles with me. You could have ten per cent with no trouble.'

'Aha,' Wokulski interposed, 'I paid my fellow investors fifteen per cent without any trouble, even to myself,'

'But times are hard now . . . Well, I'll gladly pay you fifteen per cent, if you'll leave me your firm.'

'Neither the firm, nor the money,' Wokulski replied impatiently. 'Would to God the firm had never existed, and as for the money . . . I have so much that the interest which the papers alone give is enough. Too much, indeed.'

'So you want to withdraw your capital by Midsummer Day?' asked Szlangbaum.

'I can leave it with you until October, without interest – on condition you keep the men who want to stay in the store.'

'That's a difficult condition, but . . .'

'As you choose . . .'

A moment of silence followed. 'What are you thinking of doing with the trading firm?' Szlangbaum inquired, 'for you speak as though you wanted to withdraw from that too.'

'That's very likely.'

Szlangbaum turned red, wanted to say something, but left well alone. They chatted for a while of unimportant matters and Szlangbaum left after bidding him goodbye very cordially.

'Evidently he intends to take over everything from me.' thought

Wokulski. 'Well, let him . . . The world belongs to those who take it.'

Szlangbaum talking to him of business interests at this moment seemed comical. 'Everyone in the store complains of him,' he thought, 'they say he is stuck-up, that he's exploiting them. Though it's true they used to say the same of me.'

His glance again fell on the desk where the letter from Paris had been lying for several days. He picked it up, yawned, but finally broke the seal. It was a letter from the Baroness with diplomatic contacts, also several official documents. He glanced through them and realised they were proofs of the death of Ernest Walter, otherwise Ludwik Stawski, who had died in Algeria.

Wokulski reflected: 'If I'd received these papers three months ago, who knows what might have happened? Stawska – pretty and above all, so noble . . . so noble. Goodness knows but perhaps she really loved me? Stawska me, and I – that other one. The irony of fate!'

He cast the papers to the desk and recalled that small, tidy drawing-room in which he had spent so many evenings with Mrs Stawska, and where he had felt so tranquil.

'Well,' he thought, 'and I rejected happiness which fell into my hands of its own accord. But can anything that we don't want be called happiness? And if she suffered even for a single day as I've suffered?'

The order of the world, in which two people unhappy for the same reason, cannot help each other, is cruel.

The papers regarding Stawski's death lay there several days, but Wokulski could not decide what to do with them. At first he didn't think about them at all, but later, when they began catching his eye with increasing frequency, he began experiencing pangs of conscience. 'After all,' he thought, 'I obtained them for Mrs Stawska, so they must be given to her; but where is she? I don't know . . . It would be diverting if I married her. I'd have company. Helena is a sweet child . . . I'd have a purpose in life. Well, but she herself wouldn't get much out of it. What could I tell her, after all? That I'm ill, need a nurse, and so am offering thousands of roubles a year . . . I'll even let you love me, though as for me . . . I've had enough of love.'

Day followed day, but Wokulski could not conceive a way of sending the papers to Mrs Stawska. He would have to find out where she was living, write a registered letter, have it taken to the post office . . . Finally he realised that the simplest way would be to summon Rzecki (whom he had not seen for several weeks), and hand the papers over to him. But to summon Rzecki he would first have to ring for the butler, send him to the store . . .

'Oh, never mind,' he muttered.

He took to reading again, this time travel books. He visited the United States, China – but Mrs Stawska's documents gave him no peace. He knew something must be done but felt that he couldn't do it himself. This state of mind began surprising him. 'I'm thinking logically,' he said, 'well, as long as memories don't interrupt. I feel in accordance with logic . . . even too much so. Only . . . I don't feel like settling this business, and in any case . . . This, therefore, is today's fashionable sickness of the will. A splendid invention! But I never followed fashion, after all. What's fashion to me?'

He had just finished a journey to China when it occurred to him that if he had will-power then he would sooner or later be able to forget certain incidents and certain persons. 'But it tortures me so . . . has tortured me so . . .' he whispered. He had entirely lost track of time.

One day Szuman insisted on entering the apartment. 'Well, how are you?' he inquired. 'We've been reading, I see . . . Novels? Very well . . . Travel? Excellent. Don't you feel like going out for a walk? It's a fine day, and surely you've had enough of your apartment after some five weeks.'

'You've had enough of yours for ten years,' Wokulski retorted.

'You're right. But I was busy, I was studying human hair and thinking of fame. Above all, though, I didn't have other people's and my own business on my shoulders. In a few weeks there's to be a meeting of the company for trading with the Empire.'

'I shall resign from it.'

'As you please . . . A capital idea,' said Szuman ironically. 'And, so that they learn to appreciate you better, let them take on Szlangbaum as director. He will fix things for them! As he did for me. These Jews are a race of genius, but what scoundrels they are!'

'Come now . . .'

'Don't defend them in my presence!' cried Szuman angrily, 'for I both know and can sense them . . . I'd give my word that at this moment, Szlangbaum is digging a trap for you in that company, and I'm certain he will worm his way into it, for how could Polish gentry get along without a Jew?'

'I see you don't like Szlangbaum.'

'On the contrary, I do – and would like to imitate him, but can't. Just now the instincts of my forebears are beginning to awaken in me . . . a tendency to business. Oh, Nature! How I wish I had a million roubles, in order to make another million, and a third . . . And become Rothschild's younger brother. Meanwhile, even Szlangbaum is deceiving me. I've moved for so long in your world that in the end I've lost the most valuable attributes of my own people . . . But they're a great people; they will conquer the world, and not by common sense, but by cheating and boldness.'

'So break with them and become a Christian.'

'I wouldn't dream of it. In the first place, I won't break with them even if I became a Christian, and then again, I myself am such a phenomenal Jew that I don't like trickery. In the second place, if I didn't break with them when they were weak, I won't today, now that they are powerful.'

'It seems to me that now they are weaker,' Wokulski interposed.

'Is that because people begin to hate them?'

'Come, hate is too strong a word.'

'For goodness sake, I'm not blind or stupid . . . I know what is being said about Jews in the workshops, saloons, stores, even in the newspapers . . . And I am certain that new persecutions will break out any year now, from which my brothers in Israel will emerge still more clever, still stronger and in still greater solidarity. And how they will repay you all, at some future time! They are scoundrels, but I must admit their genius and cannot rid myself of a sneaking liking for them . . . For me, a dirty Jew-boy is dearer than any well-scrubbed young lordling; and when I looked into a synagogue for the first time in twenty years and heard the singing, there were tears in my eyes, upon my word . . . But what's the use of talking? Israel in triumph is beautiful, and it's pleasant to think that this triumph of the oppressed is partly my handiwork.'

'Szuman, you seem to have a fever.'

'Wokulski, I'm certain you have a mote – not in your eye, but in your brain.'

'How can you speak of such things?'

'I do so because first of all, I don't want to be a snake in the grass, and then . . . you, Staś, won't fight against us. You're a broken man, and broken by your own people into the bargain. You've sold your store, you're abandoning the company . . . Your career is finished.'

Wokulski hung his head.

'Think, too,' Szuman went on, 'who is on your side today? I, a Jew, as despised and ill-used as you are . . . And by the same people . . . By the aristocracy.'

'You're growing sentimental,' Wokulski interrupted.

'This isn't sentimentality! They have thrown their greatness in your face, they have proclaimed their own virtues, they have told us to adopt their ideals . . . But today, just tell me, what are these ideals and virtues worth, where's their greatness which had to draw on your pocket? You only lived on equal footing with them, as it were, for a year – and what have they done to you? So just think what they must have done to us, whom they have oppressed and kicked for whole centuries? This is why I advise you to join with the Jews. You'll double your fortune, and as the Old Testament says, you'll see your enemies grovelling before you. For your firm and your good name, we will give you all the Łęckis, Starski and someone else, too, as bad. Szlangbaum is no partner for you, he's a fool.'

'And when you finish off these great lords, what then?'

'We shall of necessity join with your common folk, we shall be the intelligentsia which today they don't have . . . We shall teach them our philosophy, our politics, our economics, and they will certainly come out better with us than they have done with their leaders hitherto . . . Leaders!' he added, with a smile.

Wokulski made a gesture. 'It seems to me,' he said, 'that you, who wish to cure everyone else of dreaming, are a dreamer yourself.'

'That again?' asked Szuman.

'Yes . . . You have no ground to stand on, yet you want to seize hold of others . . . You'd better think of honest equality with other people, not of conquering the world, and don't try to cure other people's faults before curing your own, which only make more enemies for you. Besides, you yourself don't know what to hold on to; once you despised the Jews, now you evaluate them too highly.'

'I despised individuals, I respect the strength of the community.'

'Just the opposite to me, who despise the community but sometimes respect individuals.'

Szuman pondered. 'Do as you please,' he said, taking his hat, 'but the fact remains that if you leave your company, it will fall into the hands of Szlangbaum and a whole pack of wretched Jews. But if you stay, you might bring in honest and respectable people who have not many faults, and all the Jewish contacts.'

'In either case, the Jews will dominate the firm.'

'But without your help, orthodox and reactionary Jews will do it, while with your help, university-trained ones would.'

'Isn't it all the same?' Wokulski replied, with a shrug.

'Not at all. We're linked with them by race and a common position, but our views divide us. We have education, they – the Talmud; we, sense – and they, cunning; we are rather cosmopolitan, they are particularists, who see nothing beyond their synagogue and council. As far as common enemies are concerned, they are excellent allies, but when it's the progress of Judaism . . . then they are an intolerable burden to us. This is why it is in the interests of civilisation that the guidance of affairs be in our hands. The others can only dirty the world with their gabardines and garlic, but not move it ahead . . . Think of that, Staś!'

He pressed Wokulski's hand and left, whistling the air: 'Oh Rachel, when the Lord in His mysterious goodness . . .'

'So,' thought Wokulski, 'a conflict is brewing up between progressive and reactionary Jews over us, and I am to take part in it as an ally for one or the other side. A fine role! Oh, how it bores and wearies me!'

He began dreaming, and again he saw Geist's house surrounded by walls and an infinite number of steps, at the summit of which was the statue of the brass goddess, with her head in the clouds, bearing the enigmatic inscription: 'Unchangeable and pure'. For a moment, as he looked at the folds of her robe, he wanted to laugh at Izabela, at her triumphant admirer and at his own sufferings. 'Is it possible? Is it possible?' he thought, 'that I . . .?'

But at once the statue vanished and the pain returned and settled in his heart like a great conqueror no one could match.

A few days after Szuman's visit, Rzecki appeared at Wokulski's. He was very poorly, leaning on a stick, and the ascent to the second floor tired him so much that he sank out of breath into a chair and spoke with difficulty. Wokulski was shocked. 'What's the matter with you, Ignacy?' he cried.

'Oh, it's nothing. Partly old age, partly . . . Nothing at all.'

'But you need treatment, my dear man, you ought to go away somewhere.'

'I tell you, I tried to . . . I even went to the railroad station . . . But I felt so lonesome for Warsaw, and . . . for our store . . .' he added, more quietly, 'that . . . Ah, never mind! Excuse me for coming.'

'You apologise to me, my dear old fellow? I thought you were angry with me!'

'Me with you?' replied Rzecki, gazing at him fondly, 'Me with you? For goodness sake! Business and a difficult problem have brought me here.'

'Problem?'

'Just think of it – Klein has been arrested.'

Wokulski drew back.

'Klein and the other two . . . you remember? That Maleski and Patkiewicz.'

'What for?'

'They were living in Baroness Krzeszowska's house, well, and it's true they harassed that Maruszewicz somewhat. He threatened them, but they went one better . . . In the end, he went to the police station with a complaint. The police came, some trouble occurred, and all three were taken off to jail.'

'Stupid boys! Stupid boys!' Wokulski murmured.

'I said precisely the same,' Rzecki continued. 'Of course, nothing will happen to them, but it's an unpleasant business all the same. That donkey Maruszewicz is alarmed, too . . . He called on me, swore he wasn't to blame . . . I couldn't help myself, and replied: "I'm sure you're not to blame, but it's also true that these days the Good Lord protects scoundrels . . . For in reality it's you who ought to be locked up for forging signatures, not those frivolous lads." He almost burst into tears. He swore that from now on he will keep to the straight and narrow path and that if he hasn't done so hitherto, it was your fault. "I was full of the noblest intentions," he said, "but Mr Wokulski, instead of giving me his hand, instead of believing in my good intentions, put me off with contempt.'"

'An honest soul, to be sure,' Wokulski smiled. 'What else?'

'People are saying in town,' Rzecki went on, 'that you're leaving the company.'

'Yes . . .'

'And that you are handing it over to the Jews.'

'Well, after all, my fellow members are not an old wardrobe that I am throwing away,' Wokulski exploded. 'They have money, they have heads on their shoulders . . . Let them find other men, and make do.'

'Who can they find, and even if they could, whom will they trust, if not the Jews? And the Jews are seriously thinking of this business. Not a day passes but Szuman or Szlangbaum visits me, and each tries to persuade me to manage the company after you.'

'In fact, you are doing so.'

Rzecki made a gesture. 'With your ideas and your money,' he replied. 'But never mind . . . From this, I see that Szuman belongs to one party and Szlangbaum to another, and they both need a man of straw.'

'Clever of them!' Wokulski murmured.

'But I've lost my liking for them,' Rzecki replied. 'After all, I'm an old clerk, and I can tell you that as far as they're concerned, everything depends on humbug, double-dealing and trash.'

'Don't insult them too much,' Wokulski interposed, 'for after all it was we who raised them up.'

'It was not!' Rzecki cried angrily. 'Whenever one meets them — in Budapest, Constantinople, Paris, London — it's always the same principle: give as little as possible, and take as much, both materially and morally. It's deceit, always deceit.'

Wokulski began walking about the room. 'Szuman was right,' he said, 'when he said that dislike of them is mounting, if even you . . .'

'I don't dislike them . . . I'm retiring from the game . . . But just look at what is happening here! Where don't they worm their way in, where don't they open stores, what don't they reach out their hands for? And each one, as soon as he occupies some position brings in after him whole legions of his own people, by no means better than we are, often worse. You'll see what they will do to our store; what sort of clerks there will be, what merchandise . . . And hardly have they seized the store, than they are making their way into the aristocracy, and already setting about your trading company.'

'It's our own fault . . . our own fault,' Wokulski repeated. 'We can't refuse people the right to acquire positions, but we can defend our own.'

'You yourself are leaving your position.'

'But not on their account; they have behaved honourably towards me.'

'Because they needed you. They made you and your social contacts into a ladder . . .'

'Well, never mind that,' Wokulski interrupted, 'we shall never convince one another. But now . . . I have here the official papers confirming the death of Ludwik Stawski.'

Rzecki jumped to his feet. 'Helena's husband?' he asked feverishly, 'where? But this means salvation for us all!'

Wokulski handed him the documents, which Rzecki seized with a trembling hand. 'Eternal rest and . . . praise be to God!' he declared, reading. 'Well, my dear Staś, now there are no obstacles. Marry her . . . Ah, if you only knew how she loves you . . . I'll tell the poor thing immediately, and you shall take the papers to her and . . . propose on the spot. Now I see the company will be saved, and perhaps the store too. Several hundred people whom you protect from poverty and want will bless you both . . . What a woman! With her you will at last find peace and happiness.'

Wokulski stopped in front of him and shook his head. 'And will she find happiness with me?' he asked.

'She loves you distractedly . . . You can't even guess . . .'

'But does she know what it is that she loves? Don't you see that I'm nothing but a ruin, of the worst kind – a moral ruin? I can poison someone else's happiness, but not give it. If I could give the world anything, it would be money perhaps, and work . . . But not for the people of today, and as far away from them as possible.'

'Oh, stop that!' Rzecki exclaimed. 'Marry her, and you will at once see things differently.'

Wokulski smiled sadly: 'Yes, get married . . . And break a good and innocent being's heart, exploit the most noble feelings and be elsewhere in my thoughts all the time. And perhaps, in a year or two, reproach her because I abandoned great things for her sake.'

'Political things?' Rzecki whispered mysteriously.

'Goodness, no! I've had plenty of time and opportunity to grow disillusioned with all that . . . There's something more important than politics.'

'Geist's invention?'

'How do you know?'

'Szuman told me.'

'Ah, yes . . . I forgot that Szuman must know everything. That's a talent, too.'

'And a very helpful one. In any case, though, I advise you to think about Mrs Stawska, because . . .'

'You will take her from me?' Wokulski smiled. 'Do so, do! I promise you neither of you will be poor.'

'Bah! For goodness sake! We'd never hear the end of it, if an old wreck like I were to think of such a woman. But there's someone more dangerous . . . Mraczewski. He's crazy about her, I tell you, and has already left to see her, for the third or fourth time. A woman's heart is not a stone.'

'Mraczewski? Has he stopped playing with Socialism?'

'For goodness sake! He says that once a man has made his first thousand roubles and meets a pretty woman like Stawska, then politics blows out of his head.'

'Poor Klein had different views,' said Wokulski.

'What has Klein got to do with it, the hothead? A good lad, but no clerk. Mraczewski, now, was a real treasure. Handsome, with a few words of French, and how he used to look at the lady customers, how he'd twirl that moustache! He'll make his way in the world, and will seize Mrs Stawska from beneath your very nose. Mark my words!'

He started to leave, then stopped and said: 'Marry her, Staś . . . marry her. You'll make a woman happy, you'll save the company, and perhaps the store too. What's the use of inventions? I understand political plans in these times, when the most important incidents may take place. But flying machines? Although perhaps they'd be useful,' he added, on reflection. 'Ha! In any case, do as you wish, but make up your mind about Stawska, for I feel that Mraczewski won't let sleeping dogs lie. He's a dandy! Flying machines . . . Pooh!'

Wokulski was left alone. 'Paris or Warsaw?' he thought. 'There – a great purpose, though uncertain; here – several hundred people . . . Whom I can't bear the sight of,' he added, after a moment.

He approached the window and looked out into the street for a while, simply in order to gain control of himself. But everything irritated him: the traffic of carriages, the hurrying pedestrians, their worried or grinning faces . . . Most of all, the sight of women unnerved him. It seemed to him that each was the personification of stupidity and falsity. 'Each of them will find her Starski, sooner or later,' he thought. 'Each one is looking for him . . .'

Before long Szuman once again visited Wokulski.

'My dear friend,' he called from the threshold, smiling, 'even if you were to throw me out, I would continue to persecute you with my visits . . .'

'But of course, come as often as you like,' replied Wokulski.

'So you agree? . . . Splendid! . . . That is half the cure . . . Ah, what it means to have strength of mind! . . . After not quite seven weeks of severe misanthropy, already you begin to tolerate the human species, and in my person to boot . . . Ha, ha ha! . . . What would happen if one were to loose some chic woman into your cage . . .'

Wokulski paled.

'Well, well . . . I know that is too soon . . . It is high time, though, that you began to show your face again. That would complete the cure. Take me as an example,' Szuman declaimed. 'While I sat within four walls I was as bored as a devil in a belltower; and today I have barely to show myself in the world and I have a thousand diversions. Szlangbaum wishes to hoodwink me and is taken continually by surprise, becoming convinced day after day that, although I have such a naïve expression, I had in advance foreseen all his moves. It has even gained me his respect . . .'

'A modest enough sport,' put in Wokulski.

'Wait! Another pleasure is afforded me by my co-religionists in financial circles, for it seems to them that I have an exceptionally shrewd head for business, and yet despite this, that they will be able to steer me as it pleases them . . . I can imagine their painful disappointment when they realise that I am neither shrewd in business, nor stupid enough to become a pawn in their hands . . .'

'And you tried so hard to persuade me to enter into partnership with them? . . .'

'That was different. I encourage you to do so still. No one ever lost out in an agreement with intelligent Jews, at least not financially. But it's one thing to be a partner, and another to be a pawn as they wanted to make of me . . . Ah, those Jew-boys! . . . Always rogues, whether dressed in gabardines or dress-coats . . .'

'Which, nevertheless, does not prevent you from admiring them, or even from associating with Szlangbaum? . . .'

'Well, that's another thing again,' replied Szuman. 'Jews, in my opinion, are the most talented race in the world, and my race besides, so I admire them and love them as a community. And as to my agreement with Szlangbaum . . . for heaven's sake, Staś! Would it be sensible on our part to wrangle between ourselves when it is a question of saving a business as capital as a company trading with the Empire? . . . You are abandoning it, so it will either collapse, or the Germans will get it; either way the country will lose. But the other way, the country wins and we . . .'

'I understand you less and less,' interposed Wokulski. 'The Jews are great, and the Jews are rogues . . . Szlangbaum should be expelled from the trading company, and then he should be taken in again . . . First the Jews gain by it, then the country gains . . . It is complete chaos! . . .'

'You, Staś, have lost your wits . . . This is no chaos, it is the clear and simple truth . . . In this country, only the Jews create some kind

of impetus in industry and trade, and so every economic victory of
theirs is a clear gain for the country . . . Am I not right? . . .'

'I shall have to think about it,' replied Wokulski. 'Well, what
other delight do you bring? . . .'

'The greatest. Imagine, that at the first news of my future financial successes, they want to marry me off already! . . . Me, with my
Jewish mug and bald patch! . . .'

'Who? . . . To whom? . . .

'Our friends, of course, and to whom? . . . Whomsoever I wish.
Even to a Christian girl, and of a good family, if I just get christened . . .'

'And you?'

'Do you know, I am almost prepared to do it out of curiosity.
Simply in order to discover in what manner a beautiful, young,
well-brought-up, Christian girl, above all from a respectable family,
will convince me of her love? . . . Here would be a wealth of
entertainment. I would be entertained watching her vie for my
hand and heart. I would be entertained to hear her speak of her
great sacrifice for the good of her family, or maybe even of her
motherland. I would be entertained, finally, observing in what
manner she would compensate herself for her sacrifice: would she
deceive me using the old method, that is to say, in secret, or the
new, that is openly, perhaps even requiring my permission? . . .'

Wokulski clutched his head. 'Horrible . . .' he whispered.

Szuman looked at him from the corner of his eye.

'You old romantic! . . . You old romantic! . . .' he said. 'You
clutch your head, because in your sick imagination there continues
to linger the chimera of an ideal love, a woman with the soul of an
angel . . . Of those there is barely one in ten, thus you have a nine
to one chance that you will come across such a one . . . Do you
wish to know the norm? . . . Look about you at human relationships. Either the man like a cock bustles around a dozen hens, or
the woman like a she-wolf in February entices a whole pack of
addle-brained wolves or dogs after her . . . I tell you, there is
nothing more degrading than competing in such a pack, than
dependence on a she-wolf . . . In such situations are fortunes lost,
health, heart, energy, and, in the end, one's reason . . . Shame upon
him who cannot extricate himself from such a swamp!'

Wokulski sat in silence, with wide-open eyes. At last he said in a
quiet voice, 'You are right . . .'

The doctor caught him by the hand and, tugging it violently,
cried: 'Right? . . . That from your lips? . . . Well then, you are
saved! . . . Yes, you'll make a man yet . . . Spit on everything that
has passed: on your own pain and on the infamy of others . . .
Choose a goal, any goal, and begin a new life. Go on making your
fortune, or miraculous discoveries, marry Stawska or set up another

partnership, as long as you desire something and do something. Do you understand? And never let yourself be tied to a skirt . . . do you understand? Men of your energy give orders, they do not take them, they lead, they are not led . . . Whoever had the choice between you and Starski, and chose Starski, that one proved herself unworthy even of Starski . . . That is my formula, you understand? . . . And now fare you well and remain with your own thoughts.'

Wokulski did not detain him.

'You are angry?' said Szuman. 'I am not surprised, I have engendered that deep flush; and that which is left will perish of its own accord. Goodbye.'

After the doctor's departure Wokulski opened the window and unbuttoned his shirt. He found it stifling hot, and it seemed to him that he would have a stroke. He remembered Zasławek and the deceived baron, for whom he had once played almost such a role as Szuman had played for him today . . .

He began to dream, and alongside the image of Izabela in Starski's arms, there now appeared to him a pack of breathless wolves pursuing a she-wolf over the snow . . . And he was one of them! . . .

Again pain swept over him, coupled with disgust and self-loathing. 'How despicable and stupid I am! . . .' he cried out, hitting his forehead. 'To see so much, hear so much, and still sink to such degradation . . . I . . . I . . . vied with Starski and God knows with whom else.'

This time he resolutely recalled the image of Izabela; resolutely, he observed all its statuesque features, the ash-blonde hair, the iridescent eyes changing from blue to black. And it seemed to him that on her face, her neck, her shoulders and breast he saw the stamp, the traces of Starski's kisses . . .

'Szuman was right,' he thought, 'I am truly cured . . .'

But slowly, however, anger died in him, and its place was once again taken by grief and sorrow.

During the next few days, Wokulski read no more. He entered into a lively correspondence with Suzin and thought a great deal. He thought that in his present position, after being shut up in his study for almost two months, he had ceased being a man and was beginning to become something like an oyster which, stuck in the same spot, accepts from the world whatever chance happens to throw its way.

And what had accident given him?

First, he put aside the books, some of which had shown to him that he was Don Quixote, and others had aroused within him an interest in a marvellous world where men had power over the forces of Nature. So he no longer wanted to be Don Quixote, and desired power over the forces of Nature.

Then, in turn, Szlangbaum and Szuman had visited him, and he
learned from them that two Jewish parties were struggling together
to inherit his control of the trading company. There was no one
else in the whole country able to develop his ideas; no one except
the Jews, who had come forward with all their arrogance of race,
their cunning, their ruthlessness, and yet they still expected him to
believe that his decline and their triumph would be advantageous
to the country.

In view of this, he felt such a horror for commerce, trading
companies and profits of any kind that he was surprised by himself:
in what manner had he been able to mix in such things for almost
two years? 'I gained a fortune for her,' he thought, 'Commerce . . .
Commerce and I! It was I who acquired over half a million roubles
in two years, I who mixed with economic card-sharpers, bet my
life and work on a single card, well . . . And I won. I – an idealist, a
scholar, I – who understand perfectly well that a man couldn't earn
half a million roubles in a lifetime, no, not in three lifetimes . . .
And the only consolation I had from this card-sharping was the
certainty that I, at least didn't rob or cheat . . . Obviously, God
looks after the stupid.'

Then again, chance had brought him news of Stawski's death in
the letter from Paris, and from that moment on memories of Mrs
Stawska and of Geist in turn awoke within him. 'To tell the truth,'
he thought, 'I ought to return my exploited fortune to the community. Our country is full of poverty and ignorance, and these poor
and ignorant people are at the same time the most admirable
material . . . The only way to do so, however, would be to marry
Stawska. She certainly wouldn't be frightened by my plans, but
would be my most faithful helper. After all, she knows the meaning
of work and poverty, and is so noble . . .'

Thus he reasoned, though he felt differently: he despised the
people he wanted to render happy. He felt that Szuman's pessimism
had uprooted his passion for Izabela, but had also poisoned him. It
was difficult for him to deny that the human race consisted either
of hens flirting with a cockerel, or wolves chasing a she-wolf. And
that whichever way he turned, the chances were nine out of ten
that he would encounter an animal, rather than a man.

'May the devil take him, suggesting that sort of cure,' he
murmured.

Then he began thinking about Szuman. Three men had
observed strongly animal traits in the human species: he himself,
Geist and Szuman. But he believed that animals in human form
were exceptions, and that the community consisted of single
individuals. Geist, on the contrary, claimed that the human
community is animal, and good individuals are exceptions: Geist
also believed that in time, the good people would multiply and

dominate the earth – and for over a decade he had been working on an invention to bring about this triumph.

Szuman also claimed that the great majority of men are animals, but he neither believed in a better future, nor did he offer this consolation. For him, the human species was condemned to eternal animalism, in which only the Jews stood out like pike amidst minnows.

'A fine philosophy, indeed,' thought Wokulski. However, he felt that Szuman's pessimism would soon flourish in his own wounded soul, as in a freshly ploughed field. He felt that love for Izabela was dying in him, and so was his anger. For if the whole world consisted of animals, there was no good reason to be insane about one of them, or to be angry because she was an animal, no better and certainly no worse than others.

'A devilish cure!' he kept thinking. 'Yet who knows but it isn't right? I have gone catastrophically bankrupt for my views: who will promise me that Geist isn't wrong in his ideas, or that Szuman isn't? Rzecki an animal, Stawska, Geist, I myself . . . Ideals – they are painted cribs in which there is painted grass that cannot feed anyone. So why sacrifice oneself for some people, or chase after others? I must cure myself, that's all, and devour pork or pretty women by turns, and drink good wine into the bargain. Read a little, travel sometimes, go to a concert, and thus live to see old age.'

A week before the meeting that was to decide the fate of the trading company, visits to Wokulski became increasingly frequent. Merchants called, so did aristocrats, lawyers – all urging him not to abandon his position, and not to threaten an institution that was, after all, his own work. Wokulski received his callers with such icy indifference that they didn't even feel like setting out their arguments: he said he was tired and sick, and must resign. The callers left, without hope: each admitted, however, that Wokulski must be gravely ill. He had lost weight, spoke briefly and brusquely, and fever burned in his eyes.

'He has killed himself with avarice!' said the merchants.

A few days before the final date, Wokulski summoned his attorney and asked him to inform the shareholders that in accordance with the agreement he had with them, he was withdrawing his capital and leaving the company. The others might do likewise.

'And the money?' asked the attorney.

'It's already in the bank for them: I have accounts with Suzin.'

The attorney withdrew, upset. On the very same day, the Prince called on Wokulski: 'I've been hearing the most extraordinary things!' the Prince began, shaking him by the hand. 'Your attorney is behaving as though you really intended to desert us.'

'Do you think I am joking, Prince?'

'Well, no . . . I think you have observed something dishon-
ourable in our agreement, and . . .'

'And am bargaining, so as to force you to sign another, which
will lessen your interest and increase my income?' Wokulski caught
him up. 'No, Prince, I am perfectly serious about resigning.'

'You will disappoint your partners.'

'How so? You gentlemen entered into the company for only a
year, and you yourselves asked that the business be conducted so
that each partner might withdraw his investment within a month of
dissolving the agreement. That was your plain request. I, on the
other hand, have infringed it inasmuch as I will repay the money,
not within a month, but within an hour of dissolving the
company.'

The Prince sank into an armchair. 'The company will continue,'
he said quietly, 'but the Hebrews will enter in your place.'

'That is your own choice.'

'The Jews in our company!' sighed the Prince. 'They will speak
Hebrew at committee meetings . . . Our unhappy country! Our
unhappy language!'

'No fear of that,' Wokulski interrupted. 'The majority of our
shareholders are in the habit of speaking French at committee
meetings, but nothing has happened to Polish, so surely it won't be
damaged by a few phrases in Yiddish.'

The Prince blushed: 'But Hebrews, sir . . . A foreign race . . .
Now, too, there's general hostility towards them.'

'Hostility by the crowd proves nothing . . . But who is
preventing you gentlemen from collecting sufficient capital, as the
Jews do, and entrusting it, not to Szlangbaum, but to one of the
Christian merchants?'

'We don't know a single one we can trust.'

'But you know Szlangbaum?'

'In any case, we haven't sufficiently gifted men of our own
kind,' the Prince interrupted. 'They are clerks, not financiers.'

'And what was I? I was a clerk, too, even a pantry-boy in a
restaurant at one time; yet the company brought in the expected
profits.'

'You're an exception.'

'How do you know you wouldn't find more exceptions in
wine-cellars or behind counters? You must search for them.'

'The Jews come to us of their own accord.'

'So that's it!' Wokulski exclaimed. 'The Jews come to you, or
you will go to them, but a Christian parvenu cannot even come to
you, because of the obstacles he encounters on the way. I know
something of this. Your doors are so tightly closed to tradesmen
and industrialists that they must either bombard them with
hundreds of thousands of roubles in order to open them, or must

squeeze through like a bug. Open your doors a little, and perhaps you'll be able to get along without the Jews.'

The Prince covered his eyes with both hands: 'Oh, Mr Wokulski, this . . . what you say is very right, and very bitter . . . Very cruel . . . Less of this, though. I understand your resentment towards us, but surely . . . There are certain obligations towards the community.'

'No, I don't regard getting fifteen per cent annually on my capital as the carrying out of an obligation. And I don't think I'd be any worse citizen if I drew the line at five per cent.'

'But we are spending this money,' retorted the Prince, who was already offended. 'People live around us . . .'

'And I will spend money, too. I shall go to Ostend for the summer, to Paris for the autumn, and to Nice in the winter.'

'I beg your pardon . . . People live on us not only abroad . . . How many local craftsmen . . .'

'Have to wait for what they are owed for a year or longer,' Wokulski caught him up. 'Both you and I, Prince, know these patrons of Polish industry, we even have them in our company.'

The Prince jumped up. 'Ah, this is unworthy, Mr Wokulski!' he said breathlessly. 'It's true we have great faults, even sins, but we did not commit any of them towards you. You had our cordiality, our respect . . .'

'Respect!' cried Wokulski, laughing. 'Do you suppose, Prince, that I didn't know what it was based on, and what sort of position it assured me among you all? Mr Stawalski, Mr Niwiński, even . . . Mr Starski, who never did anything and got his money Heaven knows where, stood ten storeys higher than I in your estimation. What am I saying? Any foreign vagabond could get into your drawing-rooms, which I had to conquer with fifteen per cent interest on the capital entrusted to me. It is these people, not I who had your respect. Bah! They even had far wider-reaching privileges . . . Although each of these respected men is worth less than the doorman in my store, for he does something, and at least doesn't infect the community.'

'Mr Wokulski, you do us an injustice. I understand what you mean, and am ashamed, upon my word I am. But after all, we aren't responsible for the offences of individuals.'

'On the contrary, you are all responsible, for those individuals have grown up among you and what you, Prince, call "offences", are only the results of your opinions, of your contempt for all work and all obligations.'

'Resentment is speaking through you,' replied the Prince, making to leave. 'Justified resentment, but perhaps mistakenly aimed . . . Goodbye, sir. So you are leaving us as sacrifices to the Hebrews?'

'I hope you will come to a better understanding with them than with us,' said Wokulski ironically.

The Prince had tears in his eyes. 'I thought,' he said, moved, 'that you would be a golden bridge between us and those who . . . are increasingly drawing apart from us.'

'I wanted to be a bridge, but it was sawn away underneath and has collapsed now,' replied Wokulski, bowing.

'Let us return, then, to the barricades of the Holy Trinity!'

'This is not called for, yet . . . It's a partnership with the Jews, that's all.'

'So that is your view?' asked the Prince, turning pale. 'So I . . . am no longer in the company. Oh, unhappy country . . .'

He nodded and went out.

Finally the meeting to decide the fate of the company for trading with the Empire took place. First, Wokulski's committee delivered a report for the past year. It appeared that the turnover had increased the capital tenfold or more, bringing not fifteen but eighteen per cent. On hearing this, the shareholders were excited, and the Prince moved they thank the committee and the absent Wokulski by rising to their feet. Then Wokulski's lawyer took the floor and stated that his client was resigning on account of ill-health, not only from the committee, but also from the company. Everyone had been prepared in advance for this news, but it made a very depressing effect.

Taking advantage of a pause, the Prince asked for silence and informed those present that he too was resigning from the company as result of Wokulski's resignation. Having made this statement, he at once left the council room; on going out, however, he said to one of his friends: 'I never had any talent for trade, and Wokulski is the only man to whom I can entrust the honour of my name. Today he is gone, so I have nothing more to do here either.'

'But the dividends?' his friend whispered.

The Prince looked at him. 'What I did was not for dividends, but for this unhappy country,' he replied. 'I wanted to inject a little fresh blood into our sphere, and fresher views, but I must admit I lost, and it wasn't Wokulski's fault either . . . This unhappy country!'

The Prince's departure, though unexpected, created less of a stir: for those present already knew that the company would continue operations. Now one of the lawyers came forward and, in a trembling voice, read a very beautiful speech, which stated that with Wokulski's resignation, the company had lost not only its leader, but also five-sixths of its capital. 'It ought therefore to collapse,' the speaker continued, 'and to overwhelm the entire country, ruining thousands of workers, hundreds of families . . .'

Here he paused for effect. But those present behaved indifferently, knowing in advance what was to come.

The lawyer started speaking again, and appealed to those present not to lose heart: 'For an eminent citizen has been found, a professional man, a friend and partner of Wokulski, who has decided, like Atlas, to support the tottering company. This man, who wishes to wipe away the tears of thousands, to save this country from ruin, to give trade a push in new directions . . .'

At this point, all those present turned their heads in the direction of the chair on which Szlangbaum was sitting, sweating and blushing.

'This man,' the lawyer cried, 'is Mr . . .'

'My son, young Henryk!' said a voice from a corner.

Because this effect was unexpected, the entire hall shook with laughter. In any case, the committee of the trading company feigned delighted surprise, asked those present whether they wanted to accept Mr Szlangbaum as partner and director, and having obtained unanimous approval, they summoned the new director to the presidential chair. Here some confusion ensued. For Szlangbaum senior took the floor at once, and after uttering several compliments to his son and the committee, tabled a motion that the company would not guarantee its shareholders more than ten per cent dividend per annum. An uproar started, a dozen speakers took the floor at the same time, and after some very animated speeches it was resolved that the company would accept new members proposed by Mr Szlangbaum, and that the management of business was also entrusted to Mr Szlangbaum.

The final episode was a speech by Dr Szuman, who had been invited to become a member of the committee, but since he was refusing this honourable position, he permitted himself in a sarcastic manner to mock a company formed of aristocrats and Jews. 'It is like an illegitimate union,' he said, 'but sometimes geniuses are born from such unions, so let us hope that our company too will produce some unusual fruit.'

The committee was alarmed, a handful of those present took offence; but the majority gave the doctor a rousing cheer.

Wokulski was very accurately informed of the course of the meeting; during the entire week, he was visited and snowed under by letters, signed and anonymous. For himself, he had discovered he was in a new and strange spiritual mood. It seemed to him that all the bonds linking him with other people had burst, that they were now a matter of indifference to him, that he was not concerned with what concerned them. In a word, he was like an actor who, on finishing his role on the stage where he had laughed, been angry, or wept, now takes a seat in the audience to watch his colleagues acting as though they were children at play: 'Why do they rush about so? How stupid . . .' he thought.

It seemed to him that he was looking into the world from a great distance, and could see his own affairs from a new angle, which he had not observed hitherto.

For the first few days, shareholders, workers or clients of the company visited him, dissatisfied with the admission of Szlangbaum, or perhaps concerned for their own futures. For the most part, they tried to persuade him to return to the position he had abandoned but could still retake, since the contract with Szlangbaum had not yet been signed. Others presented their positions in such mournful colours, and even wept, that Wokulski was moved. But at the same time, he discovered such indifference within himself, such lack of sympathy for the misfortunes of others, that he surprised himself. 'Something has died inside me,' he thought, and sent away his petitioners empty-handed.

Then came a second wave of visitors, who pretended they wanted to thank him for his services, but who really came to satisfy their curiosity, and see what this once strong man looked like, of whom it was now said he had gone to pieces entirely. These people did not ask him to return to the company, but merely praised his past activities and said that it would be long before another man as active as he had been would turn up.

A third wave of visitors called on Wokulski, goodness knows why. For they did not even pay him compliments, merely referred more and more often to Szlangbaum, his energy and his talents.

The carter Wysocki was an exception in the crowds of visitors. He came to bid farewell to his former patron: he even wanted to tell him something, but suddenly burst into tears, kissed him on both hands and hurried from the room.

Very much the same was repeated in the letters. In some, acquaintances and unknown persons urged him not to withdraw from the business, for his withdrawal would be a disaster for the country. Others praised his past activity or pitied him; still others advised him to join Szlangbaum, as a very talented man who thought only of the community's welfare. On the other hand, he was mercilessly insulted in some anonymous letters for having ruined the country's industry a year ago by importing foreign merchandise, and today he was ruining it by selling out to the Jews. The exact price was even mentioned.

Wokulski pondered quite coolly over these things. It seemed to him he was already a dead man, watching his own funeral. He saw those who pitied him, those who praised him, those who cursed him: he saw his successor, to whom the community's admiration was starting to turn, and finally he realised that he himself was forgotten and superfluous. He was like a stone dropped into water, at first causing a whirlpool and movement, but later on, smaller and smaller waves flow away. Finally, above the place where he had fallen, a smooth mirror of water was recreated, where waves flowed again, but now originating from other places, caused by other people. 'Well, what now?' he said to himself, 'I have no one, I do nothing . . . What next?'

He recalled that Szuman had advised him to seek some other purpose in life. Good advice, but . . . How to follow it, when he himself felt no desire, had neither strength nor wishes? He was like a dead leaf, which goes wherever the wind tosses it. 'I once foresaw this state of mind,' he thought, 'but now I can see that I had no idea of what it was like.'

One day he heard a noisy argument in the hall. He glanced out and saw Węgiełek, whom the butler would not admit. 'Ah, it's you,' said Wokulski, 'come in . . . What's your news?'

At first Węgiełek eyed him uneasily; gradually, however, he became more animated, and took comfort. 'They said,' he declared with a smile, 'that you were on your last legs, sir, but I see they were lying. You have grown thin, that's true, but you don't look like a scarecrow.'

'What's your news?' Wokulski repeated.

Węgiełek told him expansively that he had a house, better than the one which had been burned down, and a great deal of work. This was precisely why he had come to Warsaw, in order to buy materials and perhaps to get two assistants. 'I could start a factory, sir, that I could,' Węgiełek concluded.

Wokulski listened to him in silence. Suddenly he inquired: 'And are you happy with your wife?'

A shadow flitted across Węgiełek's face: 'She's a good woman, sir . . . But . . . I must tell you, honestly . . . There's something . . . It's true that what the eye don't see, the heart don't grieve over; but once it sees . . .'

He wiped away some tears with his sleeves. 'What does this mean?' asked Wokulski, surprised.

'Nothing, sir. I know who it was I married, but I was easy in mind, because the woman was good, quiet, hard-working and as attached to me as a dog. Well, what of that? As long as I was easy in my mind, until I saw her former gentleman friend, or whatever he was . . .'

'Where?'

'In Zasław, sir,' Węgiełek continued. 'One Sunday, Maria and I went to the castle; I wanted to show her that stream where the blacksmith perished, and that stone you told me to put the inscription on. I noticed the carriage of Baron Dalski, who married the granddaughter of the late Duchess. She was a good woman, may God rest her soul!'

'Do you know the Baron?' asked Wokulski.

'I should say so,' Węgiełek replied. 'The Baron is now landlord of the Duchess's estate, until something is done there. And he's already had me paint rooms and repair windows. I know him! A real gent, and generous too . . .'

'So what happened?'

'So, like I was tellin' you, sir, Maria and me were in the castle, looking at the stream, when all at once the Duchess's grand-daughter comes out of the ruins, with that son-of-a-bitch Starski.'

Wokulski threw himself into a chair. 'Who?' he whispered.

'That there Mr Starski, the Duchess's grandson, who fawned on her while she was alive, but now wants to challenge her will, for he says his grandma went mad before she died . . . That's what sort of a person he is.'

He paused, then went on: 'He had the Baroness by the hand, they looked at our stone, and talked and giggled. Then Starski looked around. He saw my wife, and smiled at her a little, and she went as pale as a handkerchief. "What is it, Maria?" say I. But she: "Nothing." Meanwhile, the Baroness and that scoundrel ran down the castle hill and went into the woods. "What is it?" say I to Maria again, "only tell me the truth, for I noticed you recognised that scoundrel." And she sat down on the ground, and burst into tears: "May God punish him," she says, "it was he who first ruined me."'

Wokulski closed his eyes.

Węgiełek went on in an angry voice: 'When I heard that, sir, I thought I'd run after him and kick him to death on the spot, even in front of the Baroness. Such anger came over me . . . Then I asked myself: "Why did you marry her, you fool? You knew very well what sort of woman she was." And at that moment my heart sank, so I was afraid to leave the spot, and couldn't look at my wife at all.'

'She says: "Are you angry?" and I say: "I suppose this is where you used to meet him?" − "God be my witness that I only saw him that once." "You took a good look at one another!" say I, "would to God I'd been blinded before I saw you: would to God I'd died before I met you. . . ." And she asks me, weeping, "Why are you angry?" Then I told her, for the first and last time, "You're an animal, that's what . . ." Because I couldn't control myself any longer.'

'Then I see the Baron himself rush up, coughing till he went livid in the face, and he asks: "Did you see my wife, Węgiełek?" Something flashed through my mind then, so I said: "I saw her, Your Excellency, she went into the thicket with Mr Starski. He's run short of money for buying girls, so now he's chasing after married ladies . . ." Well, and the way he looked at me then, even though he's a Baron!'

Węgiełek wiped his eyes surreptitiously: 'Yes, that's how my life is, sir. I was easy in my mind until I caught sight of that scoundrel;

but now, no matter who I see, it seems to me that he's my brother-in-law. And it turns me against my wife, although I don't talk about it . . . It turns me against her, as if something had happened between her and me . . . I can't even kiss her like I used to, and if it weren't for the marriage vow, I can tell you, sir, that I'd have left home and gone off to the other end of the world. But it all comes from being attached to her. For if I didn't love her, it wouldn't matter. She's a careful housekeeper, cooks nicely, sews beautifully and is as quiet as a mouse at home. So – let her have suitors! But the fact is that I loved her, and on that account I suffer such pain and anger, that everything in me is being burned to ashes.'

Węgiełek trembled with rage: 'At first, sir, when we got married, I considered children differently, but it scares me, lest instead of my own son, I should see that of her lover. Everyone knows that once a she-wolf has puppies by a cur, then later on, even if she mates with the finest wolves, the cur will always speak out in the offspring, everyone can see that by looking.'

'I have to go out,' said Wokulski suddenly, 'so goodbye. Call on me again before you go home.'

Węgiełek said goodbye to him very cordially, but in the hall he said to the butler: 'Something ails your master. At first I thought he was all right, though he looked bad; but obviously he is weak . . . May God protect you all.'

'Now, you see, I told you not to worm your way in there, and not to talk so much.' the butler replied, pushing him into the porch.

After Węgiełek's departure, Wokulski fell into a profound meditation. 'They stood at my stone, and they laughed,' he murmured. 'He even had to profane a stone, a harmless stone.'

For a moment it seemed to him he had found a new purpose: all that was necessary was the choice – whether to shoot Starski dead after first enumerating to him a list of the people whose happiness he had destroyed, or whether to let him live but bring him to utter poverty and humiliation?

Then he had another idea, and it seemed childish, and even vulgar, to sacrifice his own fortune, work and peace of mind for revenge on that sort of man: 'I'd sooner consider destroying a field mouse or cockroach, for they really are pests. But a man like Starski . . . God knows what he is! In any case it's impossible that such a limited individual should be the only cause of so much misery. He's merely a spark that sets fire to tinder.'

He lay down on the *chaise-longue* and thought: 'He fixed things for me . . . Why? He had an accomplice who was entirely worthy of him, and another accomplice, too – my own stupidity. How was it possible not to recognise that woman instantly for what she is, but even to make a goddess out of her, simply because she posed as a higher being? He fixed things for Dalski too, but who can blame Dalski in his old age for going insane over a person whose morals would fit into a thimble? The cause of disasters in this world isn't the Starskis or men like him, but primarily the stupidity of their victims. Then again, neither Starski nor Izabela nor yet Ewelina were born yesterday, it's just that they were brought up in a certain sphere of society and in a given epoch, and amidst certain notions. They're like a rash, which isn't a disease, but is a symptom of sickness in society. What's the use of being revenged on them, why destroy them?'

That evening, Wokulski went out into the street for the first time, and realised how enfeebled he was. His head reeled from the rattle of droshkies and the movement of passers-by, and he dreaded going too far from home. It seemed to him he would never reach Nowy Świat Boulevard, that he wouldn't be able to find his way home, that despite himself he would cause some ridiculous incident. Above all, he dreaded meeting a familiar face.

He went home tired and agitated, but that night he slept well.

Ochocki called a week after Węgiełek's visit. He had grown manly, was tanned and looked every inch a gentleman.

'Where have you come from?' Wokulski asked him.

'Straight from Zasławek, where I sat around for nearly two months,' Ochocki replied. 'Confound it all, you'll never guess what sort of a row I got myself landed in!'

'You?'

'Yes, sir – me, and innocently into the bargain. It'll make your hair stand on end!'

He lit a cigarette, and went on: 'I don't know whether you heard that the late Duchess willed all her fortune, apart from a small amount, to charity. Hospitals, orphanages, schools, village halls and the like. And the Prince, Dalski and I are her executors . . . Very well! We'd already begun carrying out her wishes, or rather trying to probate the will, when (a month ago) Starski comes back from Cracow, and informs us that he – in the name of his ill-used family – was starting a law-suit to invalidate the will. Of course, neither the Prince nor I would hear of it; but the Baron, led on by his wife whom Starski had incited, the Baron started to soften . . . We argued several times on this account, and the Prince just wouldn't have anything more to do with him.

'What next?' asked Ochocki, lowering his voice. 'One Sunday, the Baron went with his wife and Starski on an outing to Zasław. What happened there? I don't know, but the result is as follows. The Baron insisted he would not let the will be invalidated, and that's not all . . . The Baron has decided on a separation from his adored wife (did you know that? . . . And that's not all: ten days ago, the Baron had a duel with Starski and got a bullet across the ribs. It was as though someone had ripped the skin off his chest from right to left with a hook . . . The old man is furious, he roars and curses, is feverish, but he told his wife to go back to her family immediately, though I'm certain they won't receive her . . . There's a hard fellow for you! But the old devil is so determined that he ordered his nurse, on his sick-bed, to dye his hair and beard for him, to spite his wife, and today he looks like a twenty-year-old corpse.'

Wokulski smiled. 'He did well with the woman,' he said, 'but he needn't have painted himself.'

'He needn't have got it in the ribs, either,' Ochocki put in. 'He very nearly put a bullet through Starski's brains. Bullets are always blind. I can tell you, sir, that the incident made me quite ill.'

'Where is our hero now?' asked Wokulski.

'Starski? He has bolted abroad, not so much from the coldness he began getting in society, as from his debtors. What an artist he is! He has some hundred thousand roubles of debts.'

A long silence followed. Wokulski was sitting with his back to the window, his head bowed. Ochocki pondered, whistling quietly. Suddenly he came to and began speaking, as if to himself: 'What a strange muddle human life is! Who'd have expected a booby like Starski to do so much good? And just because he's a booby!'

Wokulski raised his head and looked inquiringly at Ochocki.

'Strange, is it not?' Ochocki went on, 'and yet that's how it is. If Starski were a respectable, decent man and hadn't had an affair with the Baron's young wife, Dalski would certainly have supported his claim against the will – bah! He'd even have given him money for the law-suit, because his wife would have profited by that too. But because Starski is a booby, he offended the Baron . . . And saved the will. So even unborn generations of Zasławek peasants ought to bless Starski for flirting with the Baroness.'

'A paradox!' Wokulski put in.

'A paradox! These are facts, after all. And don't you think Starski has done the Baron a favour by ridding him of a wife like that? Between ourselves, she's not a woman, but an animal. All she thought of were clothes, parties and flirtations, and I don't know whether she ever read anything, or looked attentively at anything . . . Nothing but a lump of flesh and bone, who pretended to have a soul, but had nothing but a stomach . . . You didn't know her, you can't imagine what a dummy she is, nor how there was nothing human under that façade of humanity. By realising what she is, the Baron has won a great lottery prize.'

'Merciful Heavens!' Wokulski murmured.

'What did you say?' asked Ochocki.

'Nothing . . .'

'But the salvation of the late Duchess's bequest, and the liberation of the Baron from such a wife are only a part of Starski's services.'

Wokulski shifted in his chair.

'Pray imagine, sir, that this booby may, by his flirtation, have contributed to a really important fact,' said Ochocki. 'This is how the land lies. I sometimes urged Dalski (and, in fact, anyone with money) that it would be worthwhile to establish an experimental laboratory in Warsaw for chemical and mechanical technology. For, as you know, sir, we have no inventions in the country, primarily because there is nowhere to make them. Of course, the Baron heard my plea with one ear and let it out the other. However, something must have lodged in his brain, for now that Starski has wounded his heart and ribs, the Baron, wondering how to disinherit his wife, talks to me for days at a time about a technological workshop. What purpose would it serve? Would people really become wiser and better if they were provided with a workshop? And how much would it cost, and would I undertake to organise such an institution? When I came away, things were at the point of the Baron calling in an attorney and drawing up a document of some sort which, as far as I can make out from hints, concerns the workshop. Moreover, Dalski asked me to select for him fellows able to direct such a business. Well now, isn't this an irony of fate – that such a nonentity as Starski, a mere piece of public property for consoling bored wives, should be the source of a technological workshop? Nobody is going to convince me, after this, that there's anything superfluous in the world!'

Wokulski wiped the sweat from his face which, compared with his white handkerchief, looked almost ashen.

'But perhaps I'm tiring you?' Ochocki asked.

'Please go on . . . Although I think you overestimate the services of this . . . man, somewhat, and you entirely forget . . .'

'What?'

'That the technological workshop will grow from the sufferings, the ruins of human happiness. And you don't even ask yourself the question as to how the Baron passed from love for his wife to a workshop.'

'What's that to me?' cried Ochocki, shrugging. 'The purchase of social progress at the cost of the sufferings of individuals, however terrible – is well worth it.'

'Do you know what the sufferings of the individuals are like, at least?' asked Wokulski.

'Indeed I do! After all, I had the nail taken off my toe without chloroform, and off my big toe, into the bargain.'

'A toe nail?' Wokulski repeated thoughtfully. 'Do you know the old saying: "Sometimes the human soul rends and fights itself"?

Who knows whether that isn't worse than pulling off a toe nail, or even ripping off the entire skin.'

'Hm . . . That's some unmanly ailment,' Ochocki replied, with a grimace. 'Perhaps women experience something of the sort when having a baby . . . But a man . . .'

Wokulski laughed aloud. 'You laugh at me?' asked Ochocki.

'No, at the Baron! As for you, why didn't you undertake to organise the workshop?'

'Oh, come! I prefer travelling to established workshops, not creating a new one, the fruits of which I wouldn't live to see, and so waste myself. One needs administrative and pedagogic talents for that, and it would have nothing to do with flying machines.'

'Well?' asked Wokulski.

'What do you mean? Once I've collected the little capital I still have on a mortgage, which I haven't been able to lay hands on for three years despite my request, I shall set off abroad and start work seriously. Here a man can only idle, and grow stupid and embittered.'

'A man can work anywhere.'

'You're joking,' Ochocki replied. 'Even putting aside the absence of a workshop, we don't have a scientific climate here. This is a city of careerists, among whom a real scholar passes for a boor or madman.

'People here don't study for knowledge, but for a position; and they acquire a position and celebrity through social contacts, women, parties, goodness knows what else! I've bathed in that pond. I know genuine scholars, even men of genius, suddenly brought to a halt in their development, who have taken to giving lessons or writing popular articles which no one reads or, if they do, they fail to understand. I've talked to great industrialists, thinking I would persuade them to support research, if only for the sake of practical inventions. But do you know what I discovered? They have about as much idea of science as geese of logarithms. Do you know the sort of inventions that would interest them? Only two: one which would increase their dividends, and the other to teach them how to cheat their fellow businessmen, either in price or merchandise. As long as they thought you would perpetrate a fraud on that company for trade, they called you a genius: but today they say you have softening of the brain, because you gave your partners three per cent more than you promised.'

'I know,' Wokulski replied.

'So just try to work for science amidst such people. You will starve to death or become an idiot. But if you can dance, play an instrument, appear in amateur theatricals and – above all – amuse women, then you will forge a career for yourself. They'll call you eminent at once, and you'll gain a position in which your income will be ten times the value of your work. Parties and women, women and parties! But as I am not a footman to wear myself out at parties, and I regard women as very useful for bearing children, so I am getting away, even if I only go to Zurich.'

'Wouldn't you like to go to Geist?' asked Wokulski.

Ochocki reflected. 'I'd need hundreds of thousands of roubles there, which I don't have,' he replied. 'Besides, even if I had, I'd first of all have to be convinced as to what that invention really is. A decrease in specific gravities looks like a fairy-tale to me.'

'Yet I showed you that metal,' said Wokulski.

'So you did . . . Please let me see it again.'

A sickly flush appeared and rapidly disappeared on Wokulski's face. 'I don't have it any longer,' he said in a stifled voice.

'What happened to it?' Ochocki asked in surprise.

'Never mind . . . You may suppose it fell down a drain somewhere . . . But would you go to Geist if, for example, you had the money?'

'Certainly, but primarily to check on the facts. Forgive me, but from what I know of chemistry, it is impossible to believe in a theory of decreasing specific gravity beyond certain limits.'

Both fell silent, and soon Ochocki left.

Ochocki's visit awoke a new line of thought in Wokulski. He felt the desire and even the urge to renew his chemical experiments, and that same day he hurried into town to buy a retort, pipes and test-tubes as well as various chemicals. Still influenced by this thought, he went boldly through the streets, even got into a droshky: he looked at people with indifference, and felt no vexation on seeing that some stared at him curiously, others didn't recognise him, while yet others smiled maliciously at the sight of him.

But in the glass shop, and still more in the apothecary's, he realised how much his vitality had ebbed, along with his independence – if all that was needed was a conversation with Ochocki to remind him of chemistry which he had not interested himself in for some years. 'Never mind,' he thought, 'as long as it fills my time.'

Next day he bought a precision balance and some complex instruments, and set to work like a schoolboy at the commencement of his studies. First he obtained hydrogen, which reminded him of university days, when hydrogen had been made in a flask wrapped in a towel, using soot. What happy times they'd been! Then he recalled the balloons he had invented, and Geist, who held that the chemistry of hydrogen combines would change the history of mankind.

'Suppose a man like me were to hit upon the metal Geist is looking for?' he said to himself. 'Geist claims that the discovery will depend on testing several thousand combinations: in other words, it's a lottery, and I'm lucky . . . But if I discovered the metal, what would Izabela say?'

Rage boiled up within him at the memory. 'Ah,' he murmured, 'I should like to be famous and powerful, so I could tell her how much I despise her.'

Then it occurred to him that contempt is not manifested in rage, nor yet in the desire to humiliate someone, and he set to work again. The elementary experiments with hydrogen gave him the most pleasure, so he repeated them most often.

One day he made a glass harmonica and played so loudly upon it that the owner of the house called next day to inquire with the utmost civility whether he would mind leaving the apartment at the end of the quarter.

'Have you another tenant?' asked Wokulski.

'The fact is . . . It's like this . . . I very nearly have,' replied the landlord, embarrassed.

'In that case, I'll move.'

The landlord was somewhat surprised by Wokulski's readiness, but bade him goodbye much gratified. Wokulski laughed. 'Obviously he regards me as an eccentric,' he thought, 'or a bankrupt. So much the better! Quite honestly, I can live very well in two rooms, instead of eight.'

But a moment came when, without knowing why, he regretted his haste in yielding the apartment. Then he recalled Węgiełek and the Baron. 'The Baron,' he thought, 'has separated from his wife because she flirted with another man: Węgiełek took a dislike to his just because he saw one of her former lovers with his own eyes. So what should I do?'

Once again he set about his experiments, seeing with pleasure that he hadn't lost much of his skill.

These occupations filled his time up very well indeed. Sometimes he didn't think of Izabela for several hours at a time, and then he felt that his weary brain was really relaxing. His fear of other people and the streets died away, and he began going into town more often.

One day he went as far as the Łazienki park: he did even more, for he looked into the alley along which he had once walked with Izabela. Then the swans, alarmed by someone, spread their wings and flew to the shore, striking the water. This commonplace sight made a terrible impression on Wokulski: he recalled Izabela's departure from Zasławek . . . He fled the park like a madman, hurried into a droshky and drove home with his eyes closed.

That day he did not occupy himself with anything and in the night he had a strange dream. He dreamed that Izabela was standing before him, with tears in her eyes, asking why he had abandoned her . . . After all, that journey to Skierniewice, the conversation with Starski and the flirtation had only been a dream. He had only dreamed it.

Wokulski hurriedly sat up in bed and lit the lamp. 'Which was the dream?' he asked himself. 'The journey to Skierniewice, or her grief and reproaches?'

He could not sleep until dawn – questions and doubts of the utmost significance were tormenting him. 'Could people sitting in a badly lit compartment be reflected in the window?' he thought, 'and was what I saw merely a hallucination? Do I know enough English to be sure I didn't misunderstand the meaning of some phrases? What must she think of me, to insult her so terribly for no reason? After all, cousins who have known each other since childhood can carry on even quite outspoken conversations without betraying anyone else's confidence . . . What have I done, wretched man that I am, if I was mistaken, influenced by unjustified jealousy! Moreover, that Starski is in love with the Baroness, Izabela knew it, and surely she wouldn't degrade herself by flirting with someone else's lover . . .'

Then he remembered his present life, so empty, so terribly empty! He stopped his experiments, broke with people and no longer had anything before him. What next? Read fantastic books? Carry out pointless experiments? Travel? Marry Stawska? But whatever of these he chose, wherever he went, he would never rid himself of his grief, nor of his feelings of loneliness!

'But what of the Baron?' he said to himself. 'He married his Ewelina – and look what came of it! Today he's thinking of establishing a workshop, he who probably doesn't even know the meaning of technology.'

The daylight and a shower gave Wokulski's thoughts yet another turn: 'I have thirty or forty thousand roubles a year: I spend two or three thousand on myself; what shall I do with the rest, and with the fortune which only overwhelms me? With this money I could ensure the existence of a thousand families: but what of it, if some will be as unhappy as Węgiełek, and others repay me as the railroad man Wysocki did?'

Again he recalled Geist and his mysterious workshop in which the embryo of a new civilisation was developing. There the investment of work and a fortune would be rewarded a million times over. There was both a colossal goal and a way to occupy one's time, and the prospect of such glory and power as had never been seen on earth. Armoured ships which could rise in the air! . . . Could there be anything more immense in its consequences? . . .

'But what if, as is very probable, not I, but some other some other discovers that metal? . . .' he asked himself.

'And what of it?' he replied. 'At worst, I would belong to the few who pushed the discovery forward. Such a cause is indeed worth the sacrifice of a useless fortune and an aimless life. Is it then better to run to waste here within these four walls or stupefy oneself at cards than to reach there for unprecedented glory? . . .'

Gradually, an intention began to take shape with increasing clarity in Wokulski's soul, but the more precisely he grasped it, and the more merit he discovered in it, the more he felt that he lacked the energy, even the incentive, to execute it.

His will was totally paralysed: only a powerful shock could awaken it. But no shock came, and the daily course of events plunged Wokulski into deeper and deeper apathy.

'I am not dying, but rotting away,' he told himself.

Rzecki, who visited him with increasing infrequency, watched in alarm. 'You are doing very badly, Staś,' he would exclaim sometimes, 'Badly, badly, badly! Better not live at all, than like this . . .'

One day the servant handed Wokulski a letter addressed in a woman's hand. He opened it and read: 'I must see you, and shall expect you today at three – Wąsowska.'

'What can she want from me?' he asked in amazement.

But he left home before three. Punctually Wokulski found himself in Mrs Wąsowska's hall. Without even asking his name, the footman opened the door to the drawing-room, where the pretty widow was walking about rapidly. She wore a dark gown that set off her statuesque figure very well: as always, her auburn hair was knotted in a huge bun, but instead of hairpins, a small dagger with a golden handle was stuck in it.

On seeing her, Wokulski was filled with curious feelings of joy and tenderness: he hastened to her, and feverishly kissed her hand.

'I ought not to speak to you,' said Mrs Wąsowska, pulling her hand away.

'In that case, why have you summoned me?' he replied in surprise. It seemed to him that cold water had been poured over him.

'Pray be seated.'

Wokulski sat down in silence. Mrs Wąsowska was still walking to and fro. 'You are putting up a fine show, no doubt about it,' she began indignantly, after a moment. 'You have exposed a woman in society to gossip, her father to illness, the whole family to disagreeable incidents . . . You shut yourself up at home for months, you disappoint a dozen or more people who trusted you implicitly, and now even the worthy old Prince calls your eccentricities "a contribution to the activities of women". I congratulate you . . . If some student or other were to behave thus . . .'

Suddenly she stopped. Wokulski was terribly changed.

'Oh, what next, surely you aren't going to faint?' she said in alarm. 'I will give you some water, or wine . . .'

'No, thank you,' he replied. His face rapidly regained its natural colour and tranquil expression. 'You see, I really am not well.'

Mrs Wąsowska began regarding him attentively. 'Yes,' she said, 'you have grown somewhat thinner, but with that beard, you are not bad-looking at all . . . You should not shave it off. You look interesting.'

Wokulski blushed like a little boy. He listened to Mrs Wąsowska, and was surprised to find that he was shy of her, almost ashamed. 'What's happening to me?' he wondered.

'In any case, you ought to go to the country at once,' she continued. 'Who ever heard of anyone staying in town at the beginning of July? *Basta*, my good man! I'll take you to my place the day after tomorrow, otherwise the spirit of the late Duchess would not let me rest. From today, you are to come to lunch and dinner with me: after lunch we will take a drive, and the day after tomorrow – Farewell, Warsaw! Enough of this . . .'

Wokulski was so taken aback that he was unable to reply. He did not know what to do with his hands, and felt as though his face were on fire.

She rang. The footman came in. 'Bring some wine,' said Mrs Wąsowska, 'you know, the sweet Hungarian . . . Mr Wokulski, pray light a cigarette.'

Wokulski did so at once, praying inwardly that he would be able to control the trembling of his hands. The footman brought the wine and two glasses. Mrs Wąsowska filled both. 'Drink this,' she said.

He swallowed it at one gulp. 'Ah, I like that! Your health,' she added, drinking, 'and now you must drink to mine.'

Wokulski drank off a second glass. 'And now,' she said, 'you must drink to the fulfilment of my plans. But instantly!'

'I beg your pardon, madam,' he replied. 'but I don't want to get drunk.'

'So you don't wish to fulfil my plans?'

'Of course I do, but I must know what they are, first.'

'Really?' exclaimed Mrs Wąsowska, 'that is something entirely new . . . Very well, pray drink up.'

She began looking out of the window, tapping one foot on the floor. Wokulski pondered. The silence lasted several minutes, finally the lady interrupted it: 'Have you heard what the Baron has done? How do you like it?'

'He has done the right thing,' Wokulski replied, already quite calm.

Mrs Wąsowska turned to him. 'What's that?' she cried. 'You defend a man who has covered a woman with shame? A brute, an egoist, who didn't hesitate to use the most vile means to get his revenge?'

'What did he do?'

'So you don't know? He demanded a separation from his wife, and had a duel with Starski in order to make the scandal still more notorious.'

'I understand you,' said Wokulski, after some thought. 'For he might have shot himself in the head without saying anything, and left his fortune to his wife.'

Mrs Wąsowska burst out in anger. 'Naturally,' she cried, 'any man with a spark of nobility and feeling of honour would have done so. He would sooner kill himself than force a poor woman into the yoke of shame, a poor being it's so easy to take one's revenge on when a man has money, position and social prejudices behind him . . . But I didn't expect this from you. Ha ha ha! So this is the new man, the hero who suffers in silence . . . Oh, you men are all the same.'

'I beg your pardon, but . . . precisely what do you have against the Baron?'

A flash appeared in Mrs Wąsowska's eye. 'Did he love Ewelina or not?' she inquired.

'He was insane about her.'

'No, that isn't true, he was pretending he loved her, he was lying when he said he adored her. For at the first opportunity, he proved he didn't even regard her as a person with rights equal to his own, but as a slave girl, who for a momentary weakness, can have a halter put around her neck and be dragged into the market-place, covered with shame . . . Oh, you men of the world, you're deceivers! As long as an animal instinct blinds you, you'll cast yourselves at her feet, you're ready to commit shameful deeds, to tell lies: it's "My dearest . . . My adored one . . . I'd give my life for you." But when the poor victim believes your oaths, she starts to grow bored and if frail human nature awakens in her, you trample it underfoot. Oh, how revolting, how shameful! What have you to say to that?'

'Did not the Baroness flirt with Mr Starski?' asked Wokulski.

'Oh! So it's "flirted", is it? She did, and she had a *faiblesse* for him, besides.'

'A *faiblesse*? I didn't know the word. But if she had a *faiblesse* for Starski, why did she marry the Baron?'

'Because he went down on his knees and implored her to . . . He threatened to do away with himself.'

'Excuse me, but . . . Did he merely ask her to deign accept his name and fortune, or did he also beg her not to have a *faiblesse* for other men?'

'What about you . . . you men? What don't you do, both before marriage and after? So is a woman to . . . ?'

'Madam, they explain to us while we are still children that we are animals, and that the only way to become a man is to love a woman, whose nobility, innocence and loyalty help prevent the world from becoming totally animal. So we believe in this nobility, innocence and the like, we adore her, we fall on our knees to her . . .'

'Quite right too, for all of you are worth much less than women.'

'We admit this in a thousand ways, and we declare that although man creates civilisation, woman ennobles it and gives it ideals. But if women are to imitate us in the animal part of our nature as well, then how are they better than we are, and above all – why should we adore them?'

'For love.'

'A fine thing! If Mr Starski wins love with his moustaches and fiery glances, why should another man have to give his name, fortune and liberty for it?'

'I understand you less and less,' said Mrs Wąsowska. 'Do you admit that women are men's equals, or not?'

'Generally speaking they are, but not altogether. In intellect and capacity for work, an average woman is lower than a man: but in manners and feelings she should be as much above him as will compensate for these inequalities. At least, so they always said, and we believe it, and despite the many low attributes of women, we place them higher than ourselves. But if the Baroness renounced her virtue, and she did that long ago, as we all know, then one should not be surprised that she has lost her privileges too. Her husband got rid of her as he would a dishonest business partner.'

'But the Baron is an impotent old man!'

'Why, then, did she marry him, why did she pay any attention to his amorous paroxysms?'

'You do not understand, then, that a woman may be forced to sell herself?' asked Mrs Wąsowska, paling and blushing by turns.

'Indeed I do, for I too . . . once sold myself, though not to acquire a fortune, but out of poverty.'

'And what happened?'

'In the first place, my wife did not regard me as innocent, and I didn't promise her love, either. I made a very bad husband, though as a kept man I was the best shop clerk and her most loyal servant. I went with her to church, to concerts, theatres, I entertained her friends and in fact tripled the income of the store.'

'Did you not have mistresses?'

'No, madam. I felt my enslavement so bitterly that I simply dared not look at other women. So you must admit, madam, that I have the right to be a stern judge of the Baroness who, when she sold herself, knew that no one was buying . . . honest labour from her.'

'Horrible,' whispered Mrs Wąsowska, staring at the floor.

'Yes, madam. Trade in human beings is a horrible thing, but the sale of oneself is still more horrible. But only transactions entered into in bad faith are shameful. When such a transaction is exposed, the consequences must be very disagreeable for the unmasked party.'

For a while both sat in silence. Mrs Wąsowska was vexed, Wokulski sulky.

'No,' she cried suddenly, 'I must get a firm opinion from you!'

'What on?'

'On various questions, to which I want you to reply clearly and distinctly.'

'Is this to be an examination?'

'Something of the sort.'

'Pray continue, madam.'

One might have thought she was hesitating. However, she forced herself to ask: 'So you hold the opinion that the Baron had the right to reject and defame a woman?'

'A woman who had deceived him? Yes, I do.'

'What do you mean by deception?'

'Accepting the baron's adoration despite the *faiblesse*, as you call it, which she has for Mr Starski.'

Mrs Wąsowska bit her lip: 'And how many *faiblesses* did the Baron have?'

'As many as his desires and opportunities afforded, to be sure,' Wokulski replied. 'But the Baron didn't pose as an innocent, he didn't profess to be a specialist in the purity of morals, nor was he surrounded by tribute for that . . . Had the Baron gained someone's heart by claiming he had never taken mistresses, when in fact he had done, he too would be a deceiver. Admittedly, no one asked him.'

Mrs Wąsowska smiled: 'Capital, indeed! What woman is going to state or assure you she never had lovers?'

'So you have had them?'

'My good man!' the widow exclaimed, rising hastily. At once she recollected herself, and said boldly: 'I expect a certain consideration from you in your choice of arguments.'

'Why so? After all, we both have equal rights, and I will not be in the least offended if you ask me how many mistresses I have had.'

'I am not interested.'

She started walking about the drawing-room. Anger was seething in Wokulski, but he controlled it.

'Yes, I admit, sir,' she said, 'that I am not without prejudices. But then I am only a woman, I have a smaller brain, as your anthropologists declare: besides, I am chained by social conventions, vices and Heaven knows what beside! If I were a sensible man like you, and believed in progress as you do, I would know how to rid myself of these influences, even if only to admit sooner or later that women must be emancipated!'

'In respect of these *faiblesses*, I daresay?'

'You "daresay" . . .' she teased him, 'that is precisely what I'm talking about.'

'Aha! So why should we wait for the dubious results of progress? Already today there are many women emancipated in that respect. They have even formed a powerful party, called coquettes. But it's strange: while they have the respect of men, these women don't enjoy the benevolence of other women.'

'It's impossible to talk to you, Mr Wokulski,' the widow reproached him.

'Impossible to talk to me about the emancipation of women?'

Mrs Wąsowska's eyes gleamed and the blood rose into her face. She sat down violently in an armchair and, striking the table with one hand, exclaimed: 'Very well! I'll tolerate your cynicism and will even mention the coquettes. You must know, sir, that one must have a very low character to be able to compare those women who sell themselves for money with honest and noble women who give themselves for love.'

'Posing all the time as innocents.'

'What if they do?'

'And who deceive naive men who believe in them . . .'

'But how does the deception harm them?' she asked, looking him boldly in the eyes.

Wokulski clenched his teeth, but controlled himself and coolly said: 'If you please, madam, what would my partners have said of me if, instead of a fortune of six hundred thousand roubles, as reported, I'd only had six thousand, but never protested against the reports. It's merely a question of two noughts.'

'Let's leave financial matters aside,' Mrs Wąsowska interrupted.

'Hm! Well, and what would you have said of me, if, for example, my name had not been Wokulski, but Wolkulski, and I'd used that small change in spelling to gain the benevolence of the late Duchess, pushed my way into her house and had the honour of making your acquaintance there? What would you have called such a way of making acquaintances and gaining people's respect?'

A feeling of disgust was painted on Mrs Wąsowska's noble features. 'What has this to do with the Baron and his wife?' she countered.

'The fact that it is not allowed to appropriate titles in society. A coquette may, of course, be a useful woman and no one has the right to reproach her for her special proficiency: but a coquette masking herself behind a façade of what is called respectability is a cheat. And she deserves blame for that.'

'Monstrous!' Mrs Wąsowska burst out, 'but less of this . . . Tell me, though, what the world loses through such trickery?'

Wokulski began to hear a ringing in the ears: 'The world sometimes gains if a naive simpleton falls into the madness called ideal love, and makes a fortune by taking terrible risks in order to place it at the feet of his ideal . . . But sometimes the world loses, if this madman, on finding out the trickery, is broken and of no use for anything . . . Or if, without making a will, he throws himself under . . . That's to say, he fights a duel with Mr Starski and gets a bullet in the ribs. The world loses one happiness, one developed mind, and perhaps a man who might achieve something.'

'That man himself is to blame.'

'You are right, madam: he would be to blame if, having seen that, he didn't behave as the Baron has done and didn't break with his stupidity and shame.'

'In a word,' said Mrs Wąsowska, 'men don't voluntarily renounce their foolish privileges *vis-à-vis* women?'

'That's to say — if they don't admit the privilege of being deceived.'

'Anyone who rejects a peace treaty,' she said with excitement, 'starts a war.'

'War?' Wokulski echoed, smiling.

'Yes — a war in which the stronger side will win . . . And we shall see which is the stronger!' she exclaimed, shaking her fist.

At this moment a strange thing happened. Wokulski suddenly seized Mrs Wąsowska by both hands and placed them between three of his own fingers.

'What does this mean?' she asked, turning pale.

'Let us see who is the stronger,' he replied.

'Come . . . Enough of this joke.'

'No, madam, this is no joke. It is merely a small proof that in a battle with you, I can do as I choose. Is it so, or not?'

'Let me go,' she exclaimed, struggling, 'I'll call the servants . . .'

Wokulski let her hands go: 'Ah, so you ladies will fight us with the help of servants? I wonder what reward these allies would require, and whether they would let you evade your obligations?'

Mrs Wąsowska gazed at him, first with slight alarm, then with indignation, finally she shrugged: 'Do you know, sir, what I think?'

'That I have gone mad?'

'Something of the kind.'

'Faced with such a pretty woman and in such an argument, it would be natural . . .'

'Oh, that's a shallow compliment,' she exclaimed, with a grimace. 'In any event, I must admit you have impressed me somewhat. Somewhat . . . But you didn't keep to your role, you let my hands go, and that disappointed me.'

'Oh, I know how to keep hold of hands . . .'

'And I – to call servants.'

'And I, if you please, can shut mouths . . .'

'What? What?'

'You heard what I said.'

Mrs Wąsowska was surprised again. 'You know, sir,' she said, folding her arms à la Napoleon, 'that you're either very unusual . . . or very badly bred.'

'I was not "bred" at all.'

'Then you are really unusual,' she murmured. 'It is a pity you never let Bela know this side of your nature.'

Wokulski turned to stone. Not at the sound of that name, but on account of the change he felt within himself. Izabela seemed a matter of indifference to him, while Mrs Wąsowska had begun to interest him.

'You should have confronted her with your theories, as you have me,' she went on, 'and there would have been no misunderstanding between you.'

'Misunderstanding?' Wokulski asked, opening his eyes wide.

'Yes – for as far as I know, she's ready to forgive you.'

'To forgive me?'

'I see you are still very . . . feeble,' she said, in an indifferent tone. 'If you don't feel that your actions were brutal . . . Compared to your peculiar behaviour, even the Baron is a gentleman.'

Wokulski burst out laughing so sincerely that he himself was alarmed. Mrs Wąsowska went on: 'You laugh? I forgive you, for I understand such laughter . . . It is the highest degree of suffering.'

'I can promise you, madam, that I haven't felt so free for ten weeks . . . My God! Or even for years . . . It seems to me that during all that time, some terrible nightmare was rending my mind, and has only just vanished . . . Only now do I feel I am saved, and thanks to you.'

His voice shook. He seized both her hands and kissed them almost passionately. Mrs Wąsowska thought she perceived something like tears in his eyes.

'Saved! Liberated!' he repeated.

'Listen to me, sir,' she said coldly, removing her hands, 'I know everything that passed between you two . . . You behaved unworthily by eavesdropping on a conversation which I know down to the smallest details, and even more . . . It was the most ordinary flirtation imaginable.'

'Ah, so that was a flirtation?' he interrupted, 'which makes a woman resemble a restaurant napkin which anyone may use to wipe his mouth and fingers? That's a flirtation, is it?'

'Silence, sir,' cried Mrs Wąsowska, 'I don't deny that Bela behaved wrongly, but . . . Judge for yourself, when I say that as far as you're concerned she . . .'

'Loves me, or what?' asked Wokulski, stroking his beard.

'Oh, perhaps not yet. So far she misses you . . . I don't want to go into details, suffice it to say that I've been seeing her almost daily for the past two months . . . During this time she has spoken of no one but you, and her favourite spot for trips is Zasławek castle. Whenever she sits on that stone with the inscription, I see tears in her eyes . . . Once she even burst into tears as she repeated the couplet inscribed there: "Always, everywhere, I shall be at your side, for I have left a part of my soul there." What have you to say to that?'

'What have I to say?' Wokulski echoed. 'I vow that my only wish at this moment is that the slightest traces of my acquaintance with Miss Łęcka should disappear. And first of all, that wretched stone which moved her so.'

'If this were true, I'd have fine evidence of masculine constancy.'

'No, you would merely have evidence of a miraculous cure,' he said, with excitement. 'My God! I feel as though someone had been hypnotising me for years, that during these ten weeks I was being clumsily aroused, and that only today have I woken up.'

'Do you mean that?'

'Surely you see how happy I am? I have regained my self, and belong to myself again . . . Please believe me, madam, that this is a miracle which I don't in the least understand, but which can only be compared to a man already in his coffin awakening from lethargy.'

'And to what do you attribute this?' she asked, looking away.

'To you, in the first place . . . And then to the fact that I've finally acquired a clear view of things which I long since understood but hadn't the courage to recognise. Izabela is a woman of a different species from me, and only insanity could bind me to her.'

'What will you do, now that you've made this interesting discovery?'

'I don't know.'

'Have you ever found a woman of your own species?'

'Perhaps . . .'

'That Mrs Sta . . . Sta? . . .'

'Stawska? No. You, rather.'

Mrs Wąsowska rose from her chair with a very solemn expression.

'I understand,' said Wokulski. 'Am I to leave?'

'As you think fit.'

'Shall we not drive to the country together?'

'Oh, by no means . . . Although . . . I don't forbid you to come . . . Bela will certainly be staying with me.'

'In that case I won't come.'

'I don't promise she'll be there.'

'Should I ever find you alone?'

'I expect so.'

'And should we talk as we have done today? Should we go riding as before.'

'War would certainly start between us,' Mrs Wąsowska replied.

'I warn you I shall be the winner.'

'Really? Perhaps you would make me your prisoner?'

'Yes. I would show you I know how to rule, and then would implore you, at your feet, to accept me as your slave.'

Mrs Wąsowska turned away and made to leave the drawing-room. On the threshold, she paused a moment and, turning her head slightly, said: 'Au revoir . . . In the country.'

Wokulski left her apartment as though intoxicated. In the street he murmured: 'Of course, I am going mad.'

He looked back, and saw Mrs Wąsowska at the window, looking out from behind the curtain. 'The devil take it,' he thought, 'can I have got myself embroiled in another intrigue?'

Walking along the street, Wokulski pondered over the change that had come over him. He seemed to have extricated himself from an abyss, in which night and madness dominated, into the light of day. His pulses beat more strongly, he breathed more freely, his thoughts flowed with unusual freedom: he felt a sort of vitality throughout his entire organism, and an indescribable tranquillity in his heart. Now the traffic in the streets no longer irritated him, and he delighted in the crowds of people. The sky had a deeper colour, the houses looked brighter, even the dust, imbued with streams of light, was pretty.

But the greatest pleasure of all was that caused by the sight of young women, their graceful movements, smiling lips and inviting glances. Some looked him straight in the eye with an expression of sweetness and coquetry; Wokulski's heart beat faster, a disturbing current flowed through him from top to toe.

'Pretty creatures!' he thought. Then, however, he remembered Mrs Wąsowska and had to admit that among all these pretty women, she was the prettiest and, still better, the most attractive . . . What a figure, what marvellous ankles and bosom and eyes, holding something of diamonds and velvet . . . He could have sworn he'd caught the perfume of her body, that he could hear her convulsive laughter, and his head reeled at the mere thought of getting close to her . . .

'What a passionate woman she must be!' he murmured. 'I'd bite her . . .'

The image of Mrs Wąsowska pursued him and tormented him so, that he suddenly conceived the idea of visiting her again that day, in the evening. 'After all, she invited me to lunch and dinner,' he told himself, feeling that something was surging up in him.

'What if she shows me the door? Why did she flirt with me? I knew all along that she didn't dislike me, well and I fancy her, which is something.'

Just then, a dark girl with violet eyes and the face of a child passed him, and Wokulski realised with amazement that he liked her too.

A few yards from his apartment, he heard someone shouting: 'Hey! Hey! Staś!'

Wokulski looked around and caught sight of Szuman under the canopy of a café. The doctor abandoned an uneaten portion of ice cream, threw down a silver coin and hurried to him. 'I was on my way to see you,' said Szuman, taking his arm. 'You know, you haven't looked so well for a long time. I'll be bound that you're coming back into the firm, and will drive those Yids out . . . What a look! What an eye! At last I recognise the old Staś!'

They passed the gateway and stairs and went into the apartment. 'And I was just thinking that a new sickness was threatening me,' said Wokulski, with a smile. 'Would you like a cigar?'

'Why should it?'

'Just imagine, for perhaps an hour past, women have been making a tremendous impression on me . . . I'm shocked.'

Szuman laughed out loud: 'Capital! . . . Instead of giving a dinner party to celebrate his happiness, he's afraid . . . Do you think you were in a healthy state of mind when you were crazy about one woman? You're well today, when you like them all, and have nothing more important to do then to strive for the favours of the woman who suits your taste best.'

'Hm . . . But suppose she were a great lady?'

'So much the better . . . Great ladies are far more appetising than chambermaids. Femininity gains greatly by chic and intelligence, and by pride above all. What ideal conversations await you, what trusting looks . . . They're worth ten times more, let me tell you.'

A shadow flitted across Wokulski's face.

'Aha!' cried Szuman, 'I can see the long ears of that creature on which Christ rode into Jerusalem . . . Why do you grimace? Flirt with great ladies only, they're the ones who are interested in democracy.'

The bell rang in the vestibule and Ochocki came in. He glanced at the excited doctor and inquired: 'Do I interrupt you gentlemen?'

'No,' Szuman replied, 'you may even be helpful. For I am just advising Staś to cure himself by having a love affair, though . . . Not an ideal one. Enough of those!'

'Well, sir, I would like to attend the lecture too,' said Ochocki, lighting the cigar offered him.

'Now for an argument!' Wokulski muttered.

'Not at all,' Szuman declared. 'A man with your money could be completely happy, all that is needed for rational happiness are – to eat different dishes every day, have clean linen and to change one's residence and one's mistress every three months.'

'There wouldn't be enough women to go around,' Ochocki interposed.

'Leave that to the women, sir, and they'll make sure there is no shortage,' the doctor replied, scoffingly. 'After all, the same diet applies to women as well.'

'A quarterly change of diet?' asked Ochocki.

'Certainly. Why should they be any worse off than we?'

'But the tenth or twentieth change of diet wouldn't be interesting.'

'Prejudice! Prejudice!' said Szuman. 'You'll never notice or guess, especially if they assure you that you are only the second or fourth, and in any case you're the man they truly love and have been waiting for.'

'Weren't you at Rzecki's?' Wokulski suddenly asked Szuman.

'Well, I'm not writing him prescriptions for love,' the doctor replied. 'The old man is going to rack and ruin.'

'That's so, he looks terrible,' Ochocki put in.

The conversation shifted to Rzecki's state of health, then to politics, finally Szuman bade them goodbye.

'A cynical devil, that,' Ochocki muttered.

'He doesn't care for women,' Wokulski added, 'and besides, he sometimes has bad days, and then he talks like a heretic.'

'Not without justice, sometimes,' Ochocki said. 'He hit the mark with those observations . . . For only an hour ago I had a solemn talk with my aunt, who insists on trying to make me get married, and claims that nothing so ennobles a man as the love of a good woman.'

'He wasn't advising you, but me.'

'As I listened to his argument, I too was thinking of you. I can imagine how you'd look if you changed your mistress every three months, if at some time all the people who now work towards providing your income were to stand before you and ask: "With what are you repaying us for our labour, poverty and shortened lives, part of which we hand over to you? With work, or advice, or example?"'

'What sort of people work towards my income nowadays?' asked Wokulski. 'I have withdrawn from trade and am putting my fortune into investments.'

'If you are investing it in land mortgages, then the interest will be paid by farmhands: if in shares, then the dividends are provided by railroad workers, confectioners, weavers, goodness knows who.'

Wokulski became still more sombre. 'Pray tell me, sir,' he said, 'why should I think of that? Thousands of people live on their dividends, and don't trouble themselves with such problems.'

'But then,' Ochocki muttered, 'they are the others, not you. I have fifteen hundred roubles a year altogether, but it often strikes me that such a sum would provide subsistence to three or four people, and that some fellows are giving up their lives for me, or having to limit their own needs which are restricted enough in all conscience.'

Wokulski walked about the room. 'When are you going abroad?' he suddenly inquired.

'I don't even know that,' Ochocki replied sourly. 'My debtor won't repay the money for a year. He'll pay me off simply by getting into another debt, but that won't be easy to do nowadays.'

'Does he pay high interest?'

'Seven per cent.'

'Is it secure?'

'The next best thing after the Credit Union.'

'Suppose I gave you the cash and took over your rights, would you go abroad then?'

'In a moment!' exclaimed Ochocki, leaping up. 'Why should I settle down here? I'd marry well in sheer desperation, and later do as Szuman advises.'

Wokulski reflected. 'What would be the harm in marrying?' he said in an undertone.

'For Heaven's sake! . . . I couldn't support a poor wife, a rich one would make a sybarite out of me, and either would mean the end of my plans. What I need is some odd woman who would work in the laboratory with me, and where am I to find one?'

Ochocki seemed highly agitated, and made to leave.

'So, my dear sir,' said Wokulski, bidding him goodbye, 'we will discuss the matter of your capital. I'm prepared to pay you off.'

'As you wish . . . I am not going to ask you to do it, but should be most grateful.'

'When are you leaving for Zasławek?'

'Tomorrow, I called to say goodbye to you.'

'So the matter is settled,' Wokulski ended, pressing his hand. 'You shall have the cash in October.'

After Ochocki's departure, Wokulski lay down to sleep. He had experienced so many powerful and conflicting impressions this day that he was unable to set them in order. It seemed to him that since the moment of his break with Izabela he had entered upon some terrible elevation, surrounded by precipices, and that only today had he gained its heights, or had emerged on a second level where he could see still unclear but totally new prospects.

For some time, hosts of women moved before his eyes, and especially Mrs Wąsowska: then again, he saw crowds of labourers and workmen, asking him what he had given them in exchange for his income. Finally he fell asleep.

He woke at six next morning, and his first impression was a feeling of freedom and vitality. He didn't really want to get up, but he was not suffering and he did not think about Izabela. That's to say, he thought of her, but he didn't have to: in any case, the recollection of her did not ravage him in its previous painful manner.

Then this absence of suffering alarmed him. 'Is it a premonition?' he wondered. He recalled the events of the previous day: his memory and logic served him well. 'Perhaps I am regaining my will-power,' he murmured.

For an experiment, he decided he would get up in five minutes, bathe, dress and then go at once for a walk in the Łazienki park. He gazed at the moving hands of his watch and inquired uneasily: 'Perhaps I shan't be able to do it?'

The hand reached five minutes, and Wokulski rose without haste, but also without hesitation. He let the water into the bath himself, bathed, dried, dressed, and within half an hour was entering the Łazienki.

He was struck by the fact that all this time he had not thought of Izabela, but of Mrs Wąsowska. Obviously something had changed in him since yesterday; perhaps some paralysed cells in his brain had started functioning. The thought of Izabela had lost its domination over him.

'What an extraordinary thing,' he thought. 'Mrs Wąsowska has ejected that other woman, but any woman may replace Mrs Wąsowska. So I'm genuinely cured of my madness . . .'

He walked to the lake and gazed indifferently at the boats and swans. Then he turned down the path leading to the Orangery, where they had been together, and he told himself that . . . he would make a hearty breakfast. But as he was coming back the same way, rage overcame him and he rubbed out his own footsteps with the fierce joy of a mischievous urchin: 'If only I could erase everything thus . . . That stone, and the ruins . . . Everything!'

At this moment he felt an unconquerable urge to destroy certain things awakening in him: but at the same time he realised it was an unhealthy symptom. It also gave him great satisfaction to be able to think calmly about Izabela, and even do her justice. 'What did I get so angry about?' he asked himself. 'If it hadn't been for her, I'd never have made a fortune . . . If it hadn't been for her and Starski, I wouldn't have gone to Paris for the first time, or met Geist, and wouldn't have cured myself of my stupidity at Skierniewice. After all, they are my benefactors, the pair of them. I ought even to have acted as a go-between for the fine pair, or at least facilitated their rendezvous. And to think that Geist's metal will one day emerge from such dirt!'

It was quiet and almost deserted in the Botanical Gardens. Wokulski passed the well and began slowly ascending the shadowy hill where, over a year ago, he had talked to Ochocki for the first time. The hill seemed to him to be the foundation of those enormous stairs, at the summit of which a statue of the mysterious woman had appeared to him. He could see her now, and noticed with emotion that the clouds surrounding her head had drawn aside for a moment. He caught sight of her stern face, loose hair and under her brass brows were living, leonine eyes, gazing at him with an expression of overwhelming might. He withstood that look, and suddenly felt he was growing . . . That already his head surpassed the highest trees in the park, and almost attained the naked feet of the goddess.

Now he realised that this pure and eternal beauty was Fame, and that on her summit there is no comfort other than work and danger.

He returned home more sorrowful, yet was still tranquil. It was as though a bond had been formed during his stroll between his future and that distant past, when he as a shop assistant had constructed machines for perpetual motion, or balloons that could be steered. But the last few years had only been an interruption and waste of time. 'I must go away,' he told himself, 'I must rest, then later . . . We'll see.'

That afternoon he sent a long telegram to Suzin in Moscow.

Next day, around one o'clock, when Wokulski was eating lunch, Mrs Wąsowska's footman entered and informed him she was waiting in the carriage. When he hurried into the street, Mrs Wąsowska told him to get in. 'I am carrying you off,' said she.

'To lunch?'

'No, merely to the Łazienki. It will be safer for me to talk to you in front of witnesses, and in the open air.'

But Wokulski was sombre and said nothing.

In the park, they got out of the carriage, walked around the palace terrace and began strolling along the path adjacent to the amphitheatre.

'You must go out among people, Mr Wokulski,' Mrs Wąsowska began. 'You must rouse yourself from your apathy, otherwise a charming prize will slip through your hands.'

'Is that so?'

'Certainly. All the ladies are interested in your sufferings, and I wager that more than one would like to console you.'

'Or amuse herself with my alleged sufferings, like a cat with a hurt mouse? No, madam – I need no ladies to console me, because I'm not suffering at all, or at least not through the fault of a woman.'

'What's that?' Mrs Wąsowska exclaimed. 'Anyone might suppose you really hadn't received a blow from tiny hands . . .'

'They'd be right,' Wokulski replied. 'If anyone dealt me a blow, it was certainly not the fair sex . . . But I really don't know what . . . Fate, perhaps.'

'Through the medium of a woman, all the same.'

'Through my own naivety, above all. Ever since I was a child, I've been looking for some great and unknown thing: and since I used to see women through the eyes of the poets, who flatter them too much, I thought that woman was that great and unknown thing. I was wrong, and there lies the clue to my temporary lack of balance which, however, helped me make a fortune.'

Mrs Wąsowska halted: 'Come, sir, you surprise me! We haven't met since yesterday, but you now give me the impression of an entirely different man, a sort of old grandfather who despises women.'

'It's not contempt, but observation.'

'You mean?' asked Mrs Wąsowska.

'That there's a species of woman in this world whose purpose is to torment and excite the passions of men. In this way they confound sensible people, bring about the downfall of the honest, while fools can keep their heads. They have many admirers and because of that they exert the same influence on us as harems do in Turkey. So, madam, you see that ladies have no cause to sentimentalise over my sufferings, and no right to amuse themselves at my expense. I am outside their field of reference.'

'And you are even breaking with love, sir?' asked Mrs Wąsowska, ironically.

Anger surged up within Wokulski. 'No, madam,' he replied, 'only I have a pessimistic friend, who explained to me that it's far more profitable to purchase love for four thousand roubles – and faithfulness for five thousand – than to pay with what we call our feelings.'

'There's faithfulness for you!' Mrs Wąsowska murmured.

'At least we know what to expect.'

Mrs Wąsowska bit her lip and turned back in the direction of the carriage: 'You should start propagating your new ideas.'

'I think it would be a waste of time, madam, for some people will never understand them, and others never believe them, without personal experience.'

'Thank you for your lecture,' she said, after a moment. 'It has made such a powerful impression on me that I won't even ask you to see me home. Today you're in an exceptionally bad mood, but I trust it will pass. But . . . Here's a letter,' she added, handing him an envelope. 'Pray read it. I am committing an indiscretion, but I know you will not betray me, and I have decided once and for all to clear up the misunderstanding between you and Bela. If my plan succeeds, burn the letter: if not, bring it with you to the country, when you come. Adieu!'

She entered her carriage and left Wokulski on the garden road.

'Confound it, can I have offended her?' he said to himself. 'A pity, for she's enticing.'

He walked slowly in the direction of Aleje Ujazdowskie, and thought about Mrs Wąsowska: 'Nonsense! I'm not going to tell her I've taken a fancy to her! Besides, even if I picked a good moment to do so, what could I give her in return? I couldn't even tell her I love her?'

Not until Wokulski reached home did he open the letter from Izabela. At the sight of the once-loved writing, a lightning flash of grief passed through him: but the scent of the paper reminded him of those long-past times when she was encouraging him to arrange the ovations for Rossi. 'He was one of the beads in the rosary Izabela uses for praying,' he whispered, with a smile.

He began reading: 'Dear Kazia, I am so discouraged about everything, and still can't collect my thoughts, and only today have I found the energy to tell you what has occurred since you left.

'I know now how much aunt Hortensja has left me: it is sixty thousand roubles – so altogether we have ninety thousand roubles, which the good Baron has promised to invest at seven per cent, bringing in some six thousand a year. Never mind, we shall have to learn economy.

'I can't begin to tell you how bored I am, or perhaps I'm merely yearning . . . But that too will pass. This young engineer keeps visiting us every few days. At first he entertained me with talk about iron bridges, and now he tells me he was in love with a woman who married someone else, that he despaired, lost hope of falling in love again, and longs to regain his health by a new, better love. He also confided in me that he sometimes writes poetry, in which he only sings the charms of Nature however . . . Sometimes I want to burst into tears out of sheer boredom, but as I would die without society, I pretend to be listening and sometimes let him kiss my hand . . .'

The veins stood out in Wokulski's forehead. He paused, then read on: 'Papa is still feebler. He weeps several times a day, and whenever we are alone for five minutes, he reproaches me, in connection with you know whom! You can't think how it upsets me.

'I visit the Zasław ruins every few days. Something draws me there, I don't know whether it is the beauty of Nature, or loneliness. When I am very unhappy, I write various things in pencil on the ruined walls, and joyfully think that the first rain will wash them all away.

'But there! I was forgetting the most important thing. You must know that the marshal wrote my father a letter in which he very formally asked for my hand in marriage. I cried all night, not because I may become Her Excellency, but . . . because it may so easily happen!

'The pen is dropping from my hand. Farewell, and recall your unhappy Bela sometimes.'

Wokulski crushed the letter: 'I despise her so, and . . . I still love her,' he murmured.

His head was on fire. He walked to and fro with fists clenched, and smiled at his own dreams.

Towards evening he received a telegram from Moscow, after which he at once sent a telegram to Paris. But he spent the next day, from morning to late at night, with his lawyer and agent.

Going to bed, he thought: 'Am I committing a folly? Well, I will see how things are on the spot . . . Whether a metal lighter than air can exist is another question, but there is something in it, no doubt of that. Besides, in searching for the philosopher's stone, chemistry developed: so who knows what will be discovered next? In the end, it's all the same to me, provided I get myself out of this mud.'

Not until the following afternoon did a reply arrive from Paris, which Wokulski read through several times. A moment later he was handed a letter from Mrs Wąsowska, with a likeness of the Sphinx in place of seal. 'Yes,' Wokulski muttered, smiling, 'a human face and the body of an animal: and our imagination lends you wings.'

'Pray call on me for a few moments,' Mrs Wąsowska wrote, 'I have some very important business and hope to leave today.'

'Let us see what this important business is,' he said to himself. Half an hour later he was at Mrs Wąsowska's: trunks, ready packed, were standing in the vestibule. The lady of the house received him in her workroom, where not a single thing recalled work.

'This is very civil of you,' Mrs Wąsowska began, in an offended tone. 'I was waiting for you all day yesterday, but you didn't appear.'

'You forbade me to come here, after all,' replied Wokulski, in surprise.

'How so? Didn't I clearly invite you to the country? But never mind this, I will attribute it to your eccentricity . . . My dear sir, I have some very important business to discuss with you. I want to go abroad soon and should like your advice: when is the best time to buy francs – now, or before I leave?'

'When are you leaving?'

'Ah . . . In November . . . December,' she replied, blushing.

'Before your departure would be the best time.'

'You think so?'

'That is what everyone else does.'

'I don't want to do as everyone else does!' Mrs Wąsowska exclaimed.

'Then buy them now.'

'But what if the franc goes down between now and December?'

'Then postpone your purchase until December.'

'Well, sir, you know you're the only person who can advise me . . . Black is black, white white. What sort of man are you? A man ought to be firm all the time, or at least know what he wants . . . Well, have you brought me Bela's letter?'

Wokulski silently handed her the letter.

'Really!' she exclaimed, vivaciously, 'so you don't love her? In that case, a talk about her ought not to distress you. For I have to reconcile you both or . . . Put the poor girl out of her misery. You are prejudiced against her . . . You are doing her an injustice. That is dishonest . . . A man of honour would not behave thus, would not worm his way into her affections, then throw her aside like a faded bouquet.'

'Dishonest!' Wokulski repeated. 'Kindly tell me, madam, what sort of honesty can be left in a man who has been nurtured on suffering and humiliation, or humiliation and suffering!'

'You had other moments, too.'

'Oh, yes indeed – a few kind looks and kind words, which now have the one fault in my eyes that they were . . . trickery.'

'Today she regrets that, and if you were to return . . .'

'What for?'

'To gain her heart and her hand.'

'Leaving the other hand for both known and unknown admirers? No, madam, I have had enough of those races, in which I was outstripped by Messrs Starski, Szastalski and the devil knows how many others besides! I cannot play the role of a eunuch in the presence of my ideal, and see a happy rival or undesirable cousin in every man.'

'How low that is!' Mrs Wąsowska exclaimed. 'So for one mistake – and an innocent one, moreover – your are rejecting the woman you once loved?'

'Allow me to have my own idea of the number of the mistakes, madam: and as for innocence. . . . Merciful heavens! What a wretched position I am in, since I don't even know how far their "innocence" went.'

'Can you suppose? . . .' Mrs Wąsowska asked, coldly.

'I suppose nothing,' Wokulski replied, quietly. 'All I know is that, in my view, a flirtation of the commonest sort was going on under the cover of indifferent liking, and . . . that sufficed. I can understand a wife deceiving her husband: she may explain away her actions by the bonds which marriage has placed upon her. But that a free woman should deceive a stranger . . . Ha ha ha! That is a different kind of sport, for Heaven's sake! After all, she had the right to place Starski – and all of them – above me. But no! She also needed to have a fool in her suite of followers, a fool who truly loved her, who was prepared to sacrifice everything for her sake. And for the final degradation of human nature, it was I and I alone that she wanted to use as a screen for herself and her admirers . . . Don't you know how those people must have laughed at me, heaped with cheaply purchased attentions? And do you realise what a Hell it is, to be as ludicruous as I was, and yet at the same as unhappy, to realise my own decline and yet to know too that it was undeserved?'

Mrs Wąsowska's lips trembled: she was restraining tears with difficulty. 'Isn't it all imagination?' she interposed.

'Oh, no, madam . . . Betrayed self-respect isn't imagination.'

'Well?'

'What is the alternative?' Wokulski replied. 'I realised in time, I got myself out, and today I at least have the satisfaction of knowing that my rival's victory is not complete, as far as I'm concerned.'

'That is irrevocable?'

'If you please, madam . . . I understand a woman surrendering herself for love, or selling herself out of poverty. But I cannot conceive this spiritual prostitution, carried out without any need, in cold blood, keeping up an appearance of virtue.'

'So there are things that cannot be forgiven?' she inquired softly.

'Who is to forgive whom? Mr Starski will never take offence over such matters, and will perhaps even recommend her to his friends. For the rest, people with so many and such choice friends need not care.'

'A last word,' said Mrs Wąsowska, rising. 'May I know your intentions?'

'I wish I knew them myself.'

She gave him her hand: 'Goodbye, sir.'

'I wish you every happiness, madam.'

'Ah . . .' she sighed, and quickly went into the next room.

'It strikes me,' thought Wokulski, as he went downstairs, 'that at this moment I've settled two matters. Who knows but that Szuman wasn't right?'

From Mrs Wąsowska's he drove to Rzecki's apartment. The old clerk was very haggard and could barely rise from his armchair. Wokulski was deeply touched by the sight of him. 'Are you angry, old fellow, because I haven't been to see you for so long?' he asked, shaking him by the hand.

Rzecki shook his head sadly. 'As if I didn't know what was happening to you,' he replied. 'There's misery in the world . . . Misery . . . Worse and worse . . .'

Wokulski sat down, thoughtfully. Rzecki went on: 'You know,

Staś, I have a notion it's time for me to join Katz and my other comrades in the infantry, who are angry with me for defaulting. I know that whatever you decide to do with yourself will be wise and good, but . . . Wouldn't it be practical to marry Mrs Stawska? After all, she is your sacrifice, as it were.'

Wokulski clutched his head. 'Good God!' he exclaimed, 'when am I to pay off these women? One flatters herself I am her victim, another is my victim, a third would like to be my victim, and there are dozens of others, each of whom would accept me and my fortune as her victim . . . An amusing country, this, to be sure, where the women play first violin, and there are no matters of interest, apart from happy or unhappy love!'

'Well, well,' Rzecki replied. 'I am not forcing you. Except, d'you see, Szuman told me you urgently need romance in your life.'

'Ugh! No! I need a change of scene, and have already prescribed that medicine for myself.'

'Are you leaving?'

'The day after tomorrow at the latest I go to Moscow, and then . . . Where God wills.'

'Have you anything in mind?' asked Rzecki, mysteriously.

Wokulski pondered. 'I don't know yet: I'm as uncertain as though I were on a swing ten storeys high. Sometimes it seems to me I'll do something for this world . . .'

'As for that . . .'

'But sometimes such despair overcomes me, that I'd like the earth to swallow me up and everything I have ever touched.'

'That's foolish . . . Foolish,' Rzecki interposed.

'I know it is. Yet I wouldn't be surprised if I don't make a stir at some future time – or close all my accounts with the world.'

They sat on until late that evening. Some days later, the news spread that Wokulski had left suddenly, and for good.

All his property, from the furniture to his carriage and horses, was acquired lock, stock and barrel by Szlangbaum, at a quite low cost.

XXXVII

The Journal of the Old Clerk

FOR SEVERAL months the rumour has been circulating that on 26 June last year Prince Louis Napoleon, the son of the emperor, perished in Africa. And, what is more, that he died fighting a savage nation, about whom we know neither where they live nor what they are named. For no nation can possibly be called Zulu.

So everyone is saying. Even the Empress Eugénie was supposed to have gone over there and brought her son's body back to England. I do not know if such is the real state of affairs, for I have not read a newspaper since June and do not care to talk politics.

Politics is stupid! There were no telegrams and leading articles in days gone by, and yet the world moved forwards and every reasonable man could orientate himself in the political situation. But today there are telegrams, leading articles, and the latest news, but it all serves to confuse heads.

But they do worse than cause confusion, they deprive people of their hearts. And if it were not for Kenig or honest Sulicki, then a man would cease to believe in divine justice. Such things they write in the newspapers today!

As for Prince Louis Napoleon, then he may well have died, but he might also have hidden himself from the agents of Gambetta. I pay no attention to rumours.

Still no sign of Klein, and Lisiecki has moved to Astrakhan on the Volga. On departing, he told me that soon only Jews would remain here, and the rest would turn Jewish.

Lisiecki always was a hothead.

My health isn't what it was. I get tired so easily that I don't go into the street without my cane. There's nothing the matter with me, only sometimes I have a strange pain in the arms and get out of breath. But this will pass, and if it doesn't, then it's all the same to me. The world is changing for the worse, so that soon I shan't have anyone to talk to, or anything to believe in.

At the end of July, Henryk Szlangbaum celebrated his birthday as owner of the store and director of the trading company. Although he didn't get ahead half as well as Staś did last year, all Wokulski's friends and enemies gathered and drank the Szlangbaums' health . . . until the windows rattled.

Oh, mankind! They'd go into the sewers for a full plate and a bottle, and I don't know where – for a rouble.

Fie, fie! Today I was shown a newspaper, in which Baroness Krzeszowska was called one of the most eminent and benevolent of our ladies, for giving two hundred roubles to some orphanage. Clearly they've forgotten her court case against Mrs Stawska and those squabbles with her lodgers. Can it be that her husband has broken the old hag in?

Bad feeling against the Jews is still mounting. There are even rumours that Jews trap Christian children and bake them in matzos. My goodness, when I hear such tales, I rub my eyes and ask myself whether I'm tossing in a fever, and whether my youth was a dream? But what angers me most, is Dr Szuman's relish at the ferment.

'Serves the Kikes right,' he says, 'let them make a row, let them learn sense. They may be a race of genius, but they're such scoundrels that you won't break 'em in without using whip and spurs.'

'But, doctor,' I replied, for I had lost patience, 'if the Jews are such scoundrels as you say, even spurs won't help.'

'Maybe spurs won't improve them, but they'll drive more sense into them, and teach them to hold hands tighter,' he replied. 'Once the Jews have solidarity . . .'

That doctor is an odd fellow. Honest he certainly is, and intelligent too: but his honesty doesn't come from feelings, but from – how shall I say it? – from habit, perhaps: and his sense is of such a kind that it's easier for him to mock and destroy a hundred things than build one. Sometimes it occurs to me, when I'm talking to him, that his soul is like a sheet of ice: it may reflect fire, but will never warm of its own accord.

Staś has left for Moscow, to settle his accounts with Suzin, I suspect. He has some half million roubles with him (who would have supposed anything like this two years ago?), but I cannot imagine what he will do with so much money.

But Staś always was eccentric, and went in for surprising people. Is he going to do it again? I am almost afraid he may . . .

Meanwhile Mraczewski has proposed to Mrs Stawska and, after a brief hesitation, she accepted. If they open a store in Warsaw as Mraczewski plans, I would go into the company and live with them. And, my goodness, I'd nurse Mraczewski's children, though I used to think I would only carry out such an office with Staś's children . . . Life is painfully hard.

Yesterday I gave five roubles for a mass for Prince Louis Napoleon. Only that, for perhaps he has not died, though everyone says so . . . If, on the other hand . . . I know nothing of theology, but it is always safer to make some good connections for him in the other world. For who knows? . . .

I really am poorly, although Szuman says everything is going well. He has forbidden me beer, coffee, wine, walking fast, getting vexed . . . All very well for him! I too could write out a prescription like that: but just you try and carry it out!

He talks to me as though he suspects I'm uneasy as to Staś's fate. Comical of him! Isn't Staś a grown man, and wasn't I once parted from him for seven years? The years passed, Staś came back, and got into trouble again.

This time it will be the same: just as he suddenly disappeared, so he will suddenly return. And yet it is difficult to live in this world. Sometimes I ask myself whether there's really any plan according to which all mankind is moving towards better things, or whether it isn't all the work of chance, and whether mankind isn't going in the direction in which a greater force is pushing? If good people are on top, the world moves towards better things, but if rascals are stronger, then it goes to the dogs. And the last limit of good and evil is a handful of dust.

If this is so, I am not surprised at Staś, who sometimes said he would like to perish as soon as possible and to destroy all traces behind him. But I have a premonition it isn't so.

Although . . . Didn't I have a premonition that Prince Louis Napoleon would become Emperor of France? Hm! Let us go on waiting, because that death of his in a battle with naked black-amoors, looks strange to me, somehow . . .

XXXVIII

. . . ? . . .

MR RZECKI really was sinking: in his view from want of something to do; in Szuman's from heart disease which had suddenly developed and was proceeding apace under the influence of some mortification or other.

He had little to do. In the mornings he strolled to Wokulski's former store, now Szlangbaum's, but he only stayed until the clerks began arriving, and especially the customers. For the latter, goodness knows why, eyed him with amazement, and the clerks who were now all Jews with the exception of Mr Zięba, not only refused to show him any respect, but even treated him with contempt.

This being so, Ignacy thought more and more often of Wokulski. Not because he feared any mishap would befall him, but just because he did. In the mornings around six, he wondered whether Wokulski was getting up or still asleep at this time of day, and where he was? In Moscow, or had he perhaps already left Moscow for Warsaw? In the afternoons, he recalled those times when there had been hardly a day when Staś didn't eat his dinner with him and then, in the evenings, especially on going to bed, he would say: 'Staś is certainly at Suzin's. I bet they are enjoying themselves! Or perhaps at this moment he's on the way back to Warsaw and going to bed in a sleeping car.'

But whenever he went into the store, and he did so several times a day, despite the animosity of the clerks and the irritating civility of Szlangbaum, he always thought that it had been different in Wokulski's day. It mortified him, though not very much, that Wokulski gave no sign of life. He regarded this as nothing more than his usual eccentricity: 'He never was much of a one for writing, even when he was well, so what about now that he is so low?' he thought. 'Ach, those women, those women . . .'

On the day when Szlangbaum acquired Wokulski's furniture and carriage, Ignacy took to his bed. Not because the incident pained him, for after all the carriage and excess furniture were entirely superfluous things, but because such commerce is done only after someone has died. 'But Staś, thank God, is well,' he told himself.

One evening, as Ignacy was sitting in his dressing gown and wondering how he would arrange Mraczewski's store so as to put Szlangbaum out of business, he heard a violent ringing at the front door and a peculiar racket in the passage. The servant, who was going to bed, opened the door.

'Is your master in?' asked a voice known to Rzecki.

'He's sick.'

'How so – sick? He's hiding from people . . .'

'Perhaps, Councillor, we're being a nuisance,' exclaimed another voice.

'Nuisance, indeed! If a person don't want a nuisance at home, why don't he come to the tavern?'

Rzecki rose from his chair and at the same moment Councillor Węgrowicz and the commercial traveller Szprott appeared at the bedroom door . . . Behind them rose a curly head and not particularly clean countenance. 'The mountain wouldn't come to the Mahomets, so the Mahomets have come to the mountain,' cried the councillor. 'Mr Rzecki! Ignacy! Whatever are you doing? Since we last saw you, we've discovered a new brand of beer . . . Put it here, there's a good fellow, and come back tomorrow,' he added, turning to the sooty-faced and curly-headed individual.

At this, the curly-headed man, who wore a great apron, deposited a basket of slender bottles and three tankards on the washstand. Then he disappeared, as if he were a being composed of air and mist, not a body of some 200 pounds.

Ignacy was startled to see the slender bottles, though this feeling was in no way disagreeable.

'What has been happening to you, for Heaven's sake?' the councillor began again, stretching out his arms as if to take the entire world into his embrace, 'it's been so long since you were with us that Szprott had forgotten what you looked like, and I thought you'd taken offence at your old friend with the bees in his bonnet.'

Rzecki grew sombre.

'So this very day,' the councillor pursued, 'when I won a basket of a new brand of beer from Deklewski in a bet on your friend, I say to Szprott here: 'You know what, my dear sir, let's take the beer and call on the old boy, and maybe he'll feel better.' . . . Come now, aren't you even going to ask us to take a chair?'

'Pray do,' Rzecki replied.

'And there's a table,' said the councillor, looking around, 'and the room, I see, is cosy. Aha! We'll be able to drop in on the patient for a game of cards or two every evening . . . Szprott, young fellow, find an opener, and get to work. Let the old boy taste this new brand.'

'What was the bet you won, Councillor?' Rzecki inquired, his countenance beginning to brighten.

'On Wokulski. This is how it was. Back in January last year, when Wokulski was adventuring in Bulgaria, I told Szprott that Stanisław was crazy, that he'd go bankrupt and come to a bad end. But today, just imagine, Deklewski declares that he was the one who said that. Of course we bet a basket of beer, Szprott decided in my favour, and here we are!'

During this, Mr Szprott was arranging three tankards on the table and uncorking three bottles. 'Now, just look, Ignacy,' said the councillor, raising a brimming tankard, 'the colour of old mead, froth like cream and it tastes like a sixteen-year-old girl. Try it . . . What taste and flavour! If you shut your eyes, you'd vow it was ale . . . Ah, you see! Before drinking beer like this, a man should rinse out his mouth. . . . Tell me, now – did you ever drink anything like it?'

Rzecki drank half a tankard. 'It's good,' he said. 'But – what put it in your head that Wokulski has gone bankrupt?'

'Everyone in town is saying it. After all, if a man has money, some sense in his head and doesn't owe anyone anything, he wouldn't run away God knows where.'

'Wokulski has gone to Moscow.'

'Come now! He told you that to cover his tracks. But he gave himself away as soon as he renounced his money.'

'What money?' asked Ignacy, already agitated.

'The money he has in the bank, and the investment with Szlangbaum. It comes to some two hundred thousand roubles . . . Who'd leave that sort of money behind without any instructions, just throw it in the mud? . . . He's either crazy . . . or has something worked out, and doesn't want to wait for the payment date . . . All over town, there's unanimous indignation about that . . . that . . . I won't call him by his proper name.'

'Councillor, you forget yourself!' Rzecki exclaimed.

'You, Mr Rzecki, are going out of your mind by concerning yourself with such a man,' the councillor replied crossly. 'Just consider. Where did he go to make his fortune? To the Crimean war! The Crimean war! Do you understand the significance of those words? He made a fortune there, but in what manner? How could a man make half a million roubles in six months?'

'He had a turnover of ten million roubles,' Rzecki answered, 'so he made even less than he might have done.'

'But whose millions were they?'

'Suzin's . . . A merchant's . . . His friend.'

'Just so! But never mind that: let us suppose that he didn't do anything underhand this time. But what sort of business was he up to in Paris and later in Moscow, when he also made a great deal of money? Was it right to kill our industry in order to pay eighteen per cent interest to a few aristocrats, in order to make his way into their society? And wasn't it fine of him to sell the whole company to the Jews, then finally to bolt for it, leaving behind hundreds of people in poverty or insecurity? Is that what a good citizen and honest man does? Well, drink up, Ignacy!' he cried, clinking his tankard with his own. 'To our bachelor friend . . . To Mr Szprott, who will show you what he can do . . . Don't give the game away to our patient.'

'Hey, there!' exclaimed Dr Szuman, who had been standing for several moments on the threshold, without taking his hat off. 'Hey, there! And who may you be, my fine fellows? Are you agents for an undertaker, that you treat my patient in this manner? Kazimierz!' he called to the servant. 'Take these bottles into the passage. And I must beg you gentlemen to bid goodbye to my patient. A hospital, even for one person, is not a tavern. Is this how you carry out my instructions?' he turned to Rzecki, 'with a heart ailment, you have a drinking spree! Why not invite some young ladies too? Goodnight to you, gentlemen,' he said to the councillor and Szprott, 'and next time, don't open a beer house here, or I'll charge you with murder.'

Messrs Węgrowicz, the councillor, and the commercial traveller Szprott took themselves off so fast that, had it not been for the dense smoke of their cigars, no one would have supposed there had been anyone in the room.

'Open the window,' the doctor said to the servant. 'Oh, come,' he added, looking ironically at Rzecki, 'your face is on fire, eyes glassy, your pulse beats so that one can hear it in the street.'

'Did you hear, sir, what he was saying about Staś?' Rzecki asked.

'He was right,' Szuman replied. 'The whole town is saying the same thing, though they are wrong to call Wokulski bankrupt, for he is merely a nincompoop of the type I call the Polish Romantics.'

Rzecki gazed at him, almost alarmed.

'Don't stare at me so,' Szuman went on, in a calm tone, 'you'd do better to decide whether I am right or not. After all, the man never acted rationally once in his life. When he was a clerk, he thought about inventions and the university. When he entered the university, he got involved in politics. Later on, instead of making money he became a scholar, and came back here so poor that if it hadn't been for Mrs Mincel, he'd have starved to death. Finally he began making a fortune, not as a tradesman, but as the admirer of a young woman who had the established reputation of a coquette. That wasn't all, for as soon as he had both the girl and the money in his hands, he threw them away, again, and today what is he doing, where is he? Tell me, sir, is he wise? He's a nincompoop, an out-and-out nincompoop,' said Szuman, gesticulating. 'A thoroughbred Polish Romantic, always searching for something outside reality.'

'Will you say this to Wokulski, doctor, when he comes back?' Rzecki asked.

'I've already told him a hundred times, and if I don't tell him again, it'll only be because he isn't coming back.'

'Not coming back?' whispered Rzecki, turning pale.

'He isn't coming back, for either he'll blow out his brains somewhere, if he comes to his senses, or he'll set himself some new Utopian goal . . . Perhaps the inventions of that mythical Geist, who must be an out-and-out lunatic.'

'But did you never chase after Utopias, doctor?'

'Yes, but I was poisoned by the atmosphere that the lot of you caused. I came to my senses in time, however, and that enabled me to make a very precise diagnosis of similar cases . . . Well, take off your dressing gown, sir, let's see the results of an evening spent in jovial company.'

He examined Rzecki, told him to go straight to bed and not to turn his apartment into a tavern in future. 'You're another example of a Romantic – except that you had less opportunity to commit follies,' the doctor concluded.

After which he departed, leaving Rzecki in a very depressed frame of mind. 'That chatter of his has done me more harm than the beer,' Rzecki thought, and a moment later he added in an undertone: 'Yet Staś might at least drop me a line . . . Goodness only knows the thoughts that find their way into a man's brain!'

Confined to bed, Ignacy was excruciatingly bored. So, to pass the time, he read the history of the Consulate for goodness knows how many times, or meditated on Wokulski.

But both these pastimes, instead of calming him, only irritated him . . . The book reminded him of the marvellous history of one of the greatest of all conquerors, in whose dynasty he had placed his faith in the world's future, and which dynasty had, in his eyes, fallen under the Zulu spear. The meditations on Wokulski, on the other hand, led him to the conclusion that his much-loved friend and unusual man was on the road to some kind of moral bankruptcy at least. 'He wanted to do so much, he might have done so much, yet he did nothing,' Ignacy would repeat, with grief in his heart. 'If only he would write where he is, at least, and what his plans are . . . If only he'd let me know he is still alive!'

For some time, vague yet foreboding premonitions had been troubling Mr Rzecki. His dream after Rossi's performance when he saw Wokulski leap after Izabela from the Town-hall tower came to his mind. Then, again he recalled Staś's strange and foreboding phrase: 'I should like to die alone, and destroy all traces of my existence!'

How easily a wish of that kind may be carried out by a man who says only what he feels, and knows how to carry out what he has said!

Dr Szuman, visiting him every day, did not add to his ease of mind at all, and almost bored him by repeating one and the same comment: 'Really, a man must be either a complete bankrupt or a lunatic to leave so much money behind in Warsaw, without giving any instructions and not even letting anyone know where he is!'

Rzecki either argued with him or privately admitted he was right.

One day the doctor called on him at an unusual time, to wit, ten o'clock in the morning. He threw his hat on the table and cried: 'Well, now – wasn't I right to say he's a nincompoop?'

'What has happened?' asked Ignacy, knowing in advance to whom he was referring.

'What has happened is that that madman left Moscow a week ago and . . . Guess his destination!'

'Paris?'

'Certainly not . . . He went to Odessa, and from there he plans to go to India, from India to China and Japan, then across the Pacific to America! I can understand him taking a journey around the world, I'd have recommended it myself. But not to write a single word, leaving people who like him and some two hundred thousand roubles behind in Warsaw. To do that, my goodness, a man must have a highly developed psychosis.'

'Whence this news?' asked Rzecki.

'From the best of all sources – Szlangbaum, to whom it is very important that he should find out Wokulski's plans. After all, he has to pay him a hundred and twenty thousand roubles early in October . . . If dear Staś shoots or drowns himself, or dies of yellow fever . . . D'you see, sir? Then we may go to the Devil for the whole sum, or at least use it for six months interest-free. Surely you know Szlangbaum by this time? It was he, after all, who wanted to cheat . . . me, of all people!'

The doctor hurried about the room and gesticulated as though he himself were touched by the initial stages of a psychosis. Suddenly he stopped in front of Ignacy, gazed into his eyes and seized him by the hand: 'What's this? Your pulse is over a hundred. Did you have a temperature today?'

'Not yet.'

'Not yet, indeed! I can see . . .'

'Less of this,' Rzecki interrupted. 'Can it be that Staś has done anything like that?'

'That old Staś of ours, despite his romanticism, perhaps wouldn't have, but this Mr Wokulski, in love with her ladyship Miss Łęcka, might do anything. As you see, he's doing his best . . .'

After this visit from the doctor, Ignacy began to admit to himself that he was poorly. 'It would be absurd,' he thought, 'if I were to kick the bucket now . . . Pooh! It's happened to better men than me. Napoleon the First . . . Napoleon the Third . . . little Lulu . . . Staś. But – why Staś? After all, he's travelling to India.'

He pondered, rose from bed, dressed properly and went to the store, much to the dismay of Szlangbaum, who knew Ignacy had been forbidden to get out of bed. On this account, Ignacy felt much worse next day: so he stayed in bed twenty-four hours, and went to the store again for a few hours.

'Does he think that the store is a morgue, then?' said one of the Jewish clerks to Mr Zięba who, with characteristic sincerity, admitted that the witticism was very good.

In the middle of September, Ochocki came to Warsaw from Zasławek for a few days and visited Rzecki. At the sight of him, Ignacy regained his good spirits. 'What brings you here?' he cried, warmly embracing the beloved inventor.

But Ochocki was sombre. 'What but bad news?' he replied. 'Did you know, sir, that Mr Łęcki is dead?'

'The father of that . . . that . . .' said Ignacy, in surprise.

'None other. And who knows but it wasn't on account of her . . .'

'For Heaven's sake!' Rzecki crossed himself. 'How many men does that woman mean to destroy? To my own knowledge, and I am sure it is no secret to you either, if Staś fell upon bad times, it was entirely due to her.'

Ochocki nodded.

'Can you tell me what happened to Mr Łęcki?' asked Ignacy, curiously.

'It's no secret,' replied Ochocki, 'Early this summer the marshal proposed to Izabela.'

'Him? He's old enough to be my father,' Rzecki interposed.

'Perhaps that's why the young lady accepted him, or at least didn't refuse. So the old man collected the belongings left by his two former wives, and went into the country to stay with the Countess . . . Izabela's aunt, where she was staying with her father.'

'He must have been crazy.'

'It has happened to wiser men than he,' Ochocki went on. 'Meanwhile, though the marshal considered himself her suitor, Izabela used to go every few days – and later every day – to the ruins of the old castle at Zasław, with a certain engineer . . . She said it helped relieve her ennui.'

'And the marshal didn't react?'

'He kept silent, naturally, but the women persuaded the young lady it wasn't proper to behave in that manner. She had but one reply on such occasions: "The marshal ought to be glad I'm marrying him, but I am not getting married in order to renounce my own pleasures."'

'And I daresay the marshal caught them unawares in those ruins,' Rzecki interrupted.

'Oh no . . . He didn't even go there. Even if he had, he'd have been persuaded that Izabela was taking the naive engineer along in order to brood over Wokulski.

'That, at least, is what was supposed,' said Ochocki. 'I remarked to her myself that it wasn't proper to yearn for one admirer in the company of another. But she replied in her own way: "He should be glad I permit him to look at me."'

'That engineer must have been a proper donkey!'

'Not entirely, since for all his naivety, he too noticed what was going on, and stopped going with the young lady to brood in the ruins. At the same time, however, the marshal – jealous of the engineer – left for Lithuania in such a huff that Izabela and the Countess had hysterics and good old Łęcki, without even a word of reproach, died of apoplexy.'

On finishing his tale, Ochocki clutched his head with both hands and laughed aloud. 'And to think,' he added, 'that a woman of this kind turned the heads of so many men!'

'She is a monster!' Rzecki exclaimed.

'No. She's not even stupid or bad either, basically . . . She's only a woman like thousands of others in her world.'

'Thousands?'

'Alas, yes,' Ochocki sighed. 'Imagine, sir, a class of wealthy people who eat well and do very little. A man must use up his energies in some way: if he doesn't work, he must turn to depravity, or at least excite his nervous system . . . And for depravity and excitement he needs pretty, elegant, witty women, well-bred or rather trained in that particular direction . . . That is the only career open to them.'

'And Izabela joined their ranks?'

'They enlisted her, rather. I am sorry to say this, but I must tell you, sir, so that you may know what sort of woman Wokulski came into contact with.'

The conversation broke off – Ochocki started it again by asking: 'When is he coming back?'

'Wokulski?' replied Ignacy. 'He has left for India, China, America.'

Ochocki threw himself into a chair. 'That's impossible!' he exclaimed, then added, after thinking, 'And yet . . .'

'Have you some evidence that he hasn't gone there?' Rzecki asked in a lower voice.

'None at all. I was only surprised by his sudden decision. When I was here last time, he promised to settle a certain matter for me. But . . .'

'The former Wokulski would certainly have settled it. However, the new one has forgotten not only your business . . . But his own too.'

'I expected him to leave,' said Ochocki, as though to himself, 'but I don't like this suddenness. Has he written to you?'

'Not a word to anyone,' the old clerk replied.

Ochocki shook his head. 'It had to happen,' he muttered.

'Why did it have to happen?' Rzecki burst forth. 'Is he a bankrupt, then, or unemployed? A store like his, a company, are they nothing? Couldn't he have married a pretty, fine woman?'

'Other such women are still to be found,' Ochocki interposed, 'and they would do very well,' he said, in a more lively way, 'though not for a man with his disposition.'

'What do you mean by that?' Rzecki asked, to whom a conversation about Wokulski caused as much pleasure as though it had been about his mistress, 'what do you mean by that? Did you get to know him well?' he asked, insistently, and his eyes sparkled.

'It was easy to know him. He was, in a word, a man of wide soul.'

'Just so!' cried Rzecki, waving his hand and gazing at Ochocki with admiration. 'But what did you mean by "wide soul"? Well said! Explain yourself, though – and clearly!'

Ochocki smiled. 'You see, sir,' he said, 'people with small souls are only concerned with their own matters, they don't think beyond the present day, and they have a horror of unknown things. Providing they are at ease and well-fed . . . But a fellow like Wokulski concerns himself with the interests of thousands, sometimes he looks decades ahead, and any unknown or unresolved thing attracts him irresistibly. It isn't social benefaction, but a force. Just as iron moves to a magnet, or a bee adheres to its hive without thinking, so this kind of man is drawn to all ideas and unusual work.'

Rzecki pressed both his hands and trembled with emotion. 'Szuman . . .' he said, 'the wise doctor Szuman declares Wokulski is a nincompoop, a Polish Romantic.'

'Szuman's a fool, with that Jewish classicism of his!' Ochocki replied. 'He doesn't even suspect that civilisation wasn't created by Philistines or by businessmen, but by just such nincompoops . . . If sense was a matter of thinking about income, people would still be apes.'

'Blessed words . . . Beautiful words!' the old clerk repeated. 'But pray explain, sir, in what way a man like Wokulski might . . . so to speak . . . get involved in trouble?'

'Frankly, I am surprised it came so late, sir,' replied Ochocki, with a shrug. 'After all, I know his life and I know that this man has almost stifled here, ever since his childhood. He had scientific aspirations, but there was no way to satisfy them; he had wide social instincts, but no matter what he touched in that field, all fell through . . . Even that wretched little company he founded brought nothing but complaints and hatred down on his head.'

'You are right, sir . . . You are right,' Rzecki repeated. 'And then that Izabela . . .'

'Well, she might have satisfied him. With personal happiness, he would have come to terms with his environment more easily, and used up his energies in a way which is possible here. But he made a bad choice.'

'And what now?'

'How should I know?' Ochocki murmured. 'Today, he is like an uprooted tree. If he finds suitable soil, and he may do so in Europe, and if he still has the energy – then he will set to some kind of work, and who knows but what he won't really begin living? But if he is worn out, which is also possible at his age . . .'

Rzecki put a finger to his lips. 'Hush . . . Hush!' he interrupted. 'Staś has the energy, that he has! He will still go on . . . on . . .'

He came away from the window and, leaning against the doorpost, began sobbing. 'I'm so poorly . . .' he said, 'so upset . . . Apparently I have heart disease . . . But it'll pass, it'll pass. Only – why did he run away like this? Hide himself ? Not write?'

'Oh, I can understand so well,' Ochocki exclaimed, 'that horror a broken man feels for things which remind him of the past. How well I know it, even from my own little experience. Imagine, sir, that when I took my matriculation at the high school, I had to get through the seventh grade Latin and Greek courses in five weeks, for I'd never wanted to study them. Somehow I got through the exam, but I worked so hard beforehand that I overdid things. From then on, I've never been able to look at Latin or Greek, or even think about them. I can't bear to look at the school building, I avoided the friends who studied with me, I even had to leave the apartment where I'd studied night and day. That lasted a few months, and I really didn't get over it until . . . Do you know what I did? I threw all the Greek and Latin textbooks into the fire, and burned the horrible things. They smouldered an hour, then I had the ashes thrown into the garbage can, and recovered! Although even to this day, I get palpitations at the sight of Greek letters or Latin irregulars . . . *panis, piscis, crinis* . . . Ugh, how loathsome! So don't be surprised,' Ochocki concluded, 'if Wokulski has gone away to China. Long torment may drive a man out of his senses . . . Though even that passes . . .'

'But at the age of forty-six, sir?' Rzecki inquired.

'With his strong organism? His powerful brain? Well, I've talked too much . . . Goodbye to you, sir.'

'What, are you leaving?'

'Yes, for St Petersburg,' Ochocki replied. 'I have to look after the will of the late Duchess, which her grateful family want to have annulled. I shall probably stay there till the end of October.'

'As soon as I have news from Staś, I'll let you know. Just send me your address.'

'I'll inform you as soon as I hear something. Although I doubt . . . Goodbye!'

'Come back soon!'

The conversation with Ochocki revived Ignacy. The old clerk seemed to have regained strength by talking to a man who not only understood his beloved Staś, but also recalled him in many respects. 'He was just the very same,' Rzecki thought. 'Energetic, sober and yet always full of high impulses.'

We may say that the convalescence of Ignacy began on this day. He left his bed, changed his robe for a frock-coat, spent more time in the store and even went out frequently into the streets. Szuman was delighted with the success of his cure, thanks to which the development of heart disease had been halted. 'What the future holds,' he said to Szlangbaum, 'no one knows. But it's a fact that the old man has been better for several days. He's regained his appetite, and above all, his apathy has gone. I had the same experience with Wokulski.'

But in truth, Rzecki was encouraged by the hope that sooner or later, he'd have a letter from his Staś. 'Perhaps he's in India by this time,' he thought, 'so by the end of September I ought to have news . . . Well, it's easy for such things to be delayed: I bet anything that in October. . .'

As a matter of fact, news of Wokulski arrived at the appointed time, though very strangely. Szuman called on Ignacy one evening at the end of September, and said with a smile: 'Just look, sir, how that nincompoop interests people. A tenant in Zasławek told Szlangbaum that the late Duchess's carter saw Wokulski not long ago in the Zasławek forest. He even described how he was dressed, and what sort of horse he was riding.'

'It could well be!' exclaimed Ignacy, in relief.

'Nonsense! The Crimea, indeed, and Rome, and India – and Zasławek?' the doctor retorted. 'Better still, another Jew who deals in coal saw Wokulski in Dąbrowa, at almost the same time. What's more, he claims to have found out that this very same Wokulski bought two loads of dynamite from a coal-miner who drinks too much . . . Well, surely you won't try to defend him against such stupid behaviour?'

'Whatever can this mean?'

'Nothing. Evidently Szlangbaum has offered a reward to the Jews for information about Wokulski, so now each one of them will catch sight of Wokulski, even if he's down a mousehole. The holy rouble has created sharp eyes,' the doctor concluded with an ironic smile.

Rzecki had to admit that the rumours were meaningless, and that Szuman's explanation was entirely natural. Yet his uneasiness for Wokulski intensified.

This uneasiness changed into genuine alarm in the face of a fact which brooked no doubt. On October 1st, one of the lawyers summoned Ignacy to his office, and showed him a document Wokulski had signed before leaving for Moscow. This was a formal will and testament, in which Wokulski bequeathed the money remaining in Warsaw, seventy thousand roubles of which was in the bank, and a hundred and twenty thousand with Szlangbaum.

To strangers, these arrangements were proof of Wokulski's irresponsibility: to Rzecki, however, they seemed perfectly reasonable. The lawyer stated: the huge sum of a hundred and forty thousand went to Ochocki, twenty-five thousand to Rzecki, twenty thousand to Helena Stawska. The remaining five thousand were divided between his former servants and the poor people he had contact with. Of this sum, five hundred went to Węgiełek the joiner at Zasław, Wysocki the Warsaw carter, and the other Wysocki, his brother, the railwayman at Skierniewice.

Wokulski had asked the lawyer, in an emotional manner, that they should accept the bequests as coming from a dead man, and told him not to publish the will before October 1st.

Among the people who knew Wokulski, a quantity of talk arose, rumours flew around, insinuations, personal insults . . . In a conversation with Rzecki, Szuman expressed this view: 'I knew of your bequest long ago . . . He gave Ochocki almost a million zloty because he discovered in him a lunatic of the same species as himself . . . And I understand the gift for pretty Mrs Stawska's little daughter,' he added, with a smile, 'but one thing alone intrigues me.'

'What's that?' asked Rzecki, biting his moustaches.

'How does that railroad man Wysocki come to be among the beneficiaries?'

He made a note of the name and left, thoughtfully.

Great was Rzecki's uneasiness at what might have have happened to Wokulski, why he should have made a will, and why he spoke in it like a man thinking of imminent death? Then, however, incidents occurred which brought a gleam of hope to Rzecki, and which explained Wokulski's strange behaviour to a certain extent. In the first instance Ochocki, informed of the bequest, at once replied from St Petersburg that he accepted, and wanted to have all the cash at the beginning of November, and he also reserved the right to the interest payable on it for the month of October by Szlangbaum.

In addition, he wrote to Rzecki inquiring whether Ignacy wouldn't let him have twenty-one thousand roubles in cash, out of his own capital of twenty-five thousand, in exchange for the sum payable on Midsummer day which Ochocki had on the mortgage of his country estate. 'It is very important to me,' he concluded, 'to have everything I possess in my hands, as I absolutely must go abroad in November. I will explain why when we meet . . .'

'Why is he going abroad all of a sudden, and why is he taking all his money with him?' Rzecki asked himself, 'and why, in the end, does he postpone explaining until we meet?'

Of course he agreed to Ochocki's offer. It seemed to him that some comfort was rooted in this sudden departure and unspoken things. 'Who knows,' he thought, 'whether Staś didn't take his half million roubles to India with him? Perhaps Ochocki and he will meet in Paris, at this strange Geist's? Some kind of metal . . . some balloon or other! Evidently he is concerned to keep the secret, at least until . . .'

On this occasion, however, Szuman wrecked his hopes by saying: 'I've been having inquiries made in Paris about this famous Geist, thinking Wokulski may run foul of him. Well, Geist, who was once a very capable chemist, is today an out-and-out lunatic . . . The entire Academy laughs at his notions . . .'

The entire Academy's derision of Geist shook Rzecki's hopes very much. Surely the French Academy could evaluate those metals or balloons, if anyone could . . . But if the wise men had decided Geist was a lunatic, then surely Wokulski wouldn't have anything to do with him.

'So where and why has he gone away?' Rzecki thought. 'Well, obviously he's gone travelling, because he didn't like it here any more . . . If Ochocki had to quit his apartment for no better reason than Greek grammar, then there's all the more reason for Wokulski to quit a town where one woman tormented him . . . And she wasn't the only one! Was ever a man more slandered than he? But – why did he make a will and refer in it to death?' Ignacy added.

This question was clarified by a visit from Mraczewski. The young man came to Warsaw unexpectedly, and called on Rzecki with an embarrassed expression. He spoke brokenly, but in the end mentioned that Mrs Stawska was hesitant to accept Wokulski's bequest, and that he himself thought it worrying . . .

'You're a booby, my dear young man,' Ignacy was indignant. 'Wokulski bequeathed the twenty thousand to her, or to little Helena, because he liked her: and he liked her because he found

peace in her home during his most difficult times. Surely you know
he was in love with Izabela?'

'I know that,' replied Mraczewski, somewhat more calmly. 'But
I also know Mrs Stawska had a weakness for Wokulski . . .'

'What of it? Today Wokulski is very nearly dead to all of us, and
God knows when we shall see him again.'

Mraczewski's face brightened. 'That's true,' he said, 'that's true!
Mrs Stawska may accept a bequest from a dead man, I don't need
to fear mention of him . . .'

And he left, very pleased to think that perhaps Wokulski was
dead.

'Staś was right,' thought Ignacy, 'to word his bequests so. He
lessened the embarrassment of the beneficiaries, and above all that
of honest Mrs Stawska.'

Rzecki called at the store only once every few days, and his only
pursuit (unpaid, by the way) was that of arranging displays in the
windows, which he usually did on Saturday nights. The old clerk
loved arranging these displays, and Szlangbaum had himself asked
him to do them, in the hope that Ignacy would invest his capital in
the store at a low interest rate.

But even these rare visits sufficed for Ignacy to realise that fundamental changes for the worse had occurred in the store. The
merchandise, though showy, was of poor quality although the
prices were lower too; the clerks treated their customers in a
haughty manner and committed small frauds which did not escape
Mr Rzecki's notice. Finally, two cashiers committed a fraud of over
a hundred roubles. When Ignacy mentioned this to Szlangbaum, he
heard in reply: 'My dear sir, the public don't know nothin' about
good merchandise, as long as it is cheap . . . As for the frauds, they
happen everywhere. Besides, vere vill I get other clerks?'

Although he put a bold face on it, Szlangbaum was mortified all
the same, and Szuman mocked him mercilessly. 'It's true, Mr
Szlangbaum, that if there were no one but Jews in this country, we
should all go a-begging!' said the doctor. 'Some would bamboozle
us, and others wouldn't let themselves be caught by our tricks!'

Having a great deal of time on his hands, Ignacy pondered
much, and he wondered why he was bothered nowadays by
questions which had never formerly entered his head. 'Why has
our store declined?' he asked himself. 'Because Szlangbaum runs it,
not Wokulski. And why isn't Wokulski running it? Because,
Ochocki said, Staś was stifled here ever since childhood, and
finally even had to run away in order to get some fresh air.' And
he recalled the most significant moments of Wokulski's life.
When, still a shop assistant at Hopfer's, he wanted to study,
everyone teased him. When he entered the university, sacrifices
were demanded of him. When he returned to the country, even

work was denied him. When he made a fortune he was showered with suspicion, and when he fell in love, the woman he worshipped betrayed him in the most despicable way . . .

'One has to admit,' said Ignacy, 'that in such conditions, he made the best he could of everything . . .'

But if the power of facts had driven Wokulski from the country, why hadn't he, Rzecki, inherited the store, rather than Szlangbaum? Because he, Rzecki, had never thought of owning his own store. He had fought for the Hungarians or had waited for the Napoleons to rebuild the world. And what had happened? The world had got no better, the Napoleon dynasty had perished, and Szlangbaum became the store's owner. 'Terrible to think how many honest men are wasted here,' he thought. 'Katz shot himself, Wokulski is abroad, God knows where Klein is, and Lisiecki also went away because there was no room for him . . .'

In the face of these meditations, Igancy experienced pangs of conscience, under the influence of which a sort of plan for the future began to make itself apparent. 'I'll enter into business,' he said, 'with Mrs Stawska and Mraczewski. They have twenty thousand roubles, I have twenty-five thousand, and for that amount we could open a respectable store, even if it stood alongside Szlangbaum's.'

This plan so dominated him that it made him feel better in health. Admittedly, he kept having pains in the shoulders more often, and shortness of breath, but he paid no attention . . . 'I'll go abroad for a cure,' he thought, 'I'll get rid of this silly shortness of breath and set to work properly . . . After all, is Szlangbaum the only one to make a fortune here?'

He felt younger and more vital, although Szuman advised him not to go out, and recommended him to avoid excitement. But the doctor often forgot his own prescriptions. Once he called on Rzecki early in the morning, so indignant that he had forgotten to put his tie on. 'Do you know, sir,' he cried, 'I have found out some fine things about Wokulski . . .'

Ignacy put down his knife and fork (he was just eating a steak with mushrooms), and felt a pain in his shoulder. 'What's happened?' he asked, in a feeble voice.

'Staś is capital!' said Szuman. 'I've unearthed that railwayman Wysocki, from Skierniewice. I interrogated him and do you know what I've found out?'

'How should I know?' asked Rzecki, feeling dizzy for a moment.

'Just think of it, sir!' said Szuman, irritated, 'that creature . . . that fool . . . When he was travelling with the Łęckis to Cracow last May, he threw himself under a train at Skierniewice. Wysocki saved him . . .'

'Hm . . .' Rzecki muttered.

'No "hm" about it, that's what happened. From this I deduce that our dear Staś had suicidal mania as well as his romanticism. I'd bet my entire fortune on it that he's dead.'

Suddenly he stopped, catching sight of a terrible change on Ignacy's face. He became very confused, almost lifted him into bed and vowed he would never again bring up the matter.

But fate had it otherwise. At the end of October, the postman gave Rzecki a letter addressed to Wokulski. The letter came from Zasław, the writing was illiterate. 'Can it be from Węgiełek?' wondered Ignacy, and he opened it.

'Dear Sir,' wrote Węgiełek, 'First we thank you, Sir, for remembering us and for the five hundred roubles and all the benefits we received from your generous hands, my mother, my wife and me thank you. In the second place, all three of us inquire as to your health, and whether you got home safe. Certainly you did, else you would not have sent that wonderful gift. Only my wife is very worried about you, at night she don't sleep, and she even wanted me to go to Warsaw, just like a woman. For here, Sir, in September, on the very same day as you met my mother in the potato field as you were going to the Castle, a terrible thing happened. My mother had just come back from the field, and was cooking supper, when there were two terrible bangs in the Castle, like thunderbolts, and the window-panes rattled all over the village. My mother dropped a jug and told me right away. "Hurry over to the Castle, maybe Mr Wokulski is still there, let's hope nothing has happened to him," and so I go. Good God! I barely recognised the hill. Out of the four walls of the Castle, only one was still standing, the other three was smashed into atoms. The stone we wrote verses on last year was broken into at least twenty pieces, and on the spot where the fallen-in well had been, there was a hole, and the rubble had piled up as high as a barn over it. I think the walls collapsed out of old age, but my mother says maybe the late blacksmith I once told you of had done the damage.'

'Without telling anyone that you had gone into the Castle just then, I dug for a week in the rubble to see whether – God forbid! – any accident had happened. Only when I found no trace did I place a holy cross on the spot, made of oak not painted, so there should be a memorial that you had been spared. But my wife, just like a woman, is still worried. So I humbly beg you, Sir, to let us know you are alive and well.'

'The priest advised me to inscribe this on the cross:

non omnis moriar

so people may know that although the old Castle, an ancient monument, fell into ruins, yet not all has perished and still a great deal remains for our grandchildren to see . . .'

'So Wokulski was in this country!' cried Rzecki, comforted, and he sent for the doctor, asking him to come over at once. Within fifteen minutes Szuman appeared. He read the letter twice, and gazed in astonishment at the enlivened features of Rzecki. 'What have you to say to that?' asked Rzecki, triumphantly.

Szuman was still more astonished. 'What have I to say?' he repeated. 'Why, what I predicted to Wokulski, even before his departure for Bulgaria, has come to pass. It's clear, after all, that Staś killed himself in Zasław.'

Rzecki laughed aloud.

'But pray consider, Ignacy,' said the doctor, controlling his emotion with difficulty, 'just think: he was seen in Dąbrowa, buying dynamite, then he was seen in the vicinity of Zasławek, then in Zasław itself. I think something must have happened between him and that . . . that accursed woman, in the Castle. For he once mentioned to me that he'd like to sink into the earth as deeply as the Zasław well.'

'If he'd wanted to kill himself, he could have done so long ago. Besides, a revolver would have sufficed, not dynamite,' Rzecki answered.

'He has killed himself . . . But he was a crazy fool in all respects, and a revolver wasn't enough. He needed a railroad train . . . Suicides can be choosy, I know that!'

Rzecki shook his head and laughed again.

'What the devil do you think, then?' asked the impatient Szuman. 'Do you have some other hypothesis?'

'I do. Staś was quite simply tortured by the Castle and its associations, so he wanted to destroy it just as Ochocki destroyed his Greek grammar after overworking. It is also a reply to the young woman, who apparently used to go into the ruins to mope . . .'

'That would be childish! A man of forty-six doesn't behave like a schoolboy.'

'It's a matter of temperament,' Rzecki replied coolly. 'Some men send back keepsakes, he blew his into smithereens. Though it's a pity his Dulcinea wasn't among the rubble.'

The doctor reflected: 'A crazy fool! And where can he be, if he's still alive?'

'At this moment he is travelling light-heartedly. And he doesn't write, because obviously he is sick of the lot of us,' concluded Ignacy, more quietly. 'Besides, if he'd perished, some traces would have remained.'

'Well, I won't swear that you may not be right, although I don't believe it,' Szuman muttered. He shook his head sadly and said: 'Romantics must die out, that's clear: today's world isn't for them. Common sense means we don't believe either in the angelic nature of women, nor in the possibility of ideals. Anyone who doesn't see this must perish or give way of his own accord. But what style he had!' he concluded. 'He died under the ruins of feudalism! He perished so that the very earth shook . . . An interesting type, very!'

Suddenly he seized his hat and hurried from the room, muttering: 'Lunatics! Lunatics! They might infect the whole world with their madness . . .'

Rzecki was still smiling. 'Confound it all,' he told himself, 'if I'm not right about Staś! He bade the young lady adieu, and left . . . That's the whole secret. Once Ochocki comes back, we'll learn the truth.'

He was in such good humour that he got his guitar out from under the bed and began humming to its accompaniment: 'Spring awakens. . . . The wistful song of nightingales . . . In a green thicket . . . Two beautiful roses . . .'

A sharp pain in his chest reminded him he ought not to tire himself. Yet he felt tremendous energy within. 'Staś has set to some great work,' he thought, 'Ochocki is going to join him, so I too must show what I can do . . . Away with dreams . . . The Napoleons aren't going to set the world to rights, nor will anyone, if we go on behaving like lunatics. I'll go into business with Mraczewski, I'll bring in Lisiecki, I'll find Klein and we'll see, Mr Szlangbaum, whether you are the only one with sense! Confound it, what is easier than making money, if one has a mind to? And with such capital and such men, too!'

On Saturday, after the clerks had gone home in the evening, Ignacy took the key to the back door of the shop from Szlangbaum so as to arrange the display in the windows for the coming week. He lit one lamp, and helped by Kazimierz, took a jardinière and two Saxon vases out of the main window, replacing them by Japanese vases and an old Roman-style table. Then he told the servant to go to bed, for he was in the habit of arranging the smaller articles, especially the mechanical toys, by himself. Besides, he didn't want the simple man to know that he played with the store toys.

As always, he brought them all out, filled the entire counter with them, and wound them all up. For the thousandth time in his life he listened to the tunes of the musical snuff-boxes, watched the bear scramble up and down its pole, watched the glass water turning the mill-wheels, the cat running after the mouse, the peasants dancing and the jockey riding his horse. And, as he watched the movements of the inanimate objects, he repeated for the thousandth time: 'Puppets! . . . All puppets! They think they are doing as they choose, but they only do what the springs command, blind as they are!'

When the jockey fell over on the dancing couples, Mr Ignacy mourned. 'No one can help others be happy,' he thought, 'but they can ruin other lives just as well as people.'

Suddenly he heard a noise. He looked into the depths of the store and caught sight of a human form emerging from under a counter. 'A thief?' flashed through his mind.

'Excuse me, Mr Rzecki . . . I was just passing,' exclaimed an individual with olive face and black hair. He ran to the door, opened it hastily and disappeared.

Mr Rzecki couldn't get up: his hands were powerless, his legs refused to obey him. Only his heart was sounding within him like a cracked bell, and a darkness came before his eyes. 'What in the world am I so scared of?' he murmured, 'that was only Isidor Gutmorgen . . . a clerk here. Obviously he stole something and ran away . . . But why am I so scared?'

Meanwhile Mr Isidor Gutmorgen, after an absence of some time, came back into the store, which astonished Mr Rzecki greatly. 'What are you doing here? What do you want?' Ignacy asked him.

Mr Gutmorgen seemed very embarrassed. He lowered his head like a guilty party and rubbing one finger along the counter said: 'Excuse me, Mr Rzecki, maybe you think I was stealing? Pray search me . . .'

'But what are you doing here?' asked Rzecki. He wanted to rise from the chair, but could not.

'Mr Szlangbaum told me to spend the night here . . .'

'What for?'

'Well, sir, Mr Rzecki, you see . . . That Kazimierz comes with you, to arrange things . . . So Mr Szlangbaum told me to watch lest he takes anything . . . But because I felt poorly, so . . . I apologise, sir.'

Rzecki had already risen from his seat. 'Ah, you scoundrels!' he exclaimed in a paroxysm of fury, 'so you all regard me as a thief! Because I work for you without pay!'

'Excuse me, Mr Rzecki, sir,' put in Gutmorgen, humbly, 'but why do you work without pay?'

'May a million devils take you all!' cried Ignacy. He hurried out of the store and carefully locked the door behind him. 'Stay there until morning, serve you right for being poorly . . . You can leave your boss a souvenir,' he muttered.

Ignacy couldn't sleep all night. And as his apartment was only divided from the store by a partition, he heard a quiet knocking inside the store about two in the morning, and the stifled voice of Gutmorgen:

'Mr Rzecki, pray open the door, sir . . . I'll be back right away.'

Soon, however, all fell silent. 'Oh, you blockheads,' thought Rzecki, turning and tossing in his bed, 'so you treat me as a thief . . . Just you wait!'

Towards nine in the morning he heard Szlangbaum liberate

Gutmorgen, and then start knocking on his door. However, he did not reply, and when Kazimierz arrived, Rzecki told him never to let Szlangbaum in. 'I'm moving out of here,' he said, 'at New Year, very likely. Even if I have to live in an attic or rent a hotel room . . . They made me out a thief . . . Staś entrusted thousands of roubles to me, and that scoundrel fears for his shoddy merchandise . . .'

By noon he had written two letters: one to Mrs Stawska, suggesting she move to Warsaw and enter business with him; the second to Lisiecki, inquiring whether he wouldn't like to come back and accept a position in the new store. As he wrote and reread the letters a malicious smile never left his face. 'I can imagine Szlangbaum's expression,' he thought, 'when we open a store in competition right under his very nose . . . He he he! He gave them orders to watch me! Serve me right for letting that trickster gain power over me . . . He he he!'

At this moment he knocked the pen with his sleeve and it fell to the floor. Rzecki leaned over to pick it up, and suddenly felt a strange pain in his chest, as if someone had pierced his lungs with a thin knife. For a moment everything went dark and he felt slightly faint: so, without picking up the pen, he rose from the chair and lay down on the *chaise-longue*. 'Szlangbaum will be bankrupt within a few years, or I'm a booby,' he thought, 'I'm an old fool . . . I bothered my head with the Bonapartes and the rest of Europe, and meanwhile an old-clothesman grew up under my nose, who told them to watch me as a thief . . . Well, at least I've gained experience: enough for a lifetime . . . Now you can all stop calling me a romantic and a dreamer.'

Something obstructed his left lung. 'Asthma?' he muttered. 'I must cure myself properly . . . Otherwise I'll be a complete invalid in five or six years . . . Ah, if only I'd paid attention ten years ago . . .'

He closed his eyes, and it seemed to him he could see his whole life, from the present moment back to his childhood, unfolded like a panorama along which he was moving with a curiously tranquil motion . . . He was merely struck by the fact that each picture, as it passed, was obliterated in his mind so irrevocably that he could not possibly recall what he had been looking at a moment earlier. Here was the dinner in the Hotel Europe, on the occasion of opening the new store . . . Here the old store and Miss Łęcka talking in it to Mraczewski . . . Here was his room with the barred window, into which Wokulski had just that moment entered on his return from Bulgaria . . .

'Just a moment . . . What did I see before that?' he thought.

It was Hopfer's wine-cellar, where he had met Wokulski. And here was the battlefield, where bluish smoke was rising above lines of blue and white uniforms . . . And here was old Mincel in his armchair, pulling the strings of the Cossack in the window . . .

'Did I really see all this, or was it only a dream? Merciful God . . .' he whispered.

Now it seemed to him he was a little boy and that, while his father was talking about the Emperor Napoleon to Mr Raczek, he himself had climbed into the attic and was looking through the window at the Vistula river, over towards Praga. But gradually the image of the city faded before his eyes, and there remained only the window. First it was as large as a plate, then the size of a saucer, then it diminished to the size of a silver coin . . .

At the same time he was seized on all sides by oblivion and darkness, or rather by a profound blackness, in which only that window gleamed, like a star of ever-diminishing brightness.

Finally that last star went out, too.

Perhaps he saw it again, but never on earth.

Towards two that afternoon Ignacy's servant Kazimierz came in with a basket and plates. He laid the table noisily, and seeing that his master did not wake up, cried: 'Please, sir, your dinner will get cold . . .'

As Ignacy still didn't stir, Kazimierz approached the *chaise-longue* and said: 'If you please, sir . . .'

Suddenly he drew back, ran into the passage and began knocking on the back door of the shop, in which there was Szlangbaum and one of his clerks. Szlangbaum opened the door. 'What is it?' he asked the servant brusquely.

'If you please, sir . . . Something has happened to my master . . .'

Szlangbaum came into the apartment cautiously, looked at the *chaise-longue* and retreated: 'Run for Dr Szuman,' he exclaimed, 'I don't want to go in there . . .'

At this moment, Ochocki was with the doctor, telling him he had returned from St Petersburg that morning and that he was taking his cousin, Izabela Łęcka, to catch the Vienna express that evening, as she was going abroad. 'Just think of it,' he concluded, 'she is going into a convent.'

'Izabela?' Szuman inquired. 'Come, does she intend to flirt with the Almighty Himself, or merely to relax after all this excitement, so as to get married with a firmer step?'

'Less of that . . . She's a strange woman,' Ochocki murmured.

'They all seem strange to us,' the doctor replied in an irritable voice, 'until we find out they are only stupid or wretched . . . Have you heard anything of Wokulski?'

'As a matter of fact . . .' he began. Then he suddenly stopped and said no more.

'Do you know anything of him? Or are you going to make a state secret of it?' the doctor persisted.

At this moment Kazimierz rushed in, exclaiming: 'Doctor,

something has happened to my master. Quickly, sir!'

Szuman jumped up, Ochocki with him. They hailed a droshky and hurried to the house in which Rzecki lived. Maruszewicz, wearing a very worried look, stopped them in the gateway. 'Well, just imagine this,' he cried to the doctor, 'I had important business to discuss with him . . . It is a question of my honour . . . And now he's gone and died!'

The doctor and Ochocki, followed by Maruszewicz, went into Rzecki's apartment. In the first room they found Szlangbaum, Councillor Węgrowicz and the commercial traveller Szprott.

'If he'd drunk light beer,' said Węgrowicz, 'he'd have lived to be a hundred. But now . . .'

Seeing Ochocki, Szlangbaum seized him by the arm: 'Must you withdraw your money this week?'

'Yes.'

'Why so fast?'

'I'm leaving.'

'For long?'

'Perhaps for good,' he replied sharply, and went with the doctor into the room where the remains lay.

The others followed on tiptoe.

'A terrible thing,' the doctor exclaimed, 'men such as he perish, you others are leaving. Who will be left here in the end?'

'We will!' replied Maruszewicz and Szlangbaum, simultaneously.

'There will be no lack of men,' Councillor Węgrowicz declared.

'No, there won't . . . But in the meantime, pray be off with you,' the doctor cried.

The whole group, manifesting their indignation, retreated to the vestibule. Only Szuman and Ochocki remained.

'Just look at him, sir,' said the doctor, indicating the remains. 'The last Romantic! How they betake themselves off . . . How they betake themselves . . .'

He tugged his moustache and turned to the window.

Ochocki took Rzecki's already cold hand and leaned over as though to whisper something in his ear. Suddenly he caught sight of Węgiełek's letter protruding from the side pocket of the dead man, and he automatically read aloud the words written in large letters: '*Non omnis moriar* . . .'

'You're right,' he said, as if to himself.

'I am?' asked the doctor, 'I've known that for a long time.'

Ochocki said nothing.

Appendix

A censored passage

Most of the passages excised by the Tsarist censor have been restored to the main text. The following passage could not be restored, since Prus rewrote Chapter XIX, from which it came, introducing some new details which play a role in the subsequent narrative. It remains an interesting example of what Tsarist censorship found objectionable.

Almost at the same time that Rzecki was following the auction of the Łęcki house, two gentlemen were conferring in his own apartment: one of them was Wokulski and the other was the Moscow merchant, Suzin.

Suzin was a short giant, with a powerful head, powerful shoulders, and even more powerful hands; he gave the impression of a strong ox dressed in a badly cut frock-coat of very thin cloth. His whole form manifested immeasurable strength, and his red face with its irregular features glowed with almost disgraceful health. He had long, flax-coloured hair, now thickly threaded with grey, cut at his collar and parted at his forehead, matched by a great beard, also flax-coloured and streaked with white. His thick fingers bore a few rings with huge diamonds, and around his neck hung a gold chain to which one would be more inclined to fasten a great coin than a watch. From under his brows, reminiscent of juniper bushes, small grey eyes looked out, flashing with shrewdness.

Wokulski sat in the armchair, deep in thought. Suzin, looking through some papers and drinking soda water and cognac in the heat, said: 'Your old fogeys, Stanisław Piotrowicz, respectable Polish gentlemen, every one of them, Polish szlachta . . . but what are they compared to our own? That Jew, what do they call him, Szlajmans? . . . he looks as if he's set to take over your shop. (Fend off the Jews, Stanisław Piotrowicz! But as you wish . . .) And that Klein, he's a nihilist . . . Mraczewski's a nihilist too, but of the type that chases the girls; Klein, on the other hand, is a thin nihilist, all gaunt, and if he gets up to something – well, God forbid! . . .'

He began to read through his papers again, sipped at his water and cognac and continued: 'But I always incline towards my own people, like that Roman governor – remember? – who said, "all the same, Carthage must be destroyed!" . . . And I will carry on saying to you: go with me to Paris tonight. I can guarantee you fifteen thousand roubles straightaway, and if a certain proposition works out for me – maybe even fifty . . . Ah! Mr Wokulski, such money – what a waste . . . Take pity on yourself and on me and go today . . . Why sit here? What will you gain by it, what will you sit out? . . . You are not at all what you were; a brain-fever, no? . . . You don't drop in on Moscow, you don't reply to letters and you disdain such money! And now old Suzin is worse than a dog in your eyes. You'd call doctors, go to Karlsbad, ha? . . .'

At that moment the door opened cautiously and in came the gaunt Klein, handing Wokulski a letter in a pale blue envelope with a lithographic seal of forget-me-nots. Wokulski seized the letter quickly, paled, flushed, threw the torn envelope onto the table and began to read:

'The garland is beautiful; I return it to you now, and thank you in Rossi's name. You must, but absolutely must come to us tomorrow for dinner, for we need to talk about this.

Gratefully – Izabela Łęcka'

'Will there be a reply?' asked Klein in a low voice.
'No.'

Klein disappeared like a theatrical ghost behind the wings, and Wokulski continued to peruse the letter, a second, third, and fourth time. Suzin pushed aside his papers and with the greatest attention began to observe him with his small eyes. Then he took the pale blue envelope into his hands, examined it, and again directed his gaze towards Wokulski, smiling slightly with a hint of mild irony.

When Wokulski put away the letter, looking around the room like a man just awakened, Suzin indicated the envelope and said: 'Obviously a letter from a woman . . . the devil take these females! . . . No sooner enters a room, but you know that she is there . . . your nose tells you. An old man once told me that Adam in Eden must have eaten a forbidden fruit, because the tree on which it grew bore the scent of a woman . . . The devil take them! But all the same she must somehow have troubled you, Stanisław Piotrowicz . . .'

'Who?'

'The one who sent this envelope. I am surprised at how much you have changed. Finish with her quickly, or you'll fall victim to some misfortune . . .'

'If it could be finished . . .' sighed Wokulski.

Suzin laughed. 'Ah, dear fellow! What cannot be? Everything can

. . . I was once at an opera, by some German (say what you will, but the Germans have sense!), where the devil himself found no better means for a woman than diamonds . . . He took her some diamonds (perhaps ten, perhaps fifteen thousand roubles worth), and all was well . . .'

'What nonsense you're talking, Suzin!' whispered Wokulski, leaning his head on his hand.

'Oh, you gentleman! Oh, you addlebrained Polish gentleman!' Suzin laughed. 'Here is what causes your downfall, all you Poles: with you it's heart, all heart, for everything, for trade, politics, women, everything – and that is your folly. Have a pocket for everything, but keep your heart only for yourself in order to enjoy what your money buys. A woman is such a singular creature that you will not haggle anything out of her for a heart, nor out of a Jew for prayers . . . For she will make a trophy of your heart, and another will come along without a heart and she will fall in love with him, kissing him before your very eyes . . . Send me to her, Stanisław Piotrowicz, and I will say to her a brief word: "Hey, little madame – you have troubled that gentleman, Mr Wokulski, and taken away his good sense. Give back his reason, and I will give you – a dozen honey-cakes . . . Perhaps too few? . . . Twice as many will I give you, and *shabash*!'*

Wokulski looked so dreadful that Suzin stopped, and then changed the subject of the conversation. 'You know,' he continued, 'what Maria Siergiejewna told me about her daughter before my departure? . . . "Oh," said she, "silly Luboczka pines and pines for that scoundrel Wokulski. I explain to her: don't you go thinking about Mr Wokulski. Mr Wokulski is sitting in Warsaw playing the national anthem on the piano . . . and never spares a thought for such a foolish girl . . . but Luboczka, nothing, like a stone . . ." And then Maria Siergiejewna says: "I don't give a damn for that rotten Poland, let it perish for all I care, but I'm sorry for the child . . ."'

'Just think, Stanisław Piotrowicz: the girl's a peach, she's been through the Smolny Institute, got a medal, she'll put three million roubles down on the table at once and she dances and paints and more than one guards colonel has tried for her hand . . . Marry her, and you'll have money enough for three local ladies, as long as God gives you strength, for women have devoured better Samsons . . .'

The door opened a second time.

'Mr Łęcki is asking for you, sir,' said Klein, revealing one cuff and the top of his head.

Wokulski started. Suzin rose heavily from the sofa.

'Well, Stanisław Piotrowicz, I will go now and sleep awhile. Drop everything, I advise you, and go with me today to Paris; and if not today then tomorrow, or the day after. I'll stop off at Berlin on the way to take a look at Bismarck, and you join me . . .'

They embraced and Suzin left, shaking his head.

'Where is Mr Łęcki?' Wokulski asked Klein.

'In the study.'

'I will go at once.'

Klein went out. Wokulski quickly gathered the papers from the table and also left Mr Ignacy's apartment.

Notes

1 *Treaty of San Stefano*: Peace treaty between Russia and Turkey, signed on 3 March 1878. As a result, Romania, Serbia, Montenegro and Bulgaria – formerly parts of the Ottoman Empire – gained independence.

election of a new Pope: Leo XIII, elected on 20 February 1878.

chances of a European war: the political conflict between Britain and Russia, which arose during the Russo-Turkish war and was not entirely resolved after the treaty of San Stefano, posed the threat of a new war involving European powers.

Krakowskie Przedmieście: one of the prime business and residential streets of Warsaw.

2 *Beef Nelson*: a Polish speciality, beef in a rich mushroom sauce.

3 *He and the rest of 'em . . . Irkutsk*: Prus alludes here to Wokulski's participation in the January Uprising, 1863–4, and Wokulski's presence in Irkutsk (Siberia) suggests political exile following the collapse of the uprising – the fate of many Polish insurgents and patriots at the time.

9 *Napoleon III*: Louis Napoleon Bonaparte, born 1803, a nephew of Napoleon I; in 1848 elected President of the French Republic; in 1851 assumed a dictatorial position in the state; in 1852, after a popular referendum, assumed the title of Emperor. In 1870, after the lost war with Prussia, Napoleon III was deprived of his throne and exiled to England, where he died in 1873.

Huguenots: opera by G. Meyerbeer (1836).

10 *History of the Consulate and Empire*: a history of the rule of Napoleon Bonaparte in France by A. Thiers, published 1845–62.

the Italian war of 1859: the war between the Kingdom of Sardinia (supported by France) and Austria; a vital stage in the process of the unification of Italy.

Rakoczi March: a patriotic Hungarian march.

15 *a Napoleon has turned up*: the reference here is to Louis Napoleon's attempted *coup d'état* in 1840.

16 *The new Napoleon has been thrown into prison*: Louis Napoleon's *coup d'état* of 1840 proved unsuccessful. He was taken prisoner, sentenced to life imprisonment and on 7 October 1840 placed in the fortress of Ham in Northern France. *Cham* is Polish for 'cad'.

20 *Schublade*: the Polish word for 'drawer' is *szuflada*, so Frau Mincel

explains that *Schublade* means *szuflada*.

22 *Andrássy*: Count Julius Andrassy (1823–90), a prominent figure in the 1848 Hungarian revolution against Austrian rule. Andrassy became Prime Minister of Hungary after the formation of the Dual Monarchy in 1867.

26 *a Turkish Wallenrod*: an allusion to a long poem by Adam Mickiewicz, *Konrad Wallenrod* (1828). The poem tells the story of the medieval Lithuanians' struggle against the Teutonic Knights. The hero, Konrad Wallenrod, a Lithuanian, joins the ranks of the Teutonic Knights and works his way up to the position of Grand Master, only to orchestrate their defeat. The implication is that Wokulski, as a Pole driven by patriotic motives, had some hidden agenda of undermining Russian success while supplying the Russian military in the Russo–Turkish War.

30 *Fifteen years ago*: an allusion to the year 1863 – the date of the abortive Polish uprising in which Wokulski participated.

38 *Un-Divine Comedy*: a Romantic play by Count Zygmunt Krasiński (1835). The play paints a catastrophic vision of the future bloodshed between the old aristocracy and the rebellious masses. In it, the Holy Trinity Fortress (a historic site in the Ukraine) is the last place on earth defended by the desperate aristocrats against the victorious, barbaric rebellion.

51 *Repenting the enthusiasm of his youth*: another allusion to Wokulski's penal exile to Siberia after the defeat of the Polish uprising of 1863.

70 *Czerski, Czekanowski, Dybowski*: eminent Polish scholars exiled to Siberia after the Uprising of 1863. During their time in exile they conducted geographic, geological, biological and anthropological studies of Siberia.

111 *The years 1846 and 1847 . . . people disappeared*: the years 1846–7 brought an escalation of the activities of the Polish clandestine liberation movement against the powers occupying Polish territory. A general uprising was planned for 1846 in all three parts of Poland, occupied respectively by Russia, Prussia and Austria. In the event, uprisings took place in the Prussian and Austrian parts, while the wave of arrests and repressions by the Russian authorities prevented any further developments in the Russian part.

112 *Our journey . . . October 1849*: in 1848, about four thousand young Poles left the Russian-occupied part of Polish territory to take part in the so-called Springtime of Nations. About two thousand of them fought against Austria for the independence of Hungary. After the defeat of the Hungarian uprising, many of them emigrated to the United States, England and Turkey.

116 *General Bem*: Józef Bem (1797–1850), a Polish general; a participant of the Polish uprising against Russia in 1831; in 1848–9, the commander of the revolutionary forces in Vienna; later, the commander of the Hungarian insurgents in Transylvania and, in August 1849, the commander-in-chief of the Hungarian army. After the defeat of the Hungarian uprising he emigrated to Turkey.

121 *Haynau*: Julius Haynau (1786–1853): Austrian field marshal who quelled the Hungarian uprising in 1849.

Kossuth: Lájos Kossuth (1802–94): Hungarian politician and leader of the 1848–9 uprising.

123 *I stayed over a year in Zamość*: Zamość was the site of a large Russian prison. Prus indirectly indicates that Rzecki served a year as a political prisoner after his return to the Russian-occupied part of Poland.

136 *Nalewki or Świętojerska*: streets in Warsaw's Jewish neighbourhood.

138 *prikashchiki*: Russian salesmen.

Citadel prison: Russian political prison in Warsaw, built in 1832–40. The area around the Citadel prison was also known for its numerous brothels.

141 *Europejski Hotel*: then the most luxurious hotel in Warsaw, located on Krakowskie Przedmieście.

143 *A Romantic of the pre-1863 kind, and a positivist of the '70s*: see the discussion of Romanticism and Positivism in the Introduction, p.xiii.

178 *mundur*: Polish for 'uniform'.

255 *Halka*: an opera by Stanisław Moniuszko, first staged in Warsaw in 1858 and very popular in Poland.

318 *at this moment I passed out*: the gathering in the cellars and the strange project championed by Leon, as well as the following changes in Wokulski's behaviour, seem to allude to Wokulski's participation in underground activities directly preceding the 1863 uprising.

320 *Twardowski*: a character from a Polish legend: a nobleman who sold his soul to the devil in exchange for the devil's assistance during his life. On the way to hell, Twardowski managed to escape to the moon where he is believed to have lived ever since.

324 *And thou shalt sit upon a fierce lion without fear, and ride on a huge dragon*: a quotation from the sixteenth-century Polish translation of Psalm XCI by Jan Kochanowski, Poland's foremost poet prior to the nineteenth century.

325 *Moltke*: Helmuth Count von Moltke (1800–91), chief of the Parisian general staff and military architect of Prussia's victories in the wars with Denmark, Austria and France.

465 *Matejko*: Jan Matejko (1838–93), the celebrated painter of large historic canvases which present glorious moments in Polish history. *The Battle of Grünwald*, the most famous of all Matejko's paintings, depicts the victory of the Polish-Lithuanian forces over the Teutonic Knights at Grünwald-Tannenberg in 1410.

483 *the incident with Nobiling*: the assassination attempt against the German Emperor Wilhelm I on 2 June 1878. Wilhelm was wounded and temporarily abdicated in favour of his successor, Friedrich Wilhelm. He resumed the throne in December 1878.

679 *shabash*: obsolete Russian expression meaning 'that's enough!' or 'that'll do!' In this context, 'and there you are!' is closer to the intended meaning.

OTHER NEW YORK REVIEW CLASSICS*

* *For a complete list of titles, visit www.nyrb.com.*